# *THIS ONE SUMMER*

### Mariko Tamaki
### Jillian Tamaki

:01
First Second
NEW YORK

CRUNCH

CRUNCH

CRUNCH
CRVNCH

CRUNCH

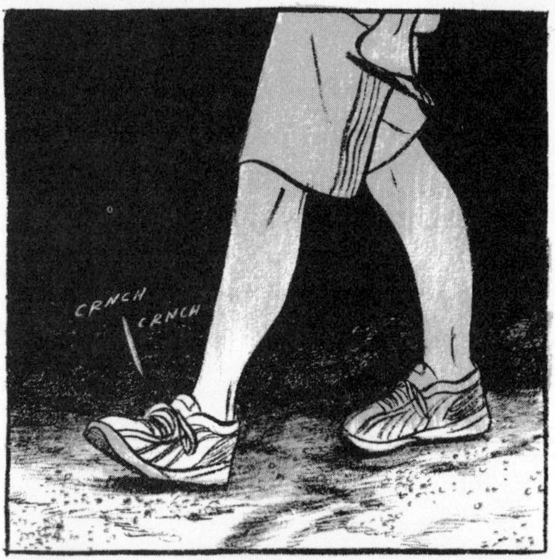
CRNCH
CRNCH

Okay.

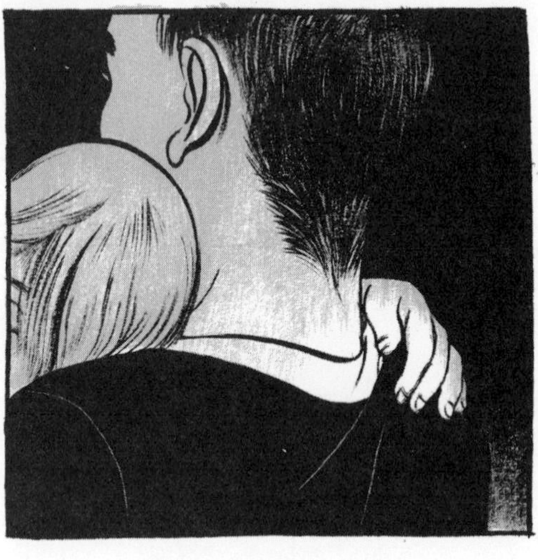

So.

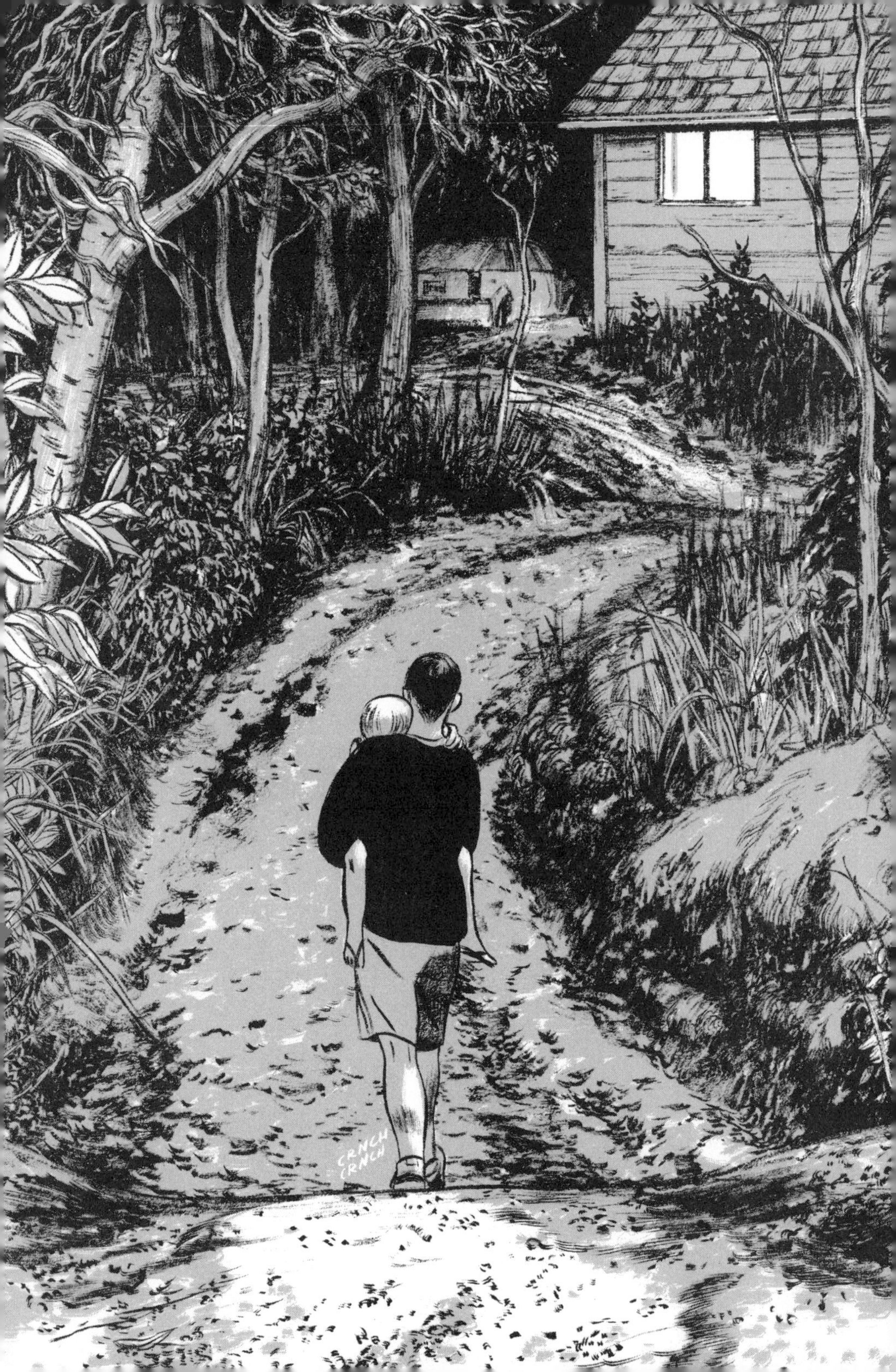
CRNCH
CRNCH

*Awago Beach is this place.*

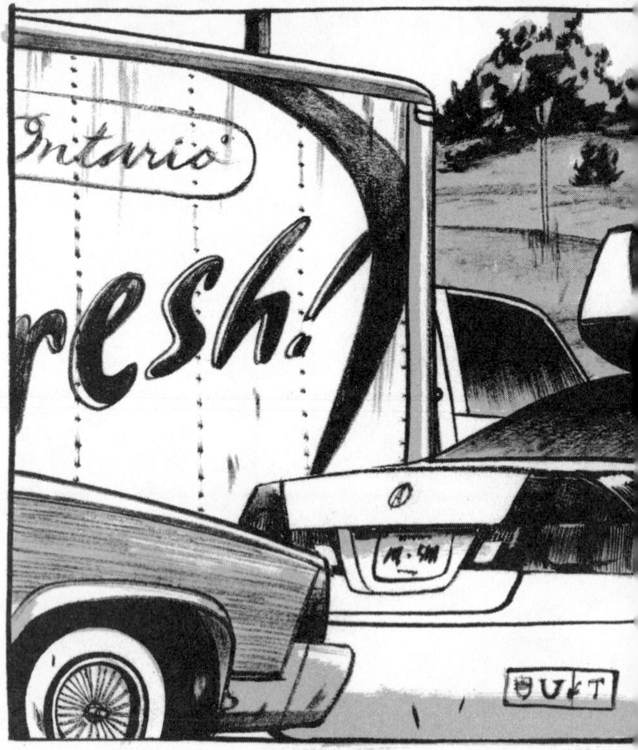

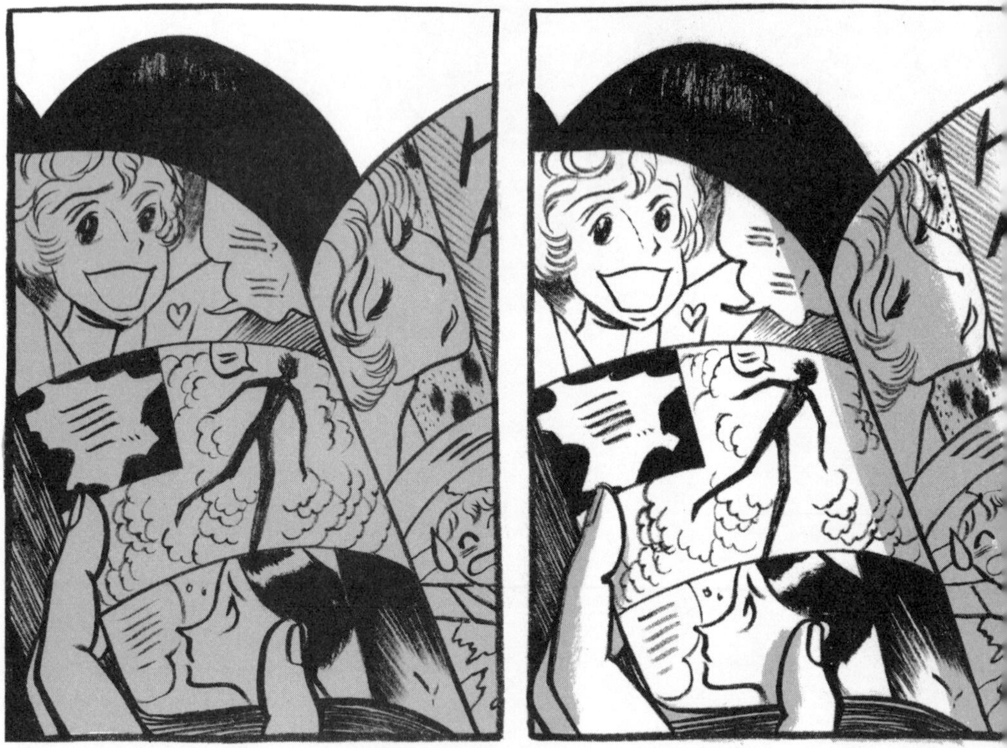

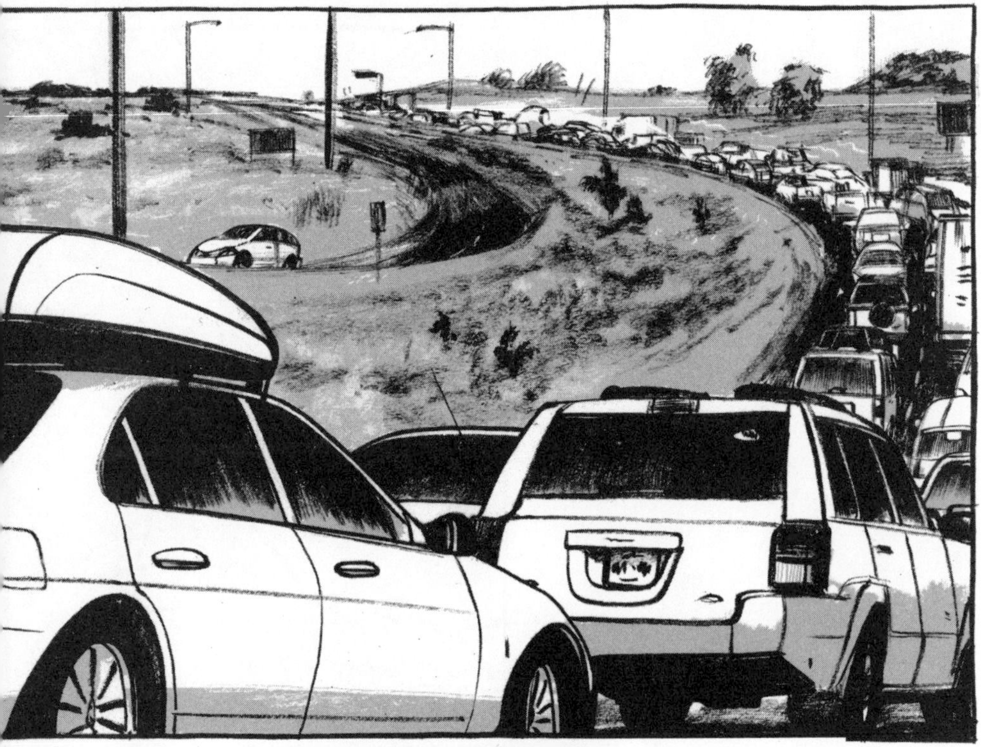

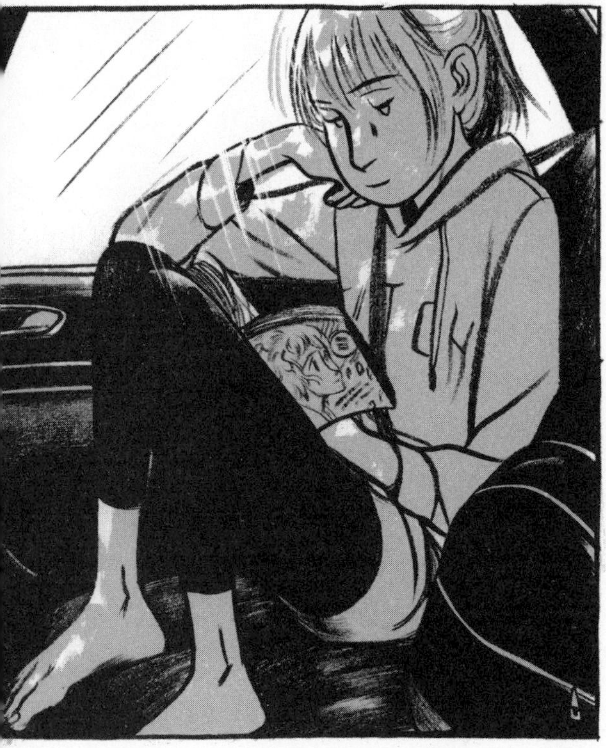

Where my family
goes every summer.

Ever since...

like...
forever.

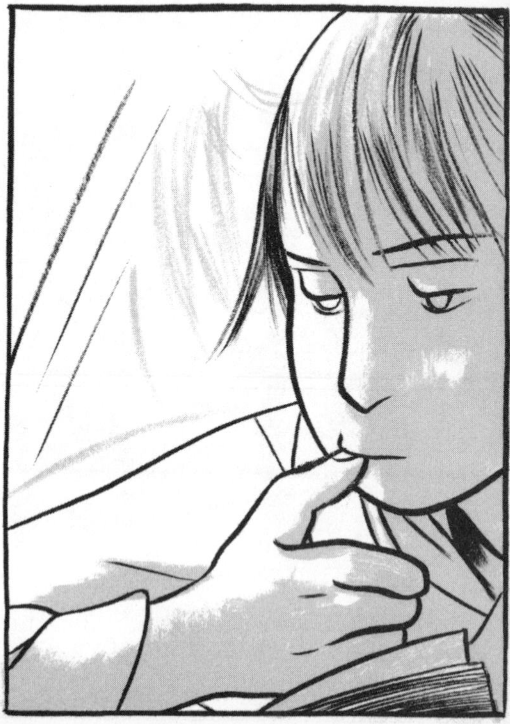

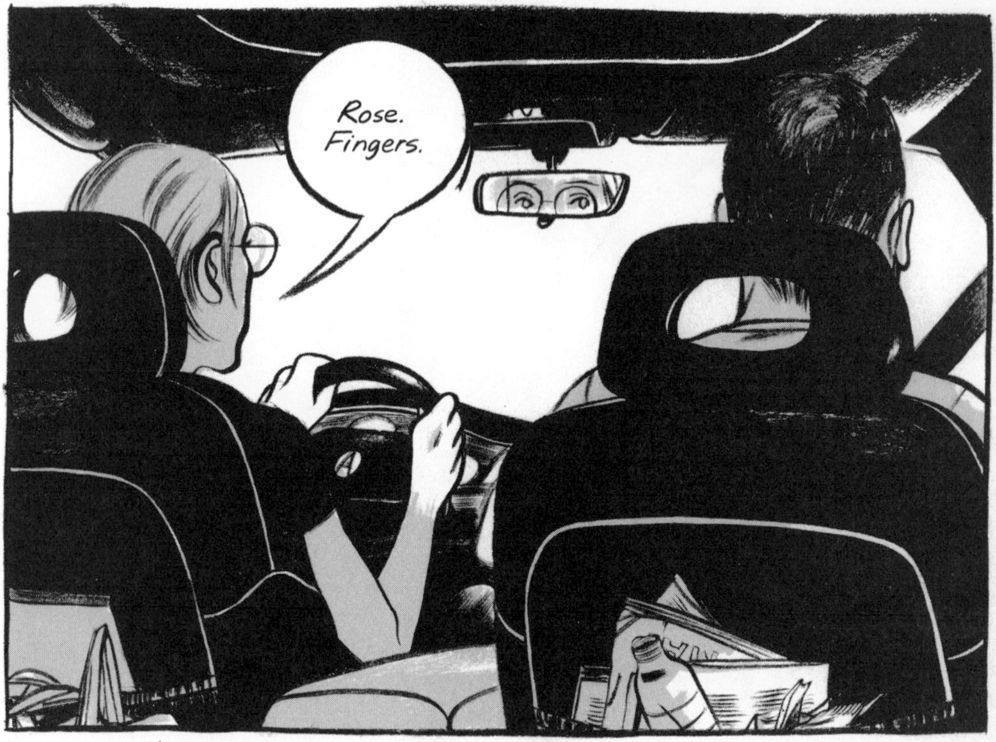
Rose. Fingers.

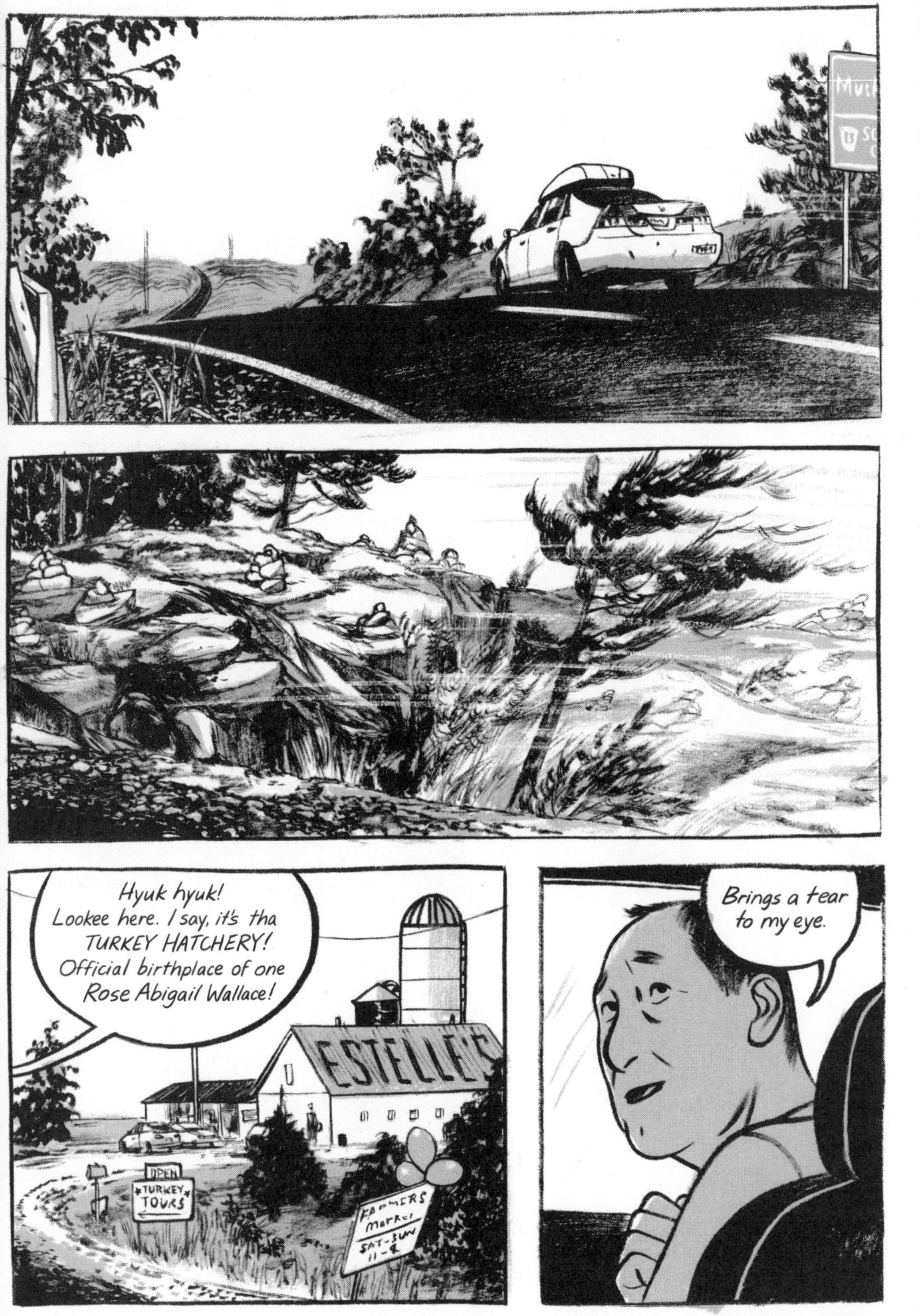
Hyuk hyuk! Lookee here. I say, it's tha TURKEY HATCHERY! Official birthplace of one Rose Abigail Wallace!
ESTELLE'S
OPEN
TURKEY TOURS
FARMERS Market
SAT-SUN
Brings a tear to my eye.

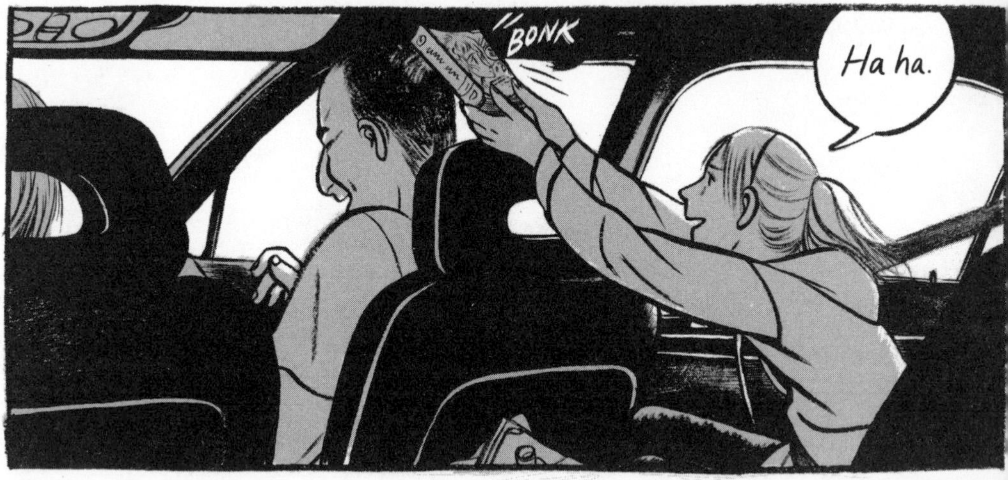
BONK
Ha ha.

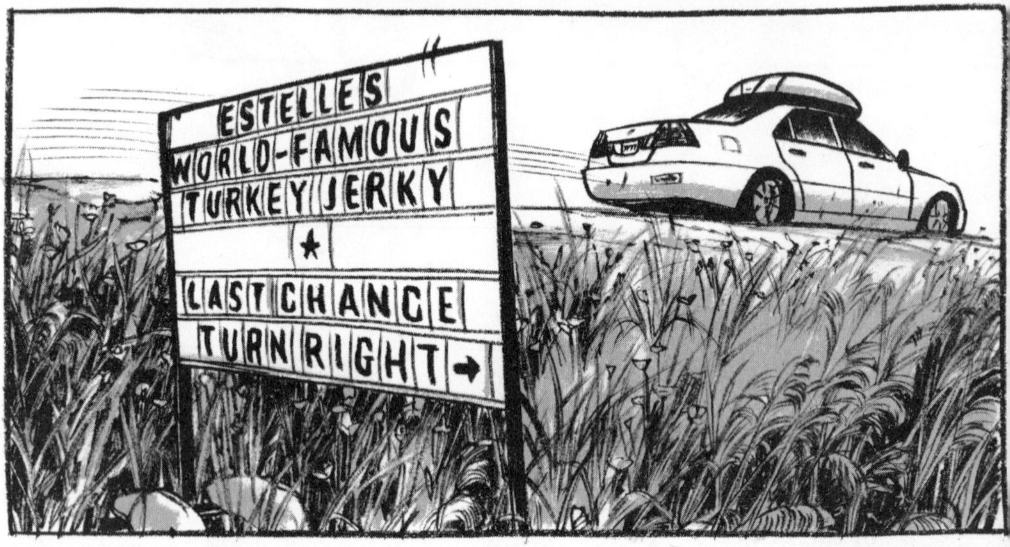
ESTELLES
WORLD-FAMOUS
TURKEY JERKY
LAST CHANCE
TURN RIGHT

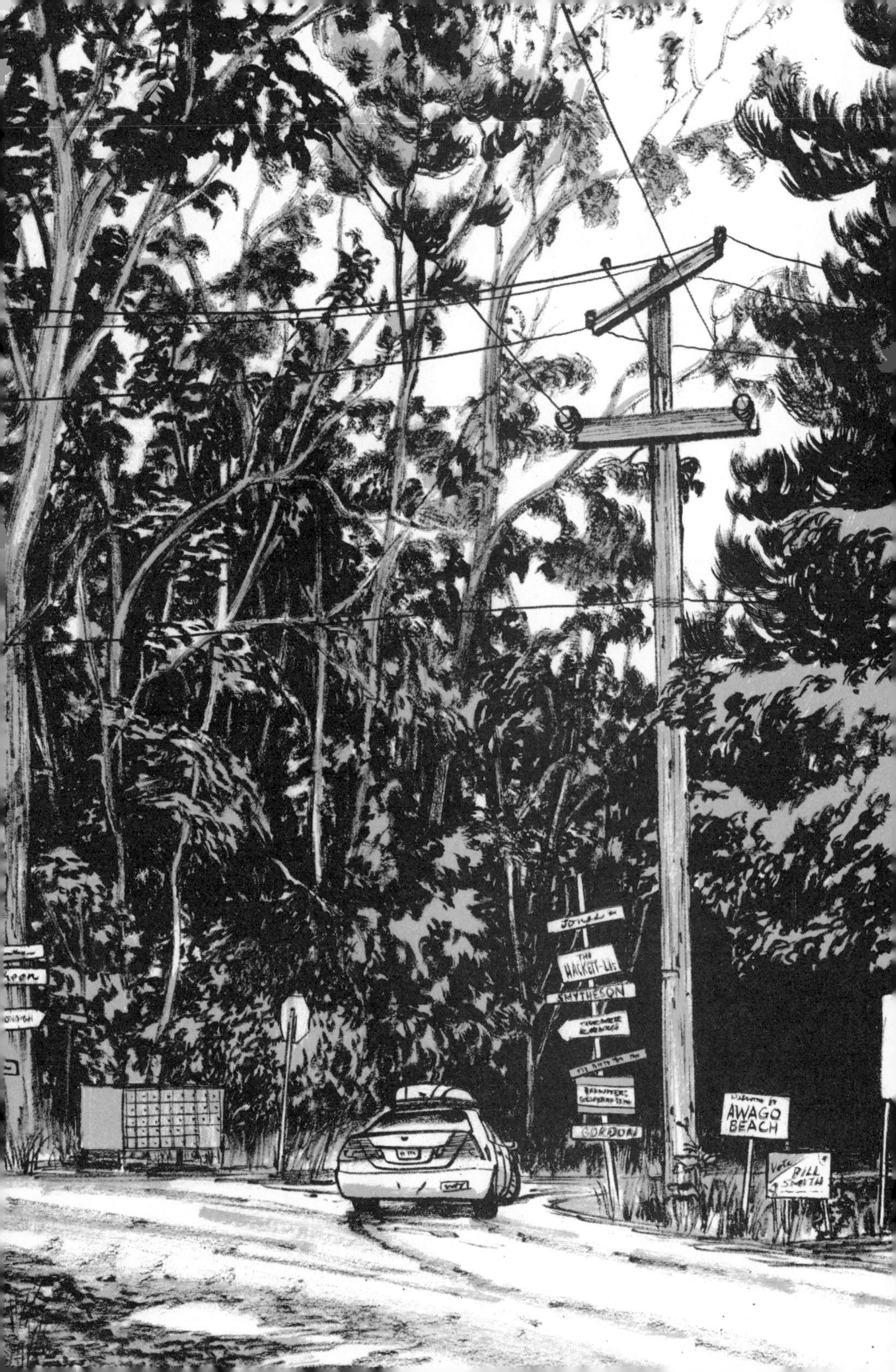

THE HACKETT-LIS
SMYTHESON
GORDON
AWAGO BEACH
Vote
BILL SMITH

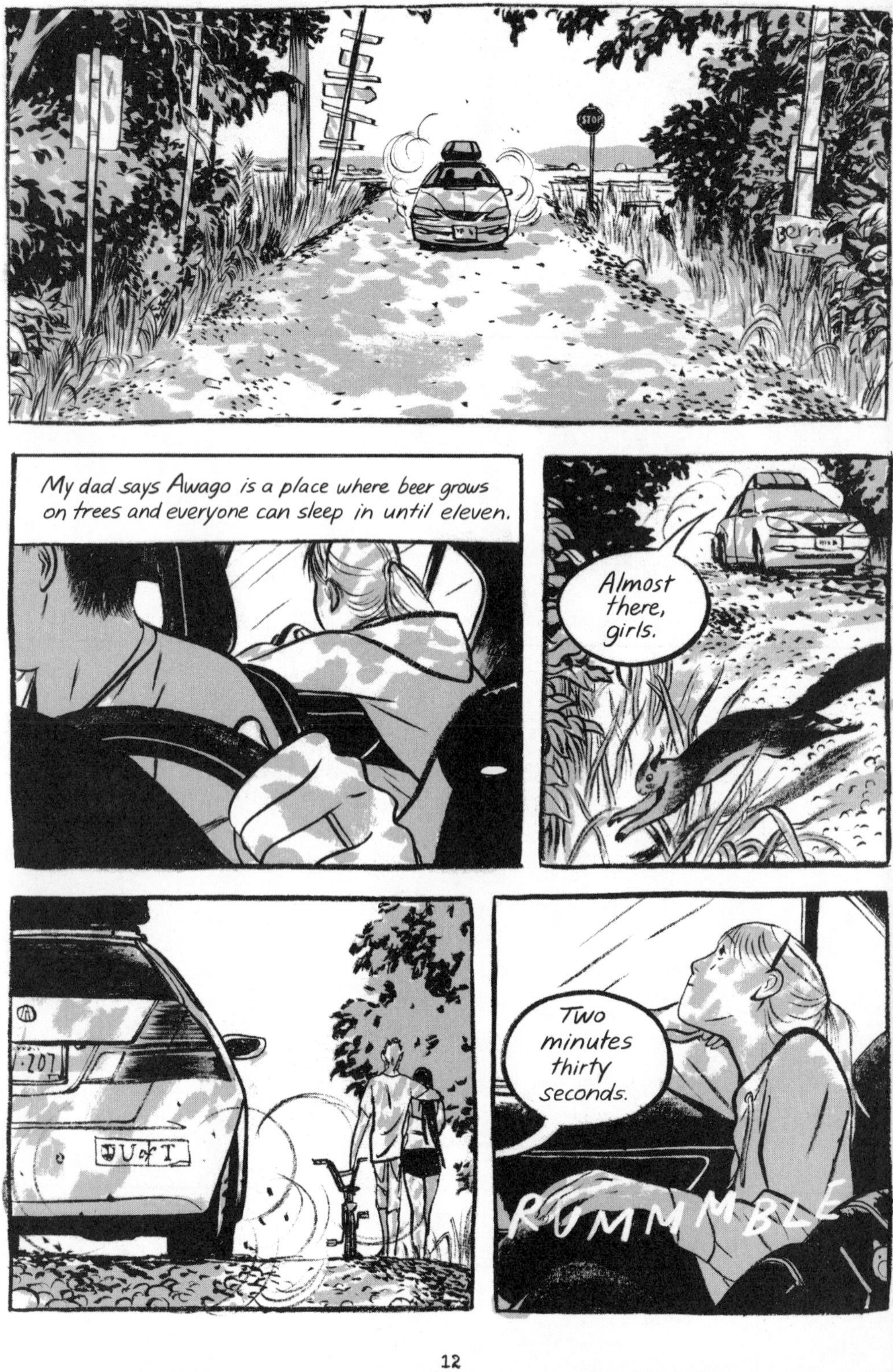
My dad says Awago is a place where beer grows on trees and everyone can sleep in until eleven.
Almost there, girls.
Two minutes thirty seconds.
RUMMMBLE

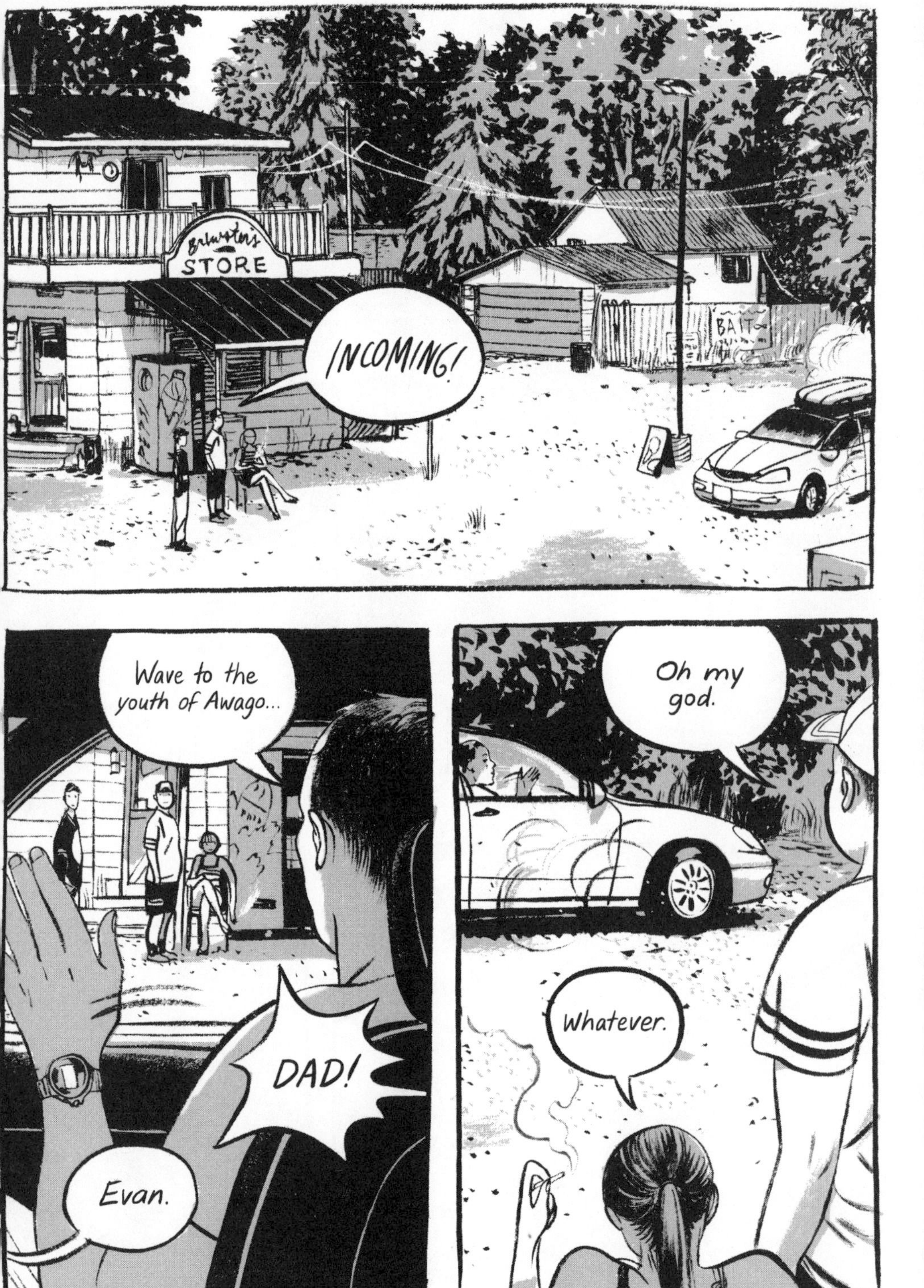
STORE
INCOMING!
BAIT
Wave to the youth of Awago...
DAD!
Evan.
Oh my god.
Whatever.

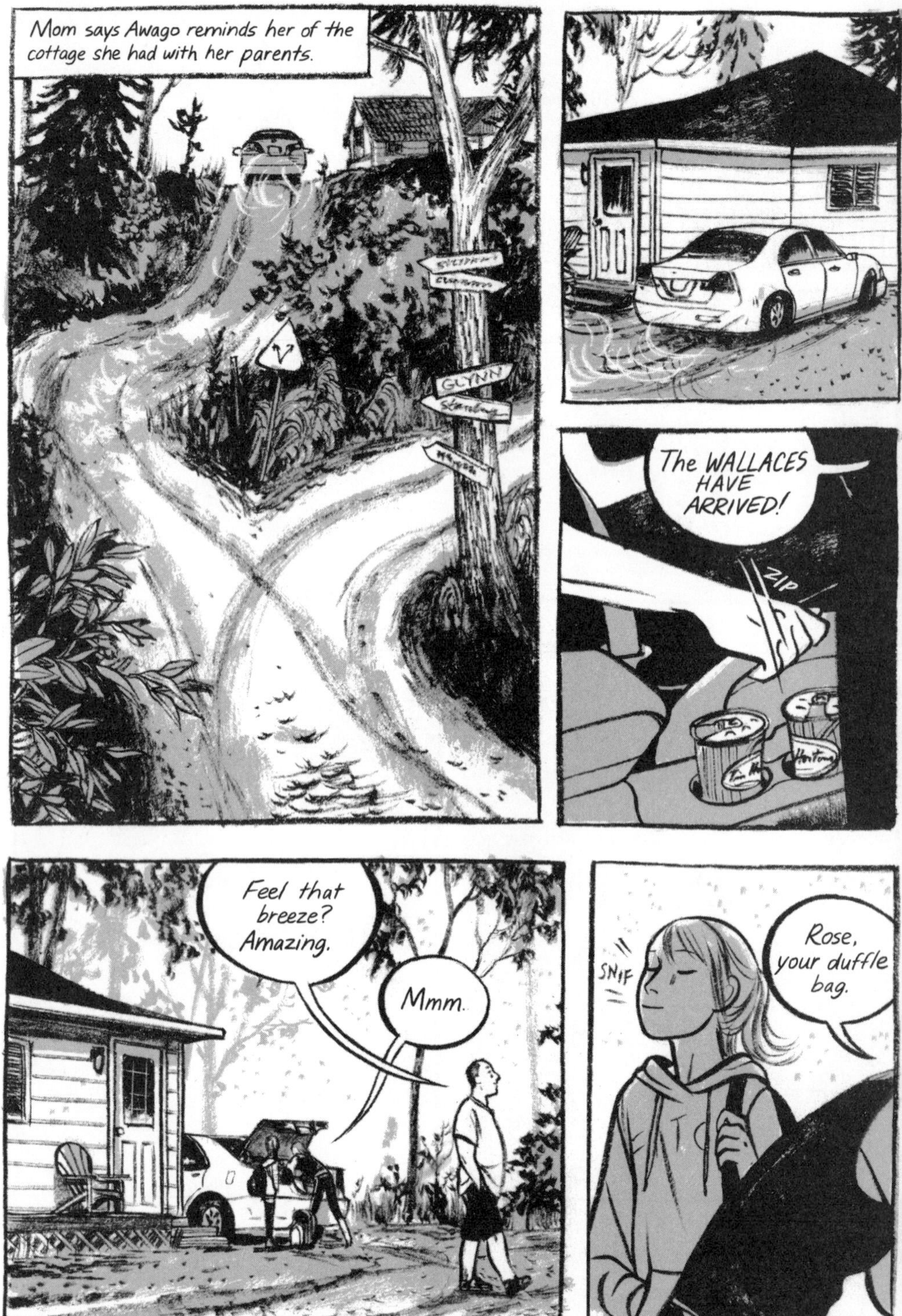
Mom says Awago reminds her of the cottage she had with her parents.
GLYNN
The WALLACES HAVE ARRIVED!
ZIP
Feel that breeze? Amazing.
Mmm.
SNIF
Rose, your duffle bag.

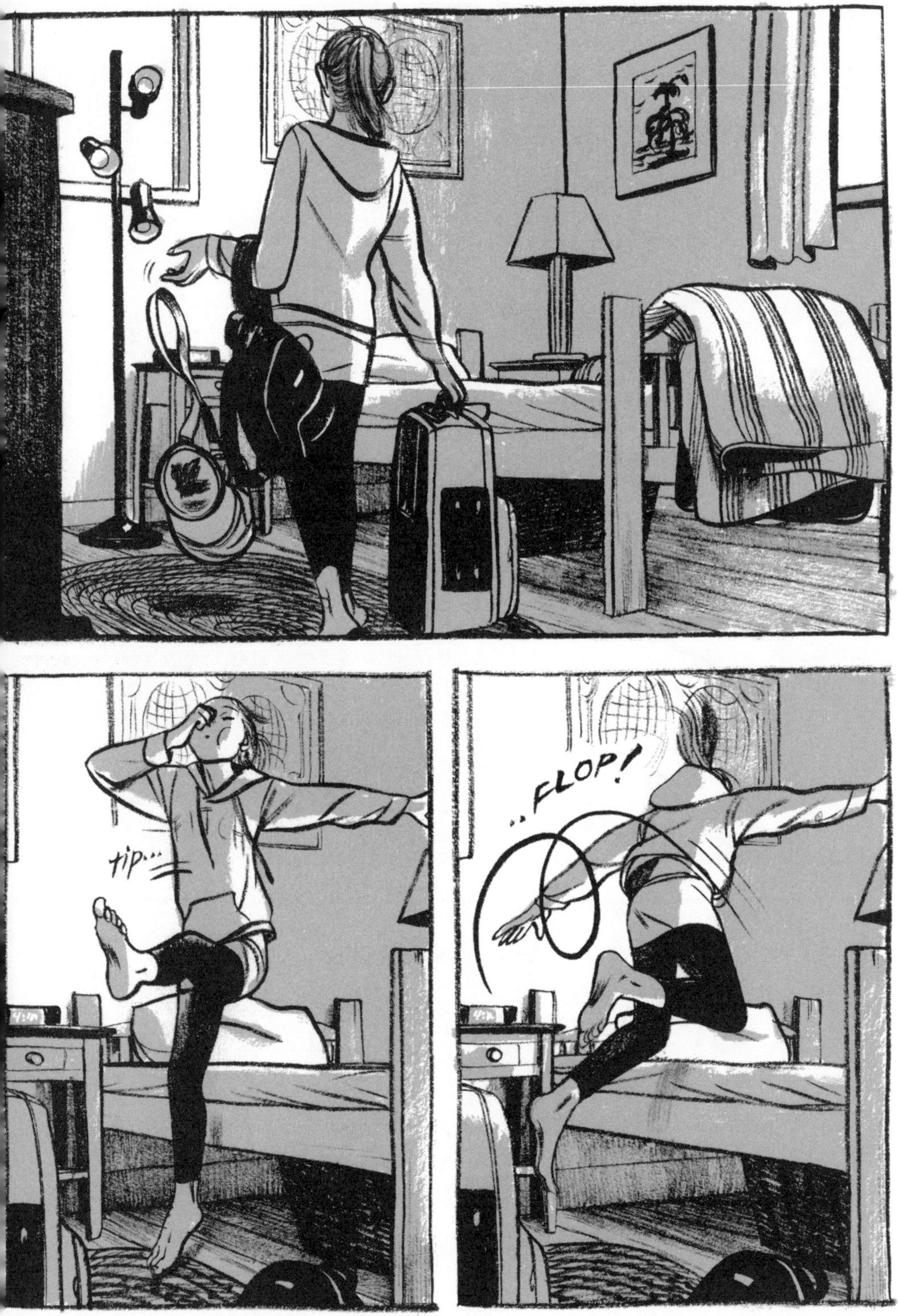
tip...
..FLOP!

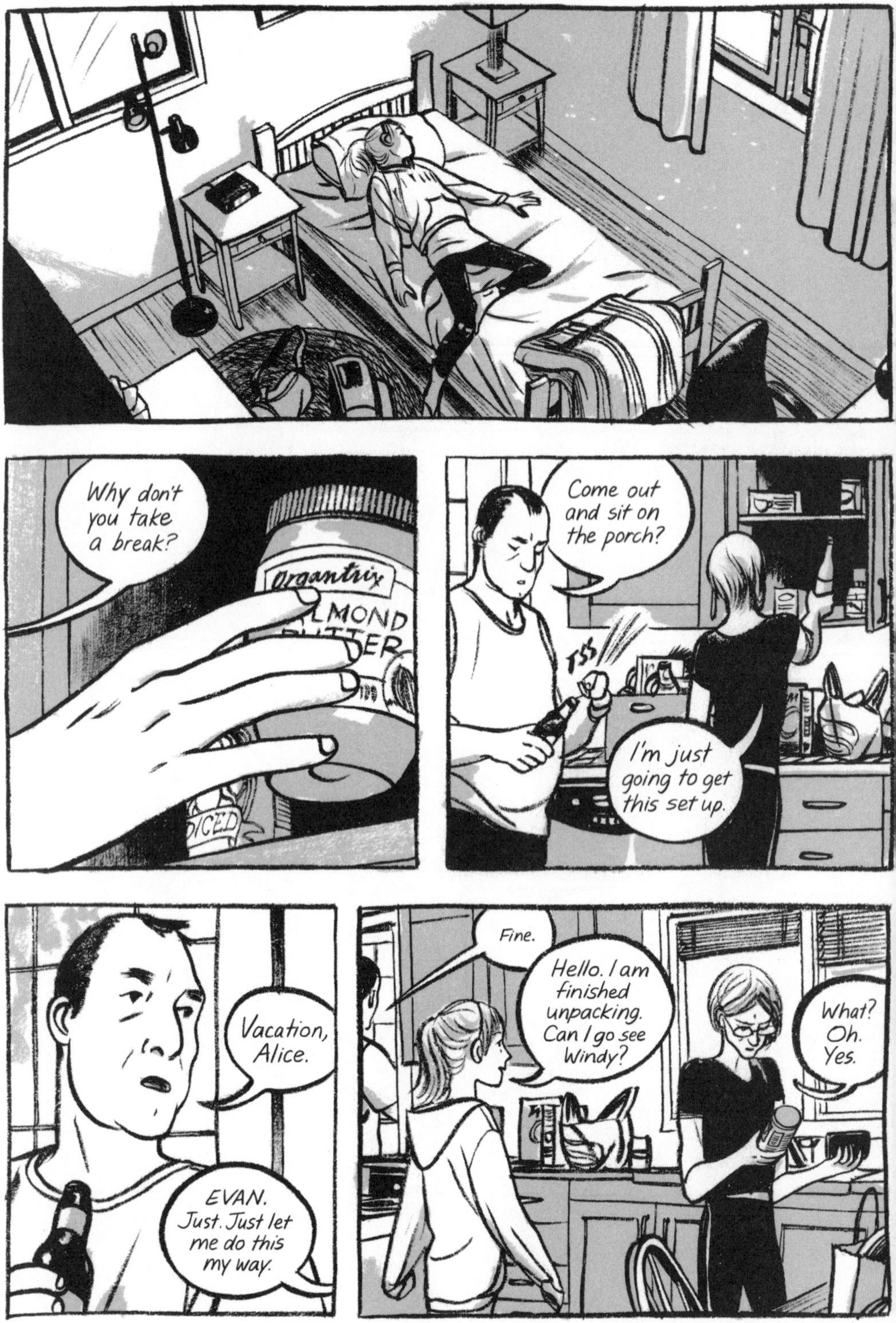
Why don't you take a break?
Organtrix
LMOND
DICED
Come out and sit on the porch?
TSS
I'm just going to get this set up.
Vacation, Alice.
EVAN. Just. Just let me do this my way.
Fine.
Hello. I am finished unpacking. Can I go see Windy?
What? Oh. Yes.

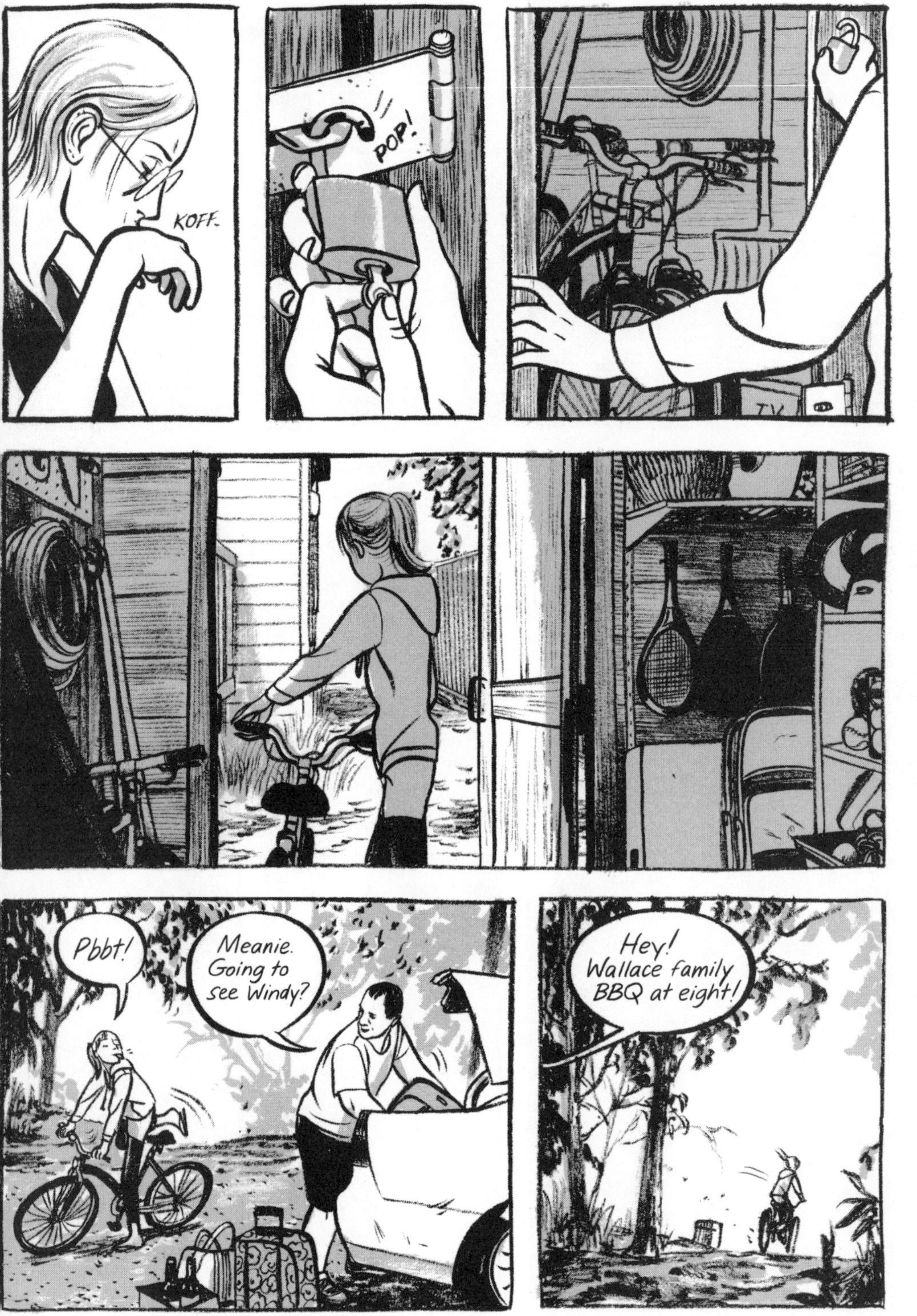
KOFF.
POP!
TV
Pbbt!
Meanie. Going to see Windy?
Hey! Wallace family BBQ at eight!

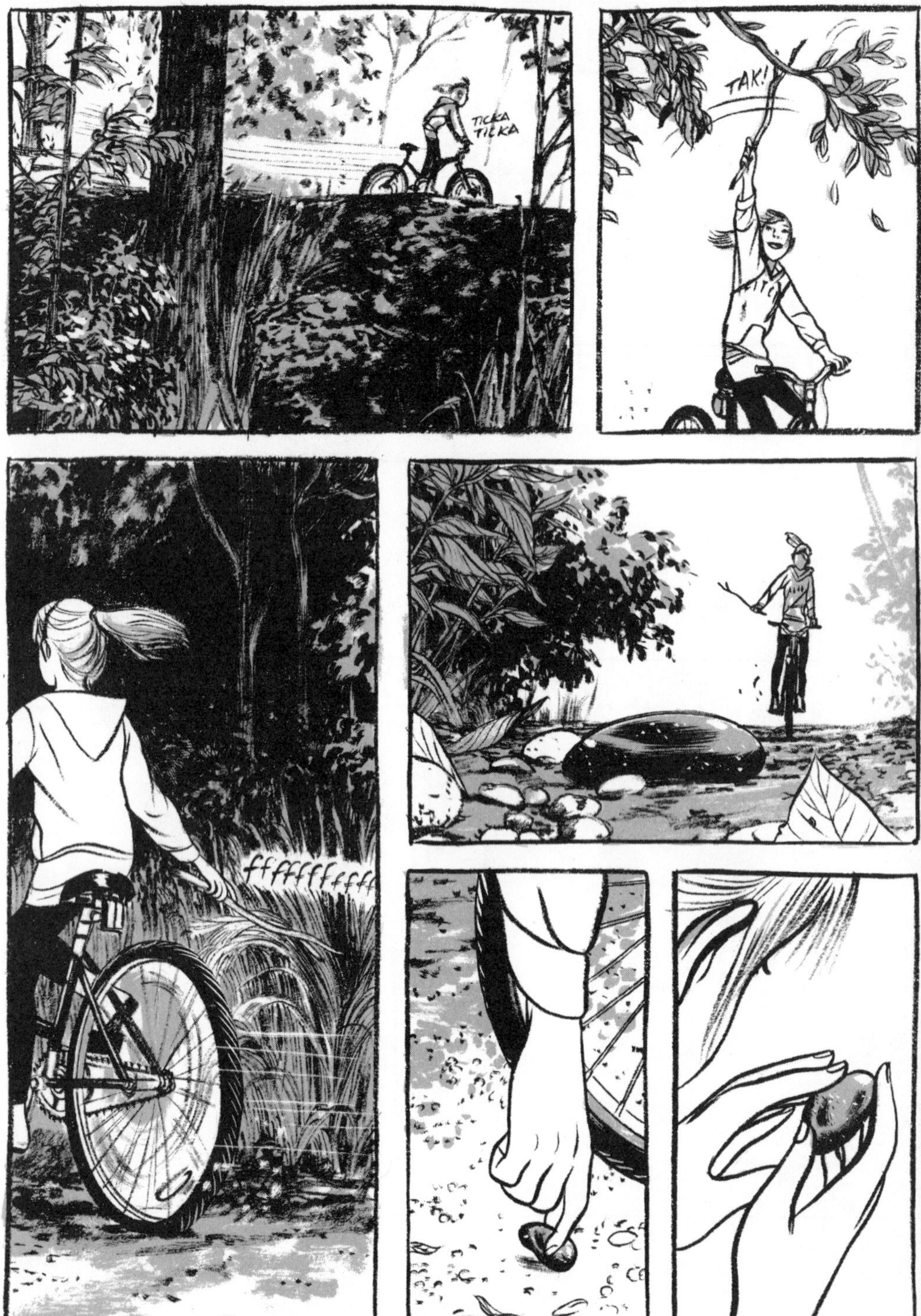
TICKA
TICKA
TAK!
ffffffffff

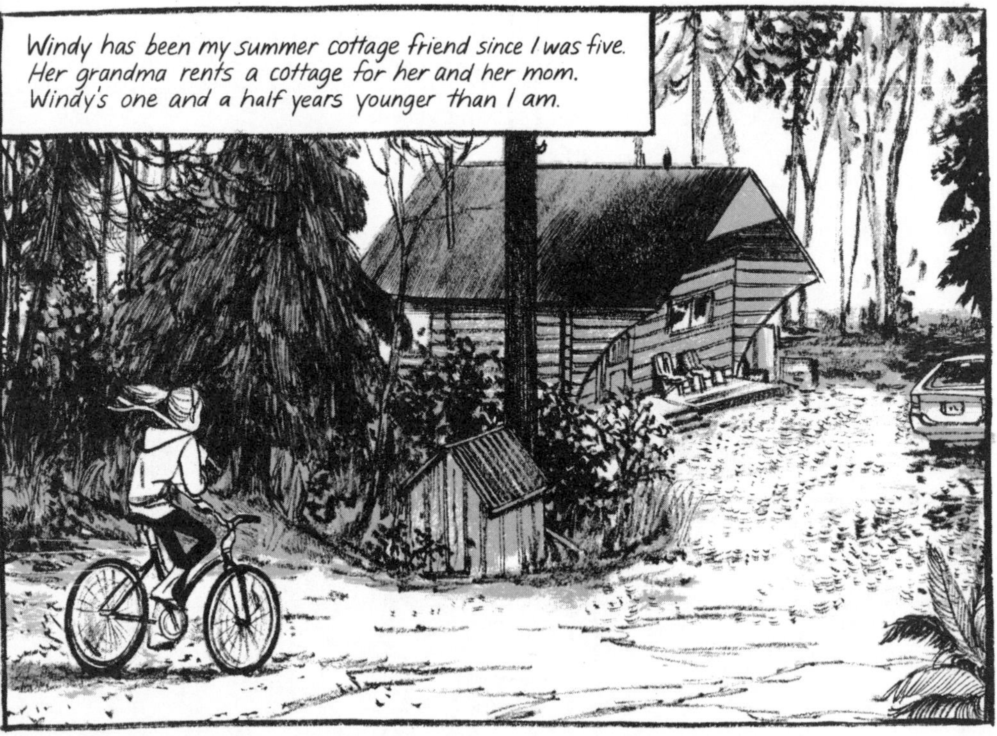
Windy has been my summer cottage friend since I was five.
Her grandma rents a cottage for her and her mom.
Windy's one and a half years younger than I am.

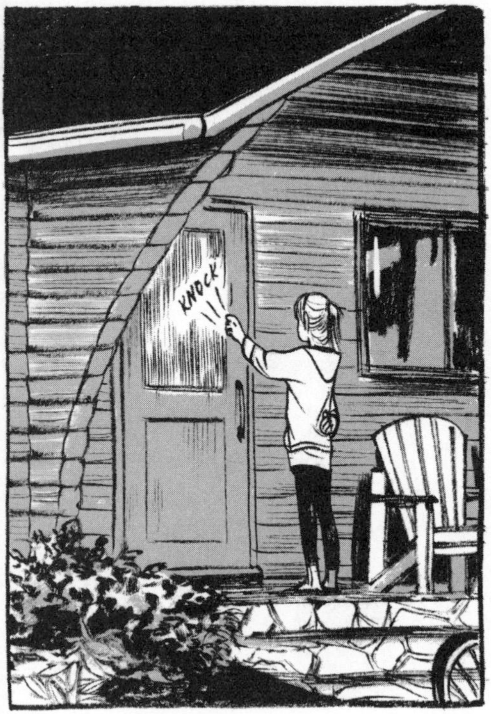
KNOCK

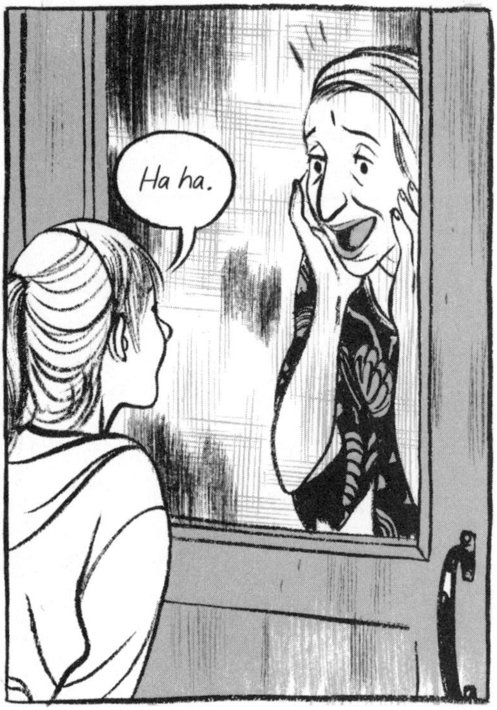
Ha ha.

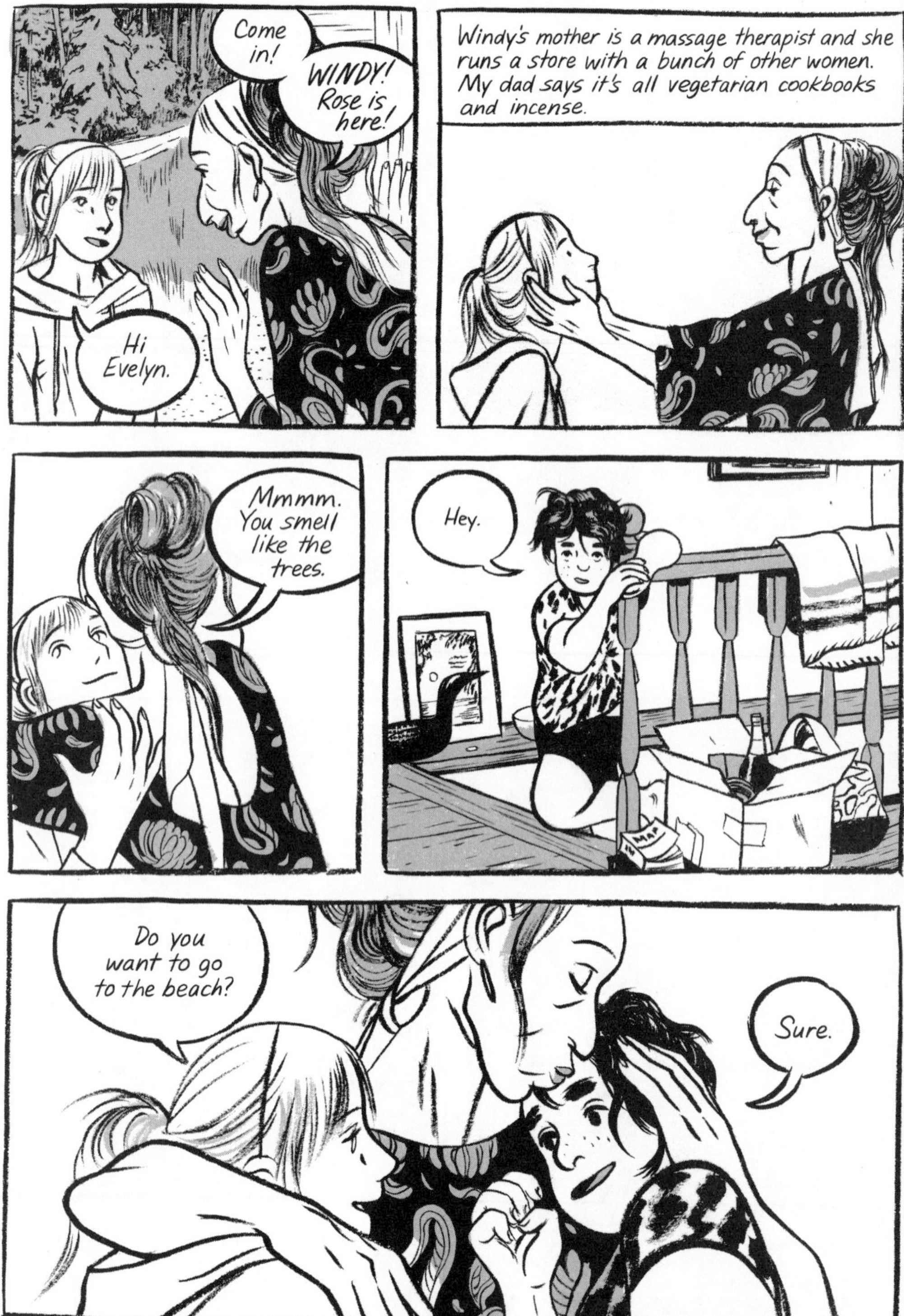
Come in!
WINDY! Rose is here!
Hi Evelyn.
Windy's mother is a massage therapist and she runs a store with a bunch of other women. My dad says it's all vegetarian cookbooks and incense.
Mmmm. You smell like the trees.
Hey.
Do you want to go to the beach?
Sure.

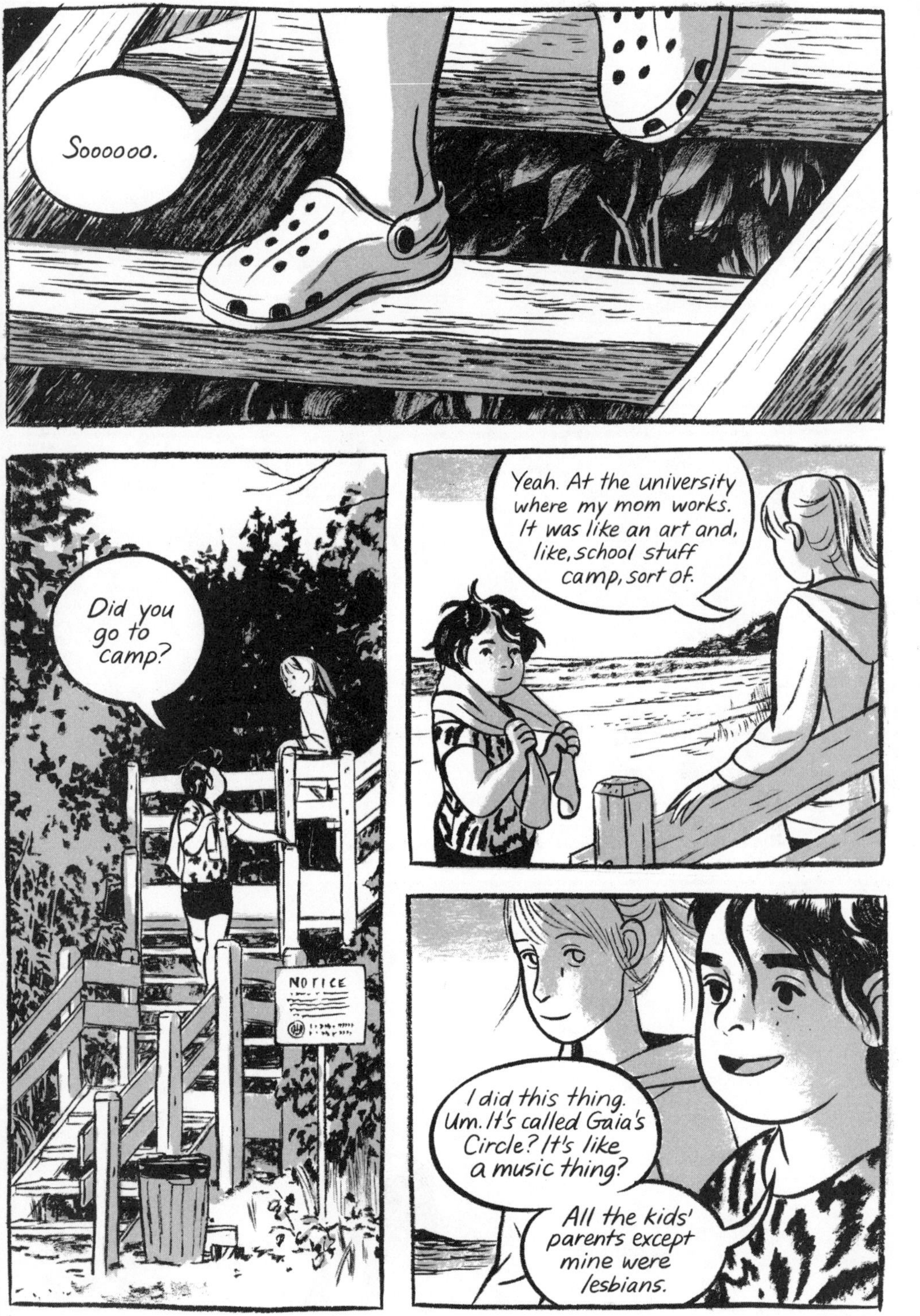
Soooooo.
Did you go to camp?
Yeah. At the university where my mom works. It was like an art and, like, school stuff camp, sort of.
I did this thing. Um. It's called Gaia's Circle? It's like a music thing?
All the kids' parents except mine were lesbians.
NOTICE

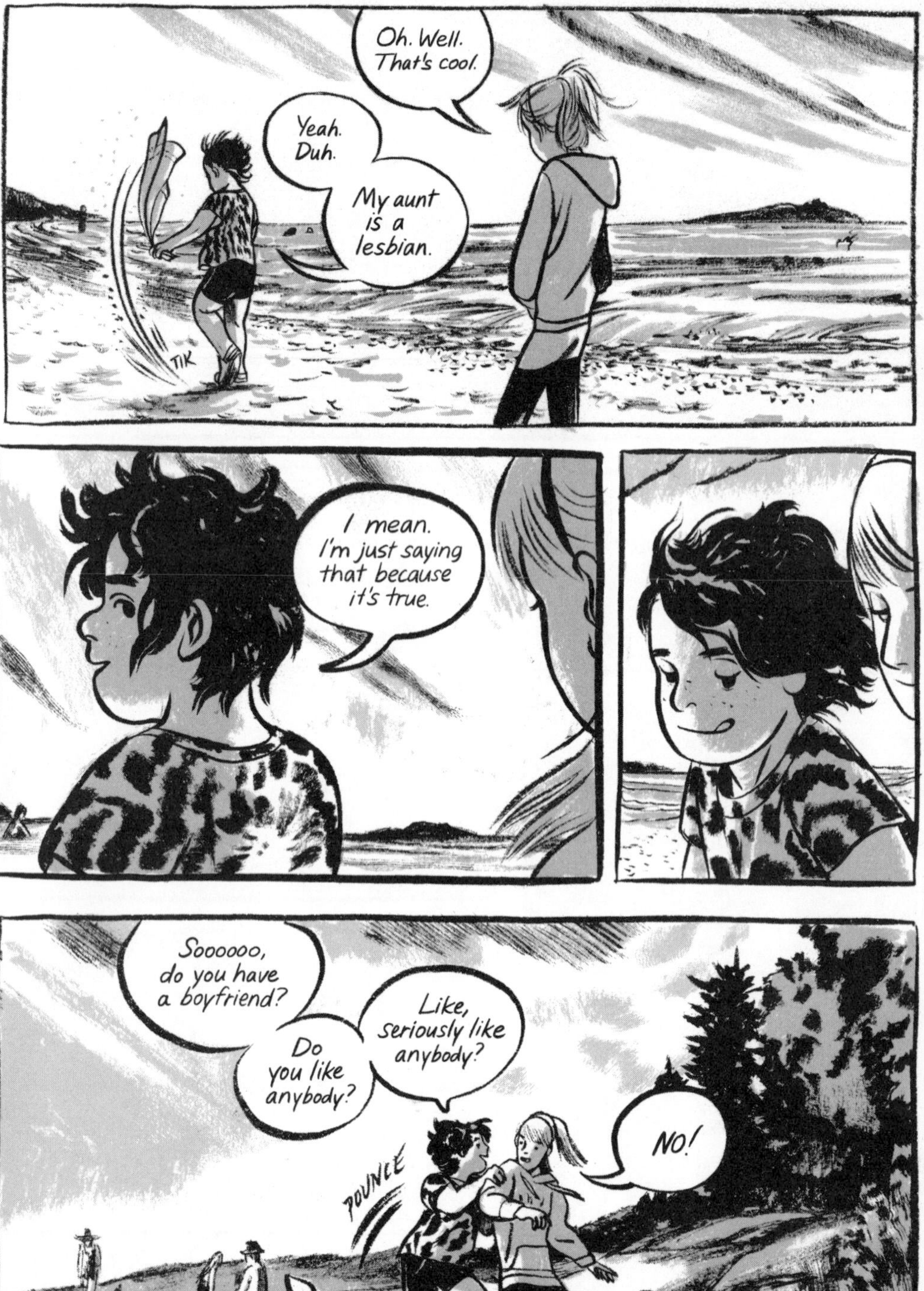
Oh. Well. That's cool.
Yeah. Duh.
My aunt is a lesbian.
TIK
I mean. I'm just saying that because it's true.
Soooooo, do you have a boyfriend?
Do you like anybody?
Like, seriously like anybody?
NO!
POUNCE

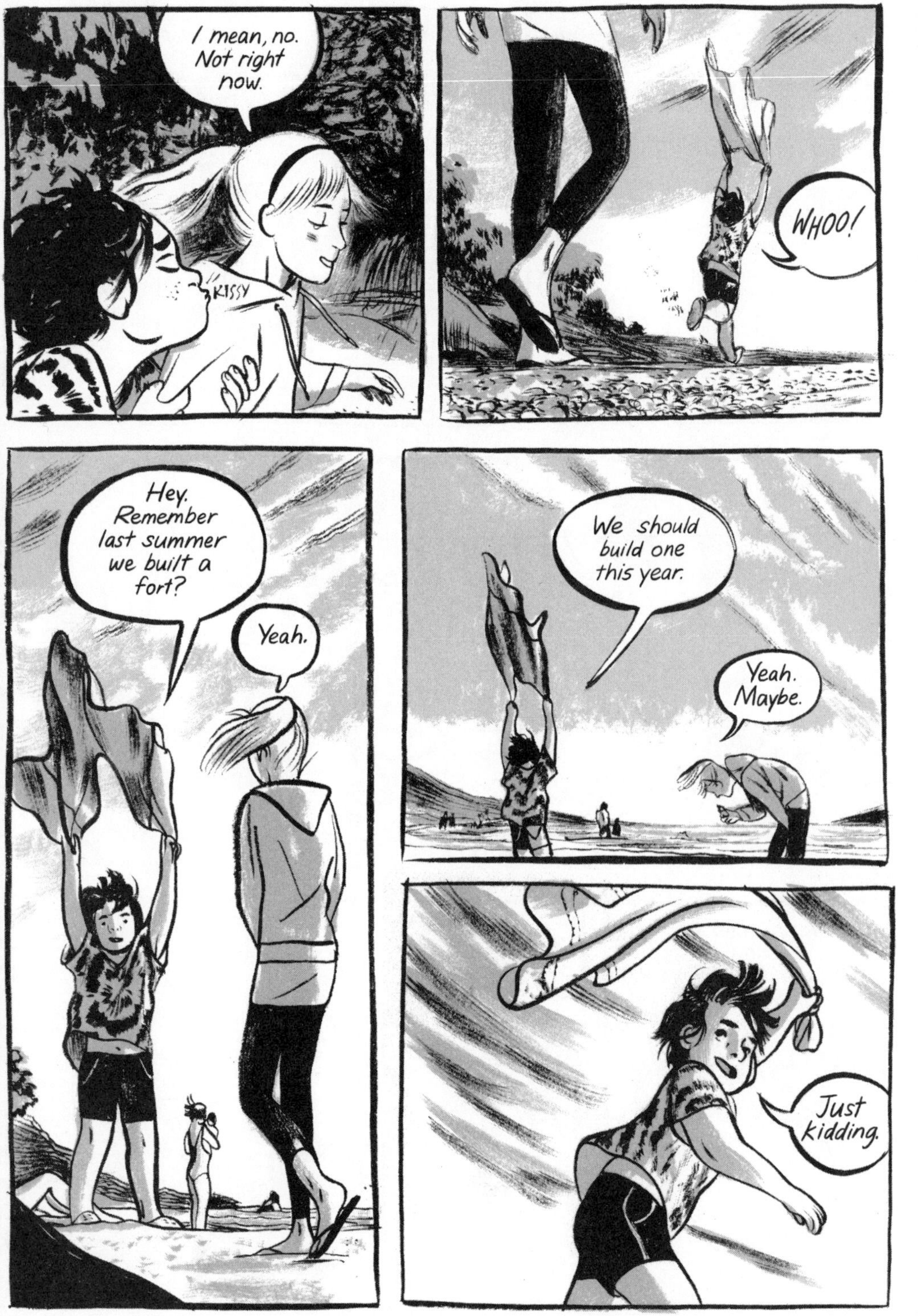
I mean, no. Not right now.
KISSY
WHOO!
Hey. Remember last summer we built a fort?
Yeah.
We should build one this year.
Yeah. Maybe.
Just kidding.

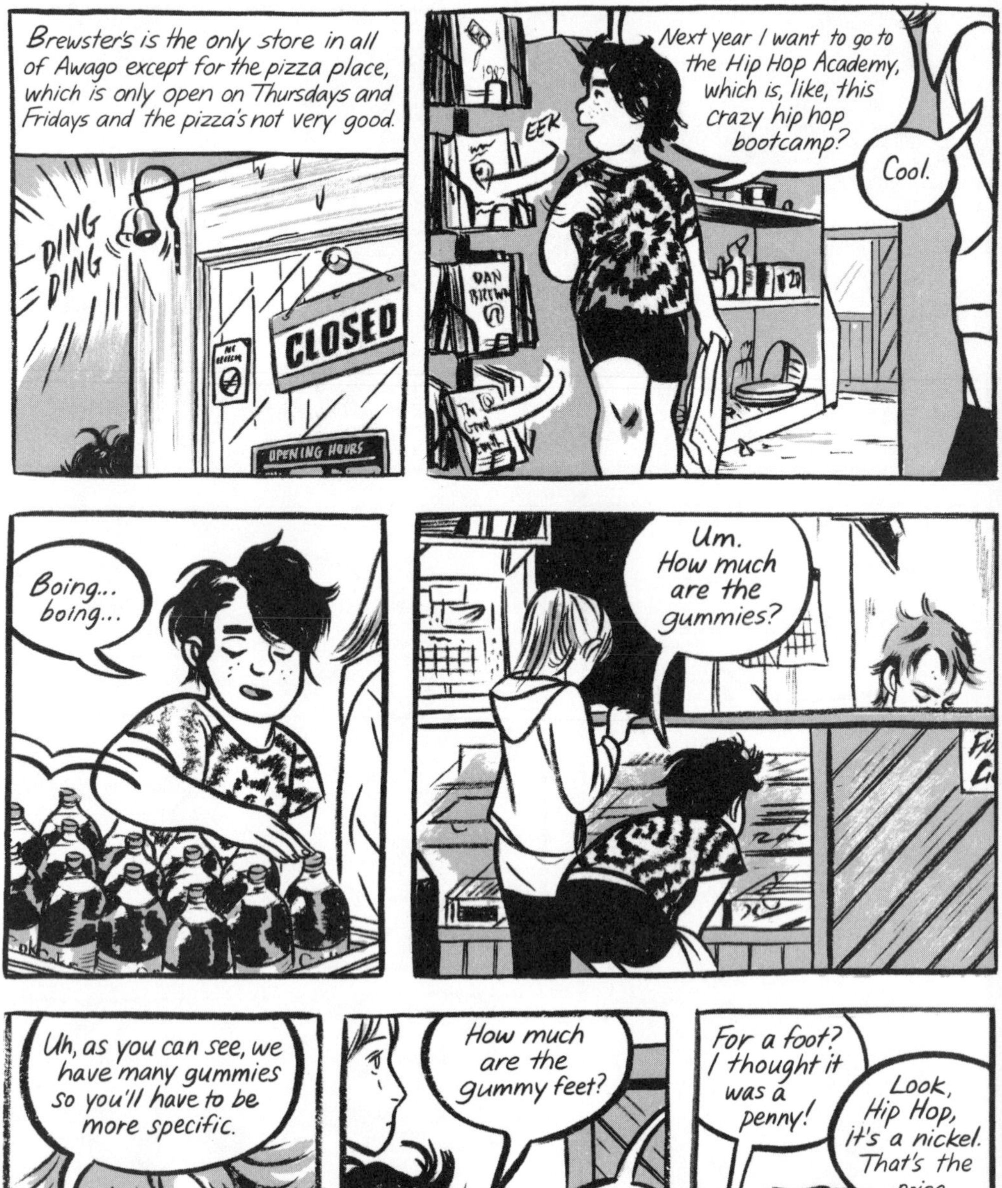
Brewster's is the only store in all of Awago except for the pizza place, which is only open on Thursdays and Fridays and the pizza's not very good.
DING DING
CLOSED
OPENING HOURS
EEK
Next year I want to go to the Hip Hop Academy, which is, like, this crazy hip hop bootcamp?
Cool.
Boing... boing...
Um. How much are the gummies?
Uh, as you can see, we have many gummies so you'll have to be more specific.
How much are the gummy feet?
Five cents.
For a foot? I thought it was a penny!
Look, Hip Hop, it's a nickel. That's the price.

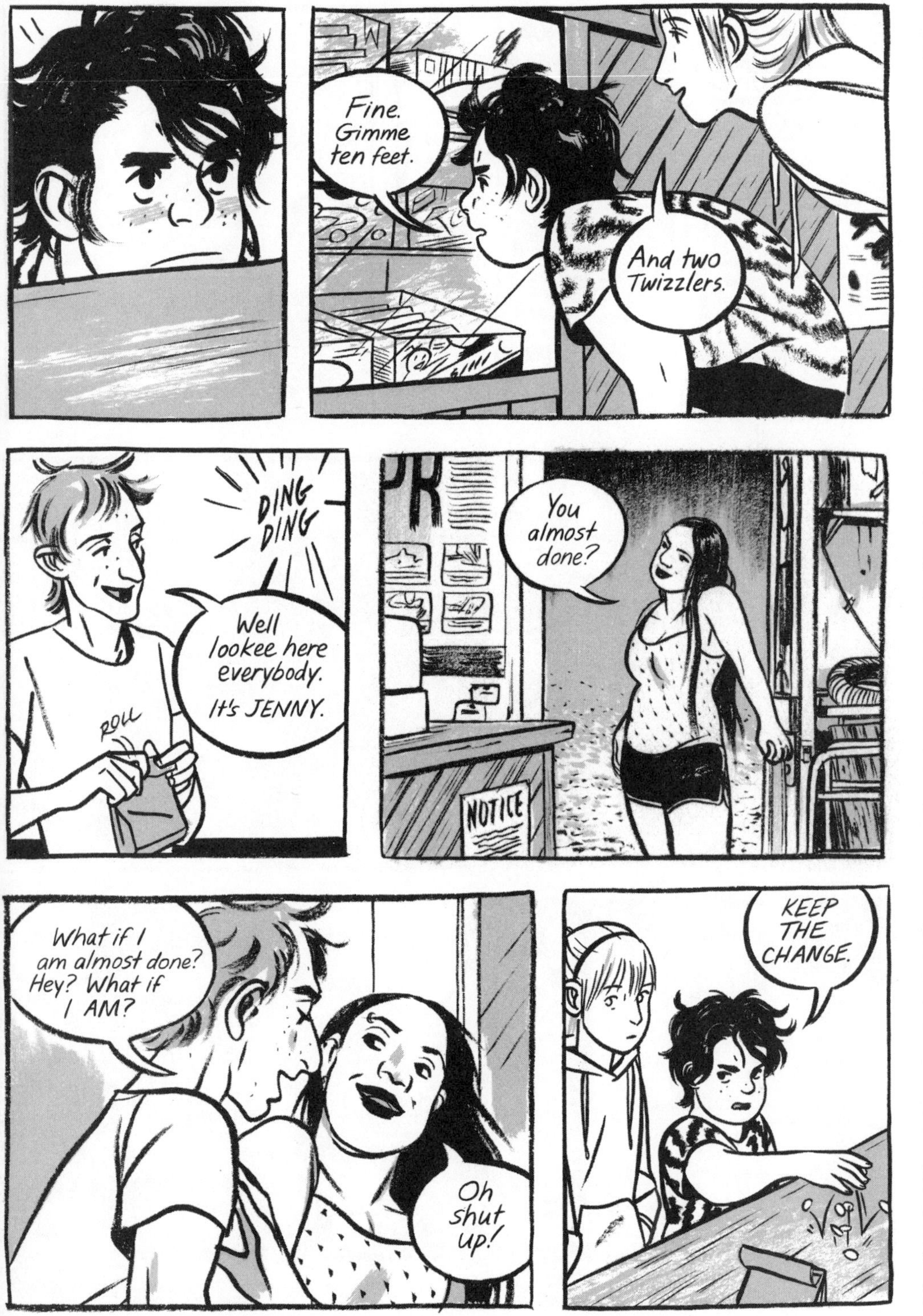
Fine. Gimme ten feet.
And two Twizzlers.
DING DING
Well lookee here everybody. It's JENNY.
ROLL
You almost done?
NOTICE
What if I am almost done? Hey? What if I AM?
Oh shut up!
KEEP THE CHANGE.

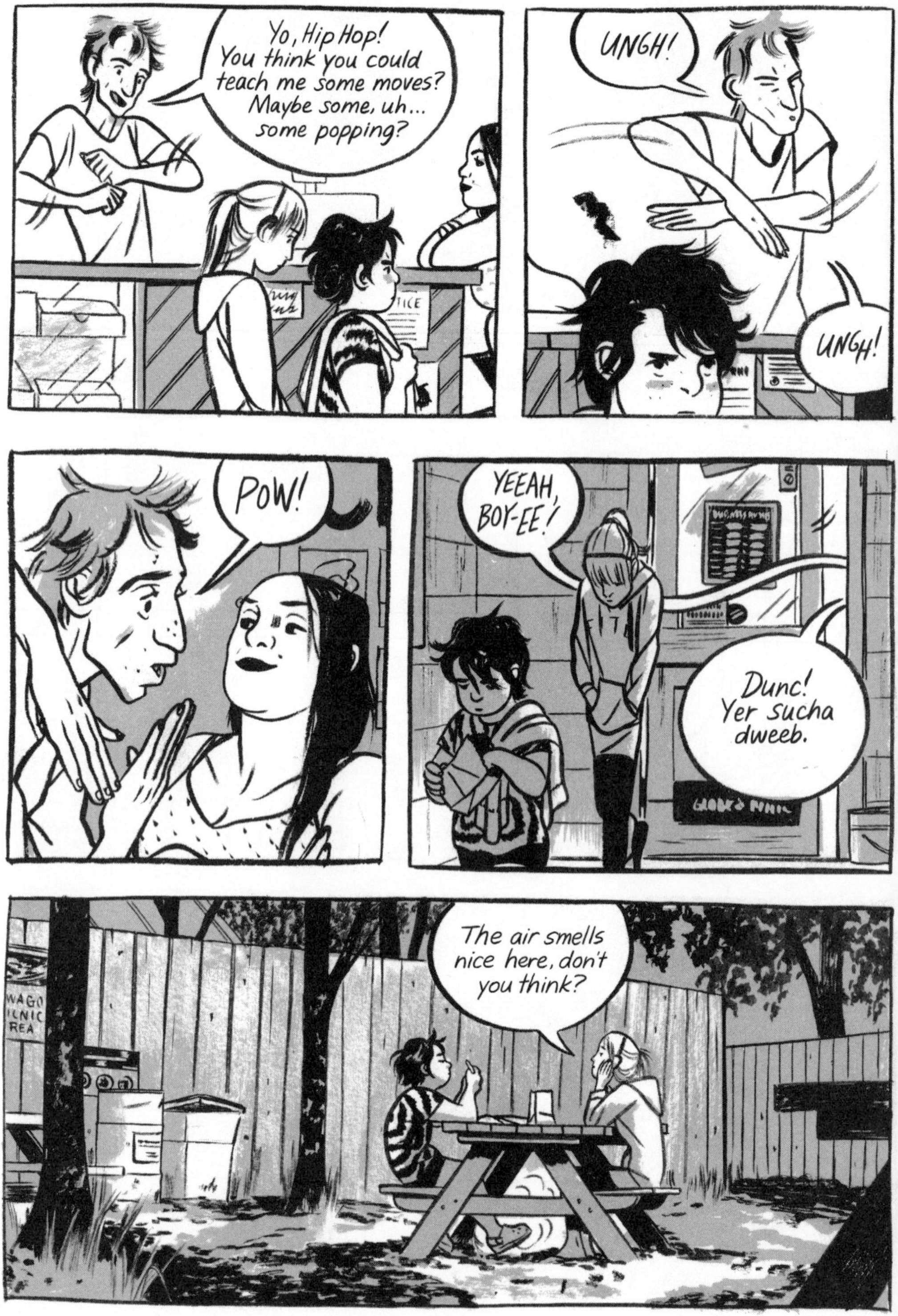
Yo, Hip Hop! You think you could teach me some moves? Maybe some, uh... some popping?
UNGH!
UNGH!
POW!
YEEAH, BOY-EE!
Dunc! Yer sucha dweeb.
The air smells nice here, don't you think?

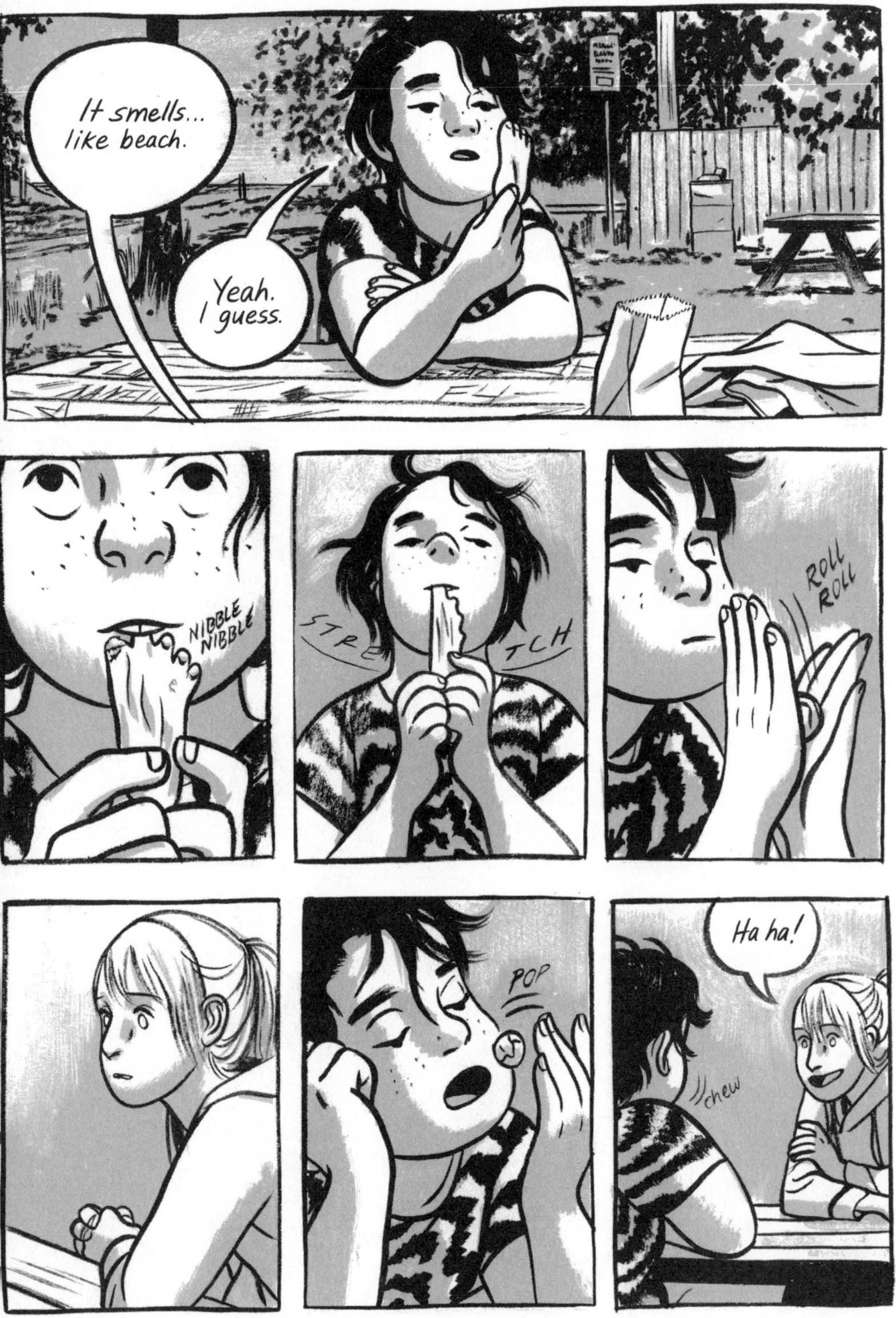
It smells... like beach.
Yeah. I guess.
NIBBLE NIBBLE
STRETCH
ROLL ROLL
POP
chew
Ha ha!

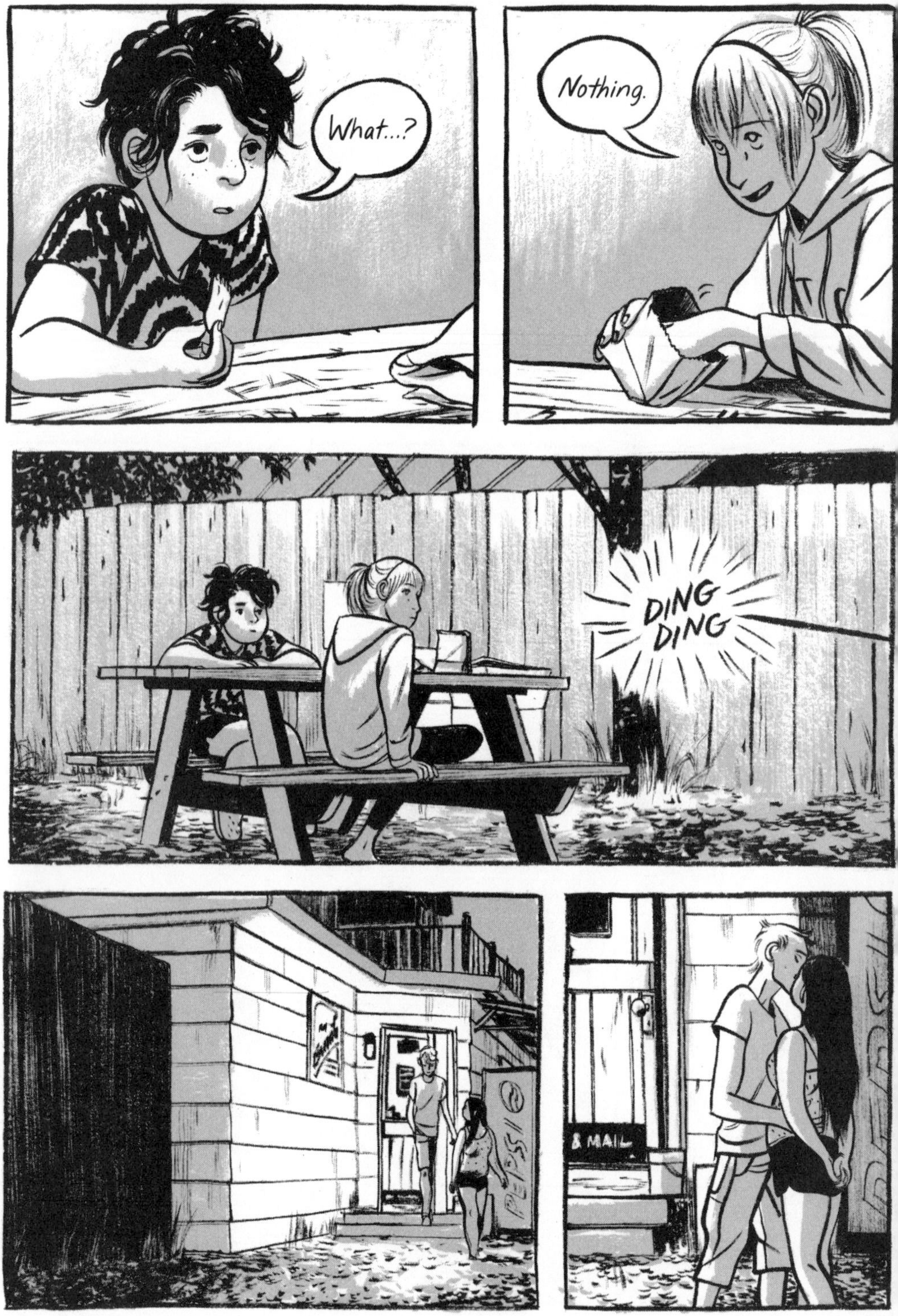
What...?
Nothing.
DING DING
& MAIL

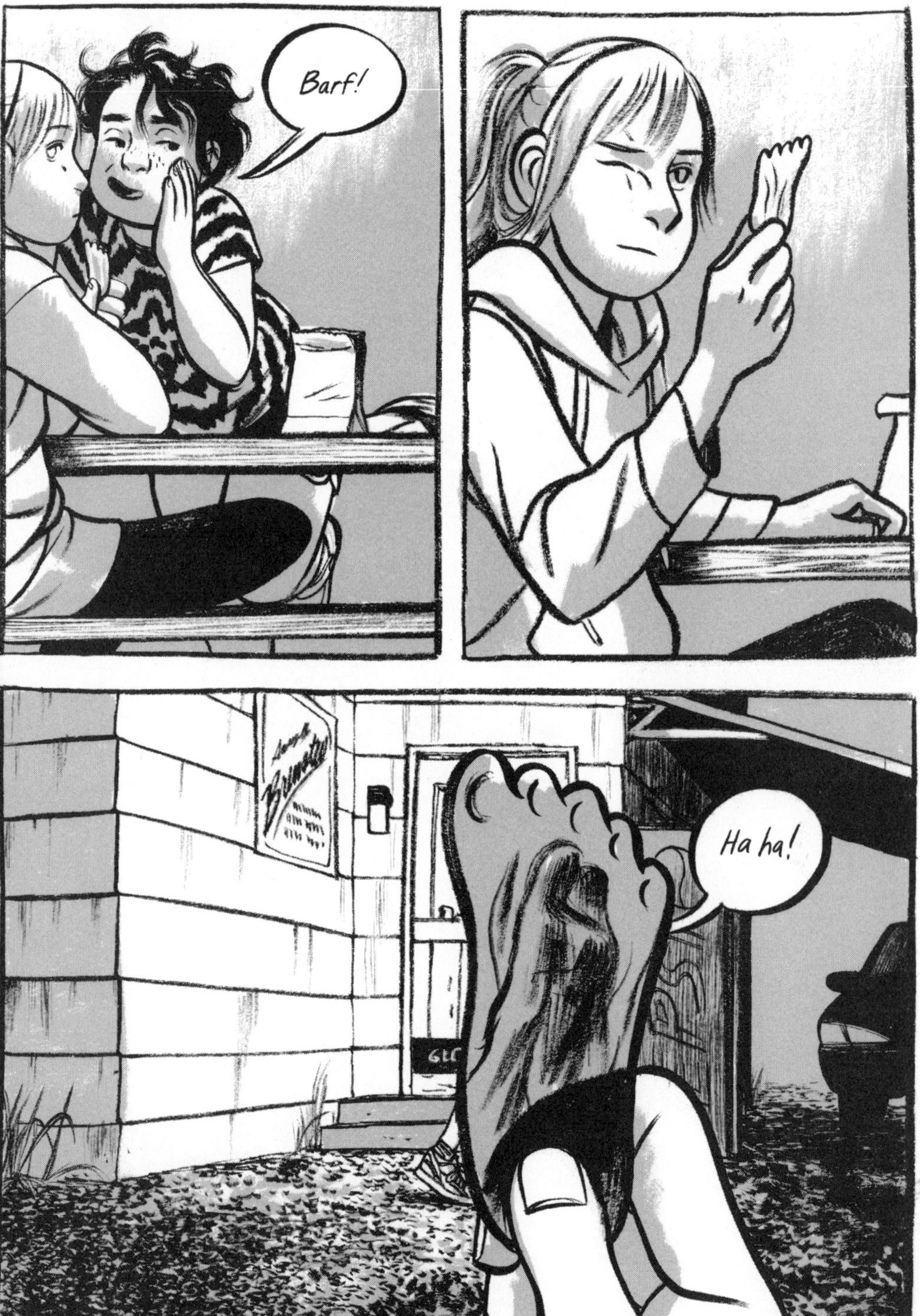
Barf!
Ha ha!

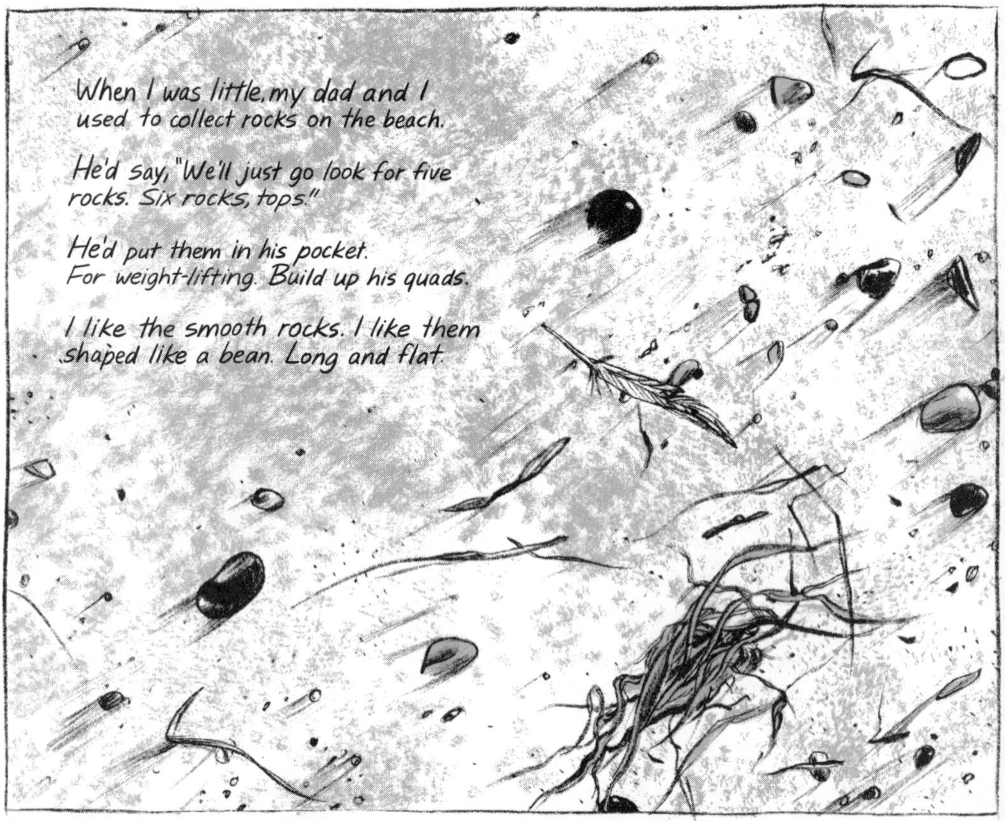
When I was little, my dad and I used to collect rocks on the beach.
He'd say, "We'll just go look for five rocks. Six rocks, tops."
He'd put them in his pocket. For weight-lifting. Build up his quads.
I like the smooth rocks. I like them shaped like a bean. Long and flat.

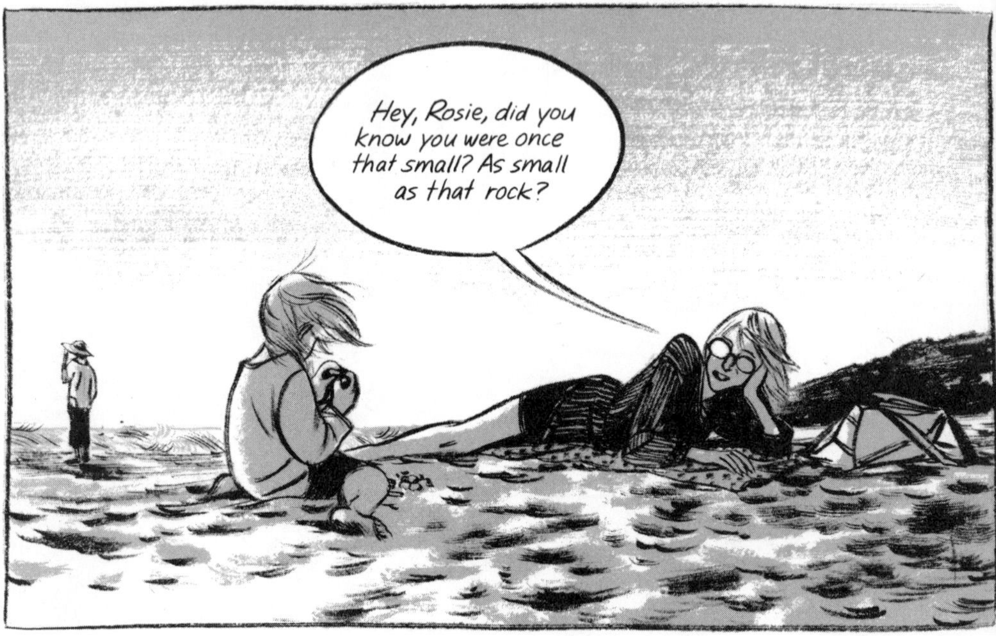
Hey, Rosie, did you know you were once that small? As small as that rock?

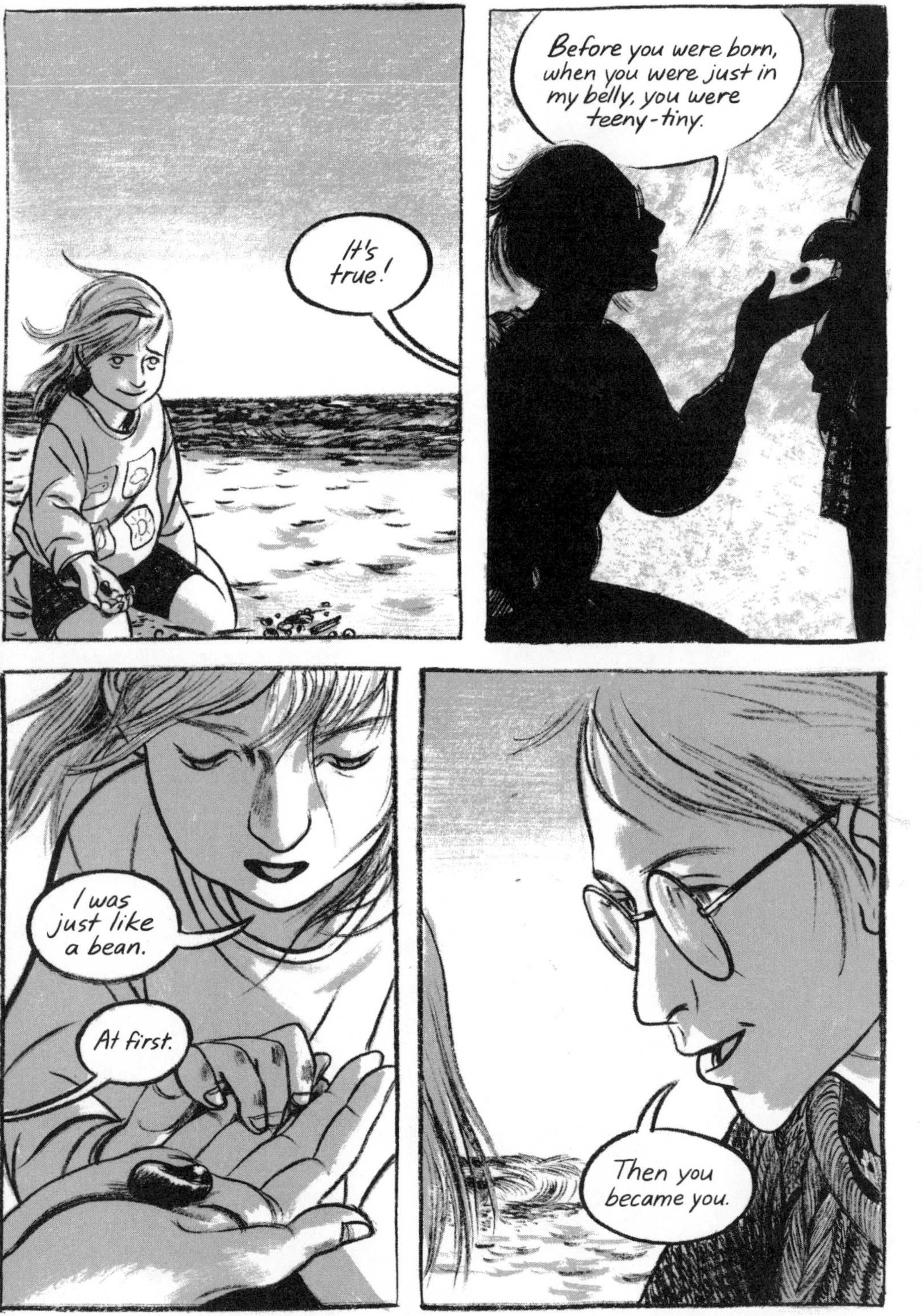
It's true!
Before you were born, when you were just in my belly, you were teeny-tiny.
I was just like a bean.
At first.
Then you became you.

The first time I ever saw
a milkweed was on the beach
at Awago. I thought they
were magic pods.

I thought that if we
ate them, the fluff would
make us grow wings.

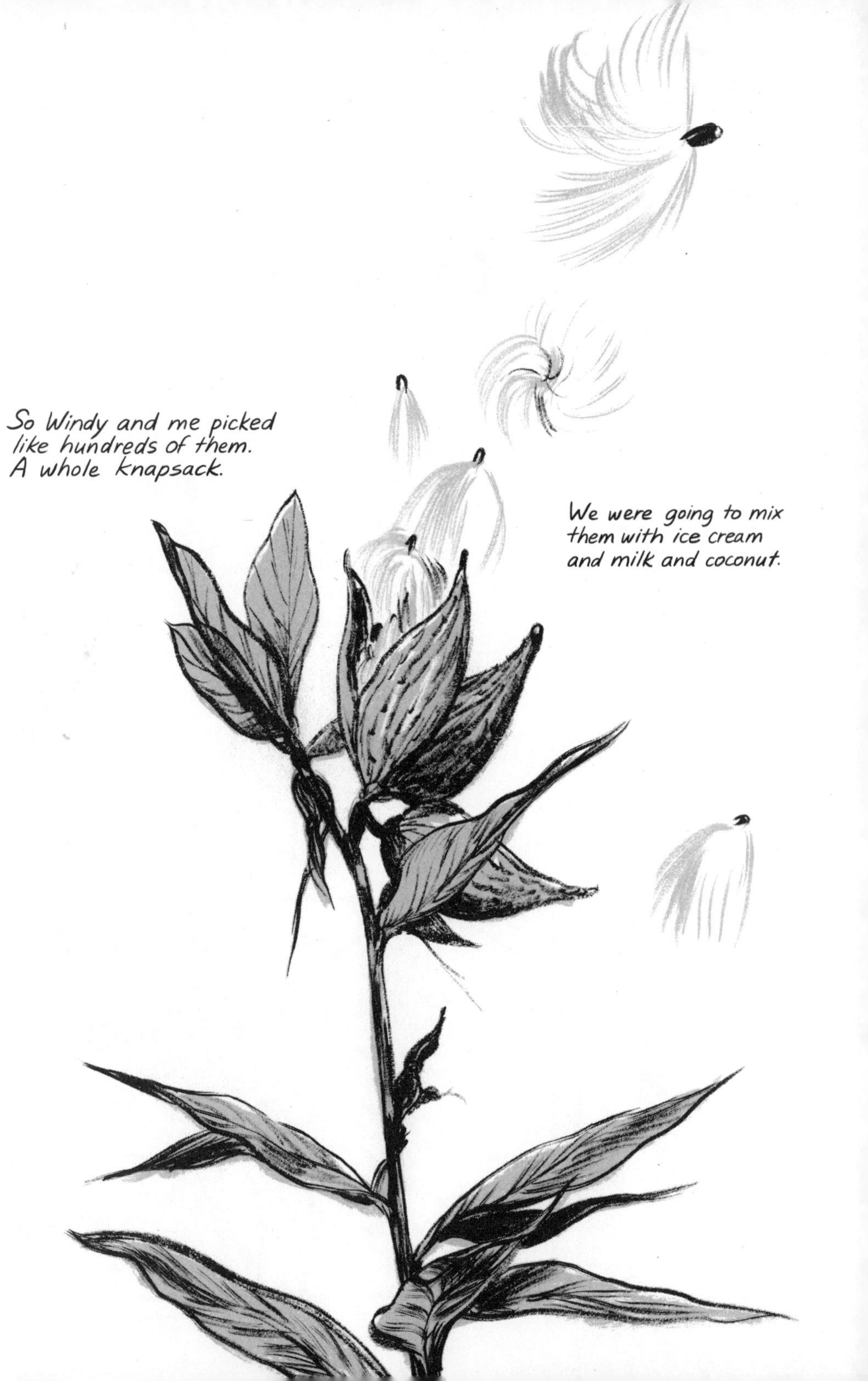
So Windy and me picked like hundreds of them. A whole knapsack.
We were going to mix them with ice cream and milk and coconut.

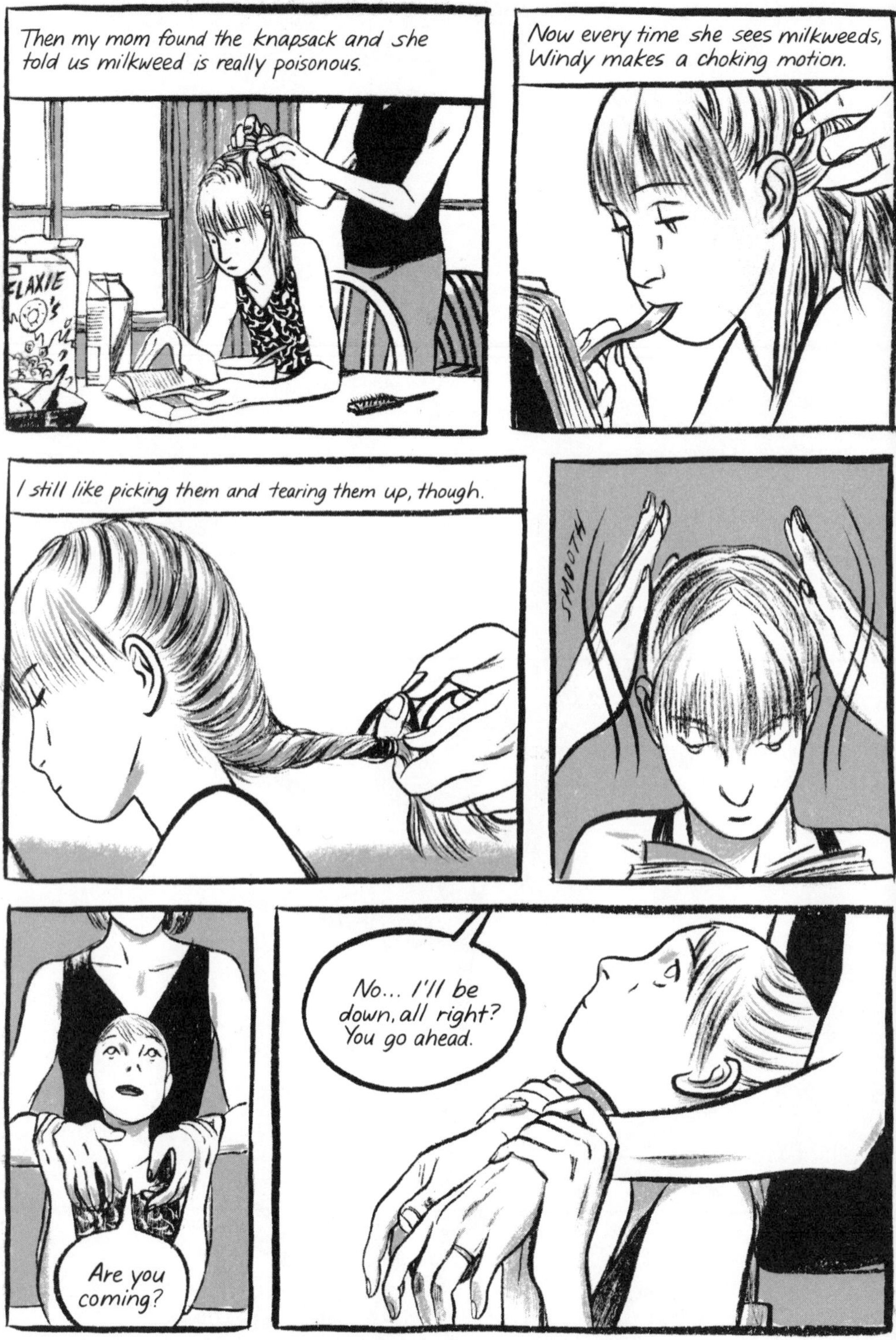
Then my mom found the knapsack and she told us milkweed is really poisonous.
FLAXIE O's
Now every time she sees milkweeds, Windy makes a choking motion.
I still like picking them and tearing them up, though.
SMOOTH
Are you coming?
No... I'll be down, all right? You go ahead.

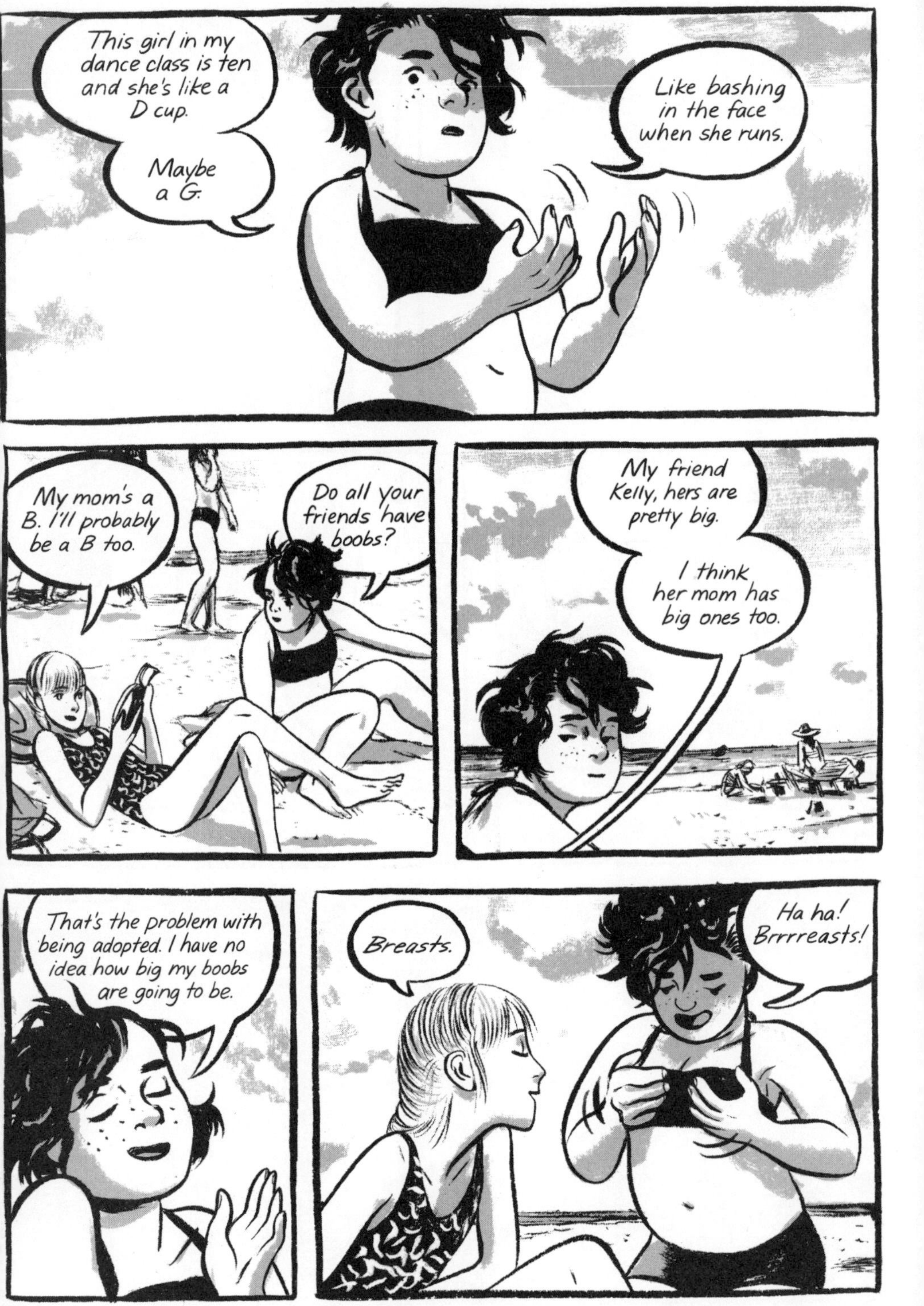
This girl in my dance class is ten and she's like a D cup.
Maybe a G.
Like bashing in the face when she runs.
My mom's a B. I'll probably be a B too.
Do all your friends have boobs?
My friend Kelly, hers are pretty big.
I think her mom has big ones too.
That's the problem with being adopted. I have no idea how big my boobs are going to be.
Breasts.
Ha ha! Brrrreasts!

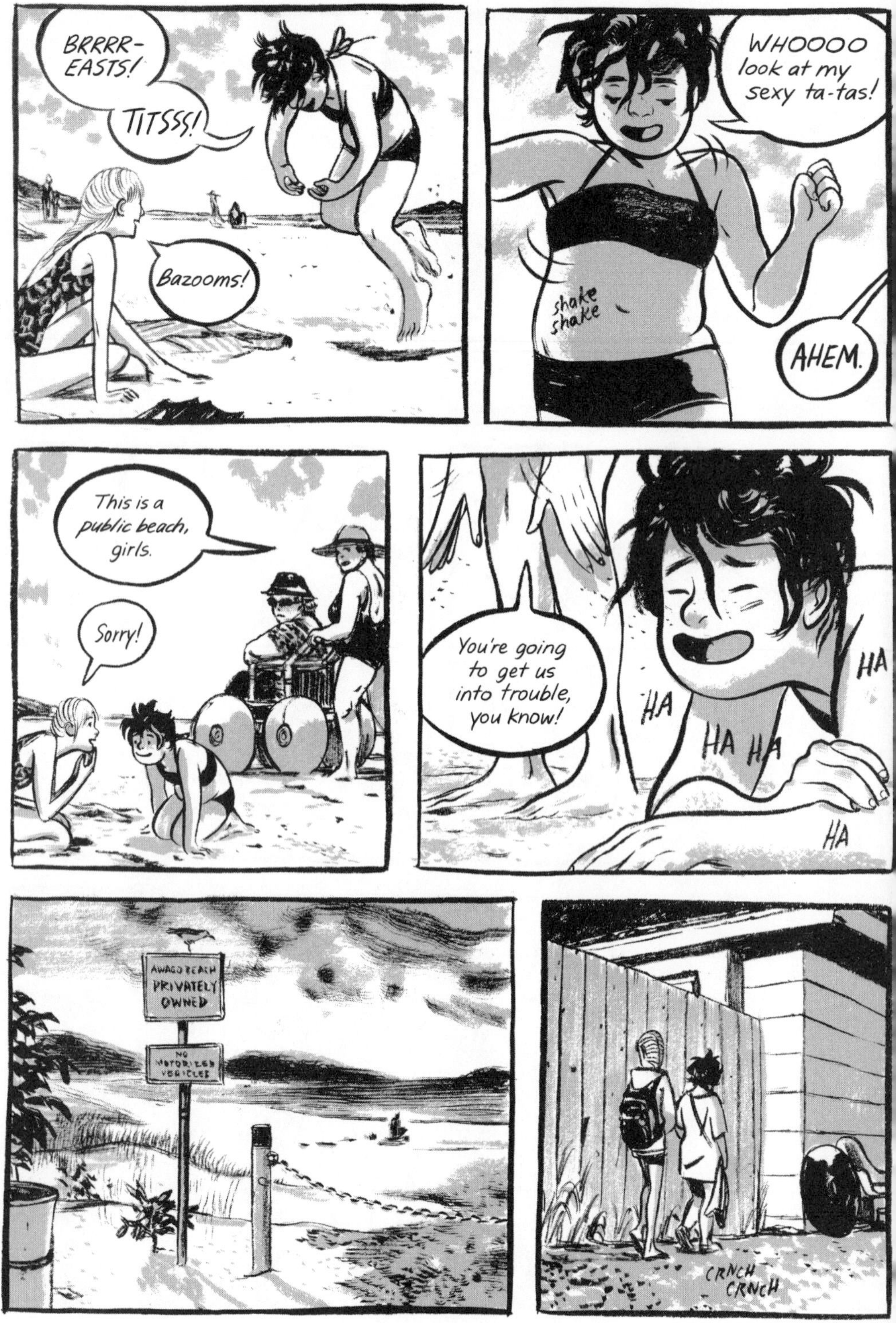
BRRRR-EASTS!
TITSSS!
Bazooms!
WHOOOO look at my sexy ta-tas!
shake shake
AHEM.
This is a public beach, girls.
Sorry!
You're going to get us into trouble, you know!
HA
HA
HA HA
HA
AWAGO BEACH PRIVATELY OWNED
NO MOTORIZED VEHICLES
CRNCH CRNCH

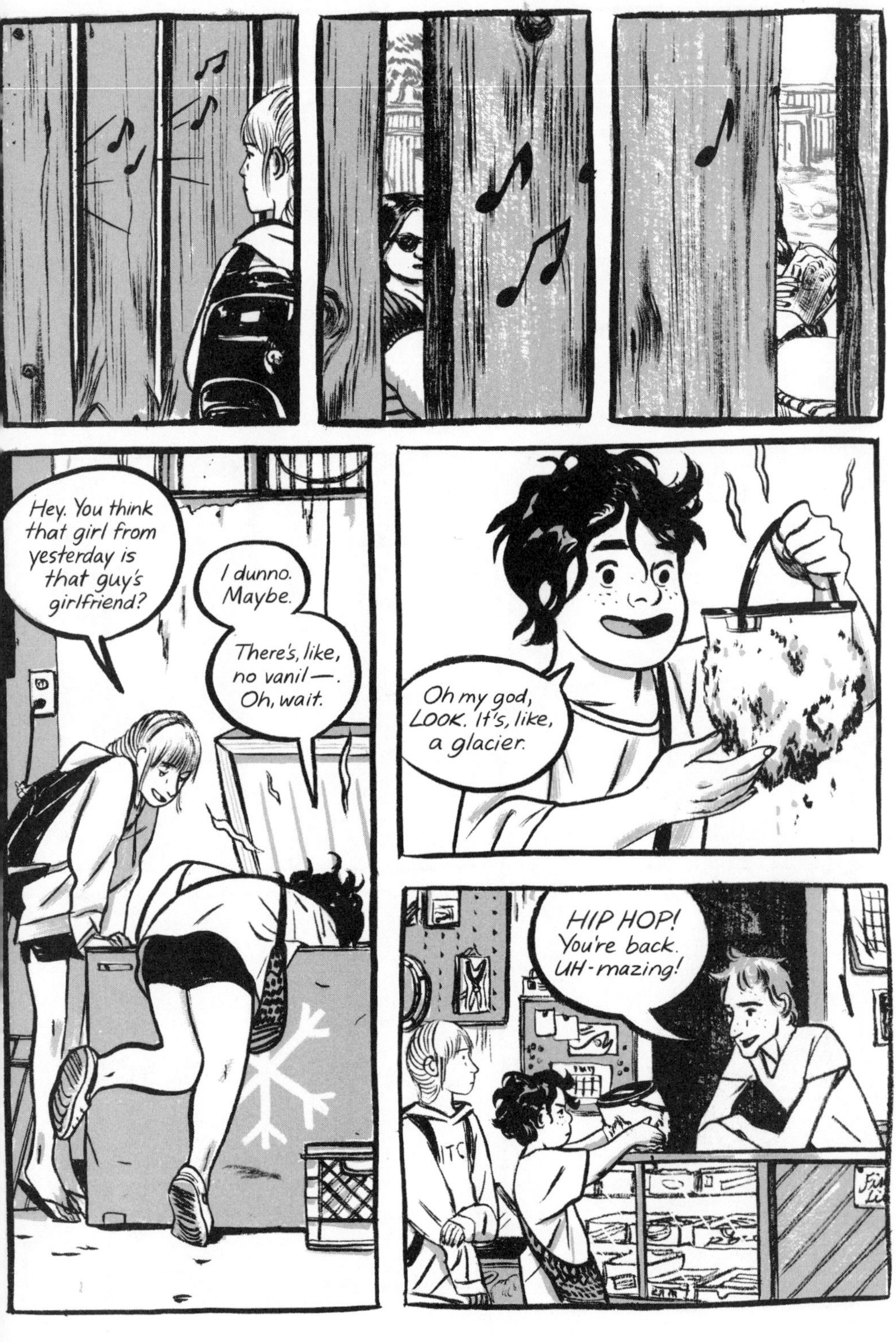

Hey. You think that girl from yesterday is that guy's girlfriend?
I dunno. Maybe.
There's, like, no vanil—. Oh, wait.
Oh my god, LOOK. It's, like, a glacier.
HIP HOP! You're back. UH-mazing!

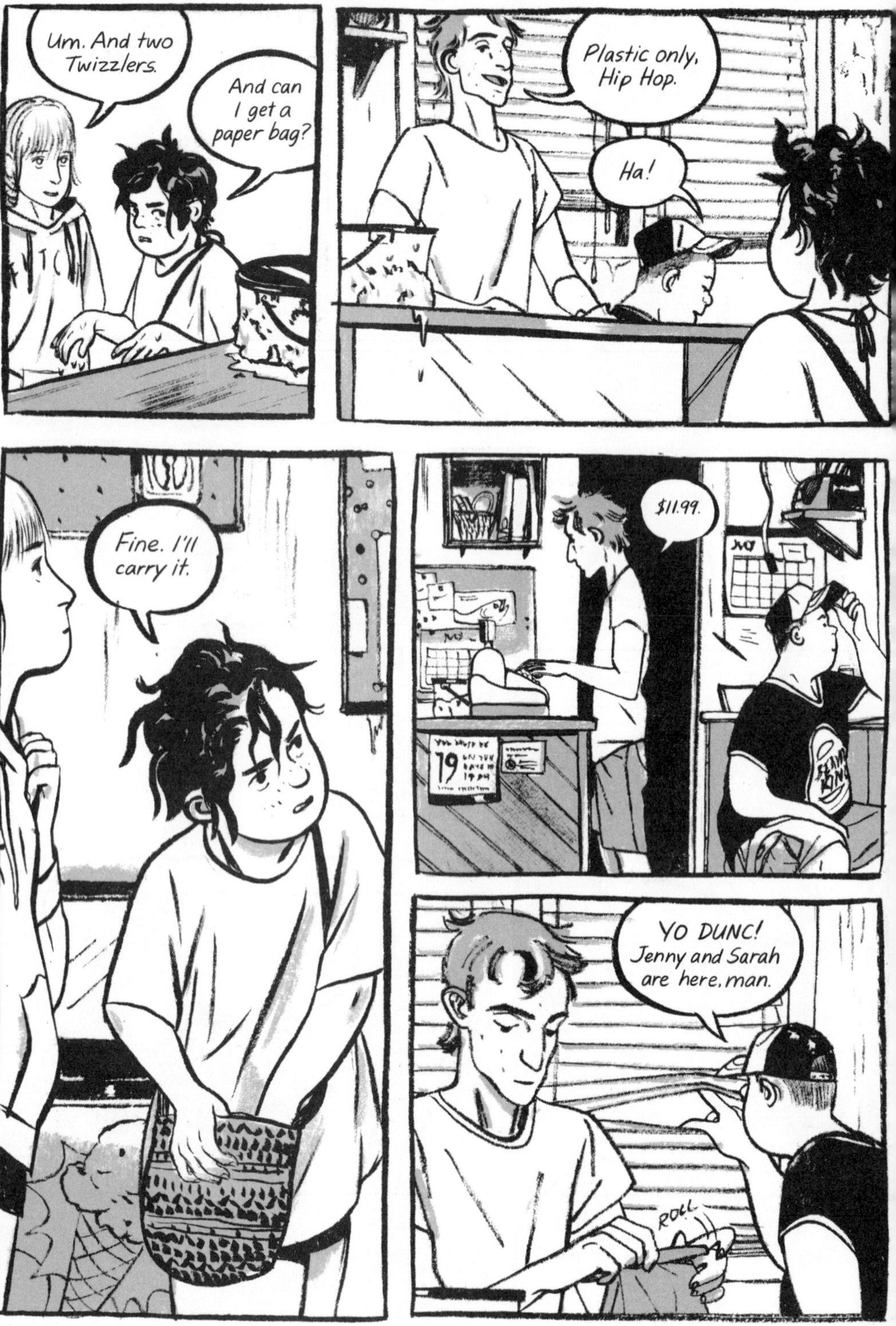
Um. And two Twizzlers.
And can I get a paper bag?
Plastic only, Hip Hop.
Ha!
Fine. I'll carry it.
$11.99.
YO DUNC! Jenny and Sarah are here, man.
ROLL

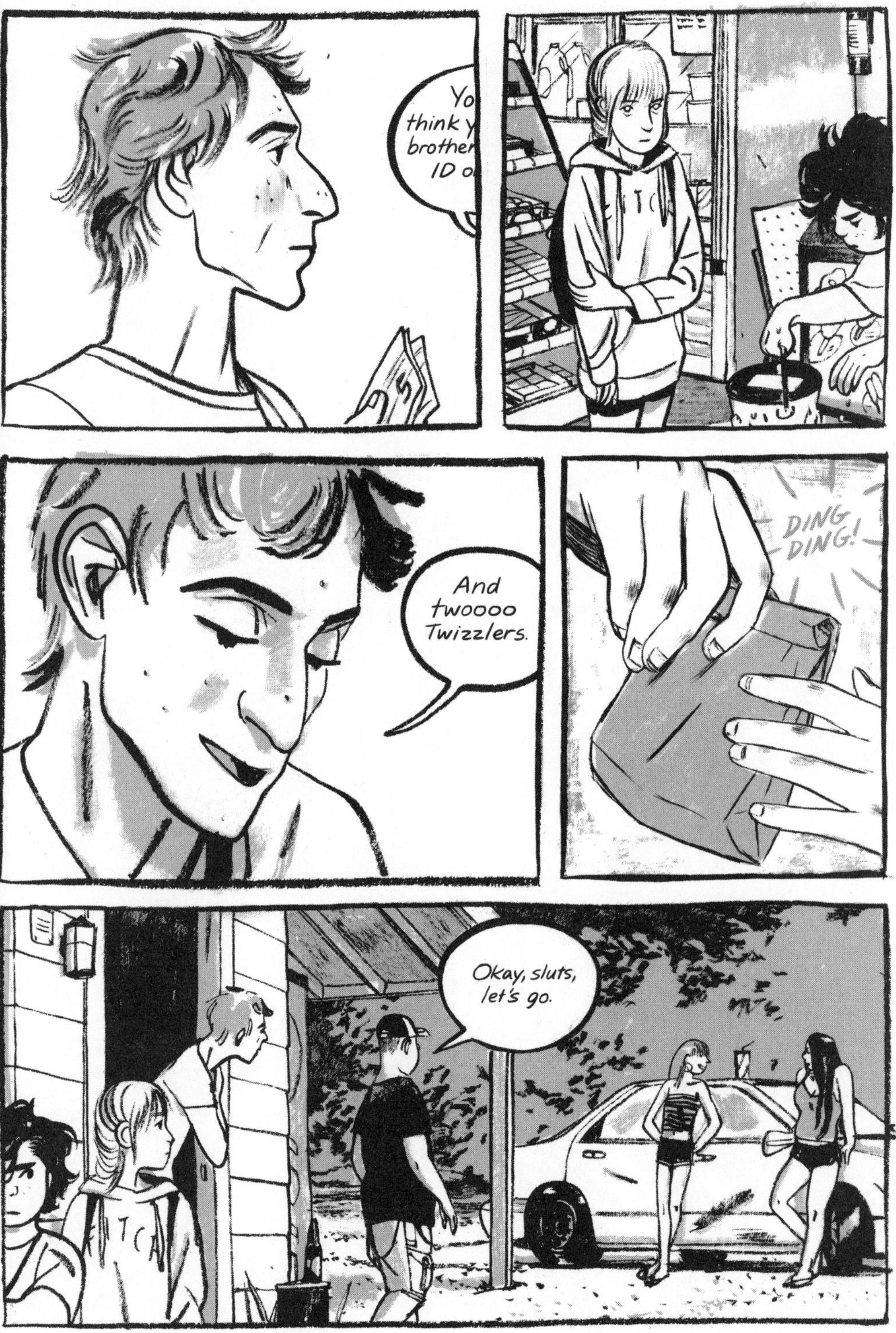
Yo
think y
brother
ID o
And twoooo Twizzlers.
DING DING!
Okay, sluts, let's go.

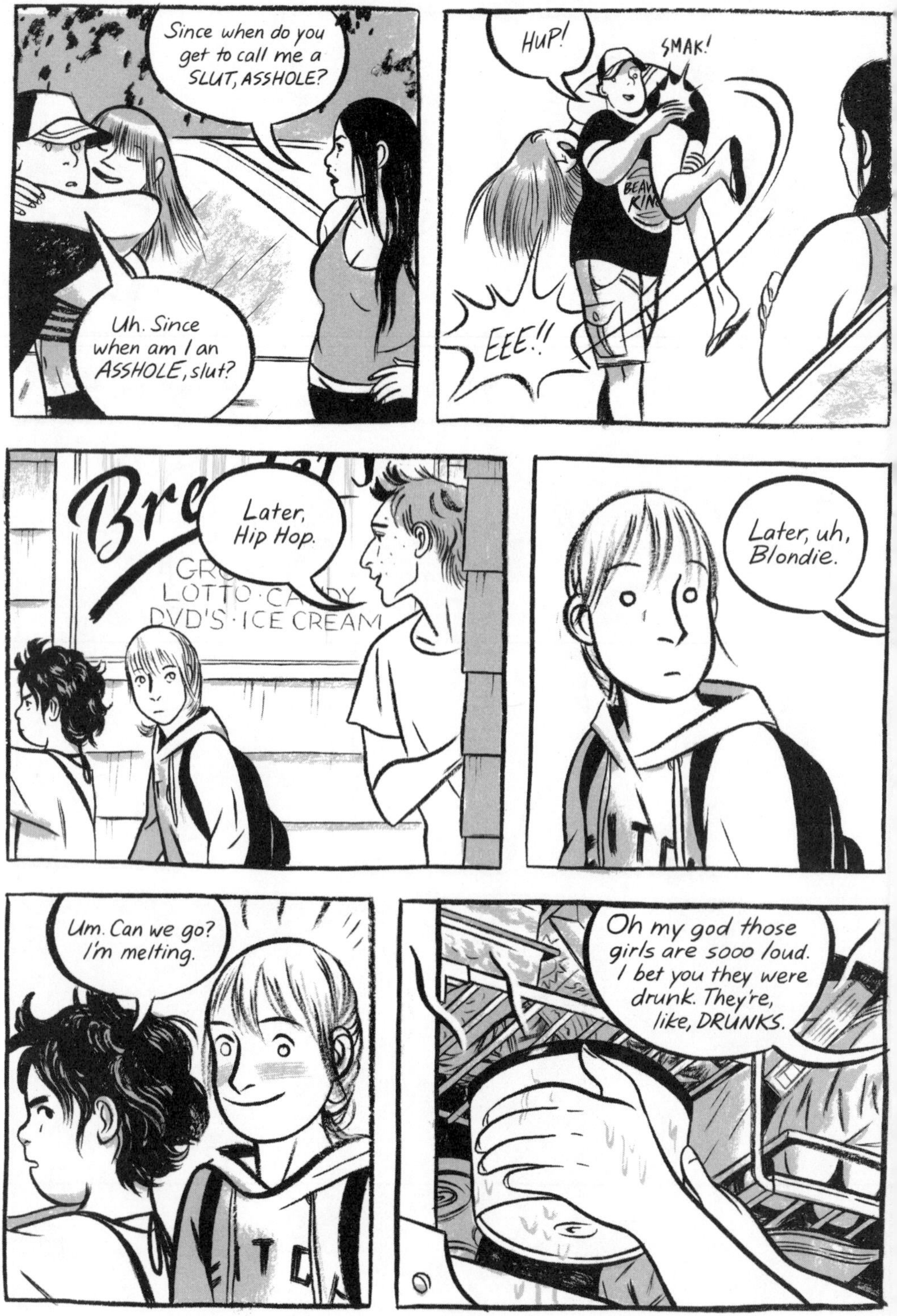
Since when do you get to call me a SLUT, ASSHOLE?
Uh. Since when am I an ASSHOLE, slut?
HUP!
SMAK!
EEE!!
BEAV KING
GRO
LOTTO · CANDY
DVD'S · ICE CREAM
Later, Hip Hop.
Later, uh, Blondie.
Um. Can we go? I'm melting.
Oh my god those girls are sooo loud. I bet you they were drunk. They're, like, DRUNKS.

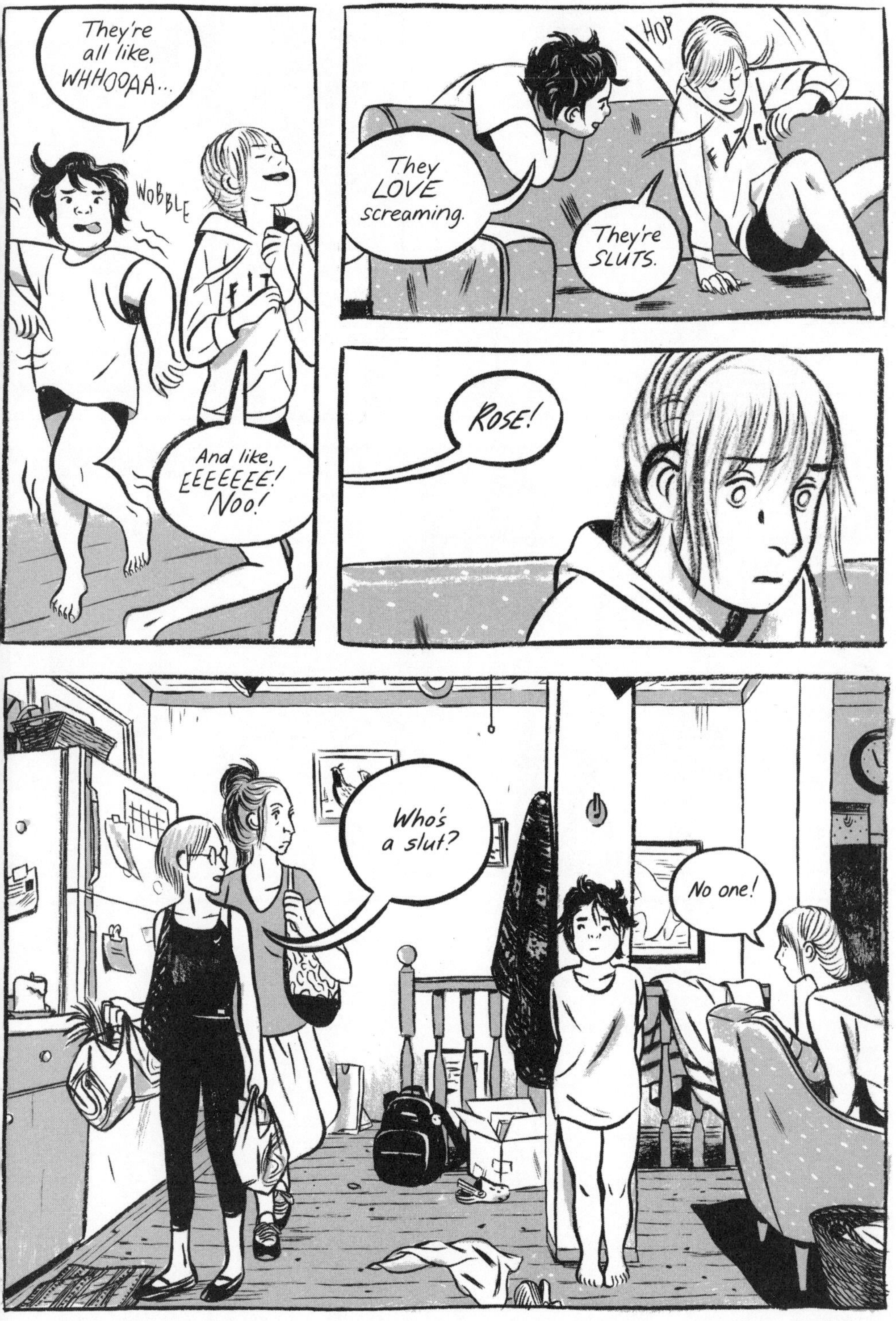
They're all like, WHHOOAA...
WOBBLE
And like, EEEEEEE! Noo!
HOP
They LOVE screaming.
They're SLUTS.
ROSE!
Who's a slut?
No one!

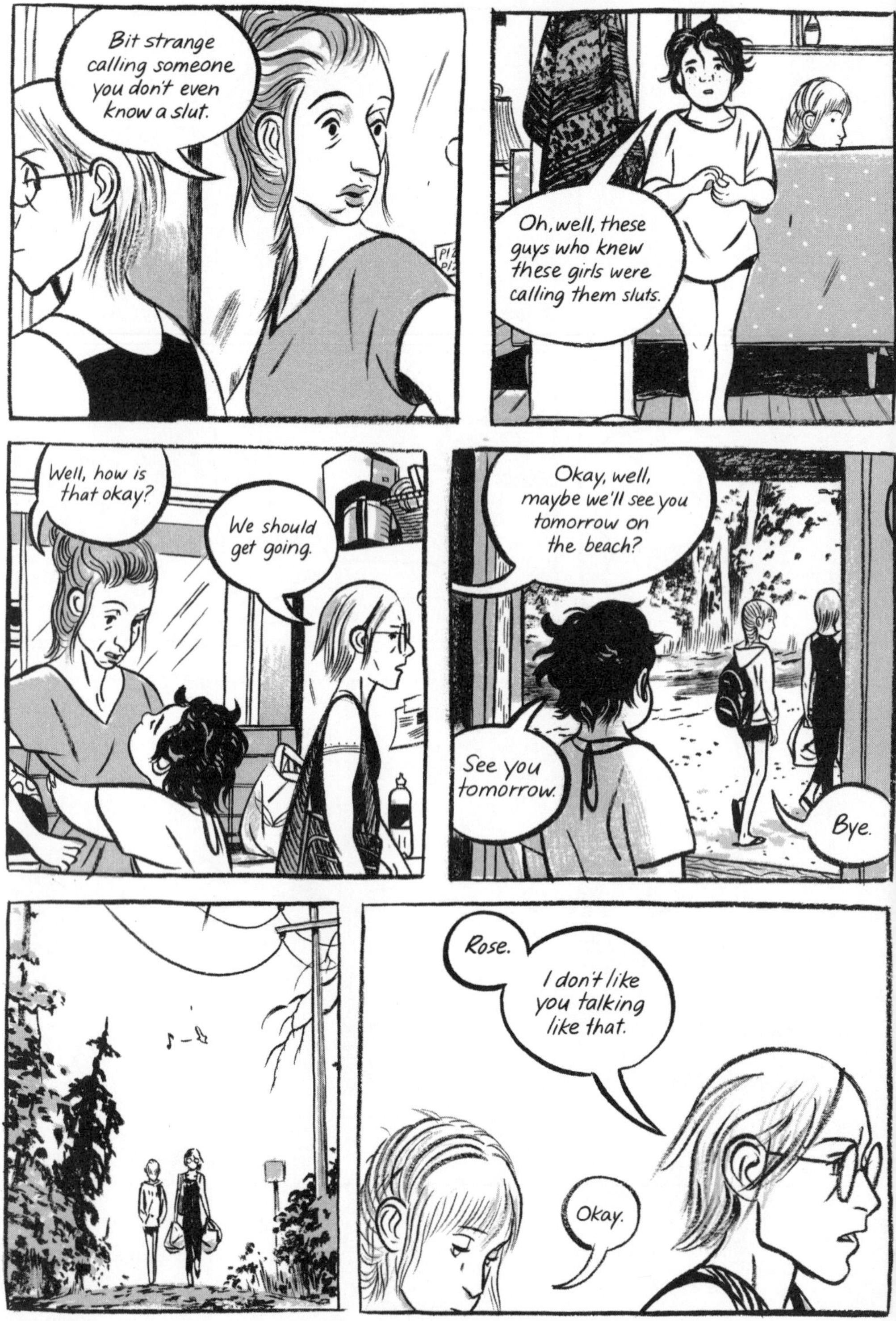
Bit strange calling someone you don't even know a slut.
Oh, well, these guys who knew these girls were calling them sluts.
Well, how is that okay?
We should get going.
Okay, well, maybe we'll see you tomorrow on the beach?
See you tomorrow.
Bye.
Rose.
I don't like you talking like that.
Okay.

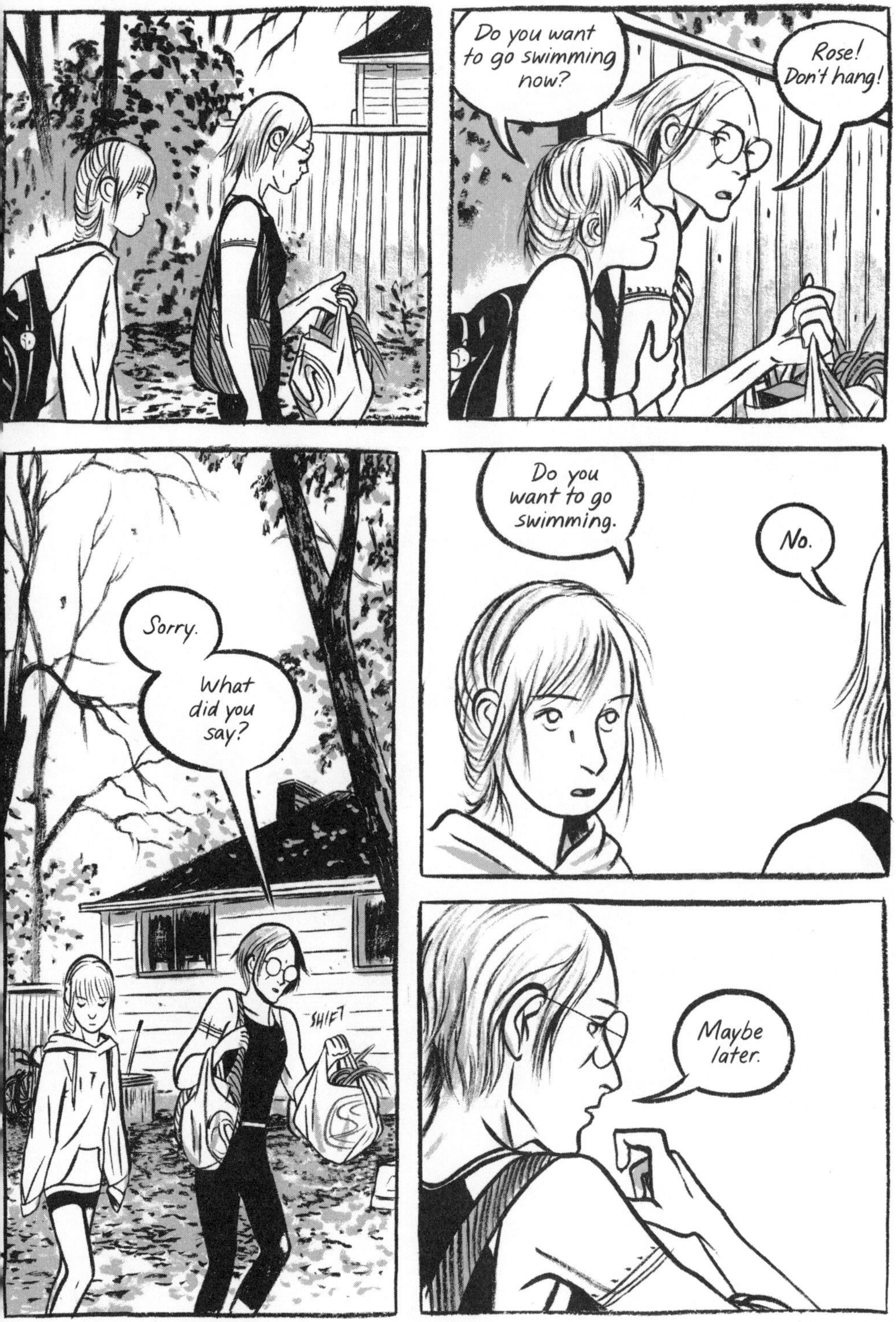
Do you want to go swimming now?
Rose! Don't hang!
Sorry.
What did you say?
SHIFT
Do you want to go swimming.
No.
Maybe later.

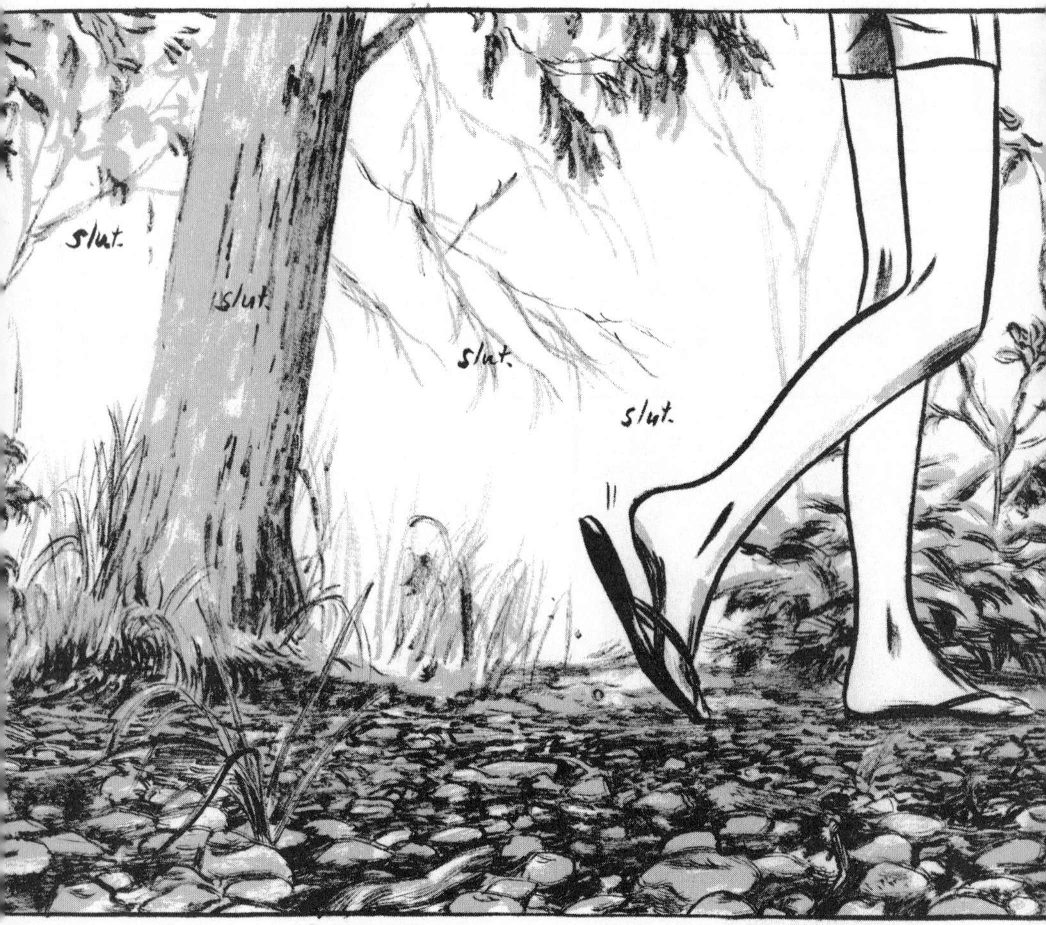
slut.
slut.
slut.
slut.

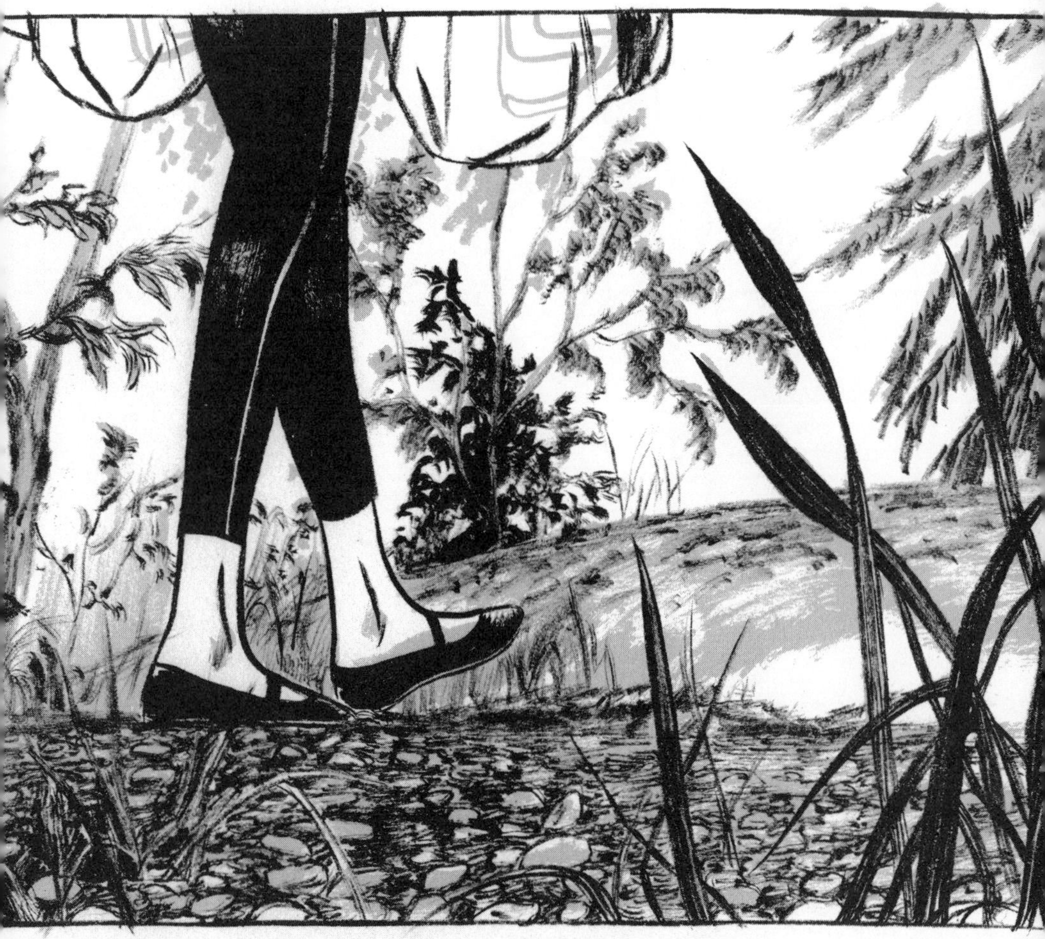

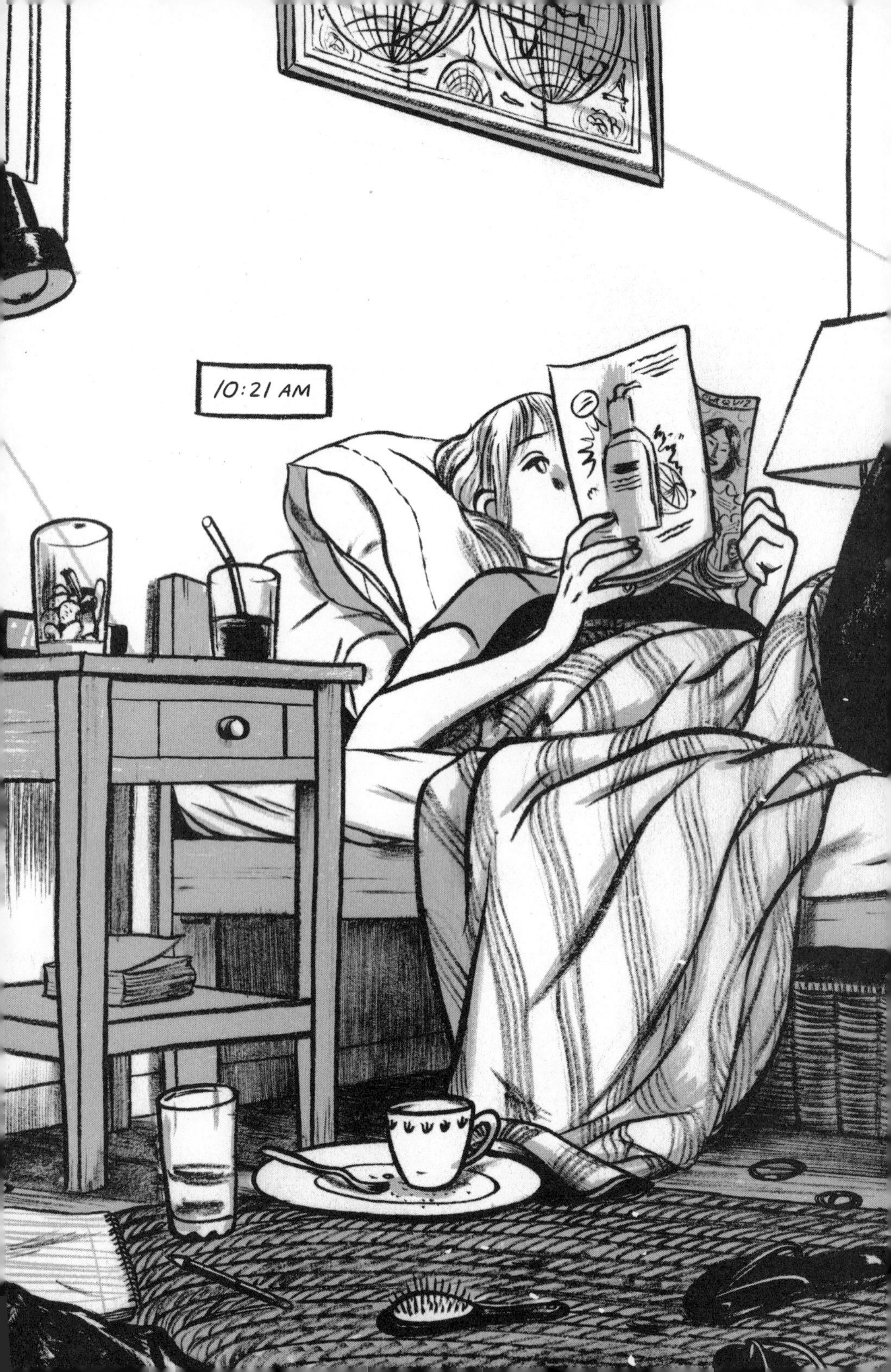
10:21 AM

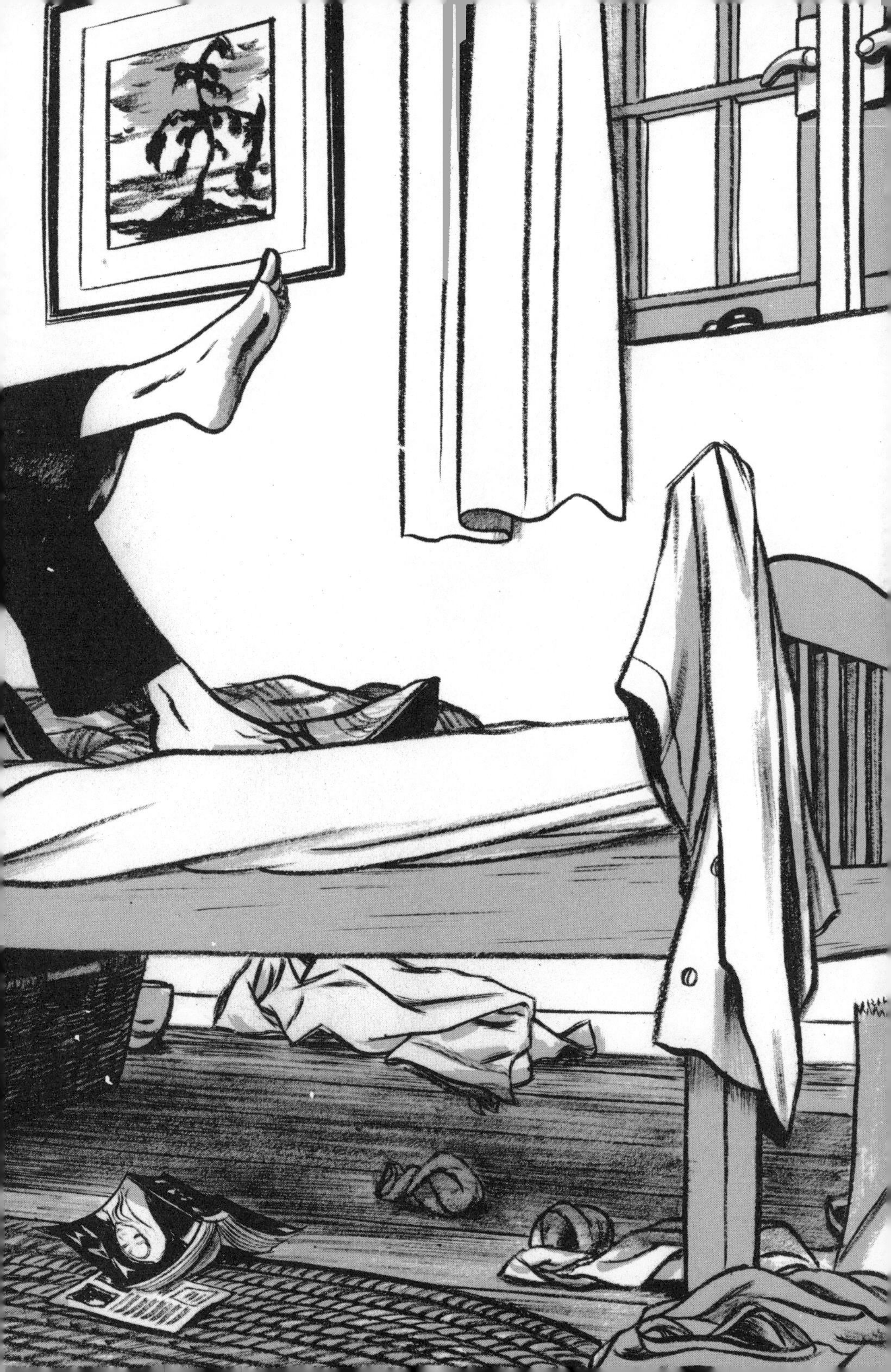

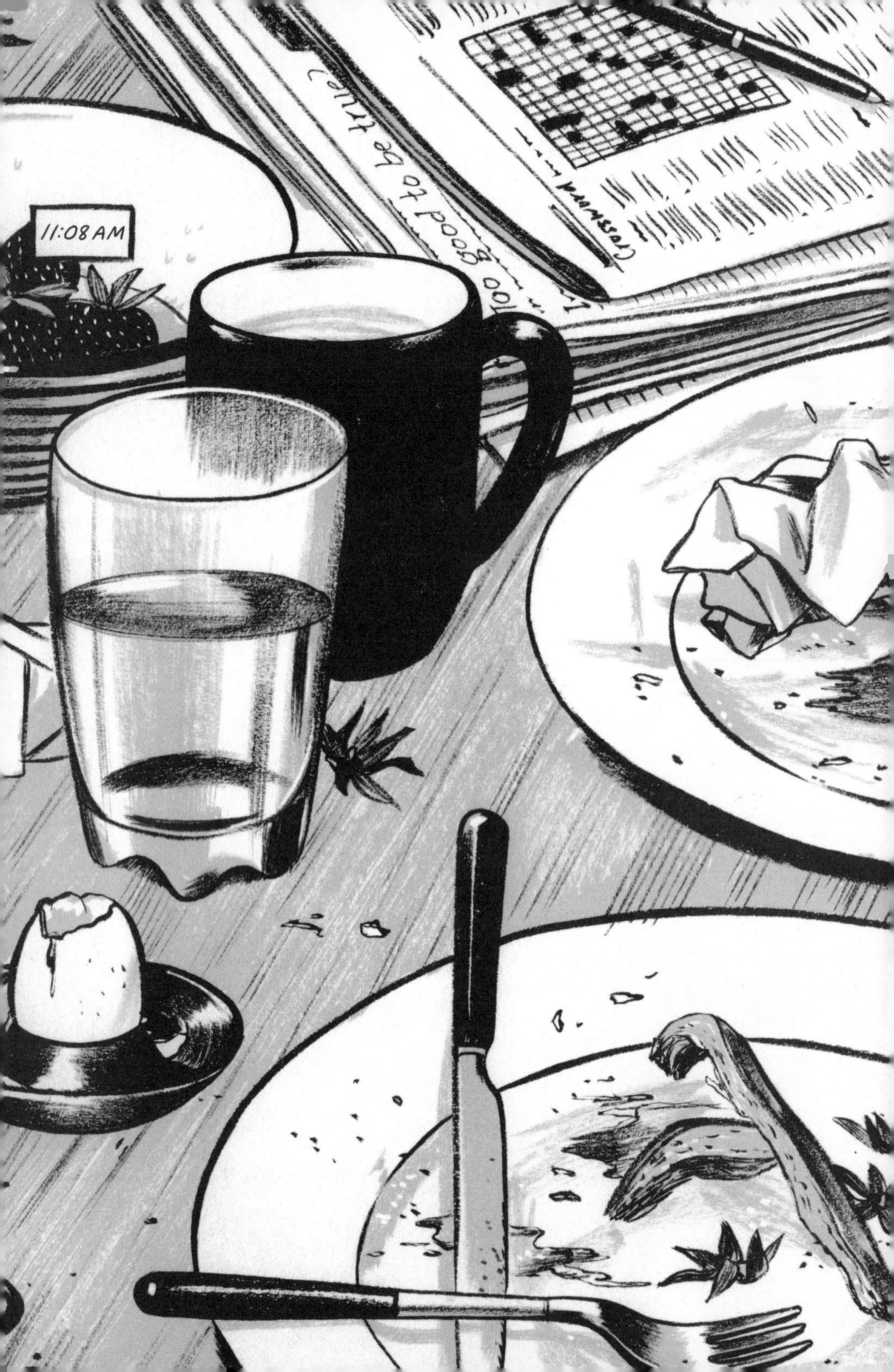

11:08 AM
Crossword

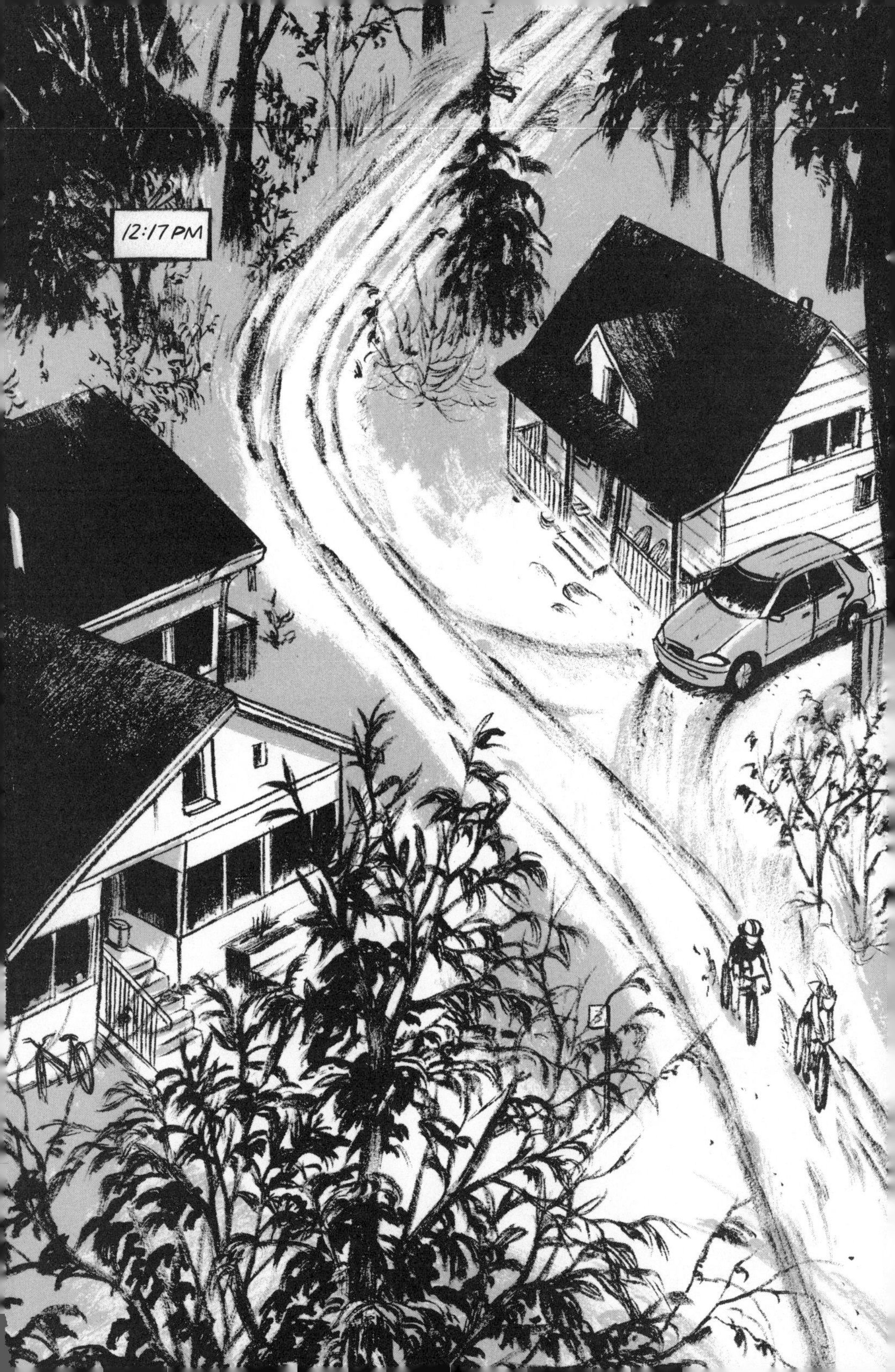
12:17 PM

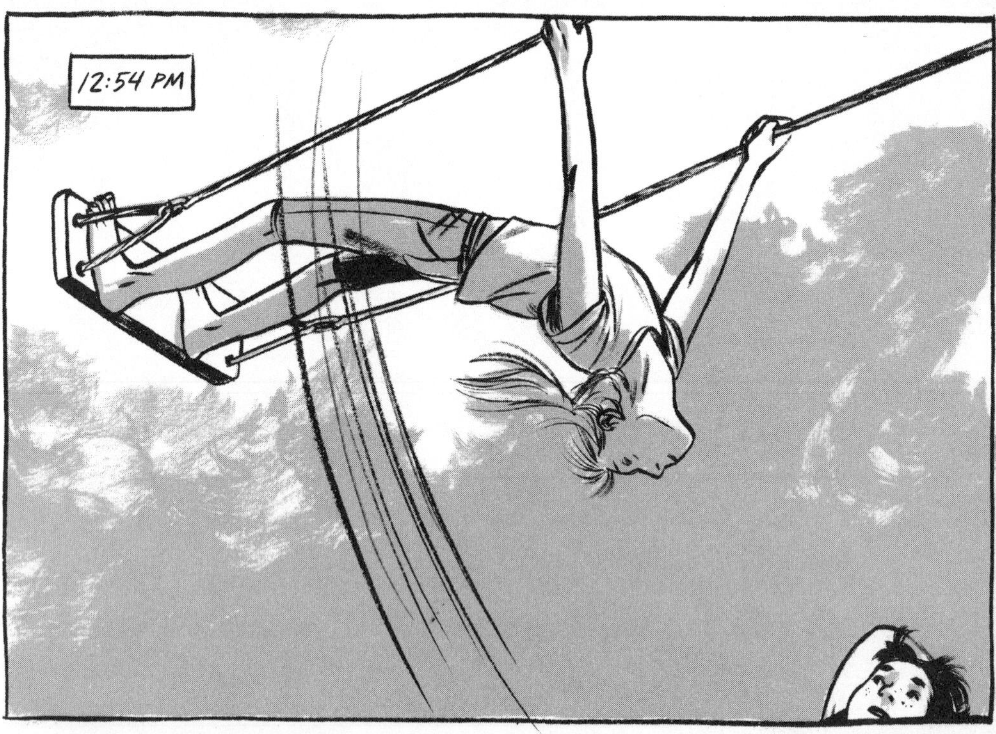
12:54 PM

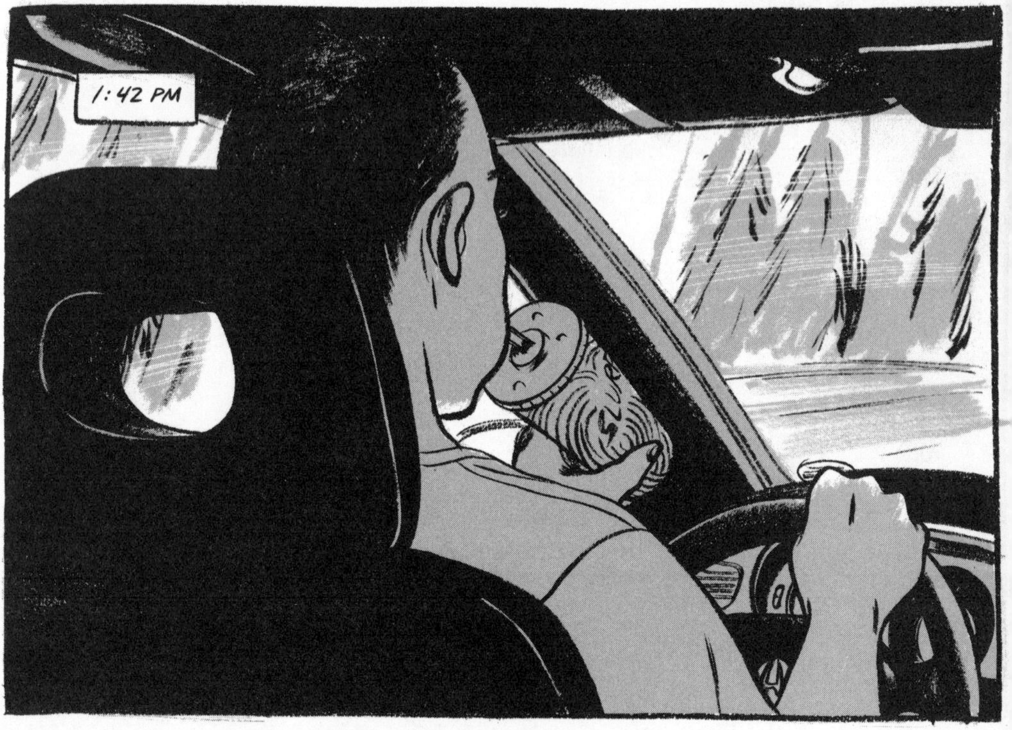
1:42 PM

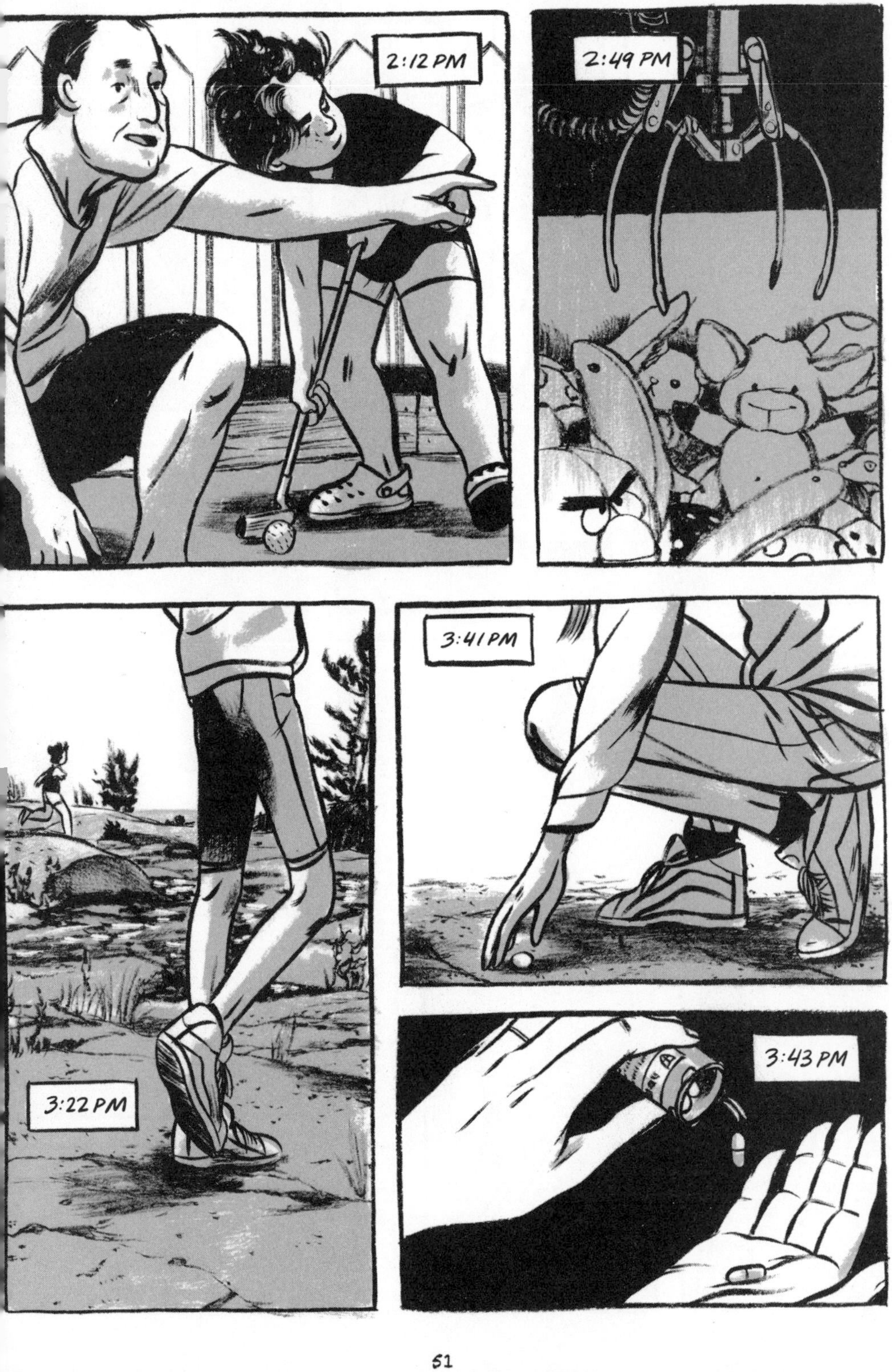
2:12 PM
2:49 PM
3:22 PM
3:41 PM
3:43 PM

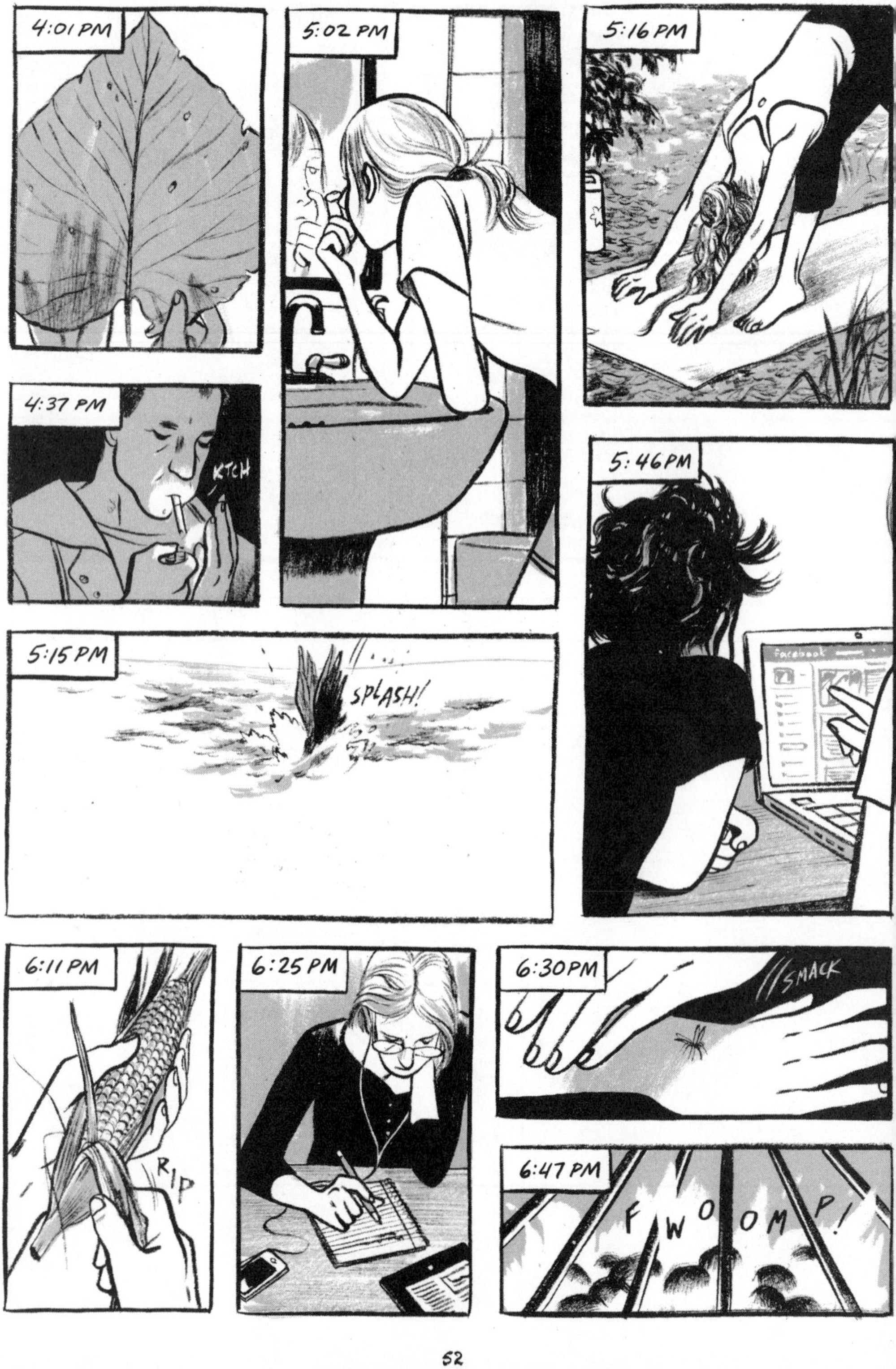
4:01 PM
5:02 PM
5:16 PM
4:37 PM
KTCH
5:46 PM
5:15 PM
SPLASH!
6:11 PM
RIP
6:25 PM
6:30 PM
SMACK
6:47 PM
FWOOMP!

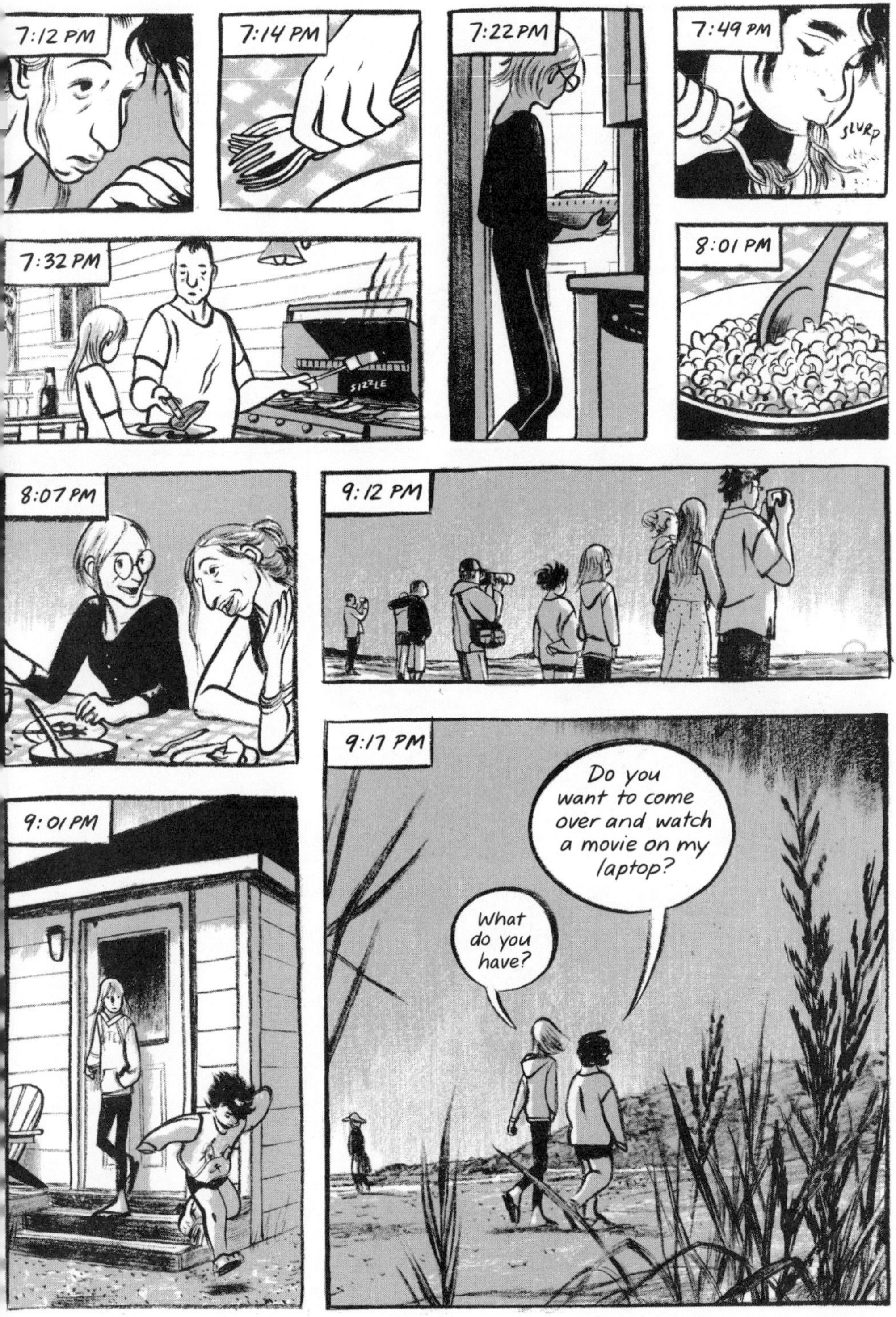
7:12 PM
7:14 PM
7:22 PM
7:49 PM
SLURP
7:32 PM
SIZZLE
8:01 PM
8:07 PM
9:12 PM
9:01 PM
9:17 PM
Do you want to come over and watch a movie on my laptop?
What do you have?

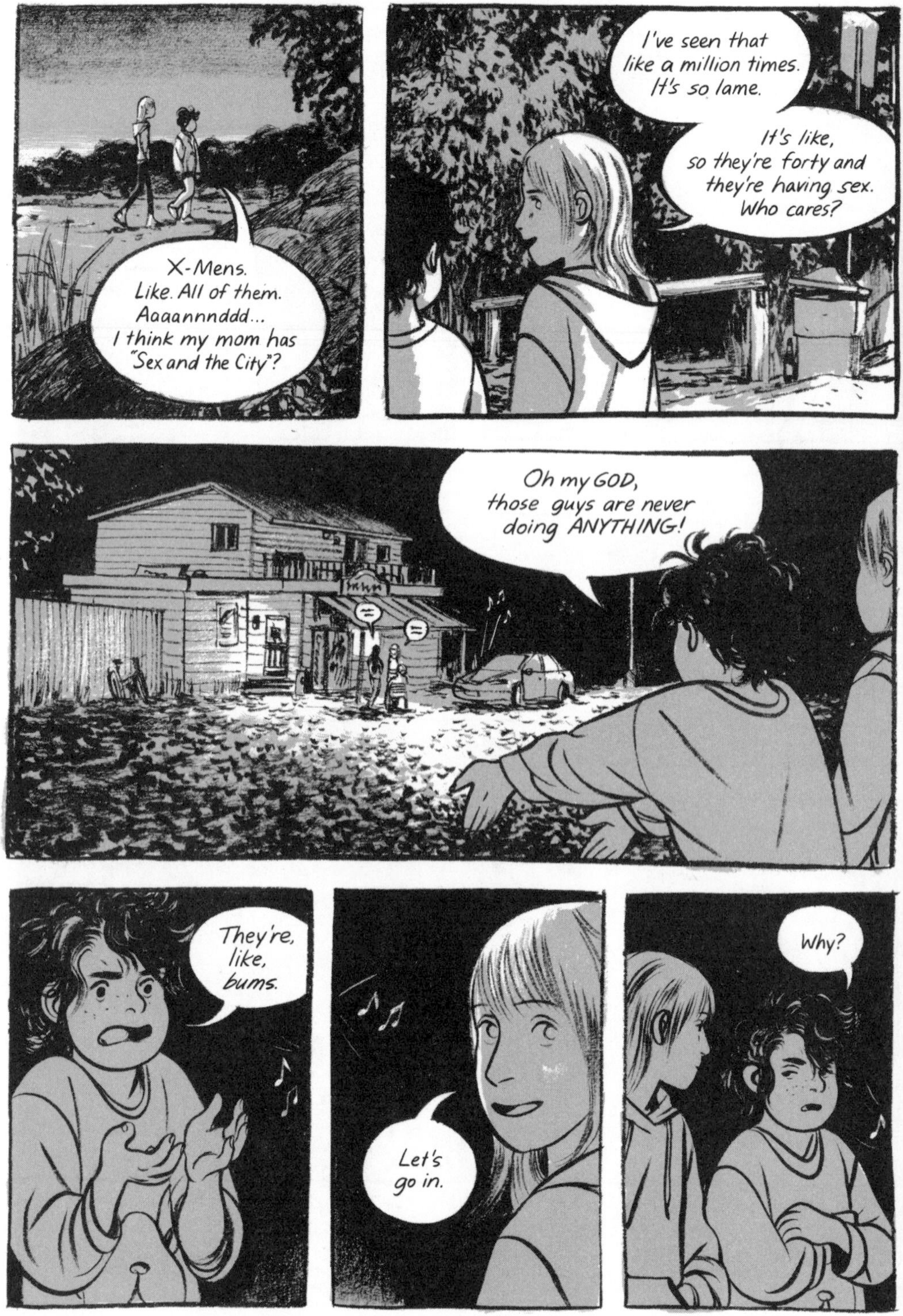
X-Mens.
Like. All of them.
Aaaannnddd...
I think my mom has "Sex and the City"?
I've seen that like a million times. It's so lame.
It's like, so they're forty and they're having sex. Who cares?
Oh my GOD, those guys are never doing ANYTHING!
They're, like, bums.
Let's go in.
Why?

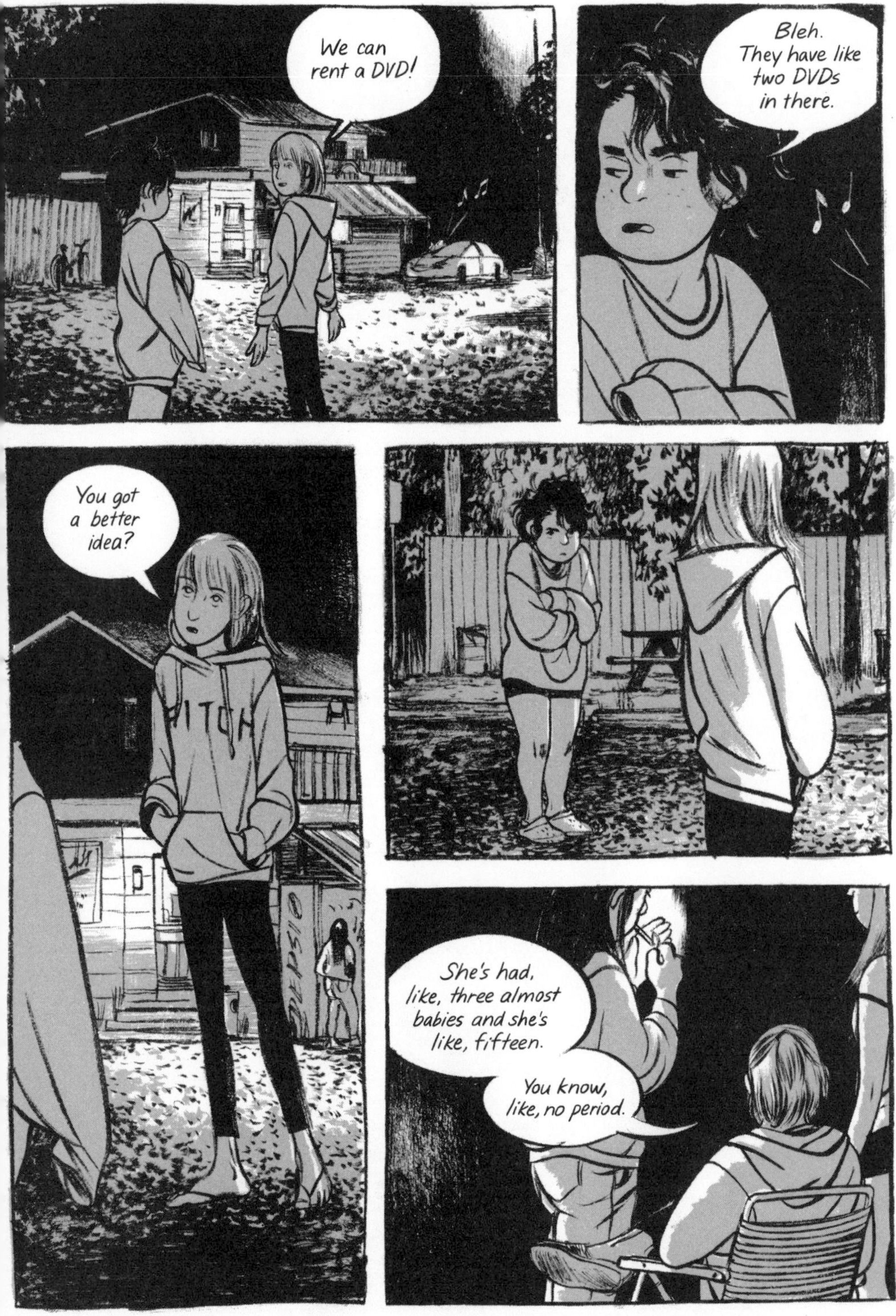
We can rent a DVD!
Bleh. They have like two DVDs in there.
You got a better idea?
She's had, like, three almost babies and she's like, fifteen.
You know, like, no period.

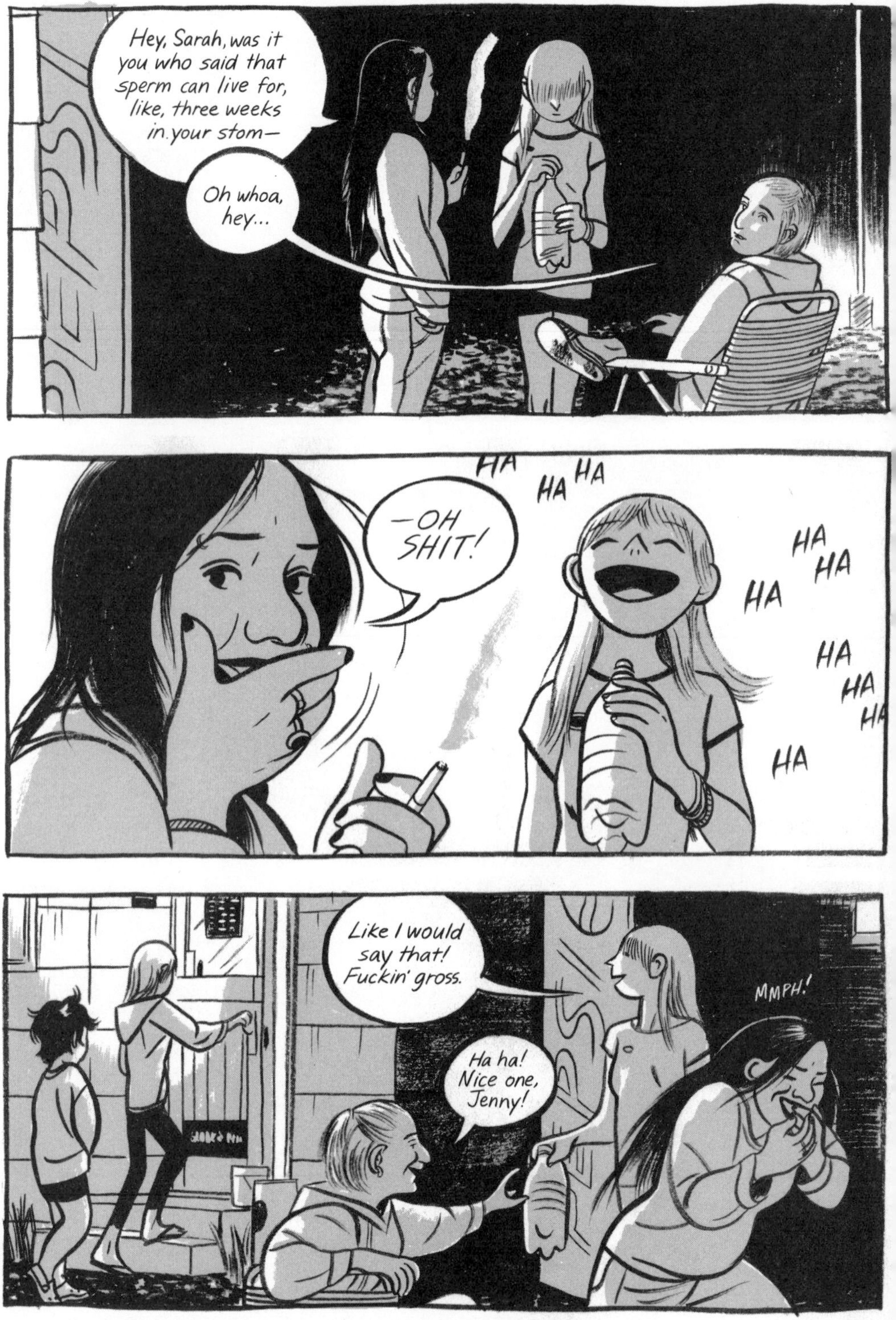
Hey, Sarah, was it you who said that sperm can live for, like, three weeks in your stom—
Oh whoa, hey...
—OH SHIT!
HA HA HA
HA HA HA HA HA HA HA HA
Like I would say that! Fuckin' gross.
MMPH!
Ha ha! Nice one, Jenny!

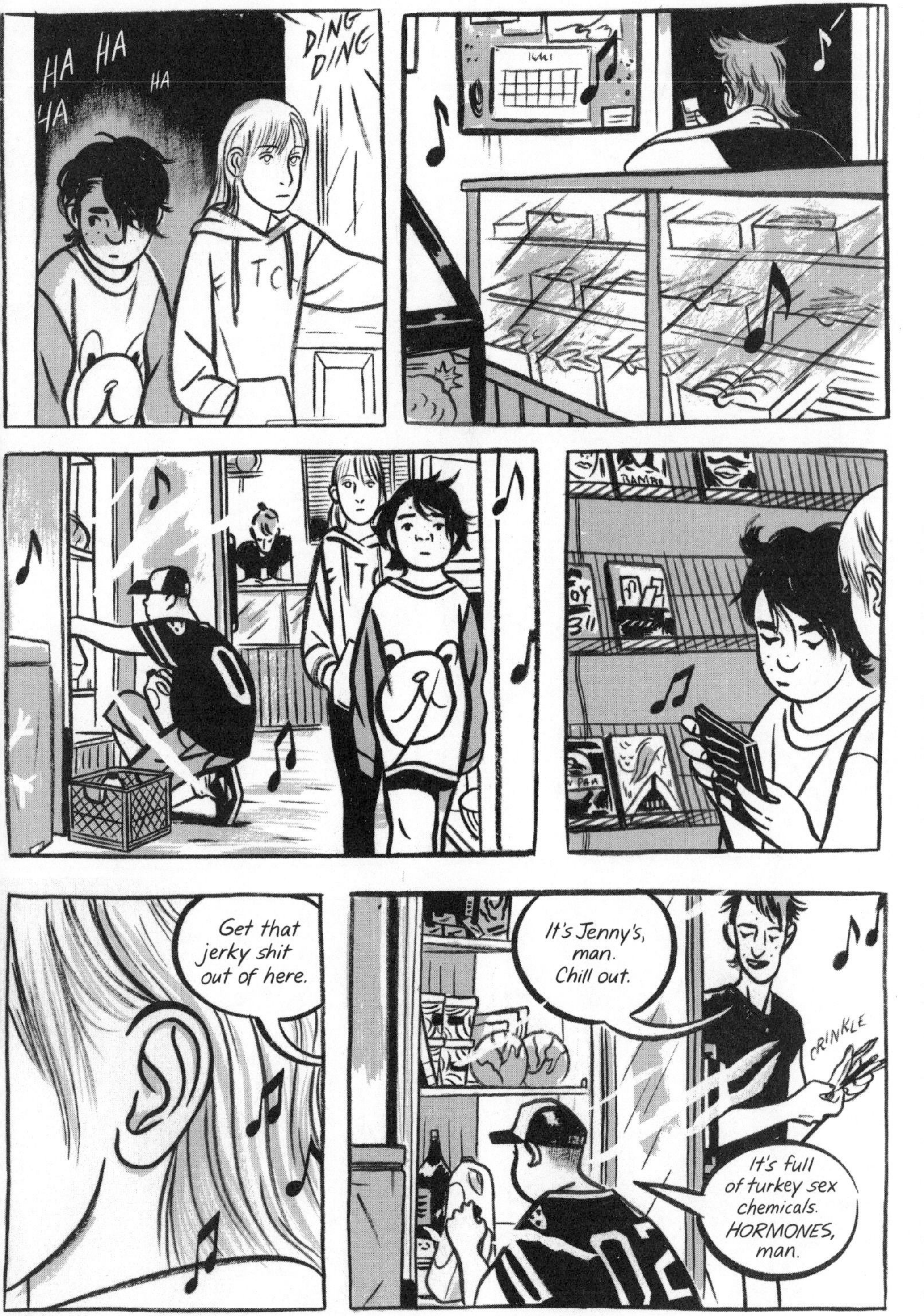
HA HA
HA
HA
DING DING
Get that jerky shit out of here.
It's Jenny's, man. Chill out.
CRINKLE
It's full of turkey sex chemicals. HORMONES, man.

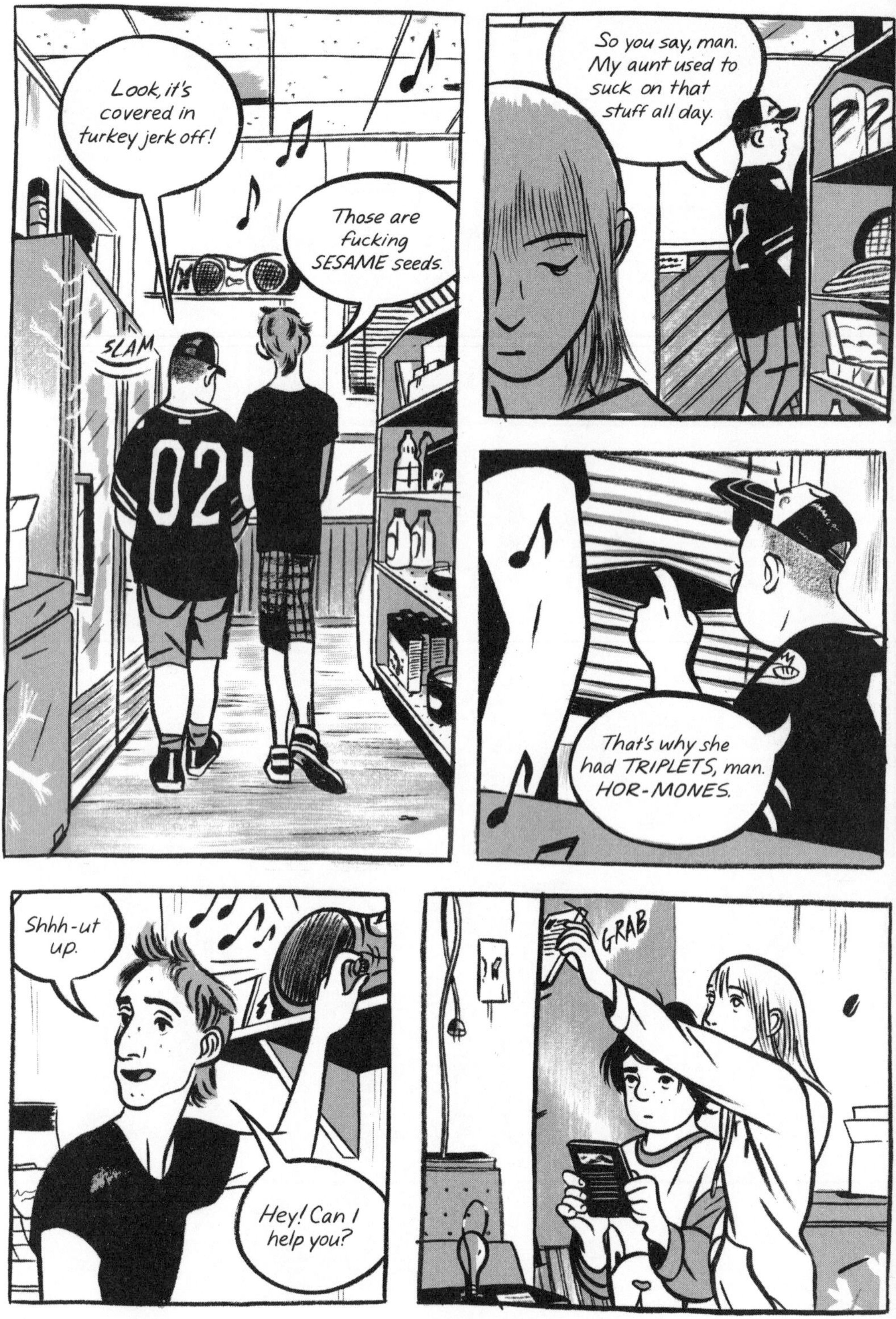
Look, it's covered in turkey jerk off!
Those are fucking SESAME seeds.
SLAM
So you say, man. My aunt used to suck on that stuff all day.
That's why she had TRIPLETS, man. HOR-MONES.
Shhh-ut up.
Hey! Can I help you?
GRAB

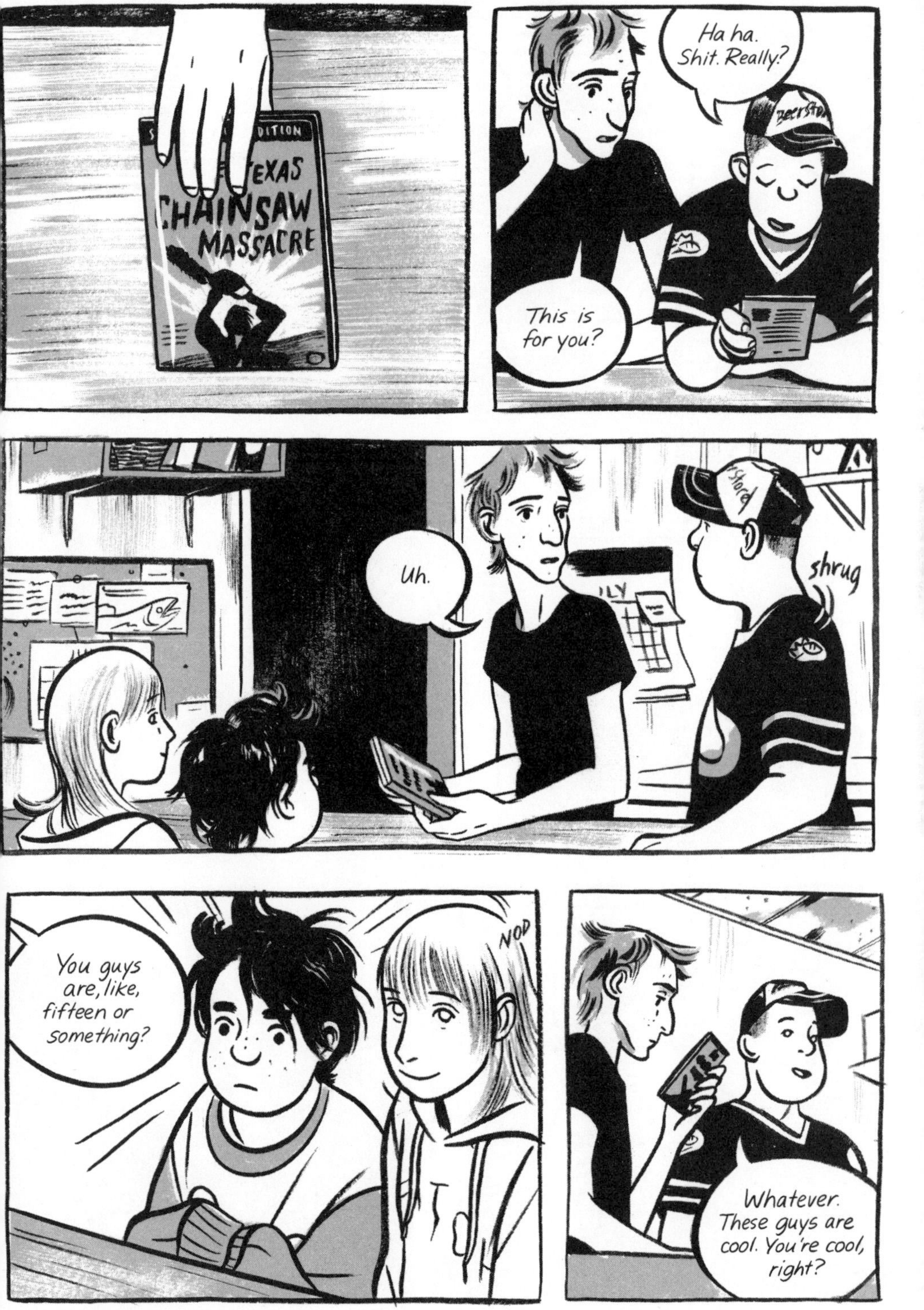

TEXAS CHAINSAW MASSACRE
Ha ha. Shit. Really?
This is for you?
Uh.
shrug
You guys are, like, fifteen or something?
NOD
Whatever. These guys are cool. You're cool, right?

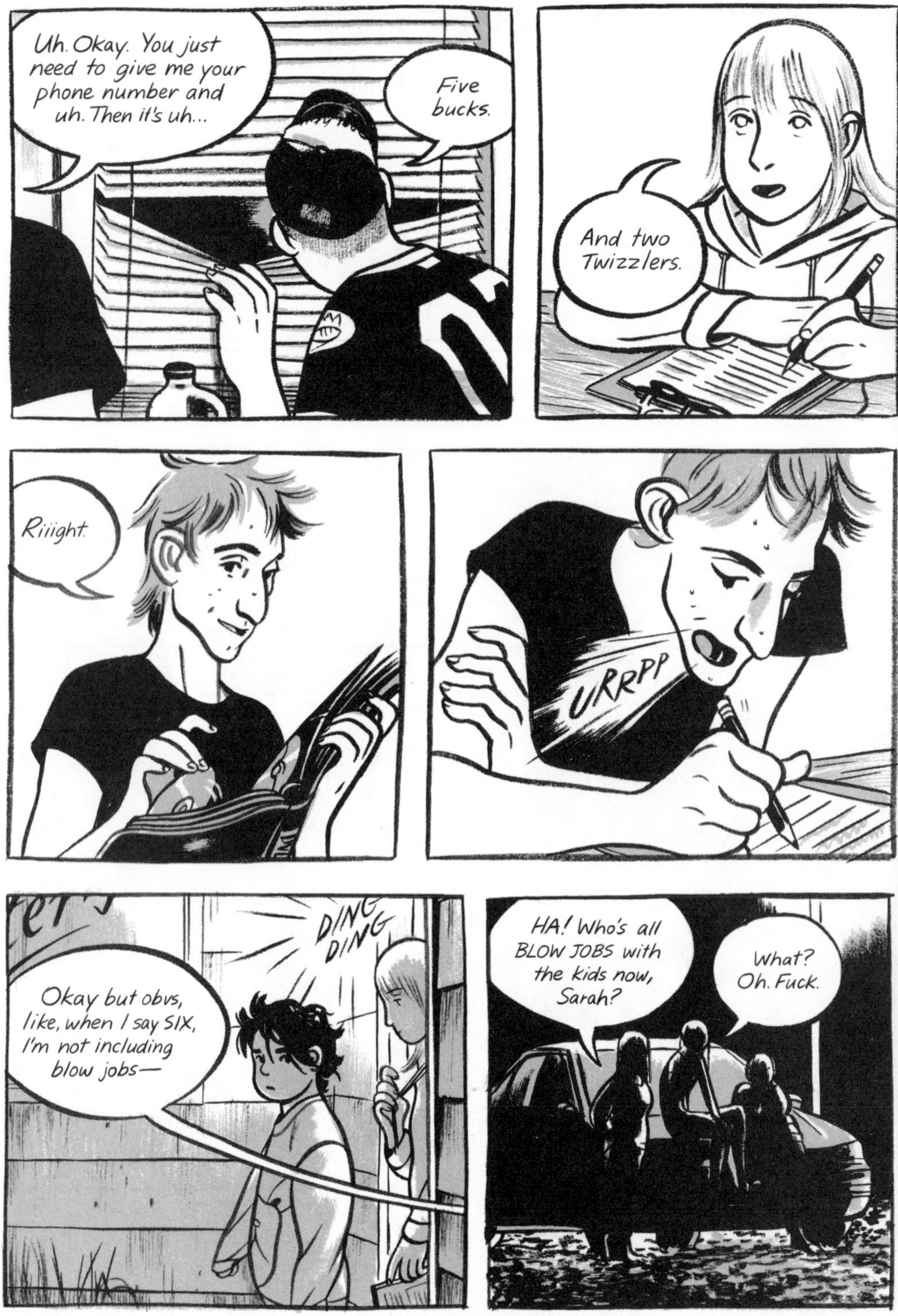
Uh. Okay. You just need to give me your phone number and uh. Then it's uh...
Five bucks.
And two Twizzlers.
Riiight.
URRPP
DING DING
Okay but obvs, like, when I say SIX, I'm not including blow jobs—
HA! Who's all BLOW JOBS with the kids now, Sarah?
What? Oh. Fuck.

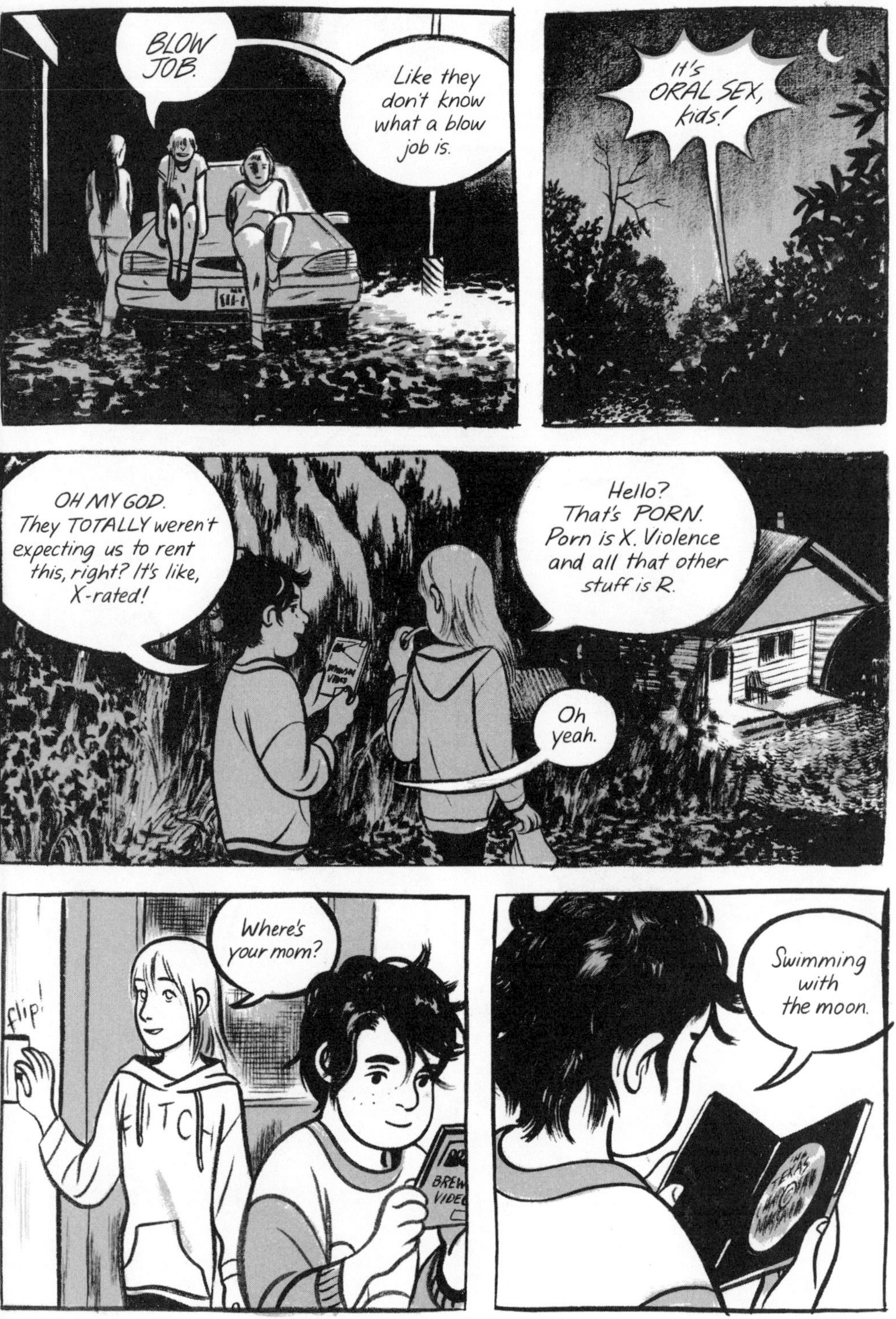
BLOW JOB.
Like they don't know what a blow job is.
It's ORAL SEX, kids!
OH MY GOD. They TOTALLY weren't expecting us to rent this, right? It's like, X-rated!
Hello? That's PORN. Porn is X. Violence and all that other stuff is R.
Oh yeah.
flip!
Where's your mom?
Swimming with the moon.

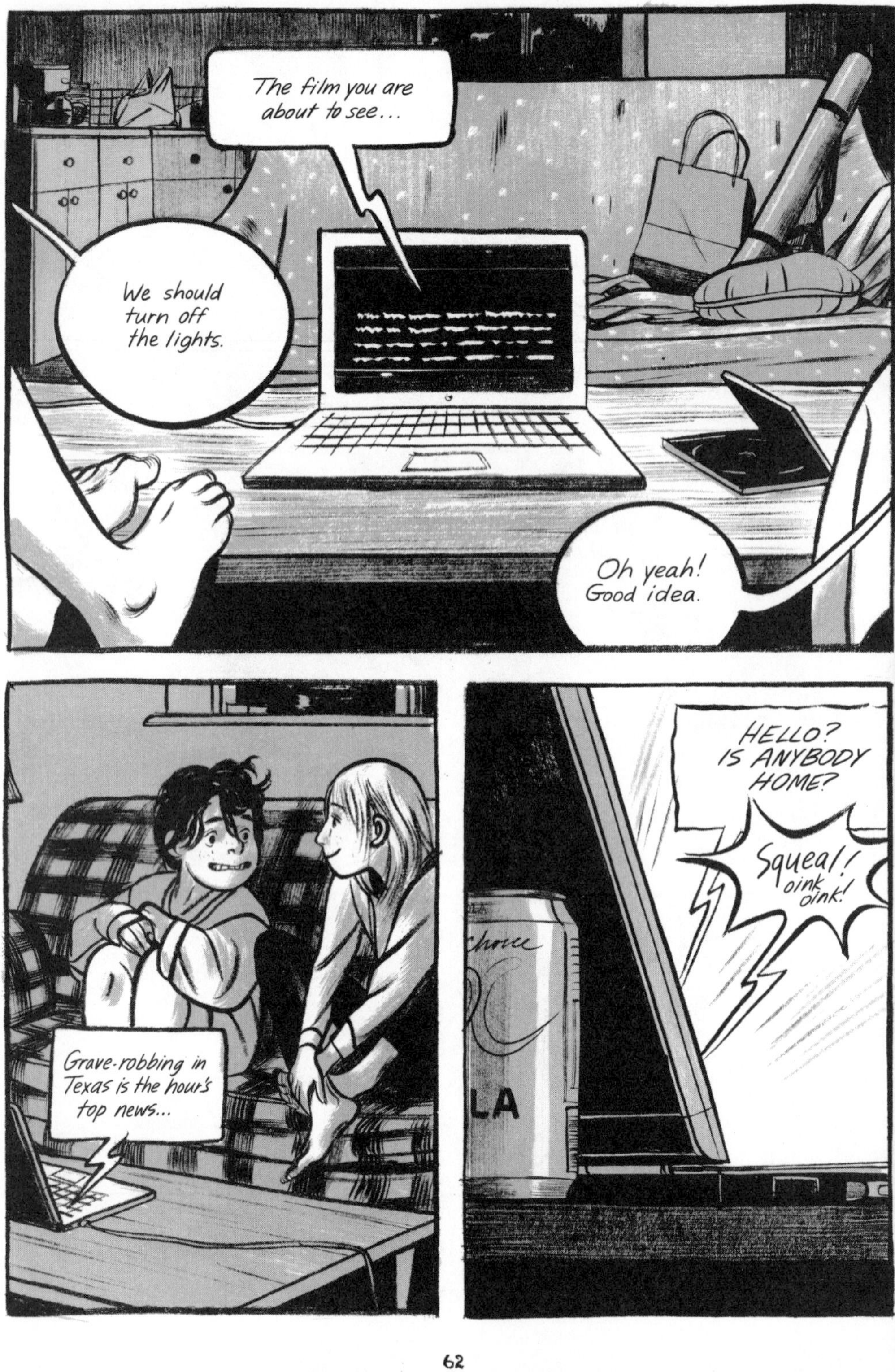
The film you are about to see...
We should turn off the lights.
Oh yeah! Good idea.
Grave-robbing in Texas is the hour's top news...
HELLO? IS ANYBODY HOME?
Squeal! oink oink!

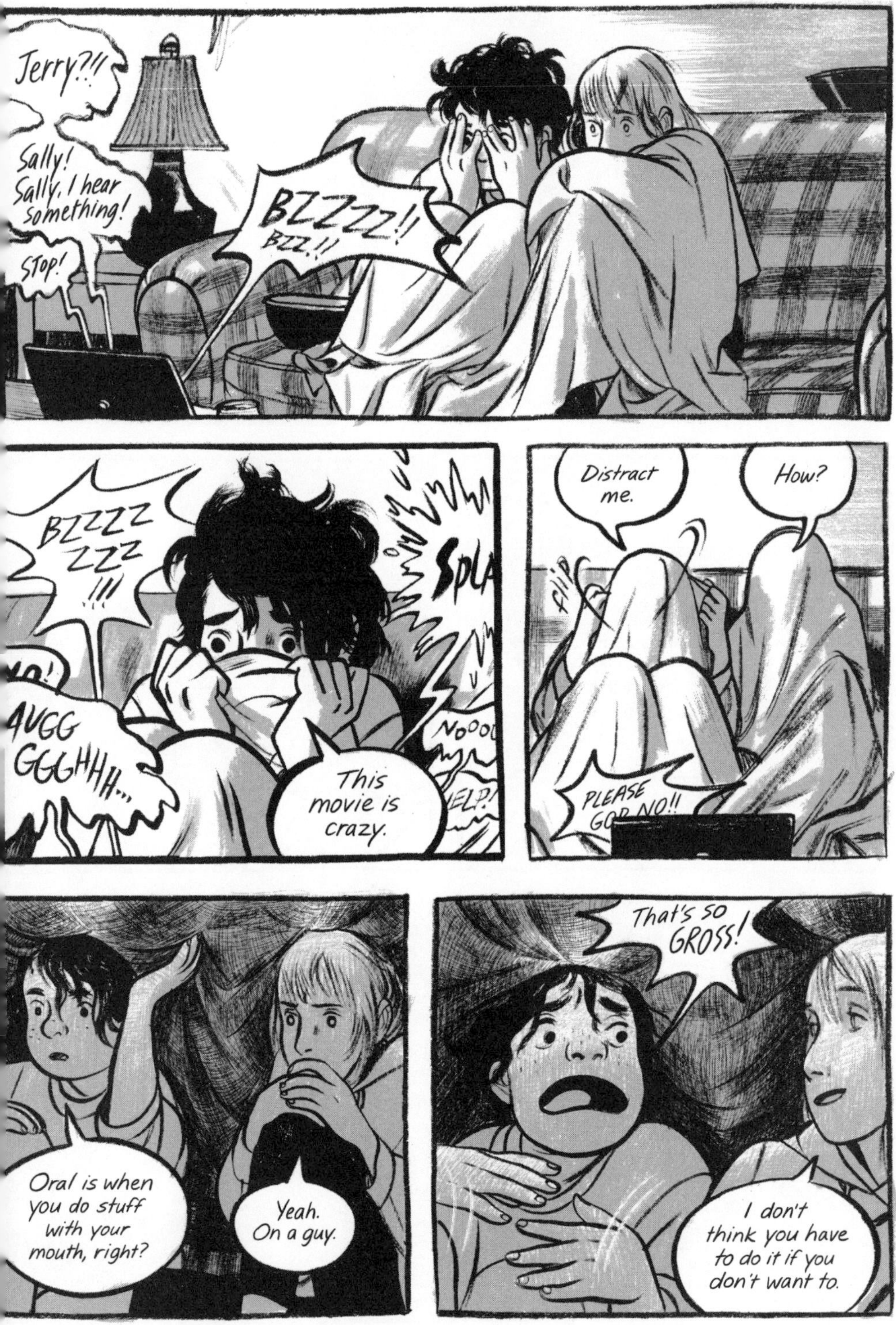

Jerry?!!
Sally! Sally, I hear something!
STOP!
BZZZZZ!! BZZ!!
BZZZZ ZZZ !!!
AUGG GGGHHH...
This movie is crazy.
Distract me.
How?
FLIP
Oral is when you do stuff with your mouth, right?
Yeah. On a guy.
That's so GROSS!
I don't think you have to do it if you don't want to.

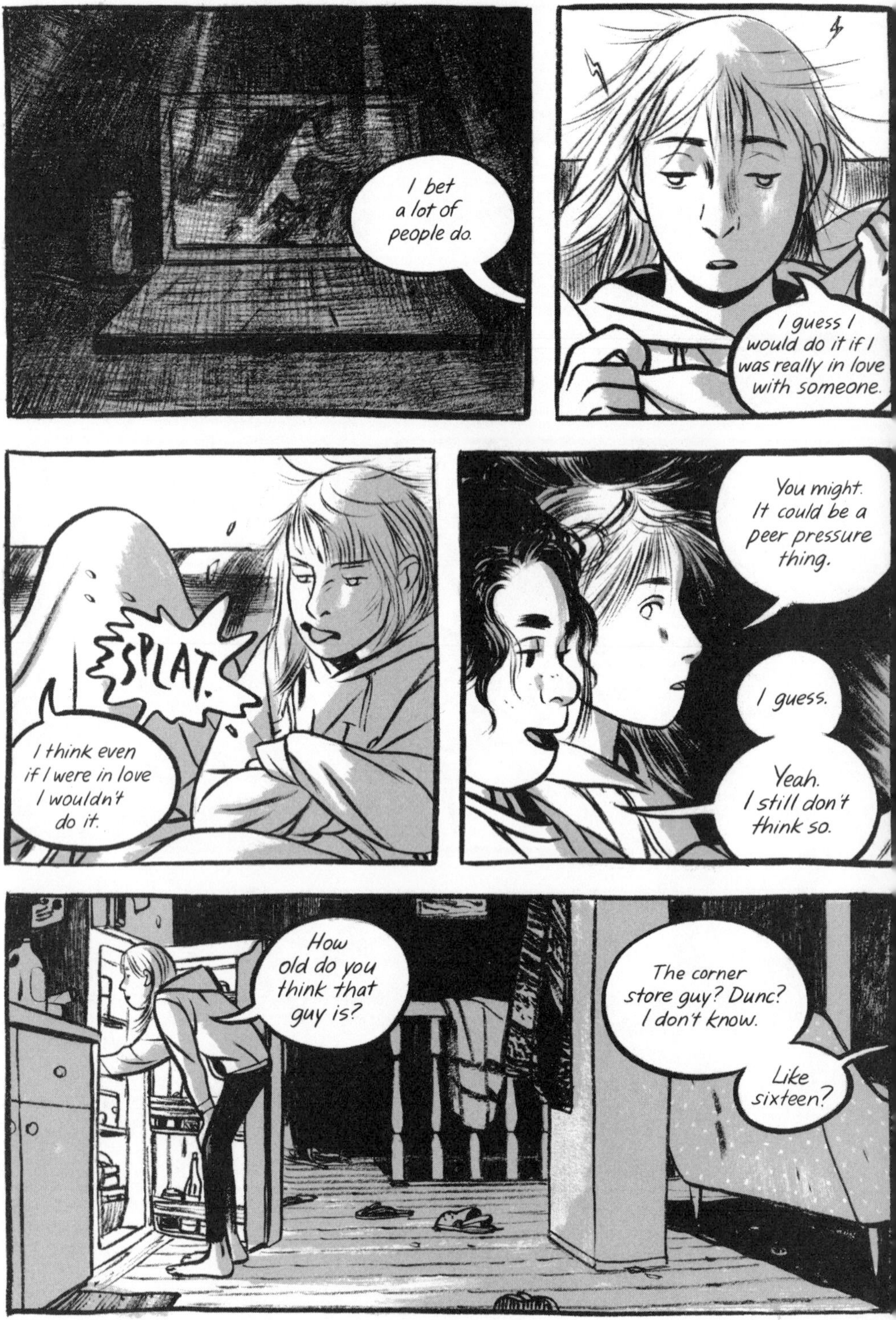
I bet a lot of people do.
I guess I would do it if I was really in love with someone.
SPLAT.
I think even if I were in love I wouldn't do it.
You might. It could be a peer pressure thing.
I guess.
Yeah. I still don't think so.
How old do you think that guy is?
The corner store guy? Dunc? I don't know.
Like sixteen?

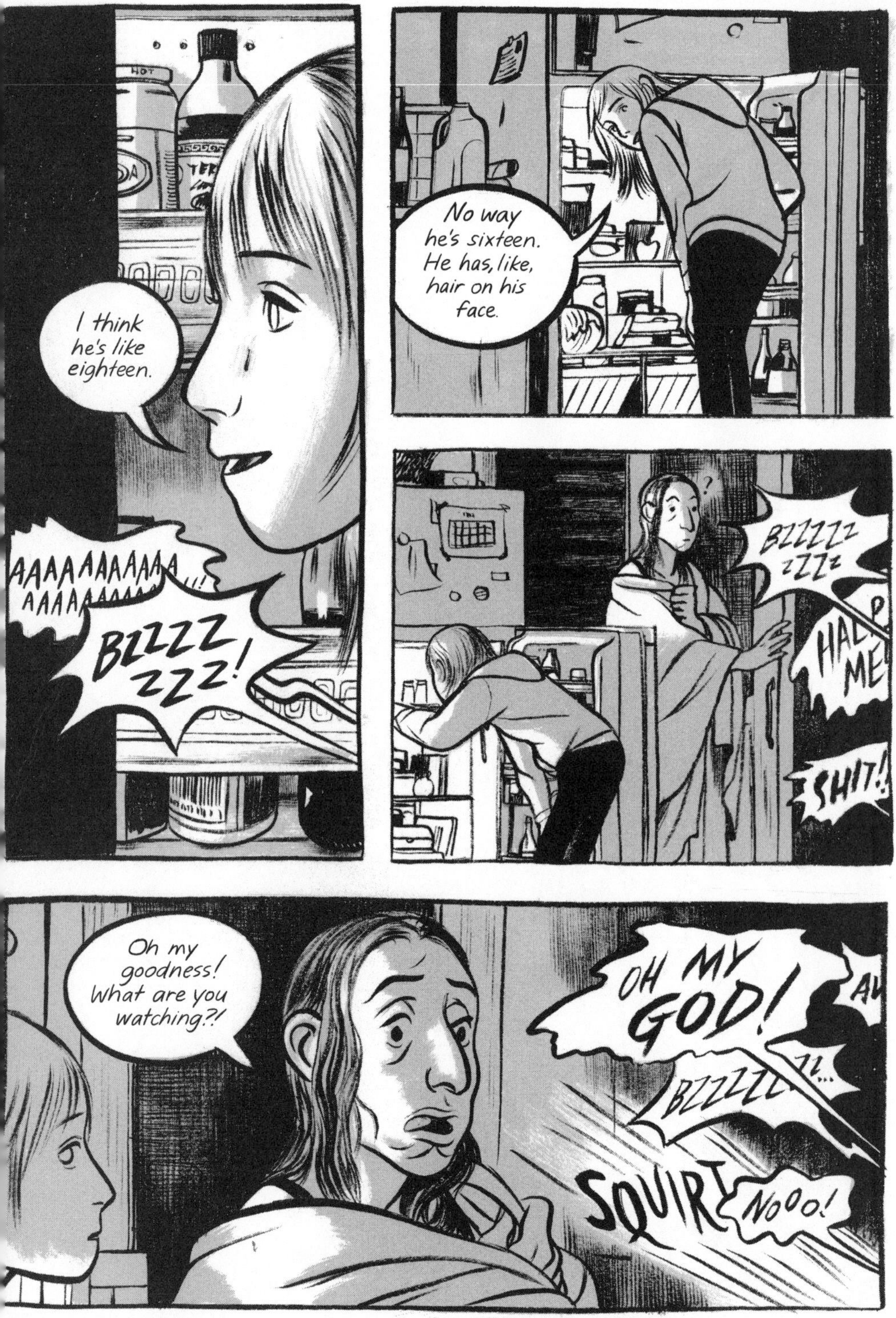
I think he's like eighteen.
BZZZZ ZZZ!
No way he's sixteen. He has, like, hair on his face.
?
BZZZZZ ZZZZ
SHIT!
Oh my goodness! What are you watching?!
OH MY GOD!
BZZZZZ
SQUIRT
NOOO!

I know a little about sex.

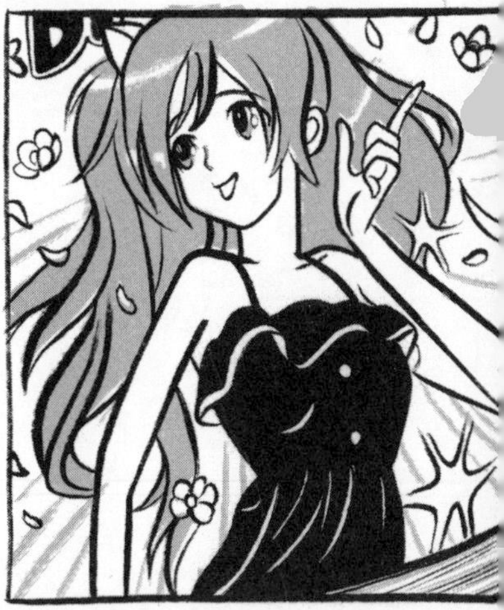

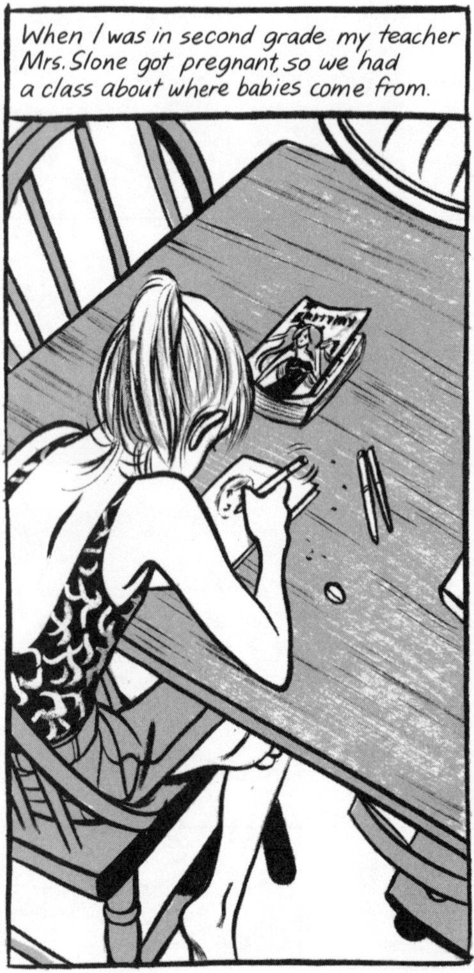
When I was in second grade my teacher Mrs. Slone got pregnant, so we had a class about where babies come from.

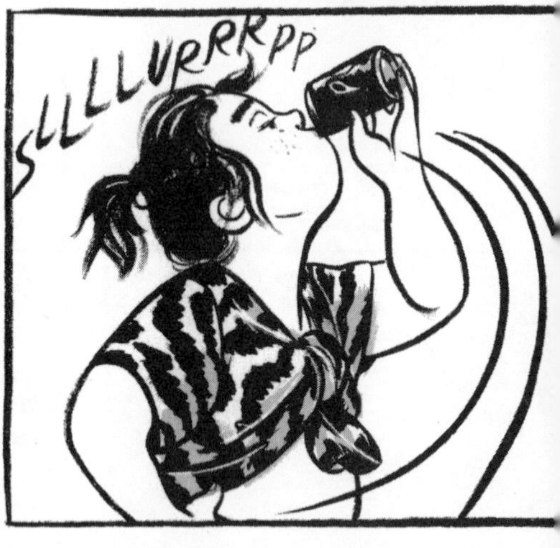
SLLLLURRRPP

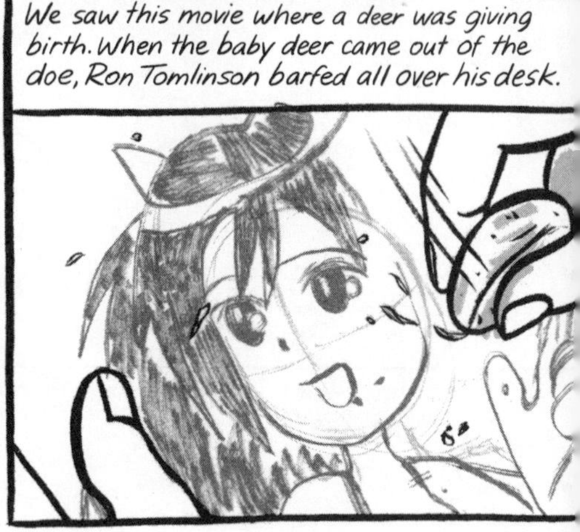
We saw this movie where a deer was giving birth. When the baby deer came out of the doe, Ron Tomlinson barfed all over his desk.

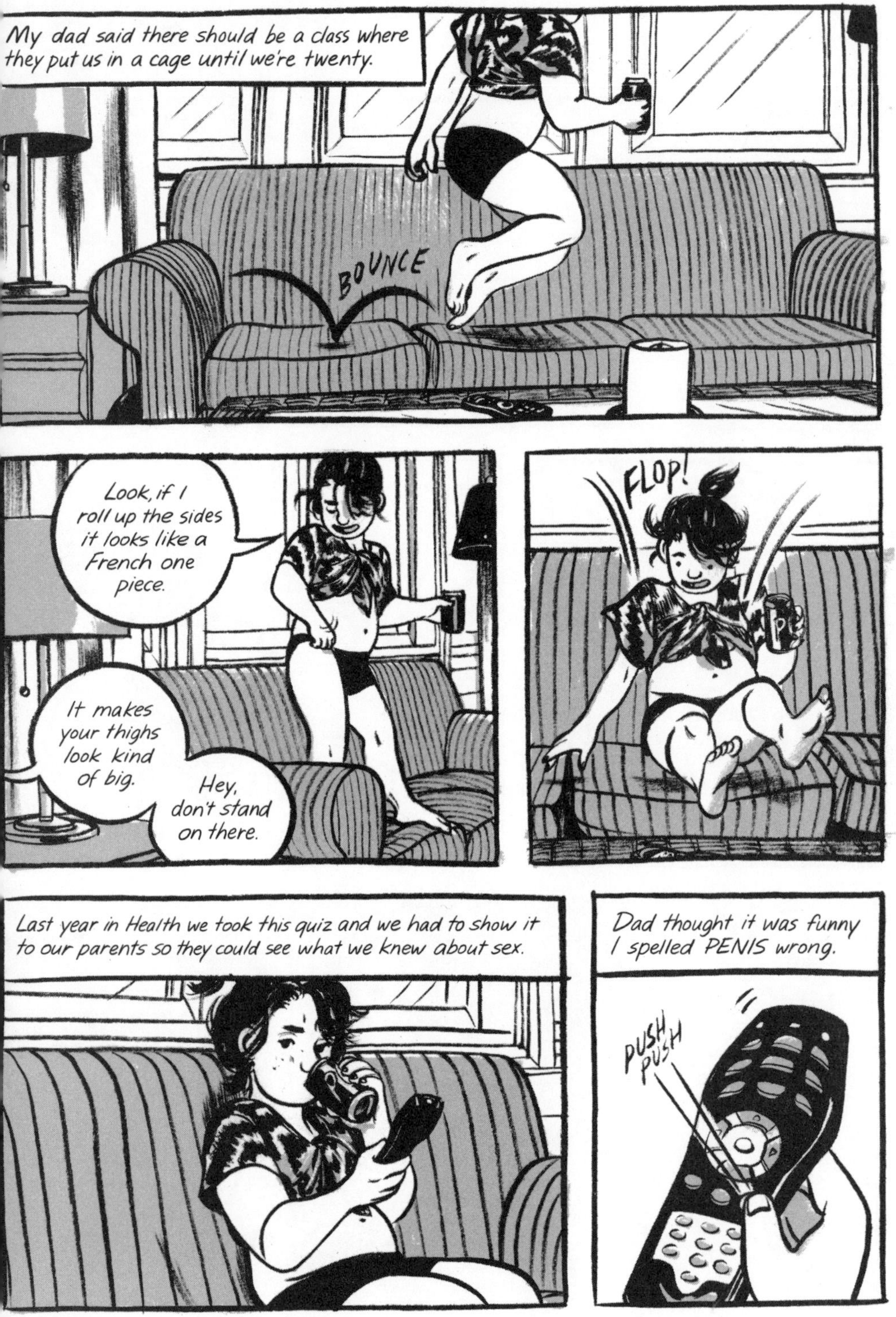
My dad said there should be a class where they put us in a cage until we're twenty.
BOUNCE
Look, if I roll up the sides it looks like a French one piece.
It makes your thighs look kind of big.
Hey, don't stand on there.
FLOP!
Last year in Health we took this quiz and we had to show it to our parents so they could see what we knew about sex.
Dad thought it was funny I spelled PENIS wrong.
PUSH PUSH

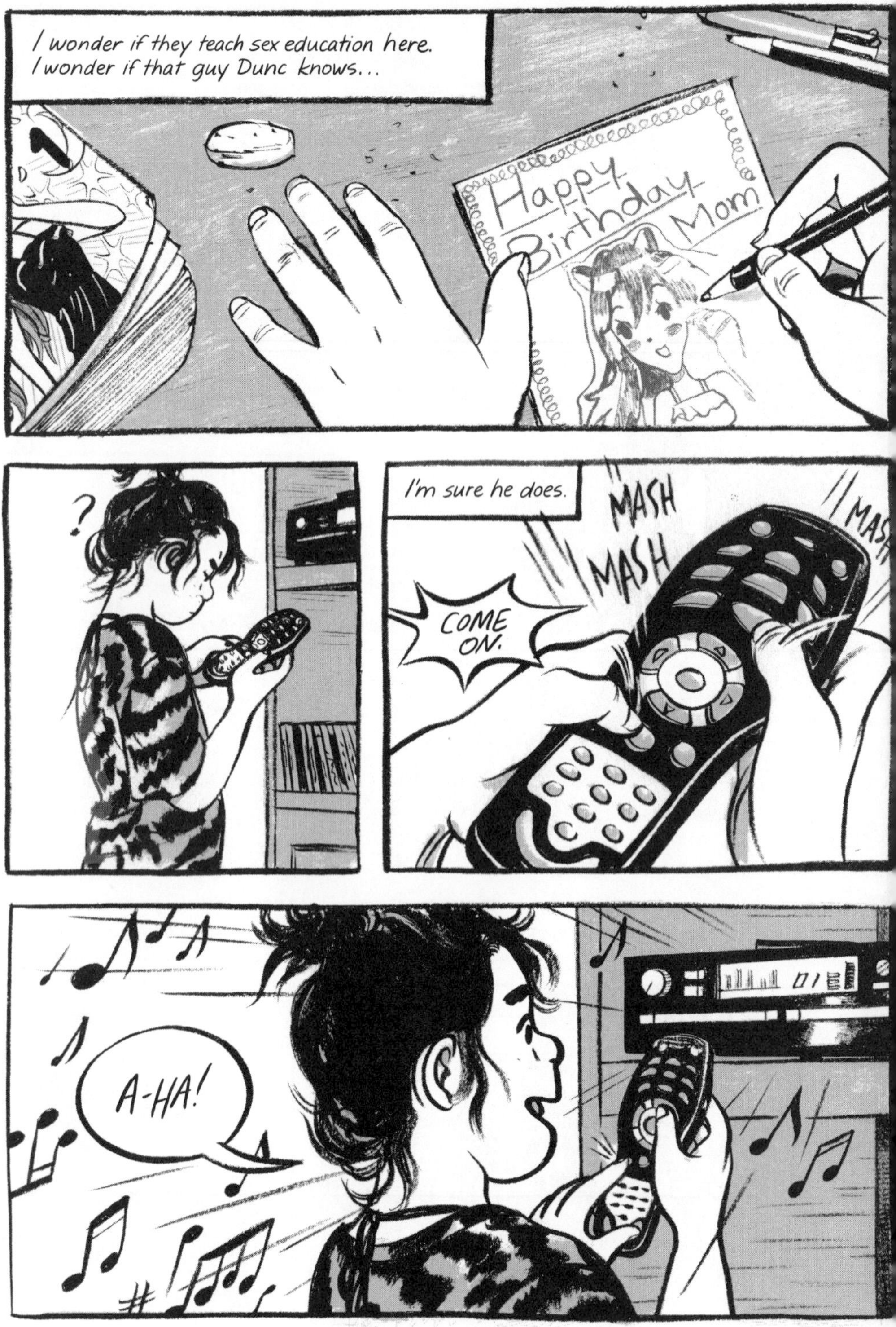
I wonder if they teach sex education here.
I wonder if that guy Dunc knows...
Happy Birthday Mom
?
I'm sure he does.
MASH
MASH
MASH
COME ON.
A-HA!

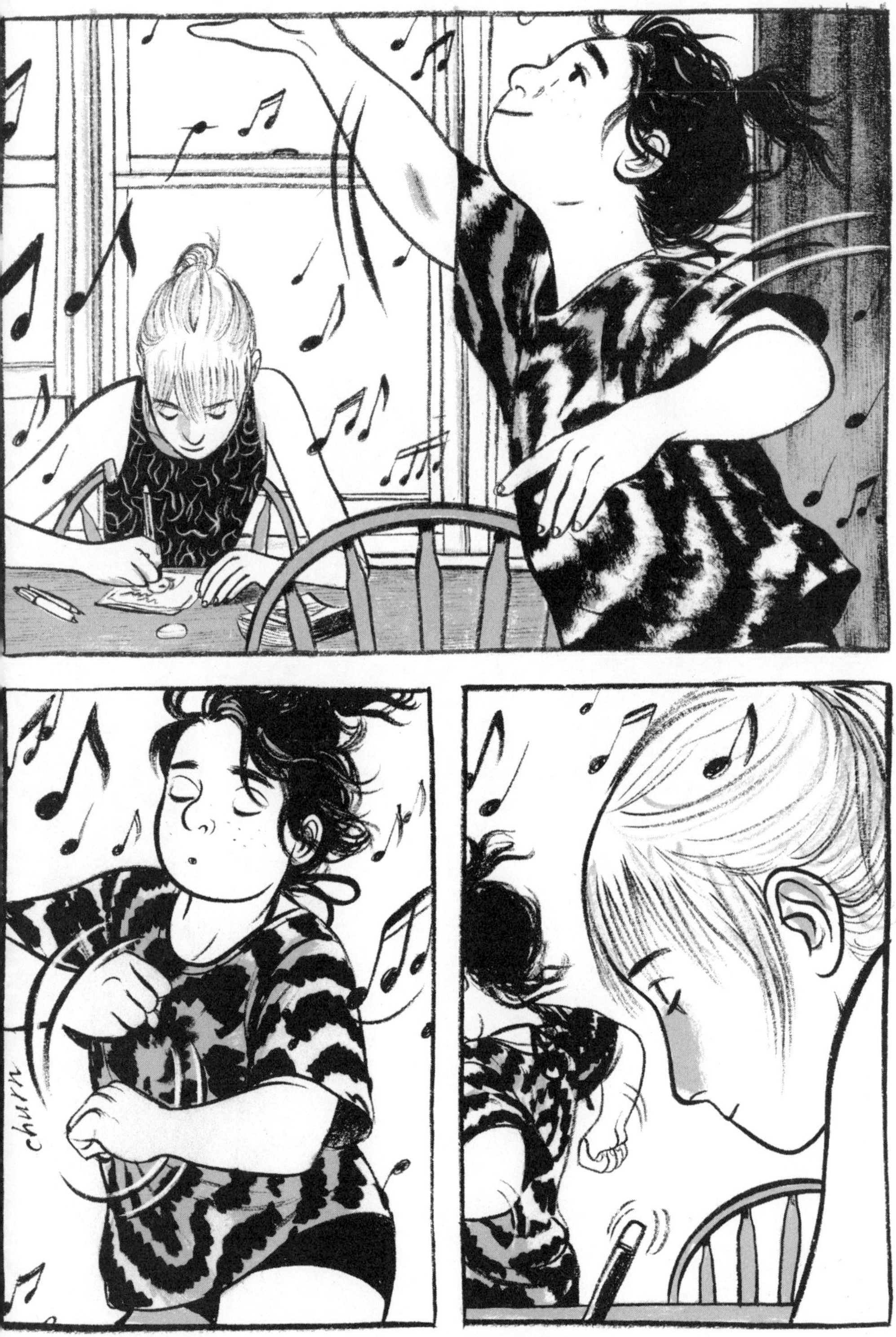
churn

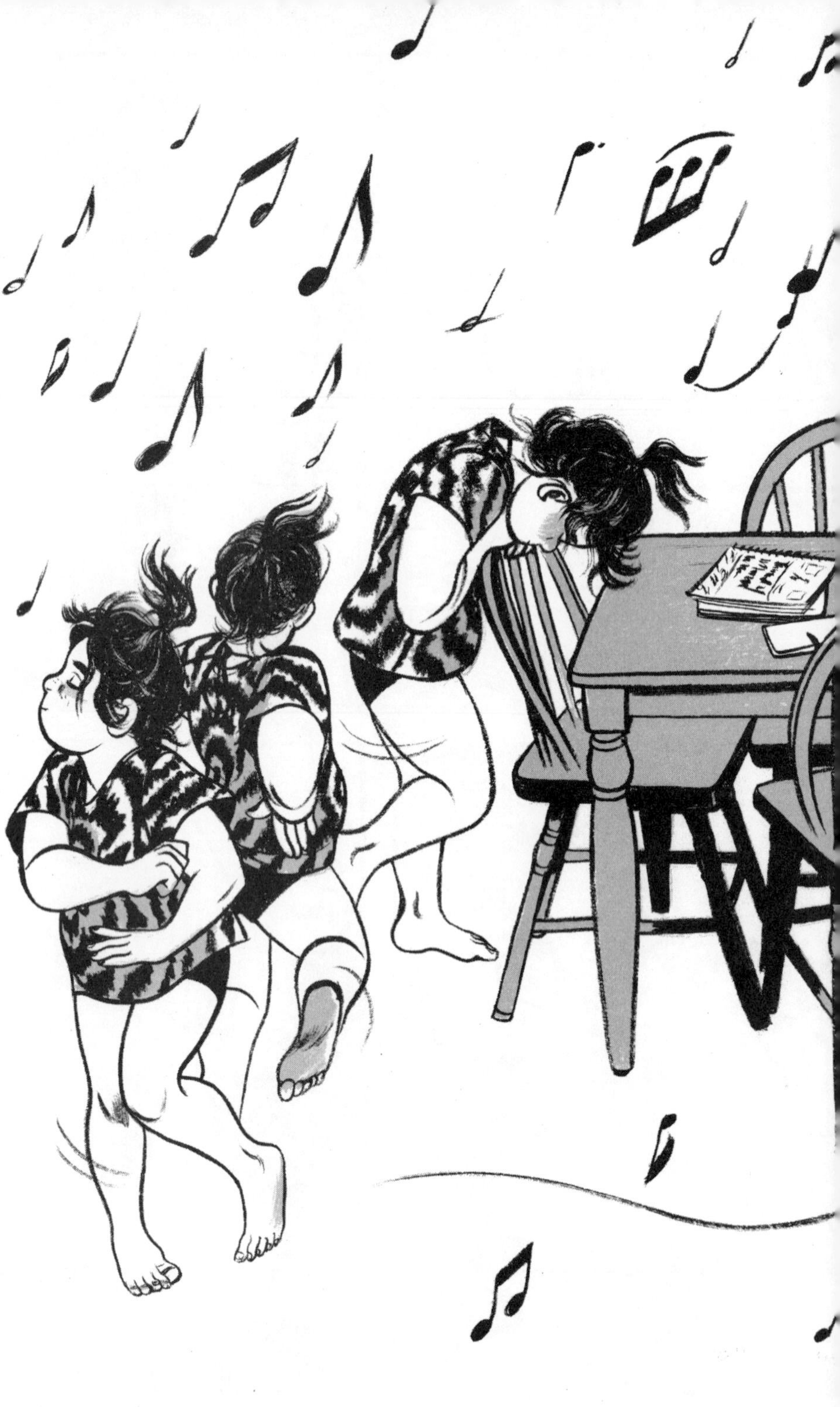

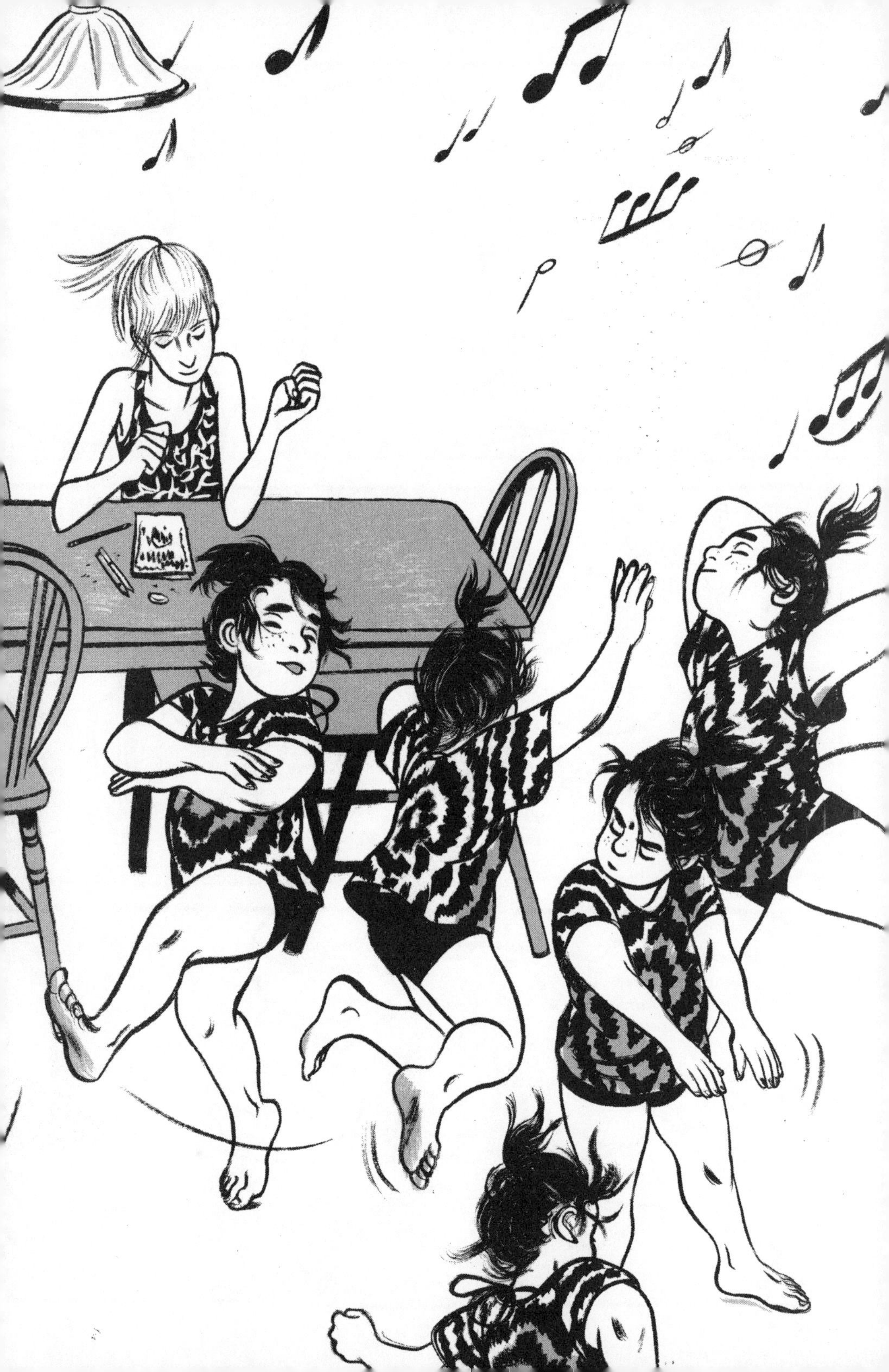

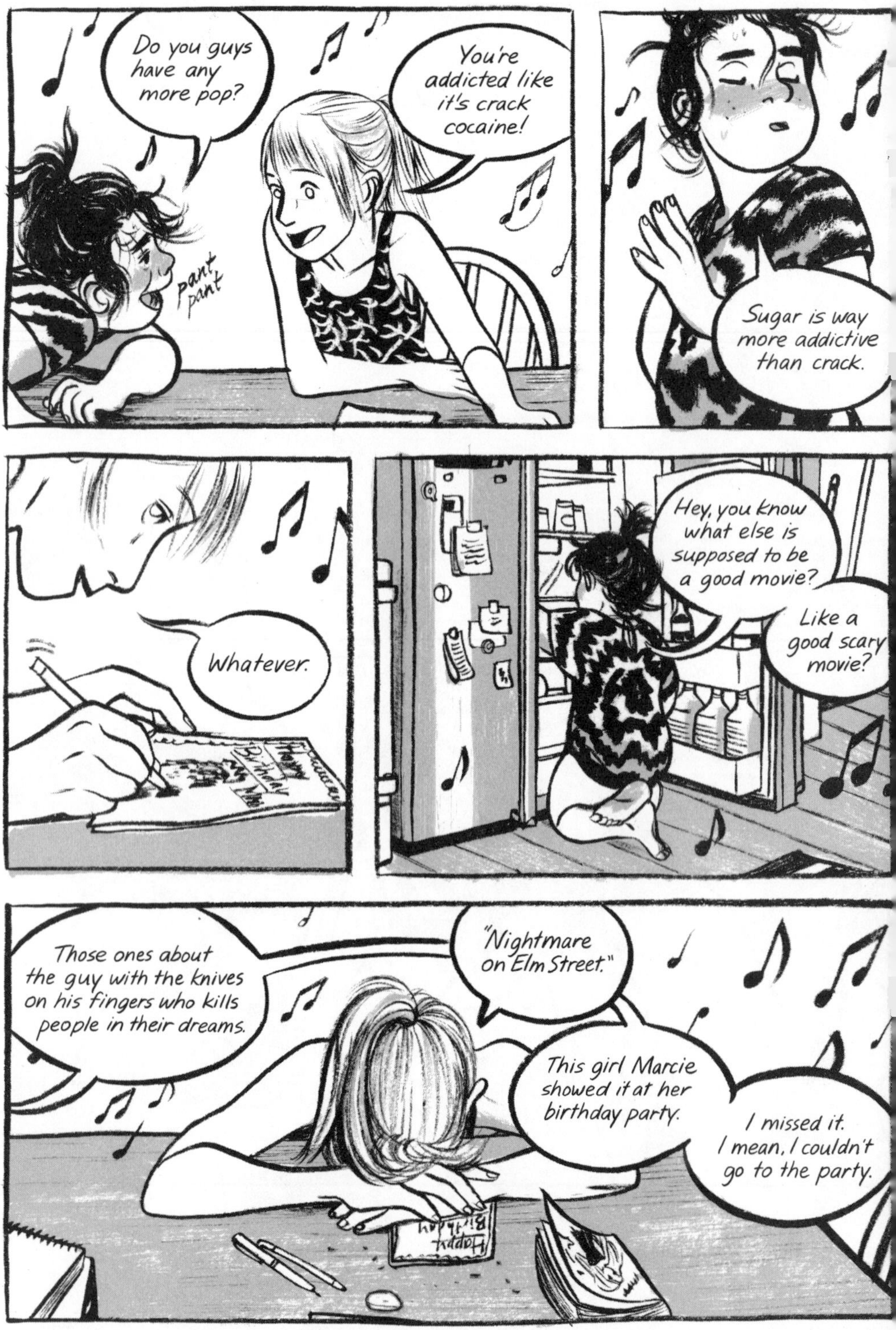
Do you guys have any more pop?
pant pant
You're addicted like it's crack cocaine!
Sugar is way more addictive than crack.
Whatever.
Hey, you know what else is supposed to be a good movie?
Like a good scary movie?
Those ones about the guy with the knives on his fingers who kills people in their dreams.
"Nightmare on Elm Street."
This girl Marcie showed it at her birthday party.
I missed it. I mean, I couldn't go to the party.

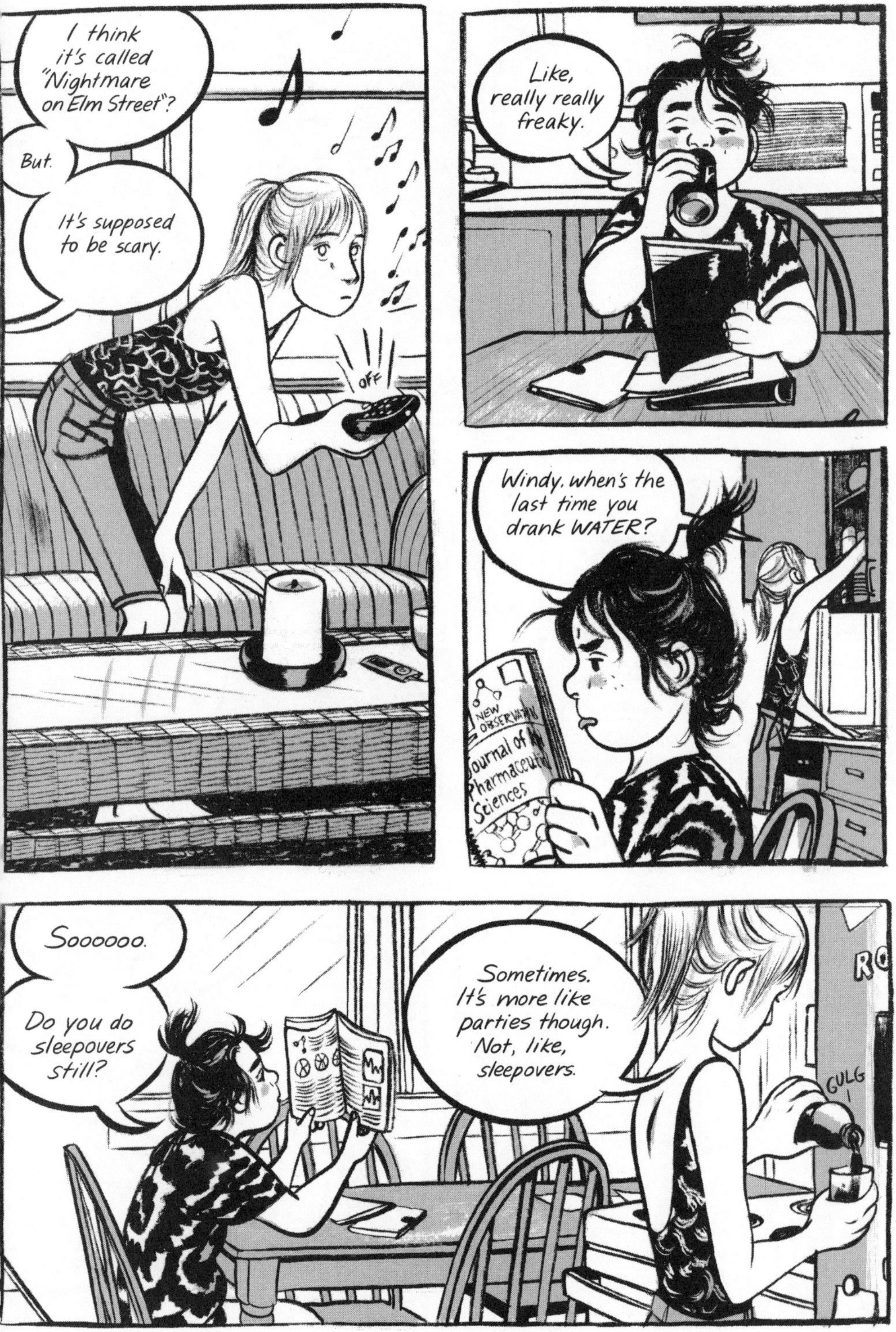
I think it's called "Nightmare on Elm Street"?
But.
It's supposed to be scary.
OFF
Like, really really freaky.
Windy, when's the last time you drank WATER?
NEW OBSERVATI
Journal of
Pharmaceuti
Sciences
Soooooo.
Do you do sleepovers still?
Sometimes. It's more like parties though. Not, like, sleepovers.
GULG

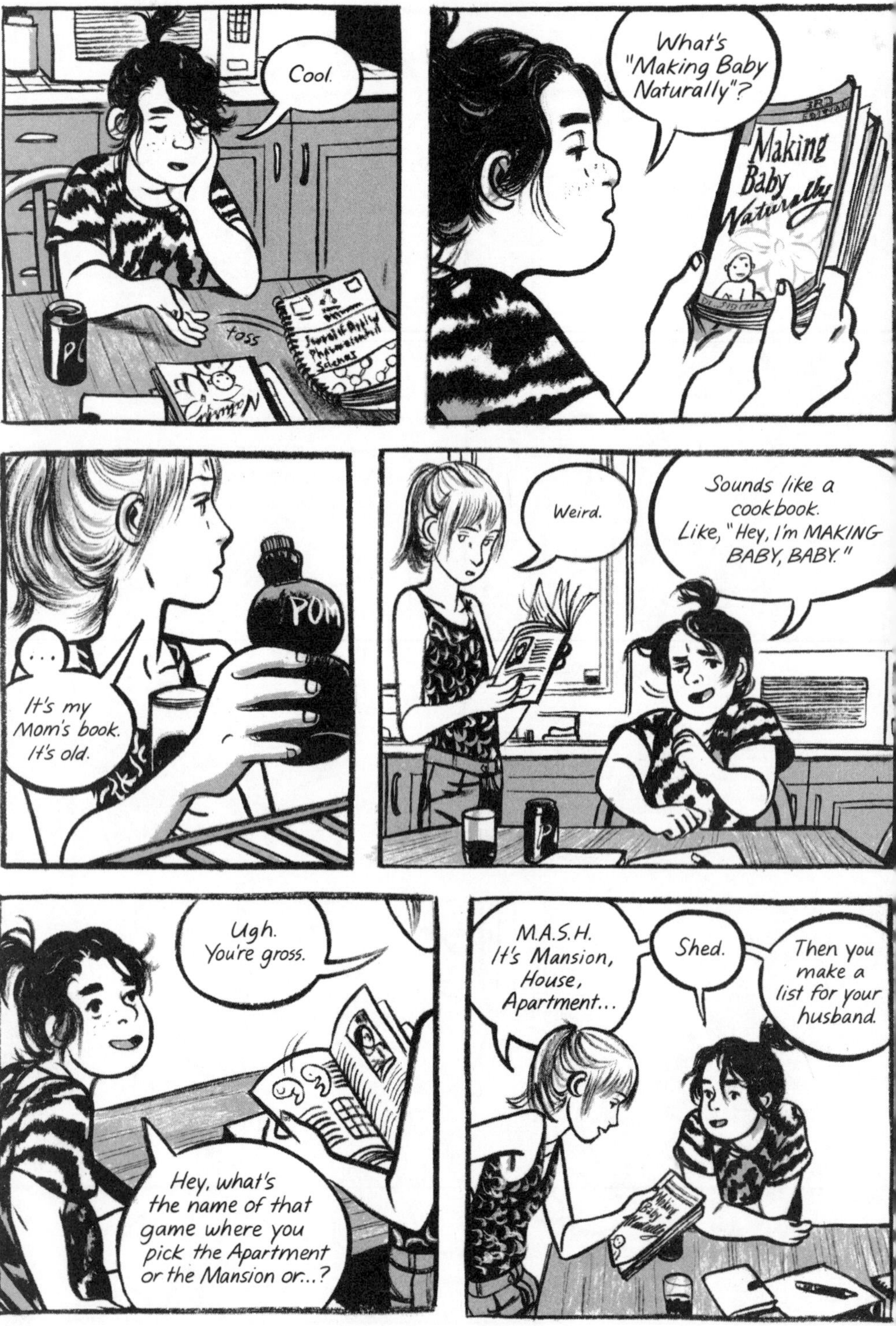
Cool.
toss
What's "Making Baby Naturally"?
Making Baby Naturally
...
It's my Mom's book. It's old.
POM
Weird.
Sounds like a cookbook. Like, "Hey, I'm MAKING BABY, BABY."
Ugh. You're gross.
Hey, what's the name of that game where you pick the Apartment or the Mansion or...?
M.A.S.H. It's Mansion, House, Apartment...
Shed.
Then you make a list for your husband.

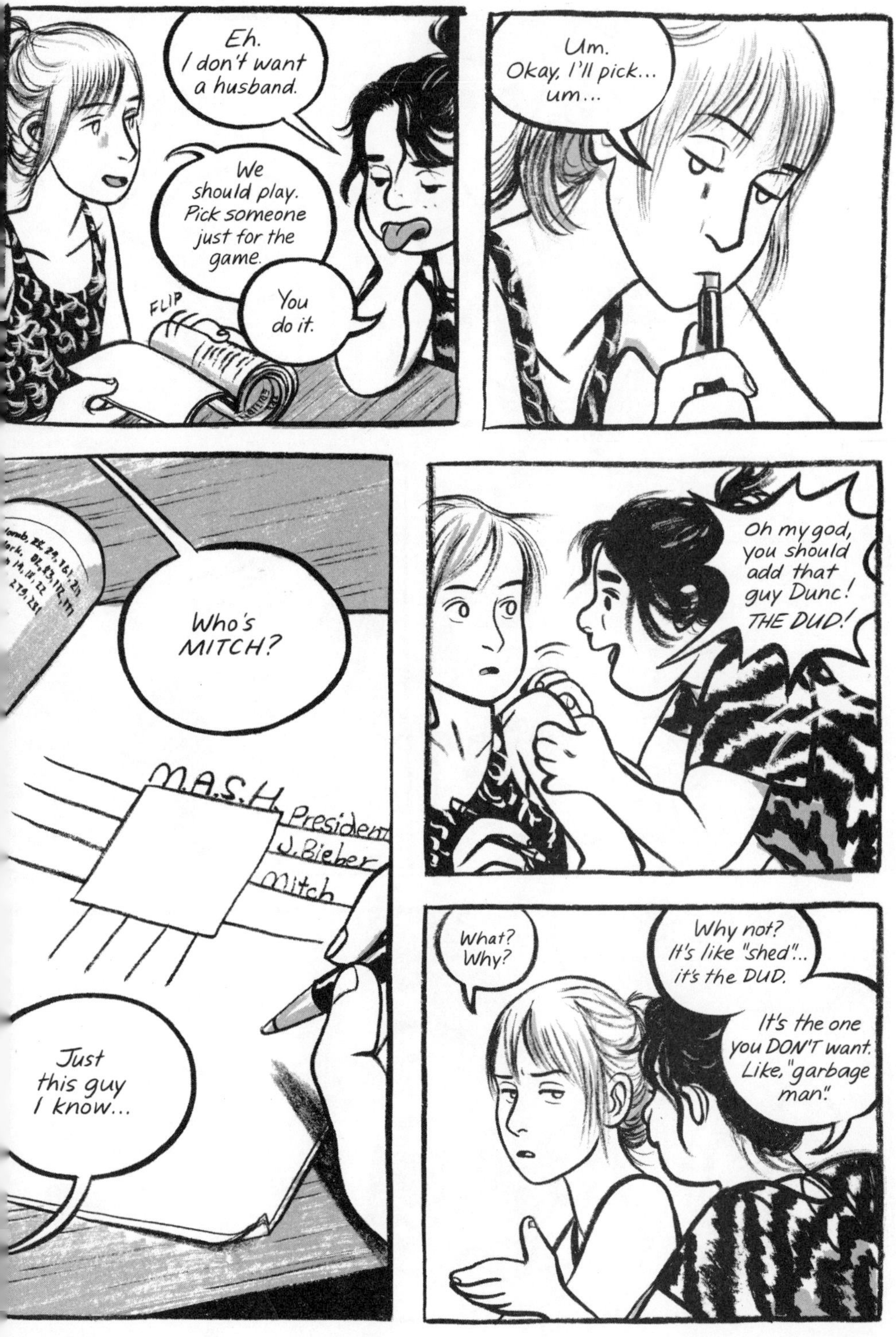
Eh. I don't want a husband.
We should play. Pick someone just for the game.
FLIP
You do it.
Um. Okay, I'll pick... um...
Who's MITCH?
M.A.S.H.
President
J.Bieber
Mitch
Just this guy I know...
Oh my god, you should add that guy Dunc! THE DUD!
What? Why?
Why not? It's like "shed"... it's the DUD.
It's the one you DON'T want. Like, "garbage man."

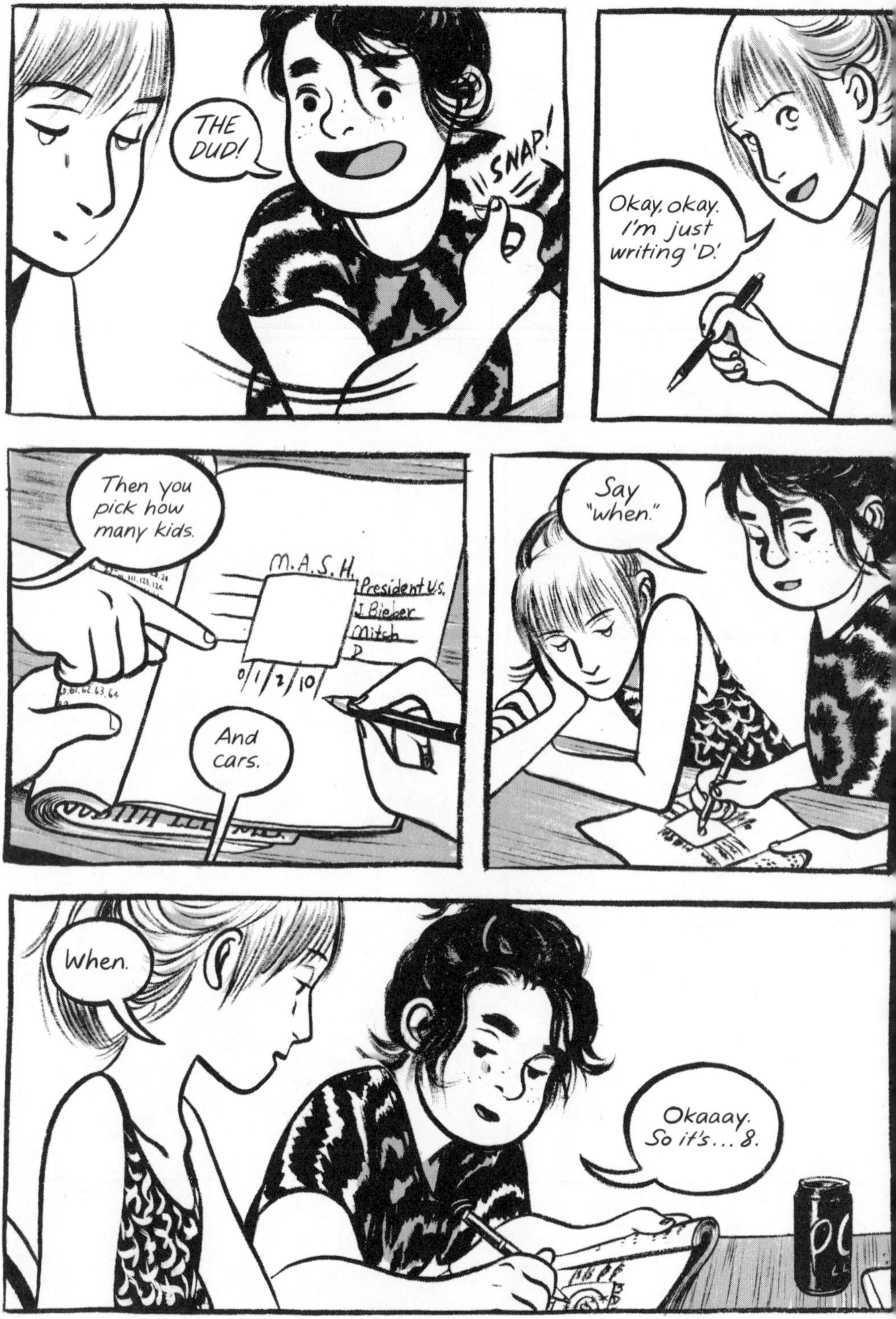

THE DUD!
SNAP!
Okay, okay. I'm just writing 'D.'
Then you pick how many kids.
M.A.S.H.
President U.S.
J. Bieber
Mitch
D
0 1 2 10
And cars.
Say "when."
When.
Okaaay. So it's... 8.

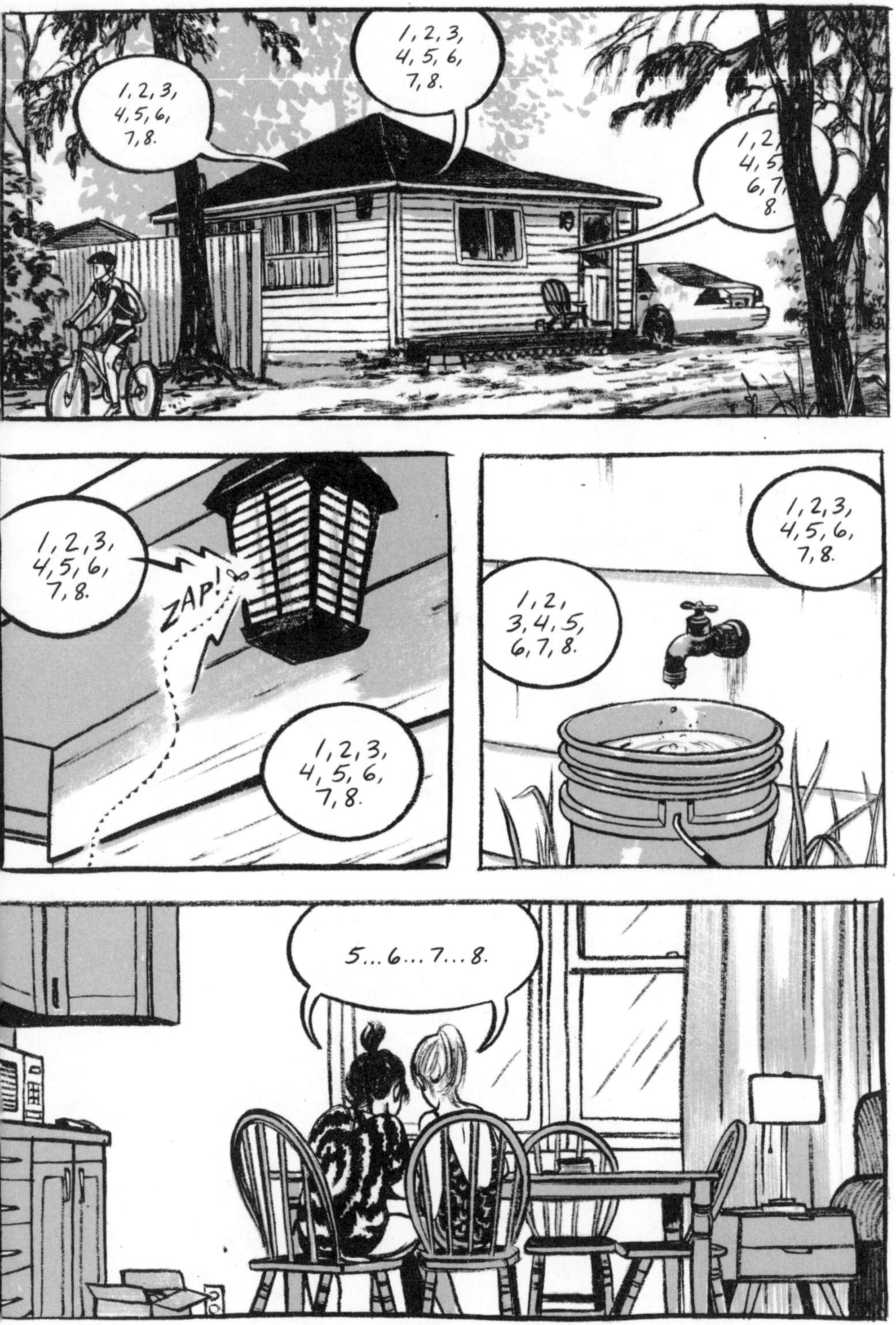
1, 2, 3, 4, 5, 6, 7, 8.
1, 2, 3, 4, 5, 6, 7, 8.
1, 2 4, 5 6, 7 8.
1, 2, 3, 4, 5, 6, 7, 8.
ZAP!
1, 2, 3, 4, 5, 6, 7, 8.
1, 2, 3, 4, 5, 6, 7, 8.
1, 2, 3, 4, 5, 6, 7, 8.
5... 6... 7... 8.

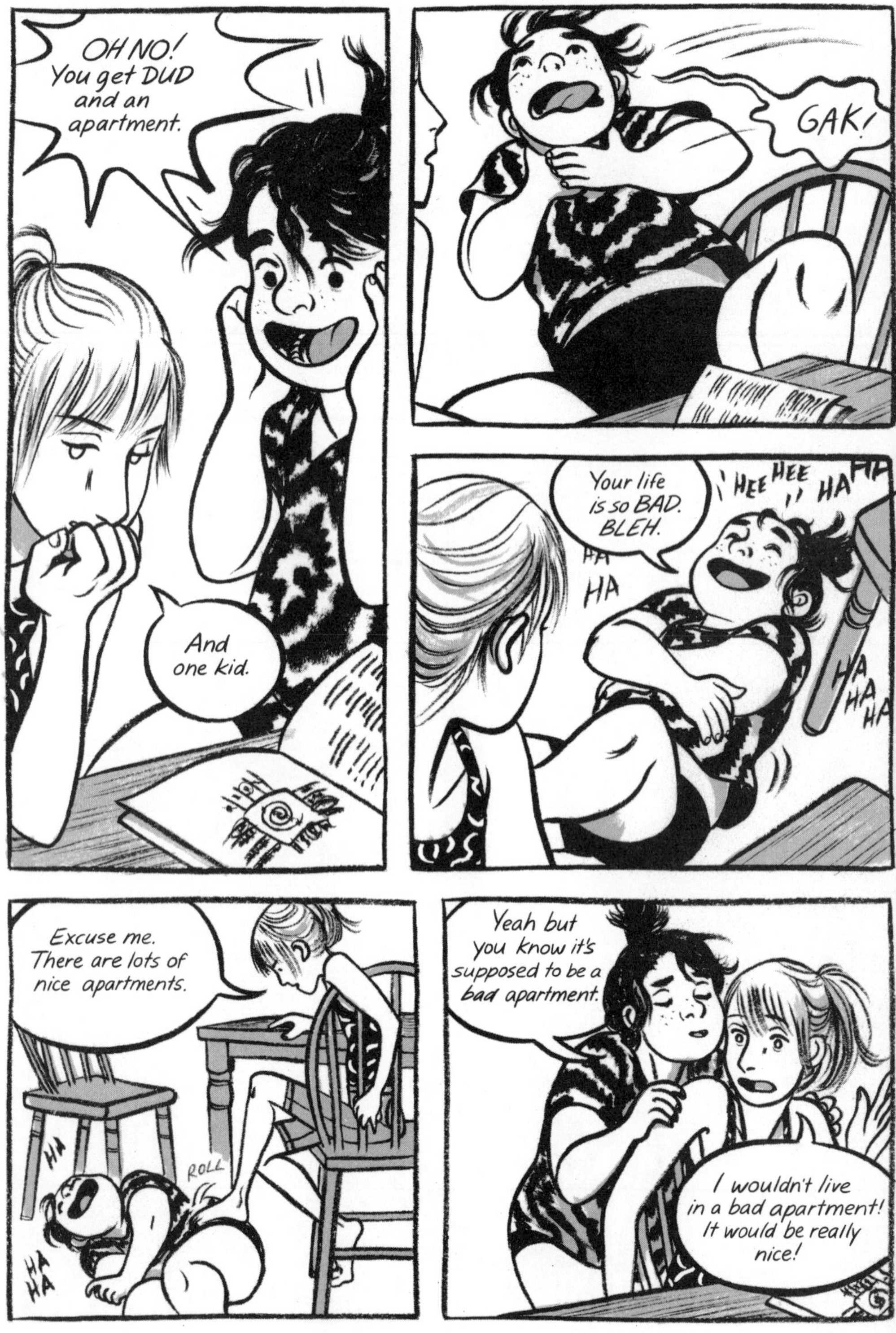
OH NO! You get DUD and an apartment.
And one kid.
GAK!
Your life is so BAD. BLEH.
HEE HEE HA HA
HA HA
HA HA HA
Excuse me. There are lots of nice apartments.
HA
ROLL
HA HA
Yeah but you know it's supposed to be a bad apartment.
I wouldn't live in a bad apartment! It would be really nice!

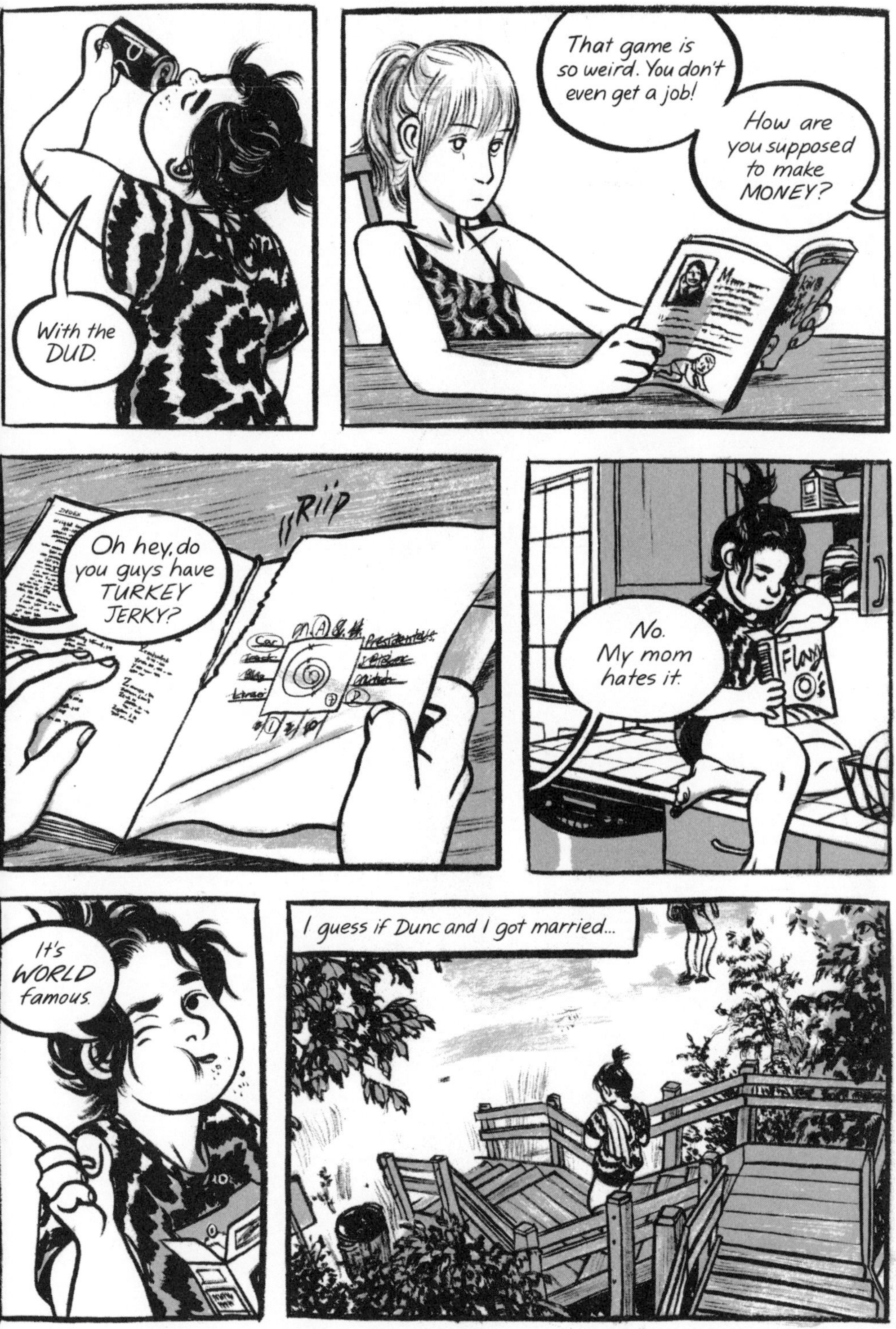
With the DUD.
That game is so weird. You don't even get a job!
How are you supposed to make MONEY?
RIIP
Oh hey, do you guys have TURKEY JERKY?
No. My mom hates it.
It's WORLD famous.
I guess if Dunc and I got married...

...we would live in an apartment first.
With regular jobs. Then.
Then we would get good jobs.
And.

And he would go to medical school.

Um.
And I would take time off to have one.

Perfect. Baby.

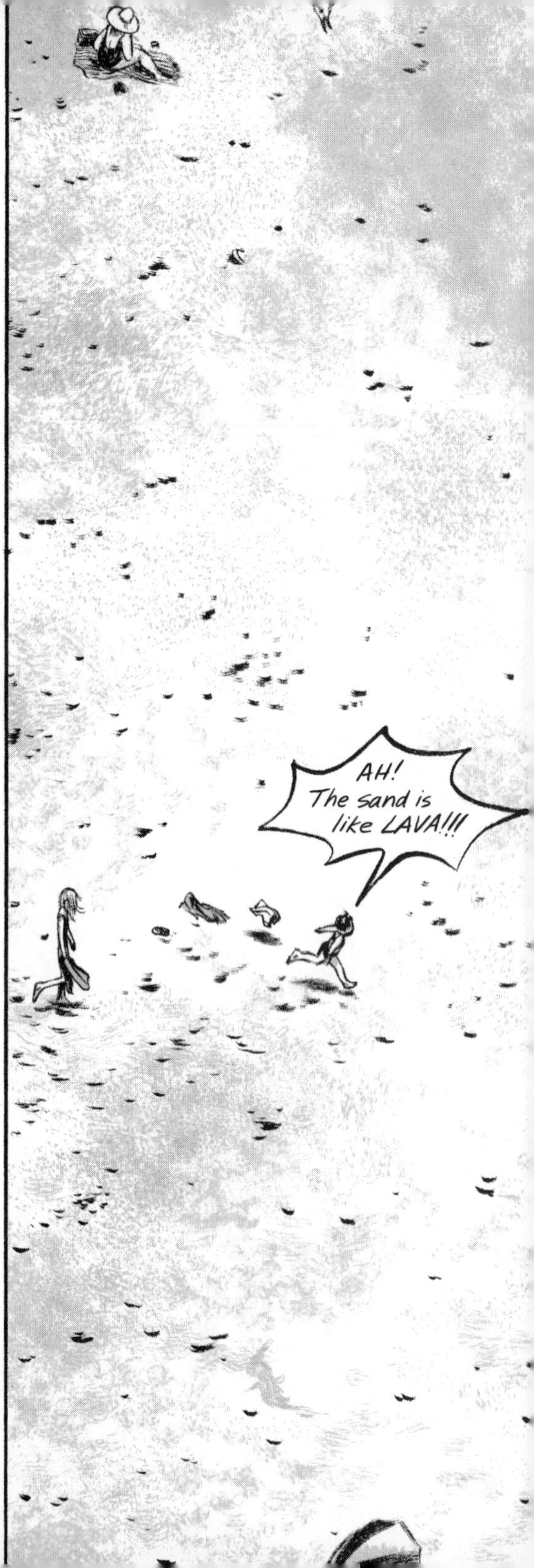
AH!
The sand is like LAVA!!!

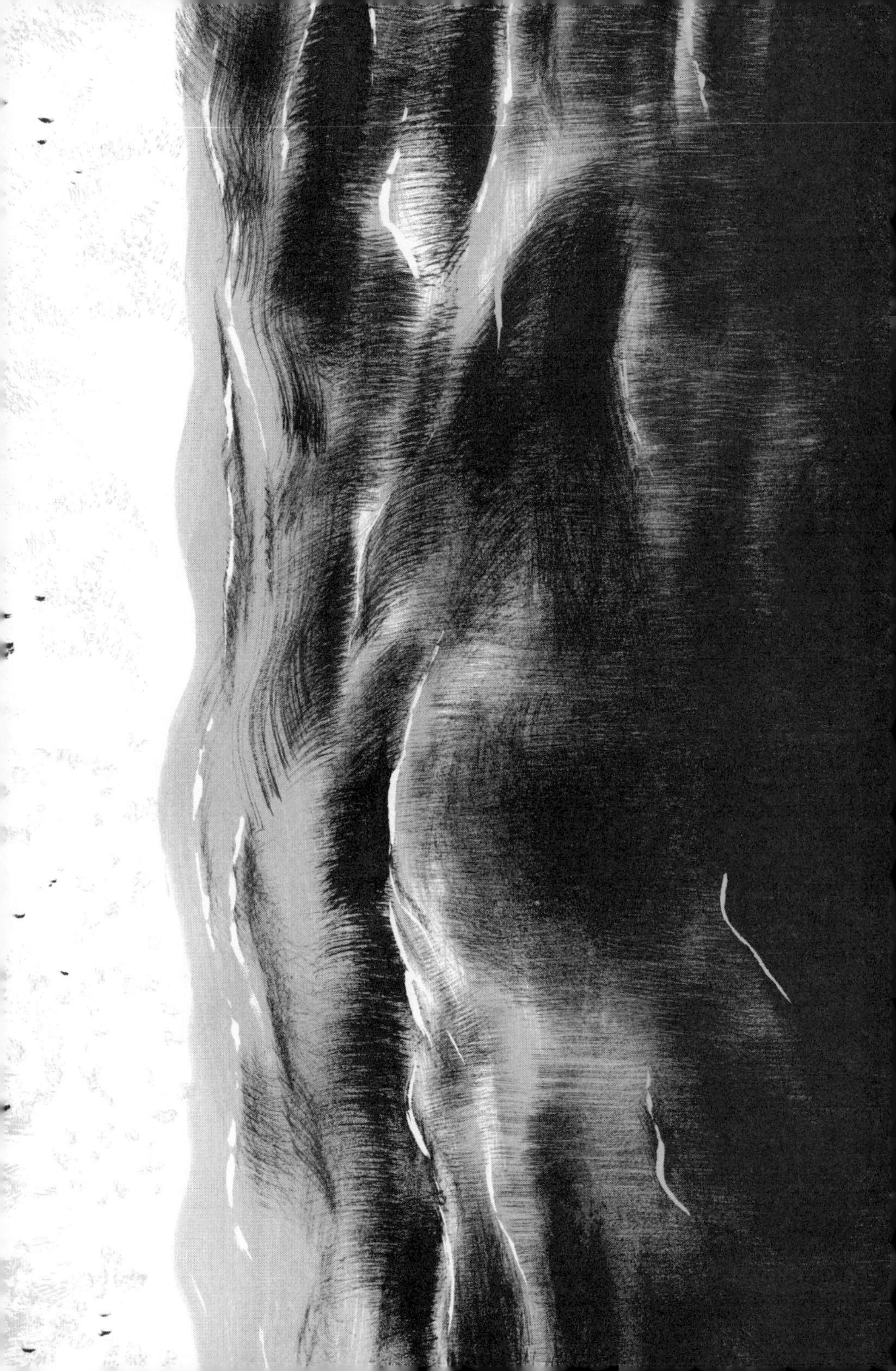

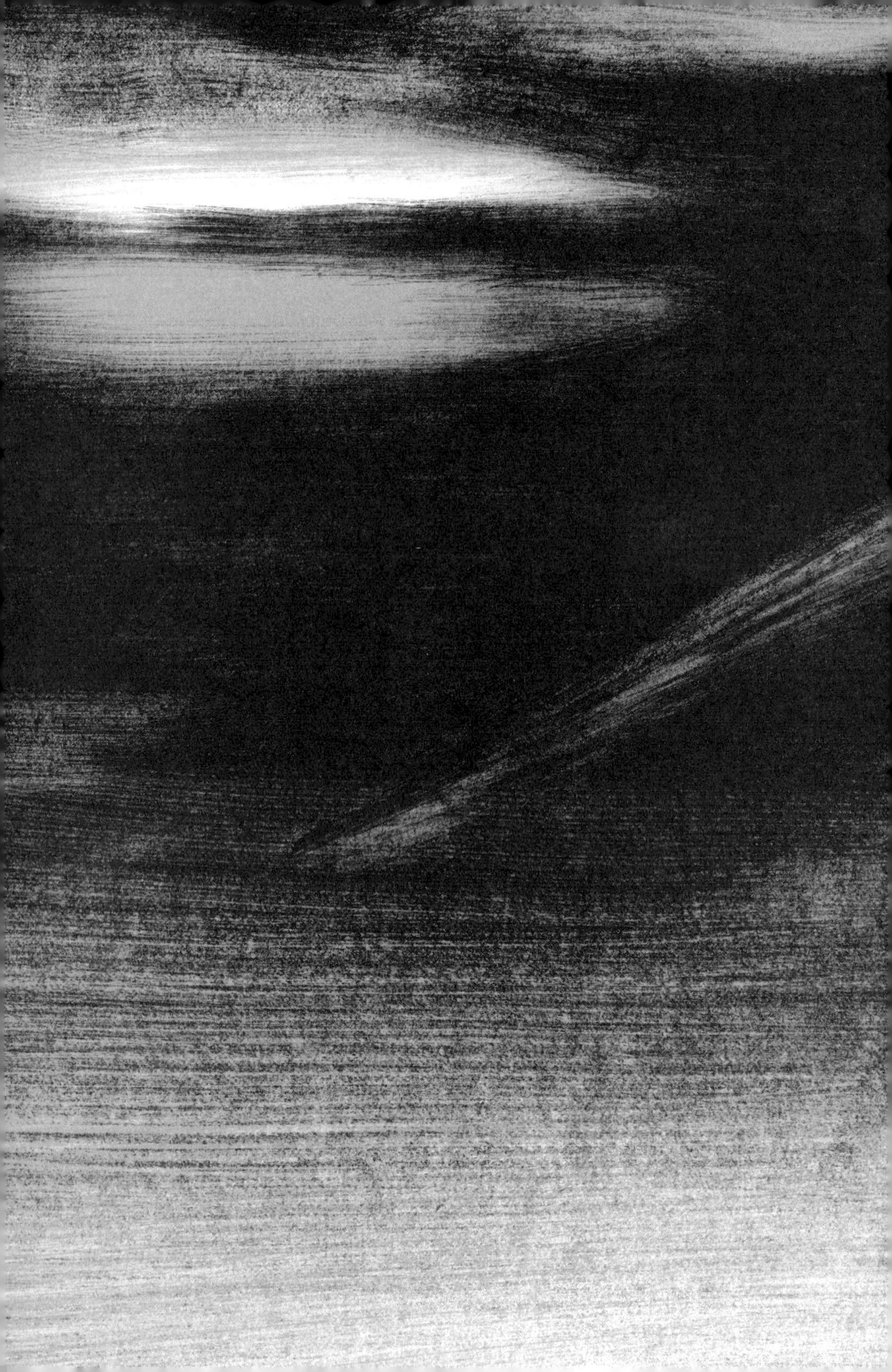

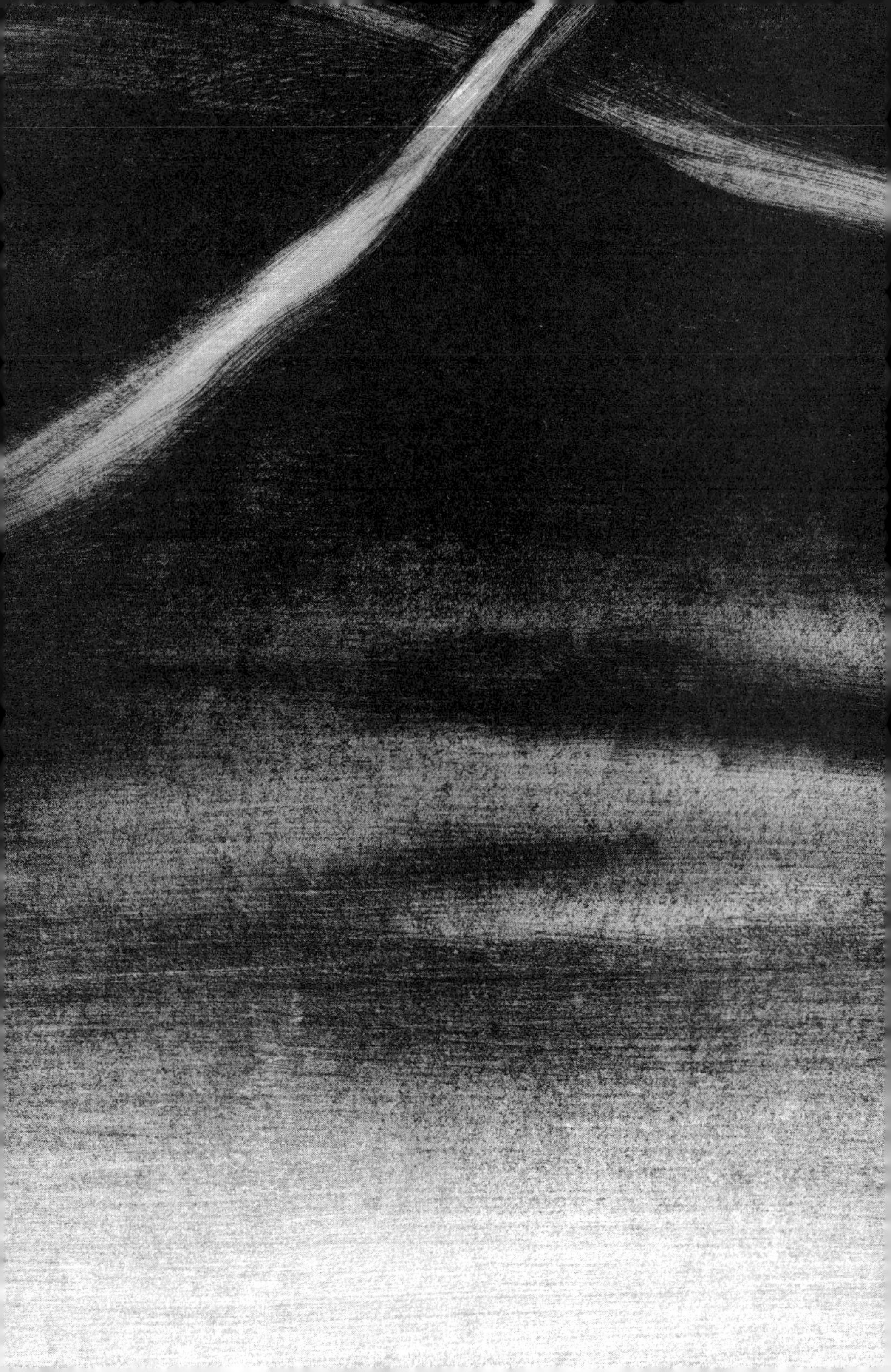

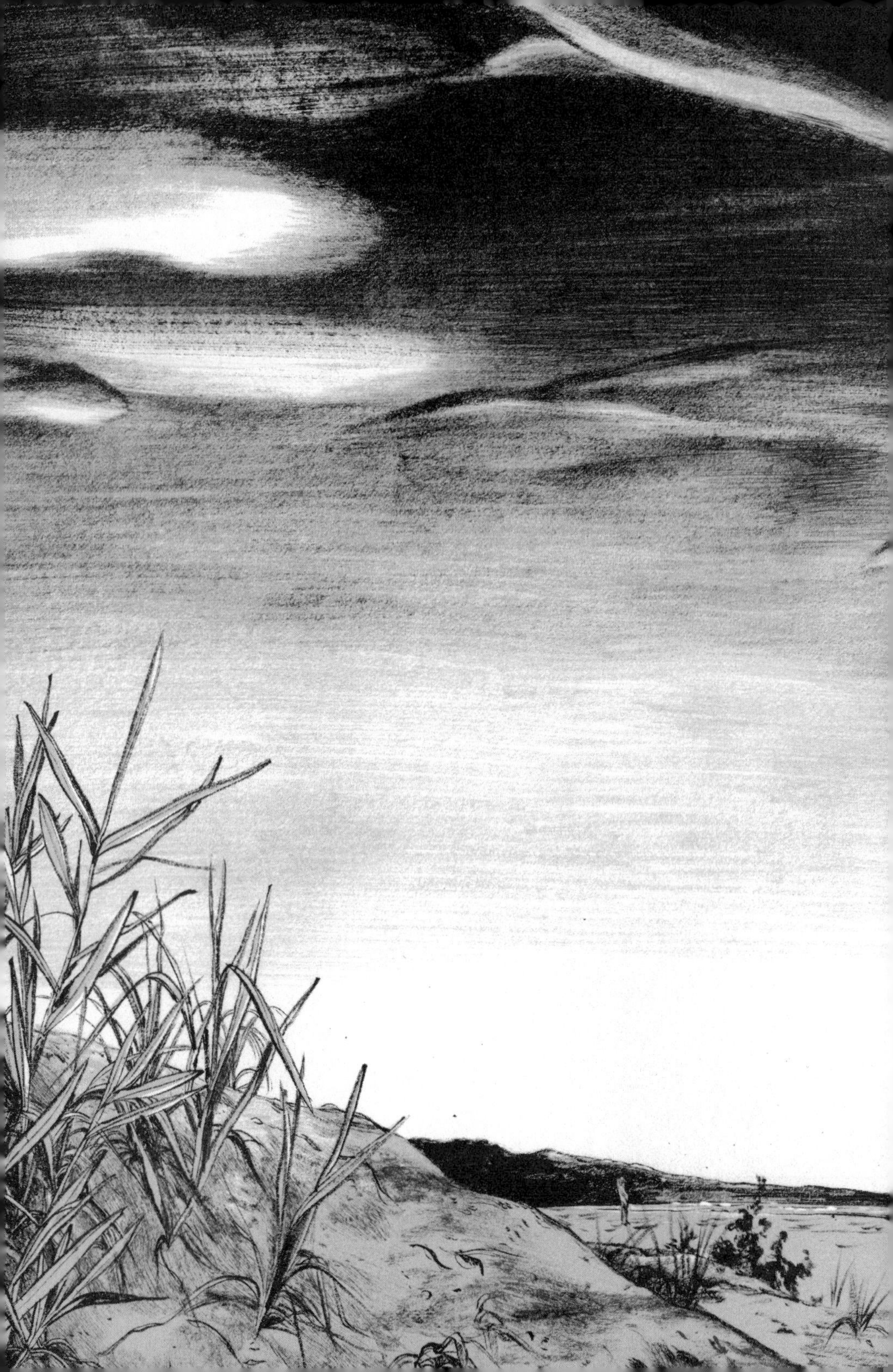

You remember that time your mom made up that ghost story about the woman who carried her heart around in her purse?

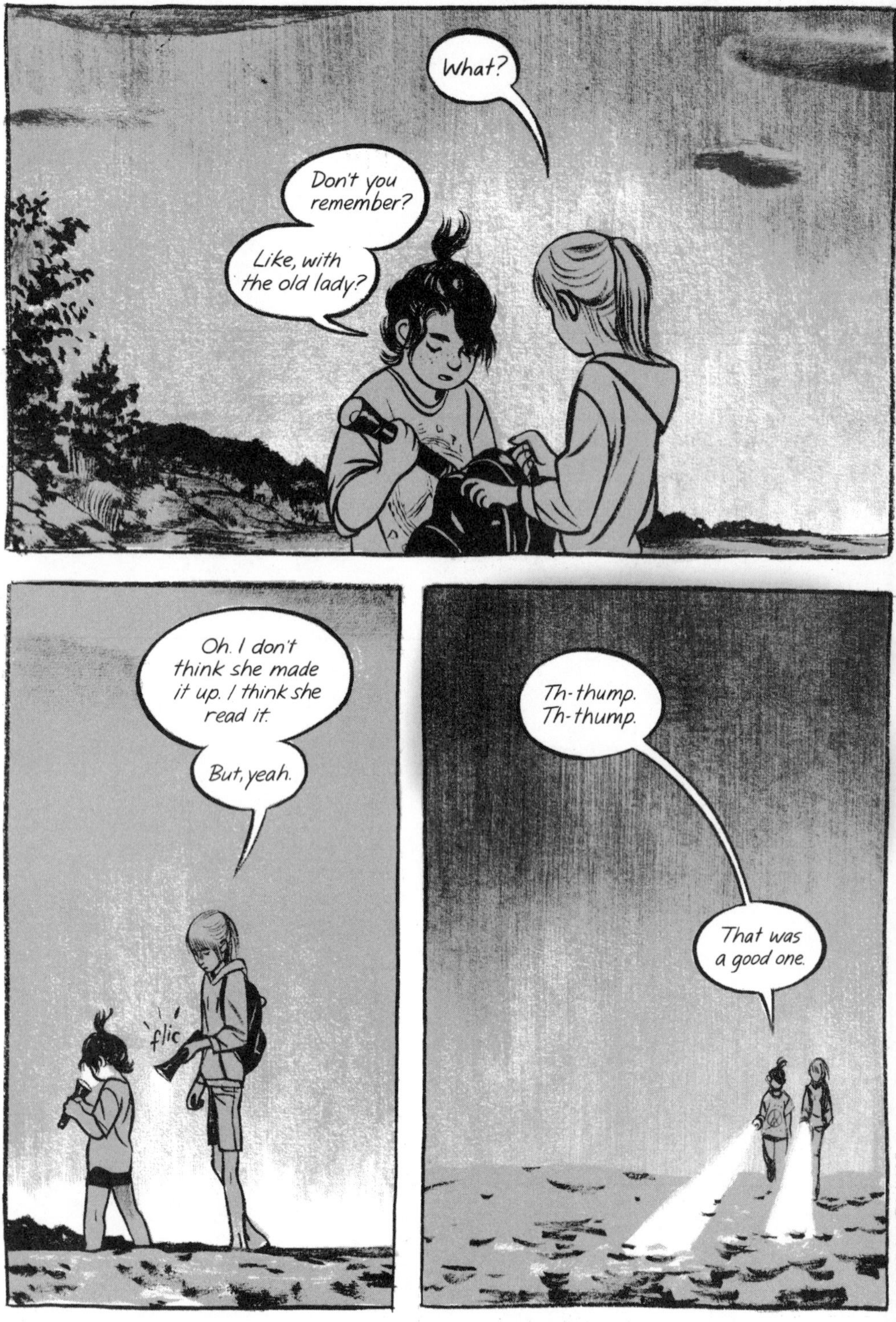
What?
Don't you remember?
Like, with the old lady?
Oh. I don't think she made it up. I think she read it.
But, yeah.
flic
Th-thump. Th-thump.
That was a good one.

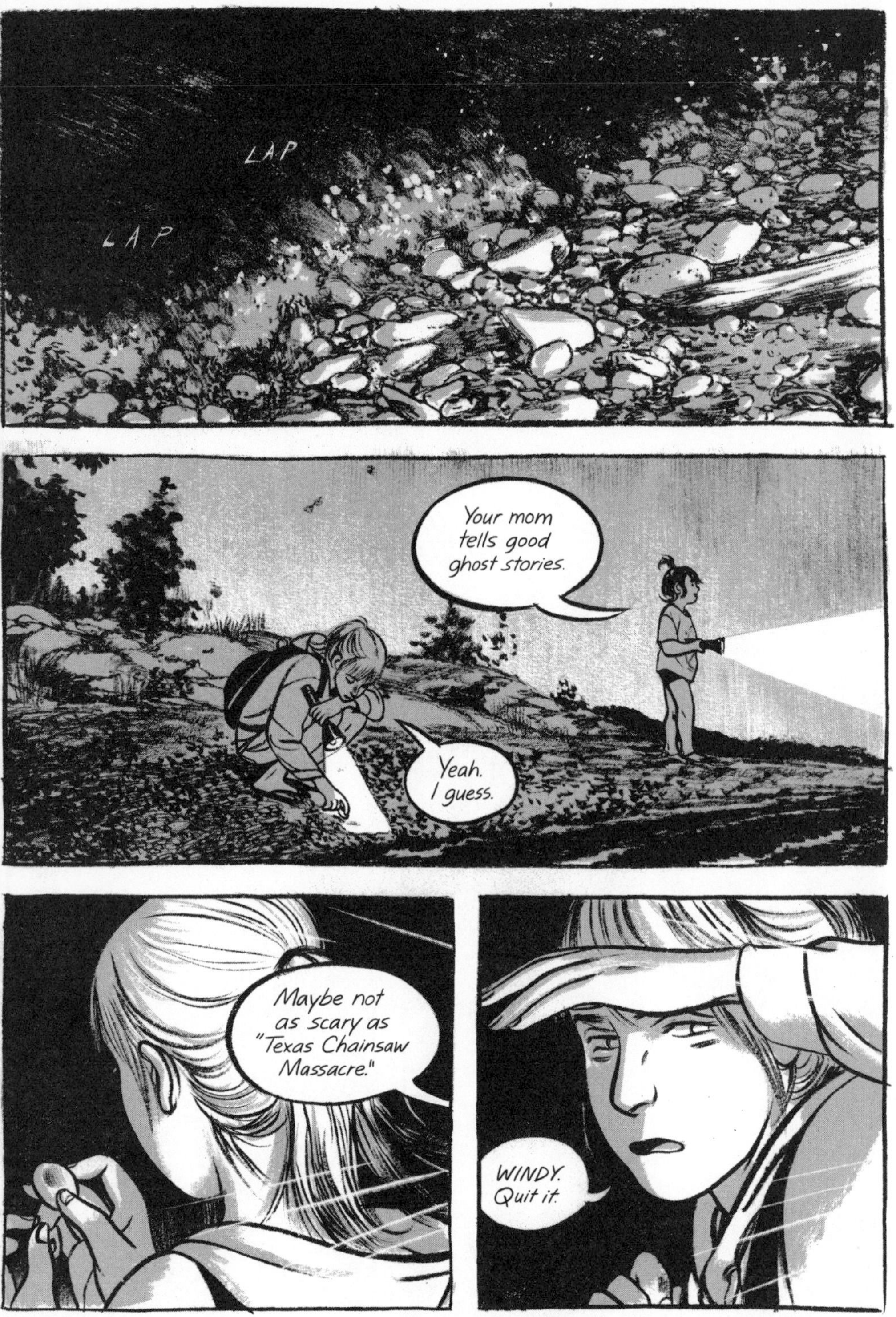
LAP
LAP
Your mom tells good ghost stories.
Yeah. I guess.
Maybe not as scary as "Texas Chainsaw Massacre."
WINDY. Quit it.

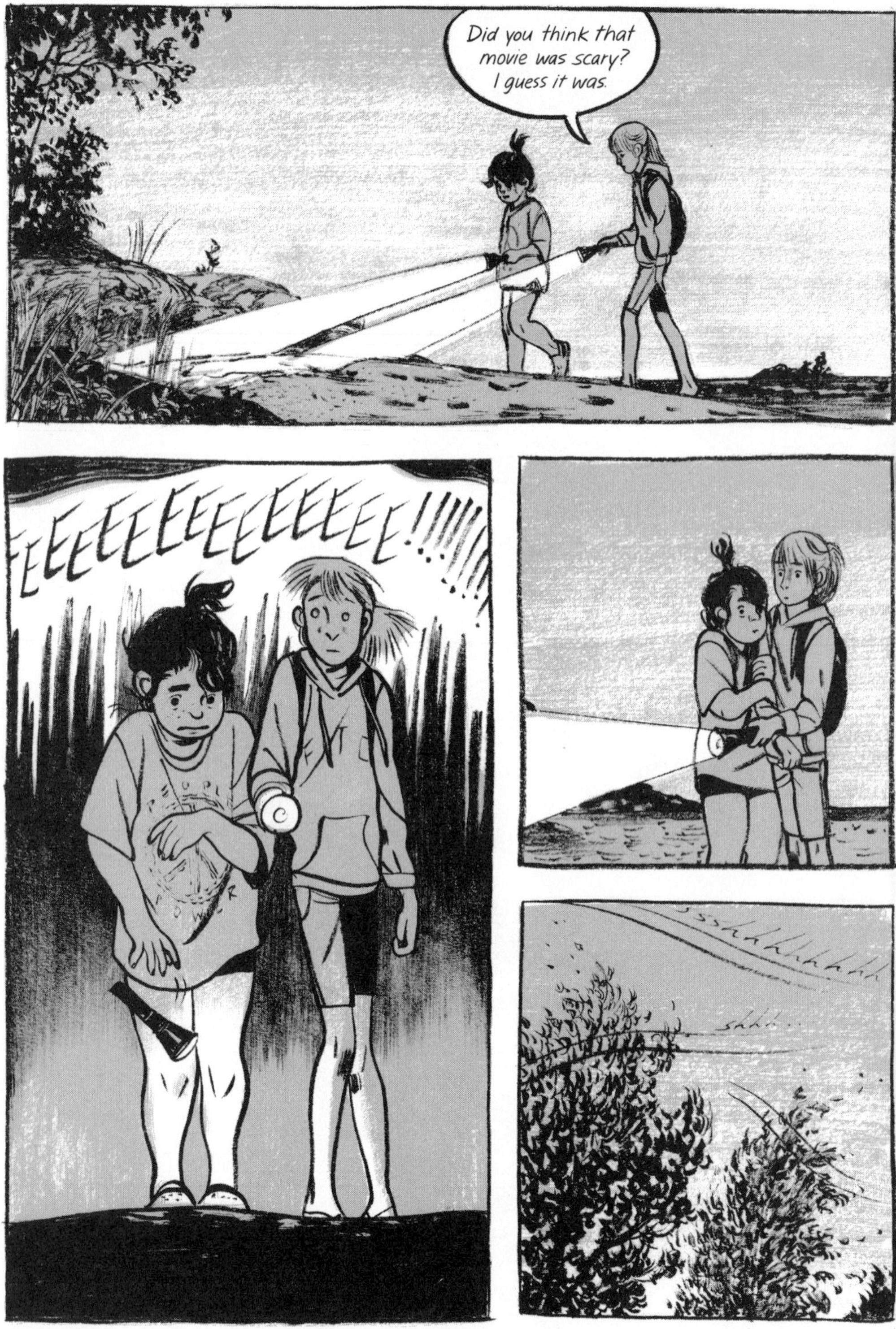
Did you think that movie was scary? I guess it was.
EEEEEEEEEEEEEE!!!!!!
ssshhhhhhhh
shhh...

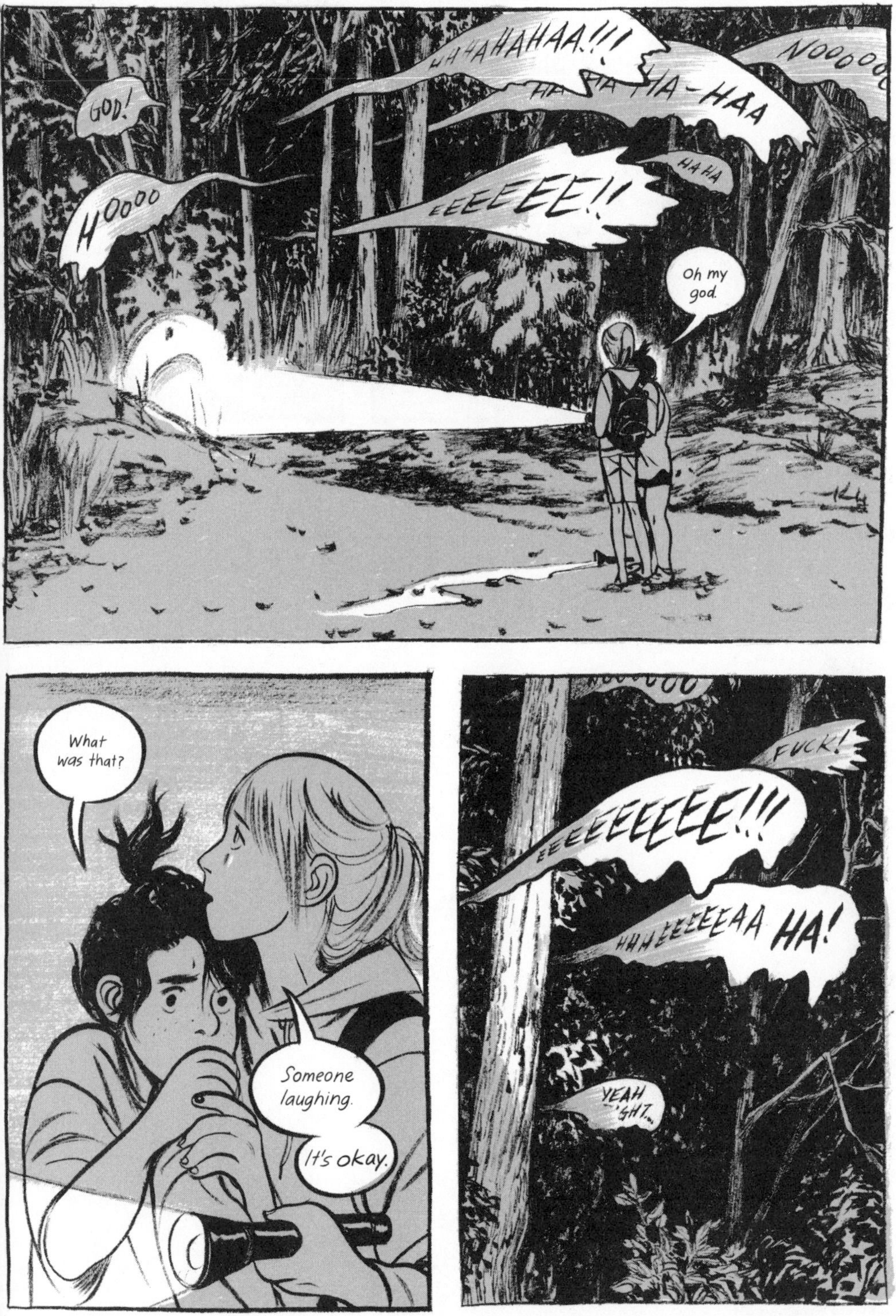
HAHAHAHAA!!!
HA HA HA-HAA
GOD!
HOOOO
EEEEEE!!
HA HA
Oh my god.
What was that?
Someone laughing.
It's okay.
FUCK!
EEEEEEEEE!!!
HHHEEEEEAA HA!
YEAH

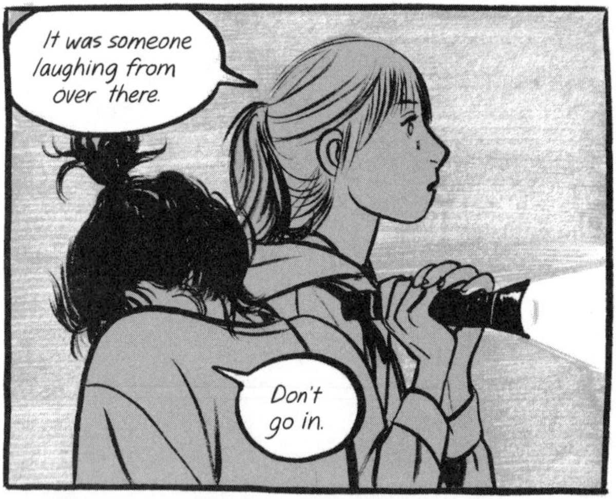
It was someone laughing from over there.
Don't go in.

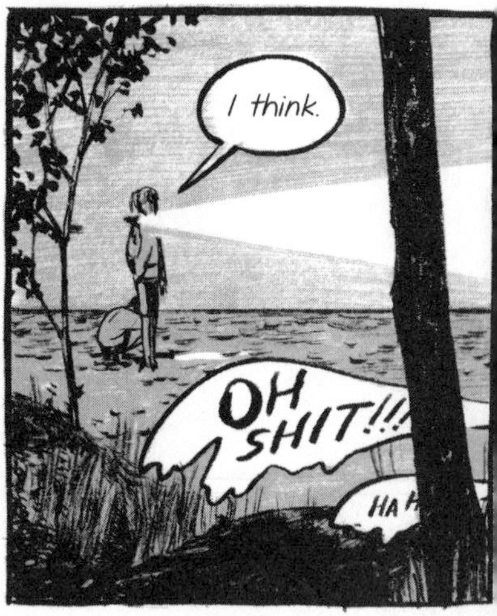
I think.
OH SHIT!!!
HA H

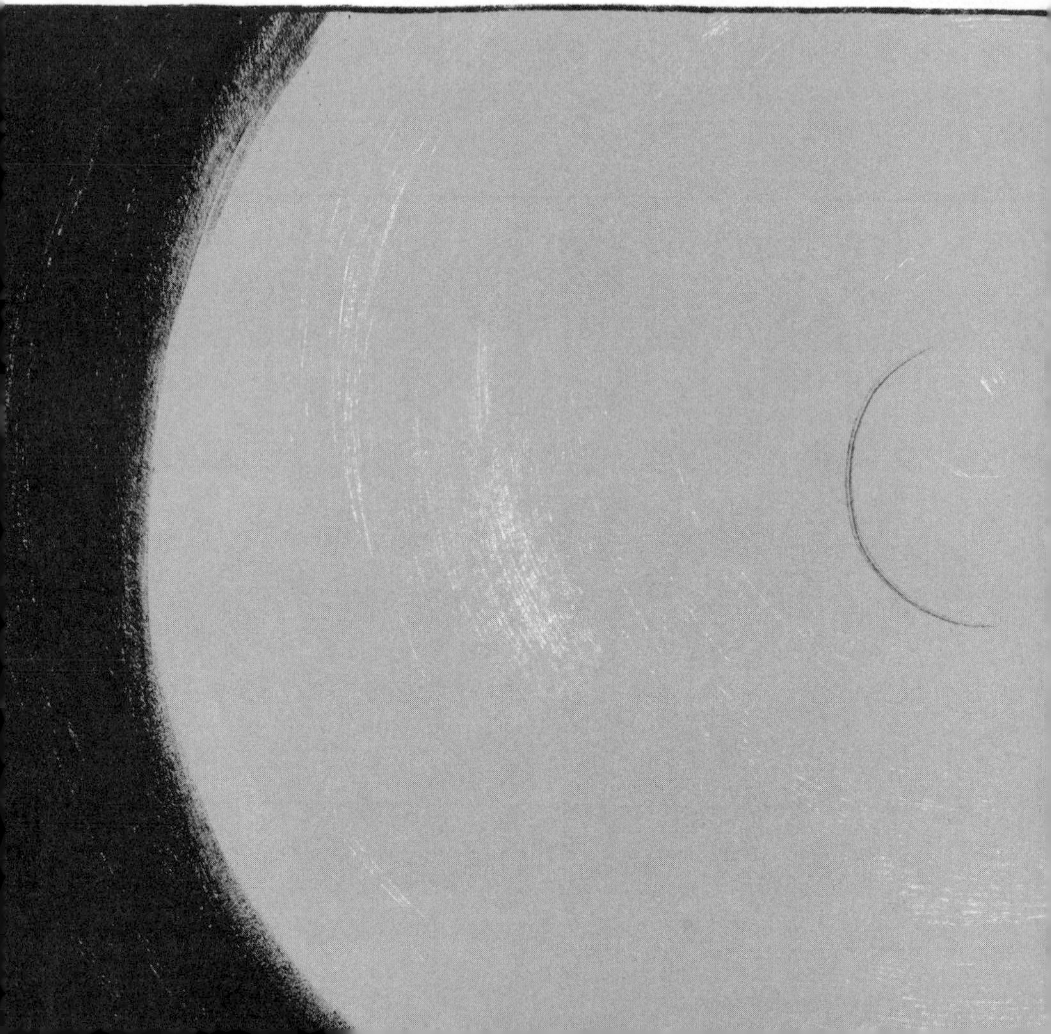

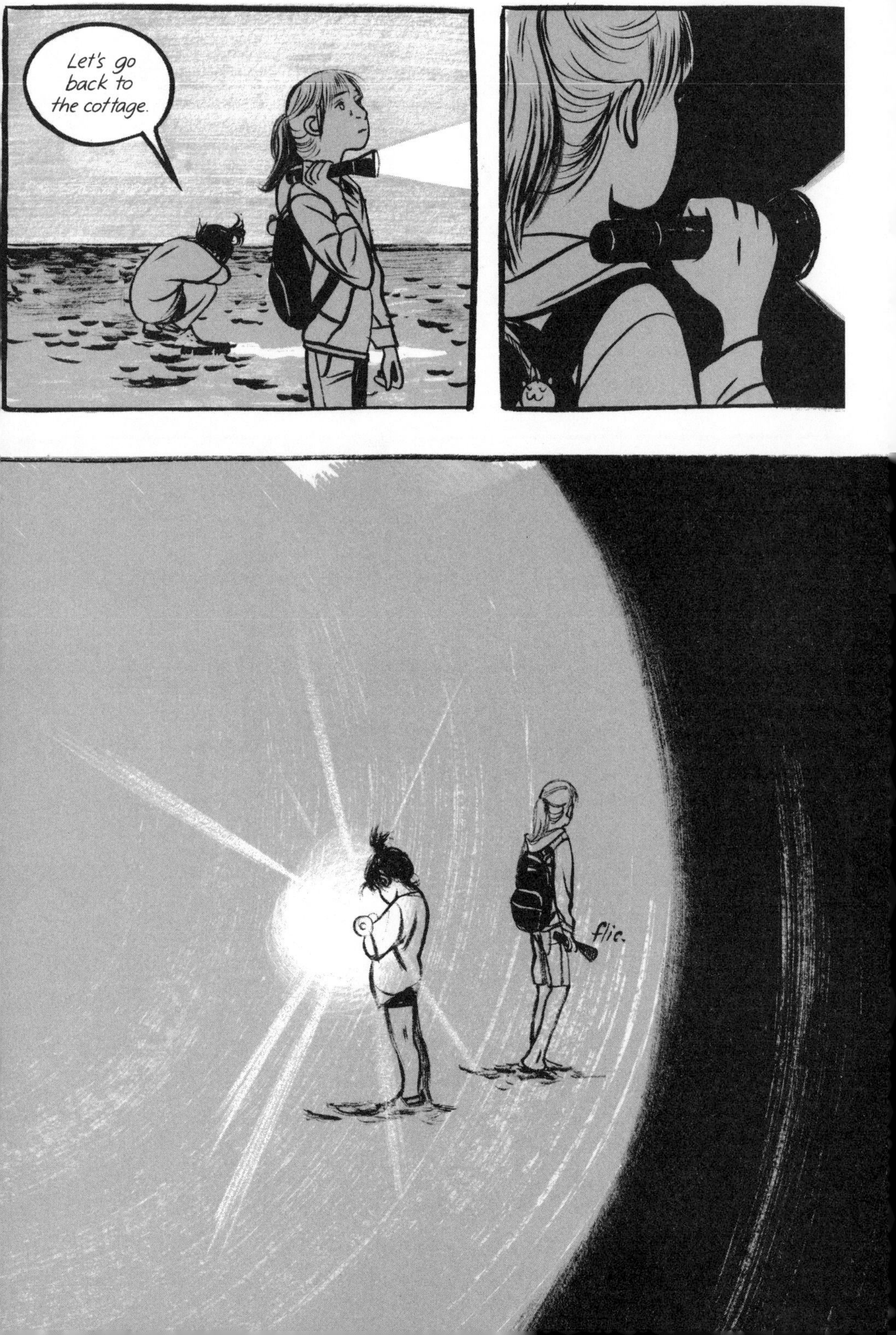
Let's go back to the cottage.
flic.

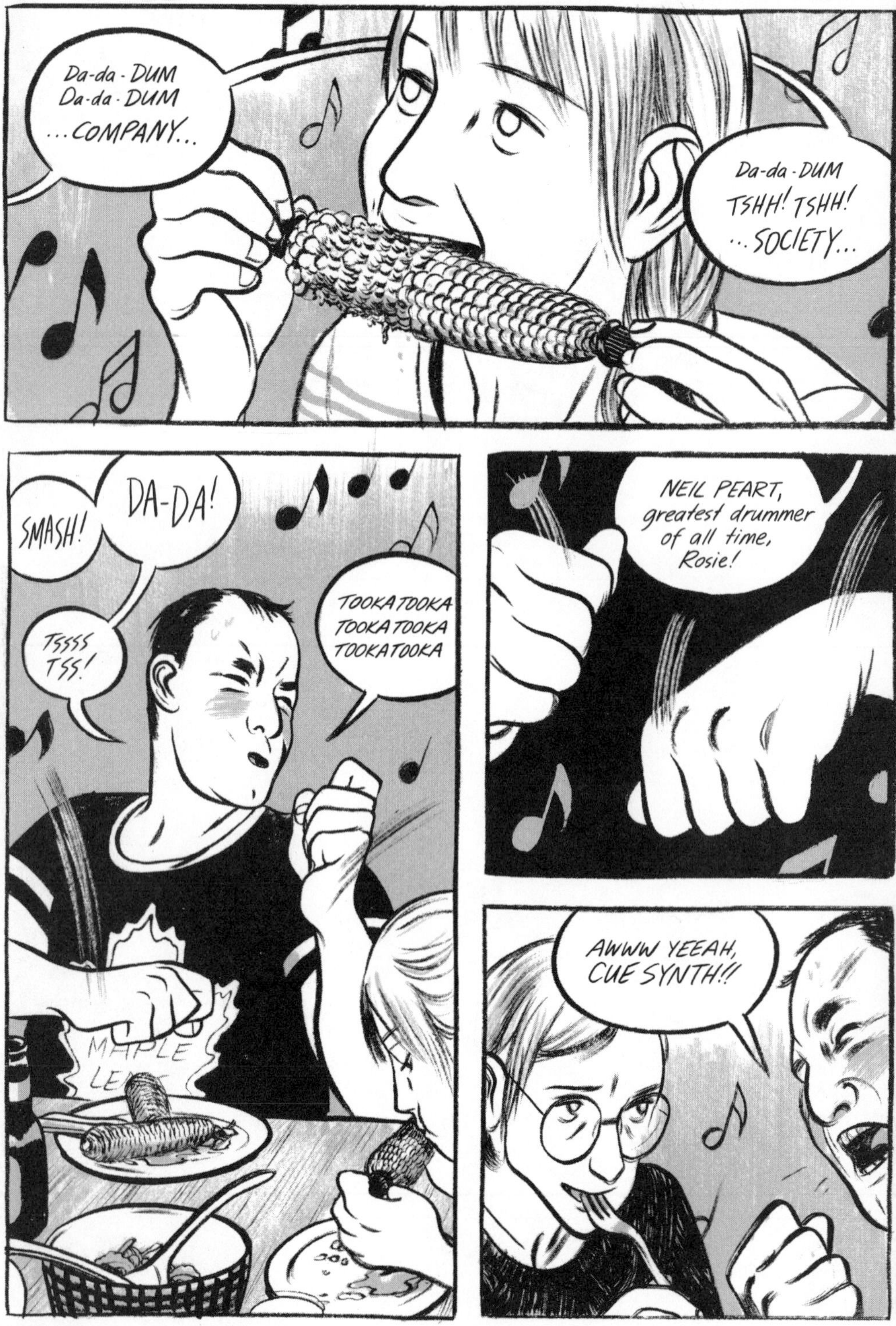
Da-da-DUM
Da-da-DUM
...COMPANY...
Da-da-DUM
TSHH! TSHH!
...SOCIETY...
SMASH!
DA-DA!
TSSSS
TSS!
TOOKATOOKA
TOOKATOOKA
TOOKATOOKA
MAPLE LE
NEIL PEART,
greatest drummer
of all time,
Rosie!
AWWW YEEAH,
CUE SYNTH!!

93

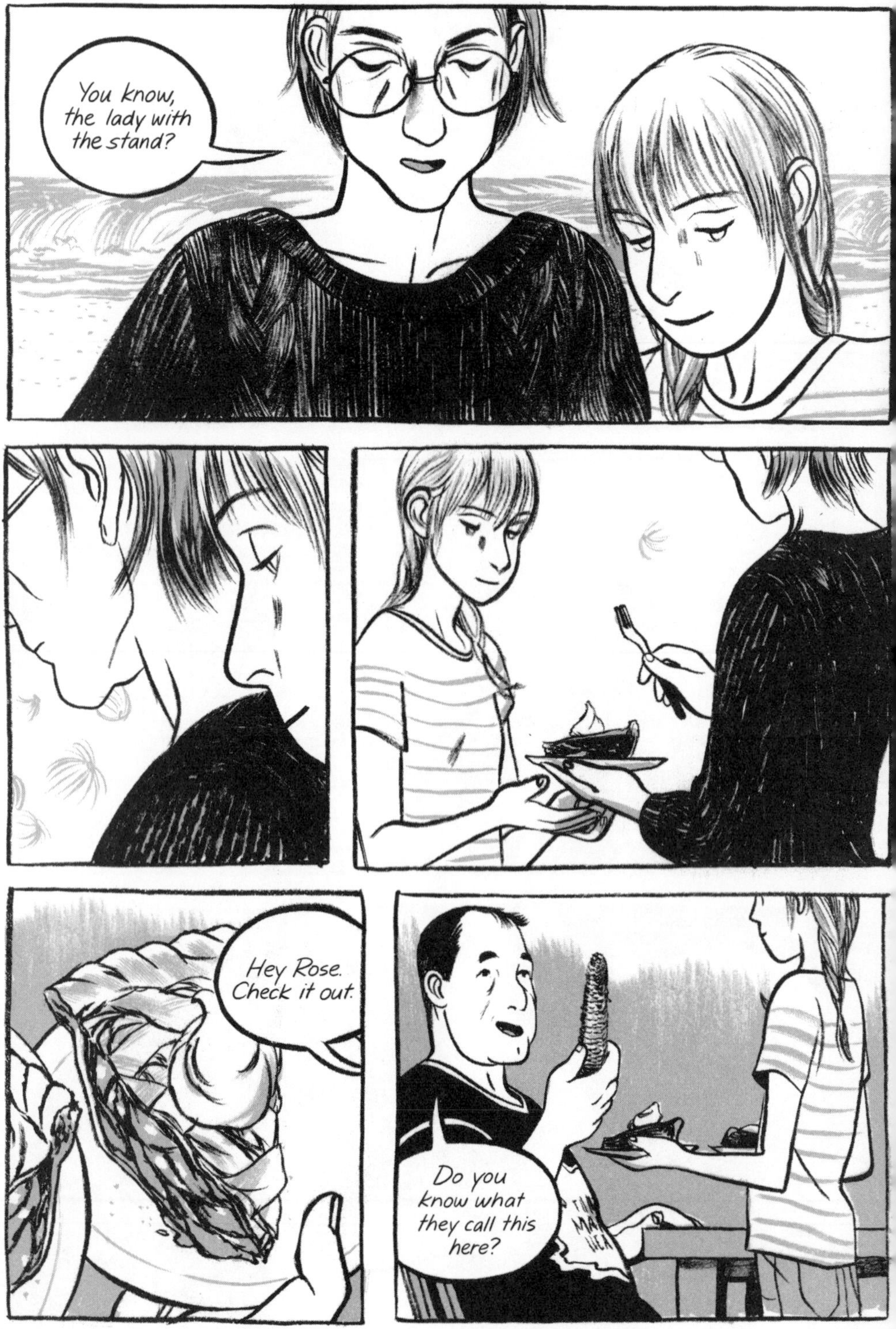
You know, the lady with the stand?
Hey Rose. Check it out.
Do you know what they call this here?

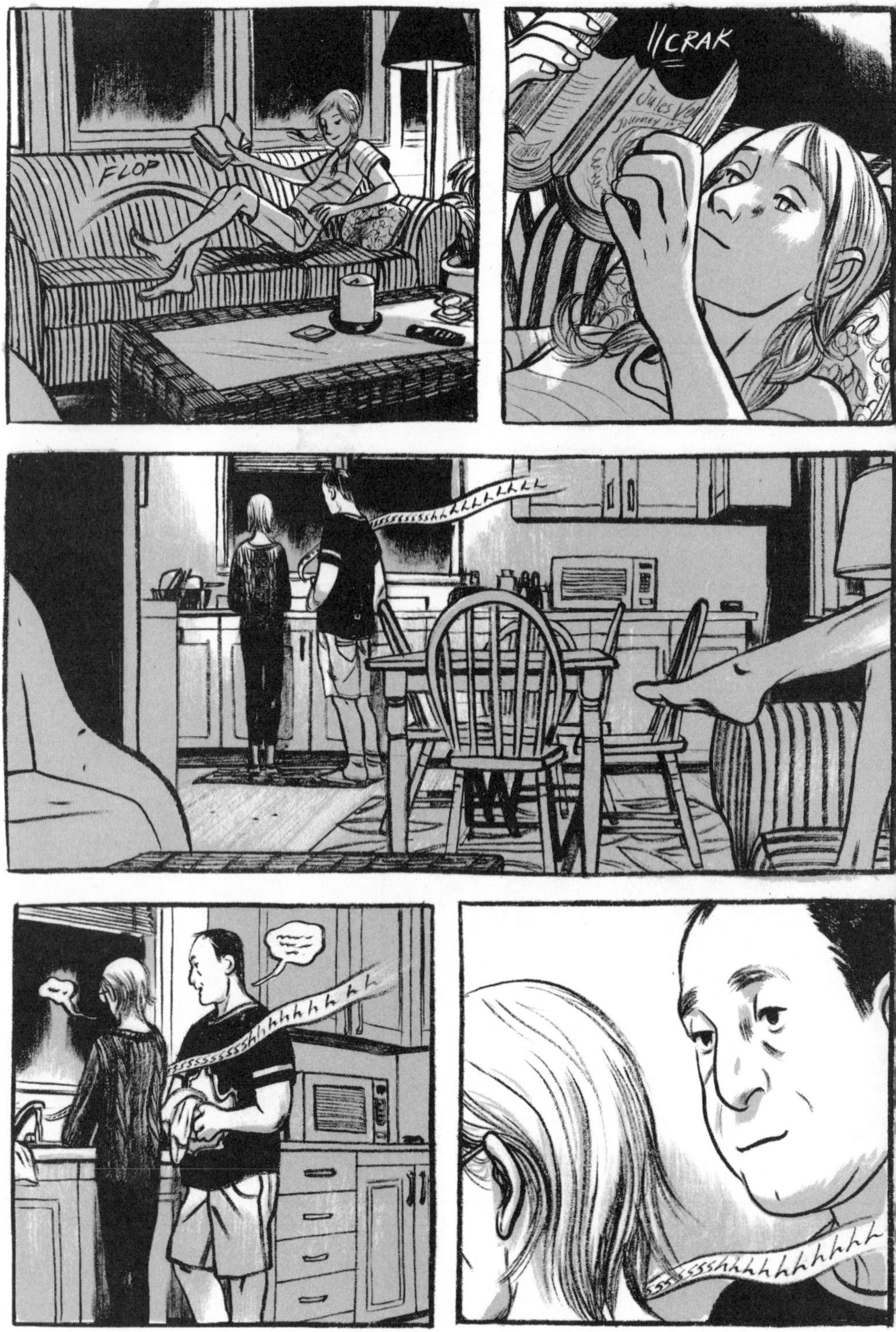
FLOP
CRAK
Jules Ve
Journey
sssssshhhhhhhhhh
sssssssshhhhhhh hh
sssssssshhhhhhhhhh

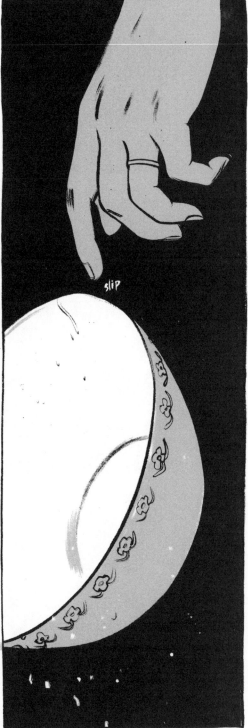

slip

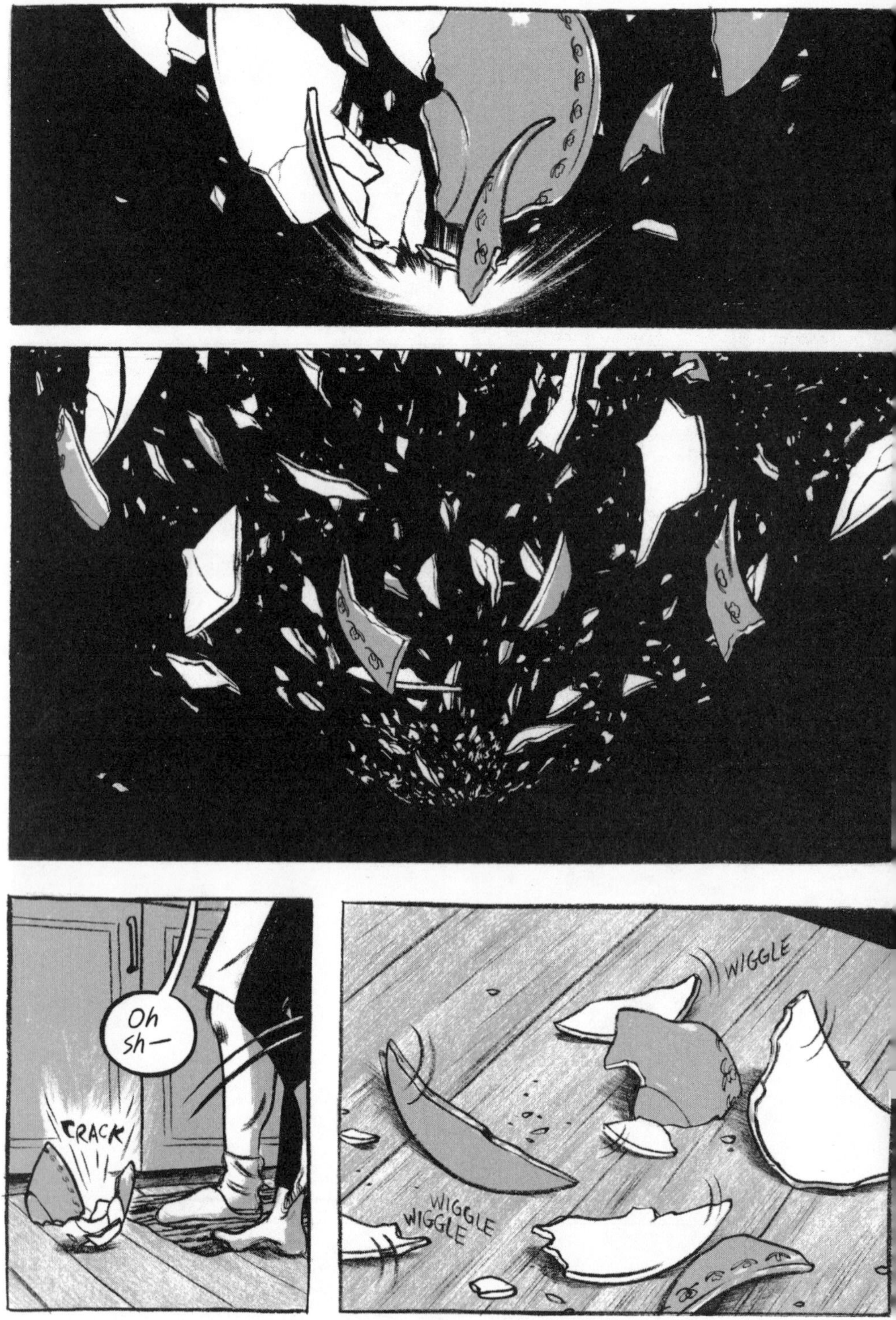
Oh sh—
CRACK
WIGGLE
WIGGLE
WIGGLE

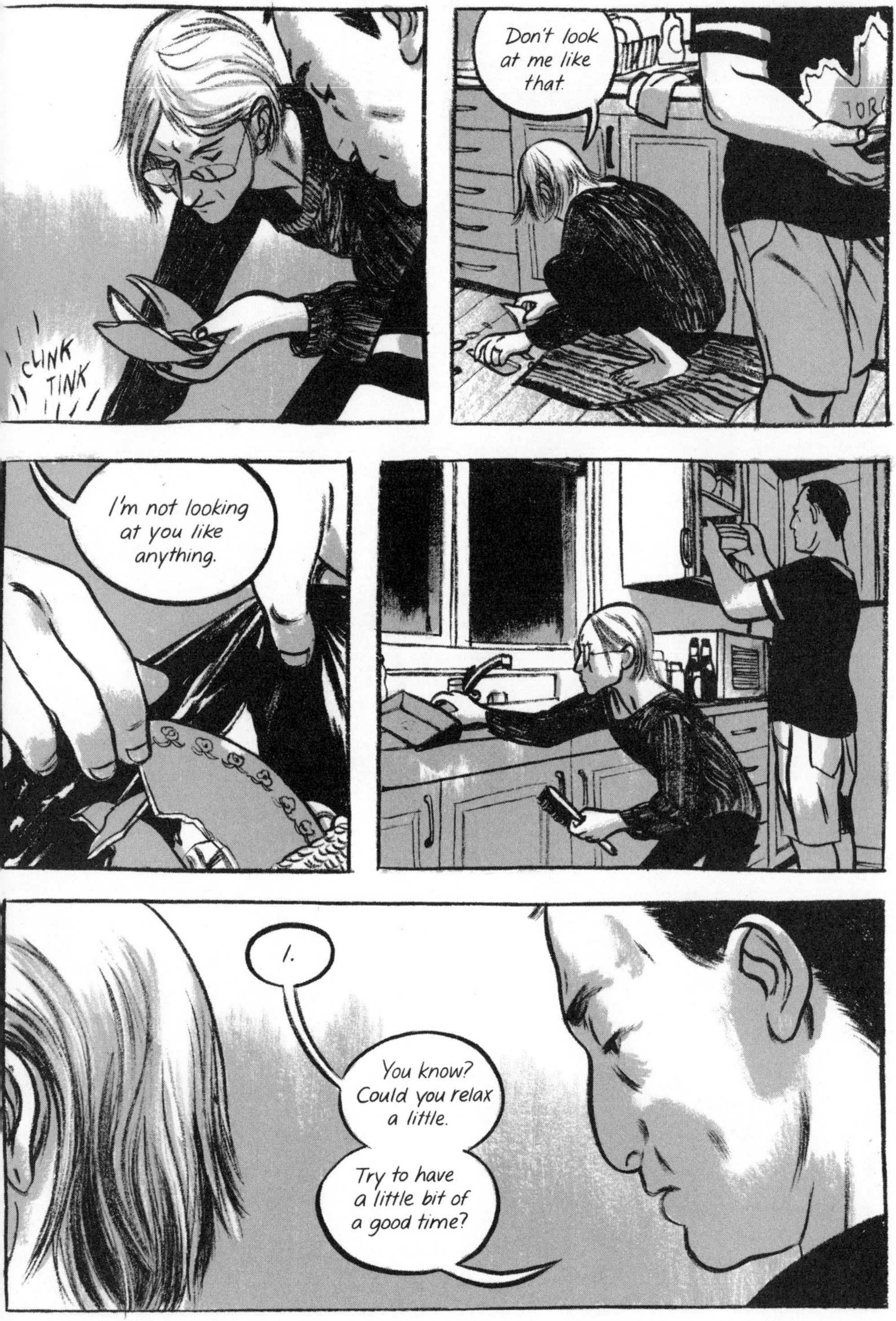
CLINK TINK
Don't look at me like that.
I'm not looking at you like anything.
I.
You know? Could you relax a little.
Try to have a little bit of a good time?

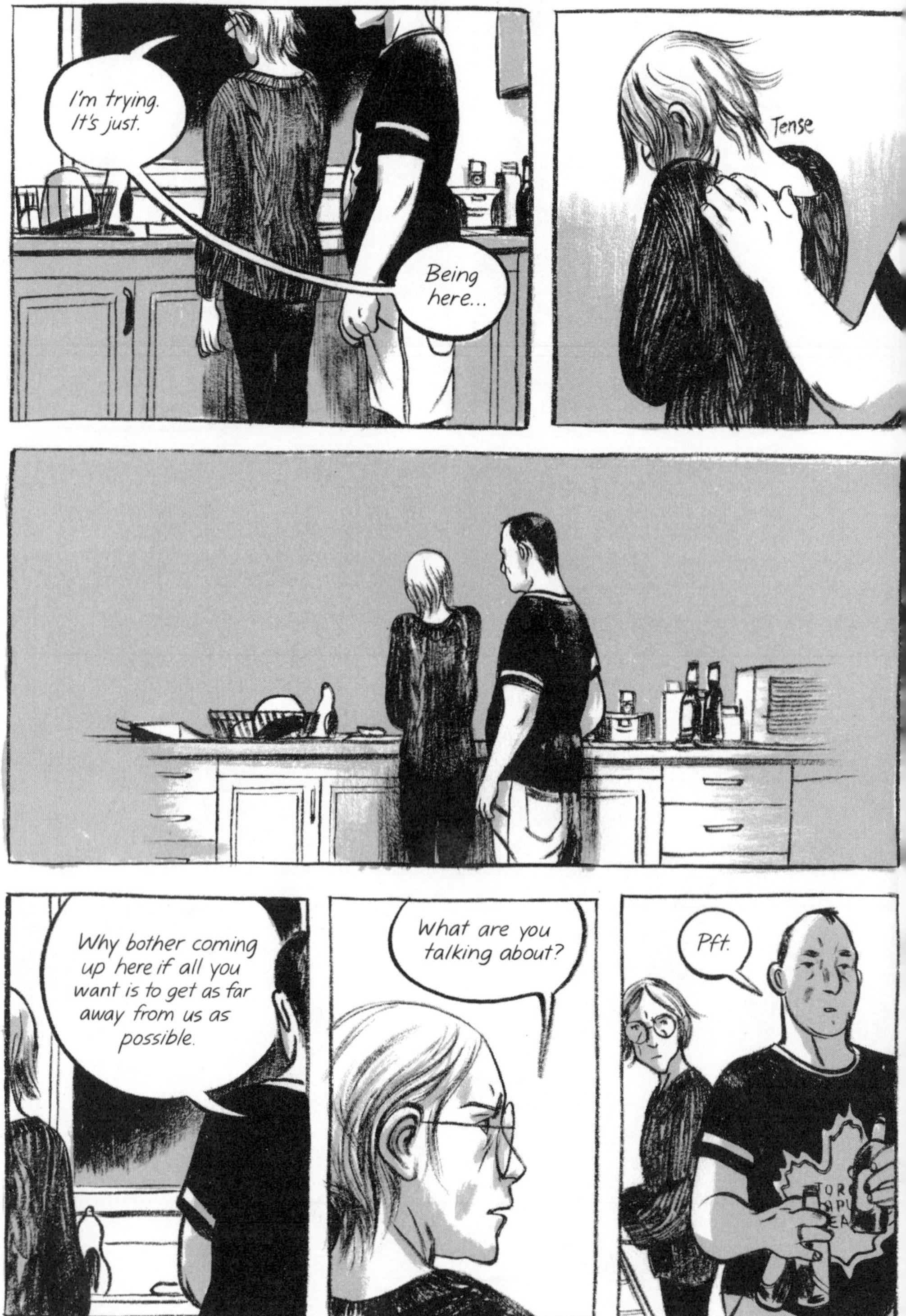
I'm trying.
It's just.
Being here...
Tense
Why bother coming up here if all you want is to get as far away from us as possible.
What are you talking about?
Pft.

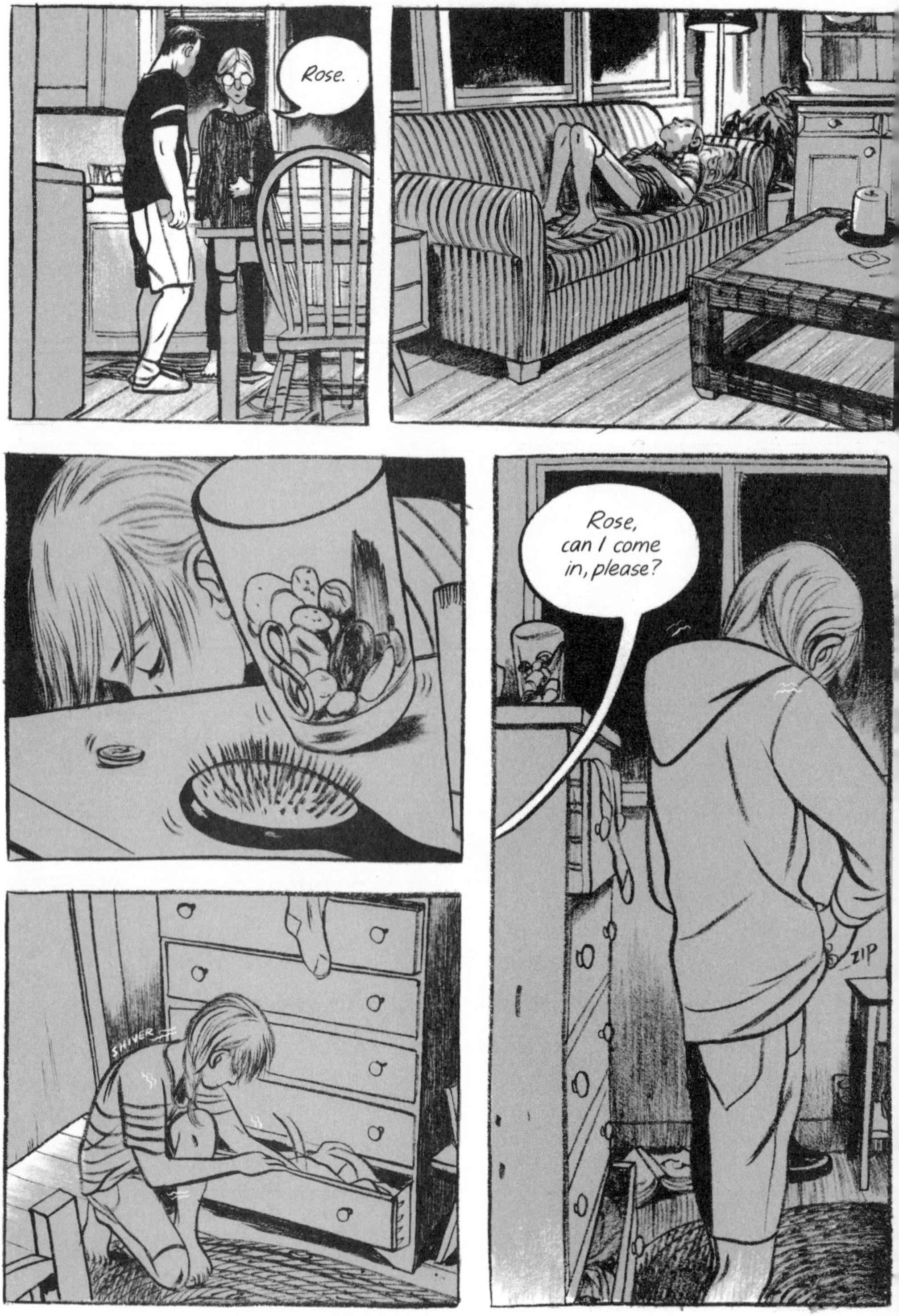
Rose.
Rose, can I come in, please?
ZIP
SHIVER

103

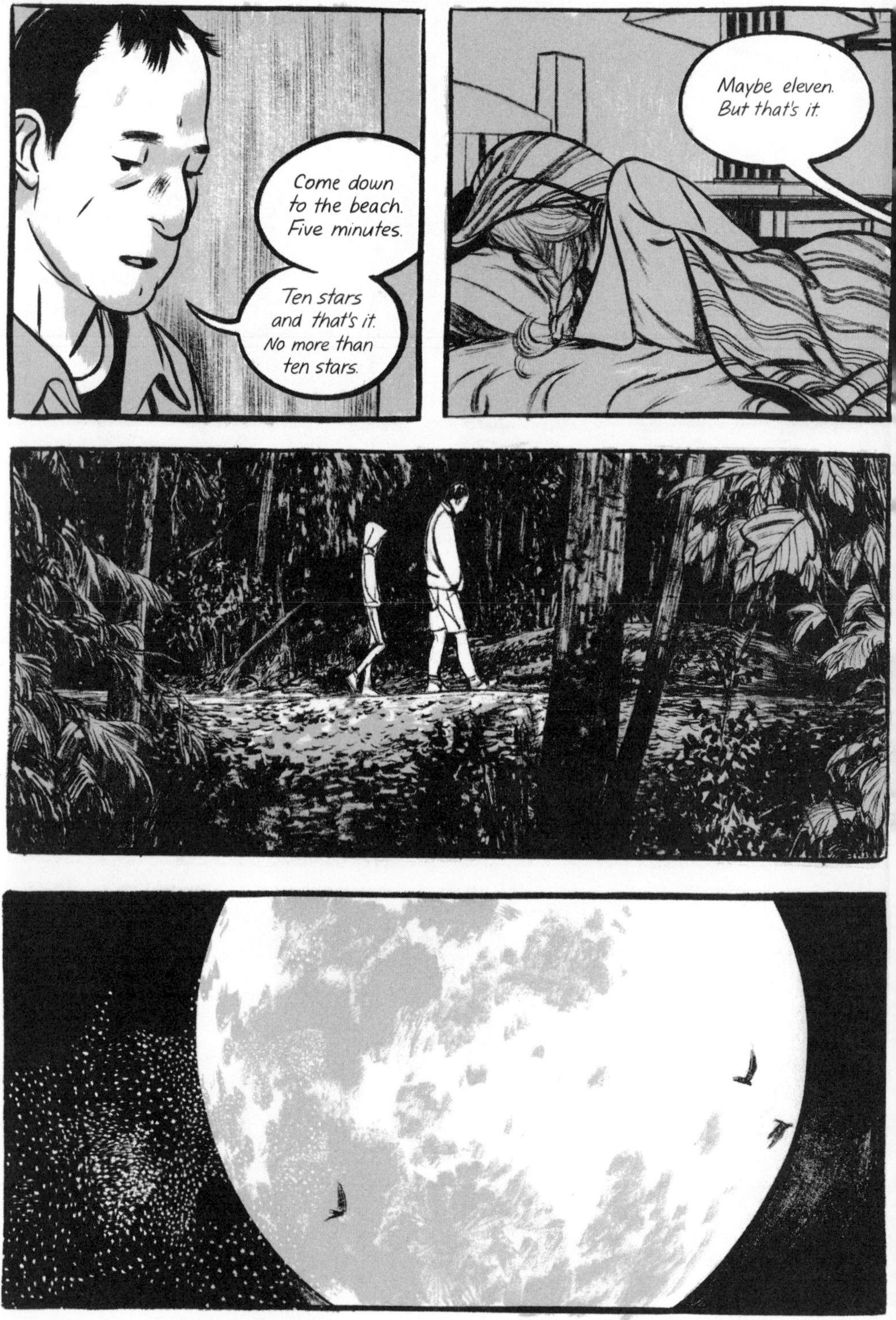
Come down to the beach. Five minutes.
Ten stars and that's it. No more than ten stars.
Maybe eleven. But that's it.

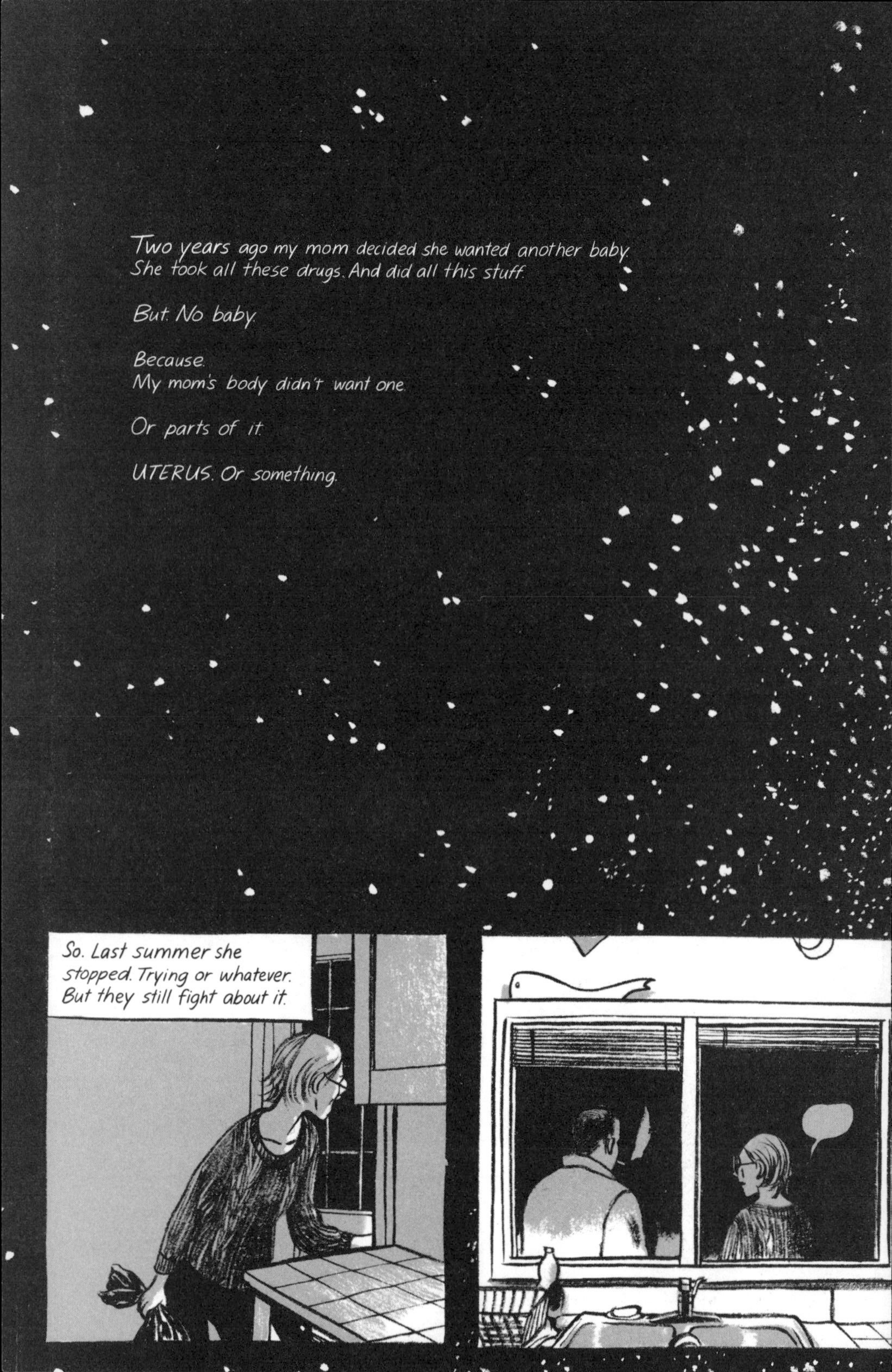
Two years ago my mom decided she wanted another baby.
She took all these drugs. And did all this stuff.
But. No baby.
Because.
My mom's body didn't want one.
Or parts of it.
UTERUS. Or something.
So. Last summer she stopped. Trying or whatever. But they still fight about it.

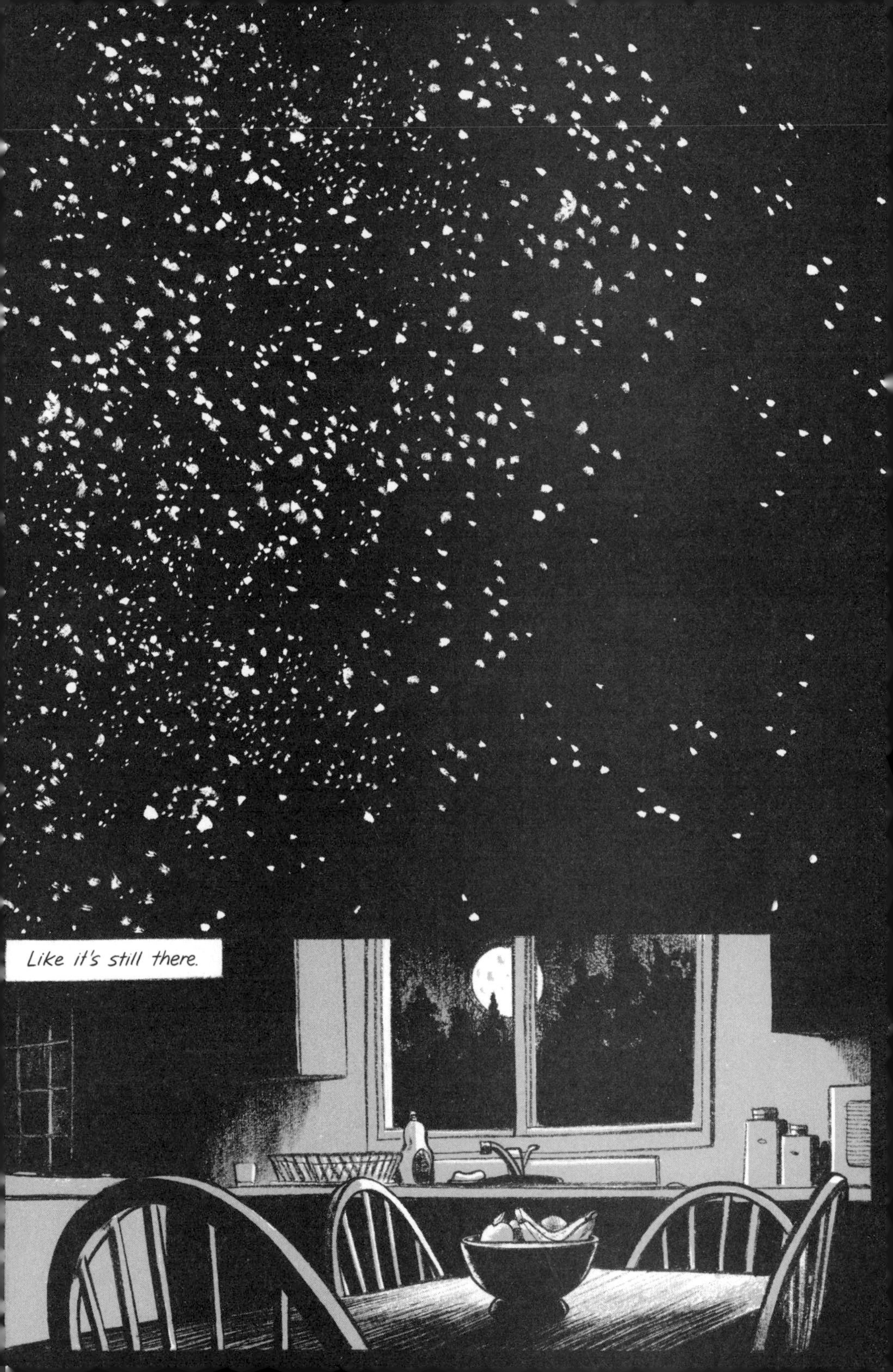
Like it's still there.

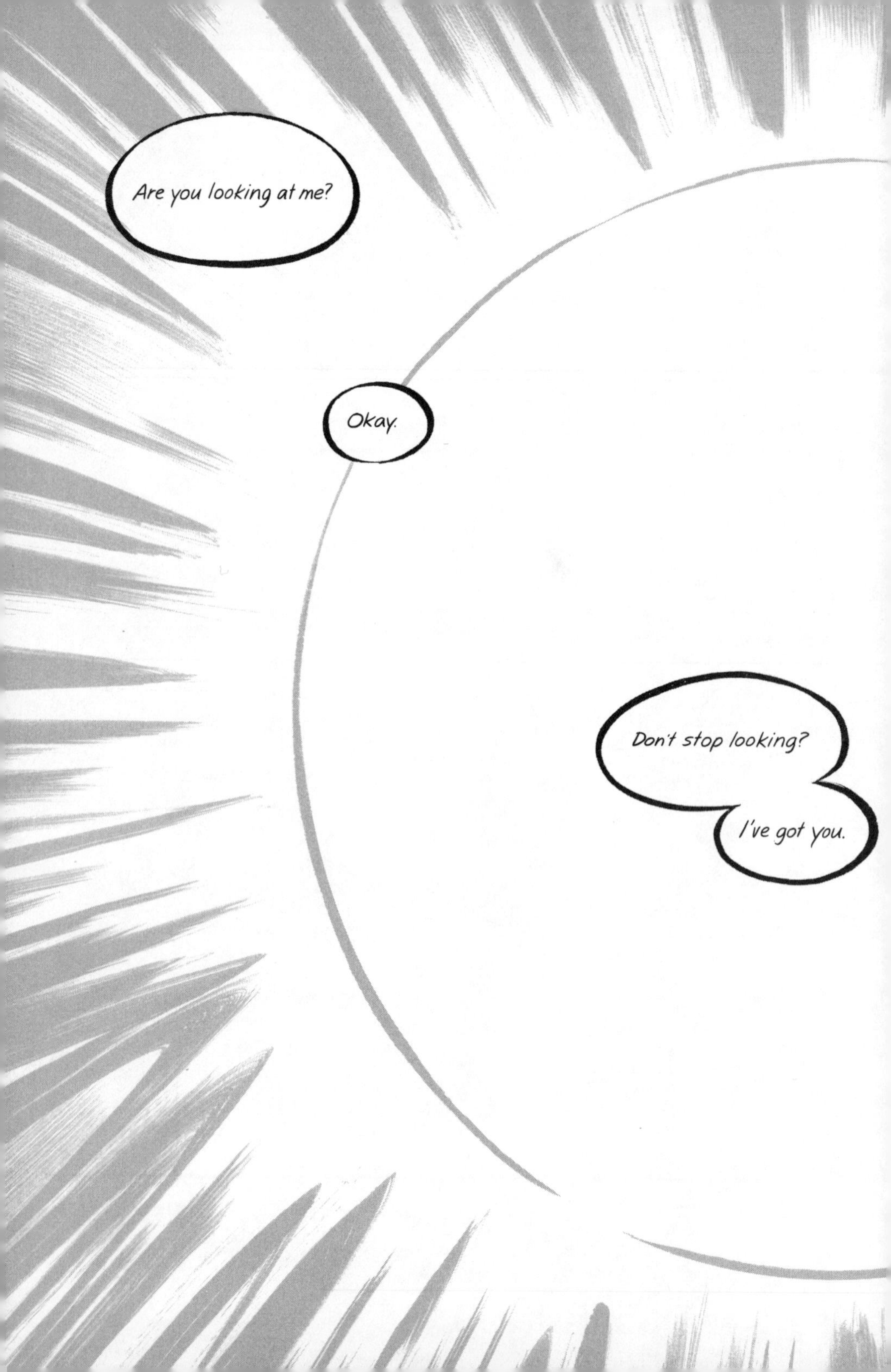
Are you looking at me?
Okay.
Don't stop looking?
I've got you.

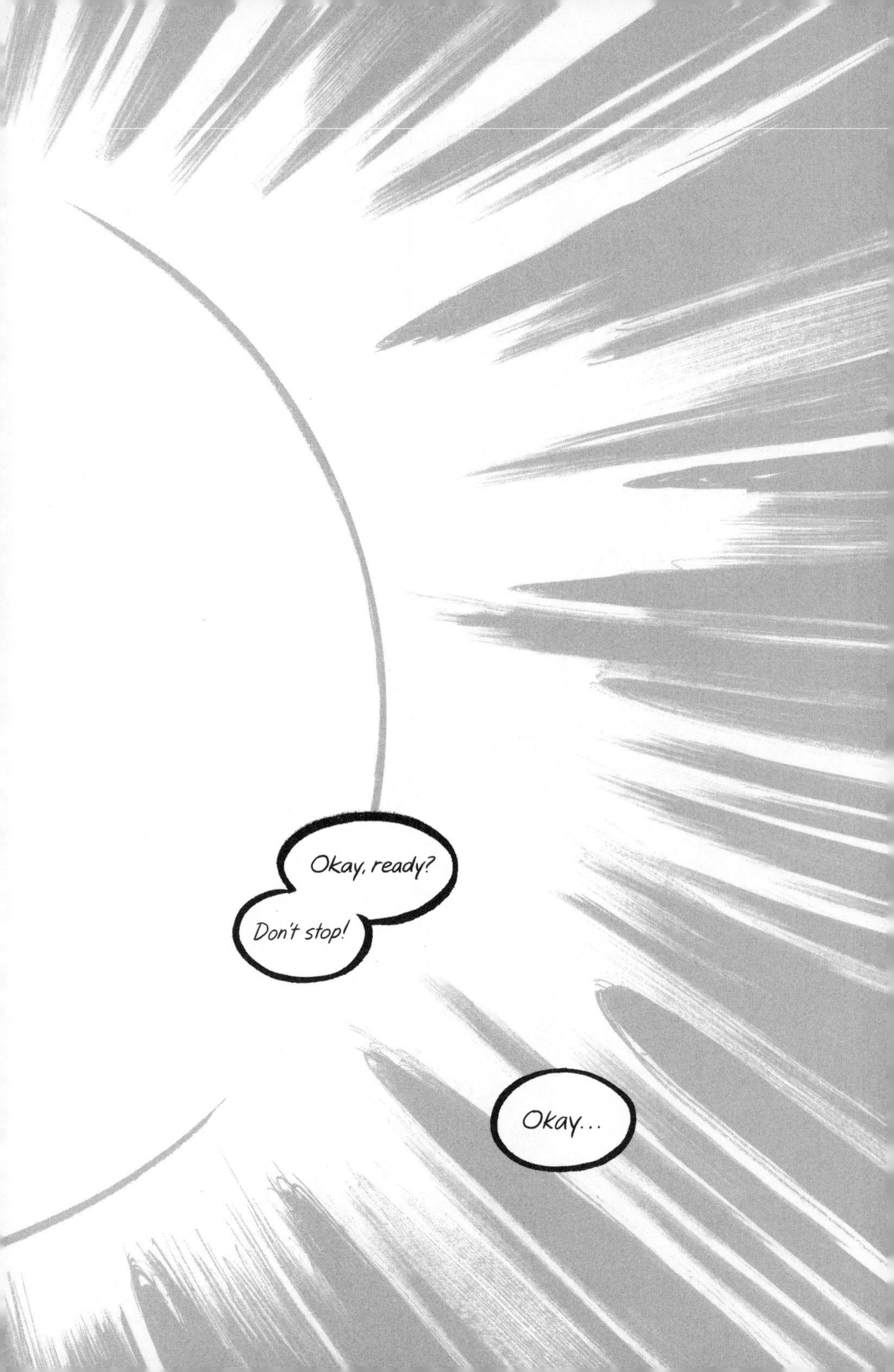
Okay, ready?
Don't stop!
Okay...

One...
Two...
Don't stop looking!
Three!

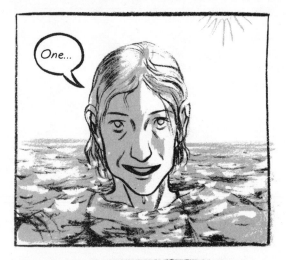

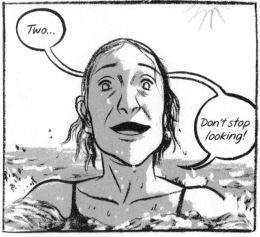

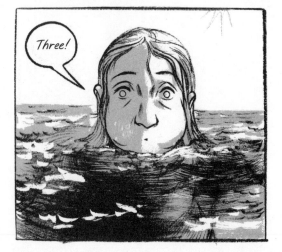

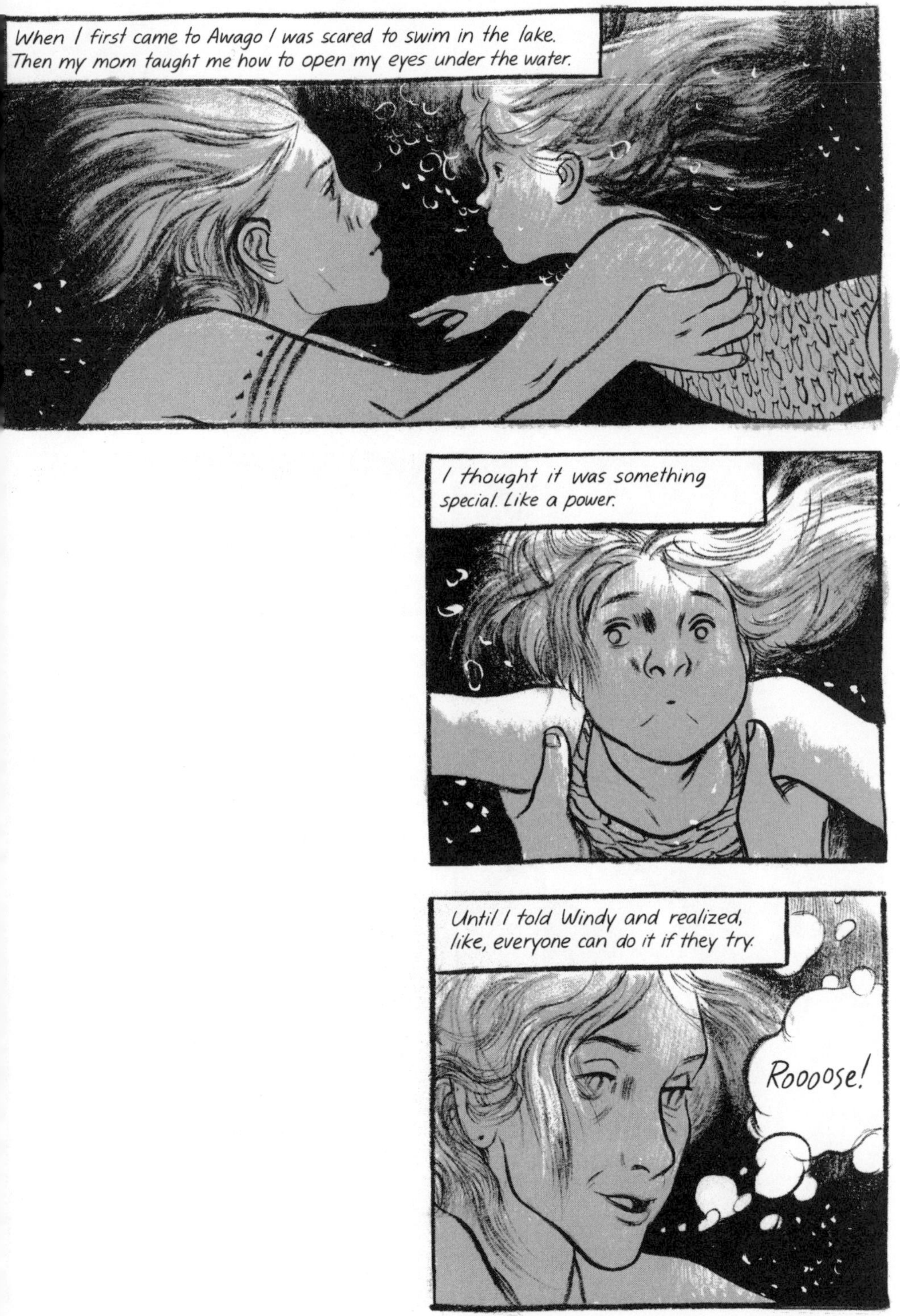
When I first came to Awago I was scared to swim in the lake. Then my mom taught me how to open my eyes under the water.
I thought it was something special. Like a power.
Until I told Windy and realized, like, everyone can do it if they try.
Rooooose!

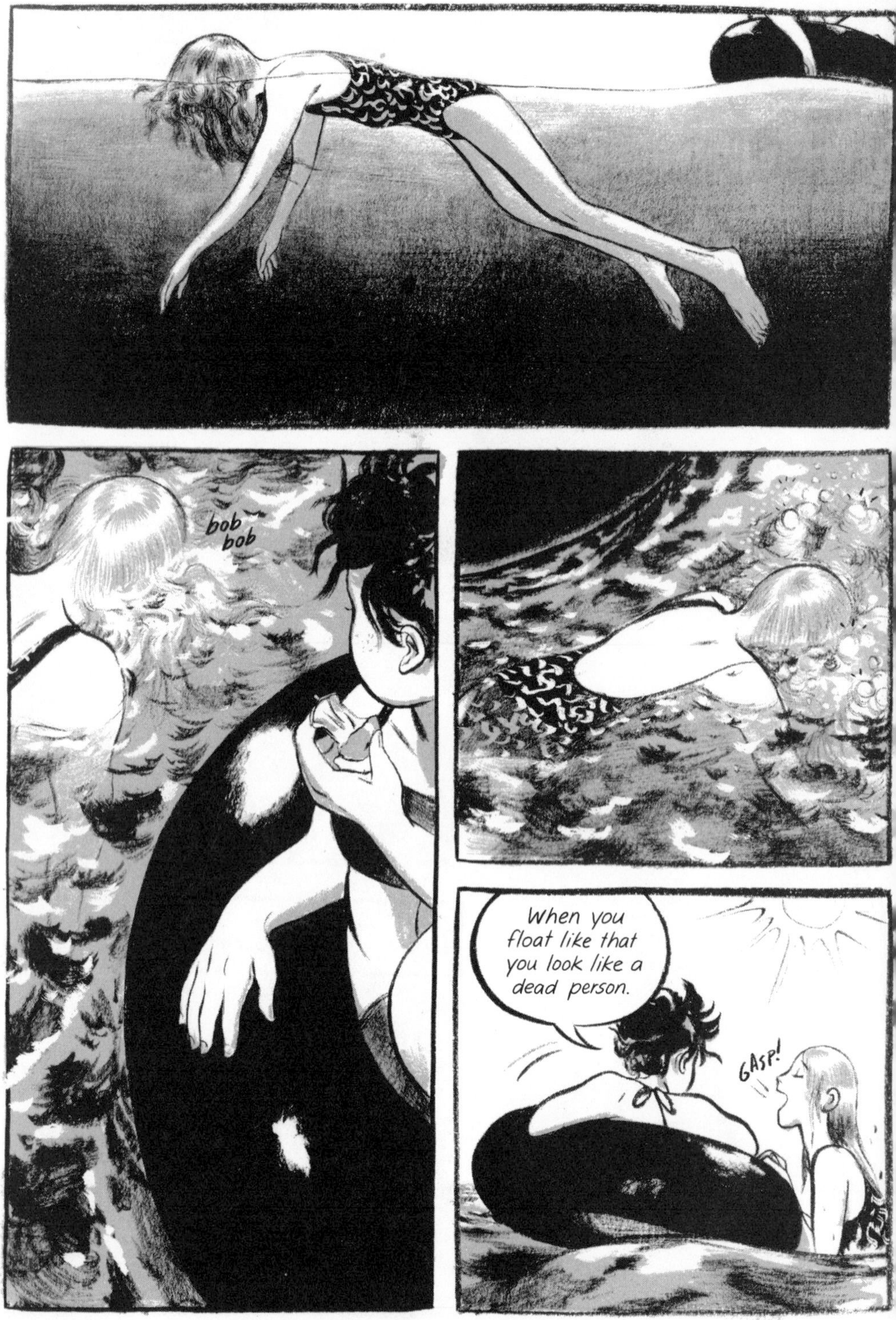
bob bob
When you float like that you look like a dead person.
GASP!

The best foods to take with you in a floatie are apples and chips in sealable containers.

Apples are better because you can just toss the cores into the water afterwards and the fish will eat them.

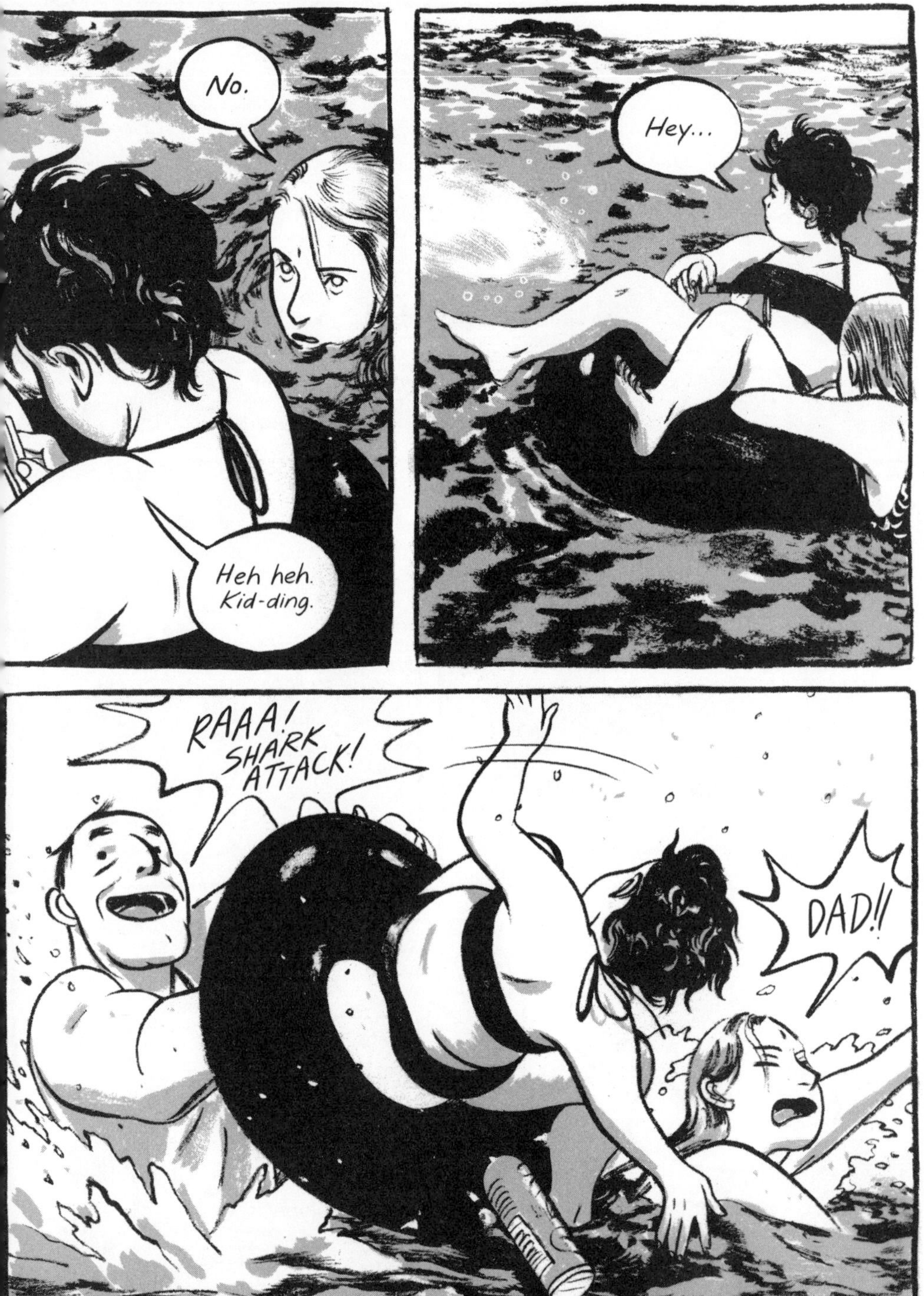
No.
Heh heh. Kid-ding.
Hey...
RAAA! SHARK ATTACK!
DAD!!

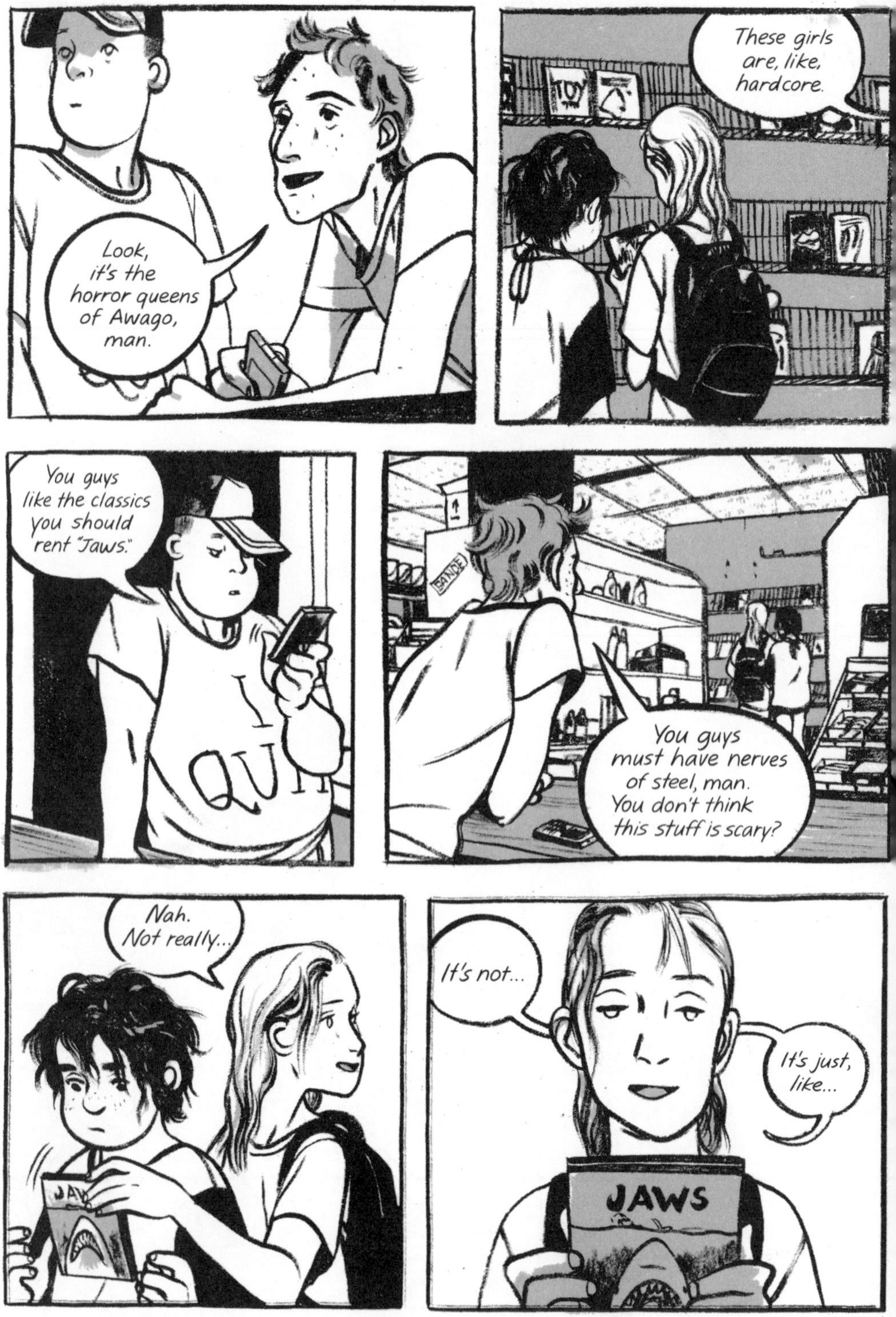
Look, it's the horror queens of Awago, man.
TOY
These girls are, like, hardcore.
You guys like the classics you should rent "Jaws."
I QUIT
BANDE
You guys must have nerves of steel, man. You don't think this stuff is scary?
Nah. Not really...
JAWS
It's not...
It's just, like...
JAWS

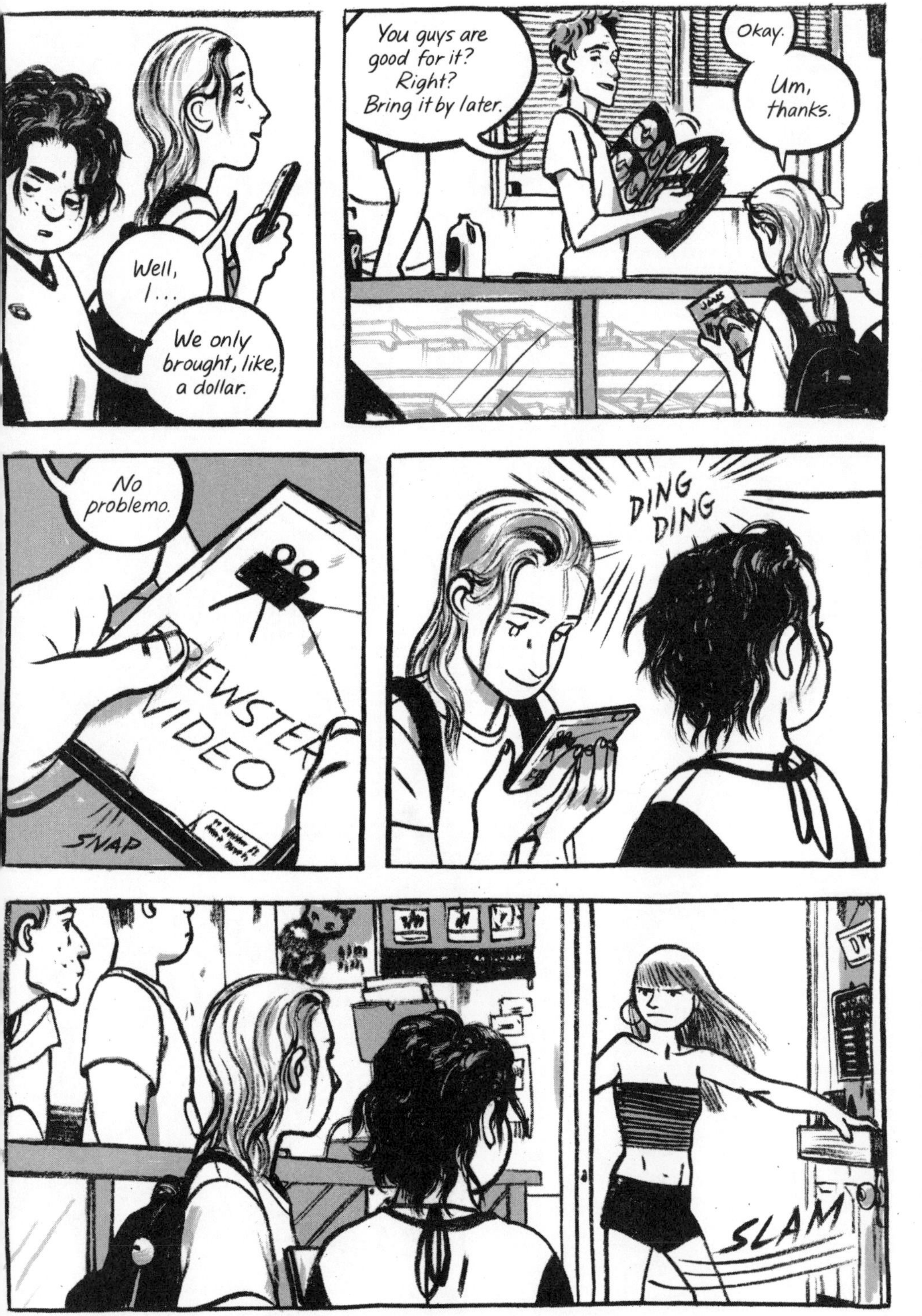
Well, I...
We only brought, like, a dollar.
You guys are good for it? Right? Bring it by later.
Okay.
Um, thanks.
No problemo.
EWSTER VIDEO
SNAP
DING DING
SLAM

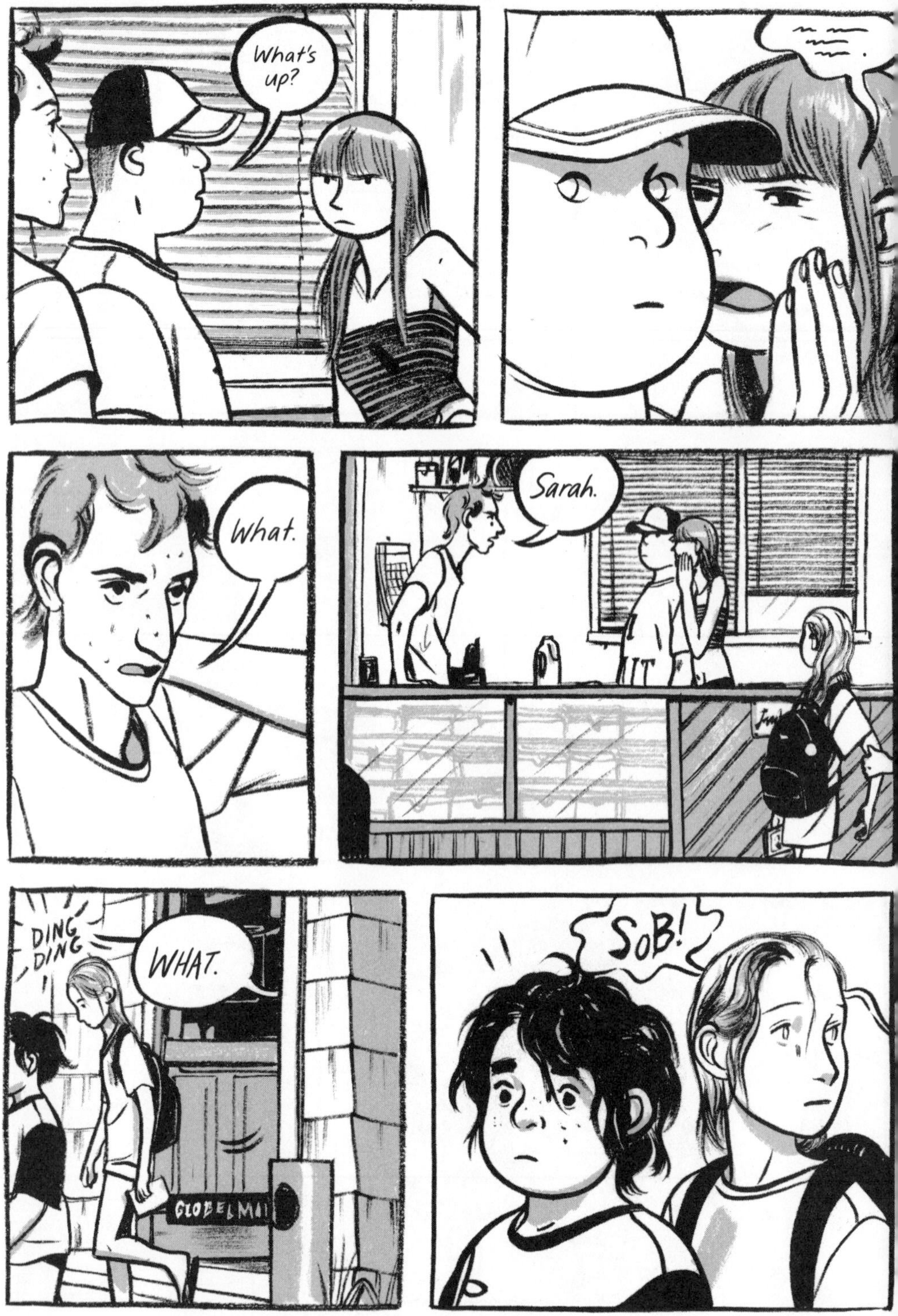
What's up?
What.
Sarah.
DING DING
WHAT.
SOB!
GLOBE&MAI

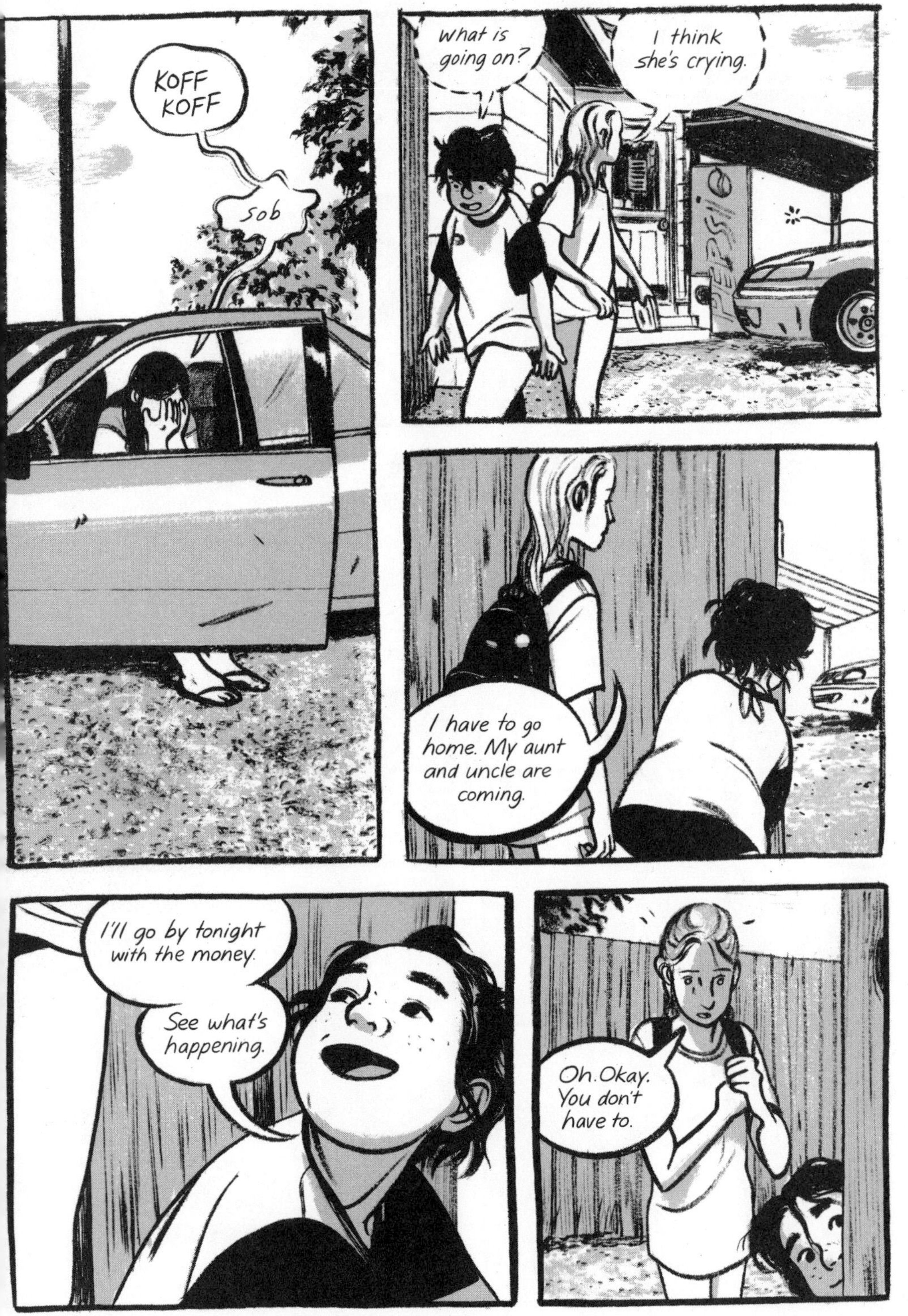
KOFF KOFF
sob
What is going on?
I think she's crying.
I have to go home. My aunt and uncle are coming.
I'll go by tonight with the money.
See what's happening.
Oh. Okay. You don't have to.

123

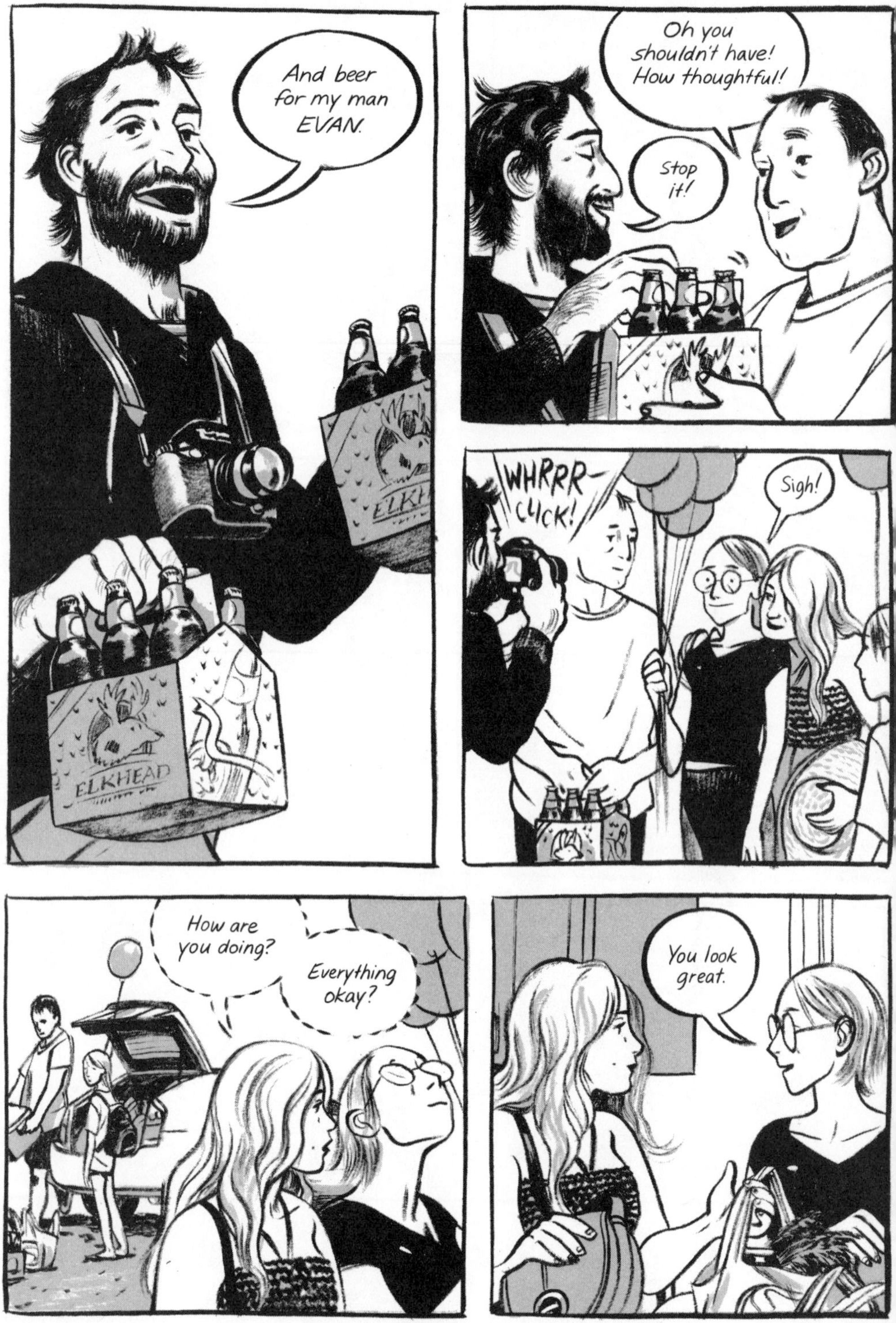
And beer for my man EVAN.
Oh you shouldn't have! How thoughtful!
Stop it!
ELKHEAD
WHRRR CLICK!
Sigh!
How are you doing?
Everything okay?
You look great.

We'll be right back.

Hey, Rosie, check it out. We brought WAGON WHEELS.

SCRAPE

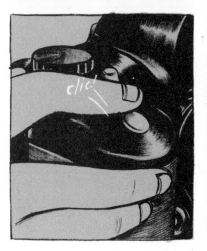

click!

SCRAPE

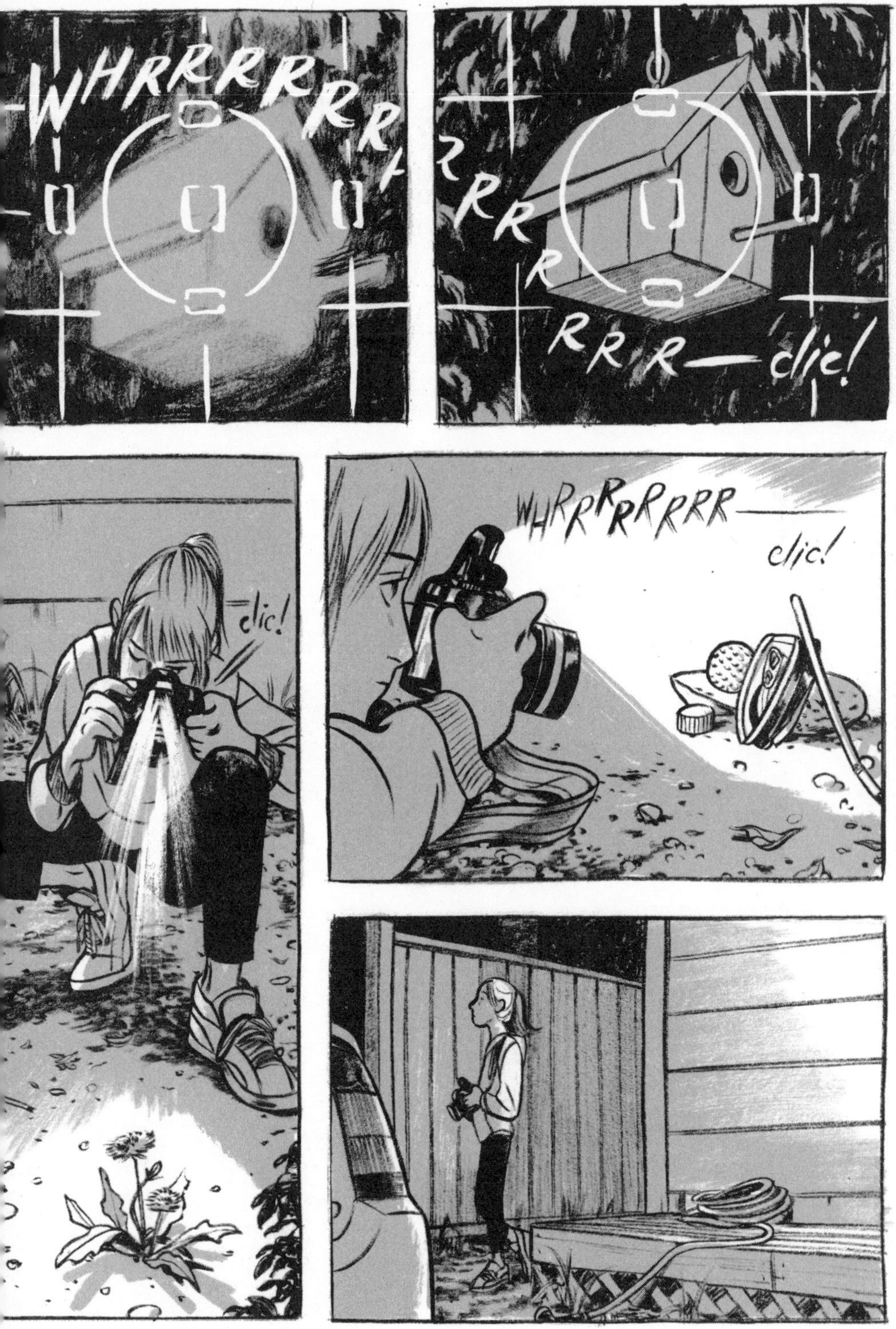
WHRRRRRRRRRRRRRR
RRR—clic!
clic!
WHRRRRRRRR—
clic!

128

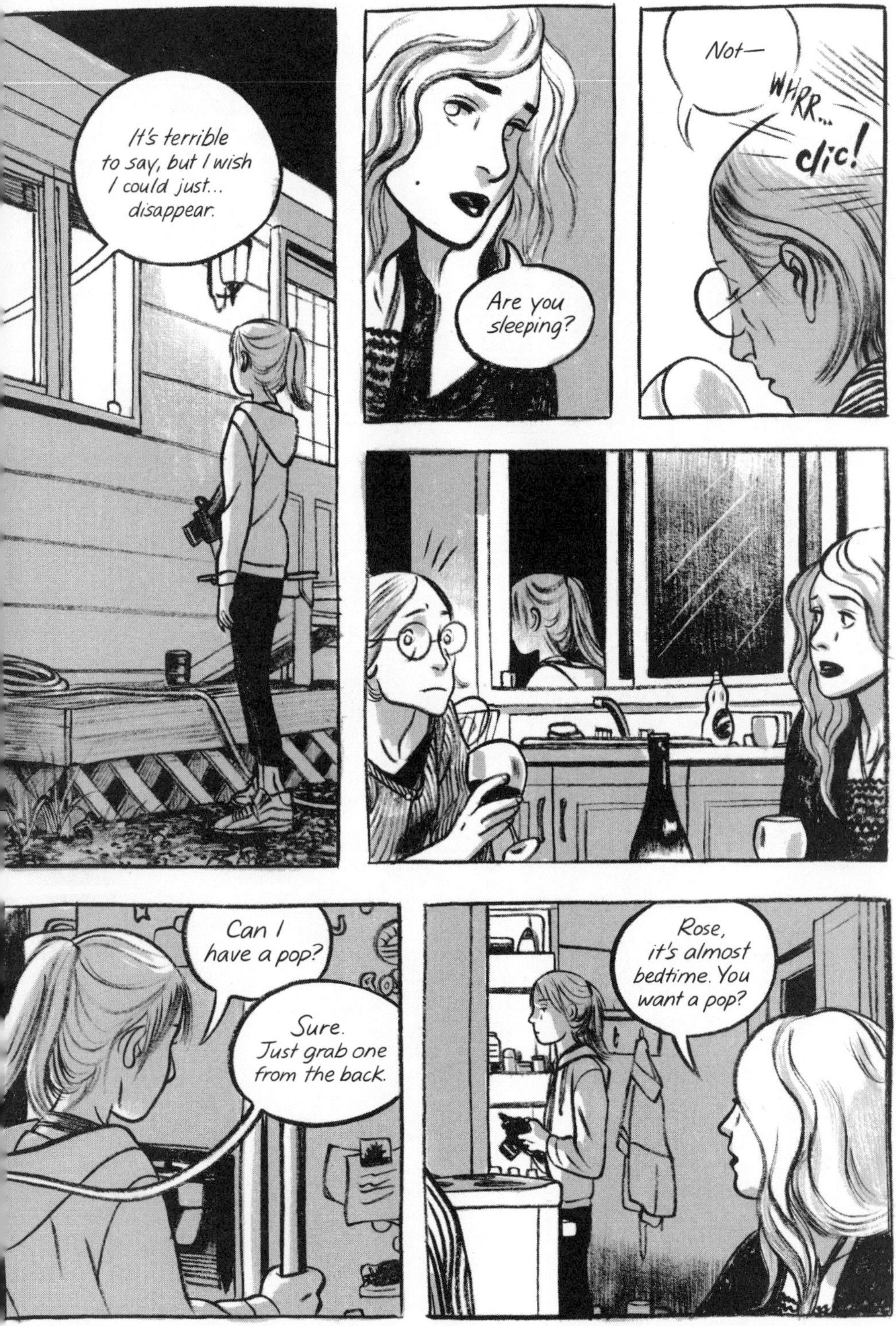
It's terrible to say, but I wish I could just... disappear.
Are you sleeping?
Not—
WHRR...
clic!
Can I have a pop?
Sure. Just grab one from the back.
Rose, it's almost bedtime. You want a pop?

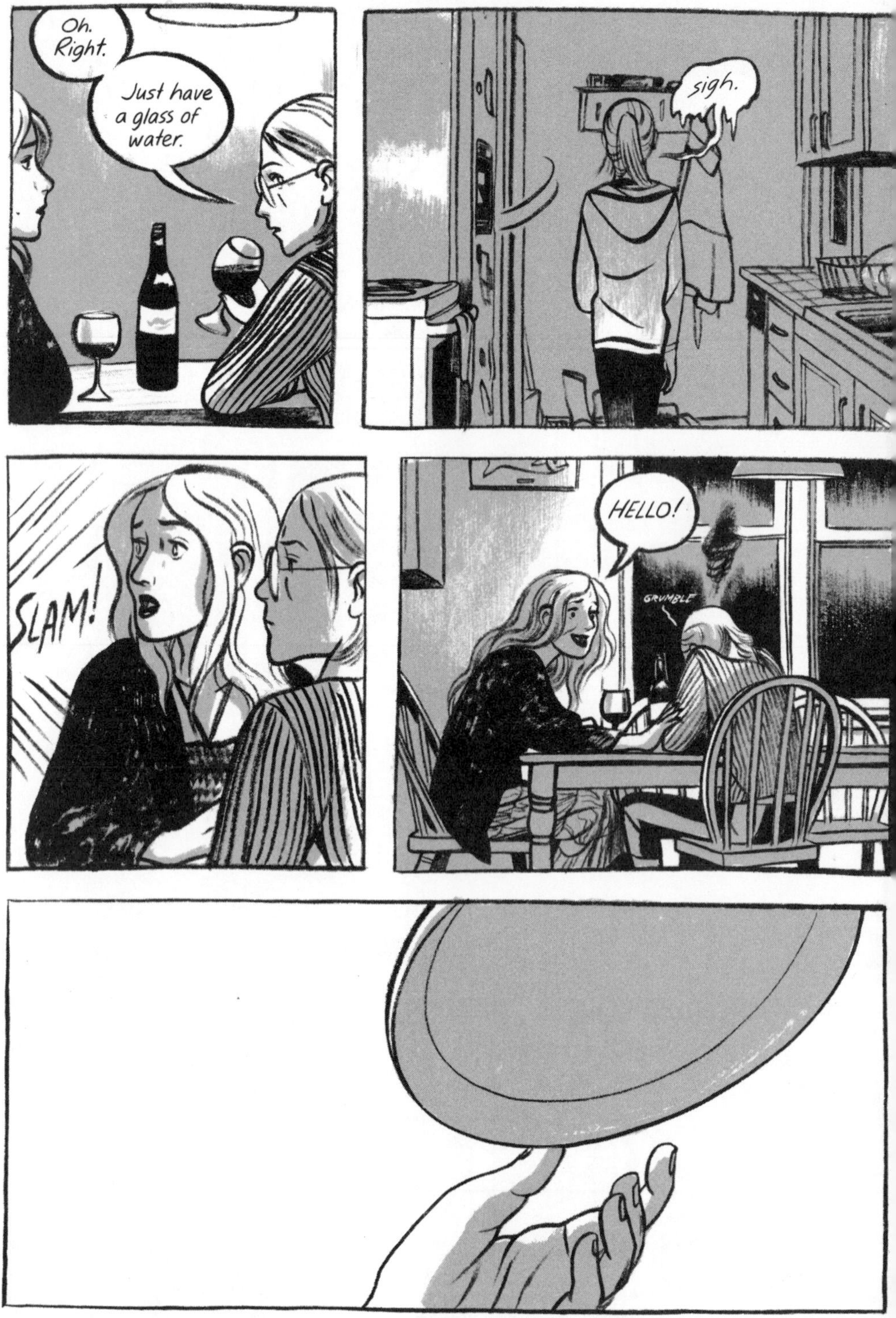
Oh. Right.
Just have a glass of water.
sigh.
SLAM!
HELLO!
GRUMBLE

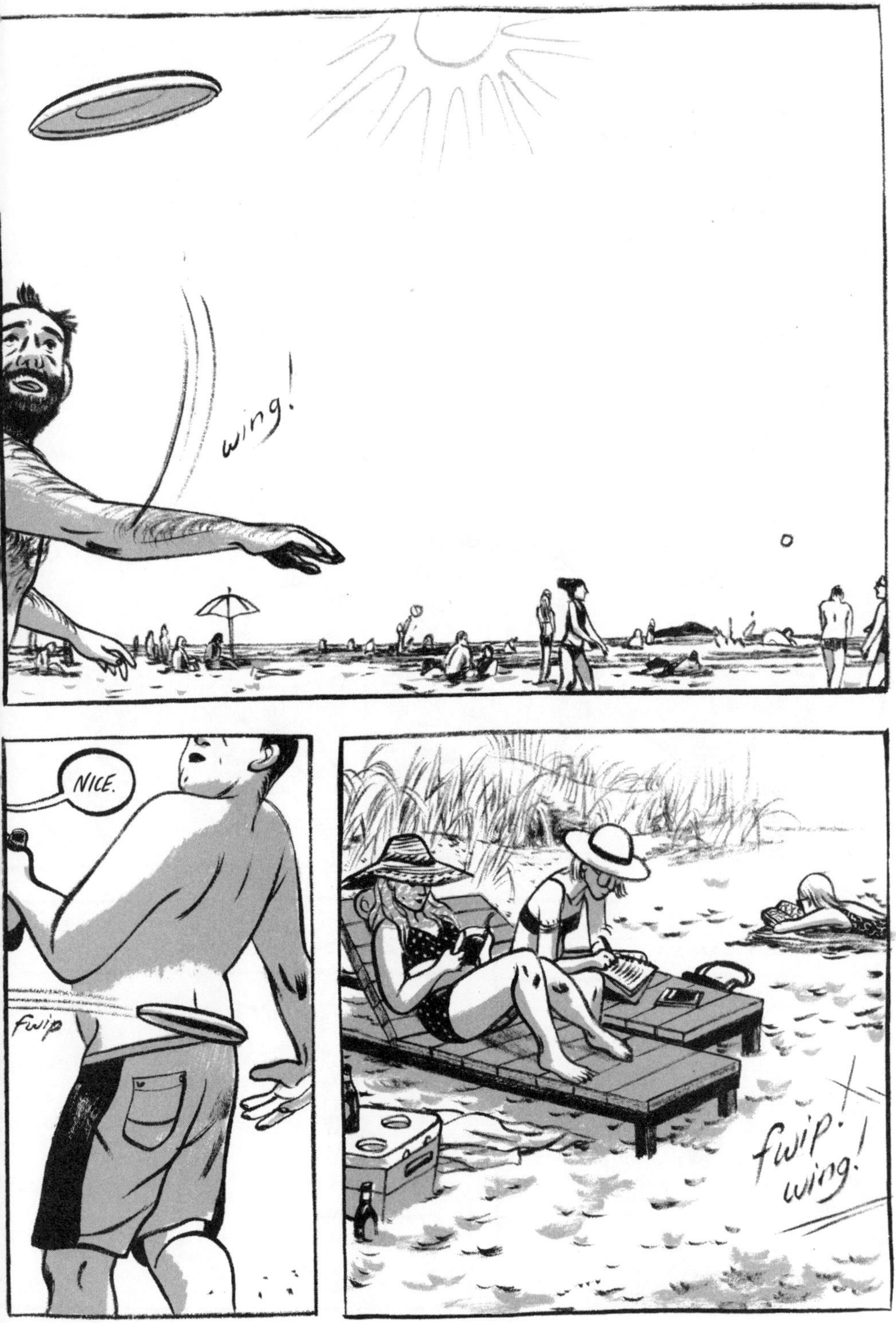
wing!
NICE.
fwip
fwip!
wing!

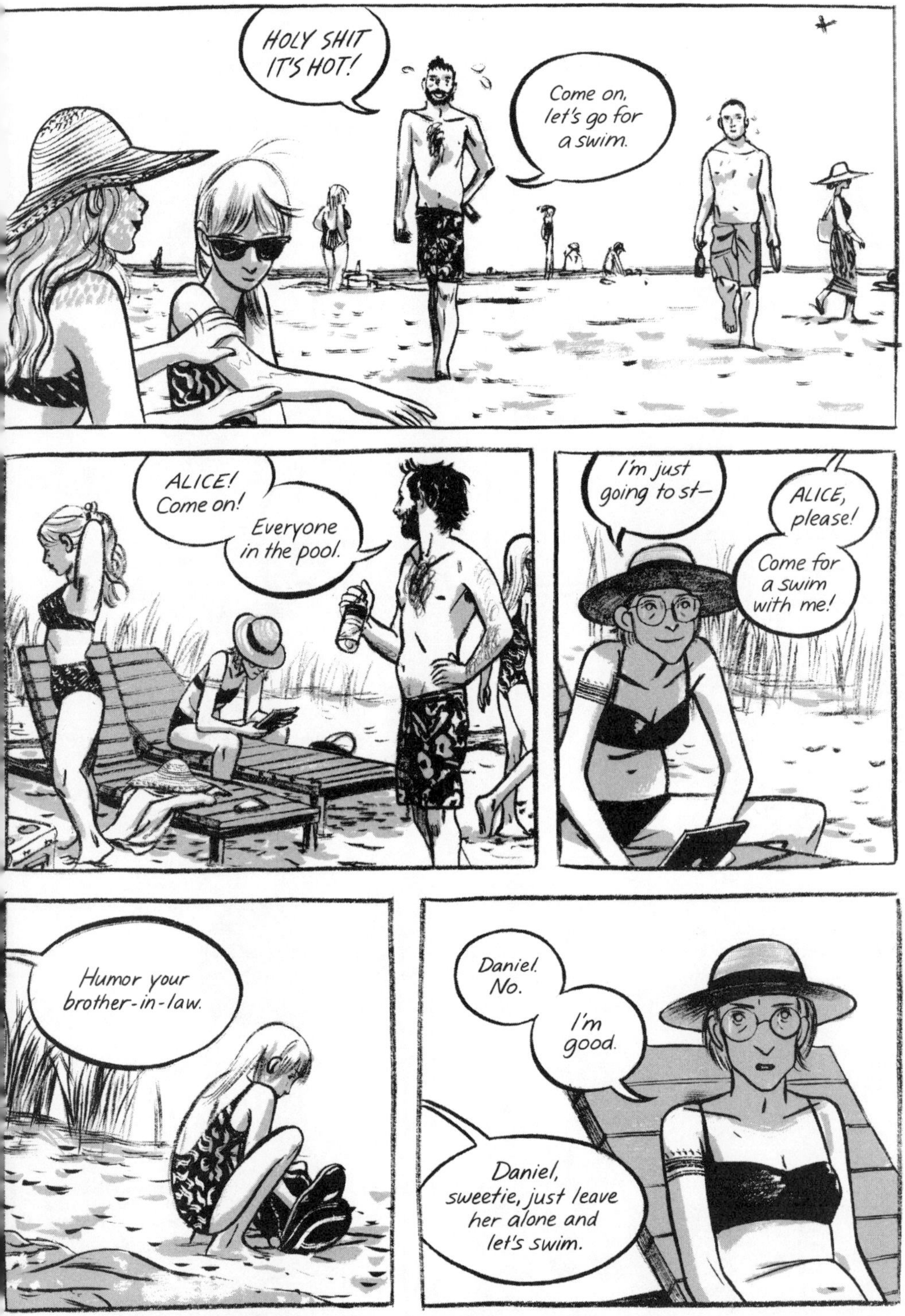
HOLY SHIT IT'S HOT!
Come on, let's go for a swim.
ALICE! Come on!
Everyone in the pool.
I'm just going to st—
ALICE, please!
Come for a swim with me!
Humor your brother-in-law.
Daniel. No.
I'm good.
Daniel, sweetie, just leave her alone and let's swim.

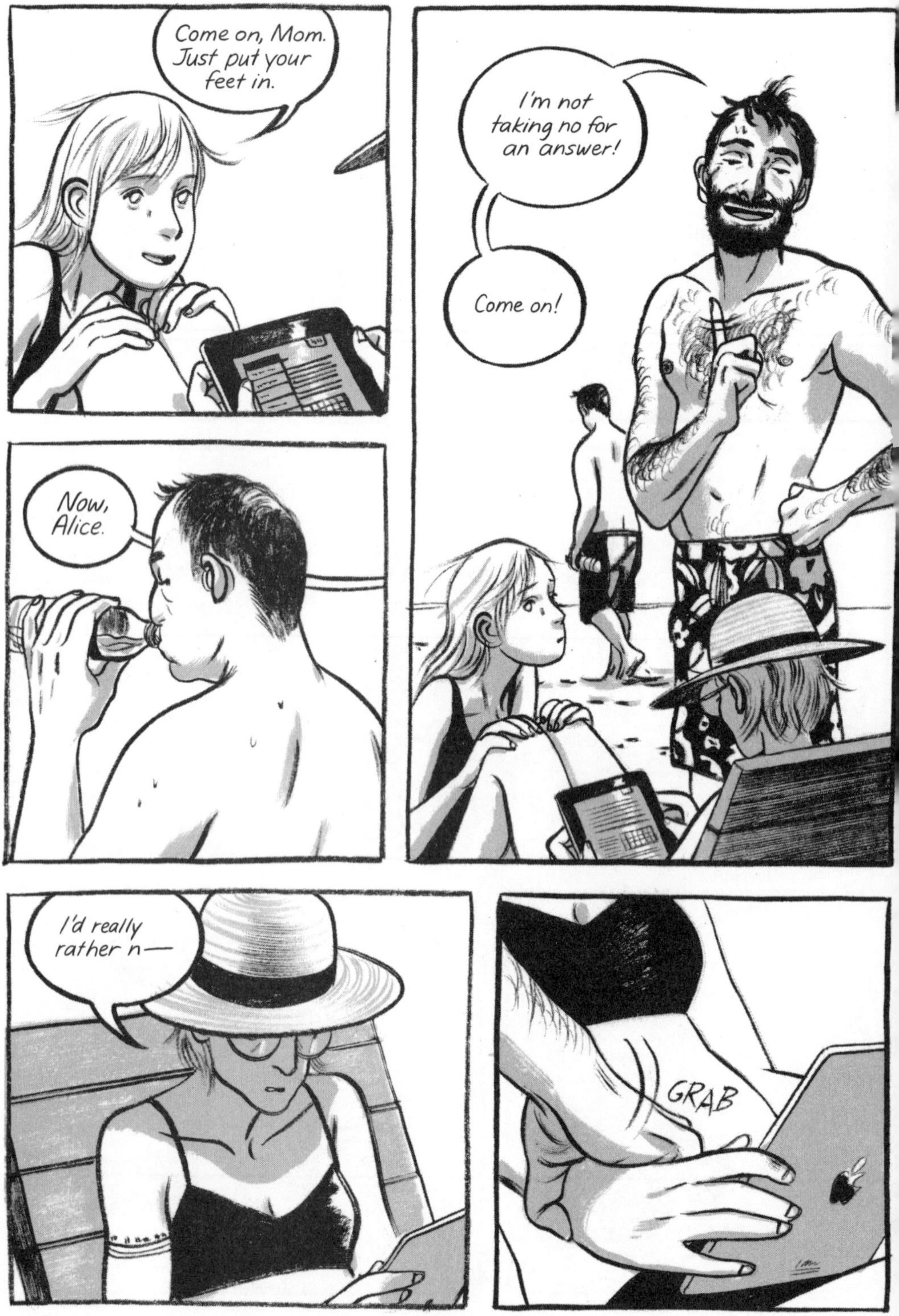

Come on, Mom. Just put your feet in.
I'm not taking no for an answer!
Come on!
Now, Alice.
I'd really rather n—
GRAB

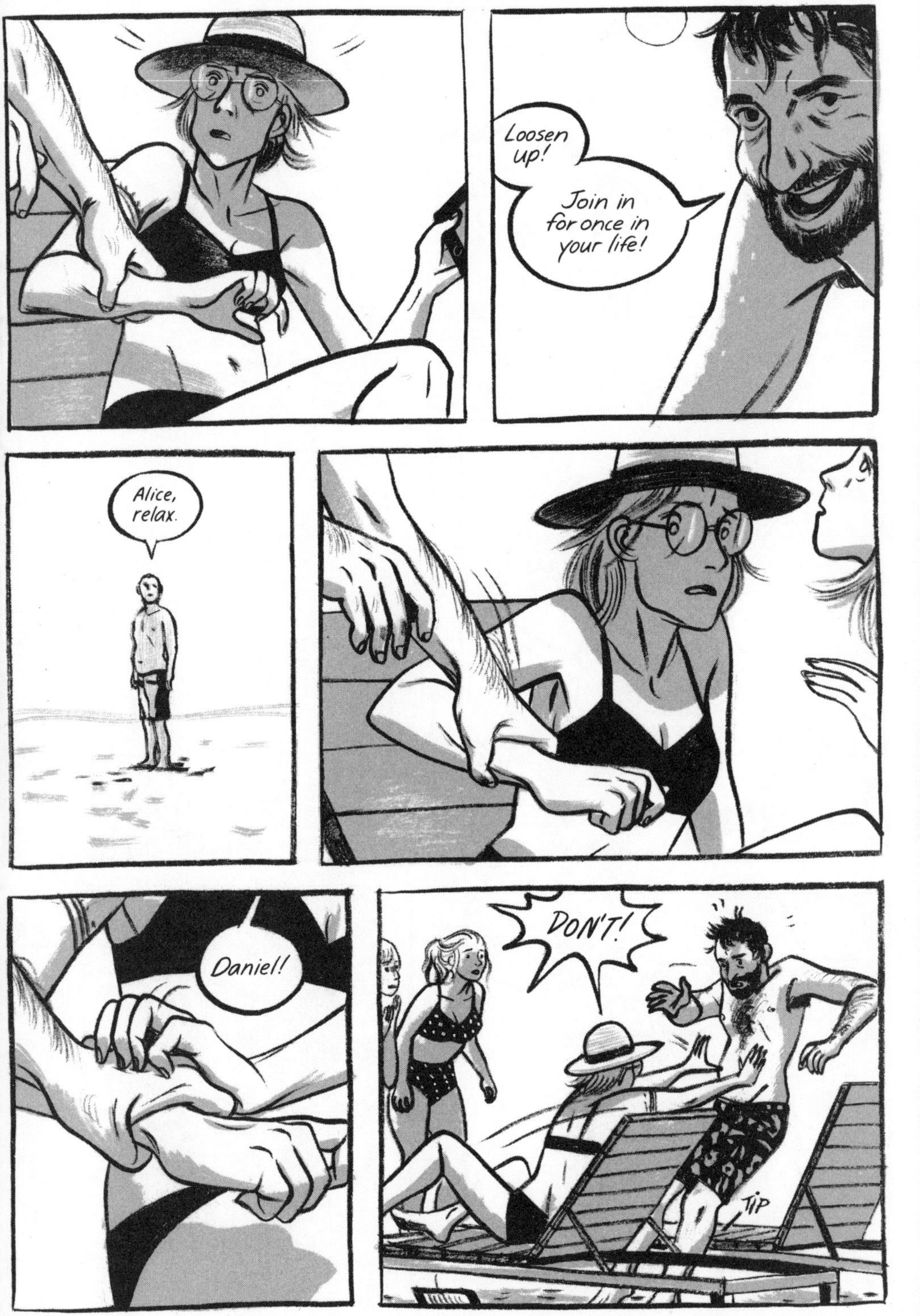
Loosen up!
Join in for once in your life!
Alice, relax.
Daniel!
DON'T!
TIP

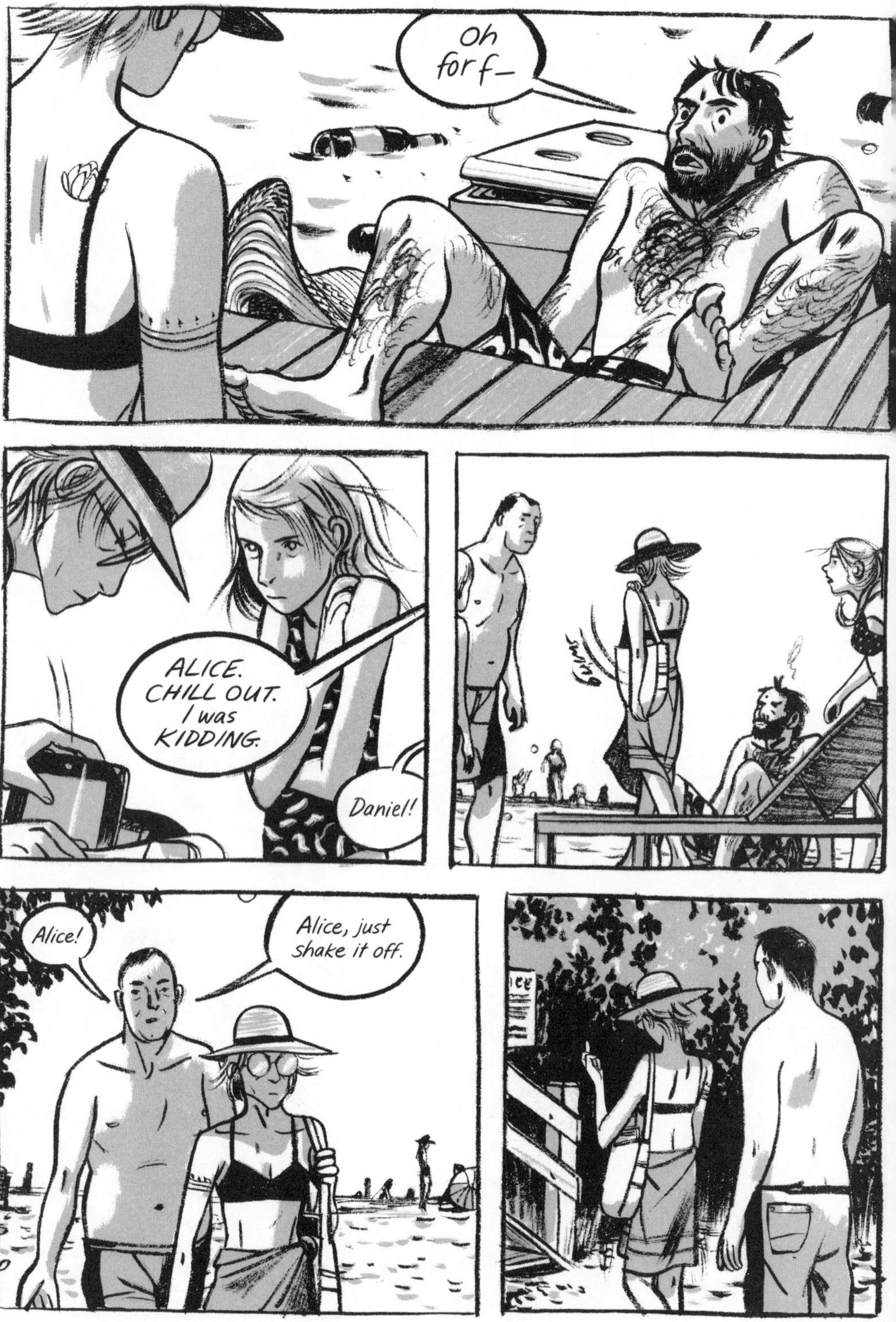

Oh forf—
ALICE. CHILL OUT. I was KIDDING.
Daniel!
Alice!
Alice, just shake it off.

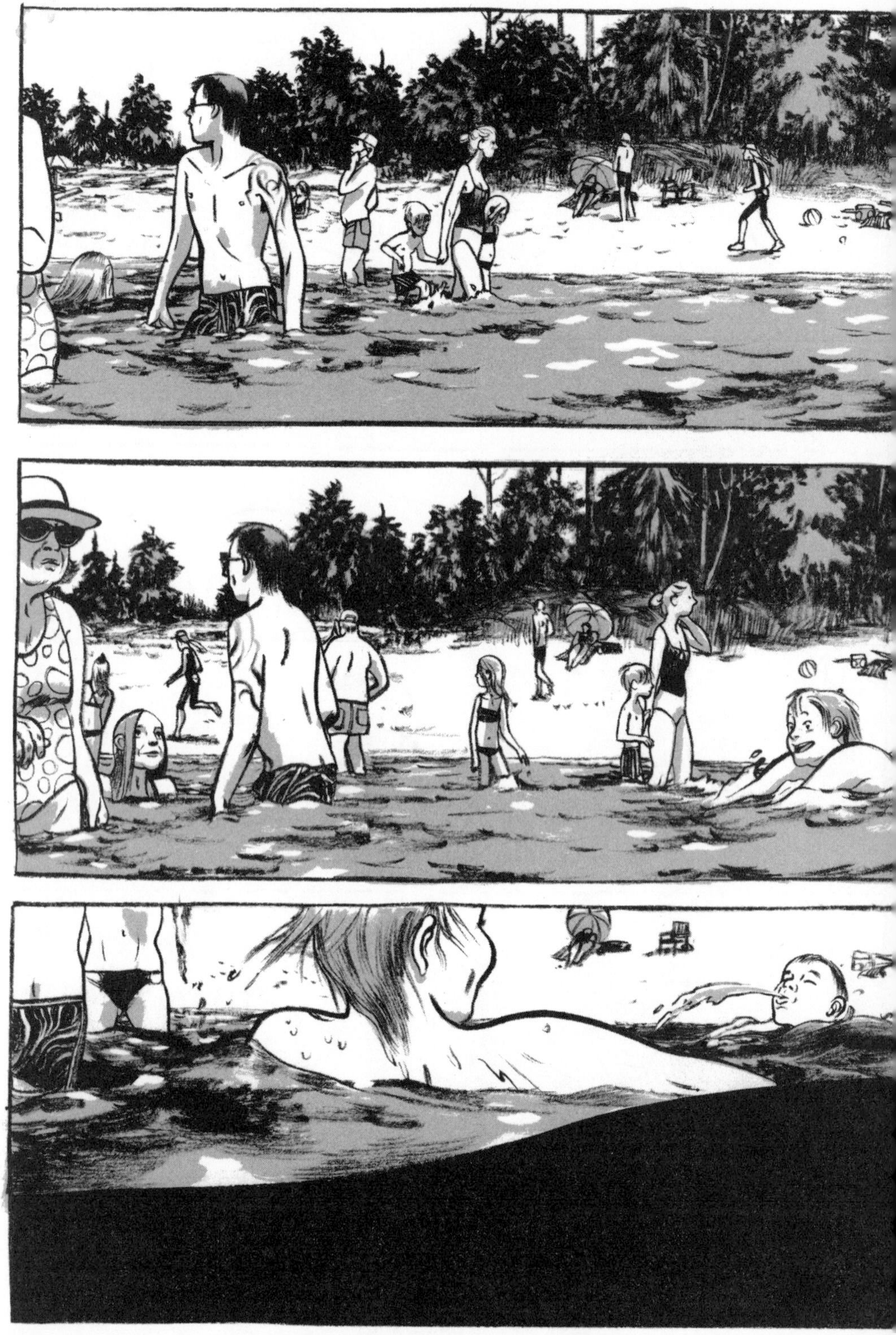

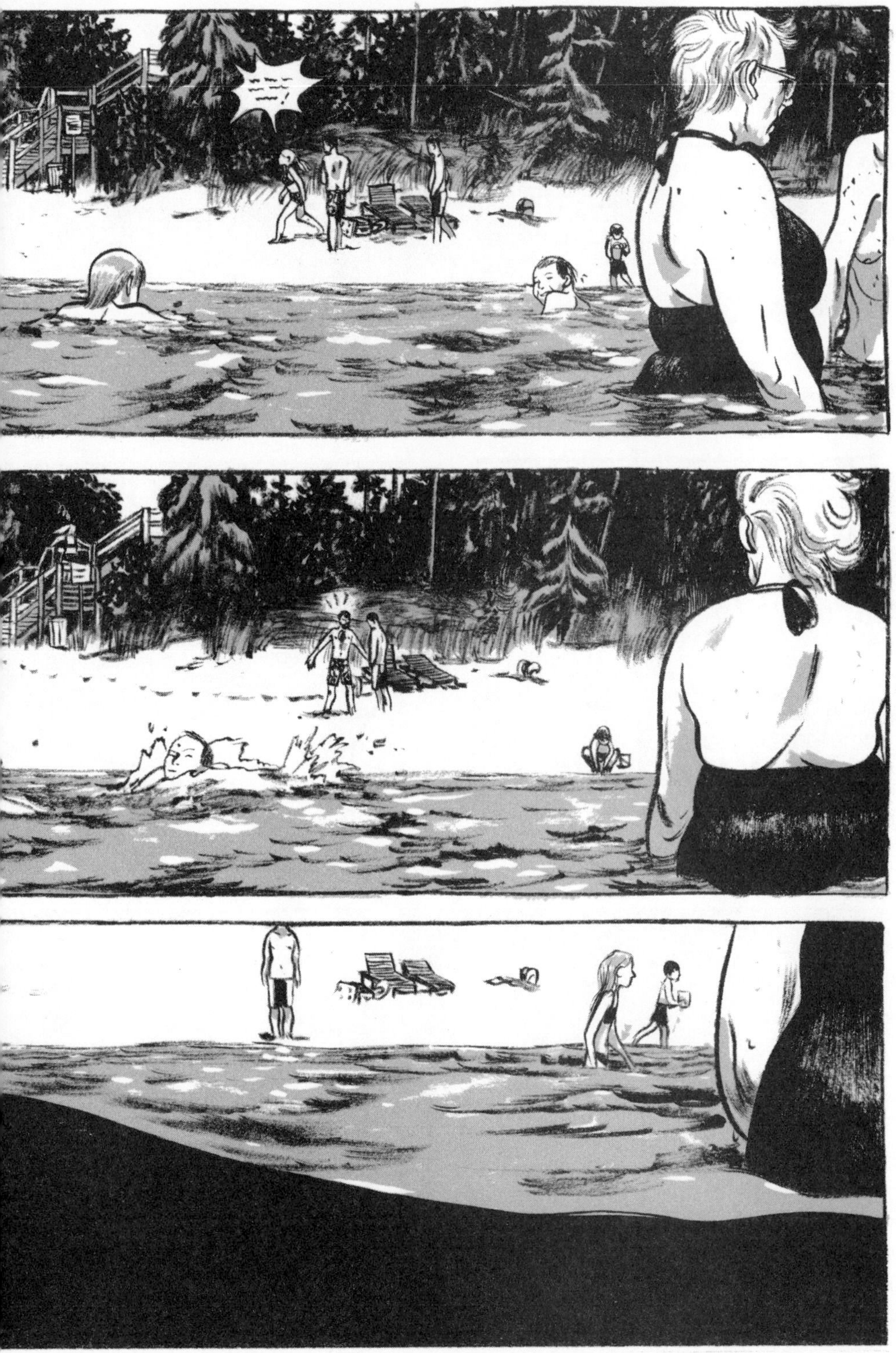

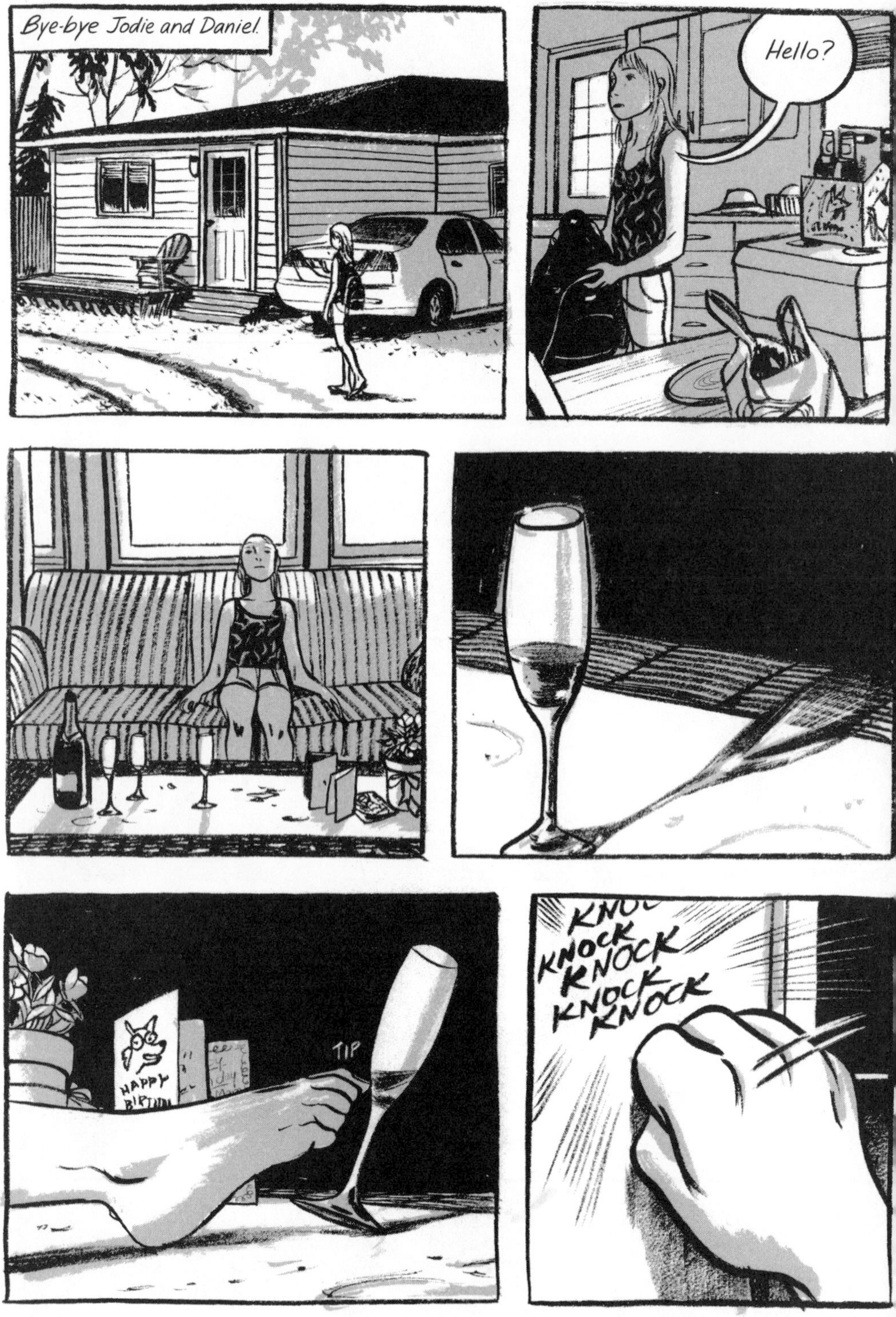
Bye-bye Jodie and Daniel.
Hello?
HAPPY
TIP
KNOCK
KNOCK
KNOCK
KNOCK

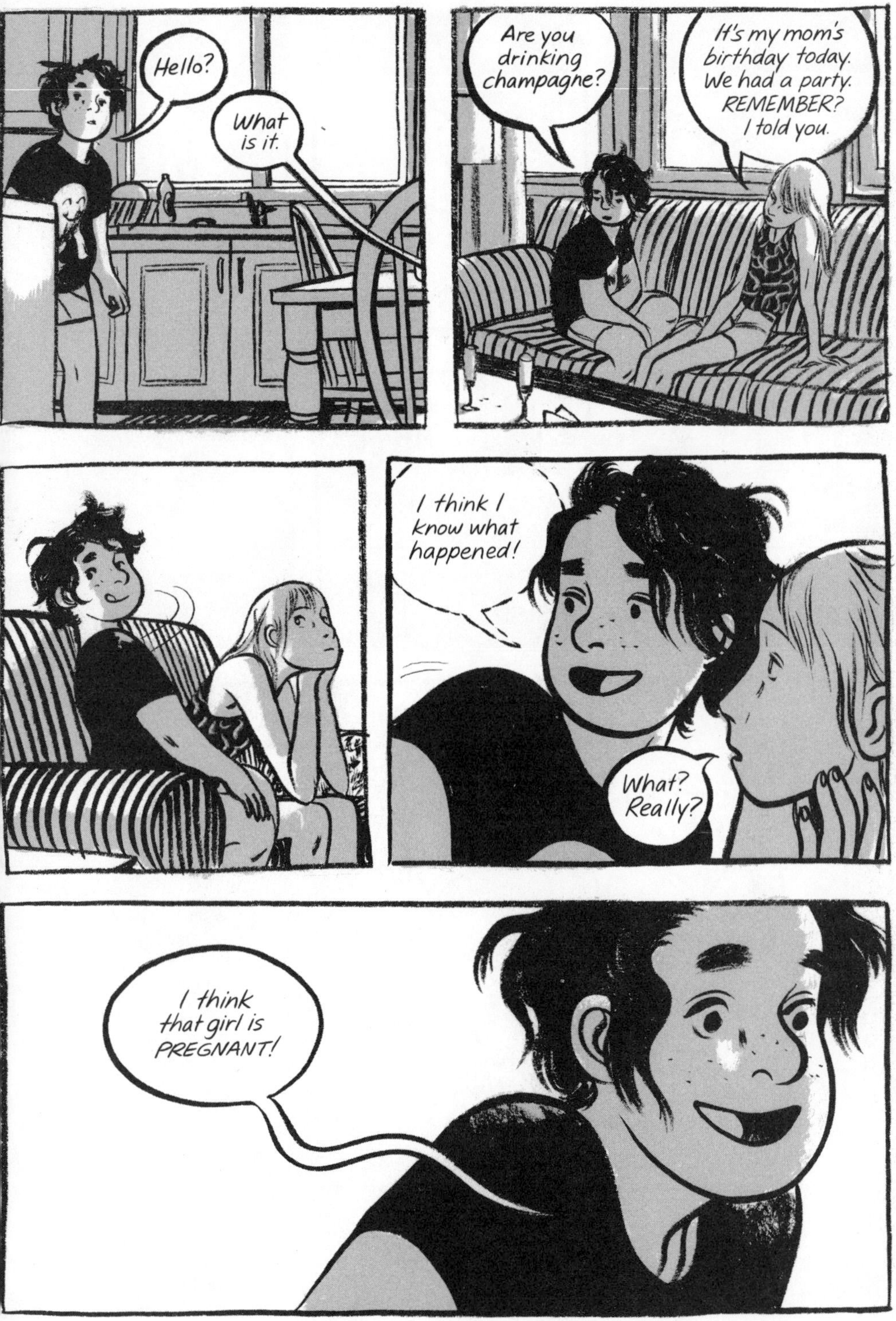
Hello?
What is it.
Are you drinking champagne?
It's my mom's birthday today. We had a party. REMEMBER? I told you.
I think I know what happened!
What? Really?
I think that girl is PREGNANT!

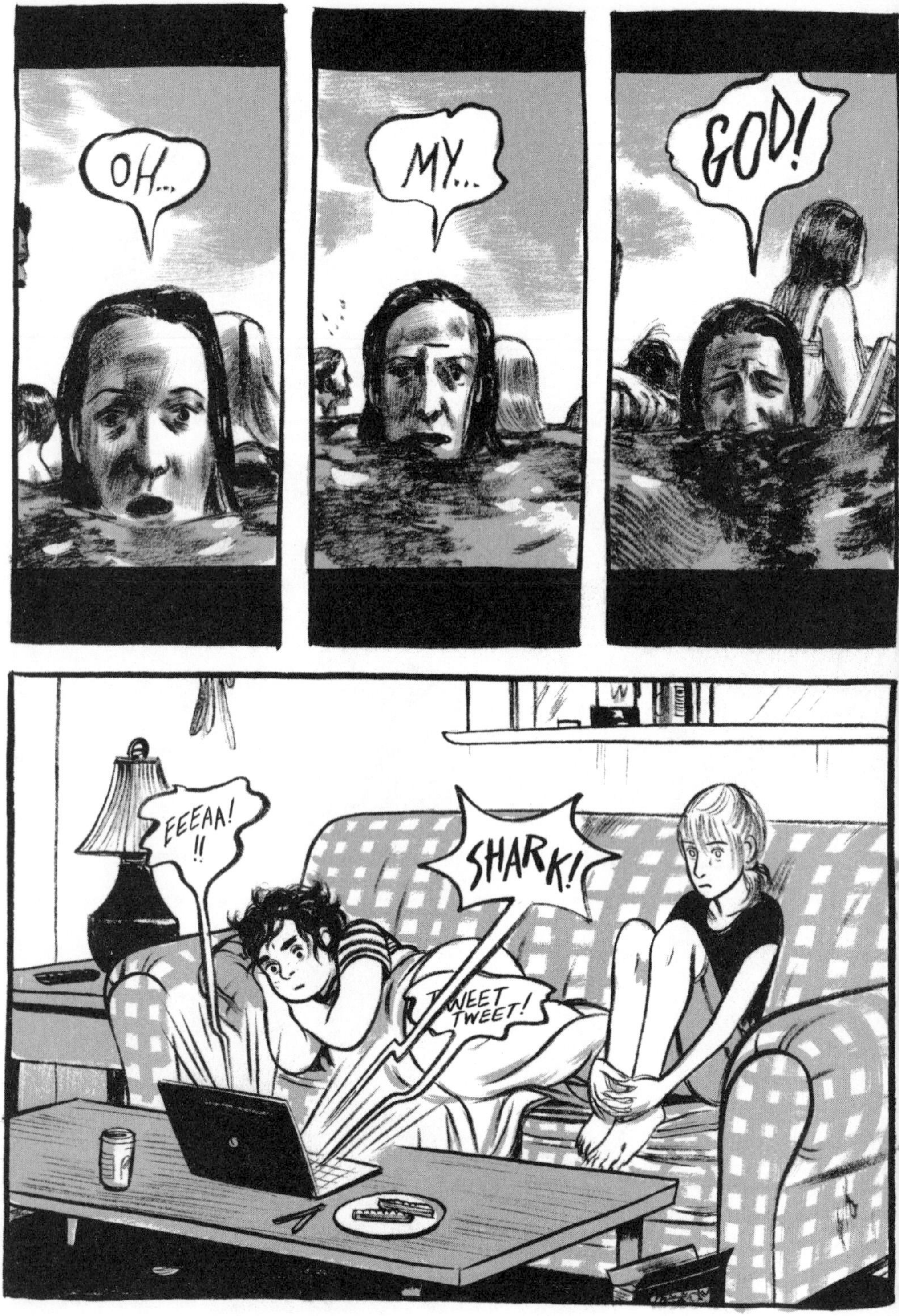
OH...
MY...
GOD!
EEEAA! !!
SHARK!
TWEET TWEET!

Yesterday, Windy went back to Brewster's to pay for the DVD and saw it all go down.

She said Dunc's girlfriend walked in and threw a plastic bag on the table.
Windy said she could see a pee stick in it.

The girlfriend didn't say anything. She just dropped the bag and walked out.

This one isn't AS scary. That shark is totally fake. It's like, RUBBER.

You can see where they put the guy with the remote control and everything.

It's sort of scary.

The sound is scary.

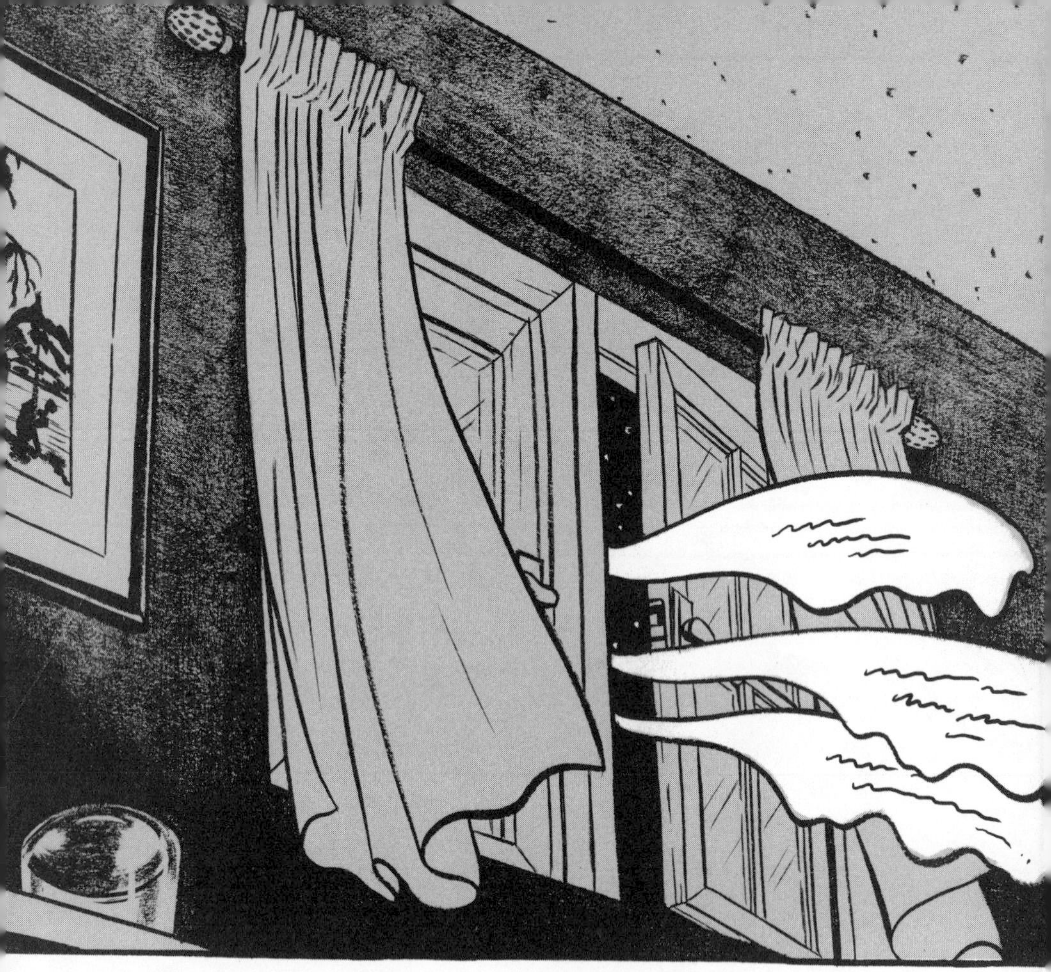

My mom screamed at my dad last night.
Like. SCREAMED. At my dad. They were outside
in the car, but I could hear her through my window.
My aunt and uncle left.

Then my mom stood outside by herself for a long time.

So today my dad is golfing and my mom is spending
quiet time in her room.

145

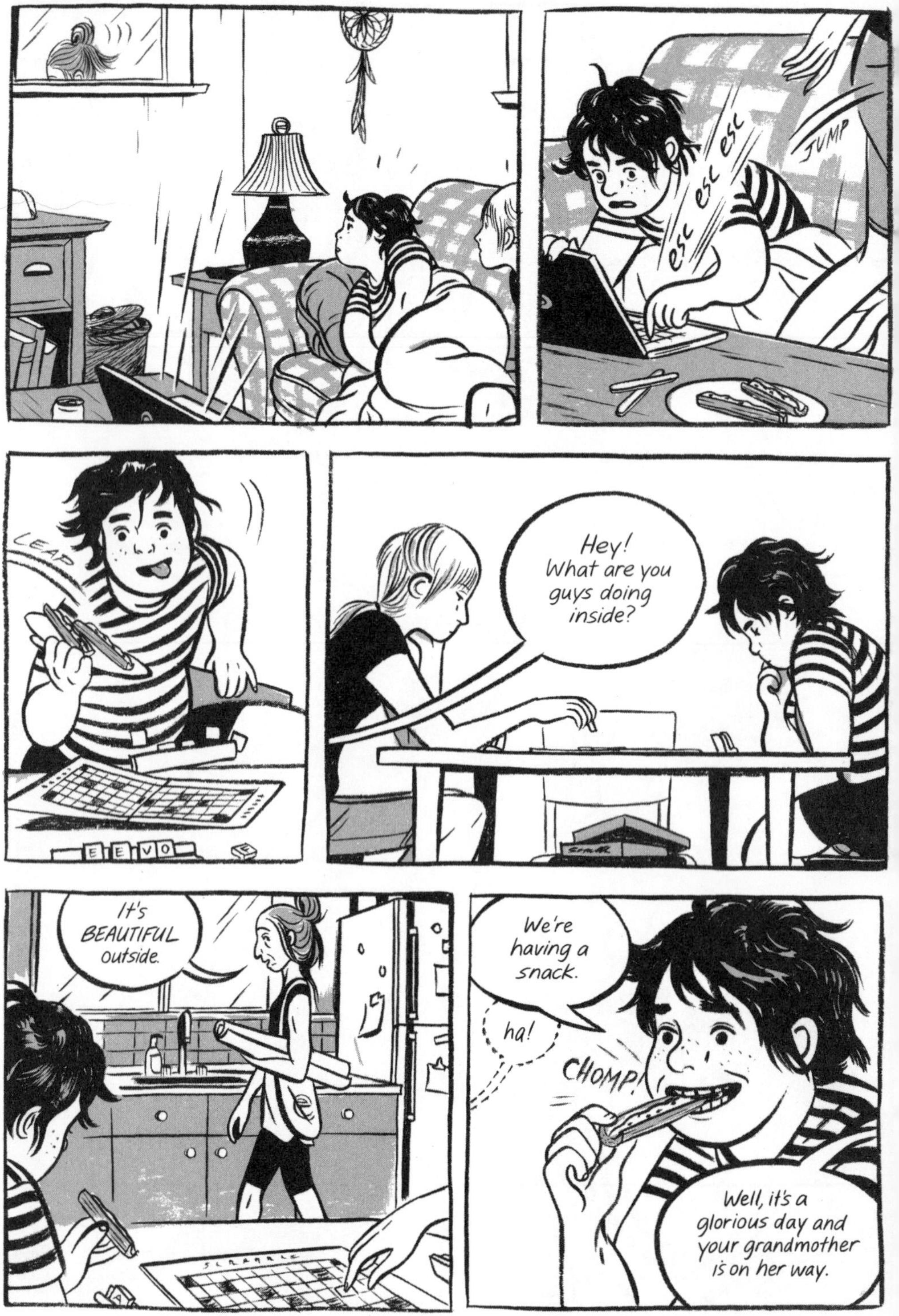

esc esc esc
JUMP
LEAP
Hey! What are you guys doing inside?
It's BEAUTIFUL outside.
We're having a snack.
ha!
CHOMP!
Well, it's a glorious day and your grandmother is on her way.

148

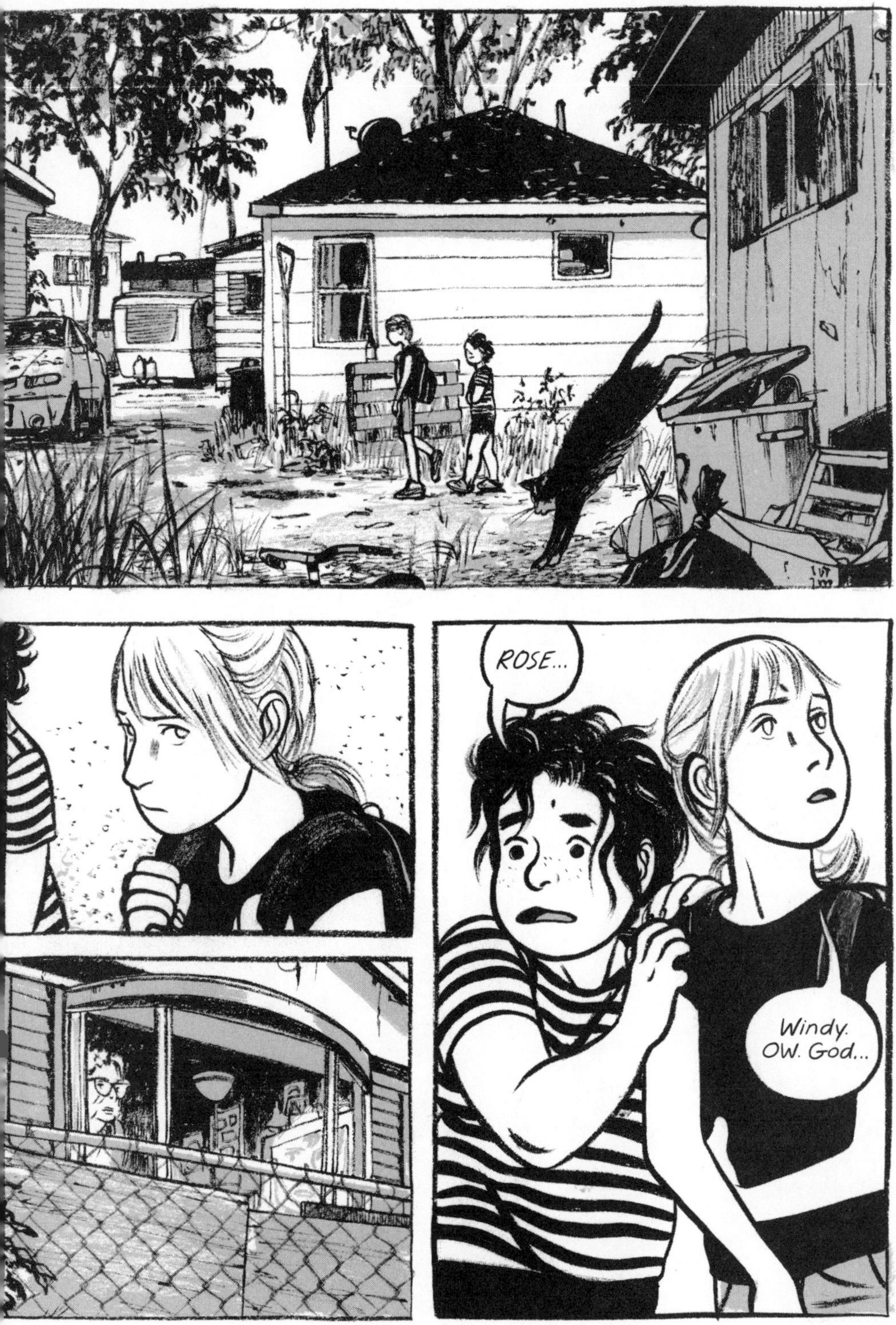
ROSE...
Windy.
OW. God...

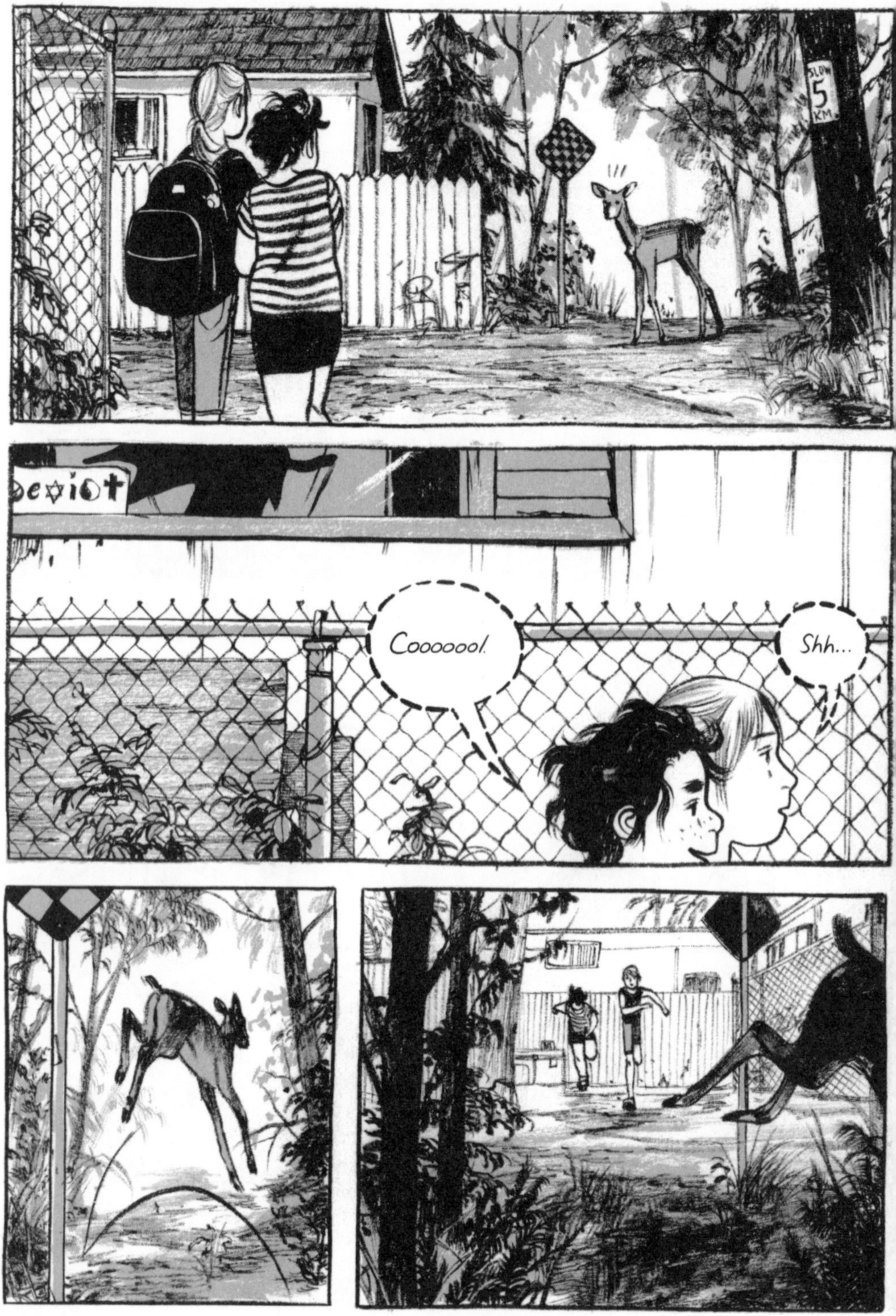
SLOW
5
KM
Cooooool.
Shh...

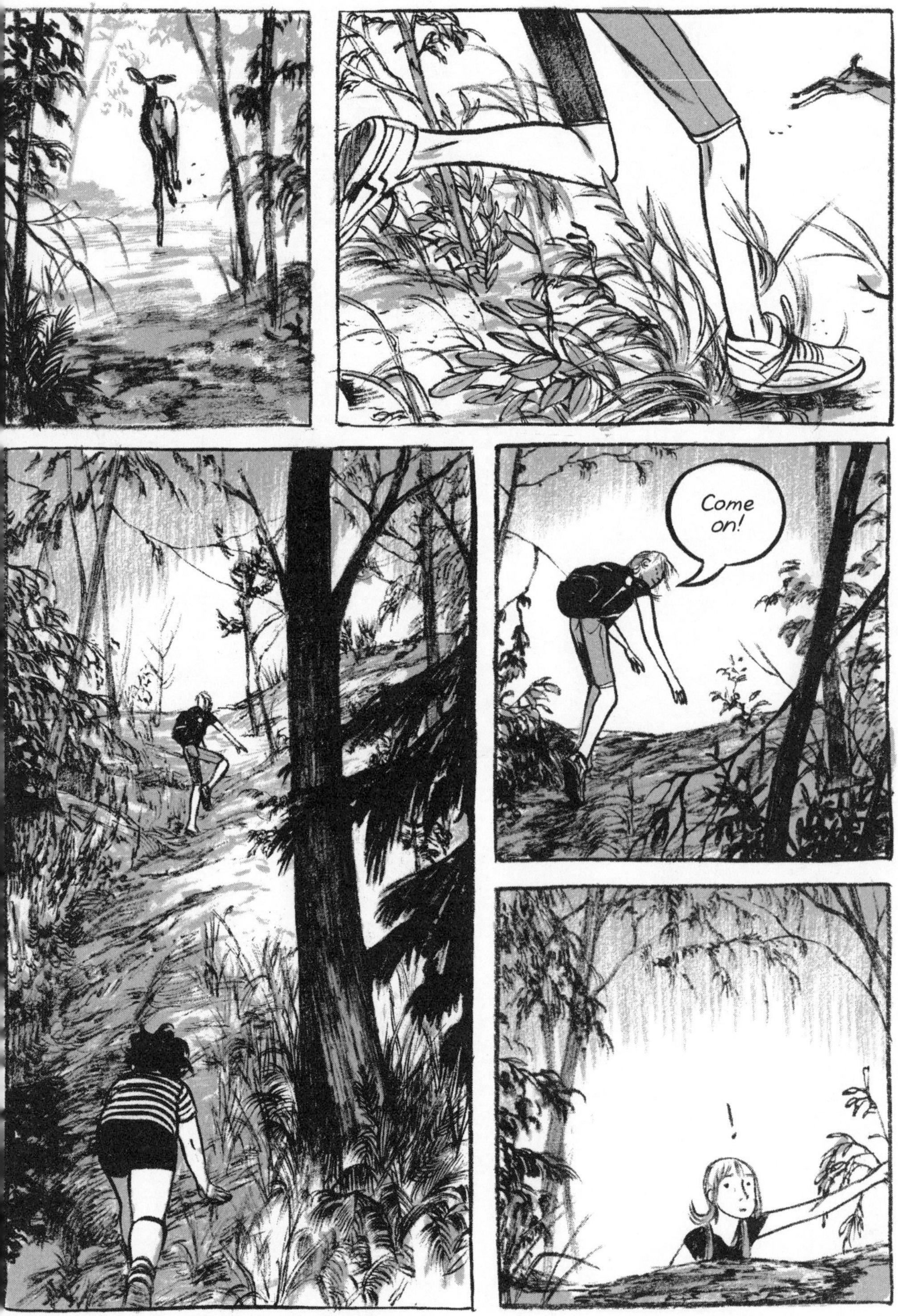
Come on!
!

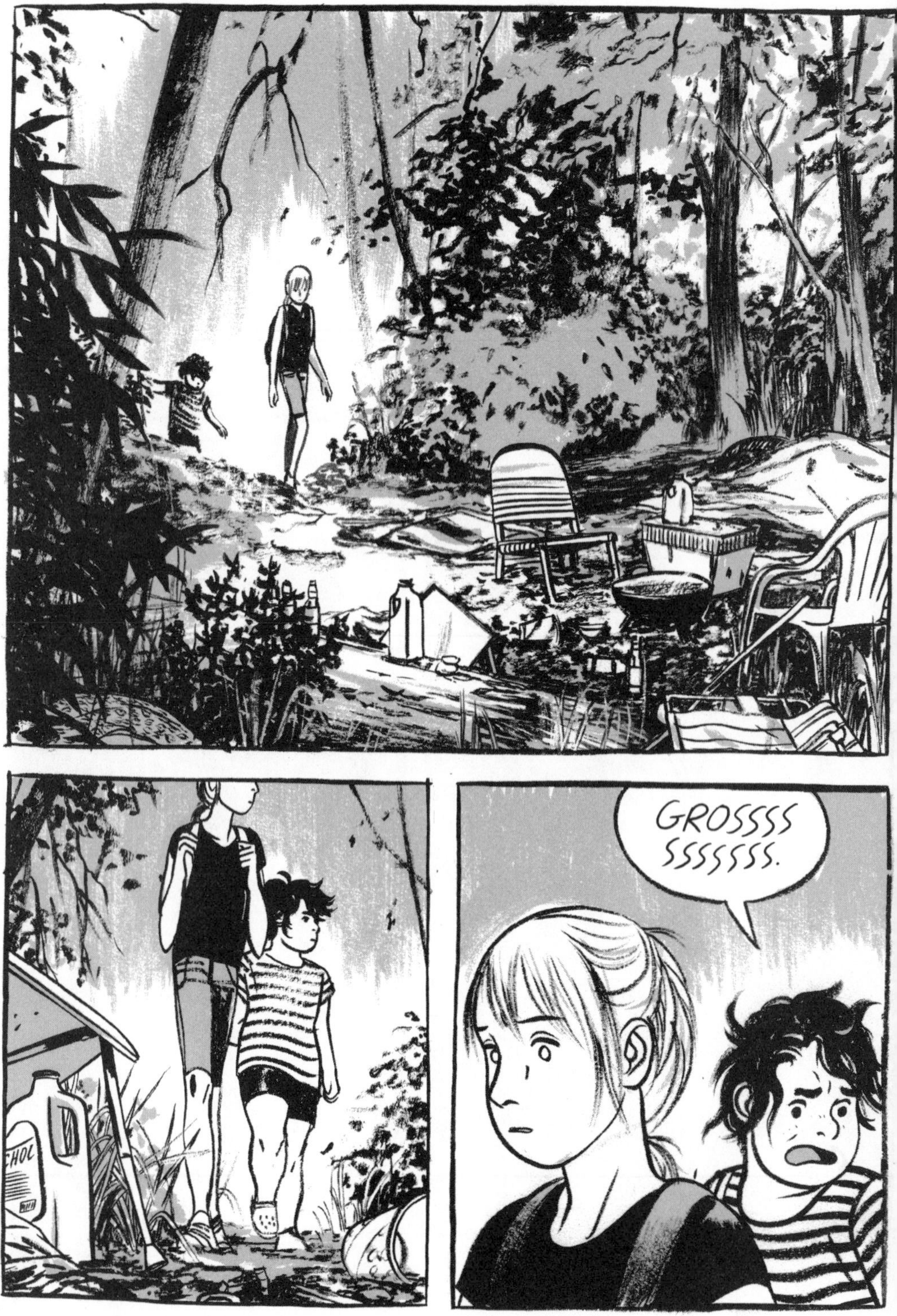
GROSSSS
SSSSSSS.

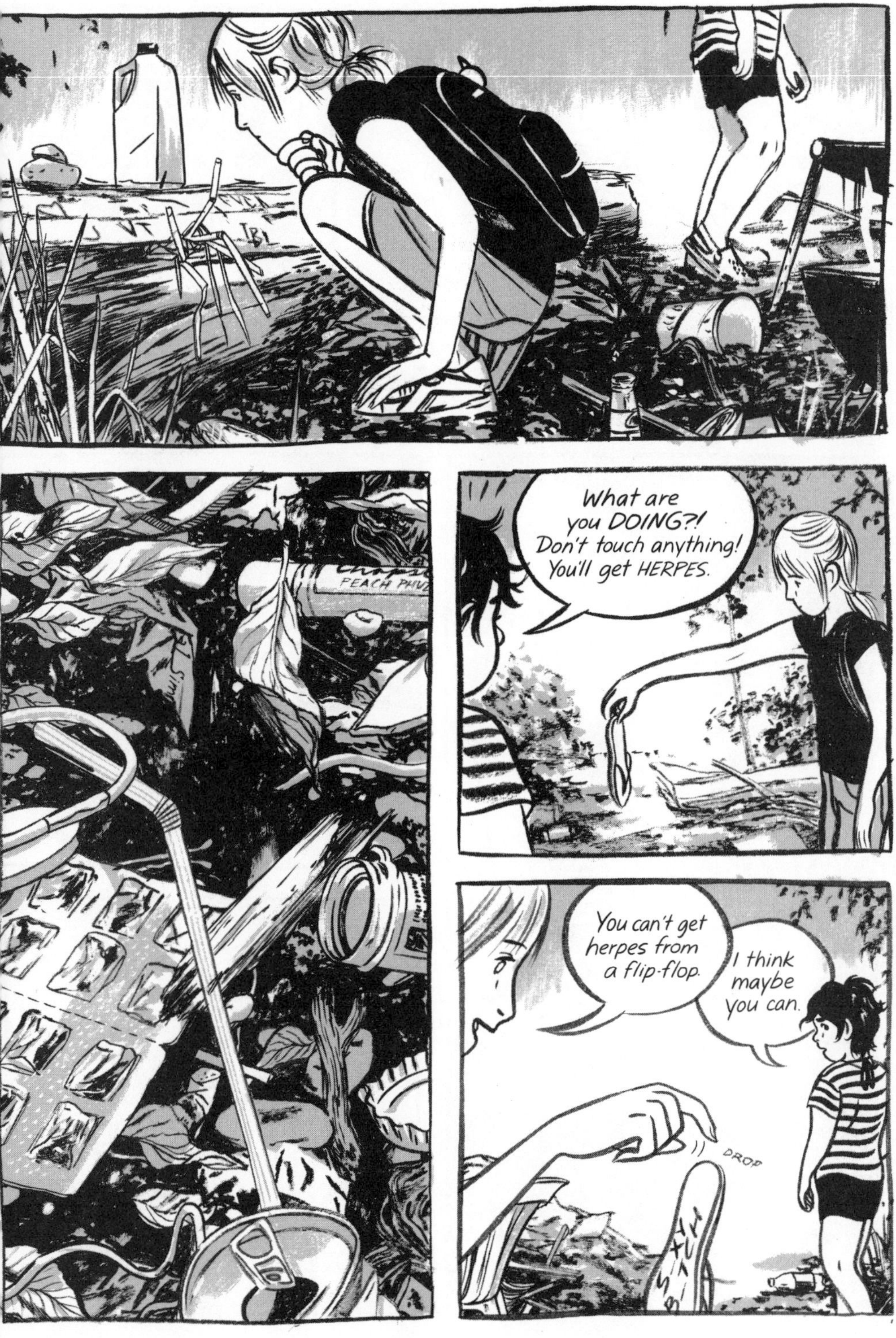
PEACH PHUZ
What are you DOING?! Don't touch anything! You'll get HERPES.
You can't get herpes from a flip-flop.
I think maybe you can.
DROP

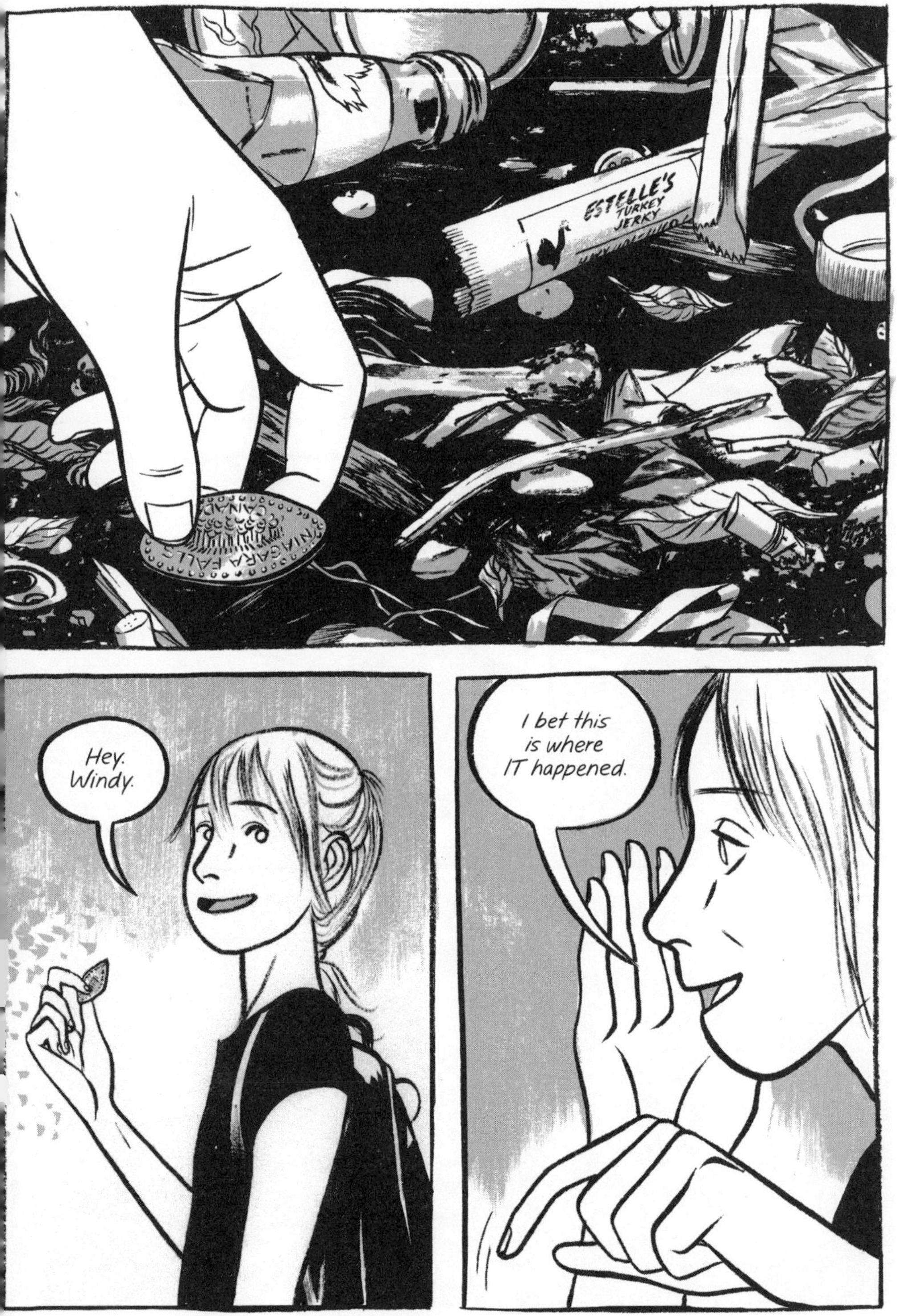
ESTELLE'S
TURKEY
JERKY
NIAGARA FALLS
CANADA
Hey. Windy.
I bet this is where IT happened.

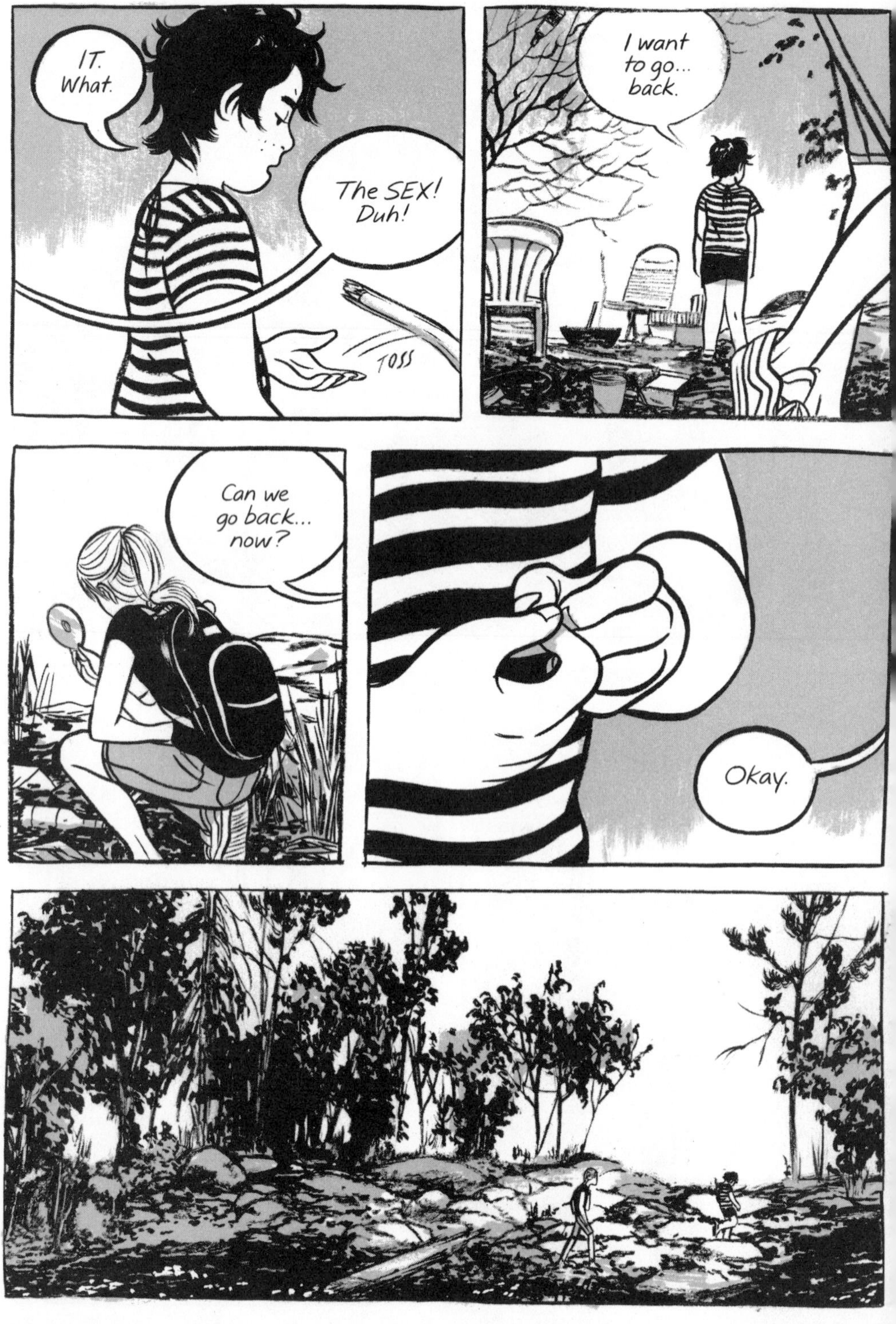
IT. What.
The SEX! Duh!
TOSS
I want to go... back.
Can we go back... now?
Okay.

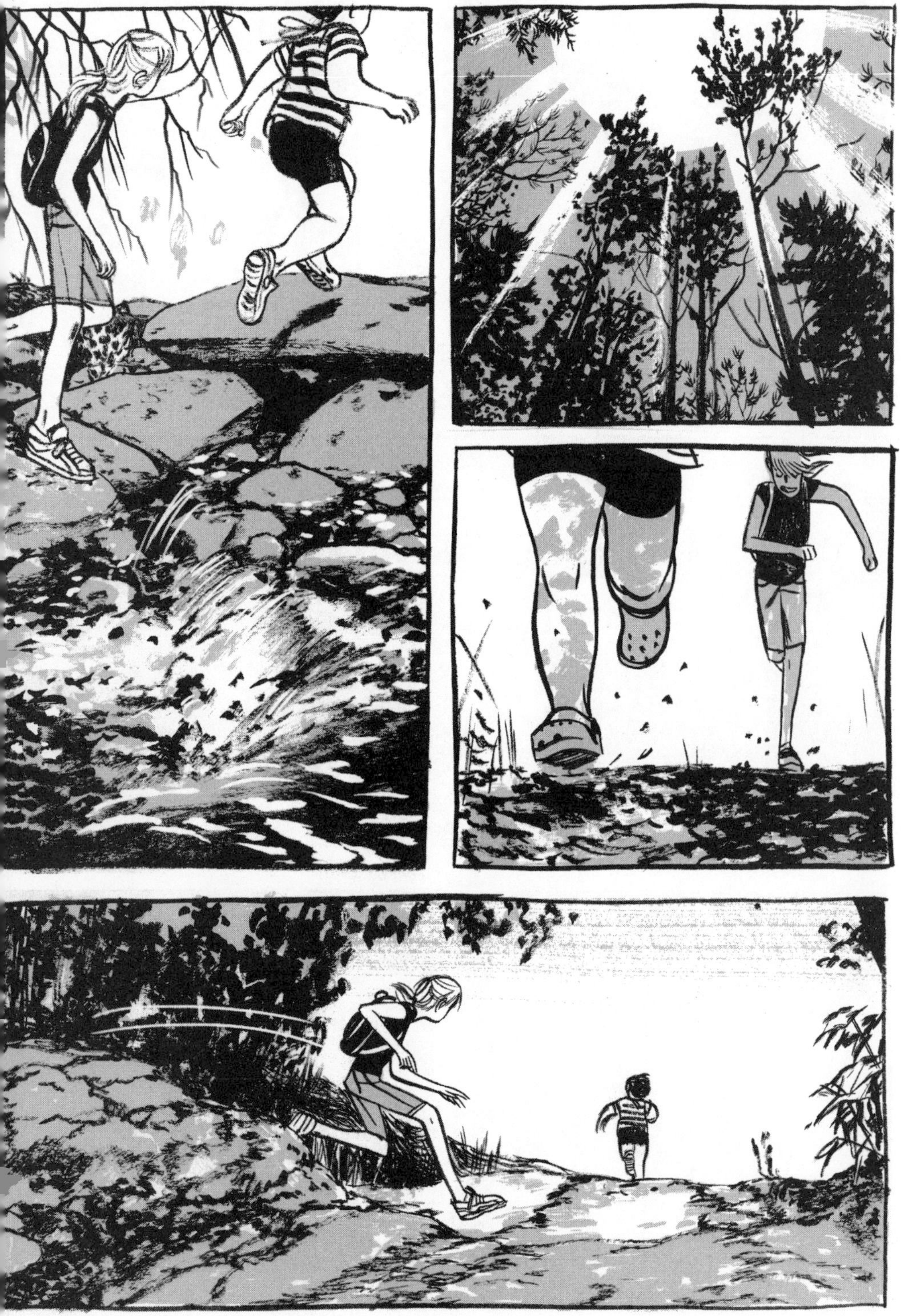

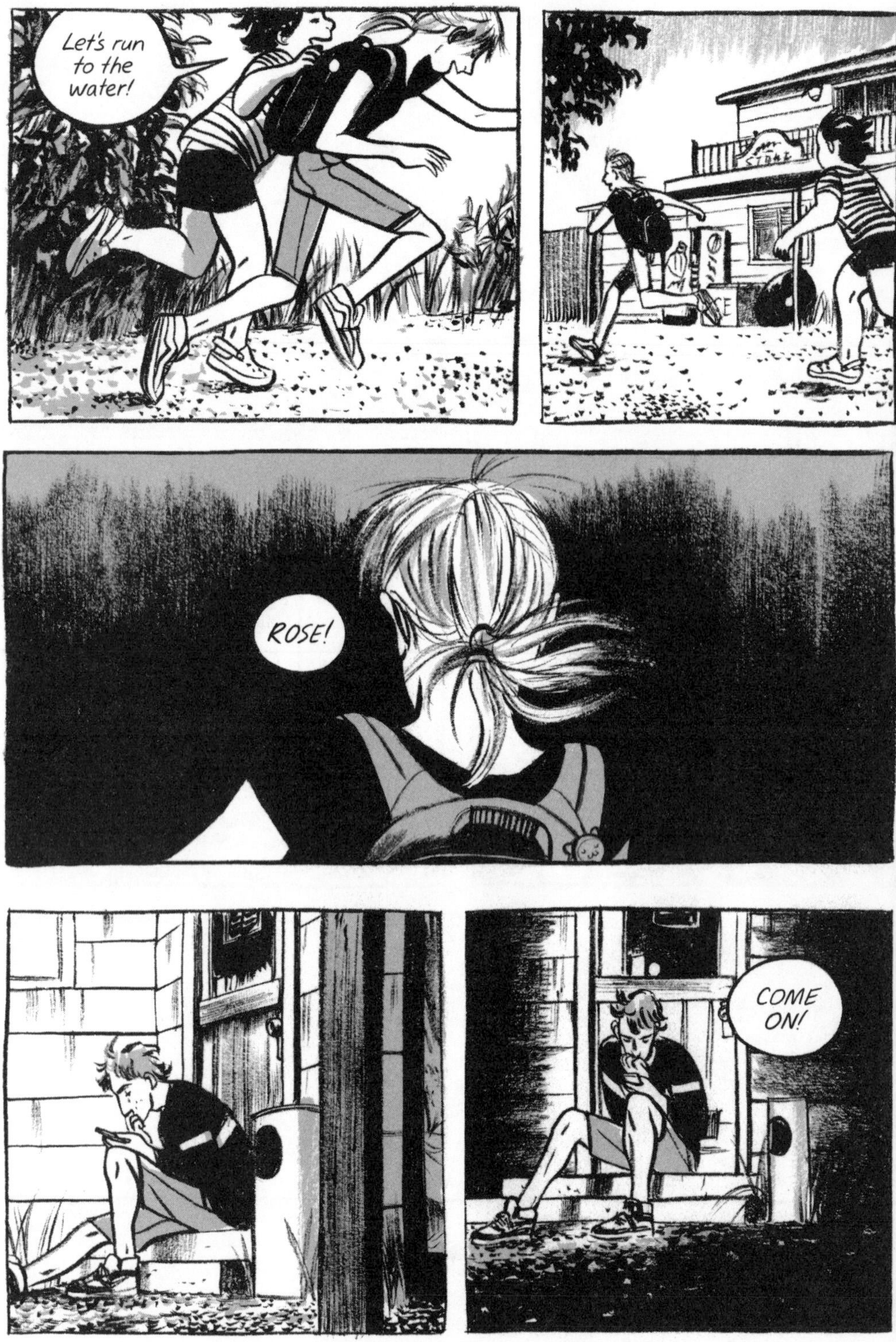
Let's run to the water!
ROSE!
COME ON!

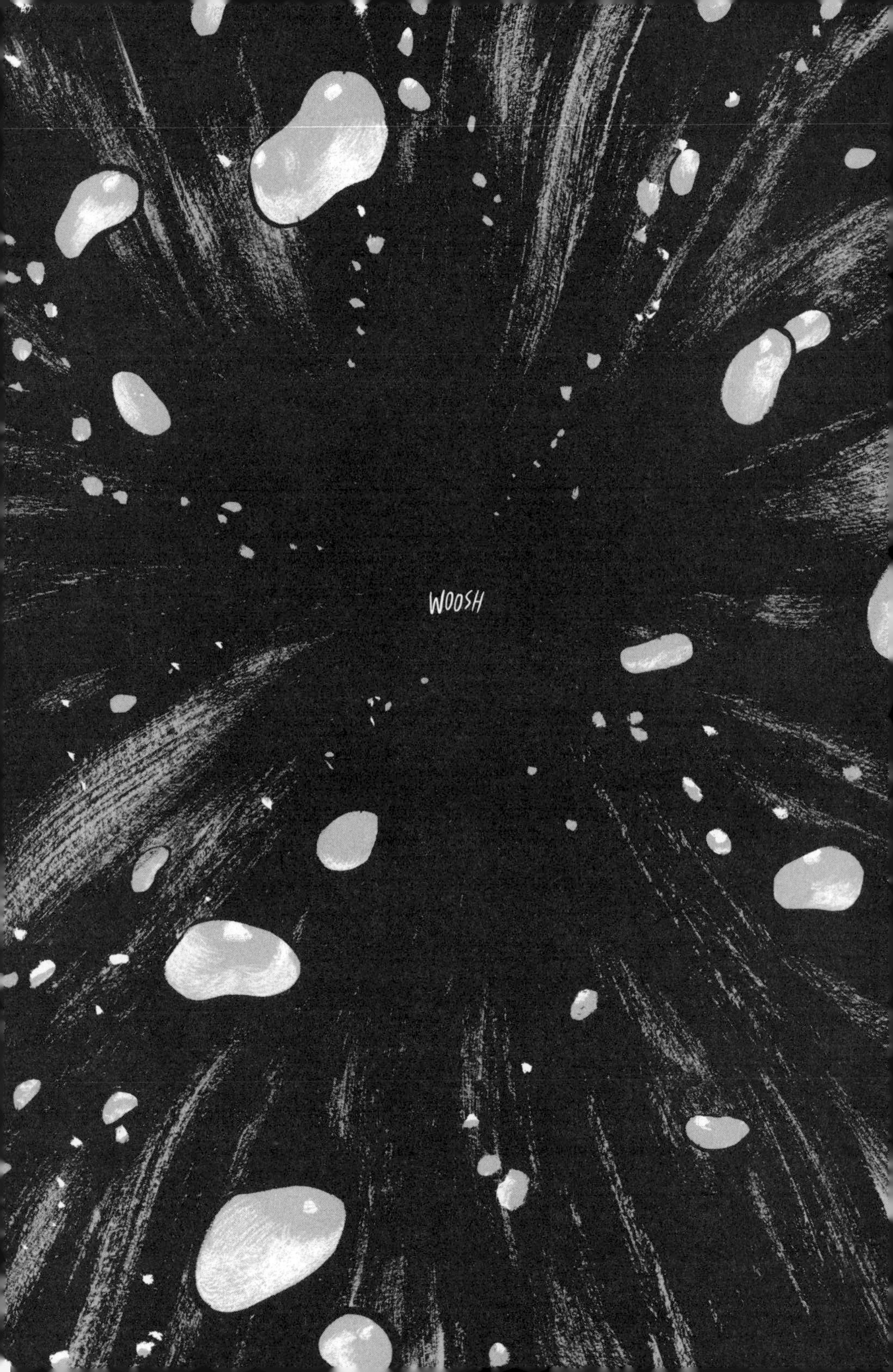
WOOSH

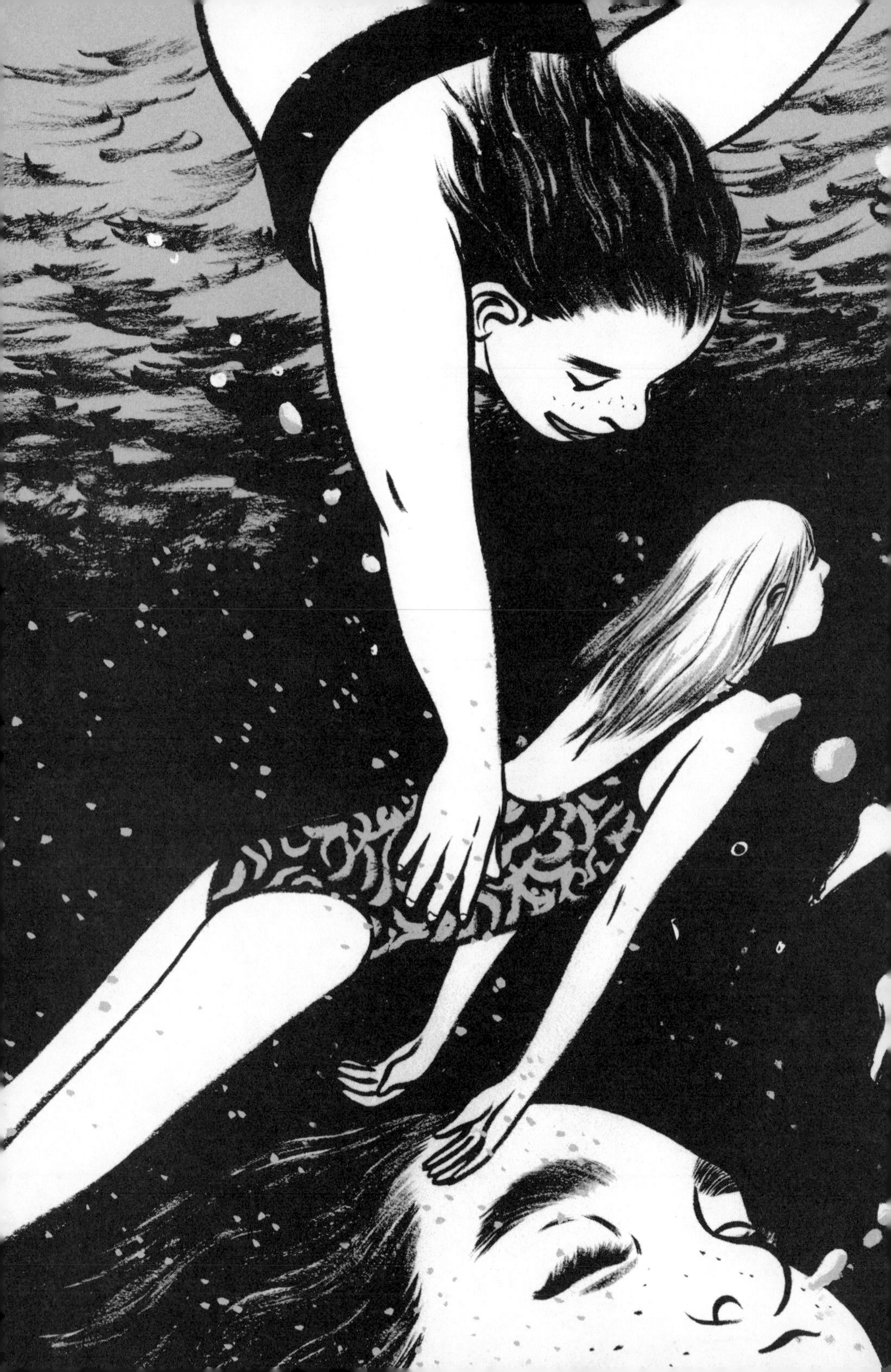

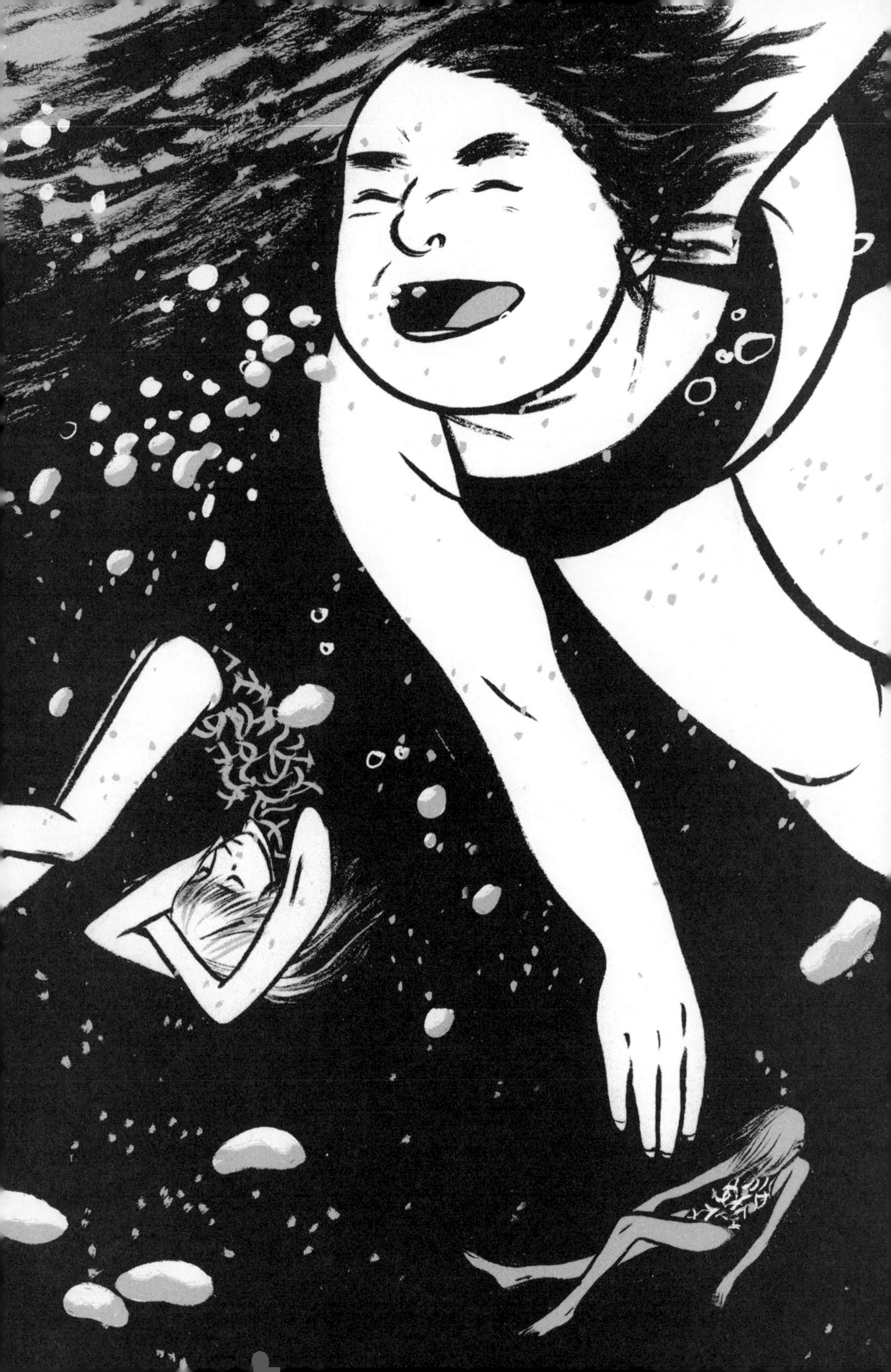

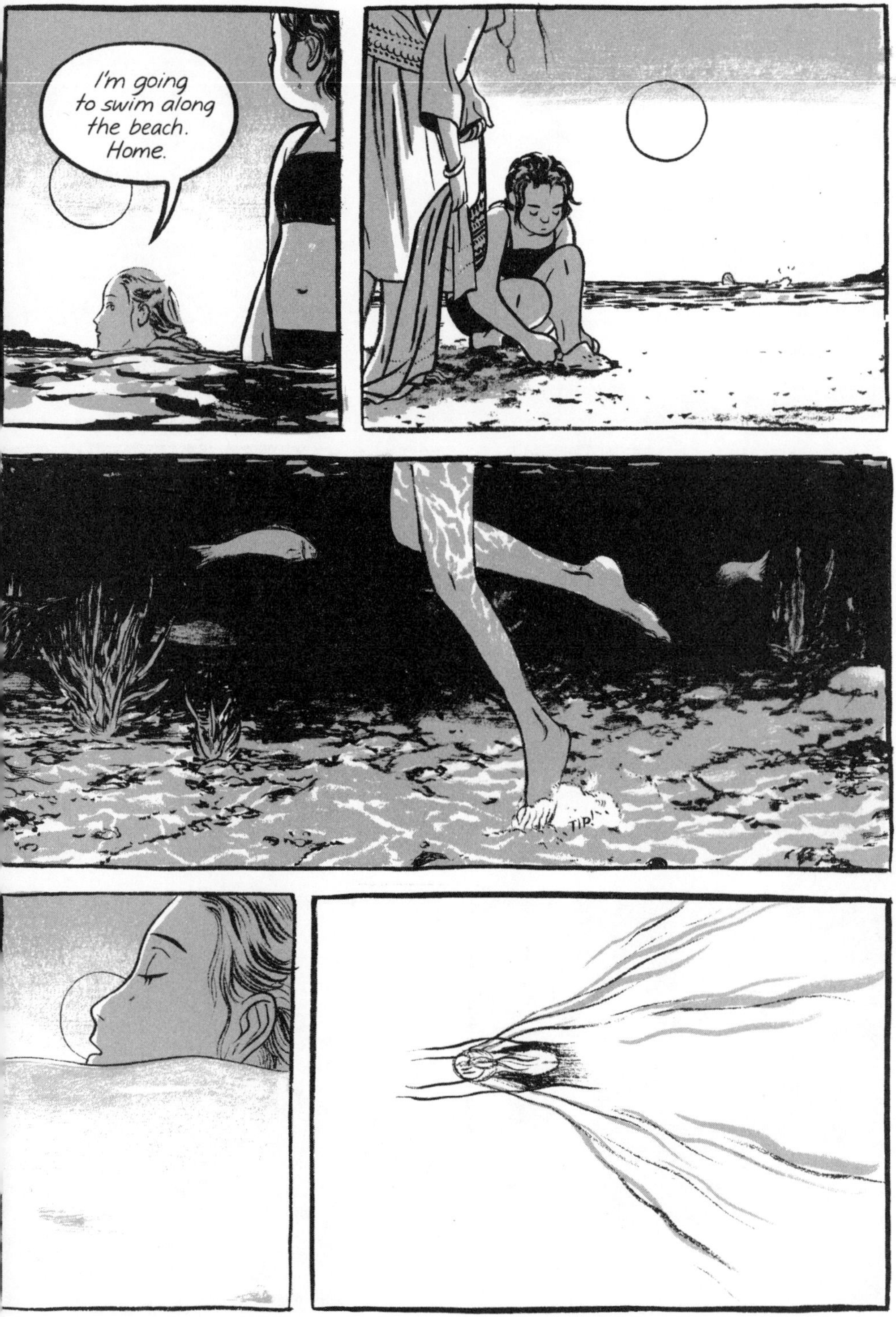
I'm going to swim along the beach. Home.
TIP!

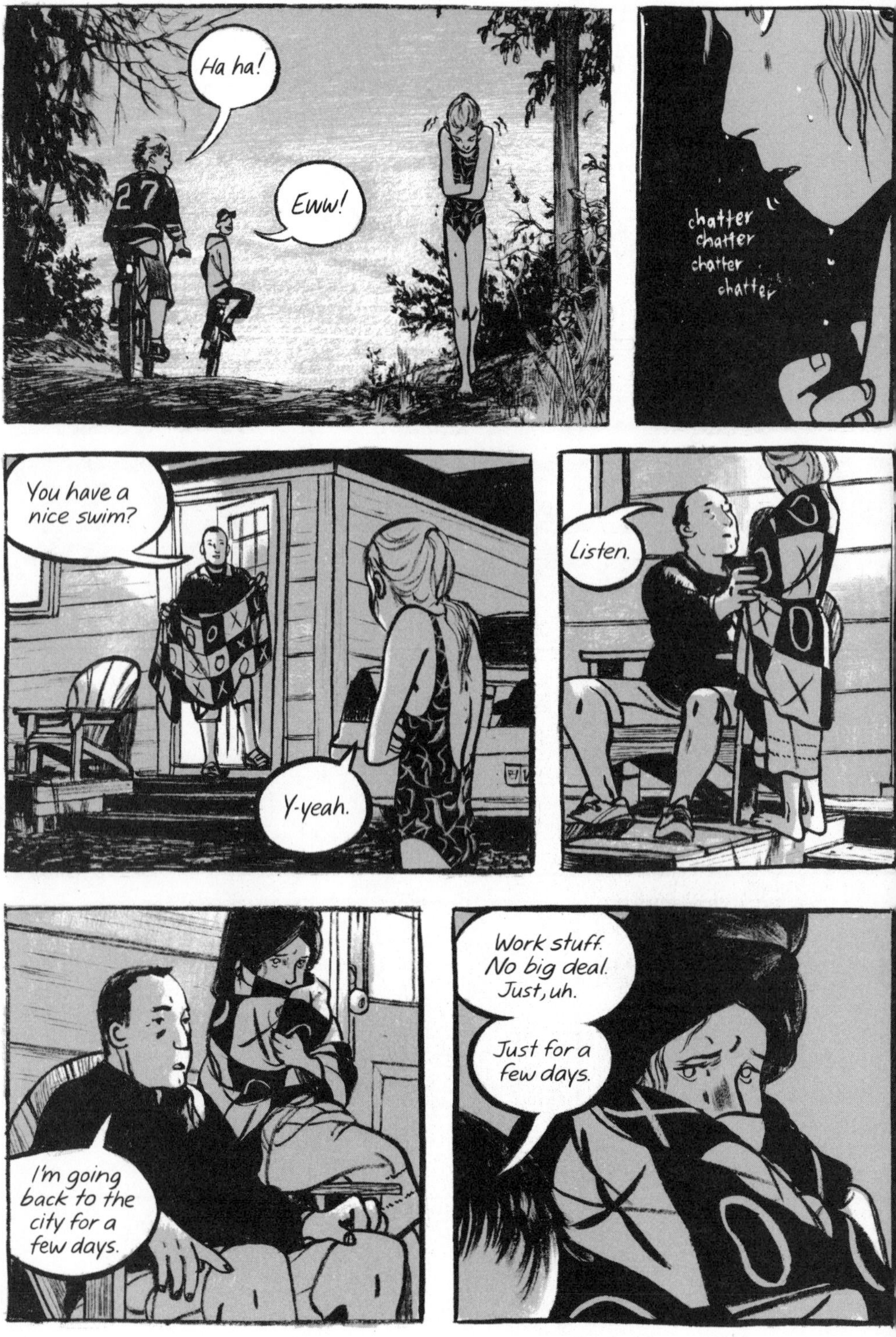
Ha ha!
Eww!
chatter chatter chatter chatter
You have a nice swim?
Y-yeah.
Listen.
I'm going back to the city for a few days.
Work stuff. No big deal. Just, uh.
Just for a few days.

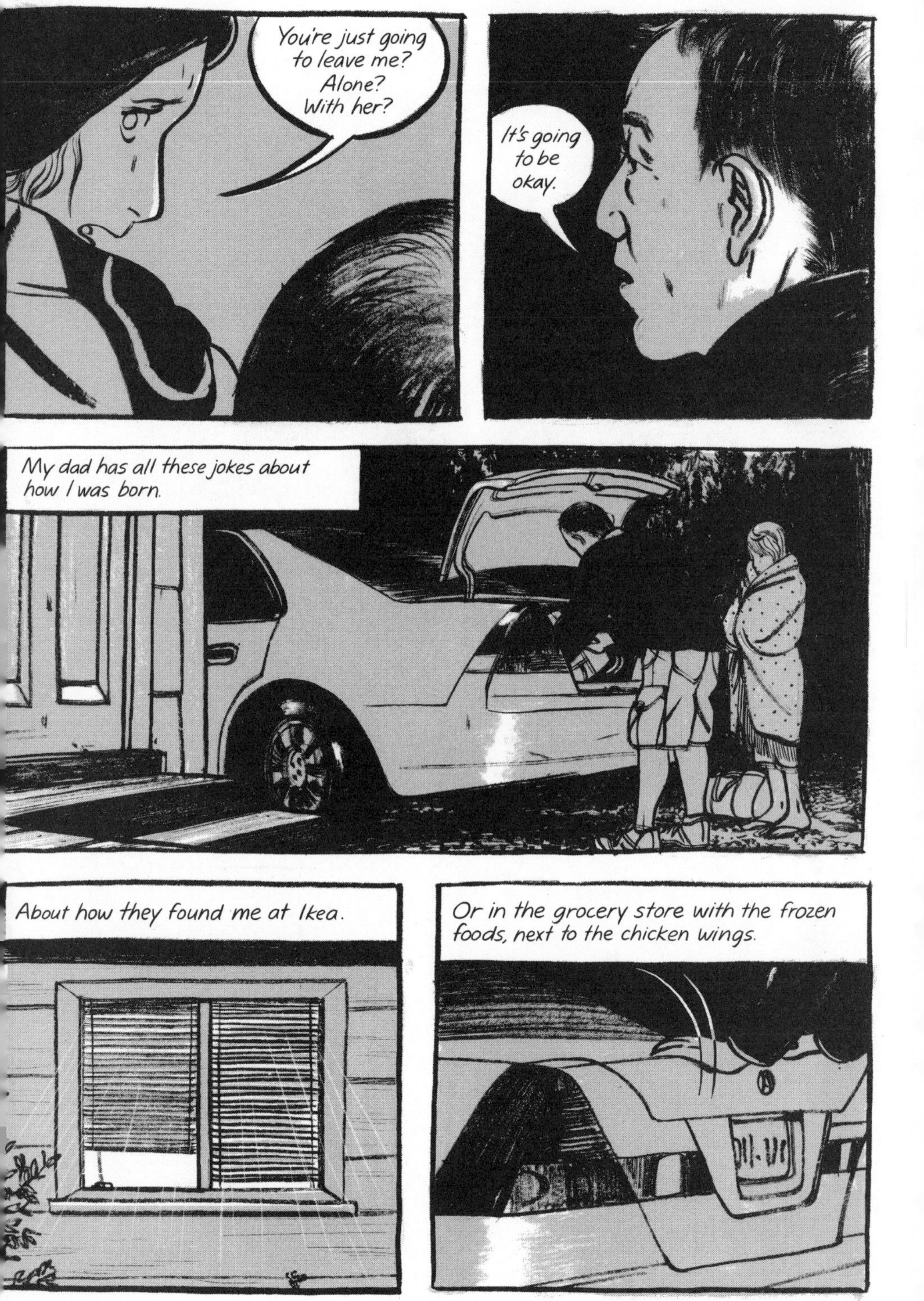
You're just going to leave me? Alone? With her?
It's going to be okay.
My dad has all these jokes about how I was born.
About how they found me at Ikea.
Or in the grocery store with the frozen foods, next to the chicken wings.

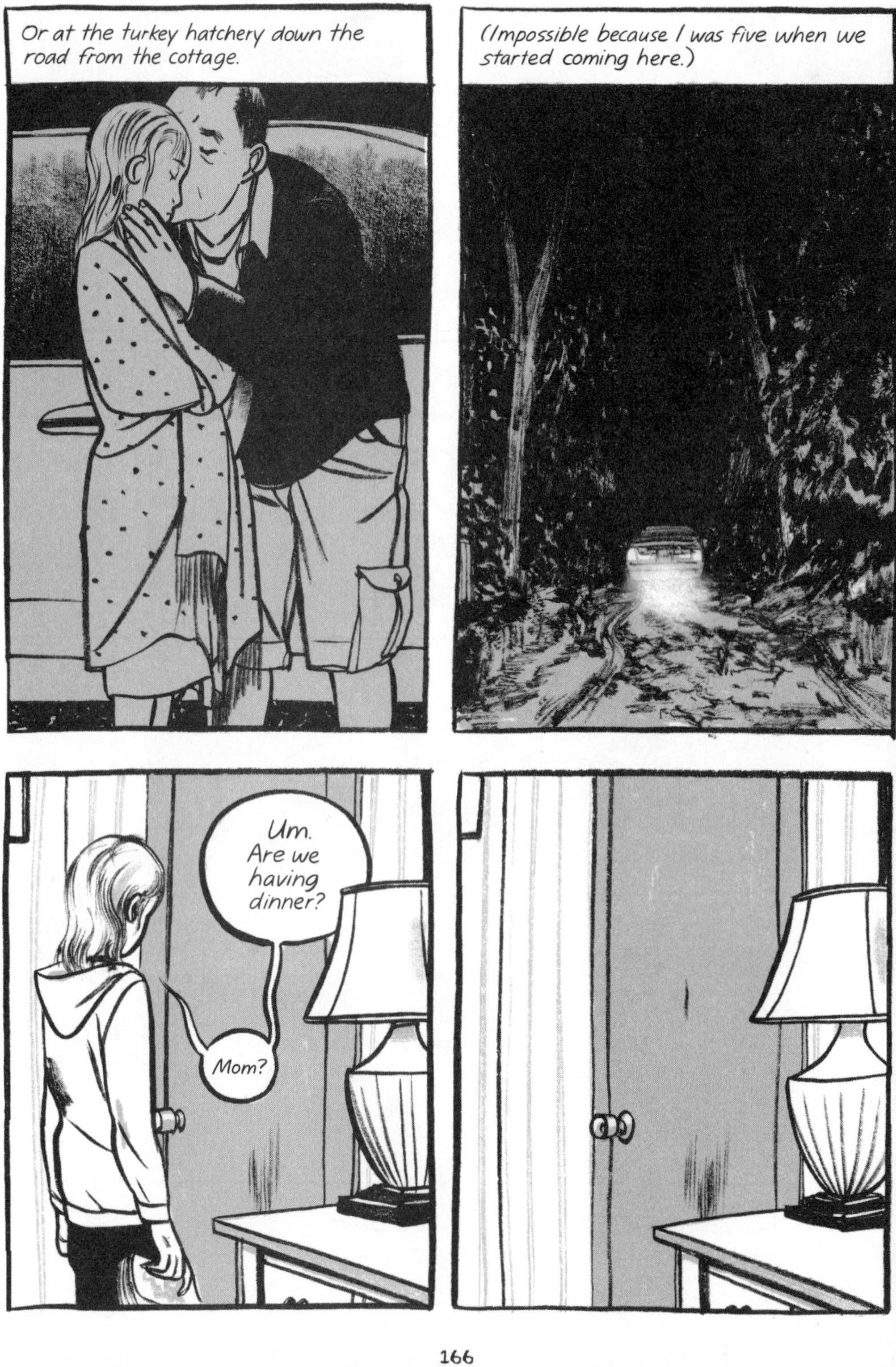
Or at the turkey hatchery down the road from the cottage.
(Impossible because I was five when we started coming here.)
Um. Are we having dinner?
Mom?

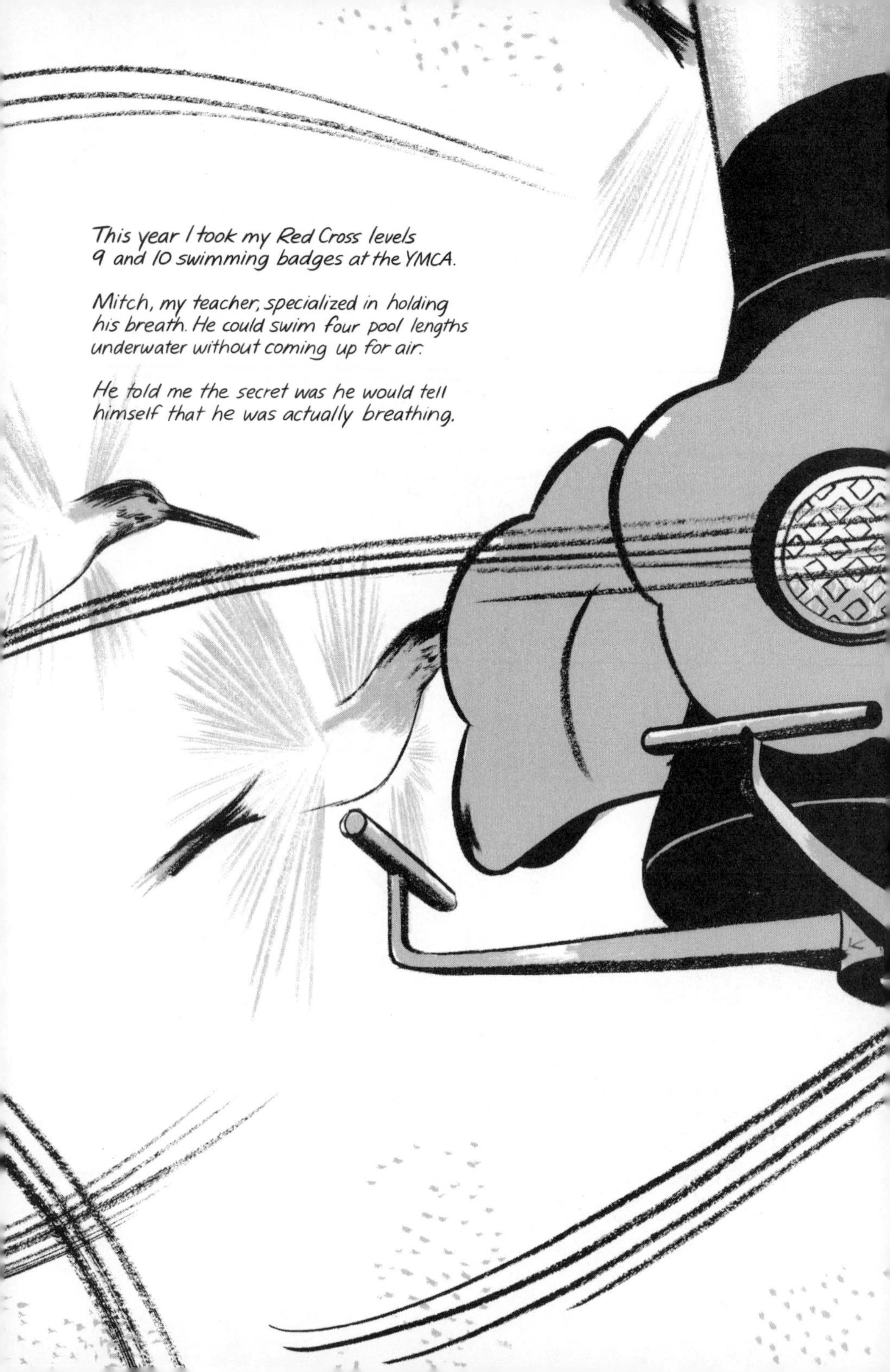
This year I took my Red Cross levels 9 and 10 swimming badges at the YMCA.
Mitch, my teacher, specialized in holding his breath. He could swim four pool lengths underwater without coming up for air.
He told me the secret was he would tell himself that he was actually breathing.

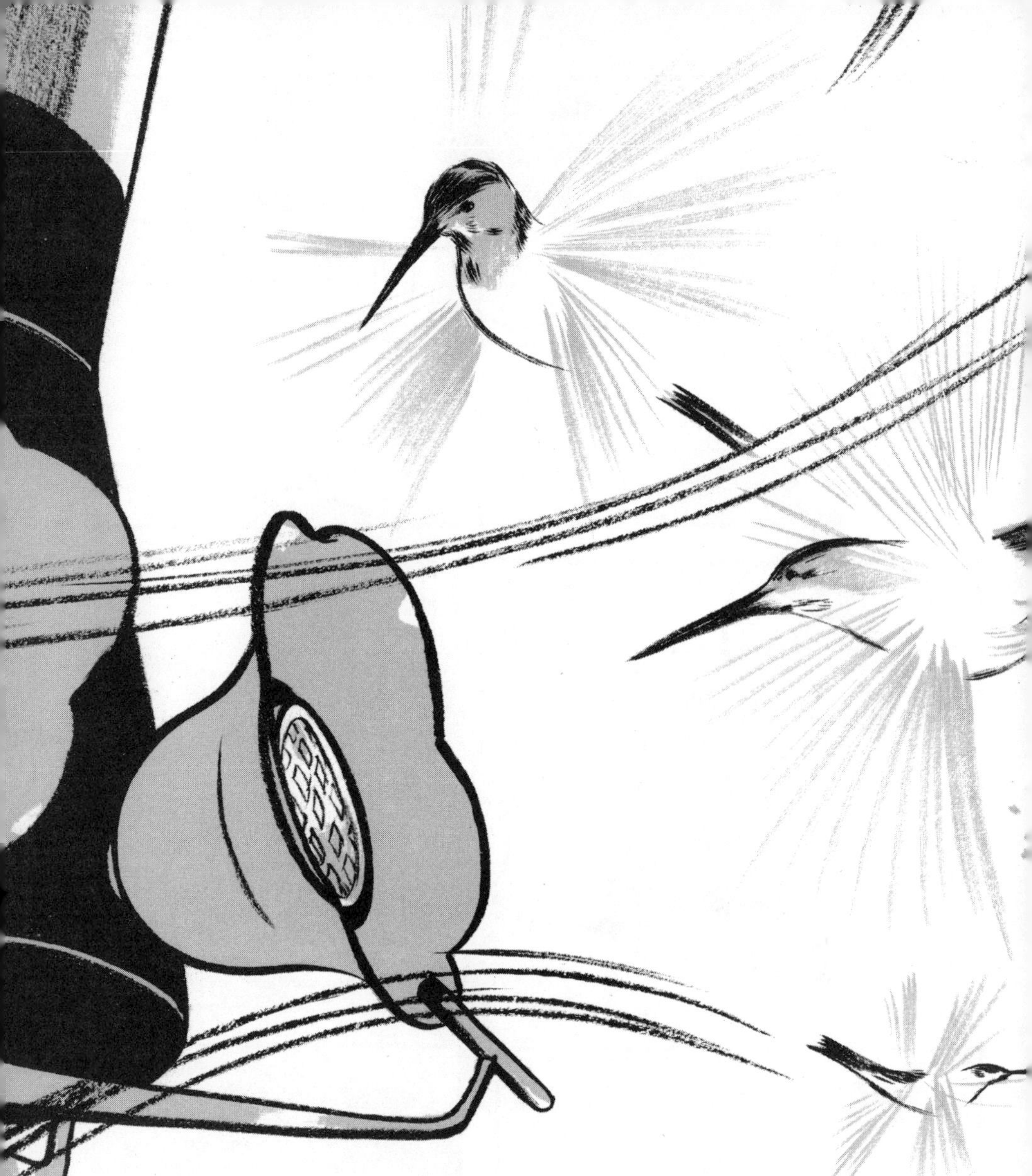

And he would just say to himself, over and over, "I'm breathing in, breathing out."

When my mom is mad at my dad, because my dad won't do something, or forgets to do something, she says, "You can say what you want, Evan, but I'm not holding my breath."

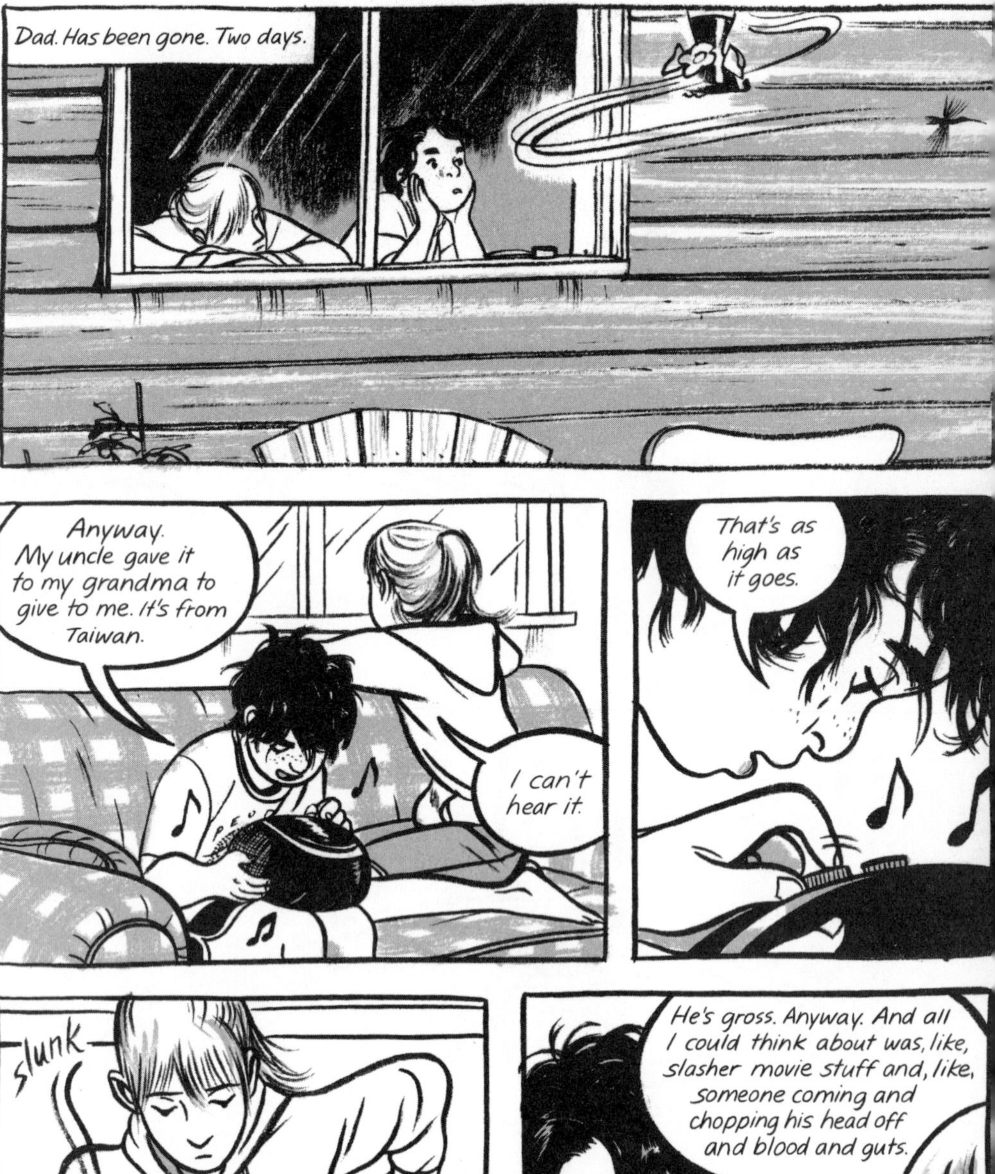
Dad. Has been gone. Two days.
Anyway. My uncle gave it to my grandma to give to me. It's from Taiwan.
I can't hear it.
That's as high as it goes.
slunk
Oh my god so, yesterday? My grandma wanted to watch this movie with, like, this guy Michael Douglas, who's her favorite actor?
He's gross. Anyway. And all I could think about was, like, slasher movie stuff and, like, someone coming and chopping his head off and blood and guts.
STAB STAB
Ha.

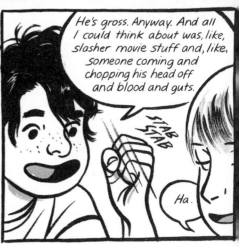

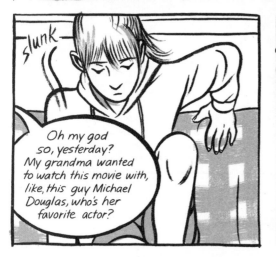

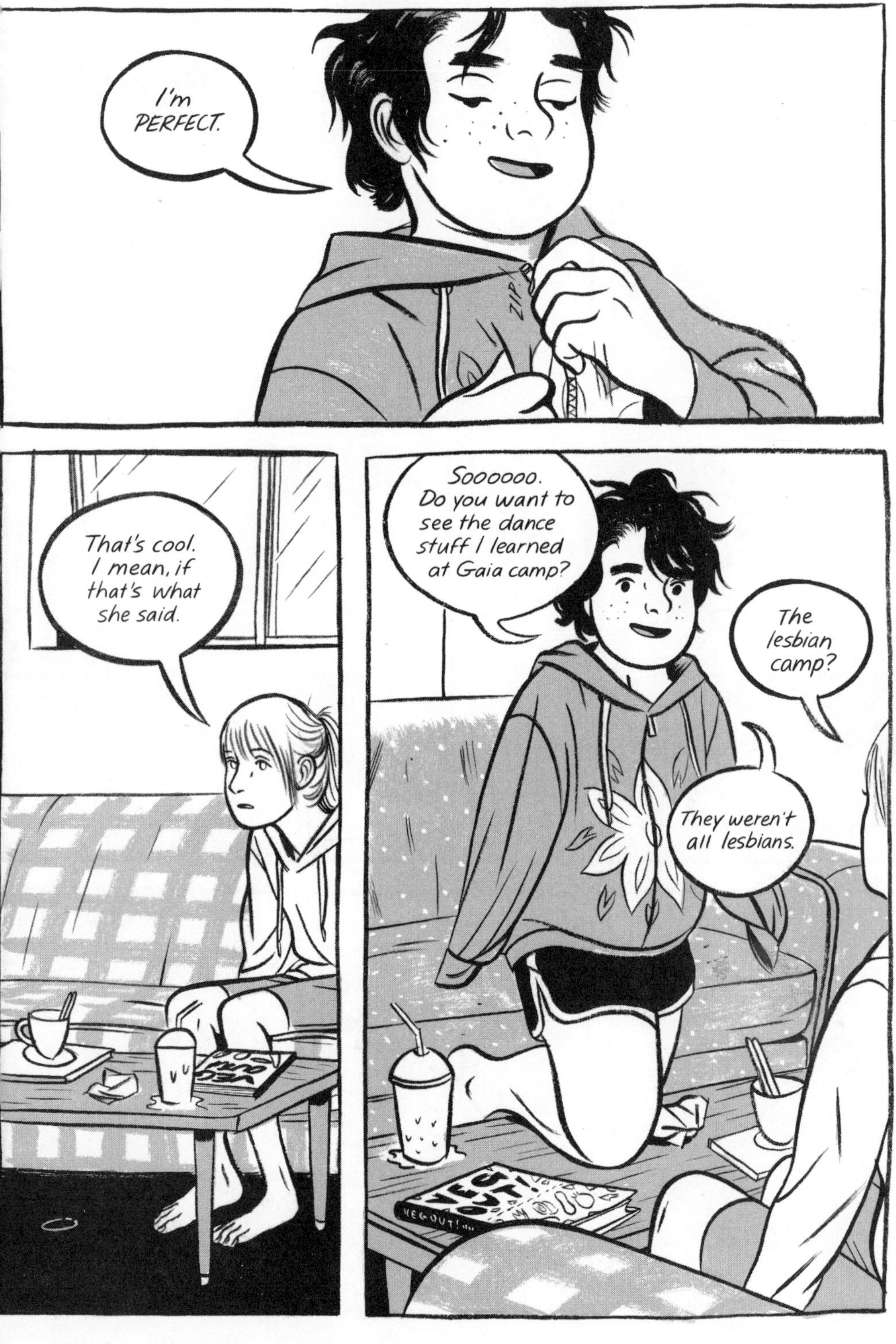
I'm PERFECT.
ZIP
That's cool. I mean, if that's what she said.
Soooooo. Do you want to see the dance stuff I learned at Gaia camp?
The lesbian camp?
They weren't all lesbians.
VEG OUT!

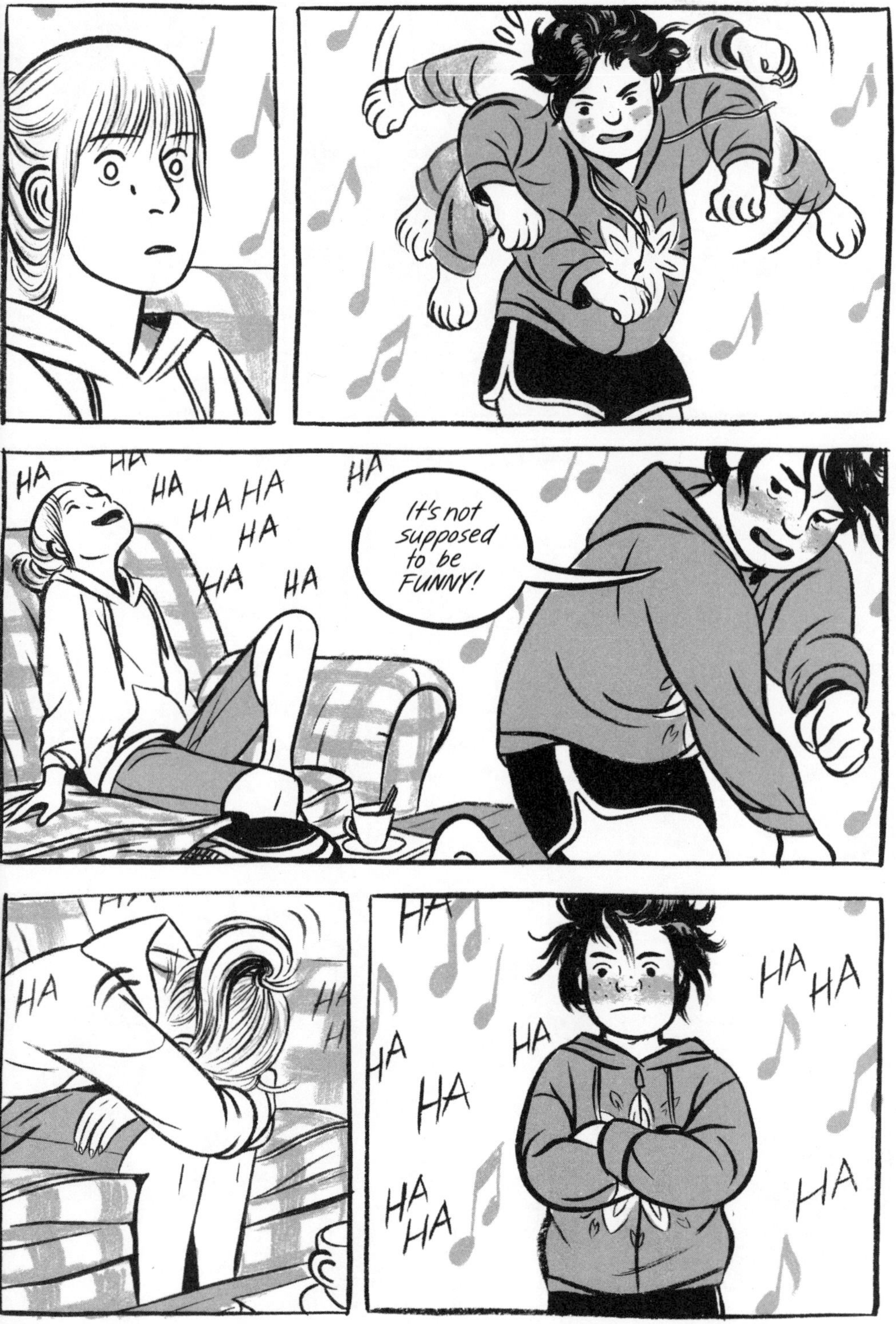
HA
HA
HA
HA HA
HA
HA
HA
HA
It's not supposed to be FUNNY!
HA
HA
HA HA
HA
HA
HA
HA
HA
HA

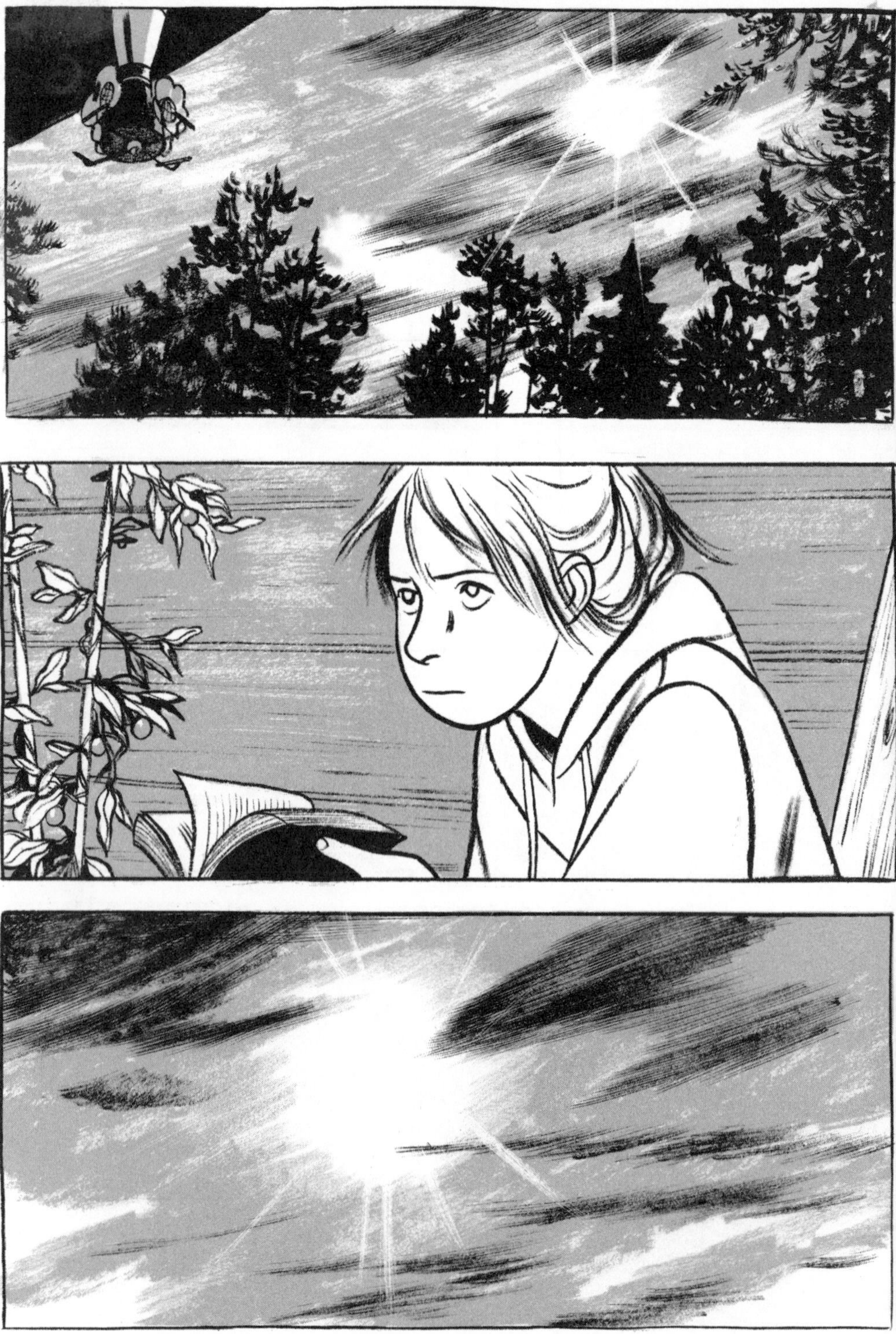

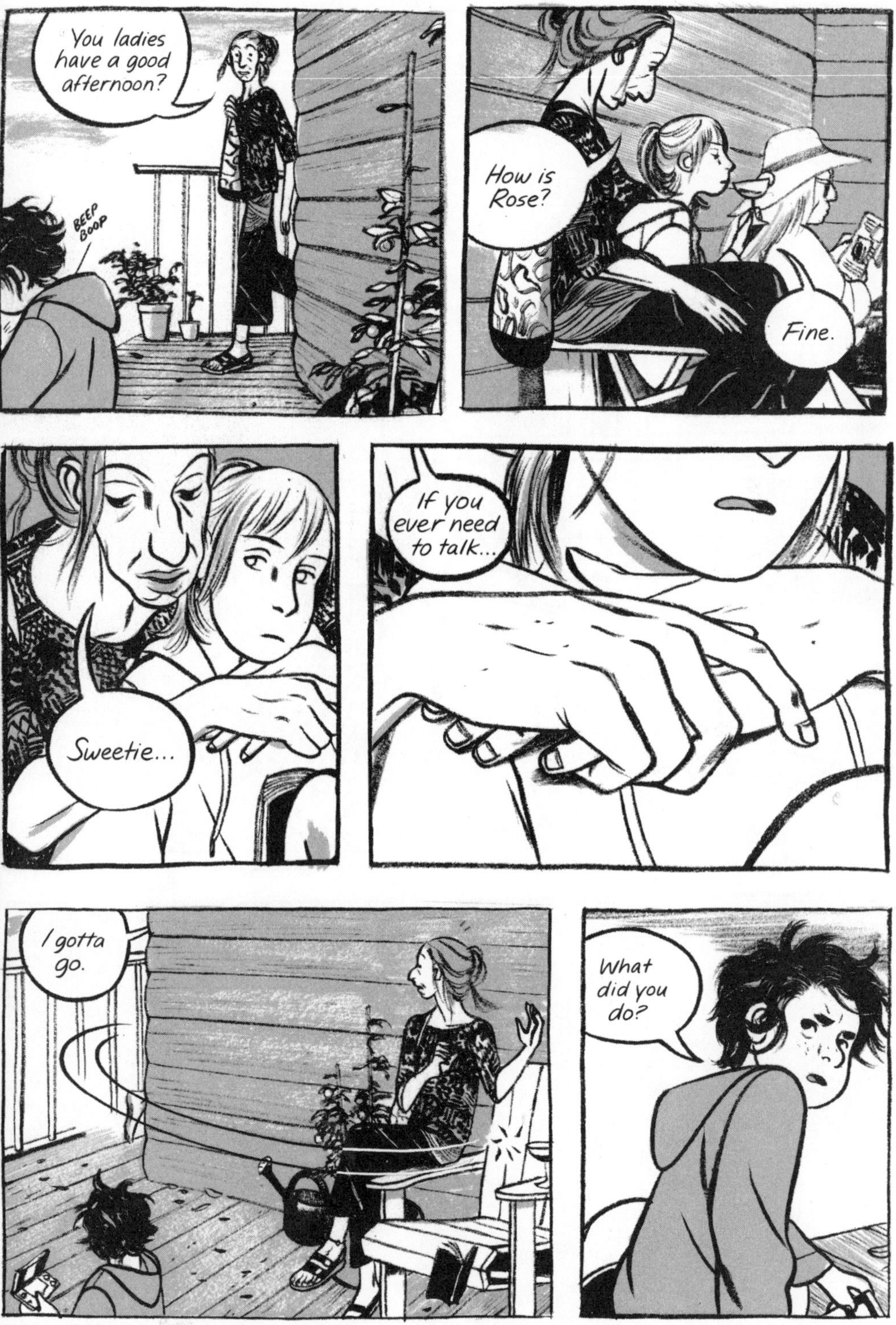
You ladies have a good afternoon?
BEEP BOOP
How is Rose?
Fine.
Sweetie...
If you ever need to talk...
I gotta go.
What did you do?

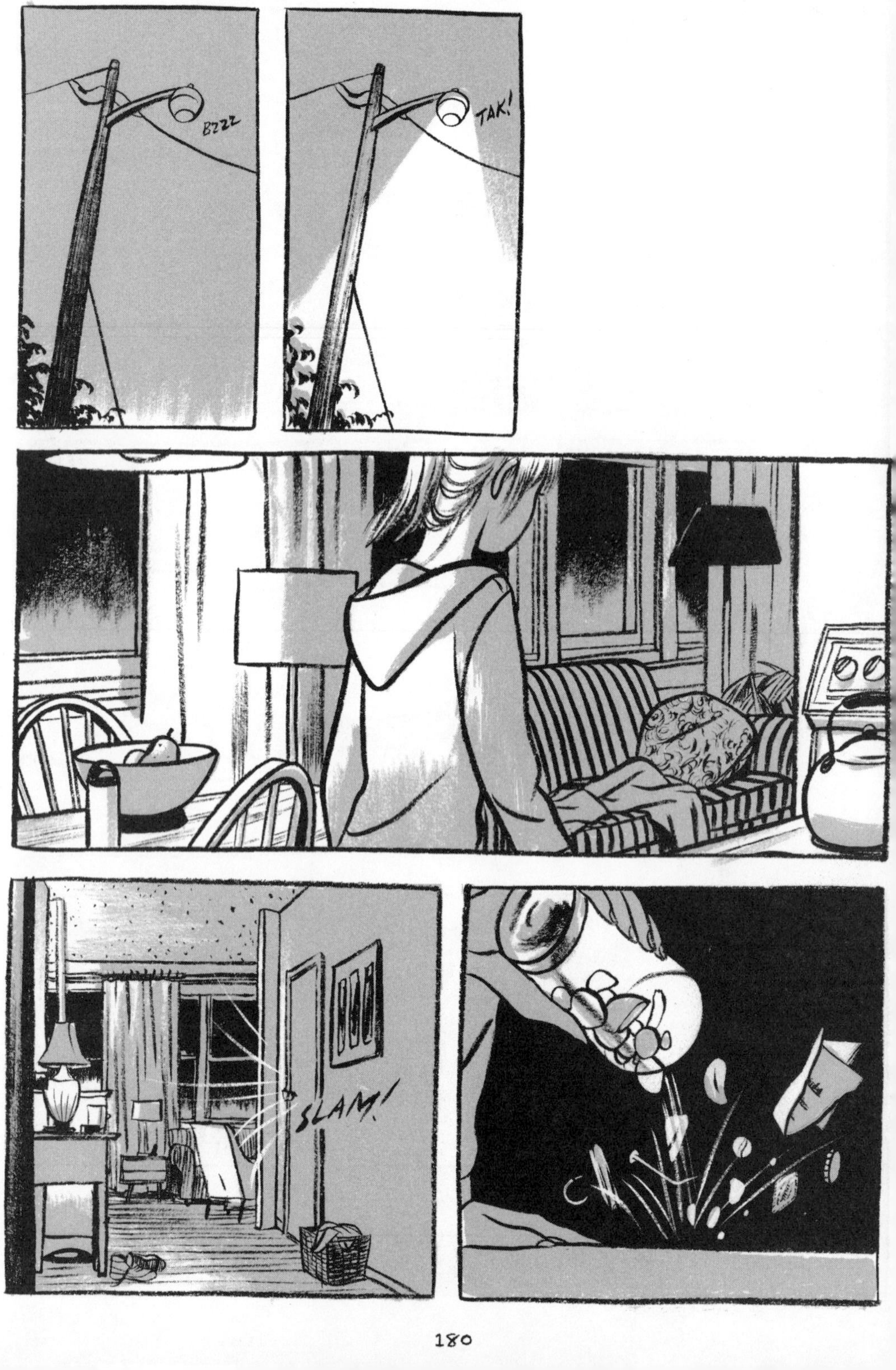
BZZZ
TAK!
SLAM!

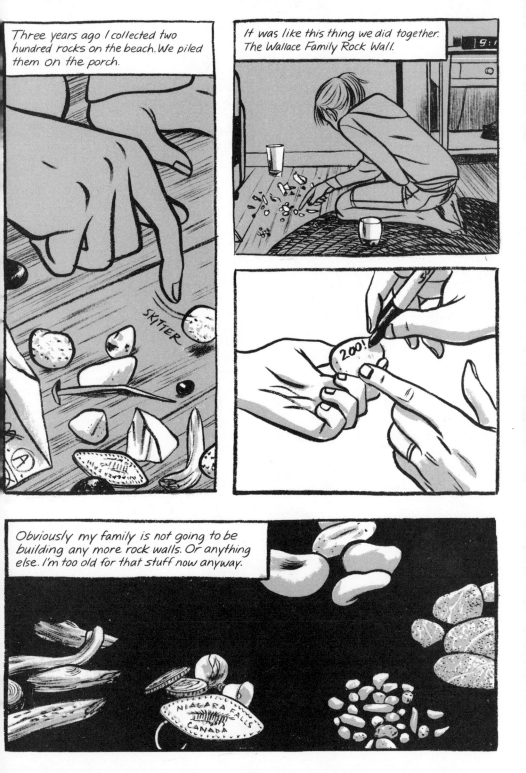

Three years ago I collected two hundred rocks on the beach. We piled them on the porch.

SKITTER

It was like this thing we did together. The Wallace Family Rock Wall.

2001

Obviously my family is not going to be building any more rock walls. Or anything else. I'm too old for that stuff now anyway.

NIAGARA FALLS CANADA

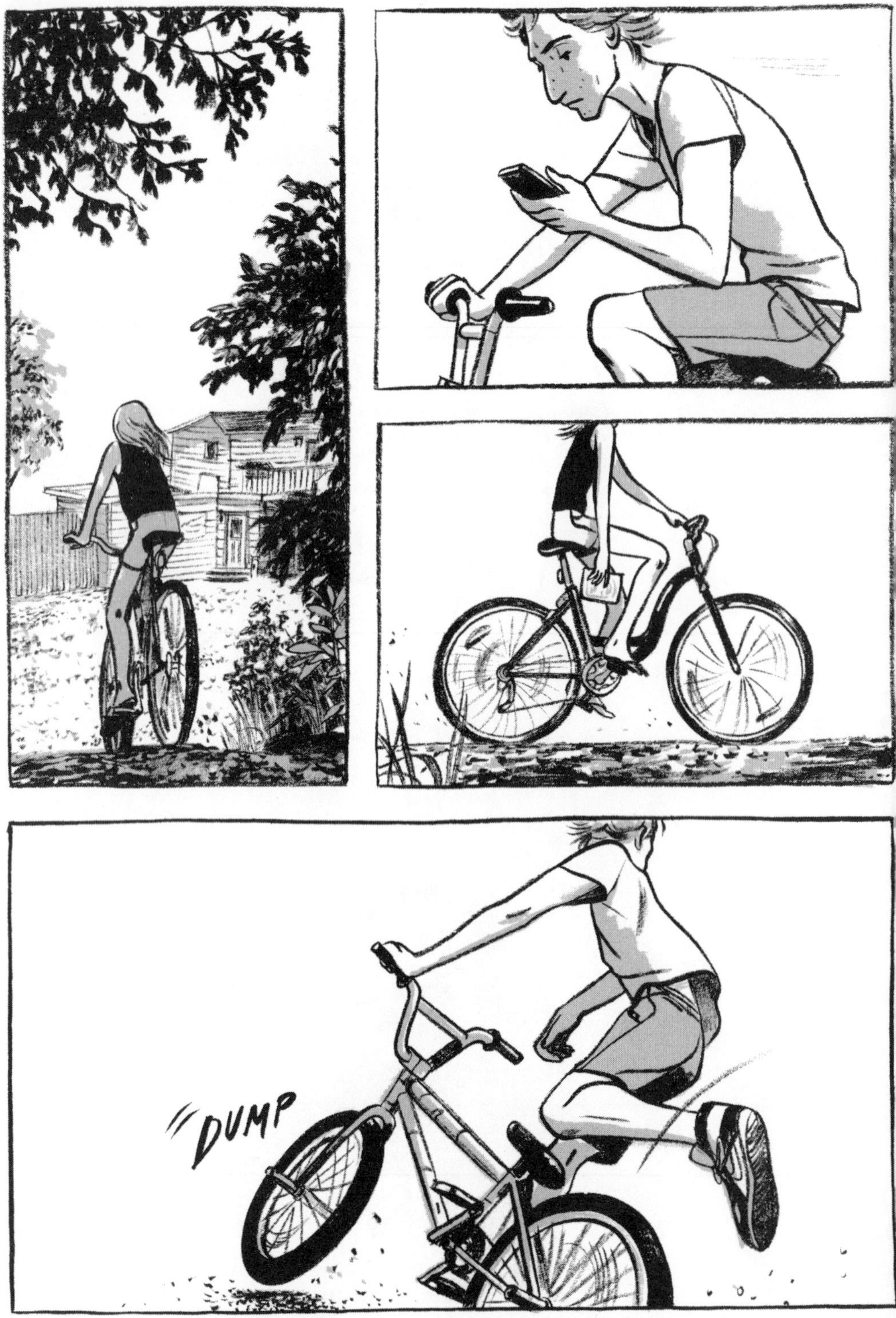
DUMP

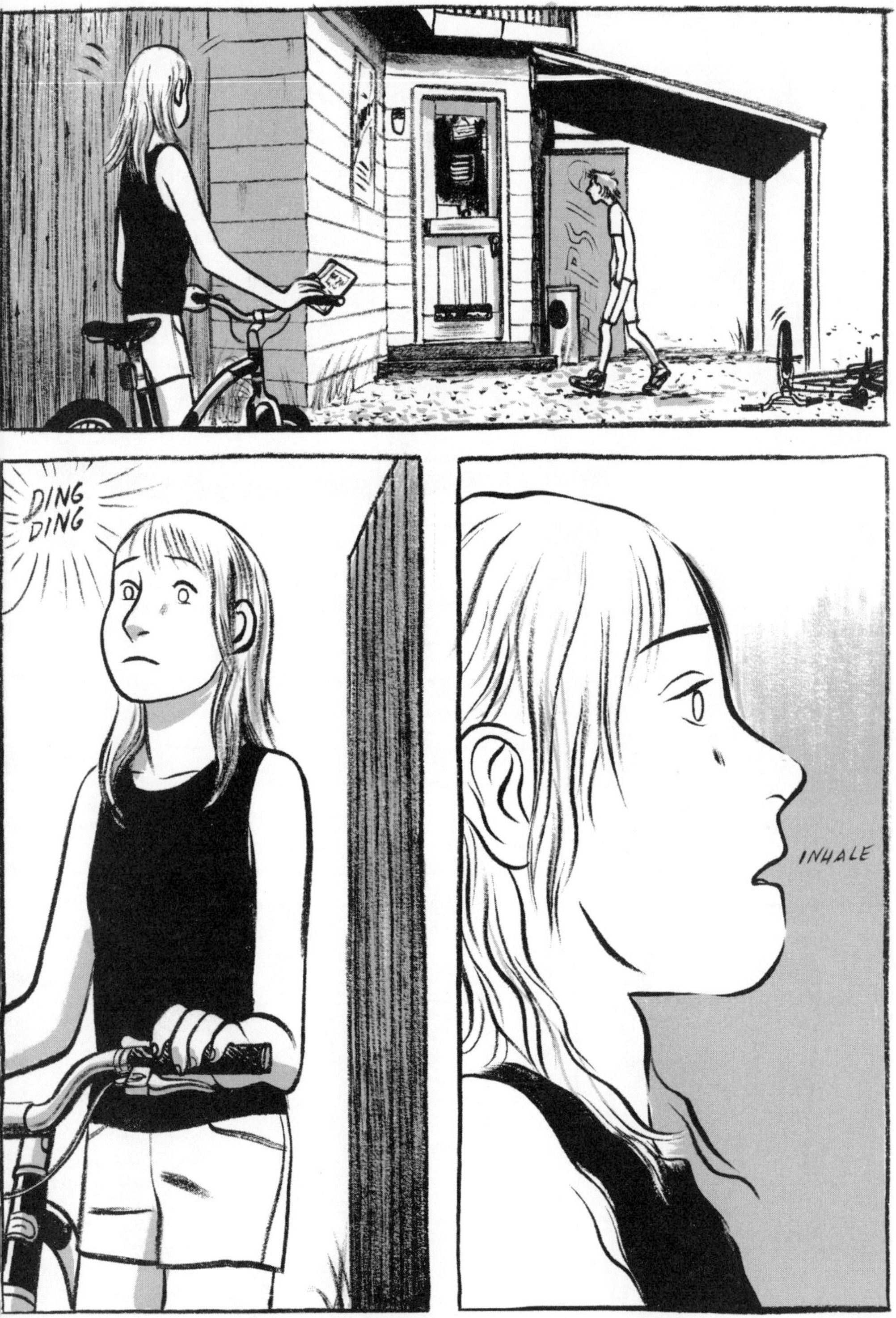
DING DING
INHALE

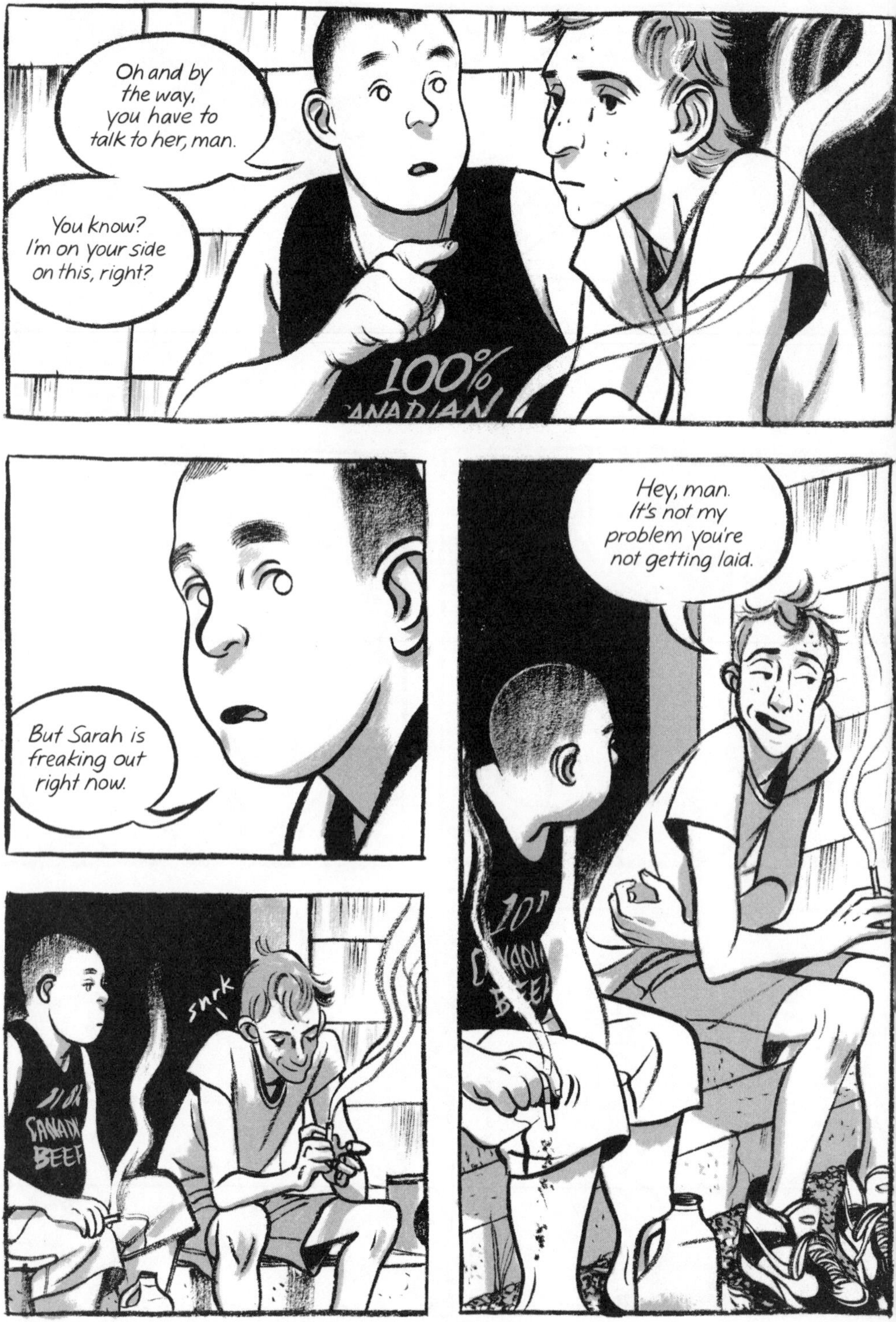
Oh and by the way, you have to talk to her, man.
You know? I'm on your side on this, right?
100% CANADIAN
But Sarah is freaking out right now.
snrk
CANADIAN BEEF
Hey, man. It's not my problem you're not getting laid.

189

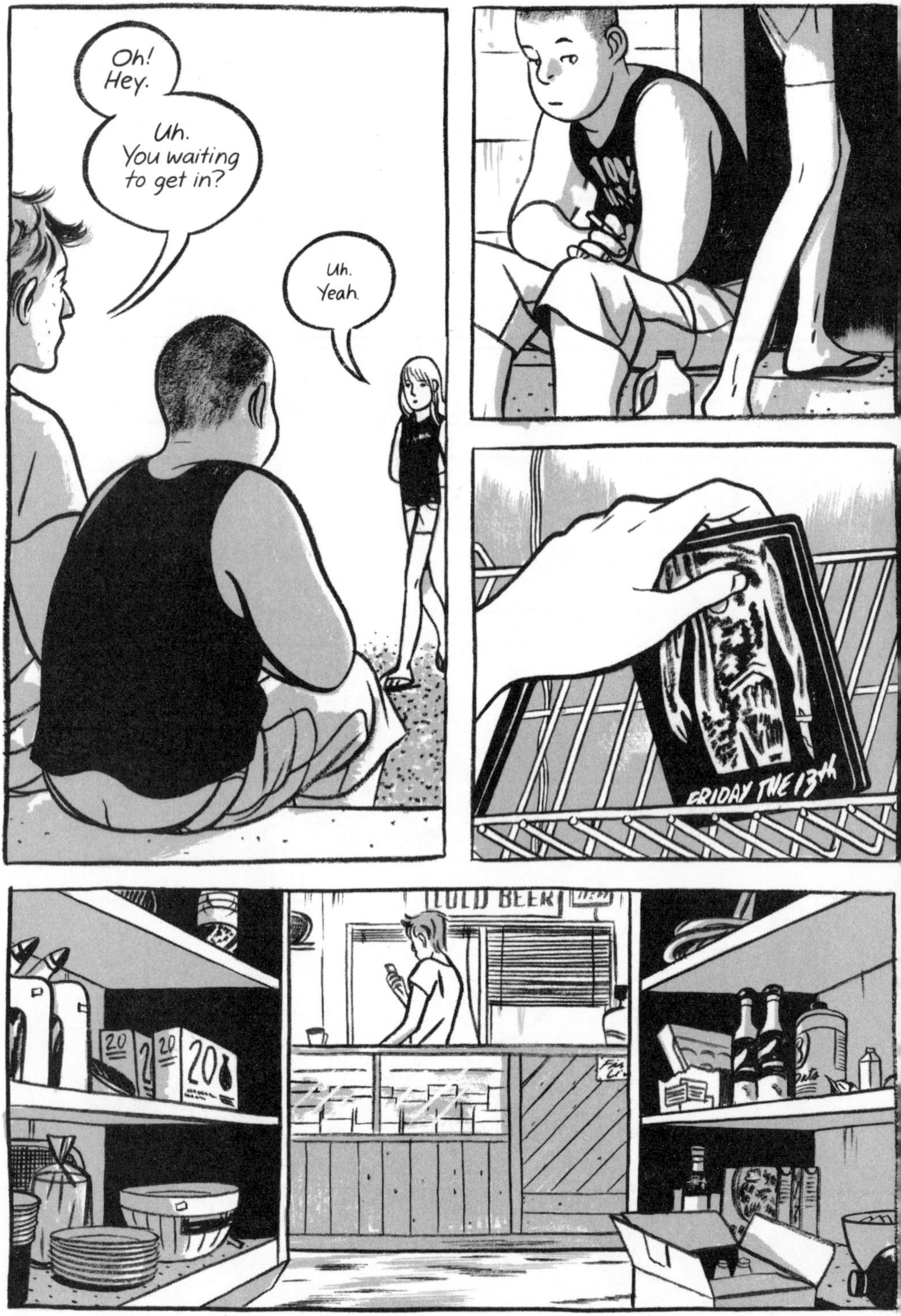
Oh! Hey.
Uh. You waiting to get in?
Uh. Yeah.
FRIDAY THE 13th
COLD BEER

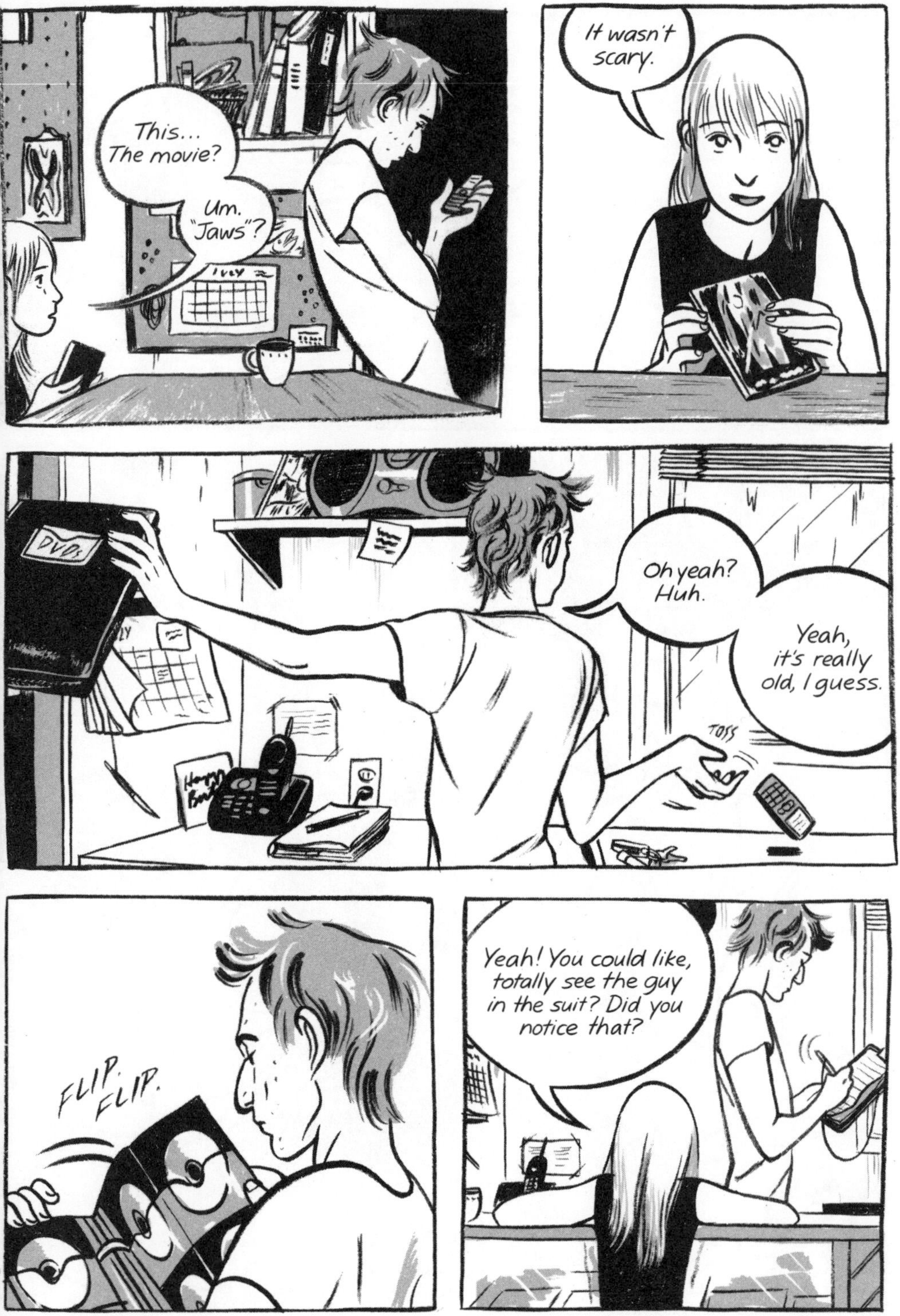

This... The movie?
Um. "Jaws"?
It wasn't scary.
Oh yeah? Huh.
Yeah, it's really old, I guess.
TOSS
FLIP. FLIP.
Yeah! You could like, totally see the guy in the suit? Did you notice that?

193

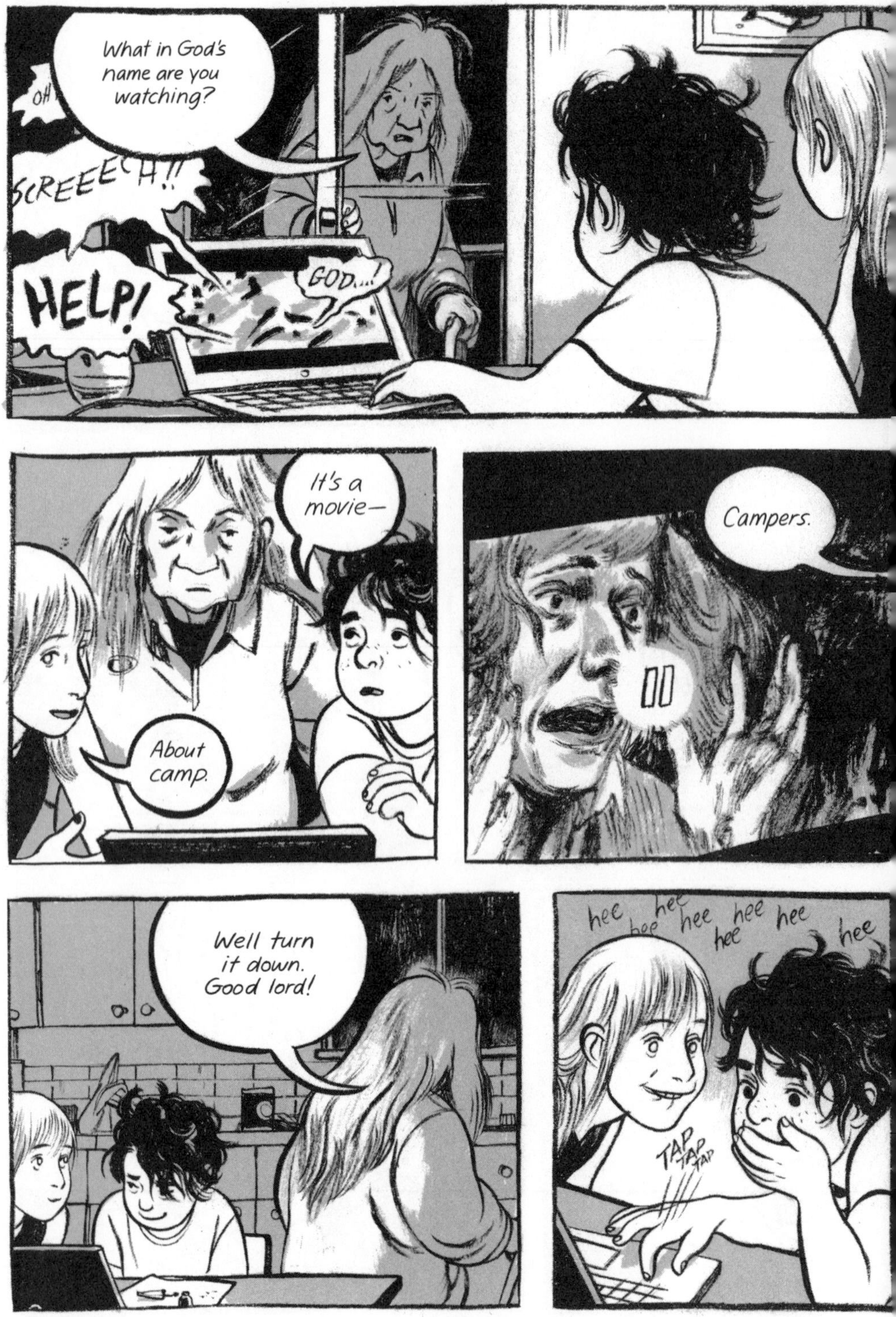
OH
What in God's name are you watching?
SCREEECH!!
GOD...!
HELP!
It's a movie—
About camp.
Campers.
Well turn it down. Good lord!
hee hee hee hee hee hee hee hee
TAP TAP TAP

195

196

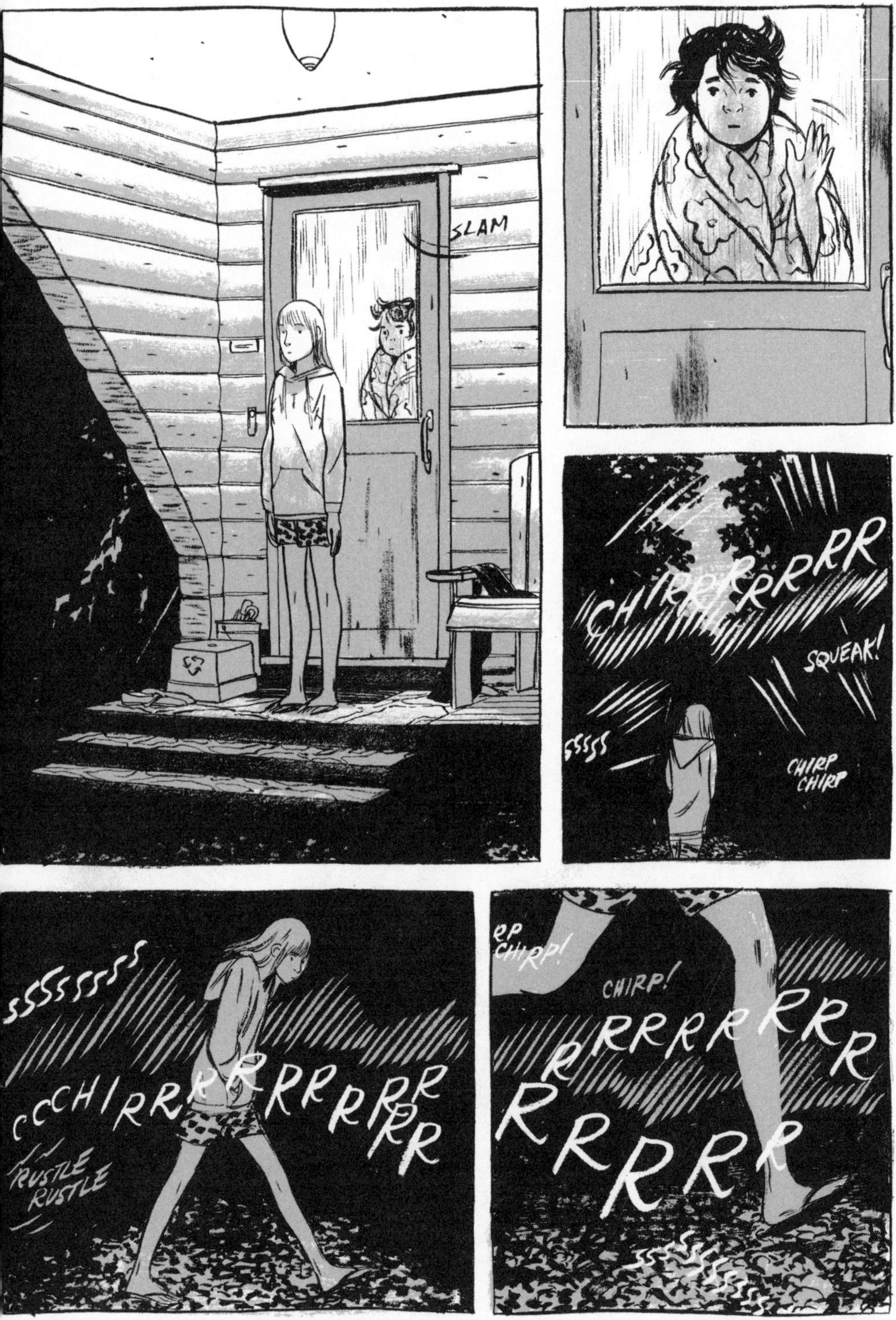
SLAM
CHIRRRRRRRR
SQUEAK!
SSSSS
CHIRP CHIRP
SSSSSSSS
CCCHIRRRRRRRRRR
RUSTLE RUSTLE
ep CHIRP!
CHIRP!
RRRRRRRRR
RRRRR
SSSSSSSS

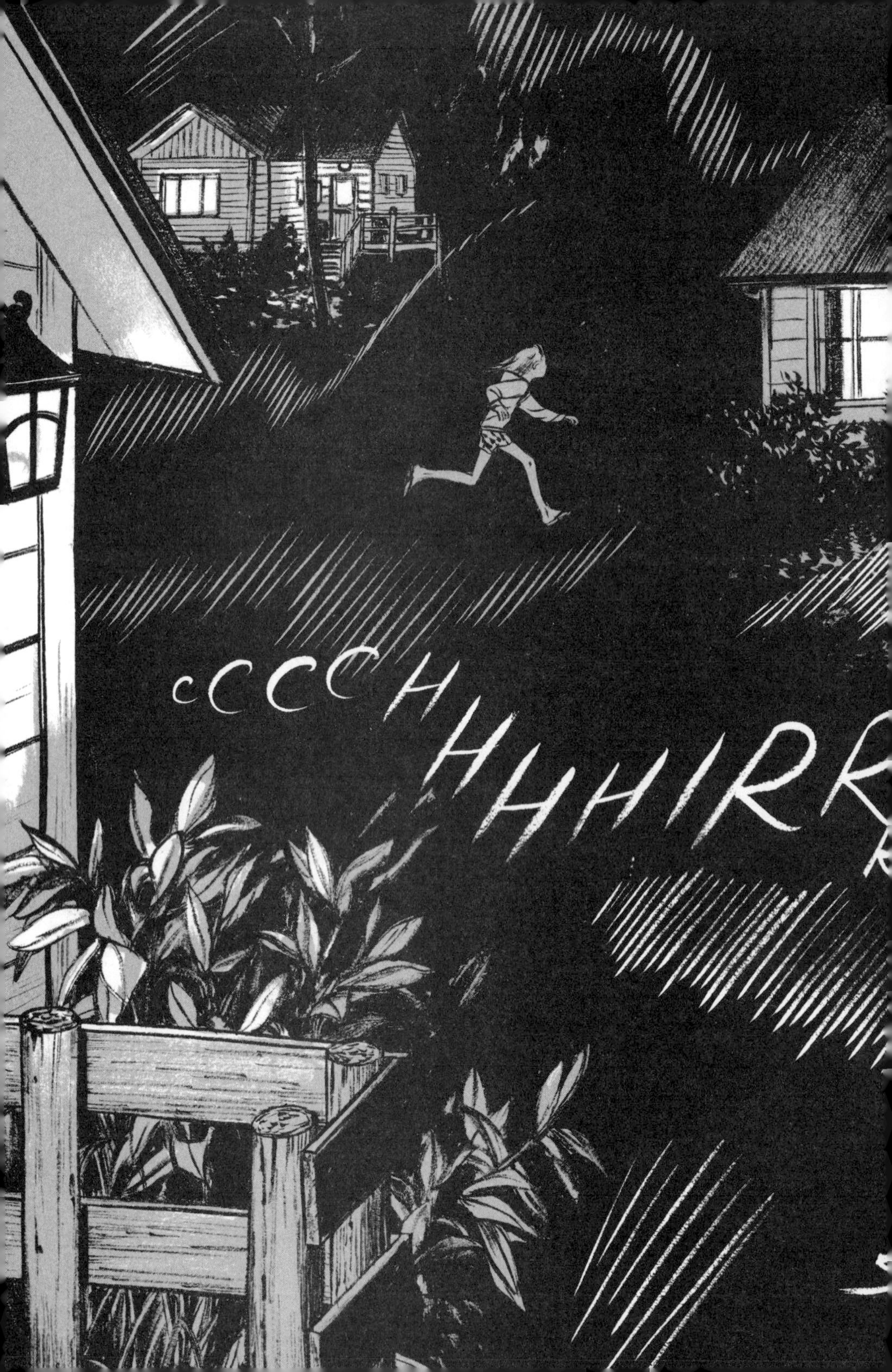

cCCCH
HHHIRR

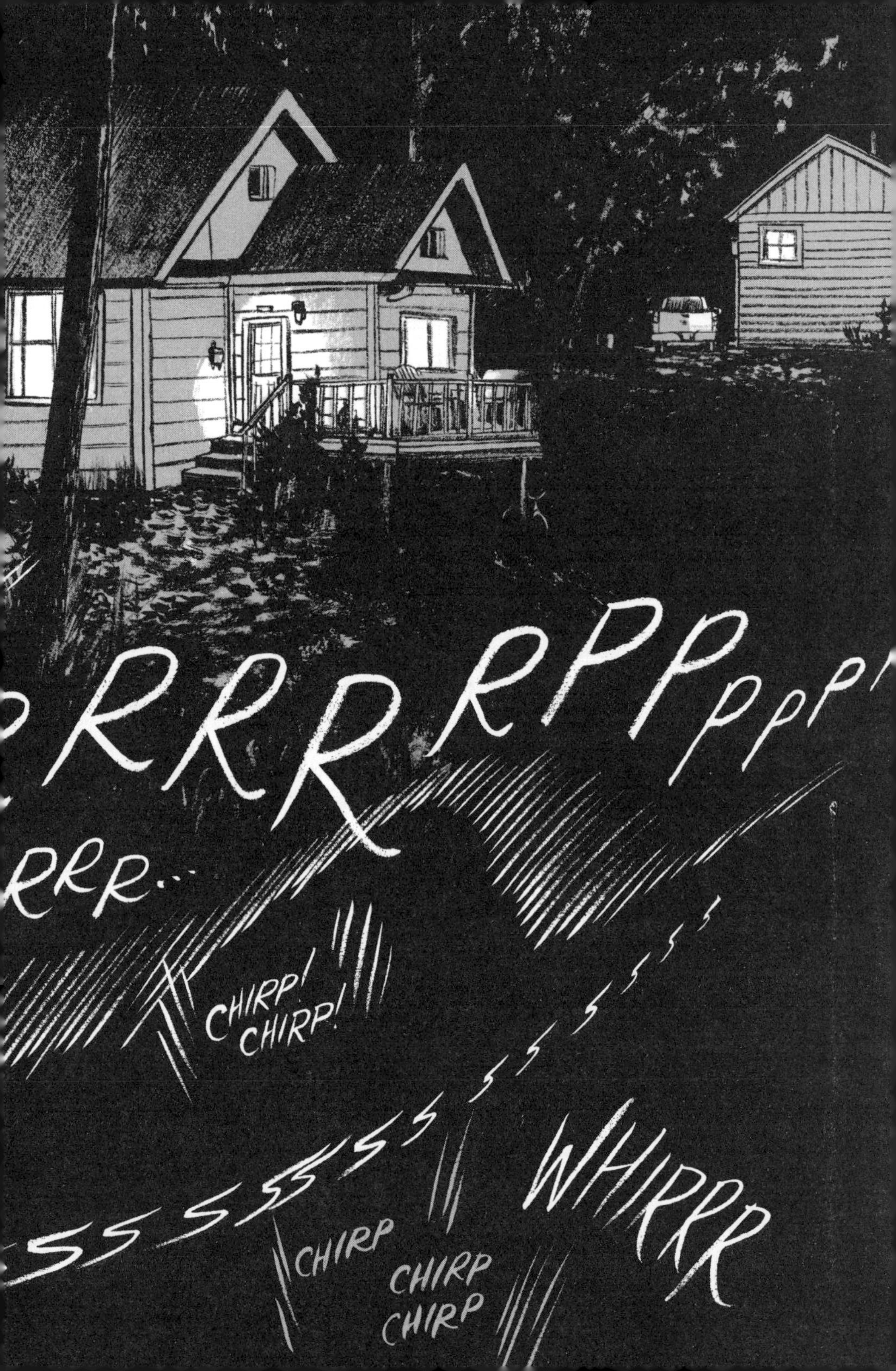

RRRRRPPppp
RRR...
CHIRP! CHIRP!
SSSSSSSSSSSSSS
WHIRRR
CHIRP
CHIRP
CHIRP

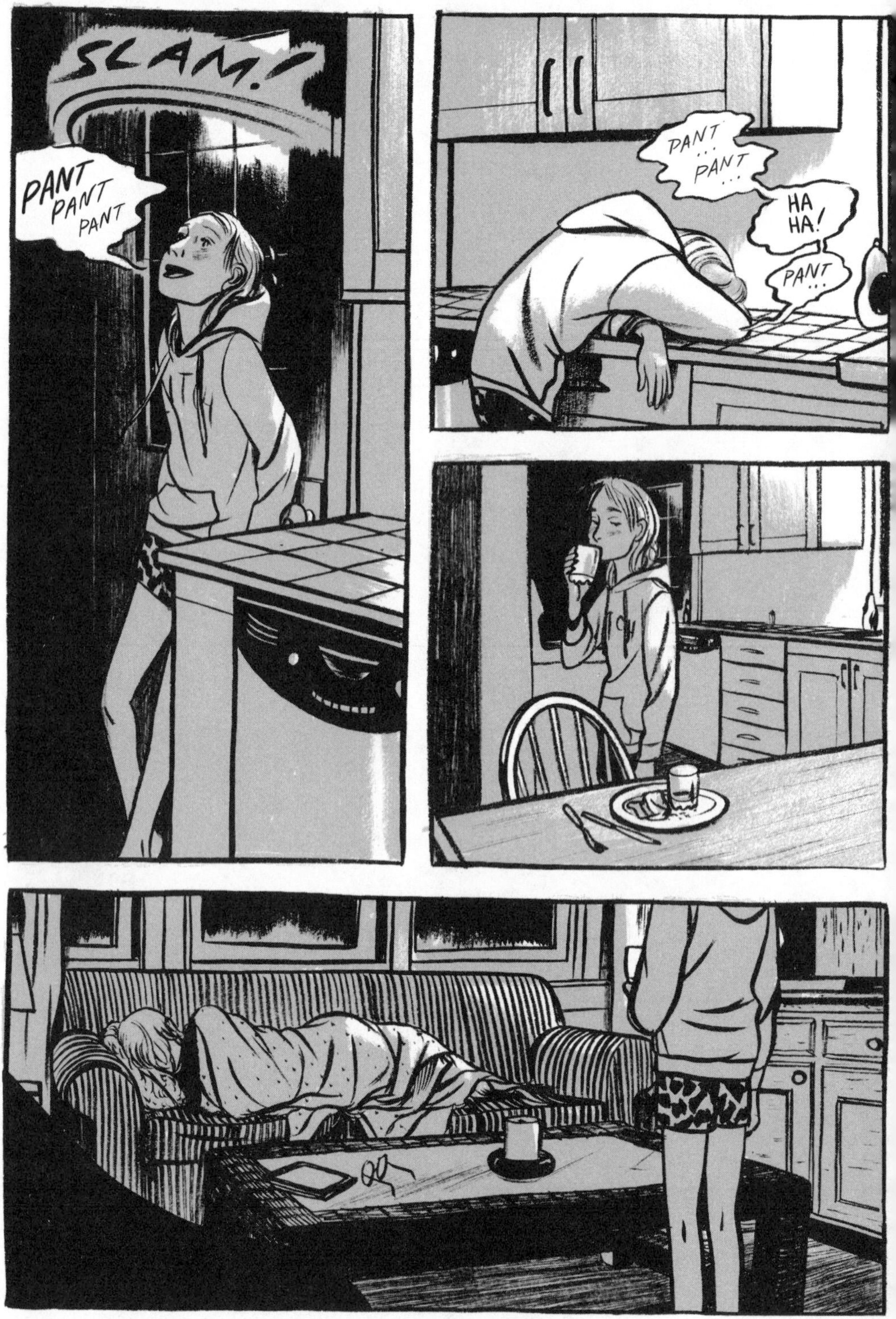
SLAM!
PANT PANT PANT
PANT ... PANT ...
HA HA!
PANT ...

BREWSTER'S DVD
Overnight rent
(1 day)
•Don't scratch disks!!!!
Handle with CARE
Clean with soft cloth
if not working
Return to:

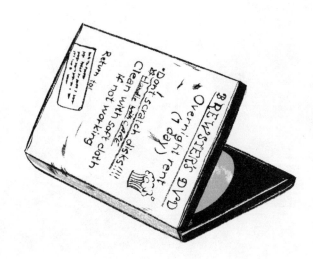

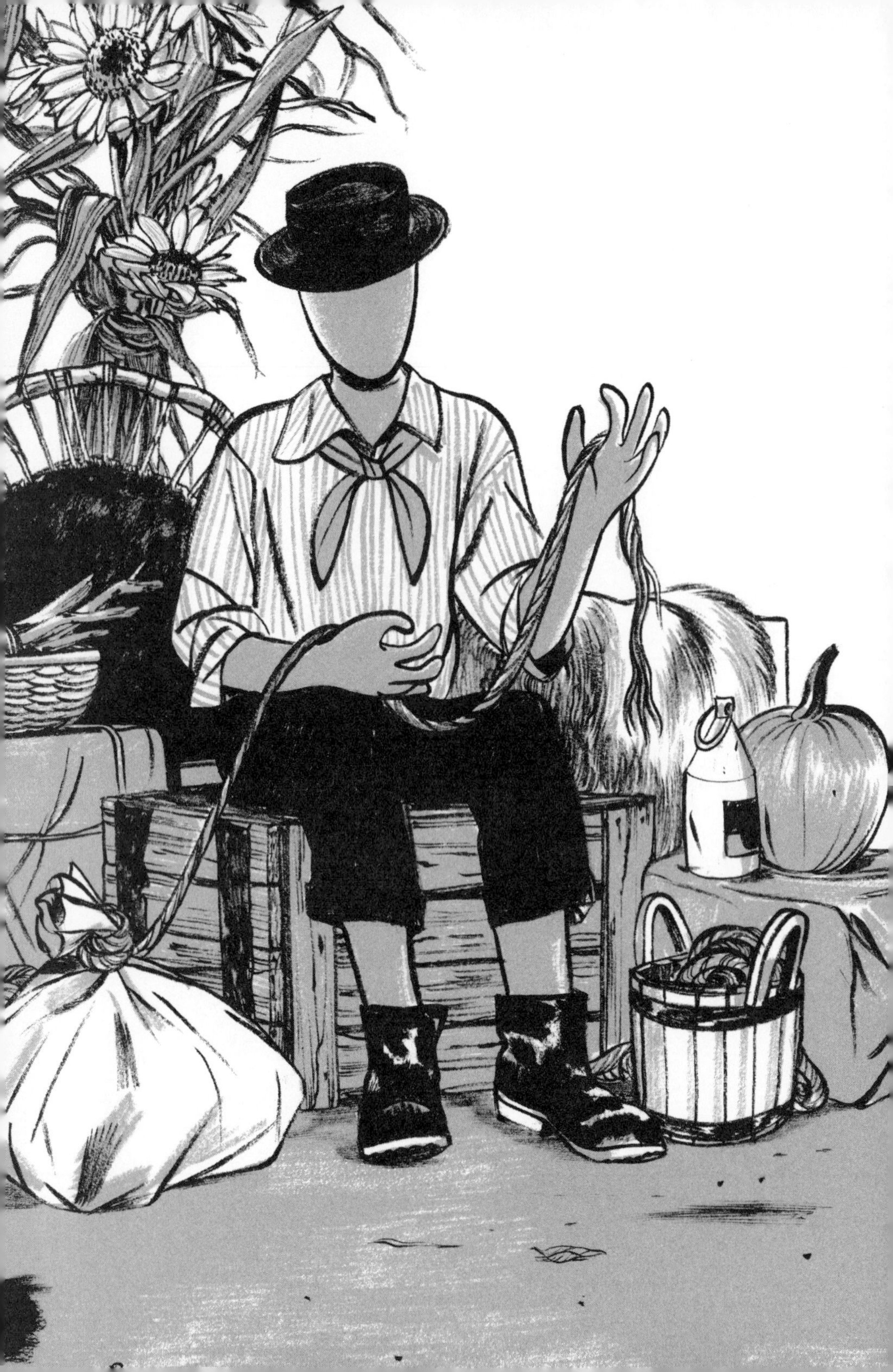

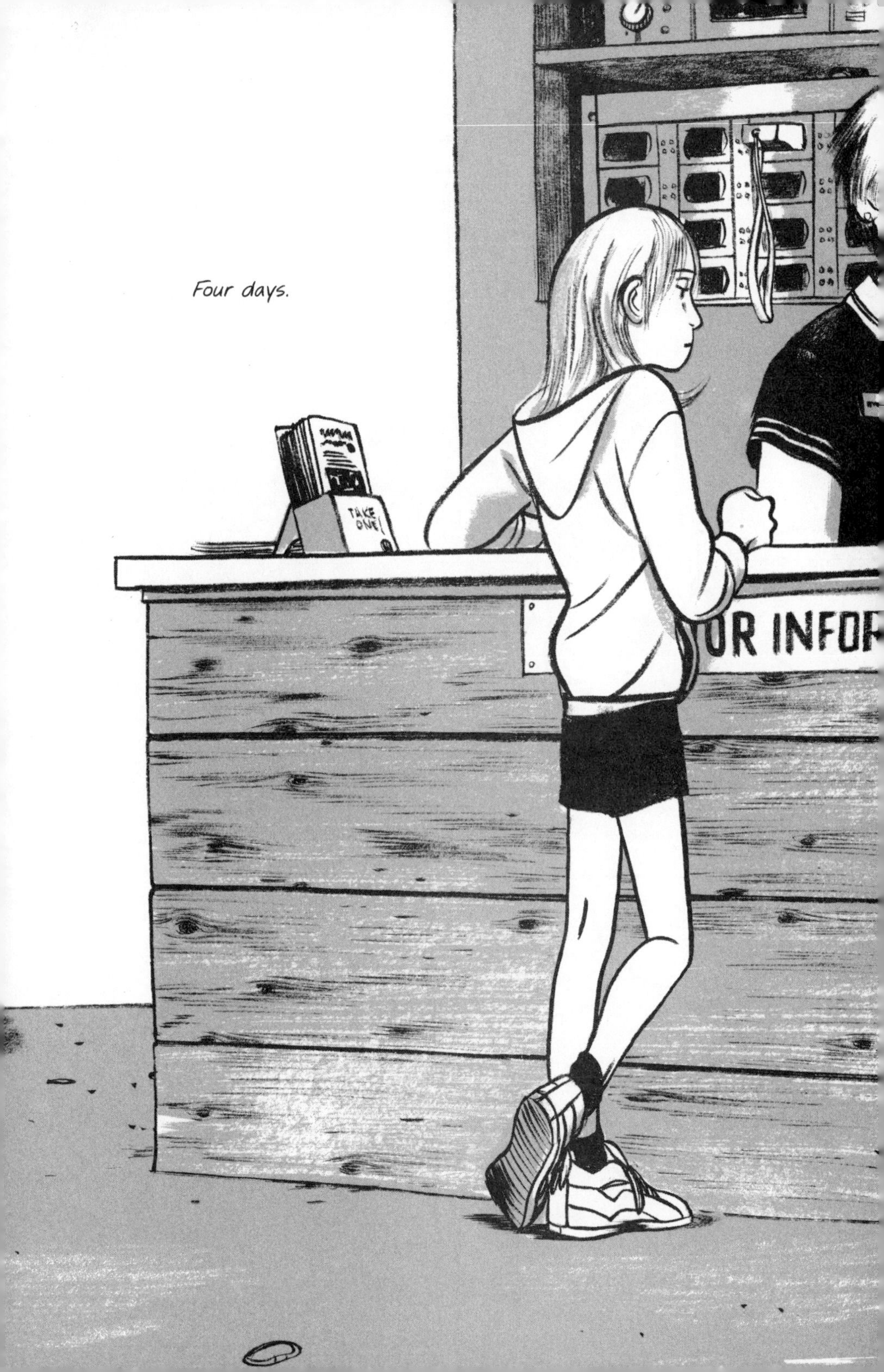
Four days.
TAKE ONE!

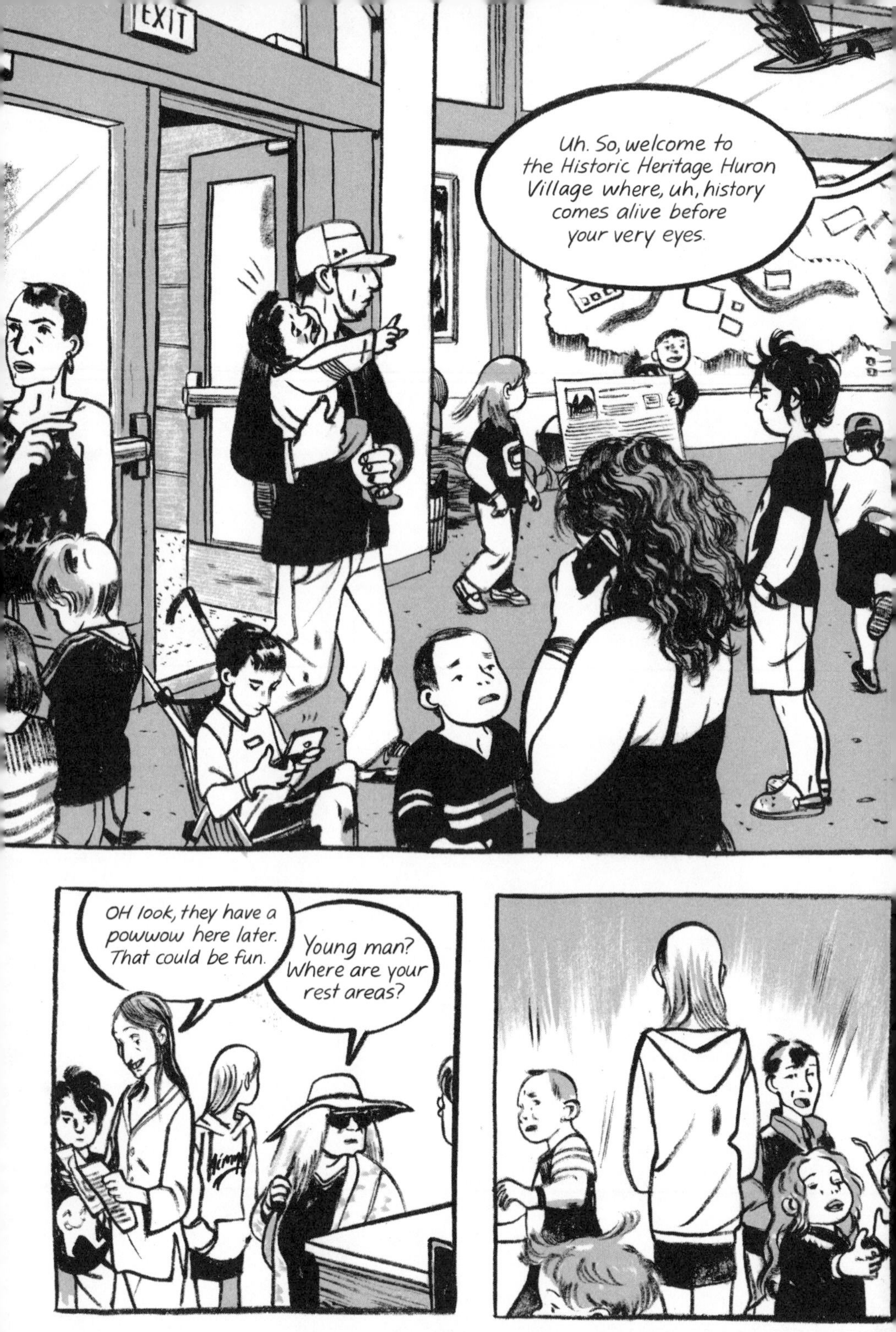
EXIT
Uh. So, welcome to the Historic Heritage Huron Village where, uh, history comes alive before your very eyes.
OH look, they have a powwow here later. That could be fun.
Young man? Where are your rest areas?

205

208

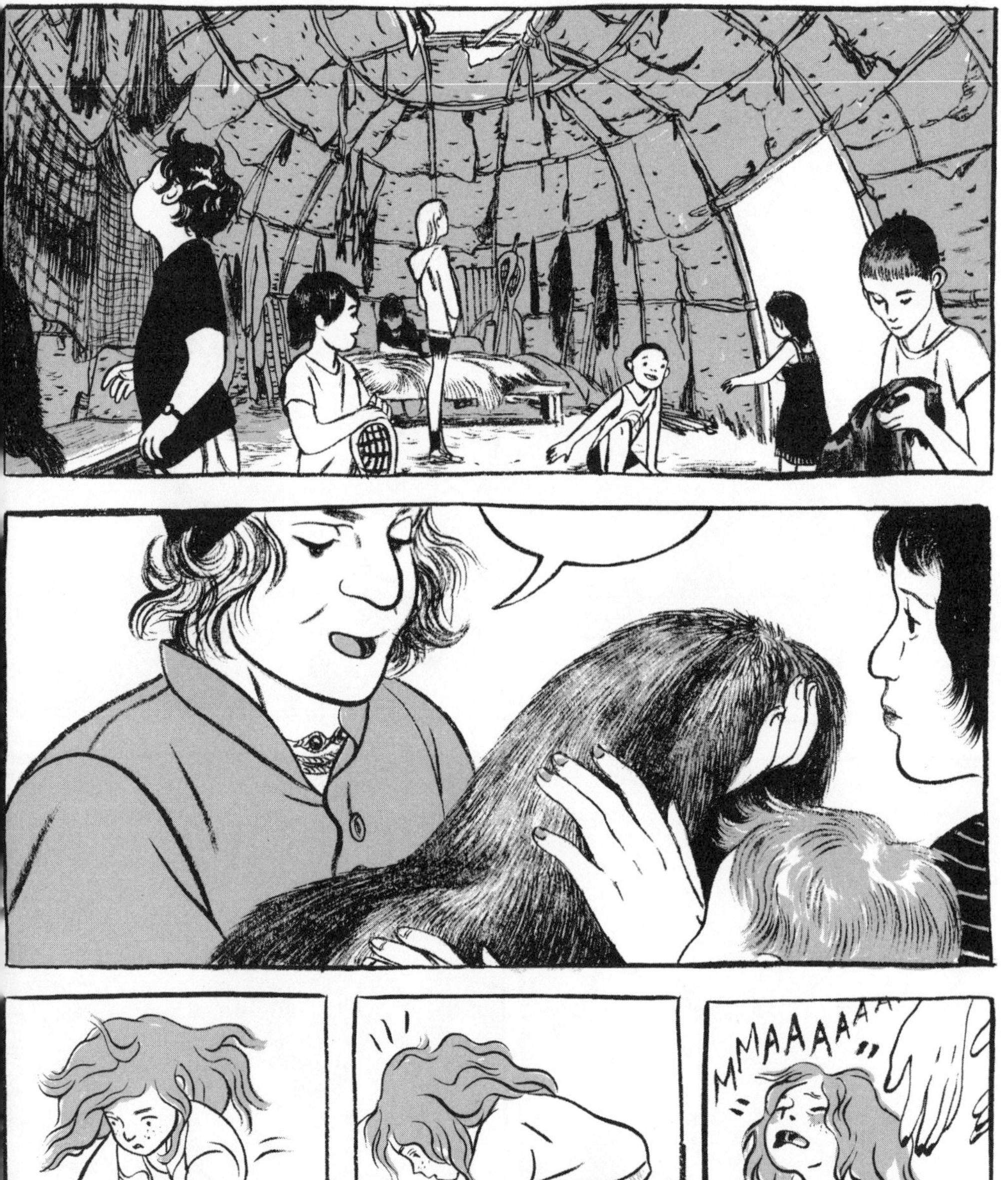
TRIP!
"MMAAAAAAA"

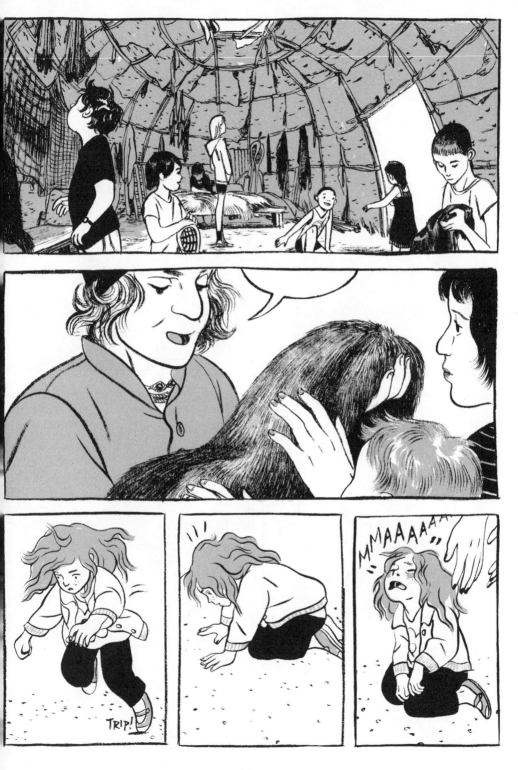

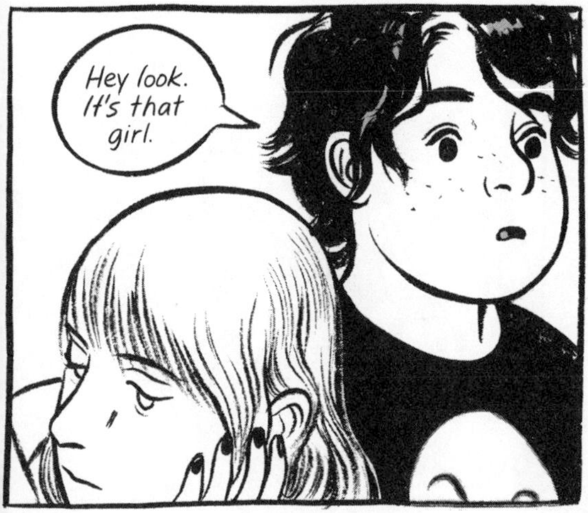
Hey look. It's that girl.

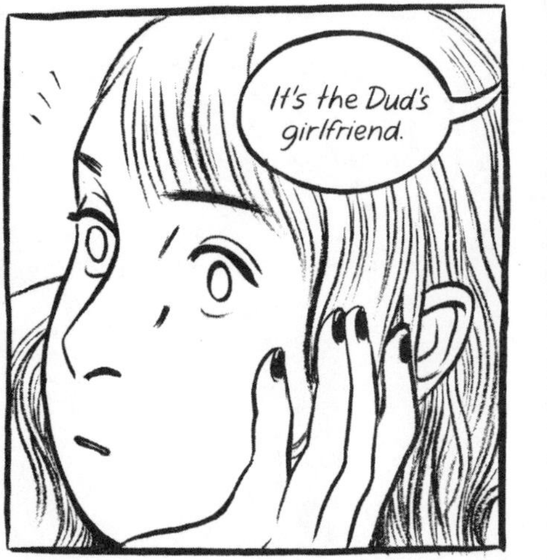
It's the Dud's girlfriend.

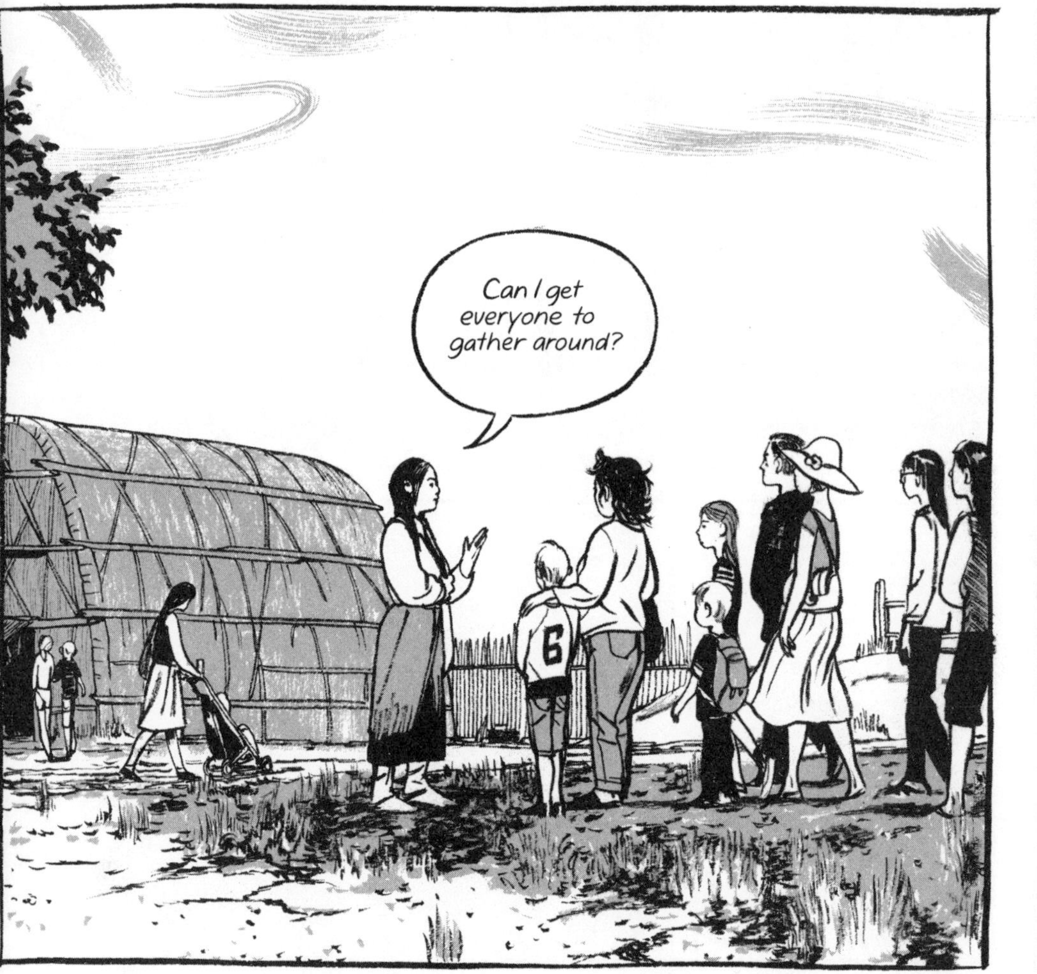
Can I get everyone to gather around?
6

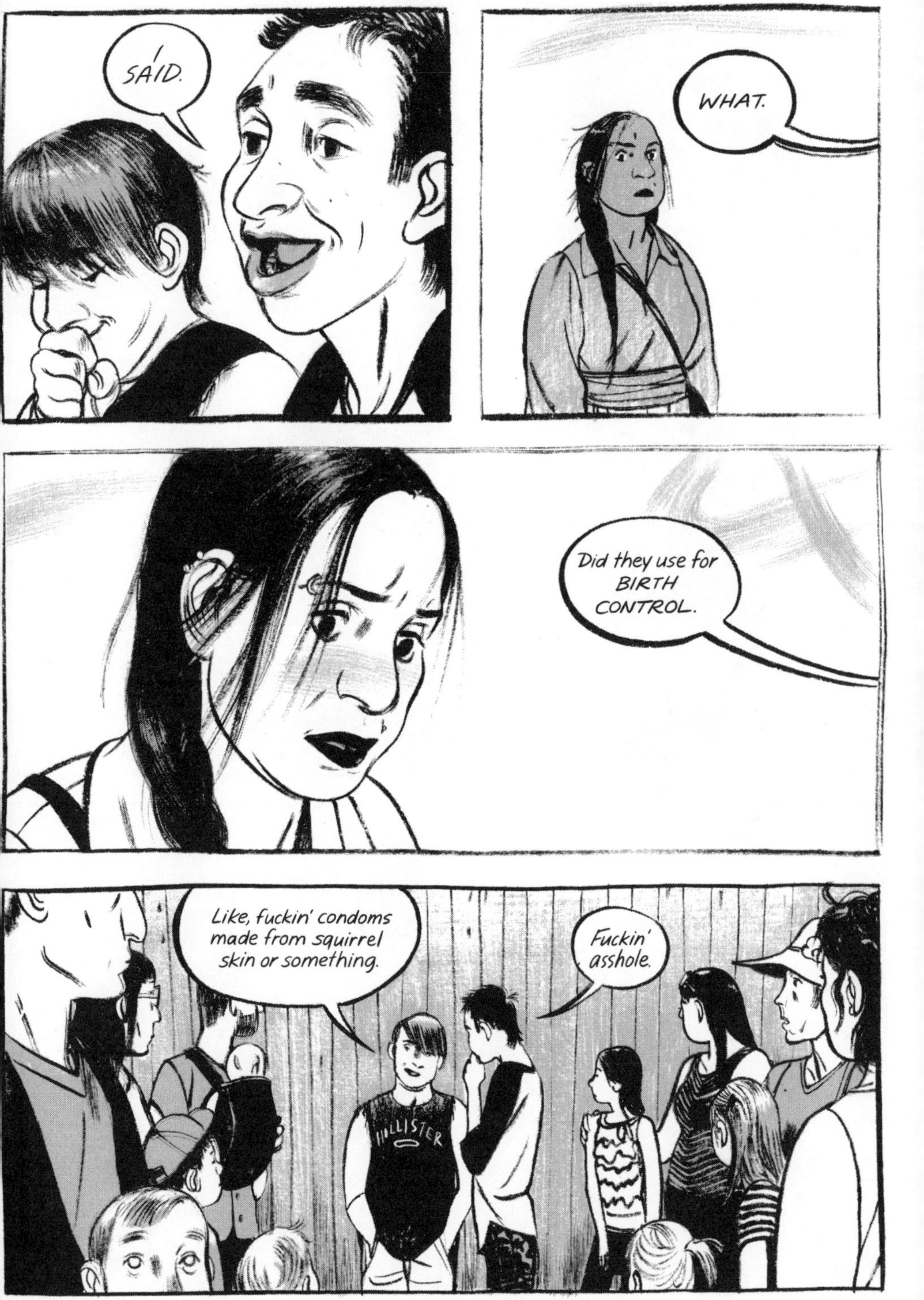
I SAID.
WHAT.
Did they use for BIRTH CONTROL.
Like, fuckin' condoms made from squirrel skin or something.
Fuckin' asshole.
HOLLISTER

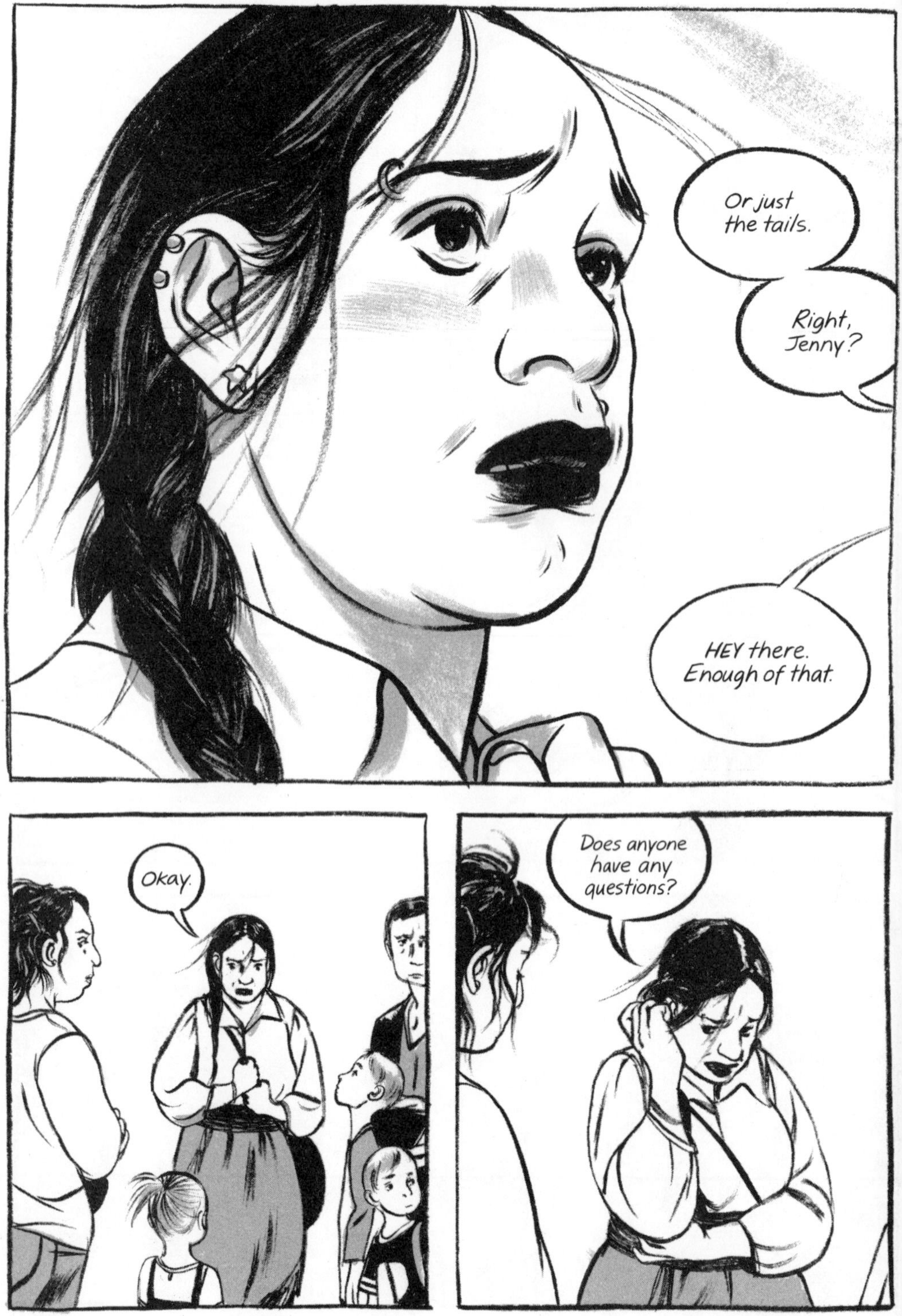
Or just the tails.
Right, Jenny?
HEY there. Enough of that.
Okay.
Does anyone have any questions?

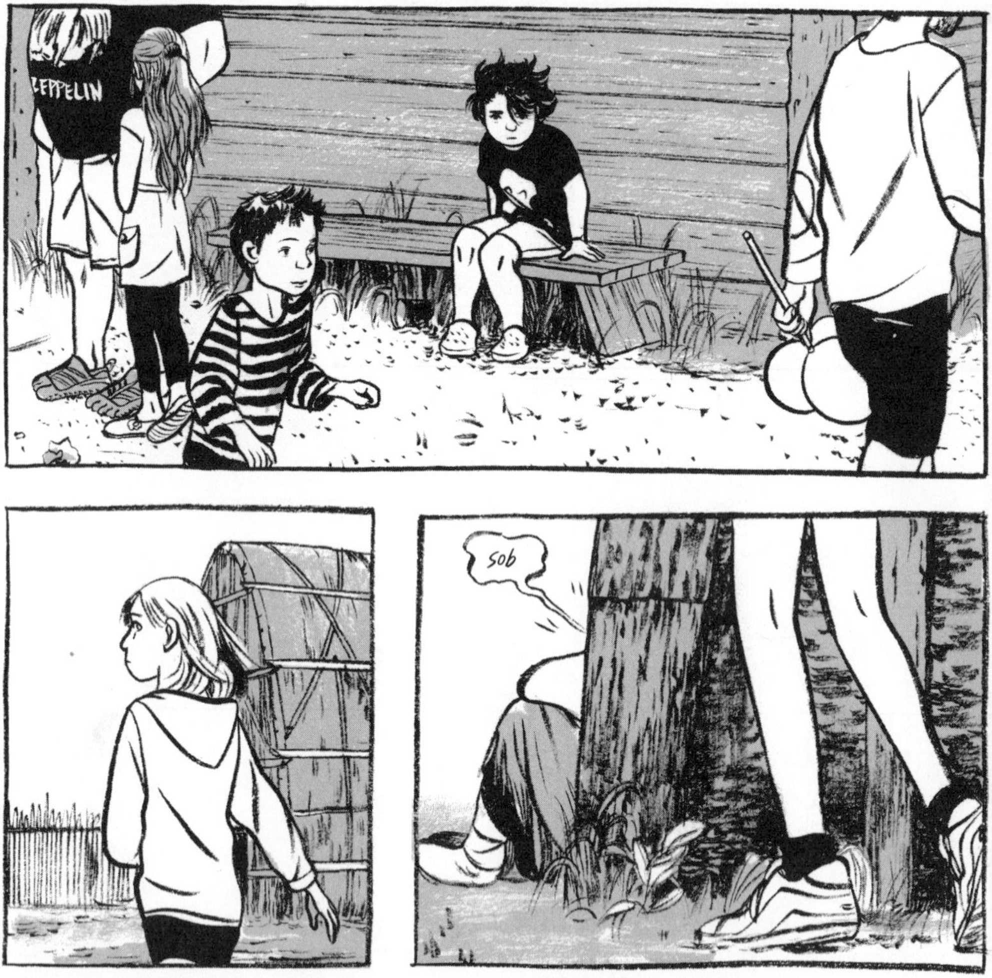
ZEPPELIN
sob

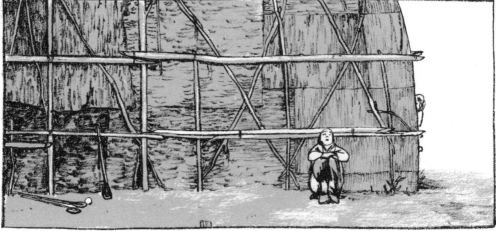

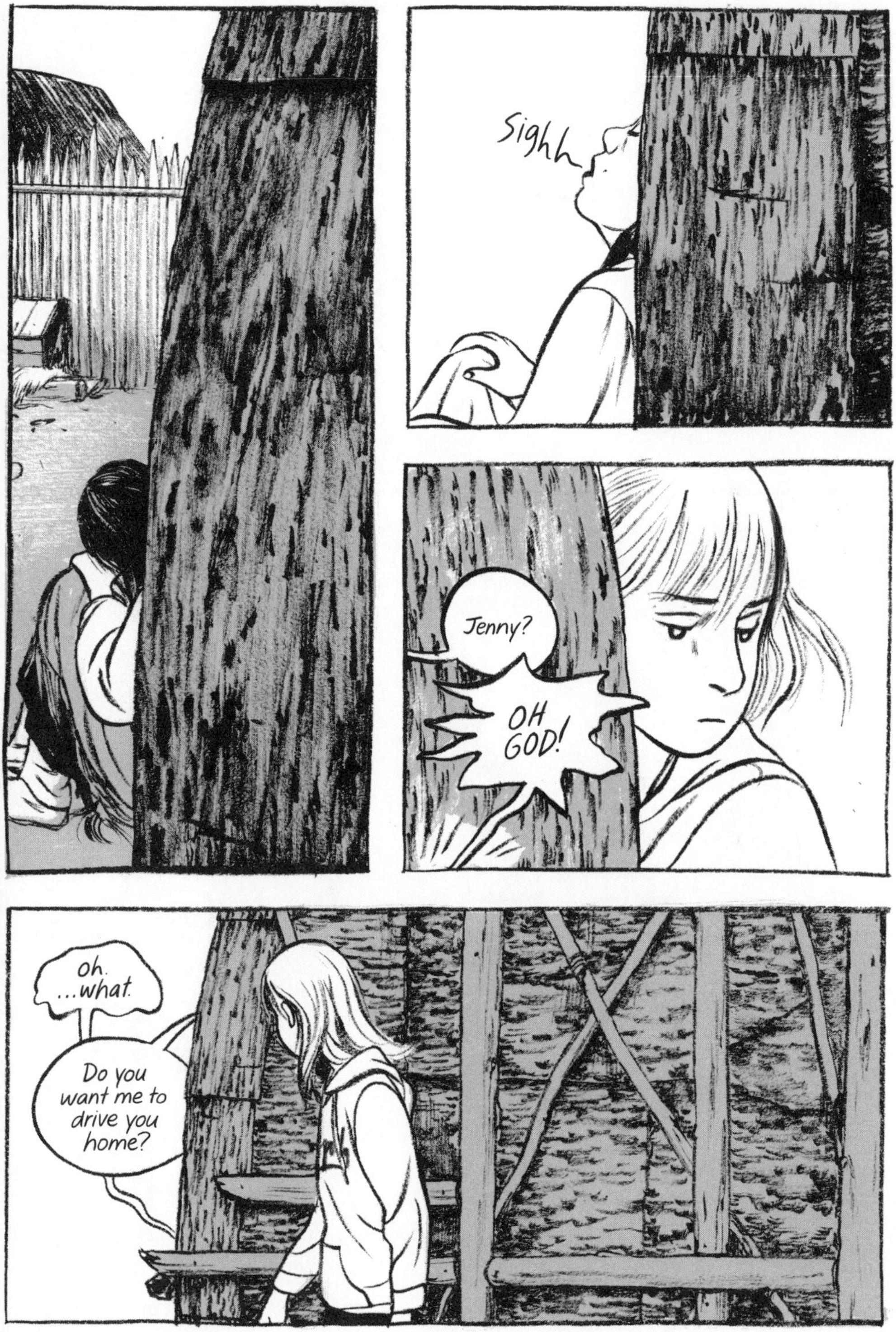
Sighh
Jenny?
OH GOD!
Oh. ...what.
Do you want me to drive you home?

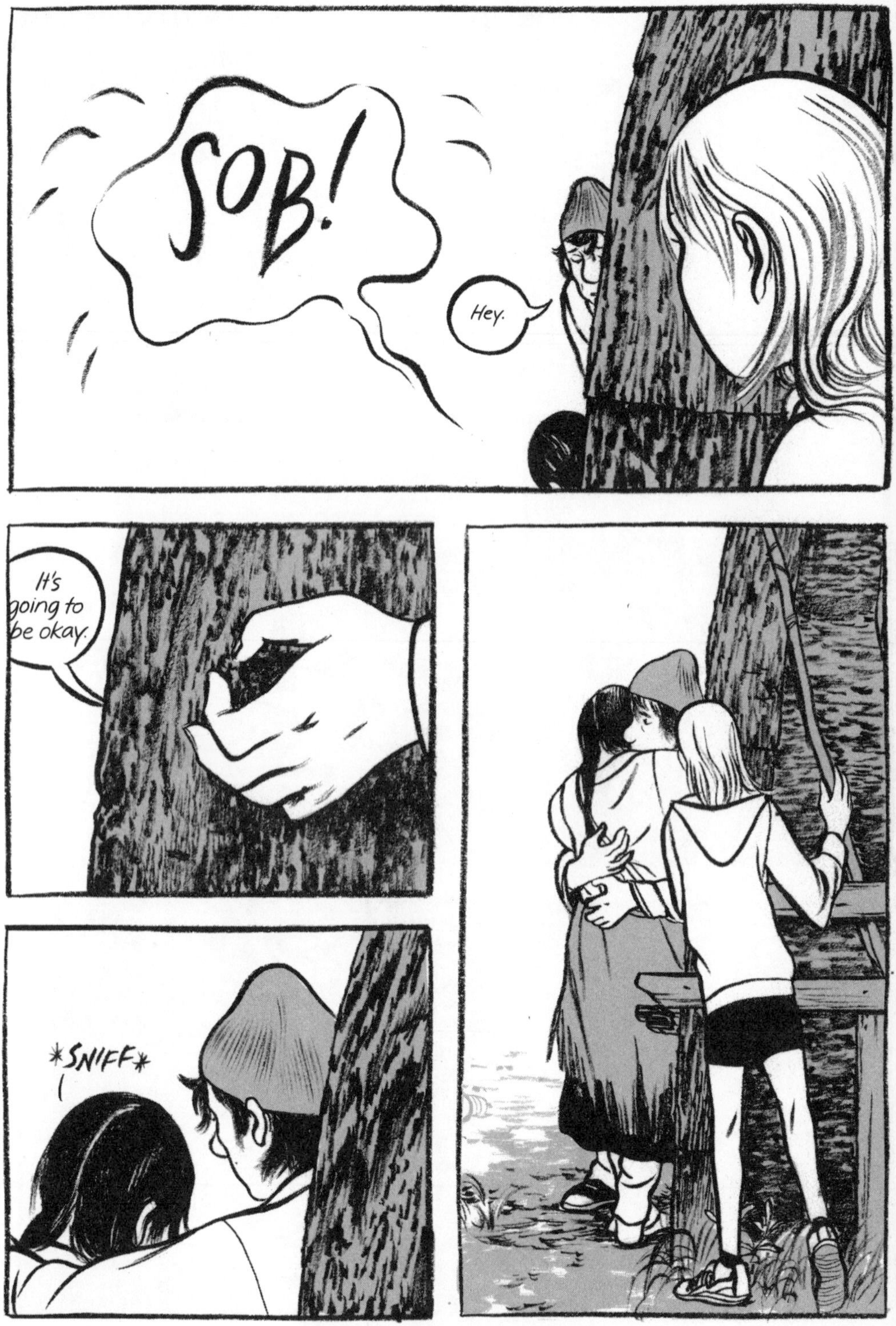
SOB!
Hey.
It's going to be okay.
*SNIFF*

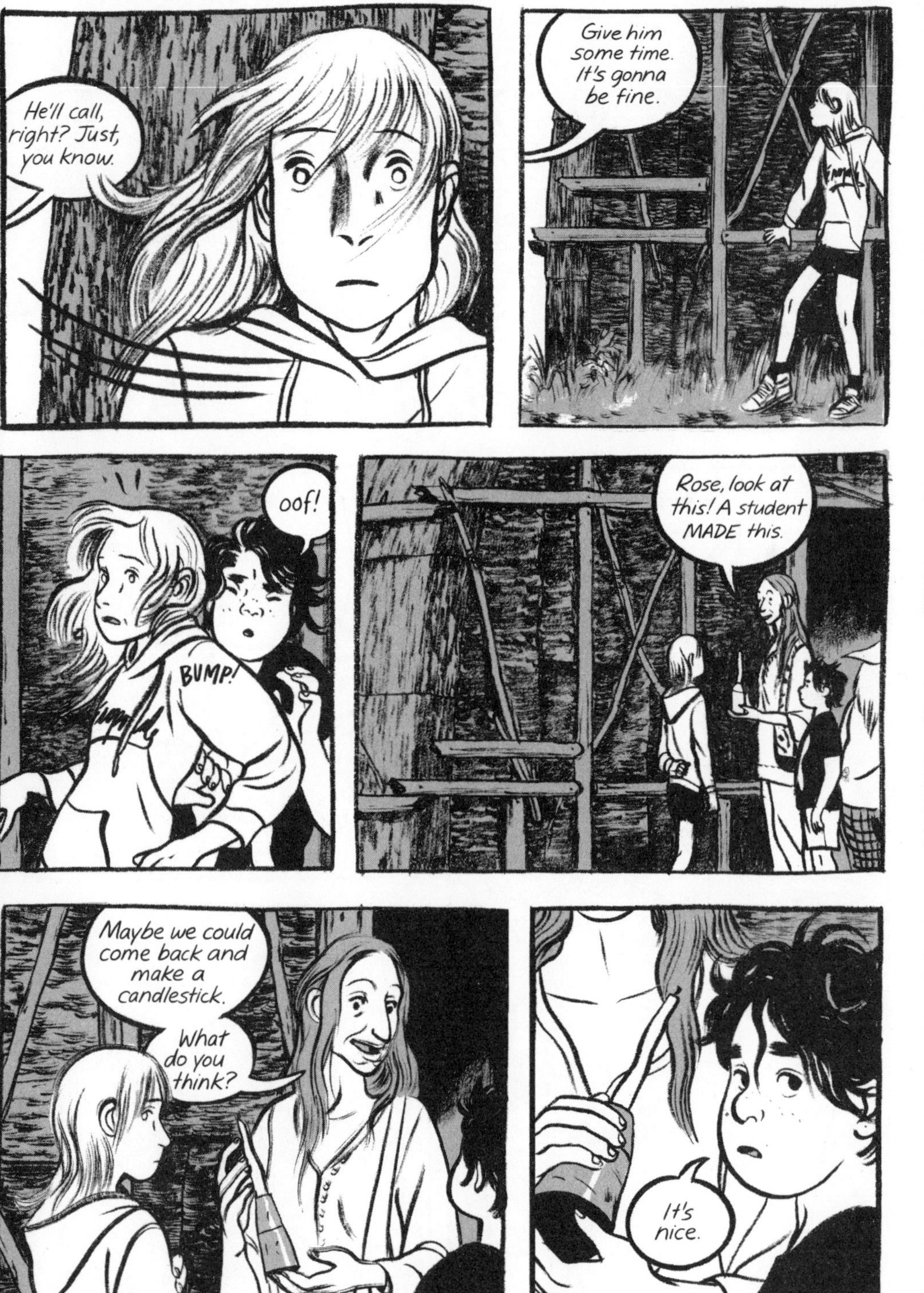
He'll call, right? Just, you know.
Give him some time. It's gonna be fine.
oof!
BUMP!
Rose, look at this! A student MADE this.
Maybe we could come back and make a candlestick.
What do you think?
It's nice.

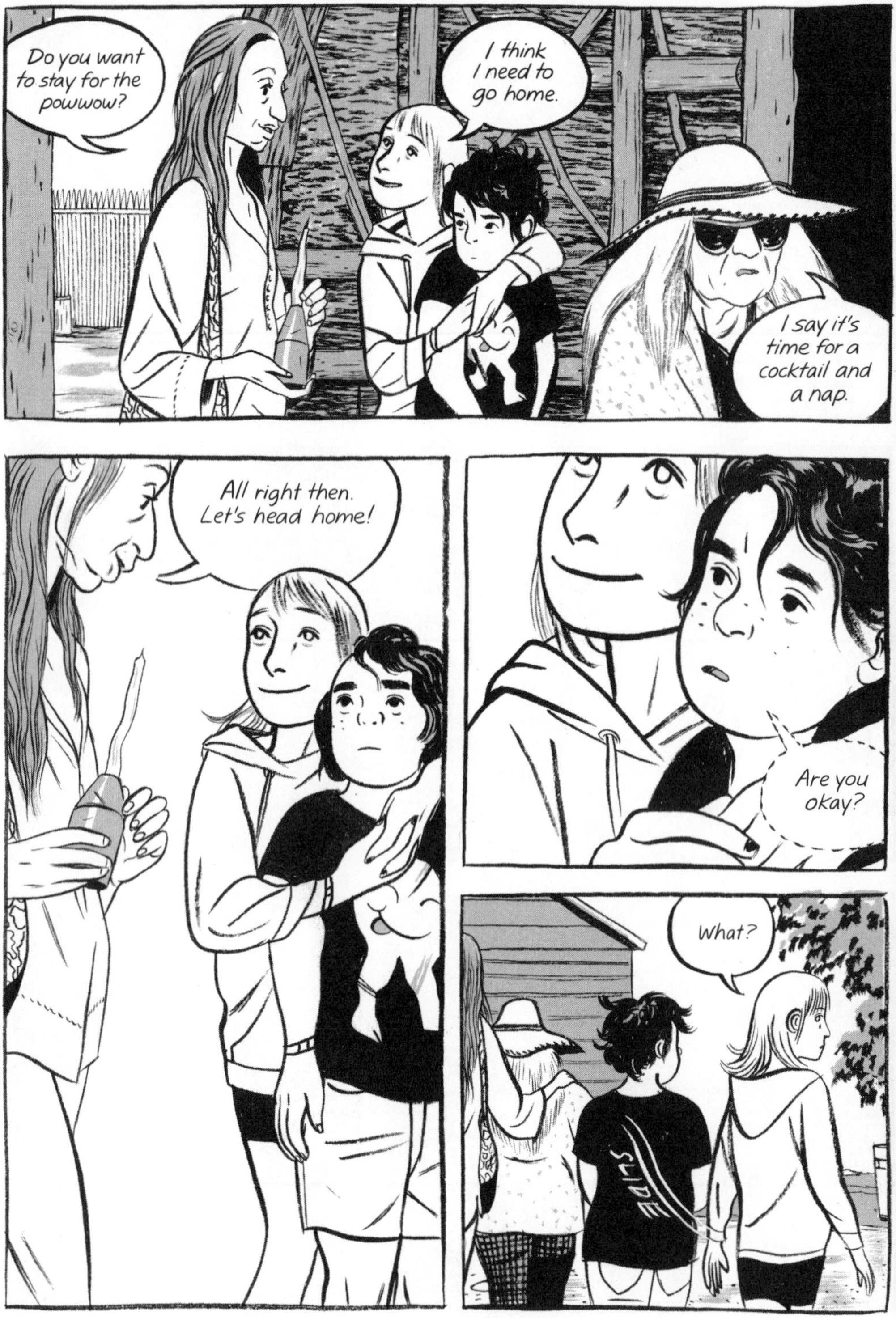
Do you want to stay for the powwow?
I think I need to go home.
I say it's time for a cocktail and a nap.
All right then. Let's head home!
Are you okay?
What?
SLIDE

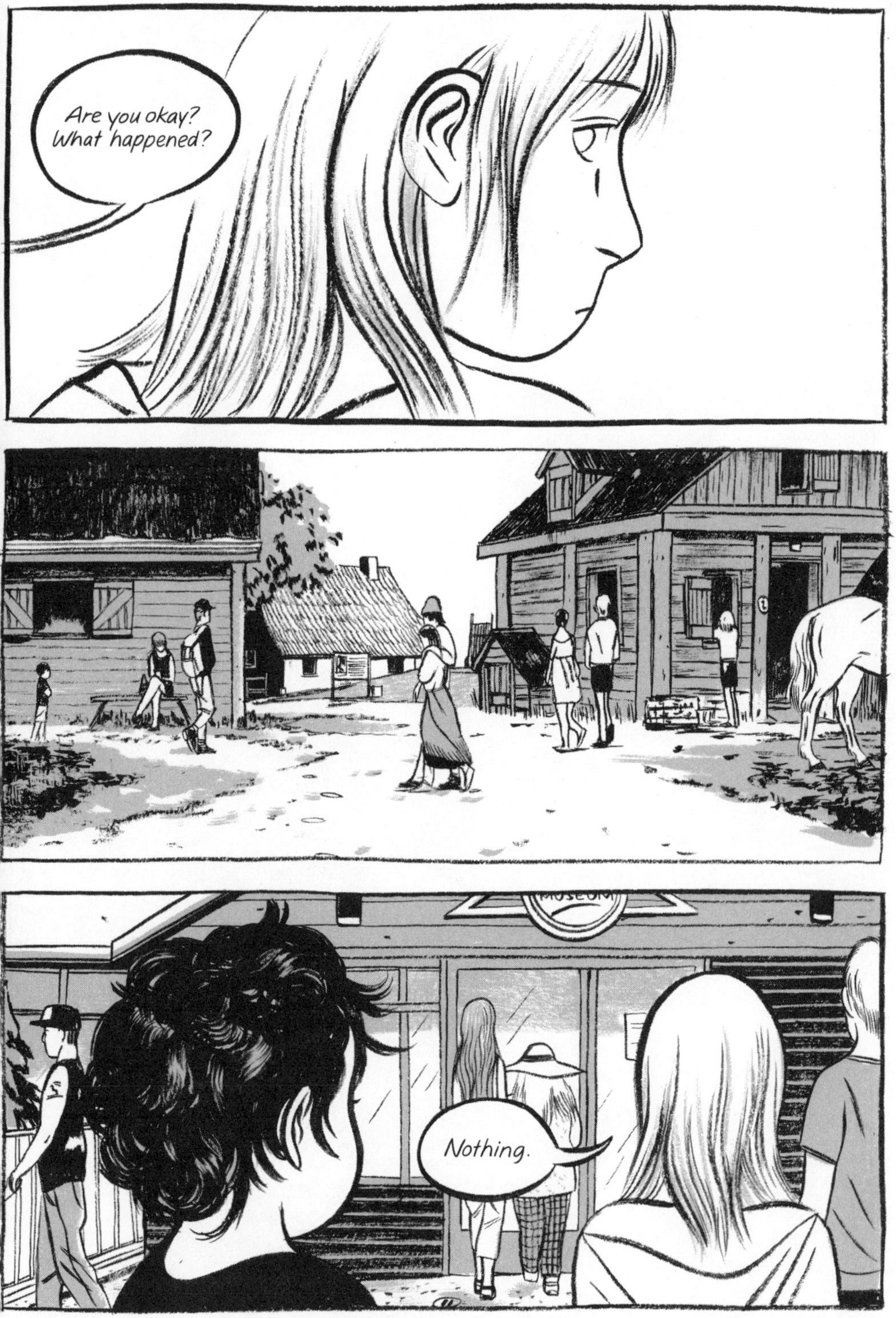
Are you okay? What happened?
MUSEUM
Nothing.

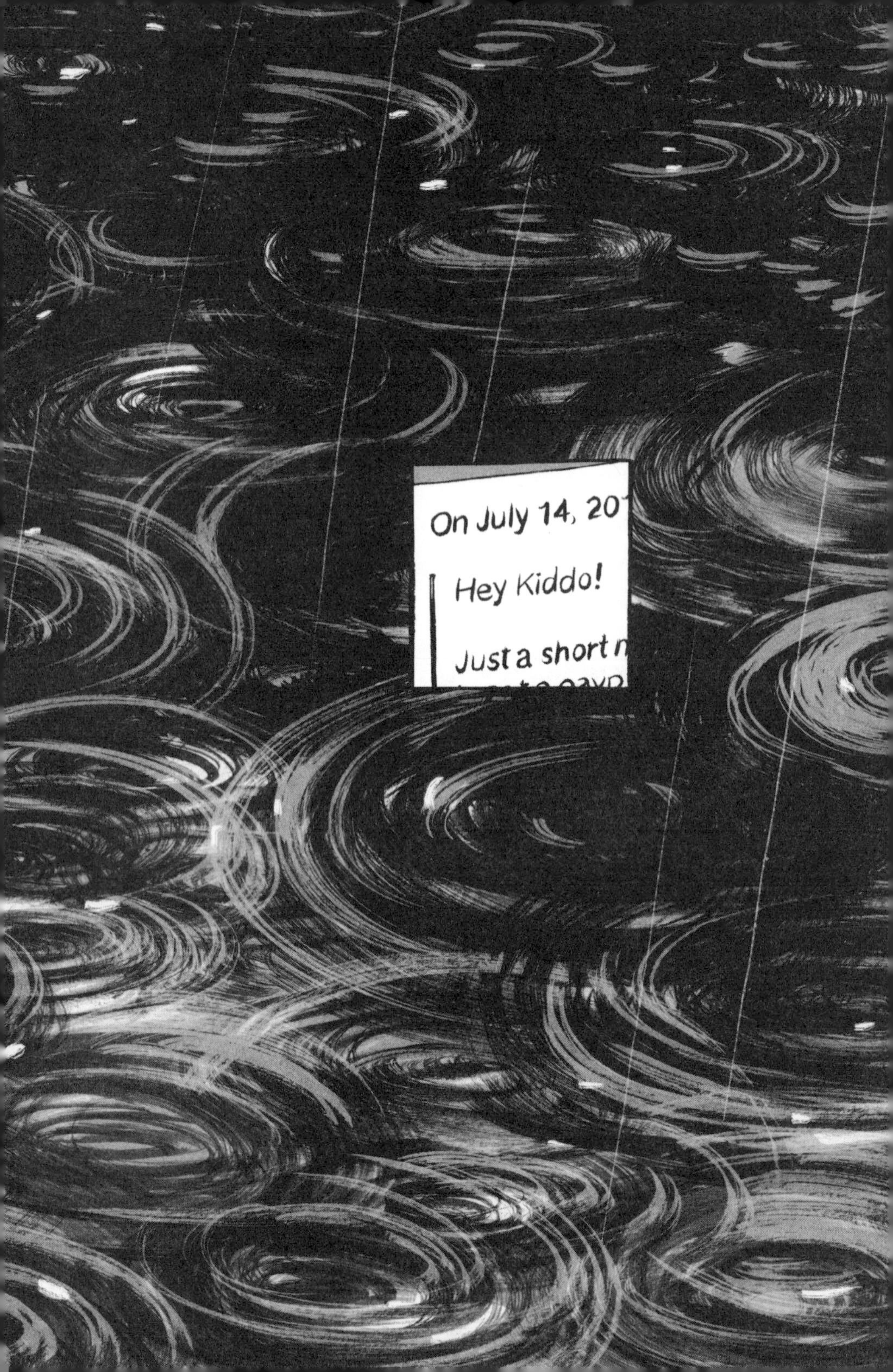
On July 14, 20
Hey Kiddo!
Just a short

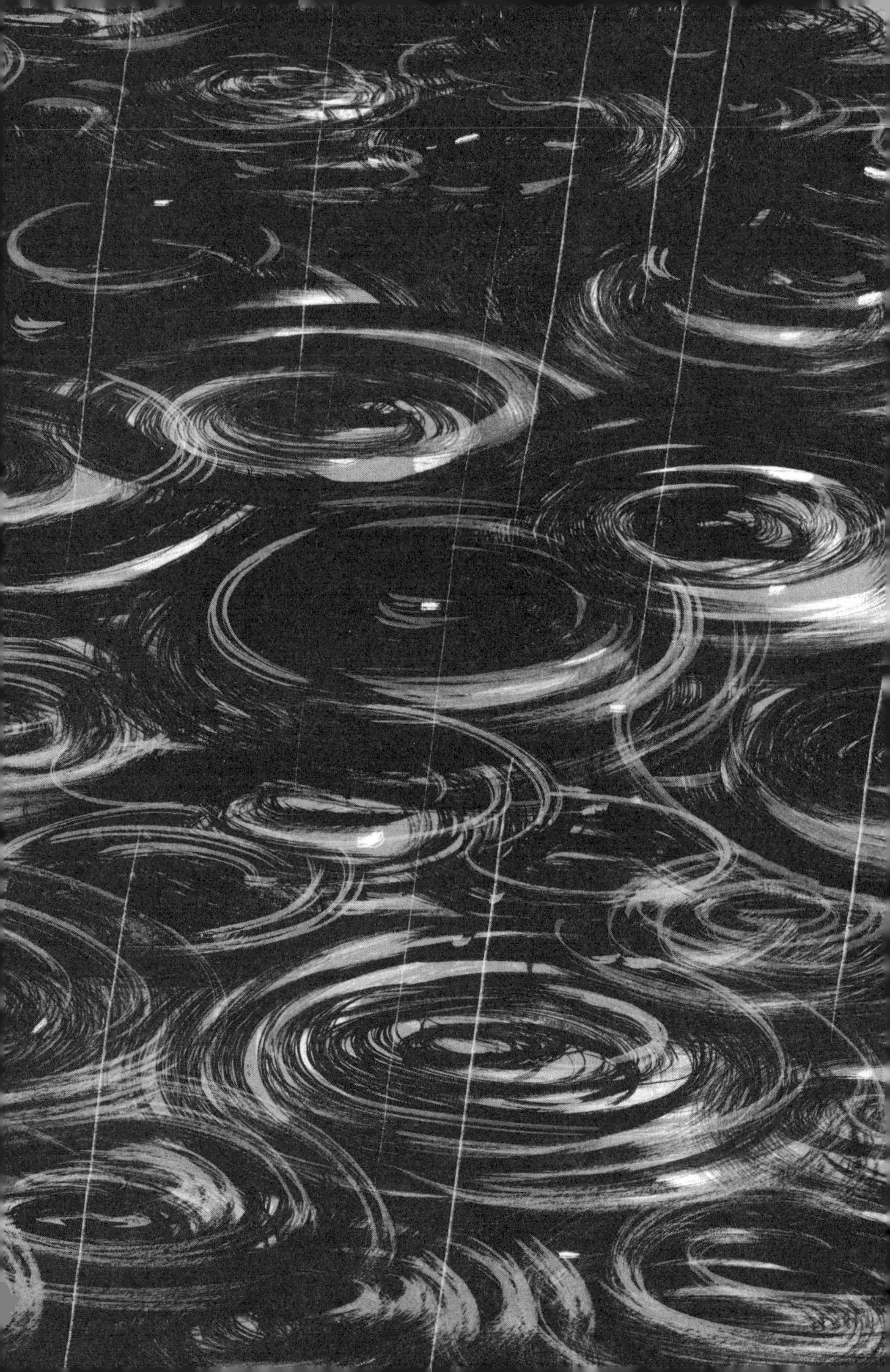

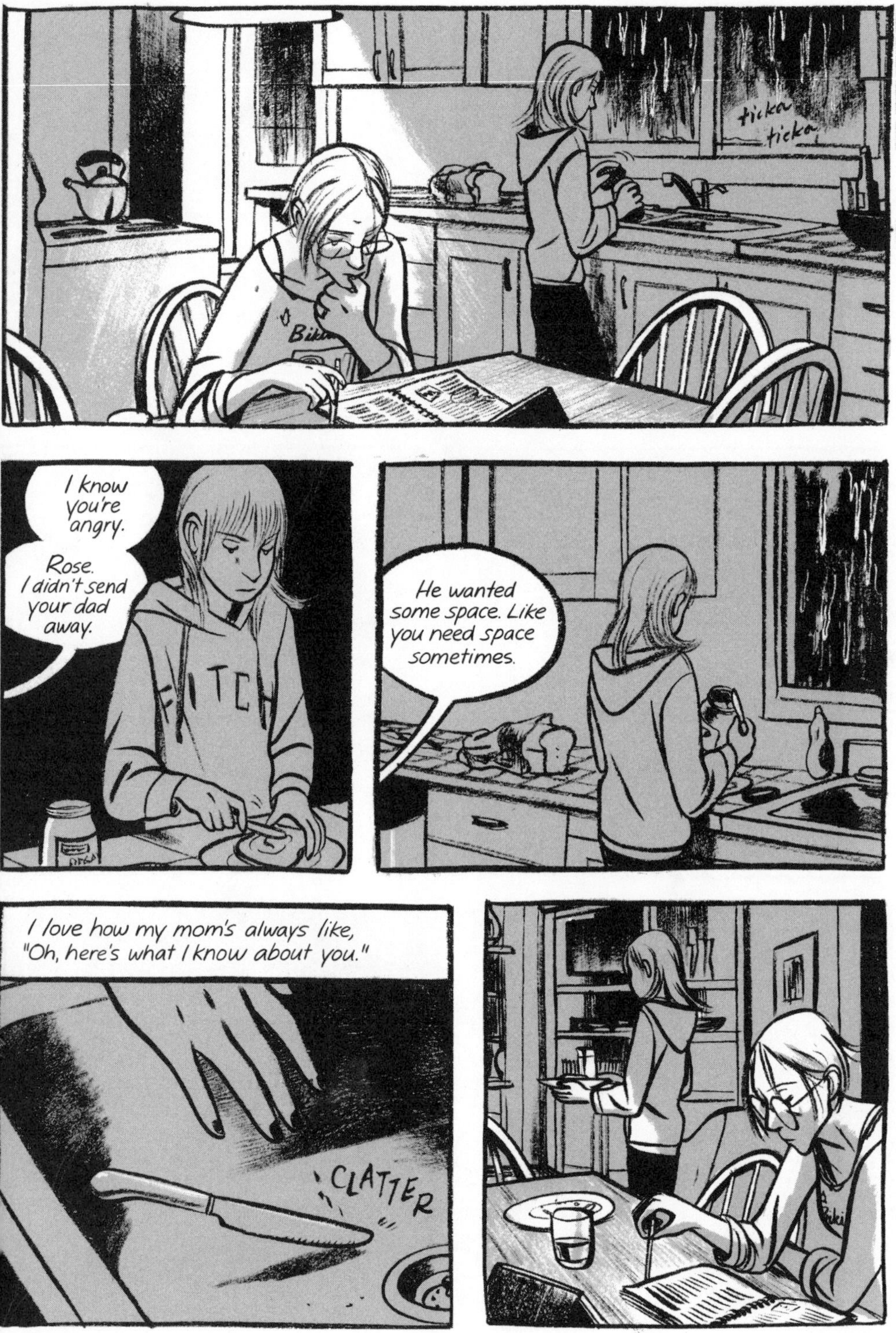
ticka ticka
I know you're angry.
Rose. I didn't send your dad away.
He wanted some space. Like you need space sometimes.
I love how my mom's always like, "Oh, here's what I know about you."
CLATTER

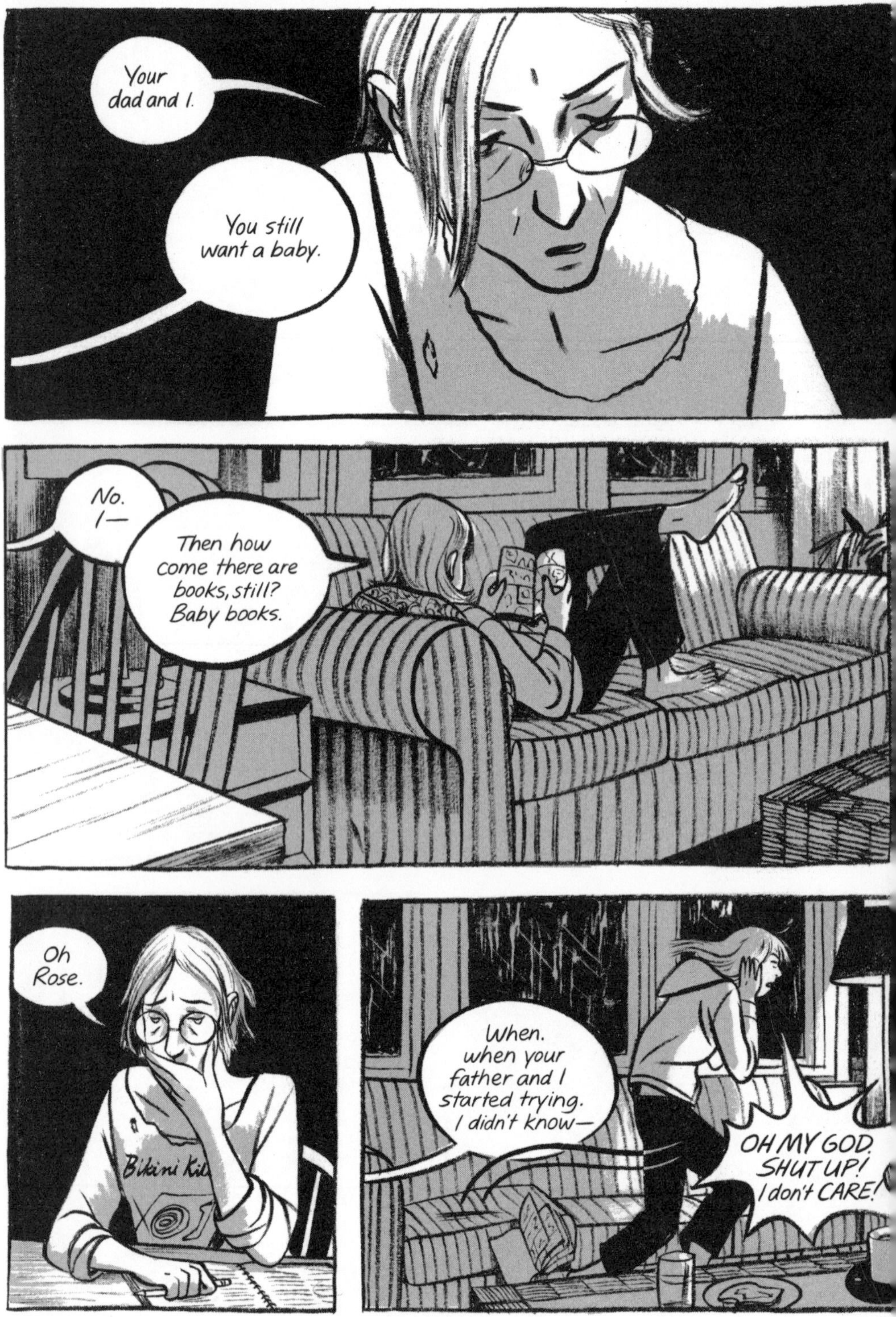
Your dad and I.
You still want a baby.
No. I—
Then how come there are books, still? Baby books.
Oh Rose.
Bikini Kil
When. when your father and I started trying. I didn't know—
OH MY GOD. SHUT UP! I don't CARE!

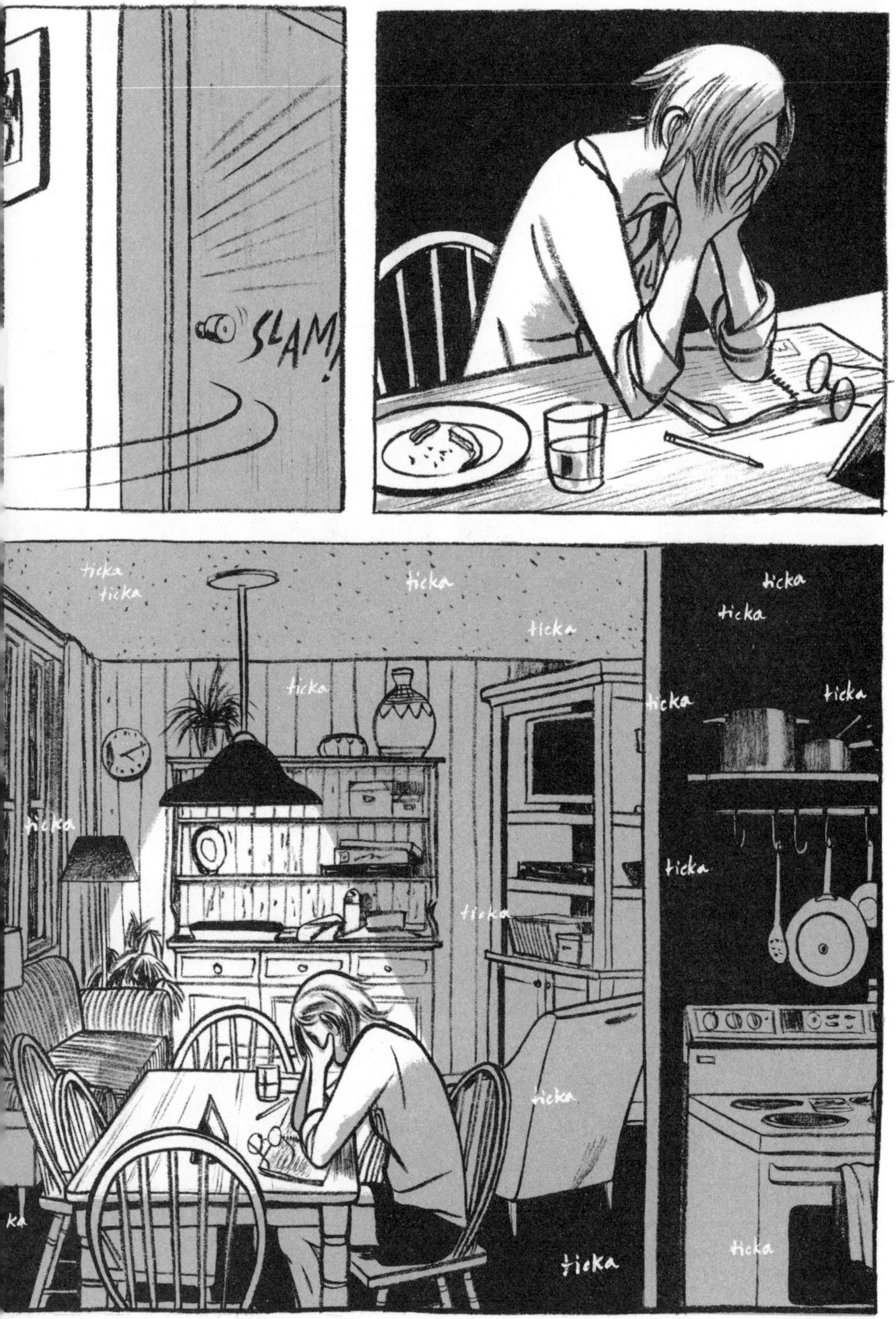
SLAM!
ticka
ticka
ticka
ticka
ticka
ticka
ticka
ticka
ticka
ticka
ticka
ticka
ticka
ka
ticka
ticka

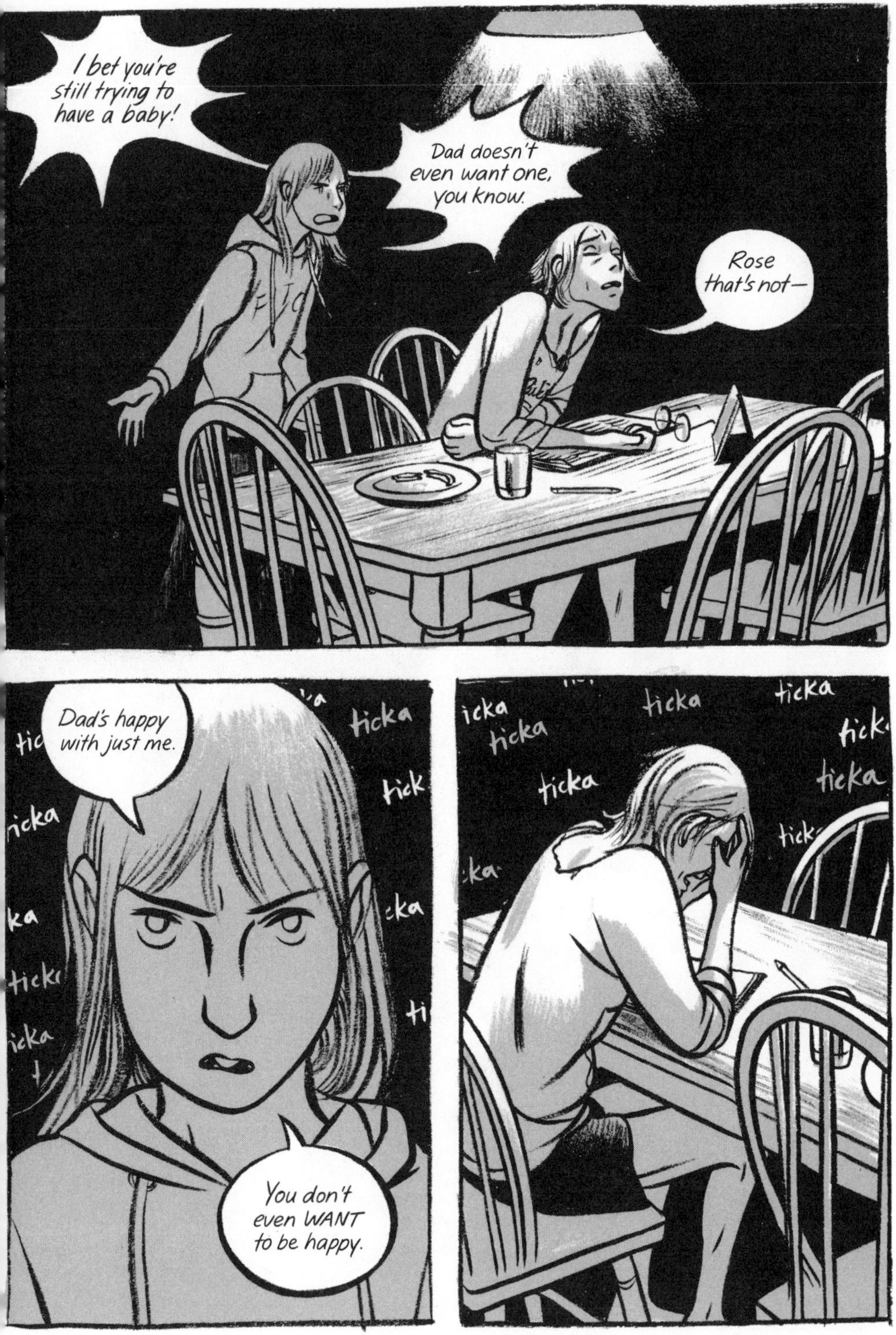
I bet you're still trying to have a baby!
Dad doesn't even want one, you know.
Rose that's not—
Dad's happy with just me.
You don't even WANT to be happy.
ticka
ticka
ticka
ticka
ticka
ticka
ticka

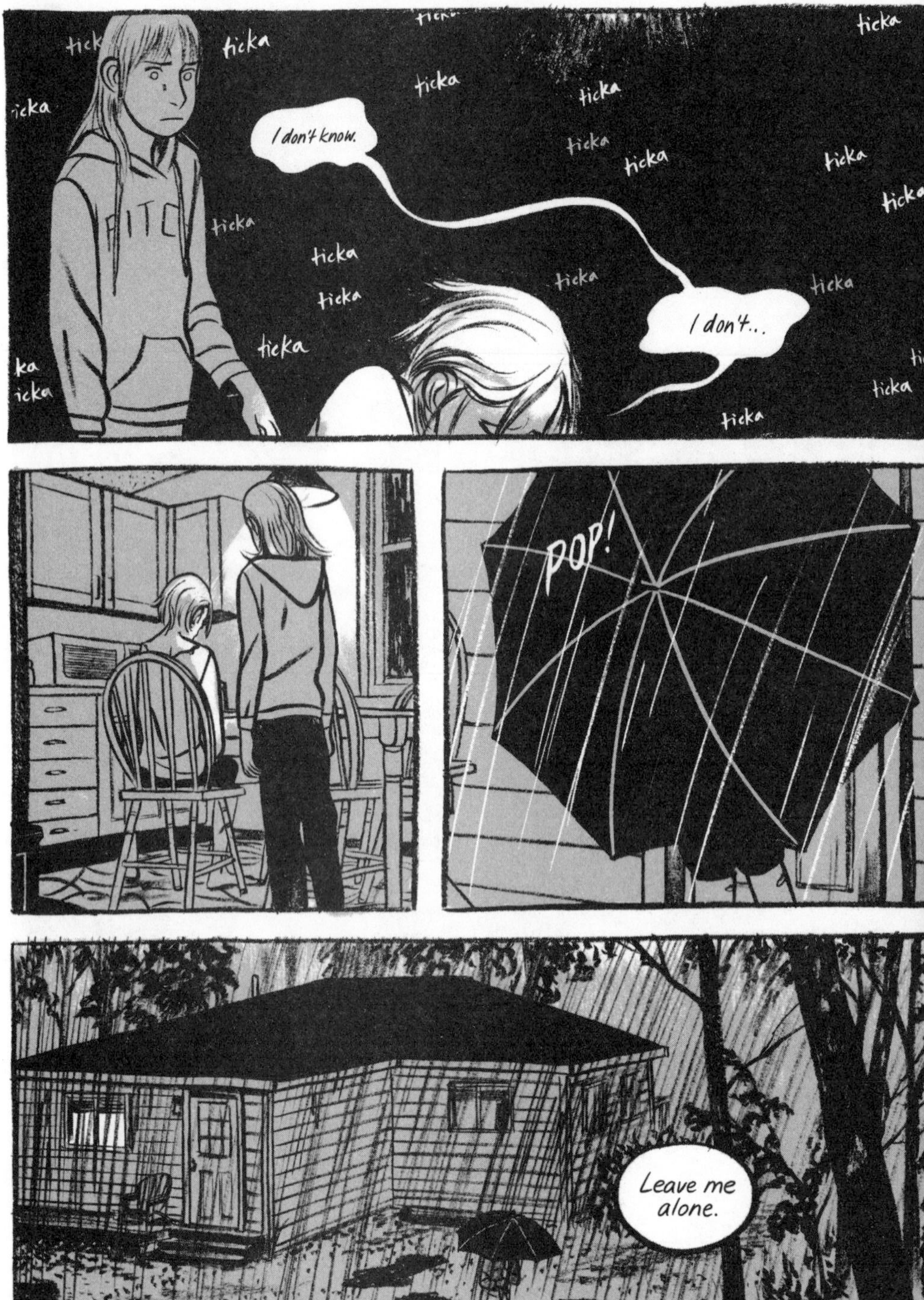
ticka
I don't know.
I don't...
POP!
Leave me alone.

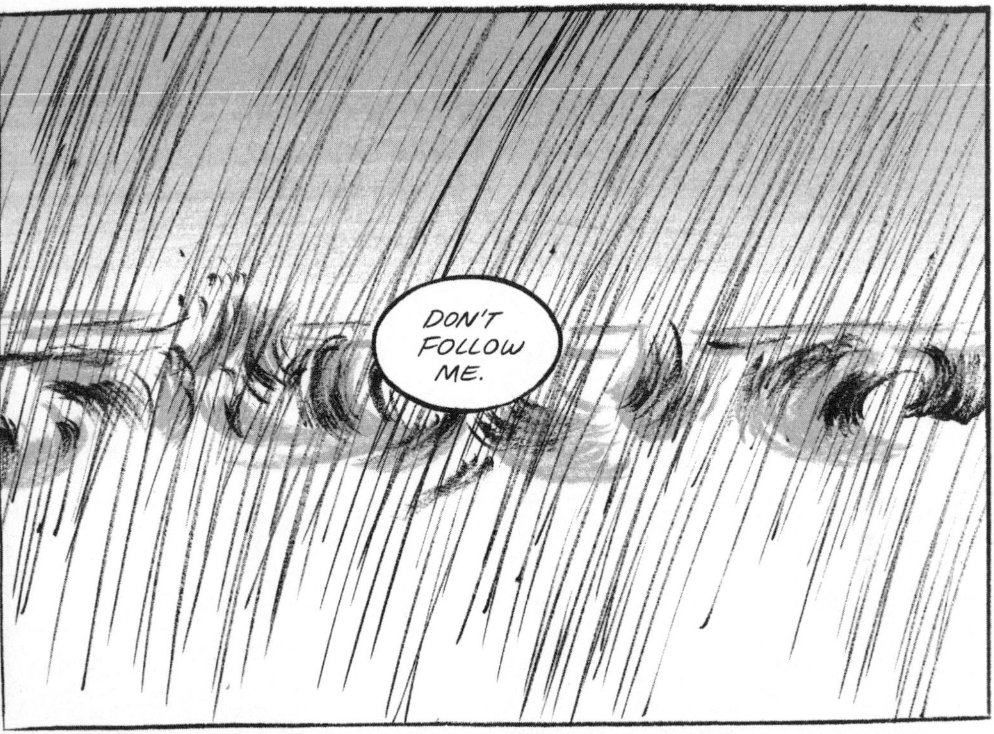
DON'T FOLLOW ME.

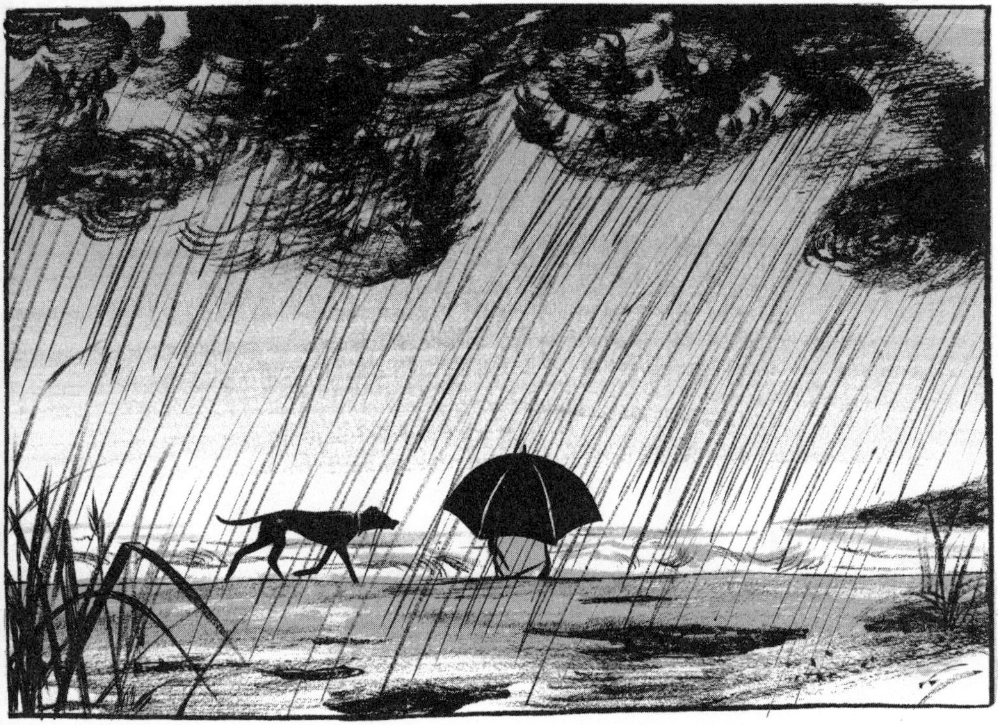

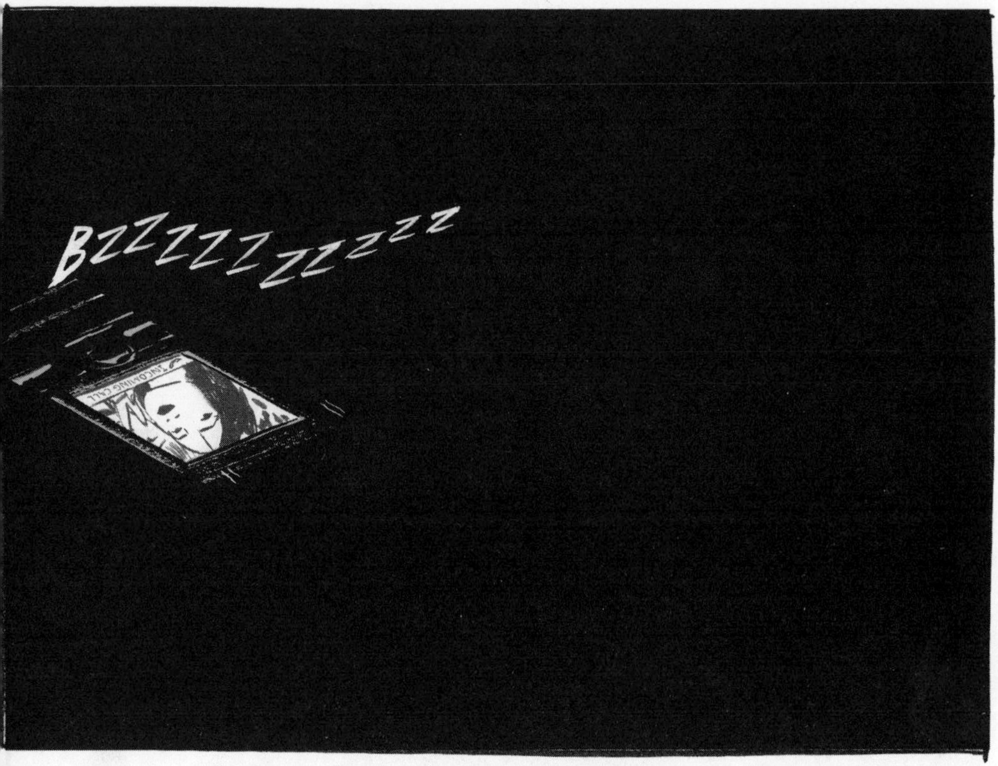
BZZZZZZZZZZ
INCOMING CALL

Yesterday at Windy's we watched a movie where this guy enters people's dreams and kills them. He had skin like Swiss cheese.

Dunc wasn't there when we went to rent the movie. Just the other guy. He had a T-shirt on that said, "FBI: Federal Boobie Inspector."

Windy pointed at it, which was totally embarrassing.

After the movie Evelyn said I could sleep over. Even though Windy was scared she fell asleep right away. I couldn't sleep.

EEEEE!!

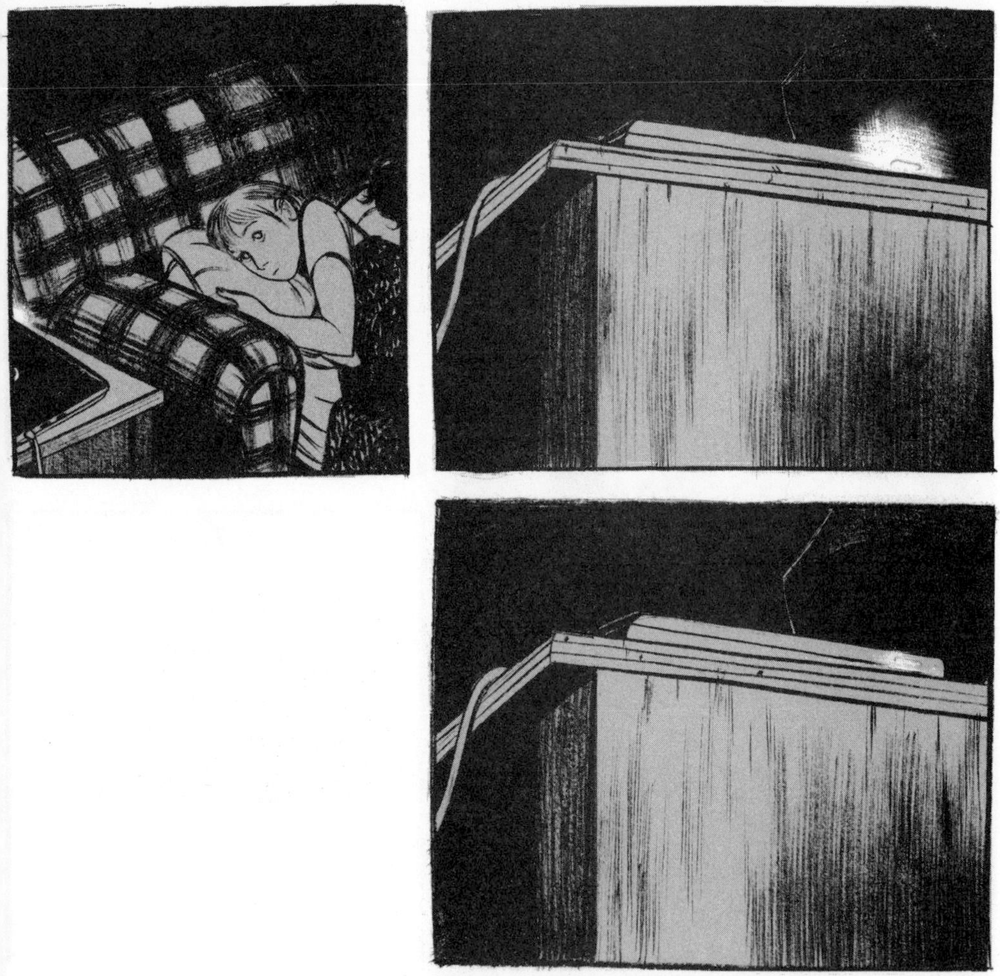

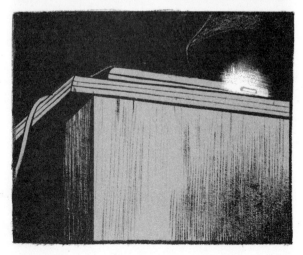

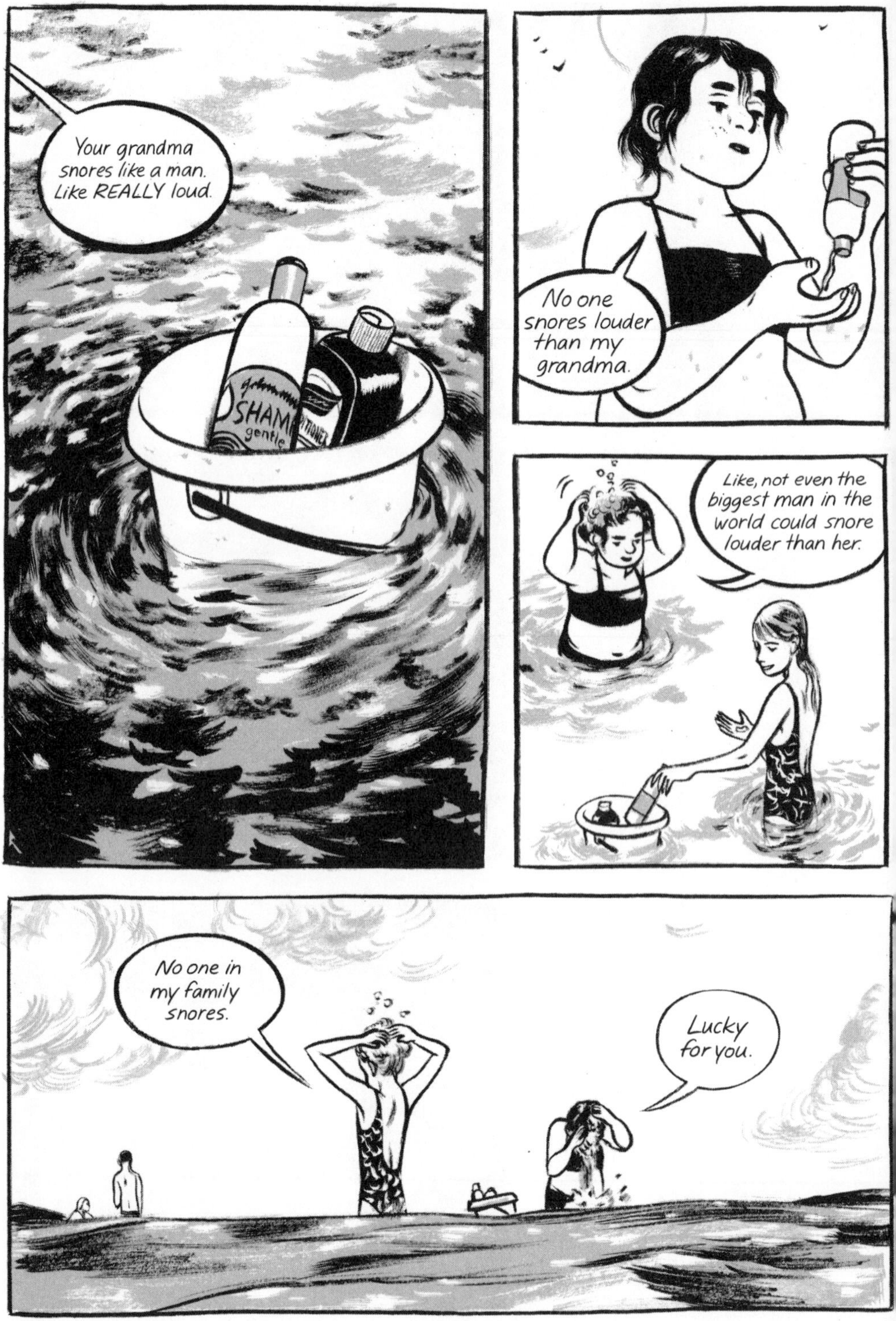
Your grandma snores like a man. Like REALLY loud.
SHAM
gentle
No one snores louder than my grandma.
Like, not even the biggest man in the world could snore louder than her.
No one in my family snores.
Lucky for you.

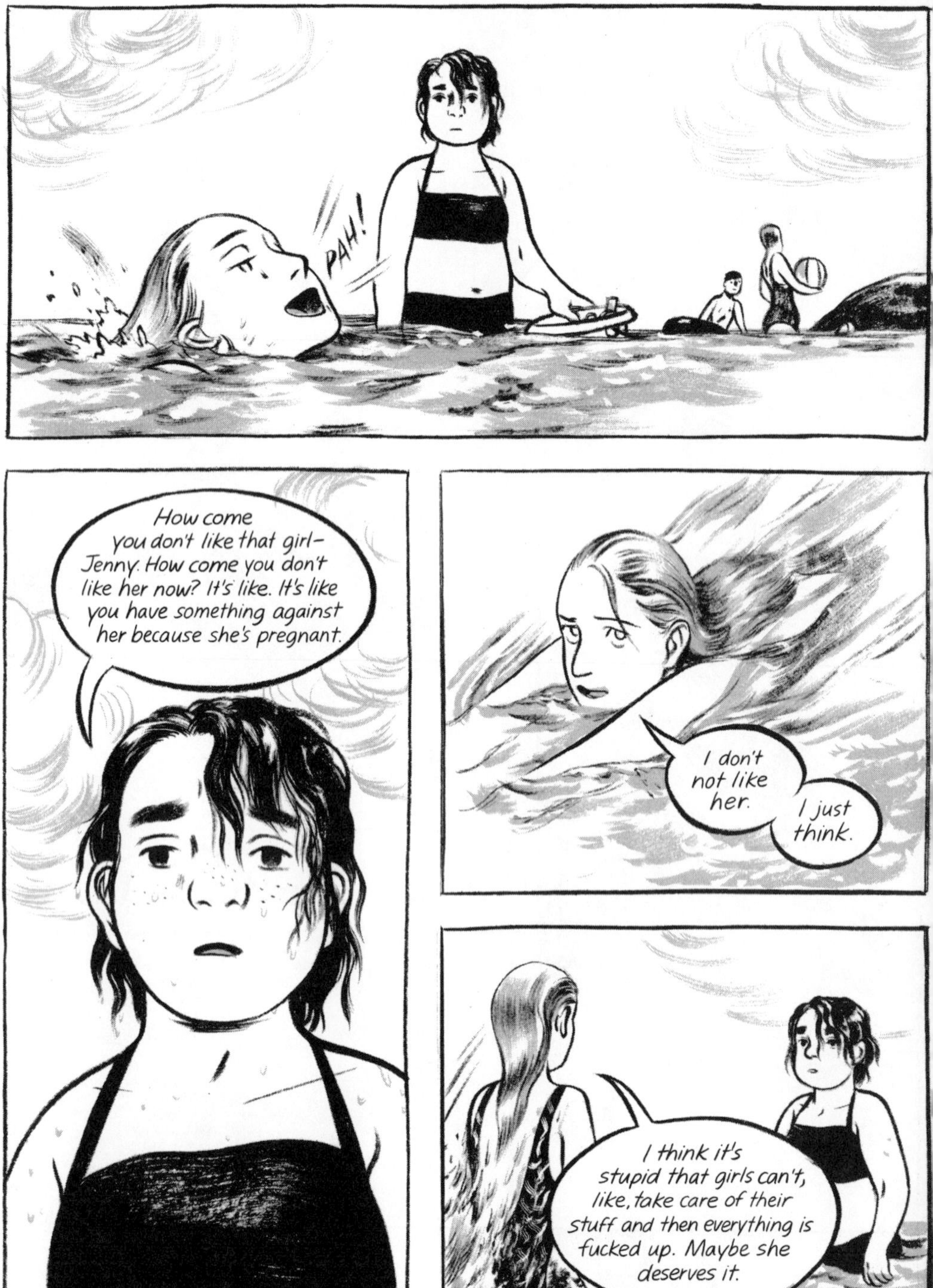
PAH!
How come you don't like that girl– Jenny. How come you don't like her now? It's like. It's like you have something against her because she's pregnant.
I don't not like her.
I just think.
I think it's stupid that girls can't, like, take care of their stuff and then everything is fucked up. Maybe she deserves it.

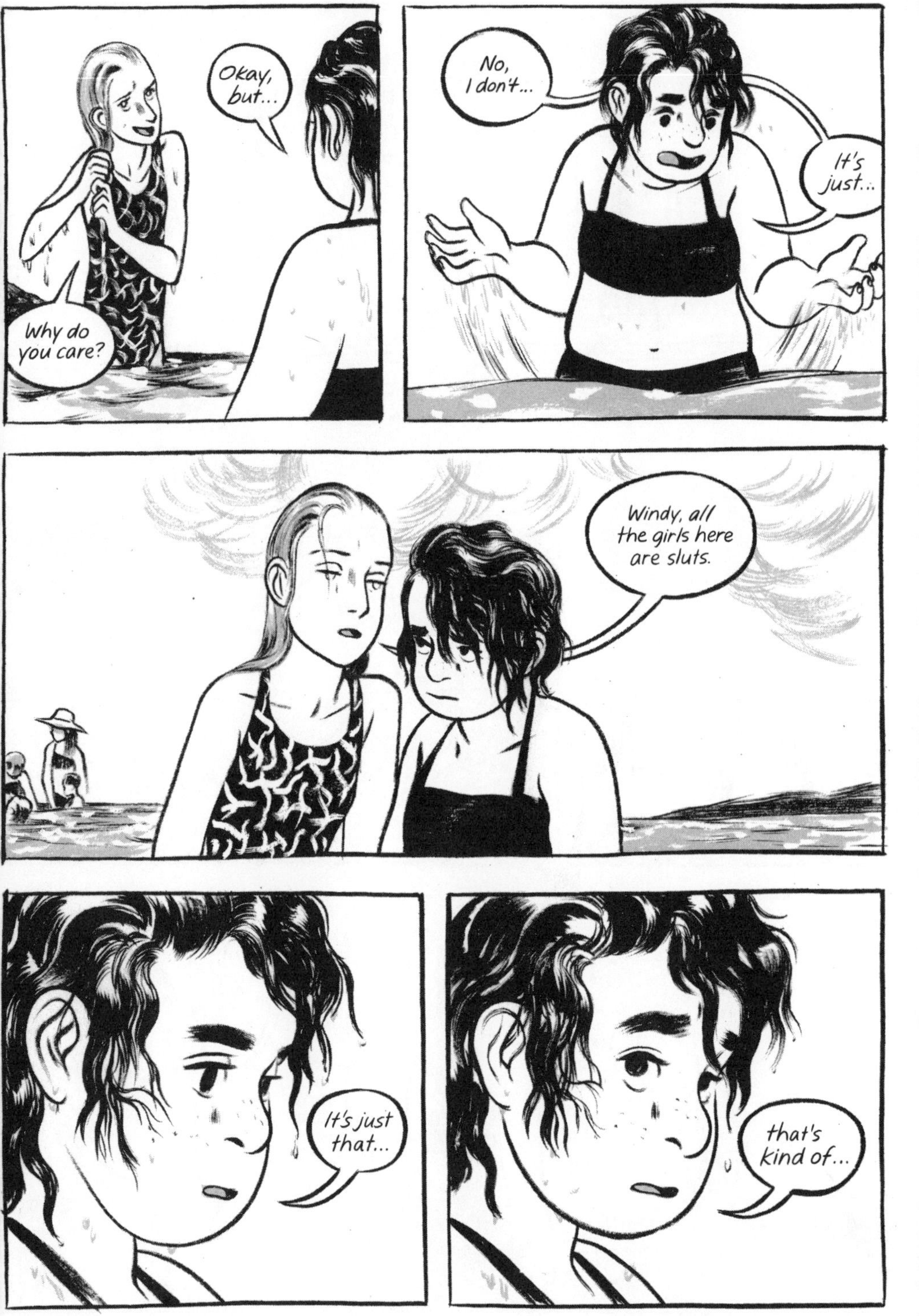
Okay, but...
Why do you care?
No, I don't...
It's just...
Windy, all the girls here are sluts.
It's just that...
that's kind of...

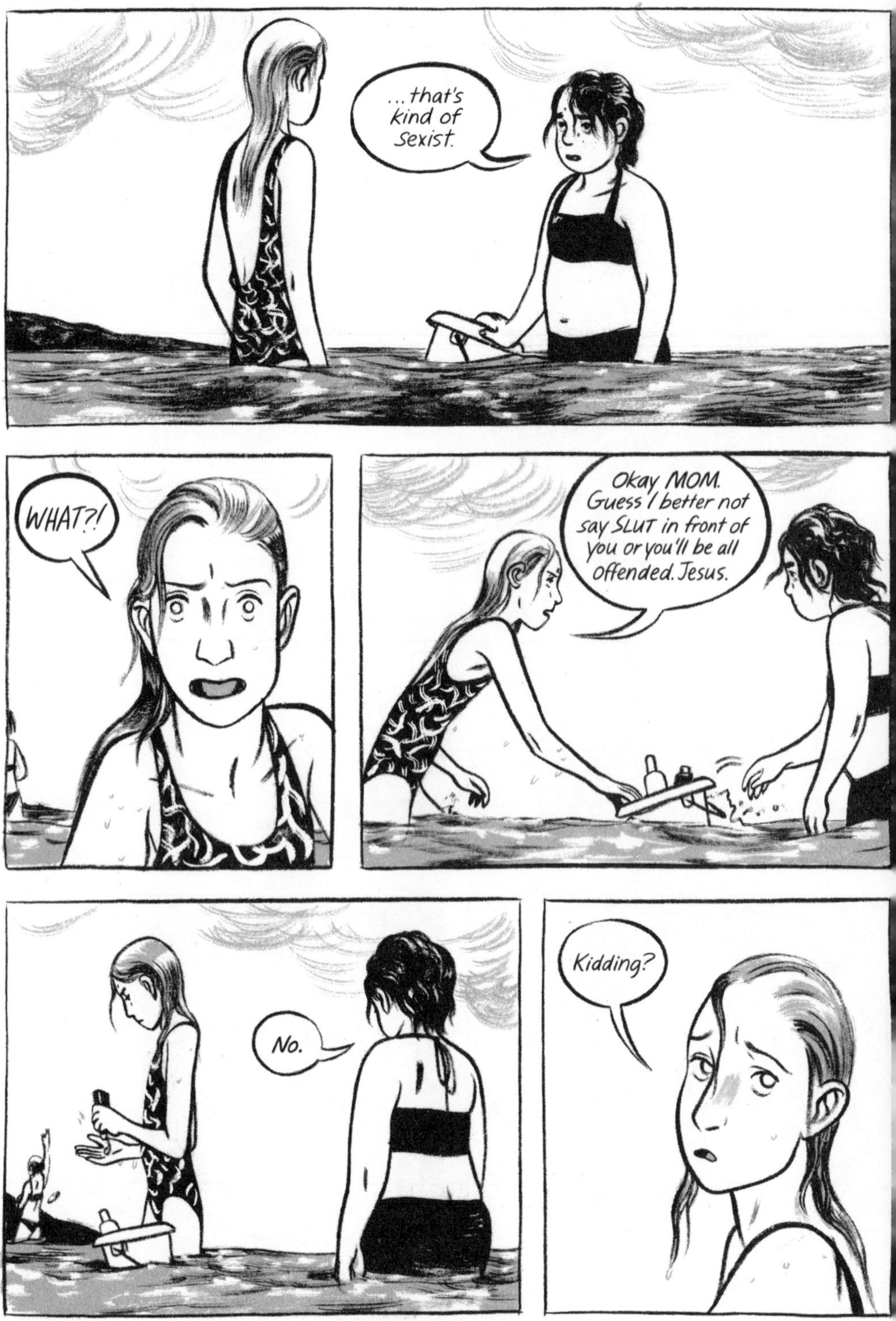
...that's kind of sexist.
WHAT?!
Okay MOM. Guess I better not say SLUT in front of you or you'll be all offended. Jesus.
No.
Kidding?

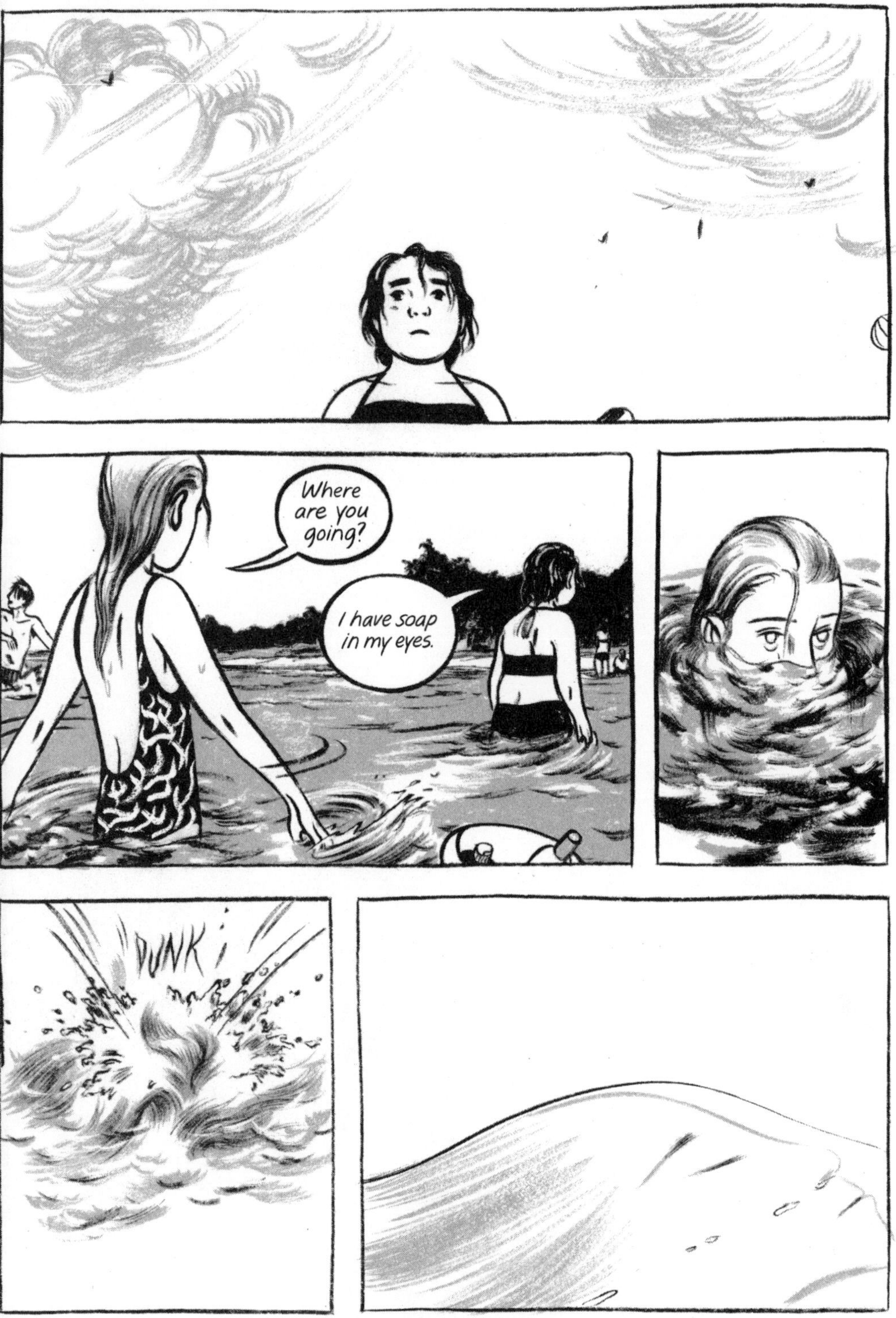
Where are you going?
I have soap in my eyes.
DUNK

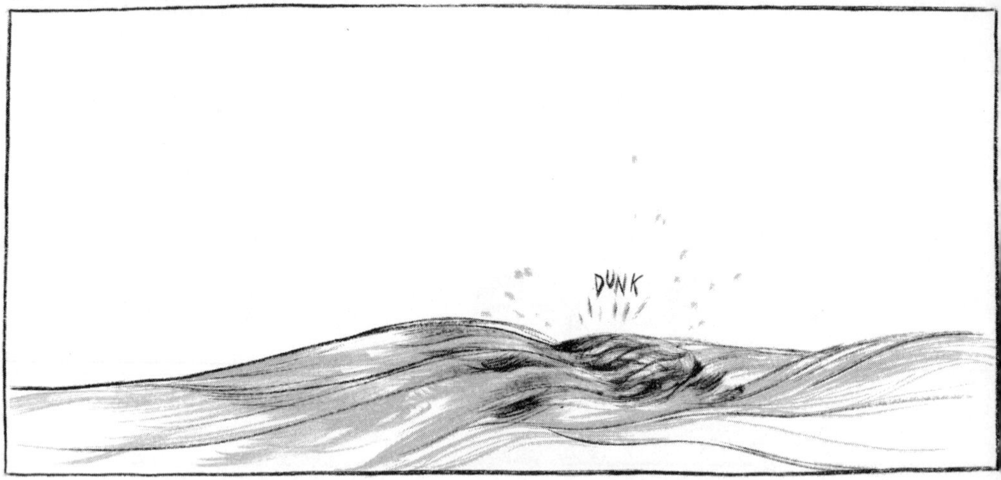
DUNK

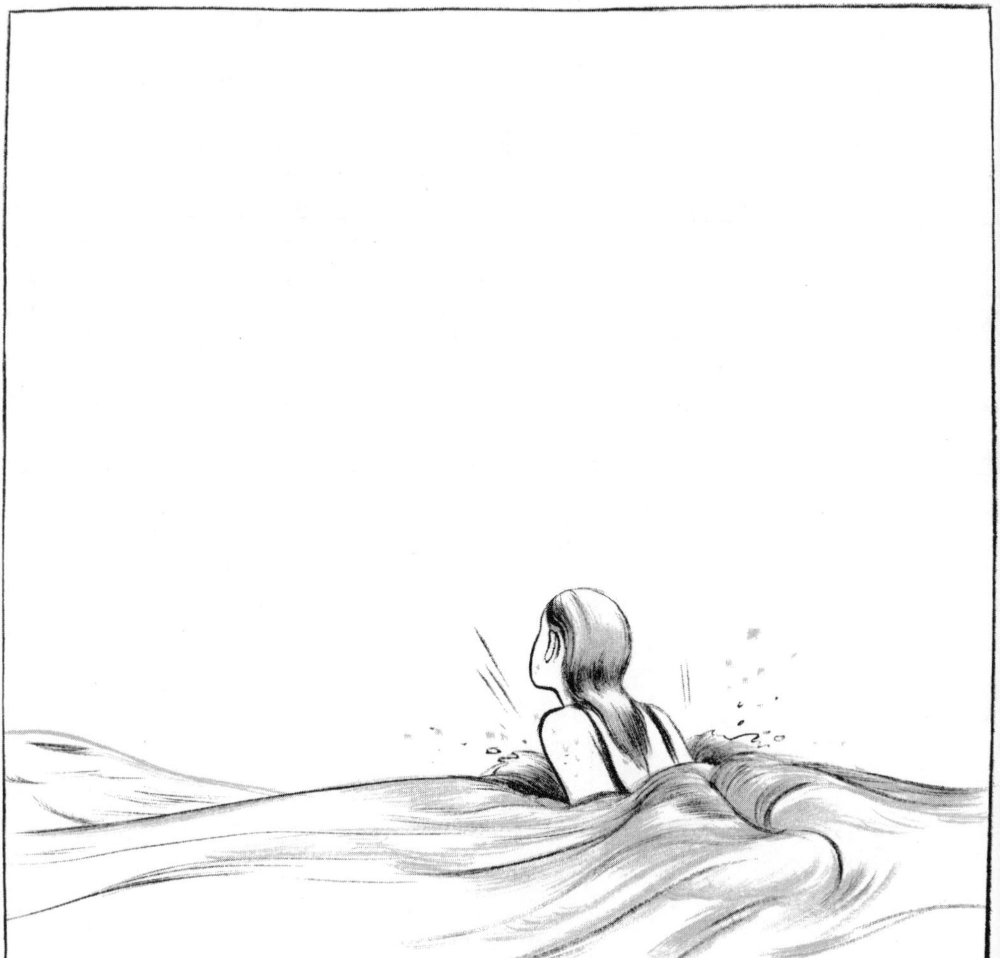

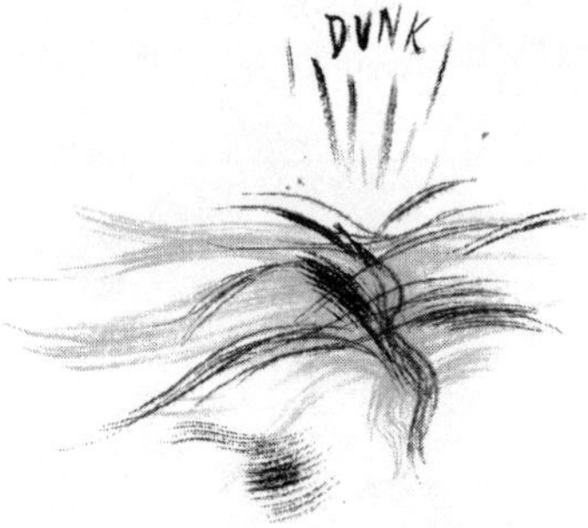
DUNK

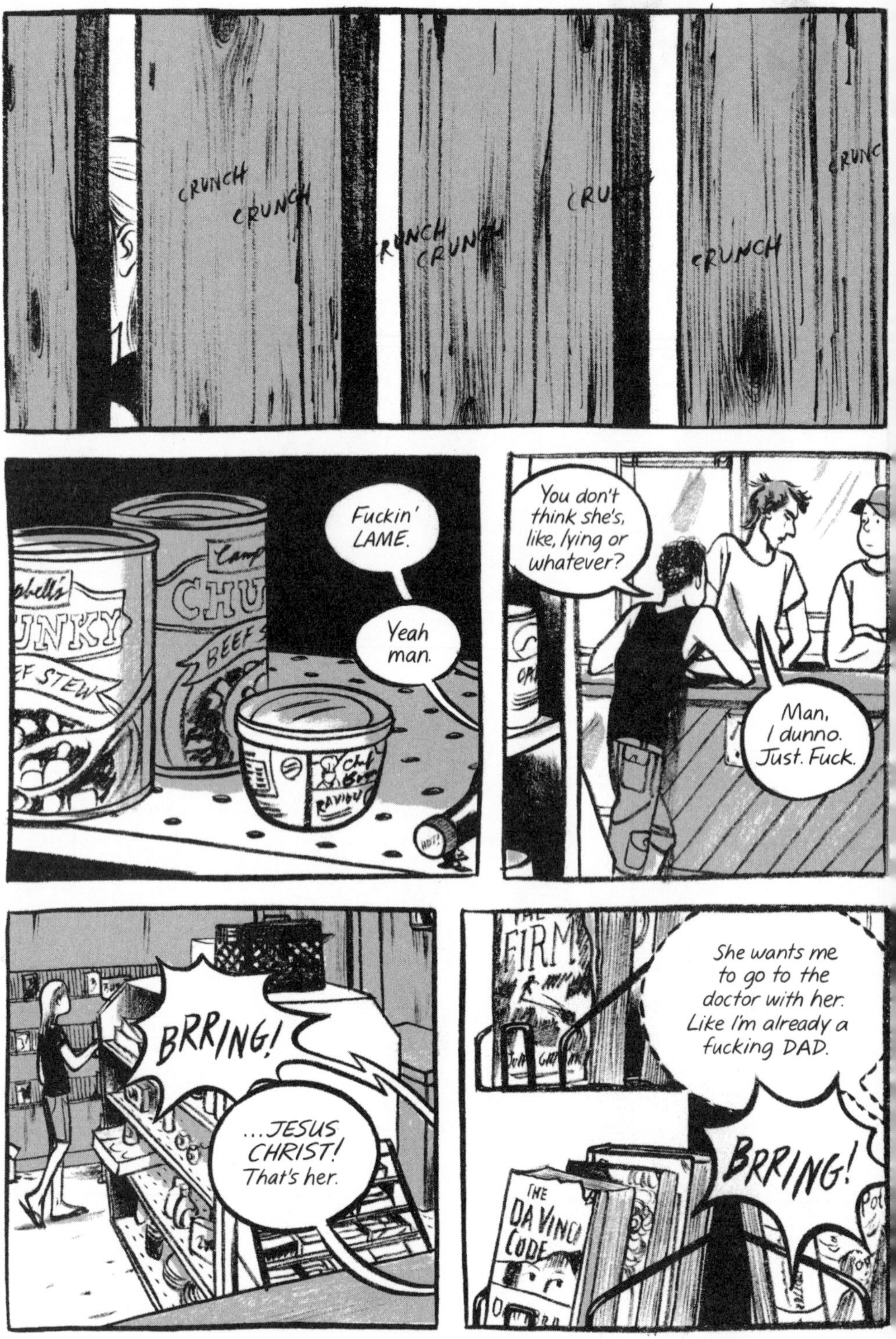

CRUNCH
CRUNCH
CRUNCH
CRUNCH
CRUNCH
Fuckin' LAME.
Yeah man.
You don't think she's, like, lying or whatever?
Man, I dunno. Just. Fuck.
BRRING!
...JESUS CHRIST! That's her.
She wants me to go to the doctor with her. Like I'm already a fucking DAD.
BRRING!

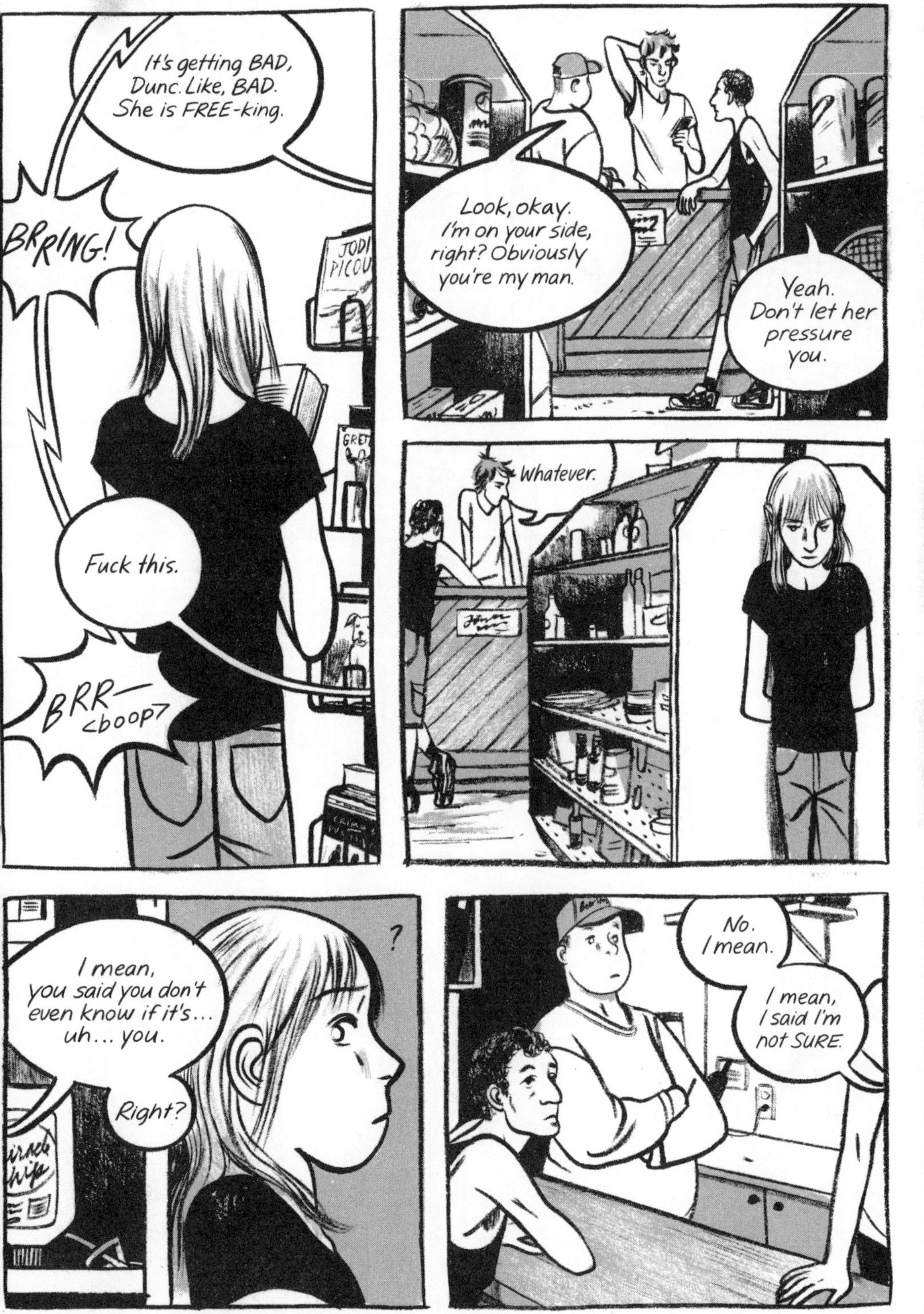
It's getting BAD, Dunc. Like, BAD. She is FREE-king.
BRRING!
JODI PICOU
Look, okay. I'm on your side, right? Obviously you're my man.
Yeah. Don't let her pressure you.
Fuck this.
BRR—
<boop>
Whatever.
?
I mean, you said you don't even know if it's... uh... you.
Right?
No. I mean.
I mean, I said I'm not SURE.

248

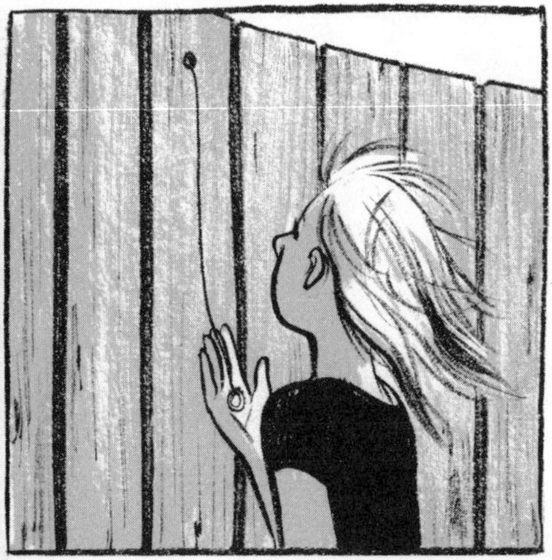

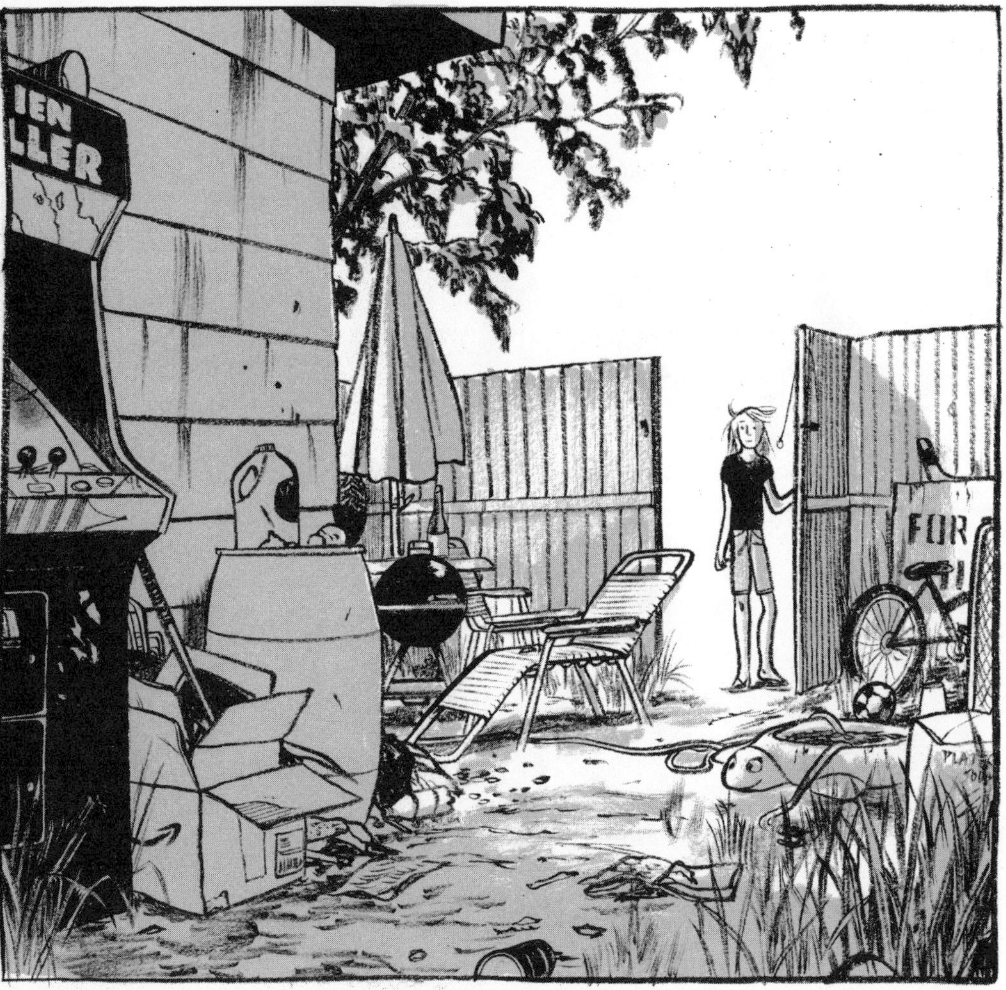
IEN
LLER
FOR

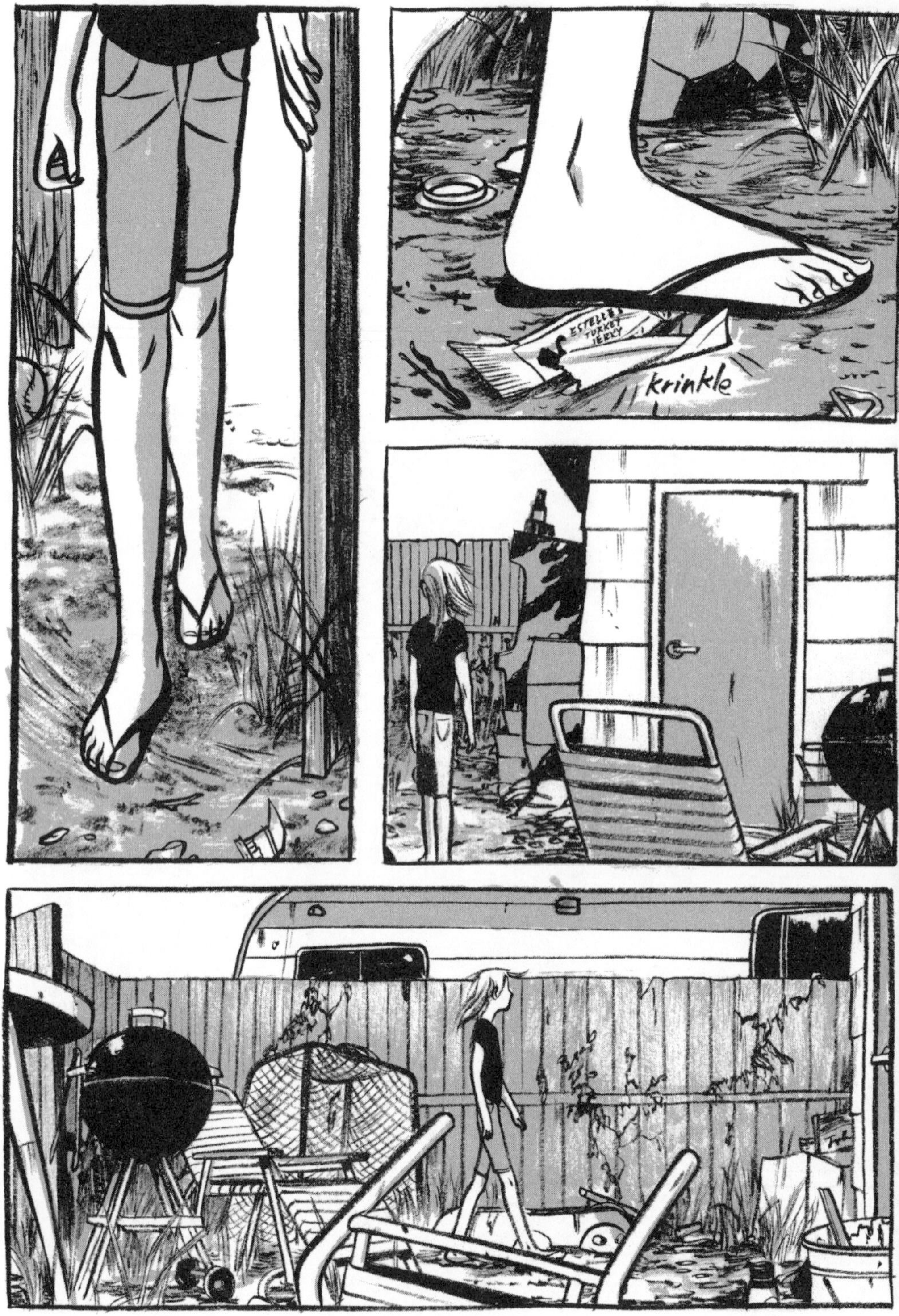
ESTELLE'S TURKEY JERKY
krinkle

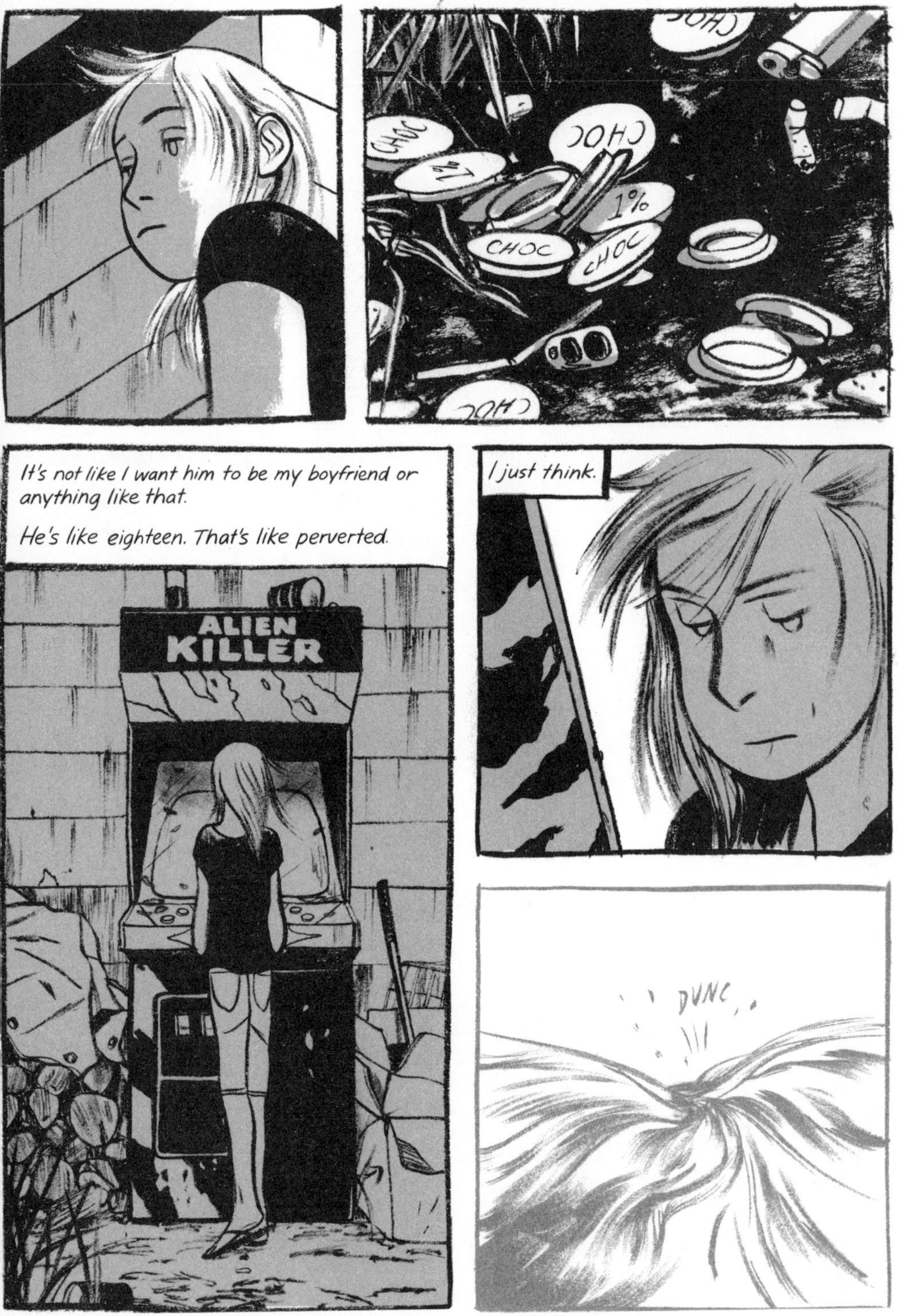
CHOC
CHOC
1%
CHOC
CHOC
It's not like I want him to be my boyfriend or anything like that.
He's like eighteen. That's like perverted.
ALIEN KILLER
I just think.
DUNC

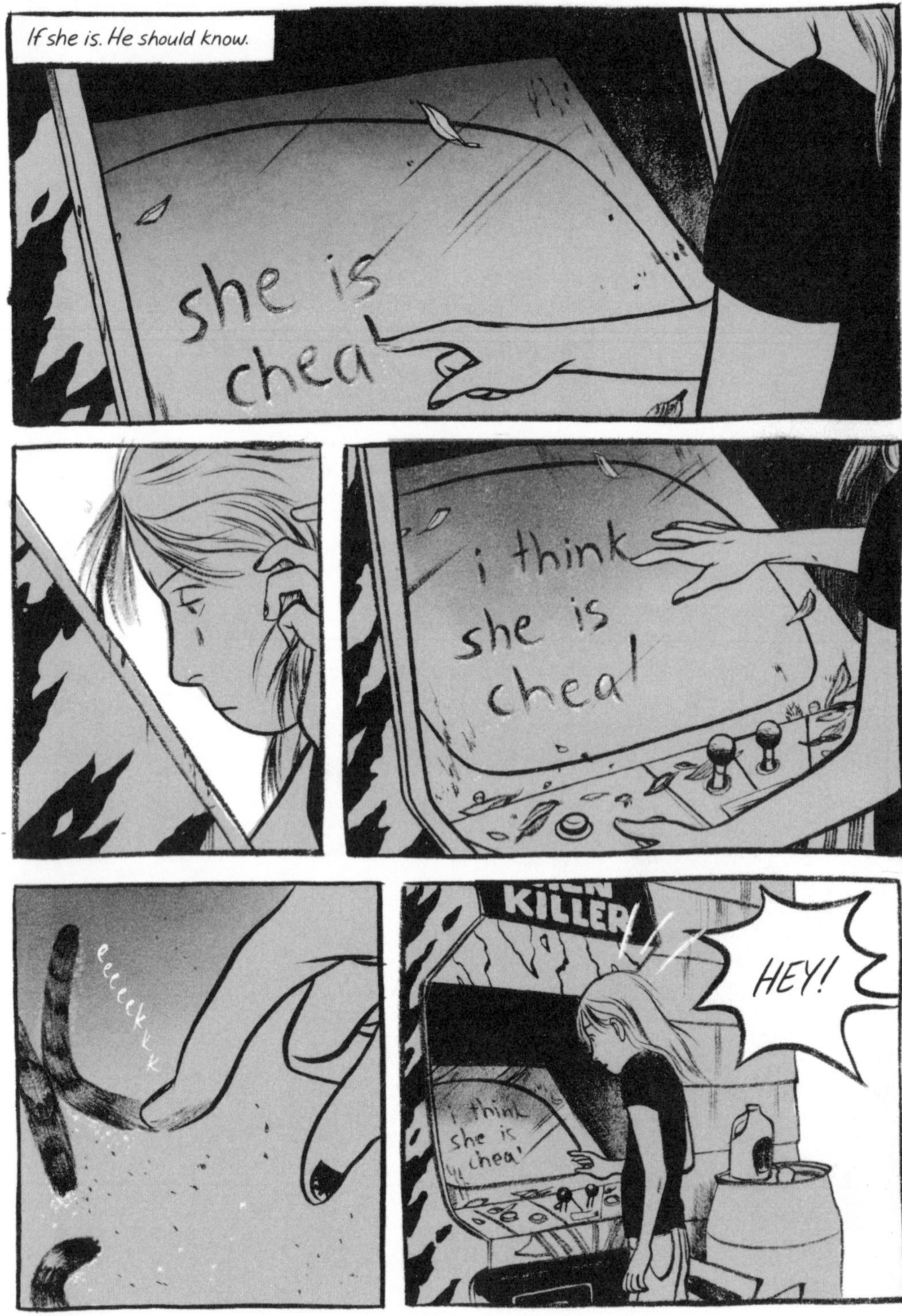
If she is. He should know.
she is chea
i think she is chea
eeeeekkk
KILLER
i think she is chea
HEY!

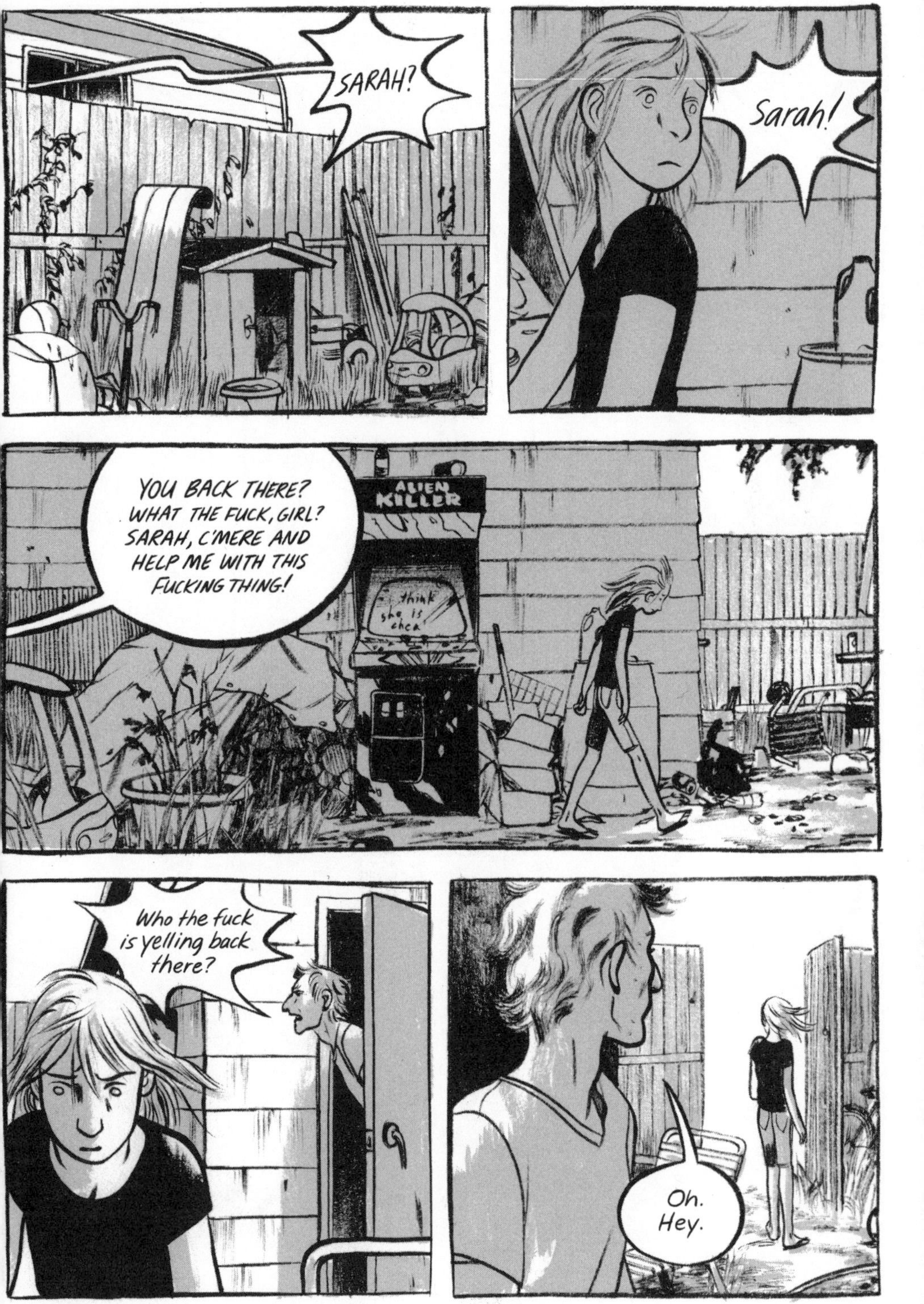
SARAH?
Sarah!
YOU BACK THERE? WHAT THE FUCK, GIRL? SARAH, C'MERE AND HELP ME WITH THIS FUCKING THING!
ALIEN KILLER
Who the fuck is yelling back there?
Oh. Hey.

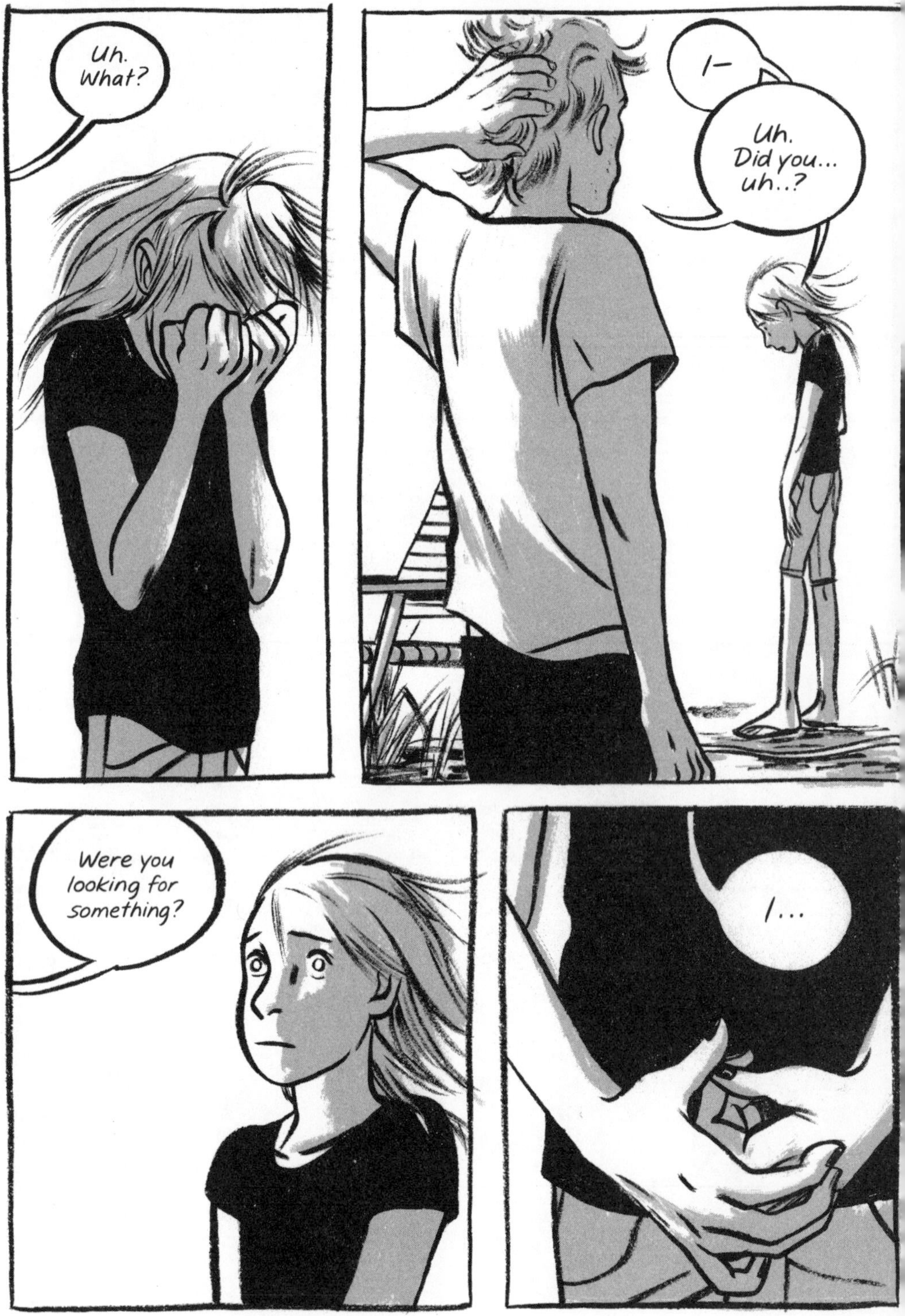
Uh. What?
I–
Uh. Did you... uh..?
Were you looking for something?
I...

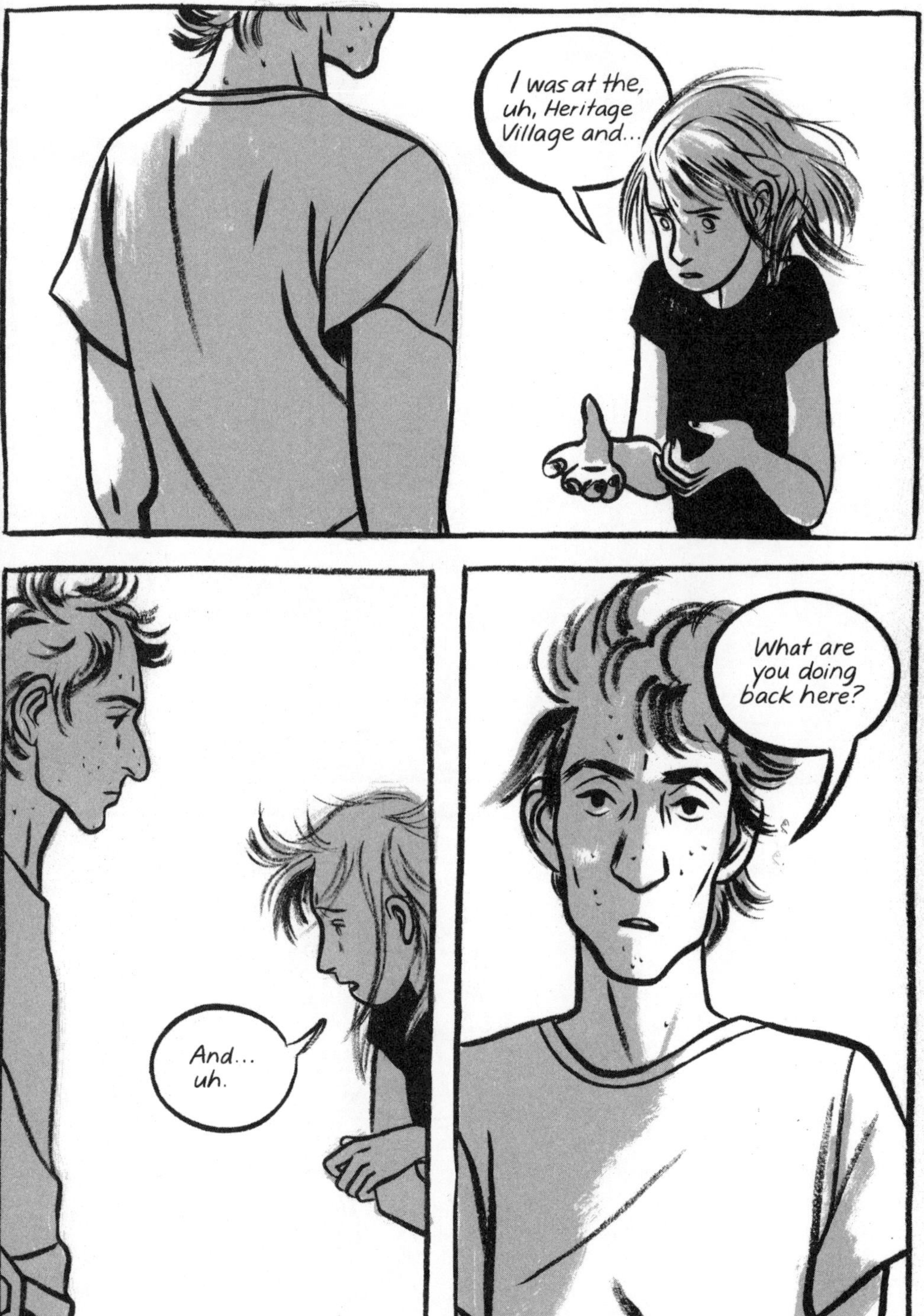
I was at the, uh, Heritage Village and...
And... uh.
What are you doing back here?

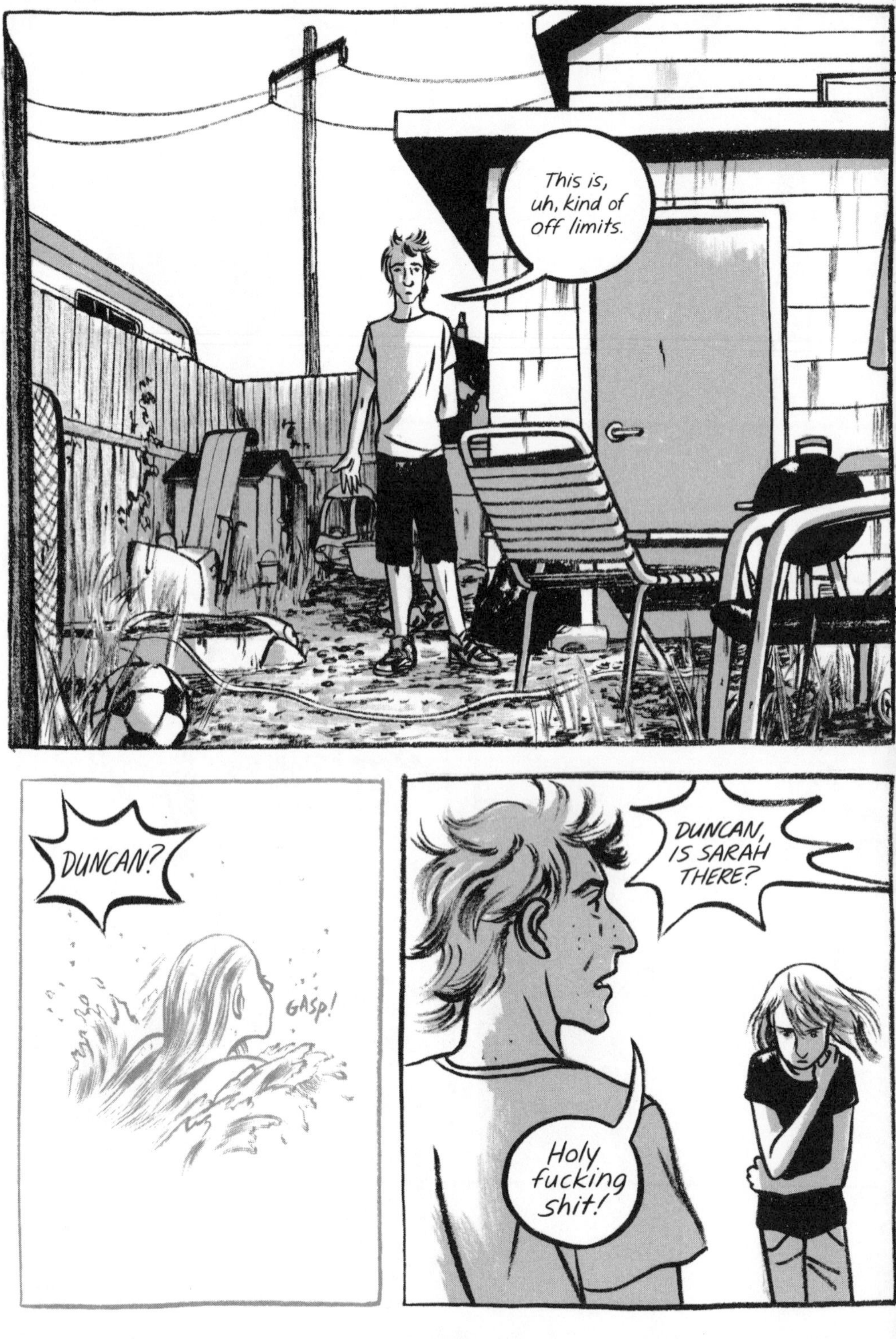
This is, uh, kind of off limits.
DUNCAN?
GASP!
DUNCAN, IS SARAH THERE?
Holy fucking shit!

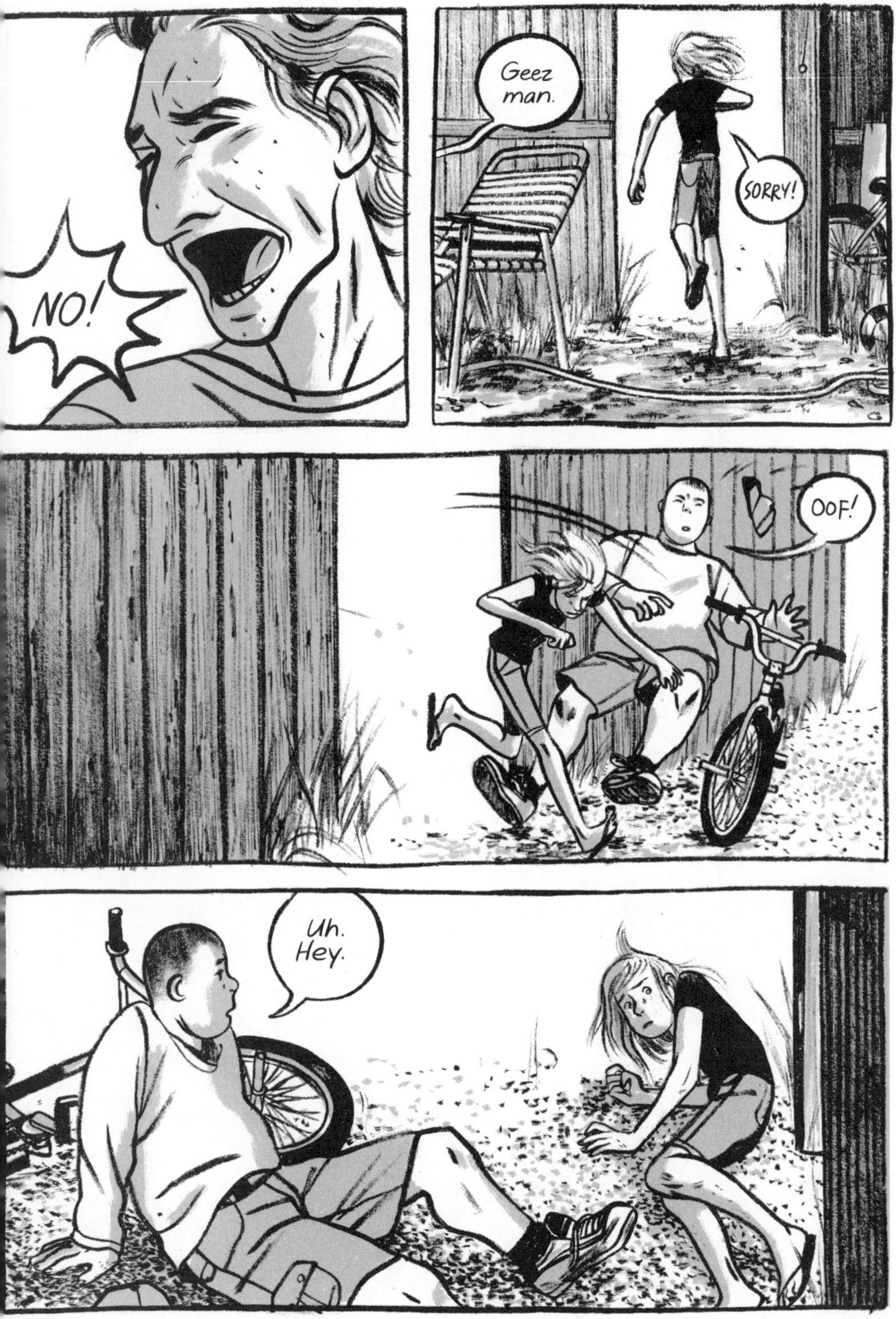
NO!
Geez man.
SORRY!
OOF!
Uh. Hey.

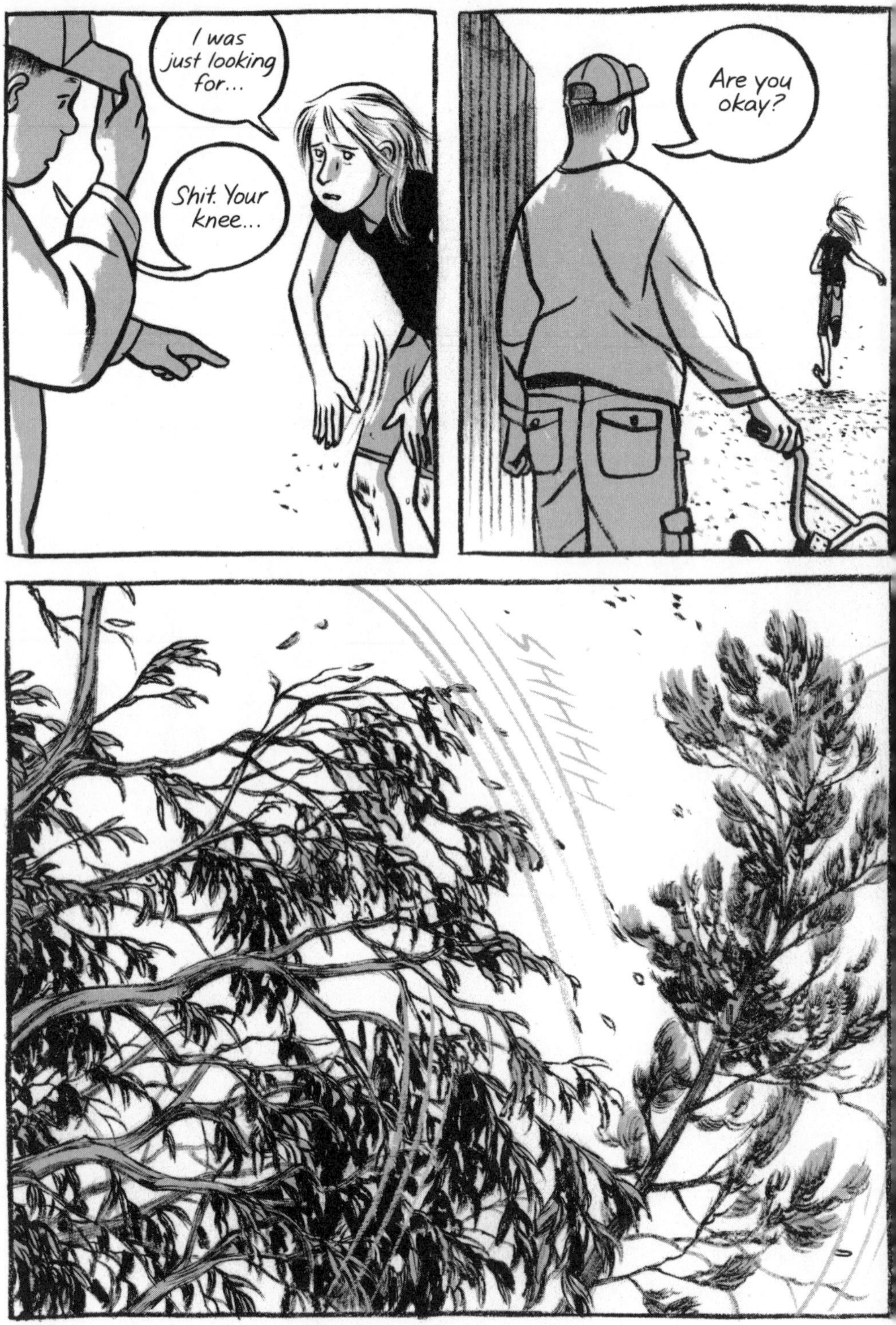
I was just looking for...
Shit. Your knee...
Are you okay?
SHHHH

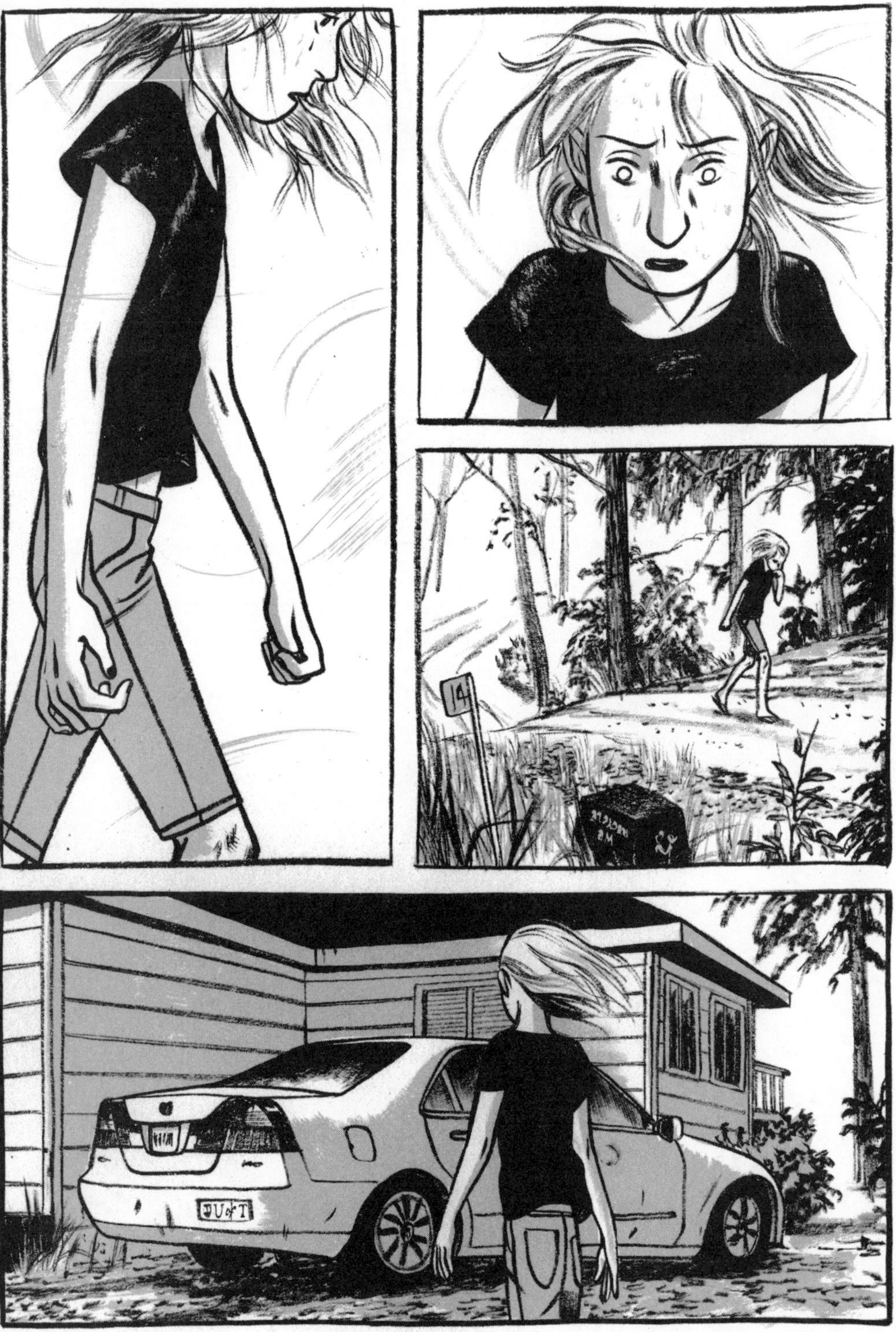

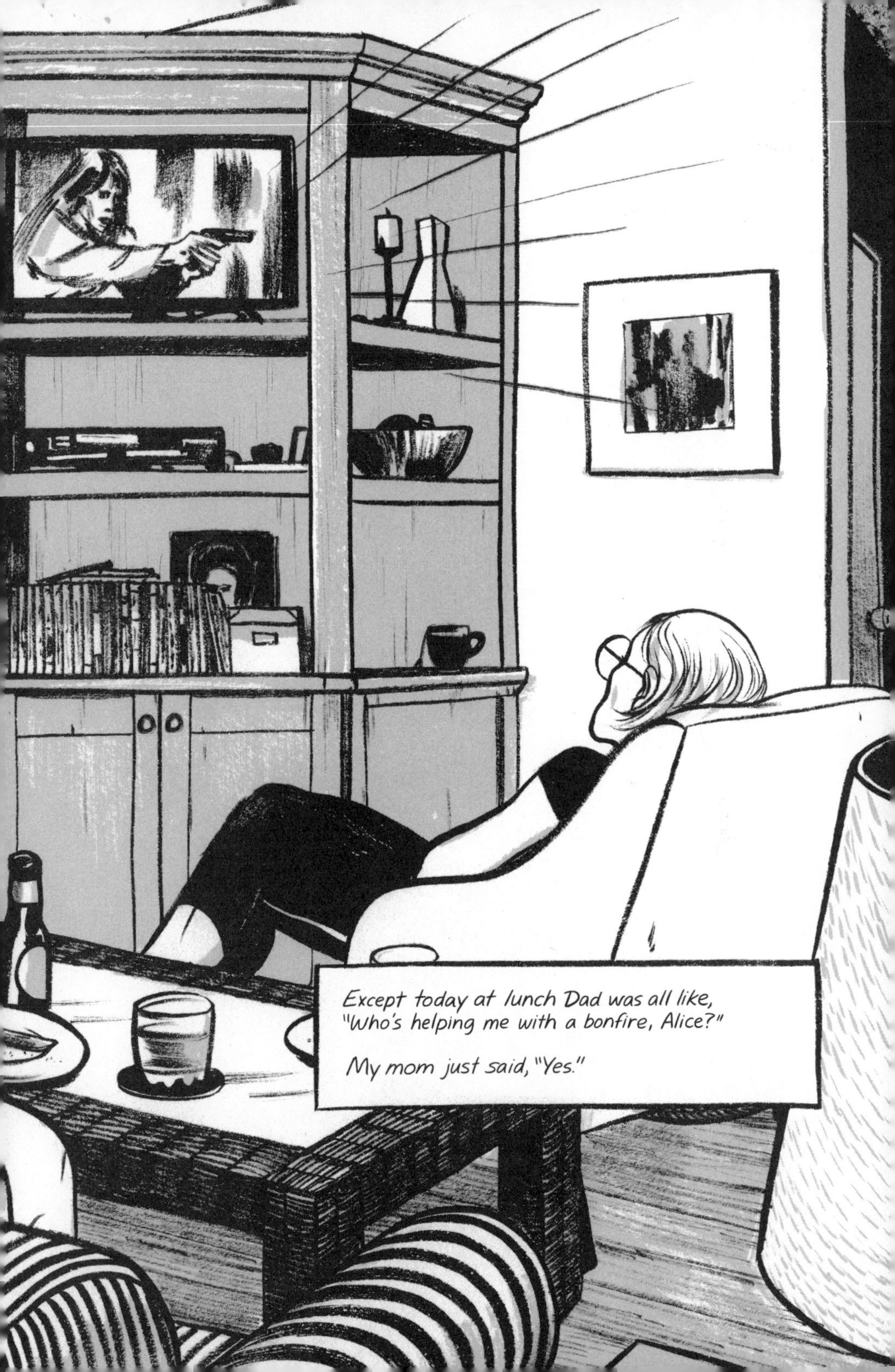
Except today at lunch Dad was all like, "Who's helping me with a bonfire, Alice?"
My mom just said, "Yes."

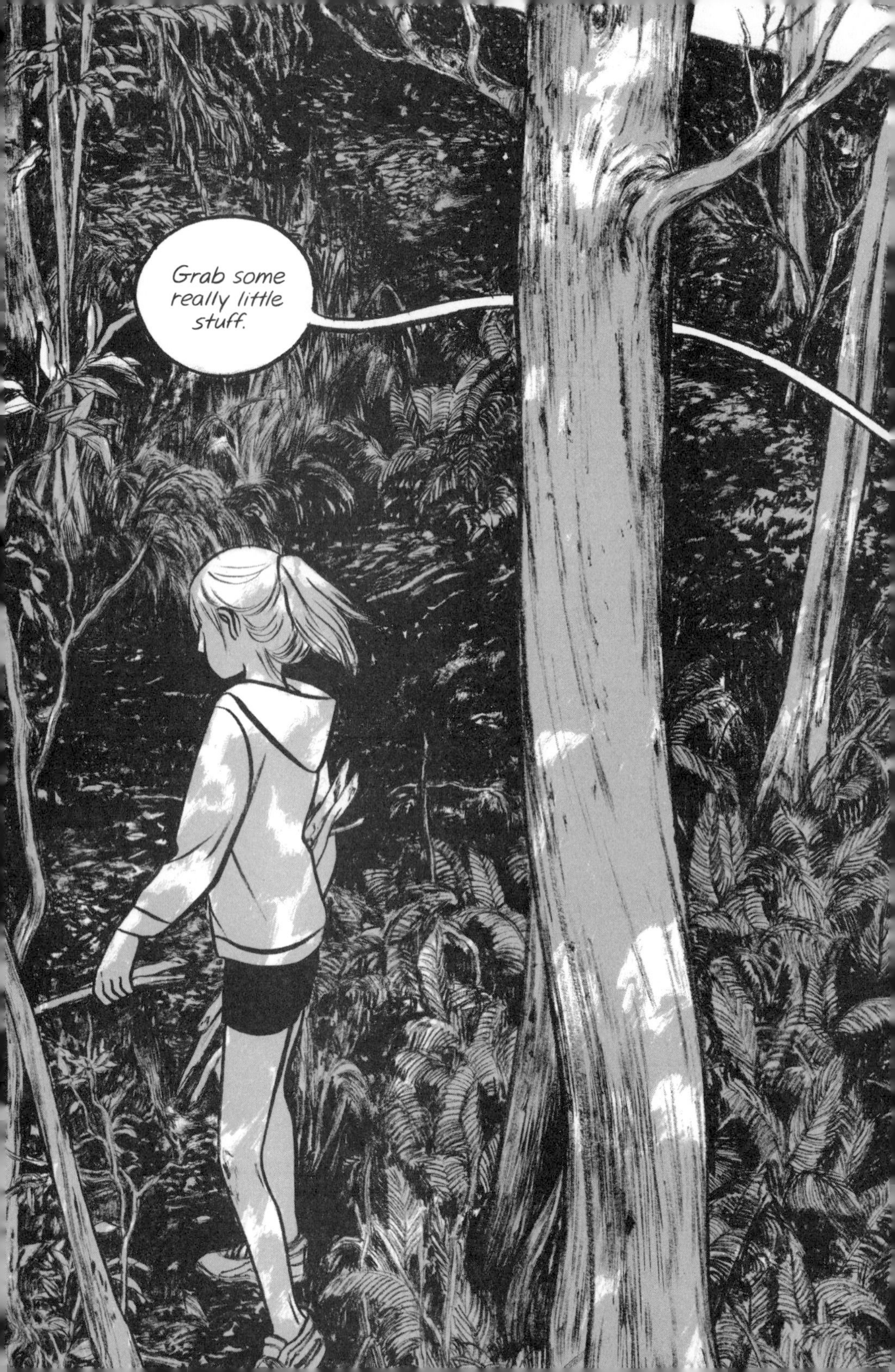
Grab some really little stuff.

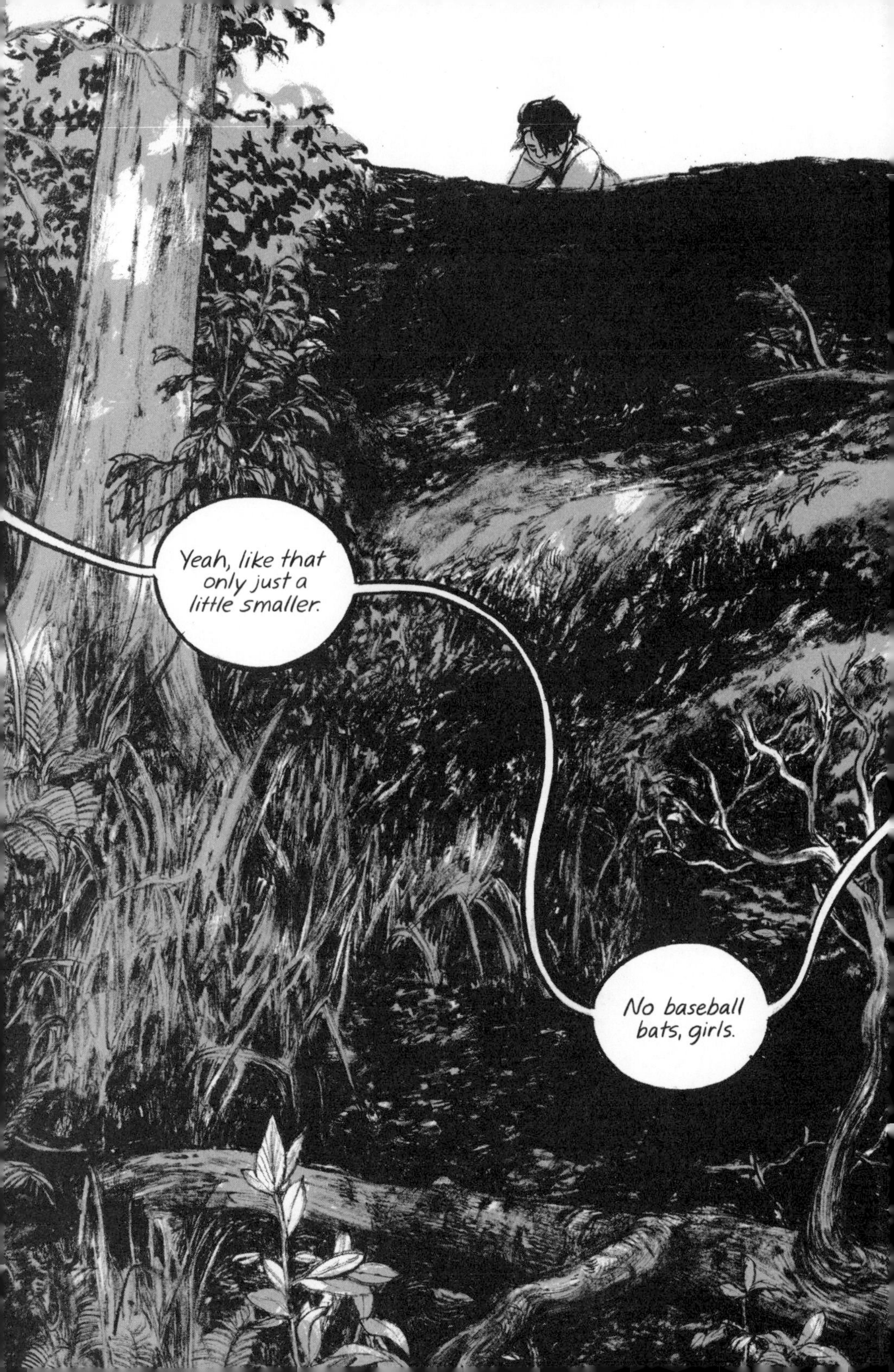
Yeah, like that only just a little smaller.
No baseball bats, girls.

265

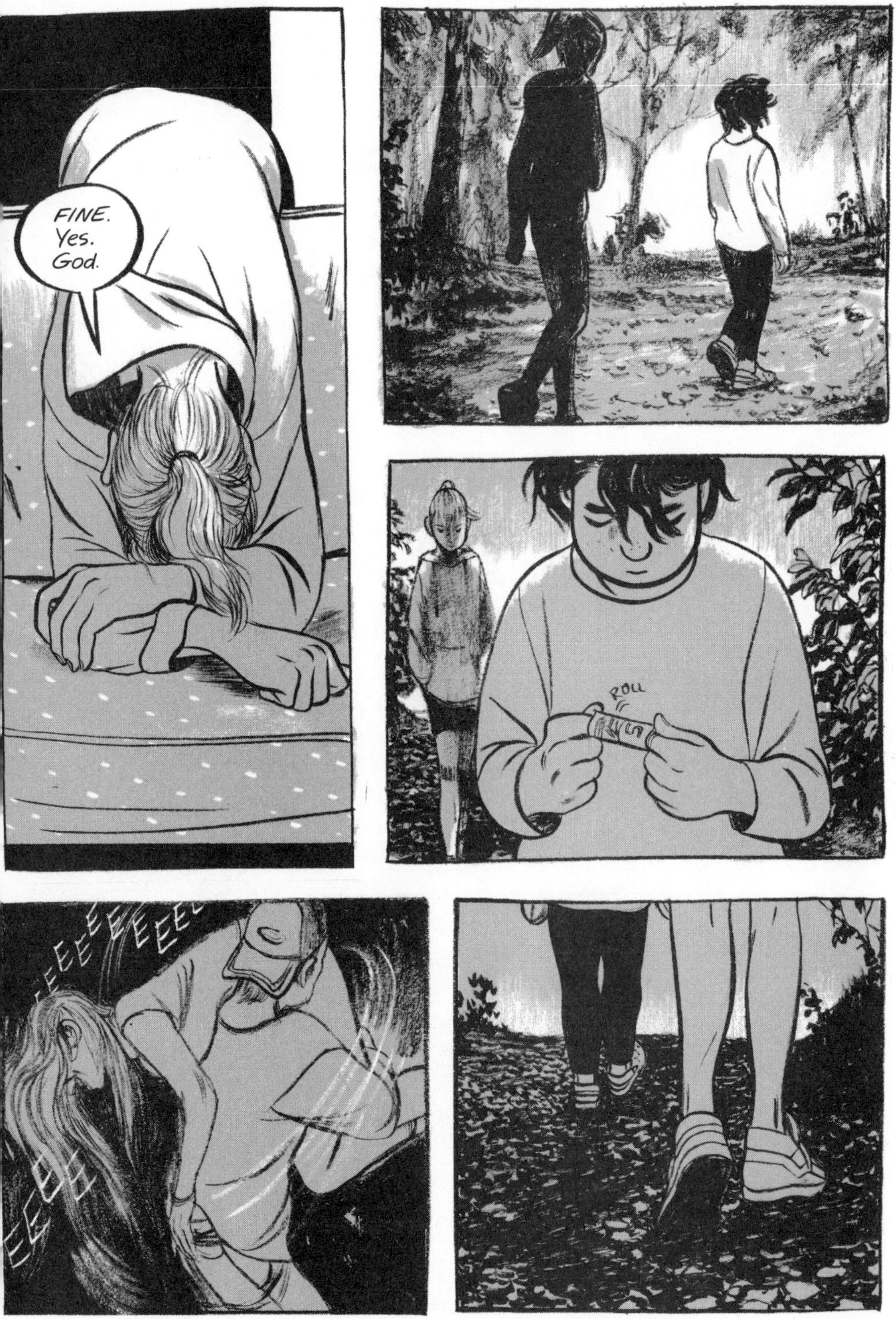
FINE. Yes. God.
ROLL

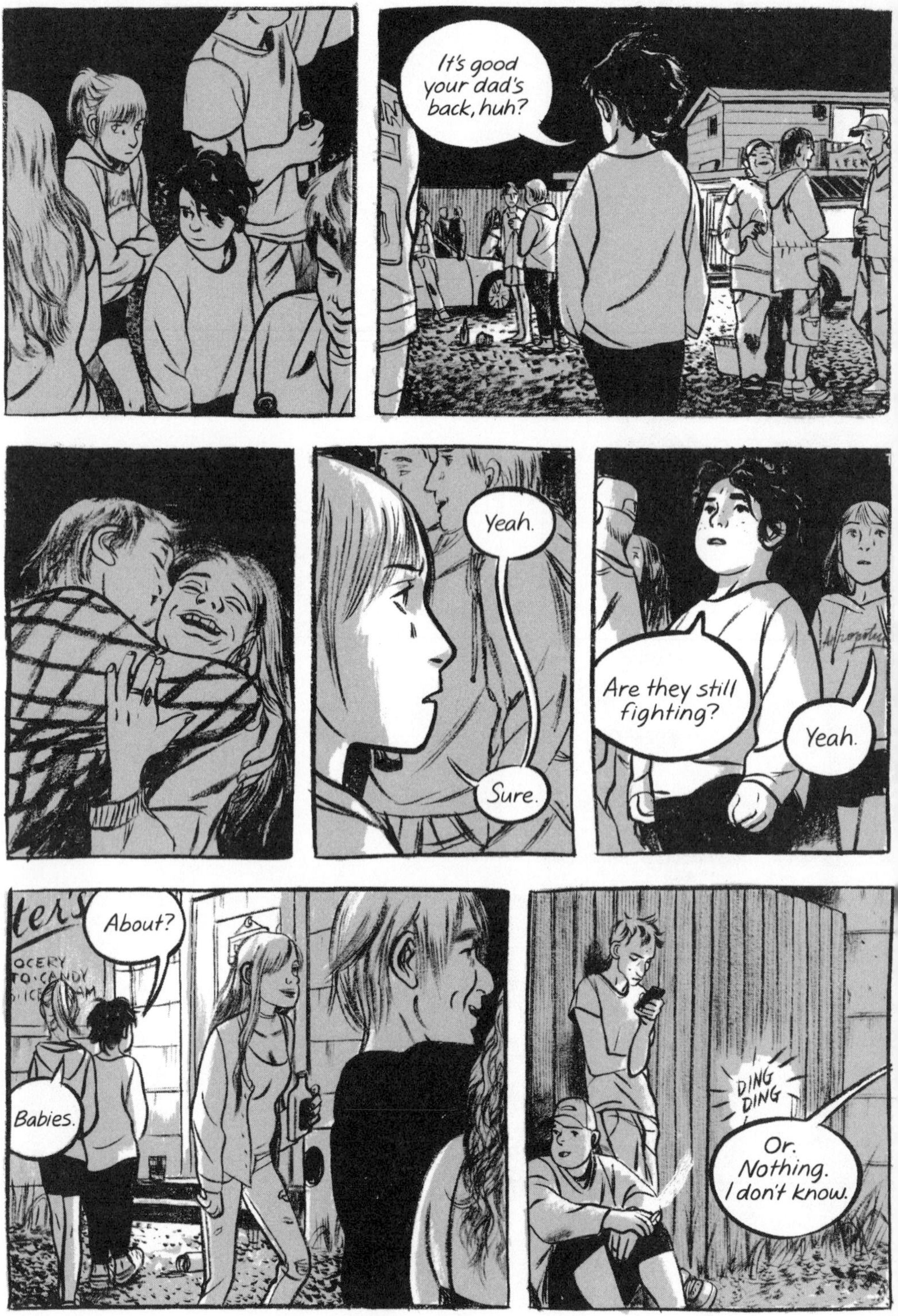
It's good your dad's back, huh?
Yeah.
Sure.
Are they still fighting?
Yeah.
About?
Babies.
DING DING
Or. Nothing. I don't know.

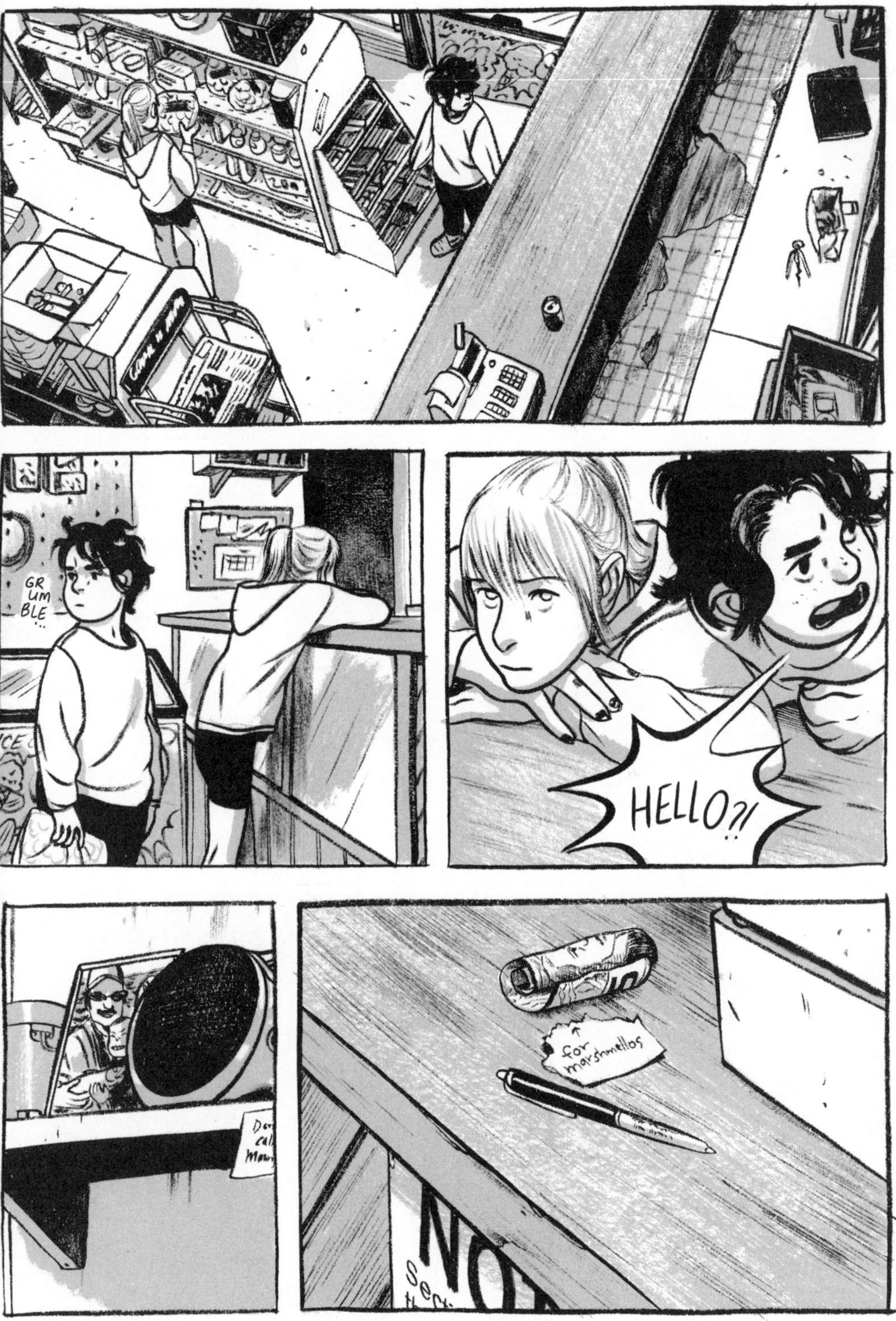
GRUMBLE...
HELLO?!
for marshmellos

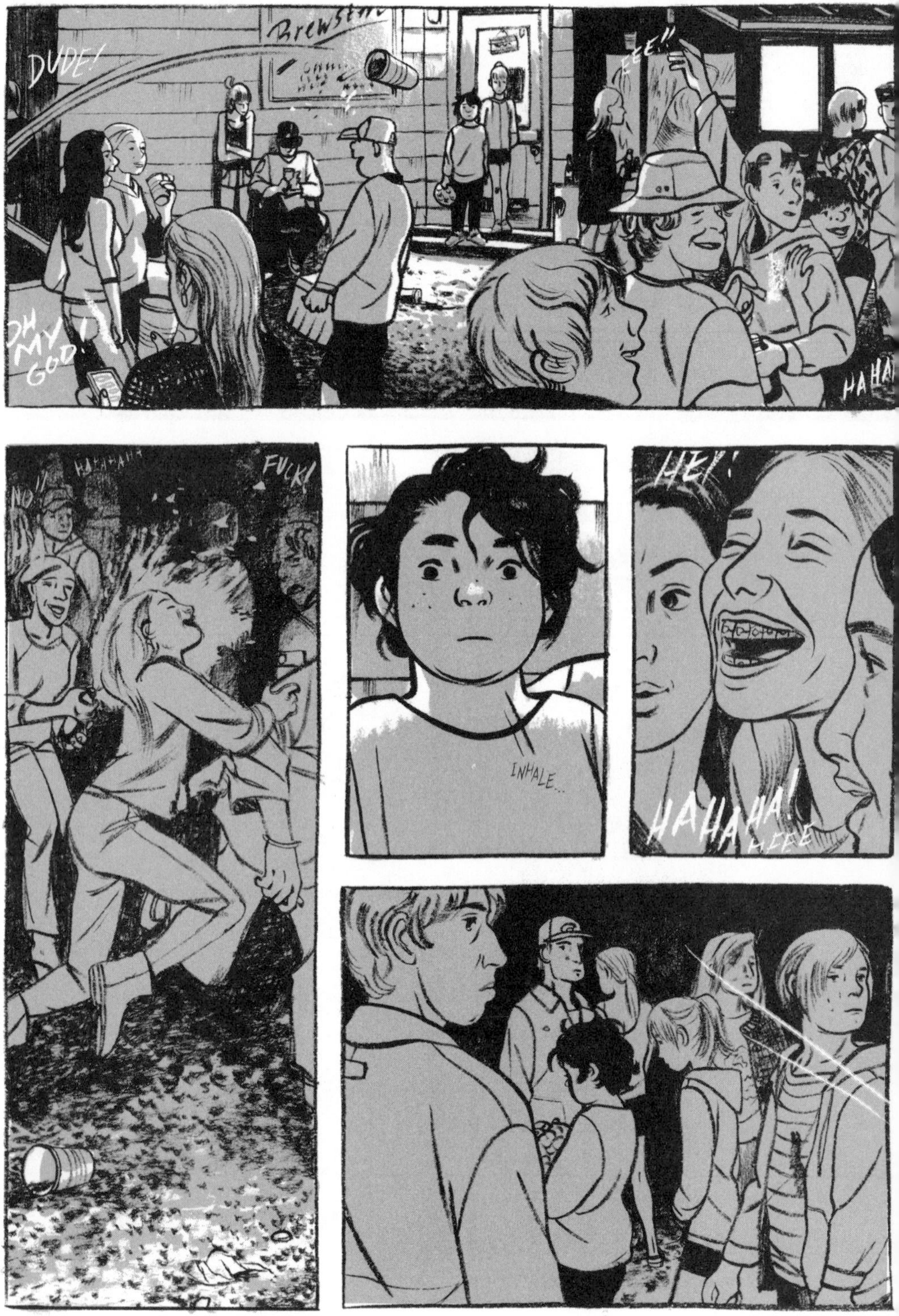
DUDE!
EEE!!
OH MY GOD!
HAHA
NO!!
HAHHAHA
FUCK!
INHALE...
HEY!
HAHAHA!
HEEE

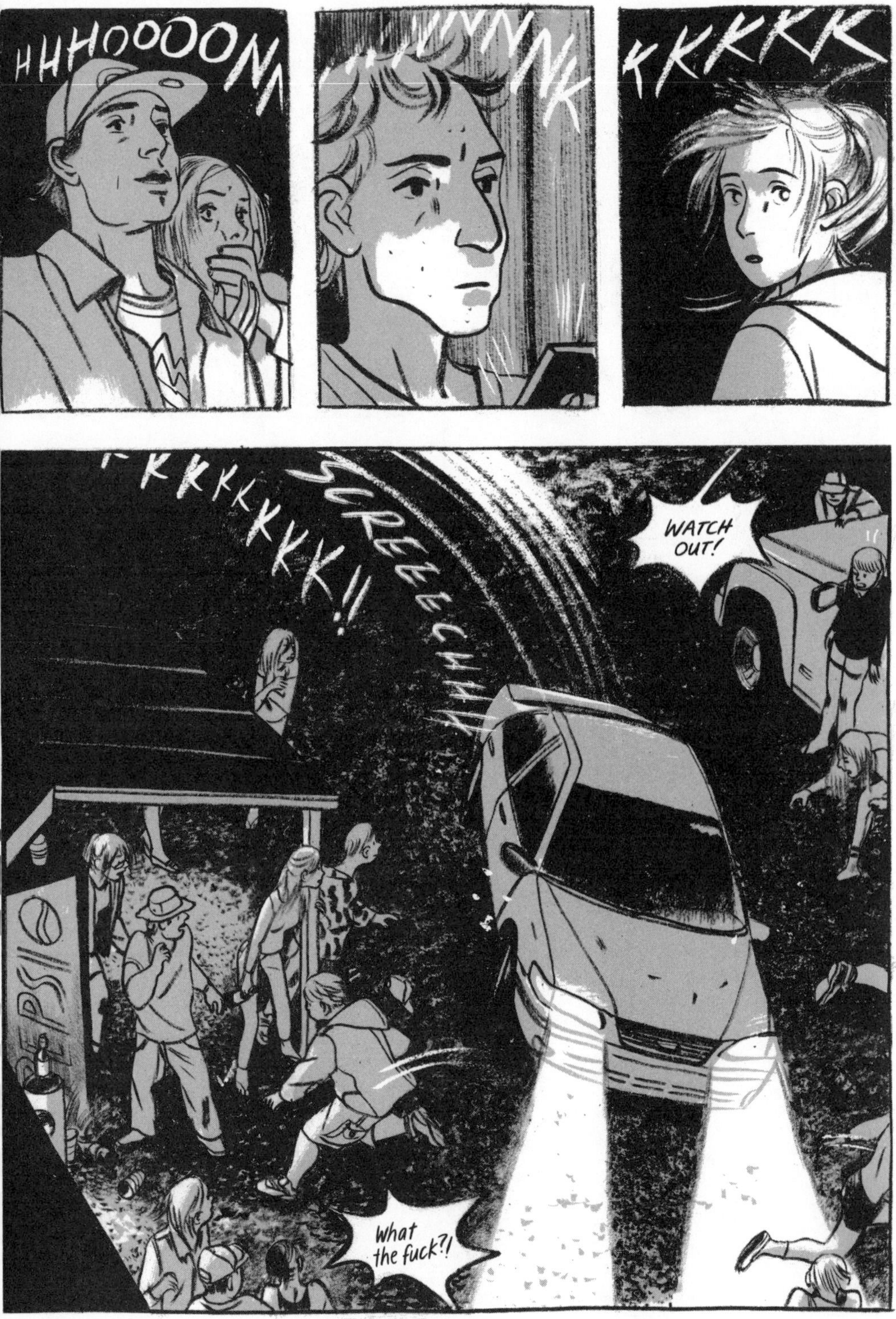
HHHOOOOM
NNNNK
KKKKK
RKKKKKKKKK!!
SCREEECHHH
WATCH OUT!
What the fuck?!

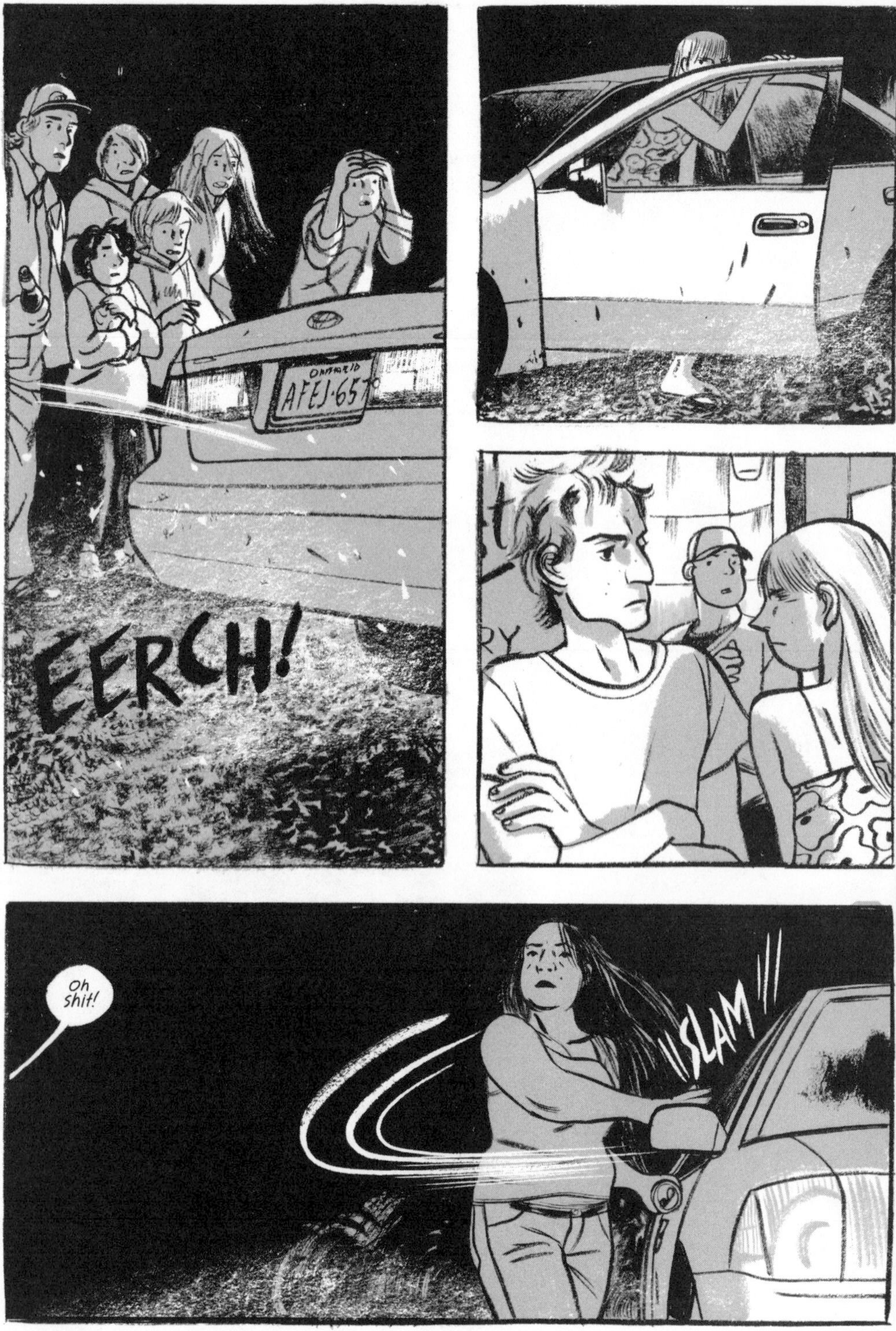
EERCH!
Oh shit!
SLAM

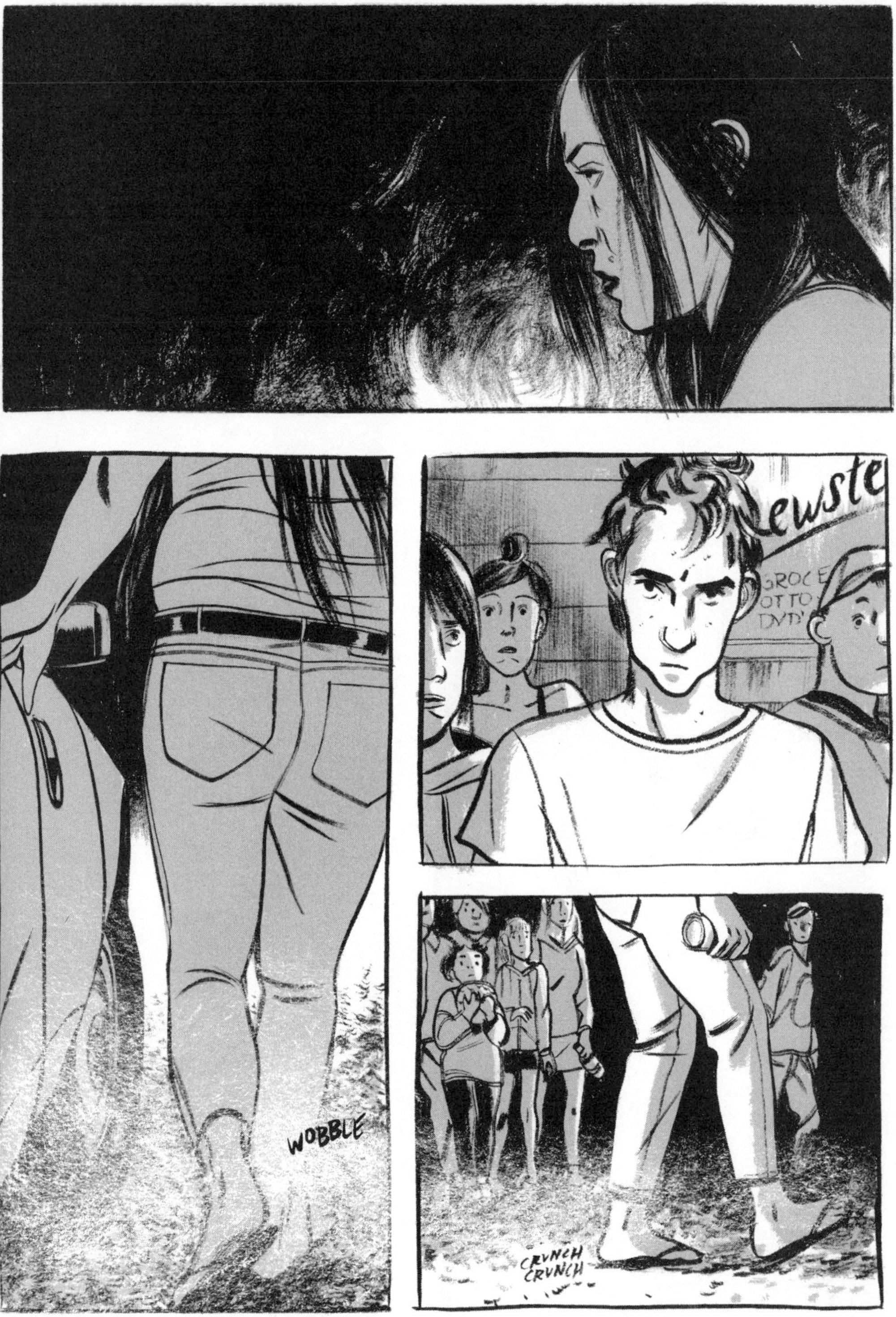
WOBBLE
CRUNCH CRUNCH

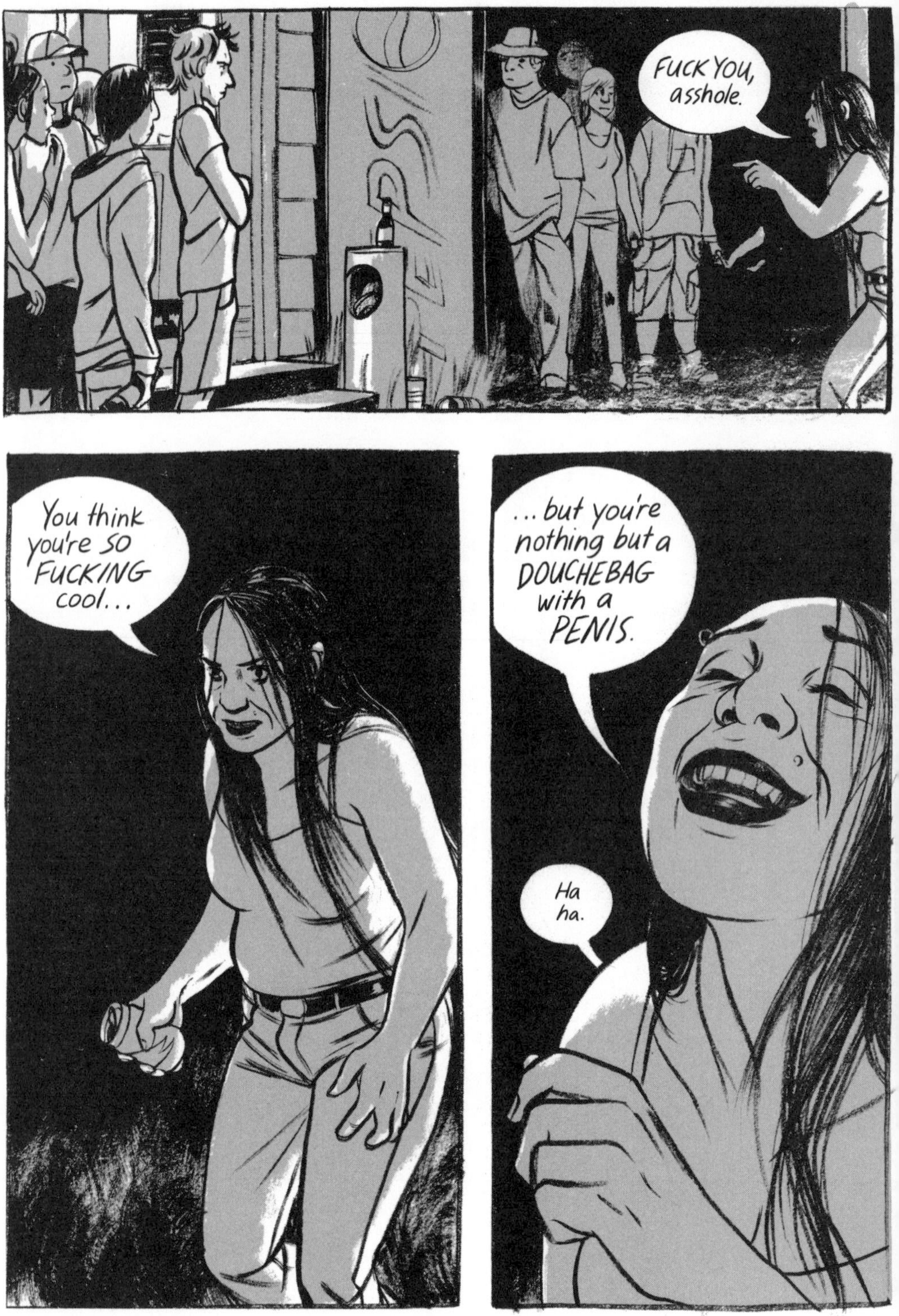
FUCK YOU, asshole.
You think you're SO FUCKING cool...
...but you're nothing but a DOUCHEBAG with a PENIS.
Ha ha.

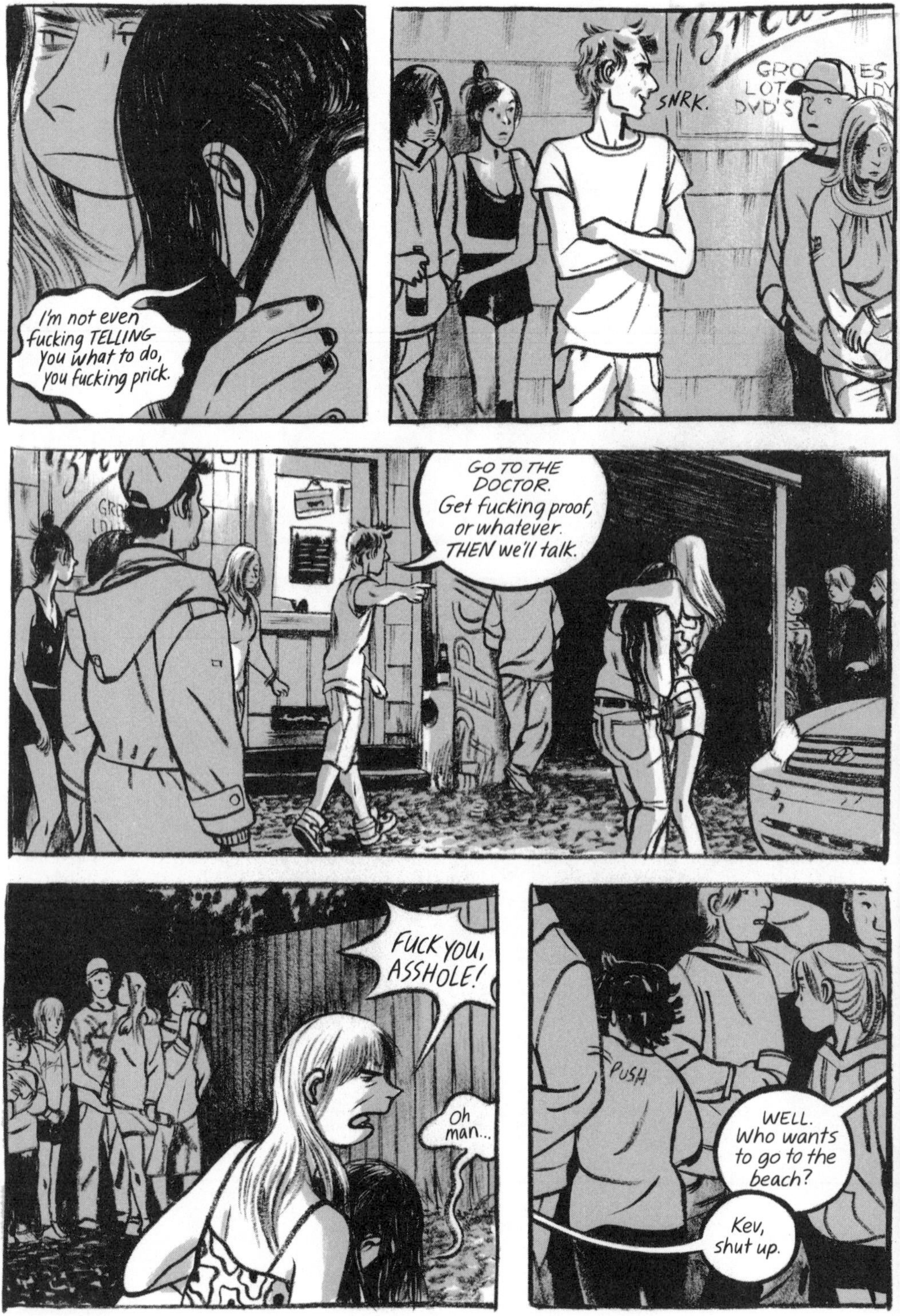
I'm not even fucking TELLING you what to do, you fucking prick.
SNRK.
GROCERIES
LOT
DVD'S
GO TO THE DOCTOR. Get fucking proof, or whatever. THEN we'll talk.
FUCK YOU, ASSHOLE!
Oh man...
PUSH
WELL. Who wants to go to the beach?
Kev, shut up.

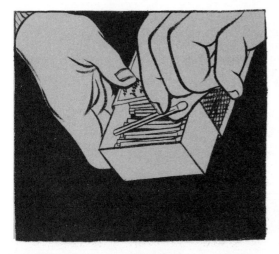

ftch

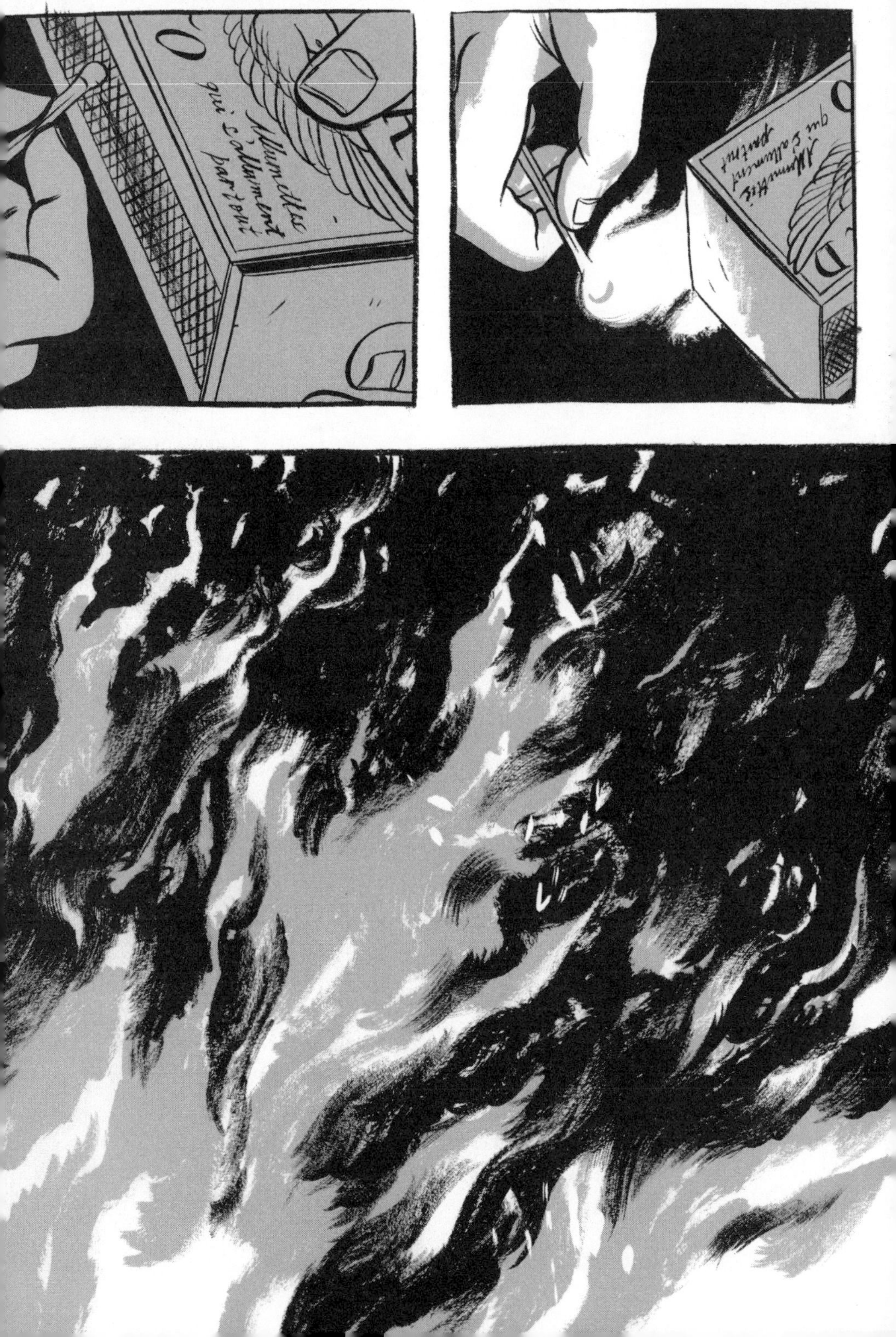
Allumettes qui s'allument partout
Allumettes qui s'allument partout

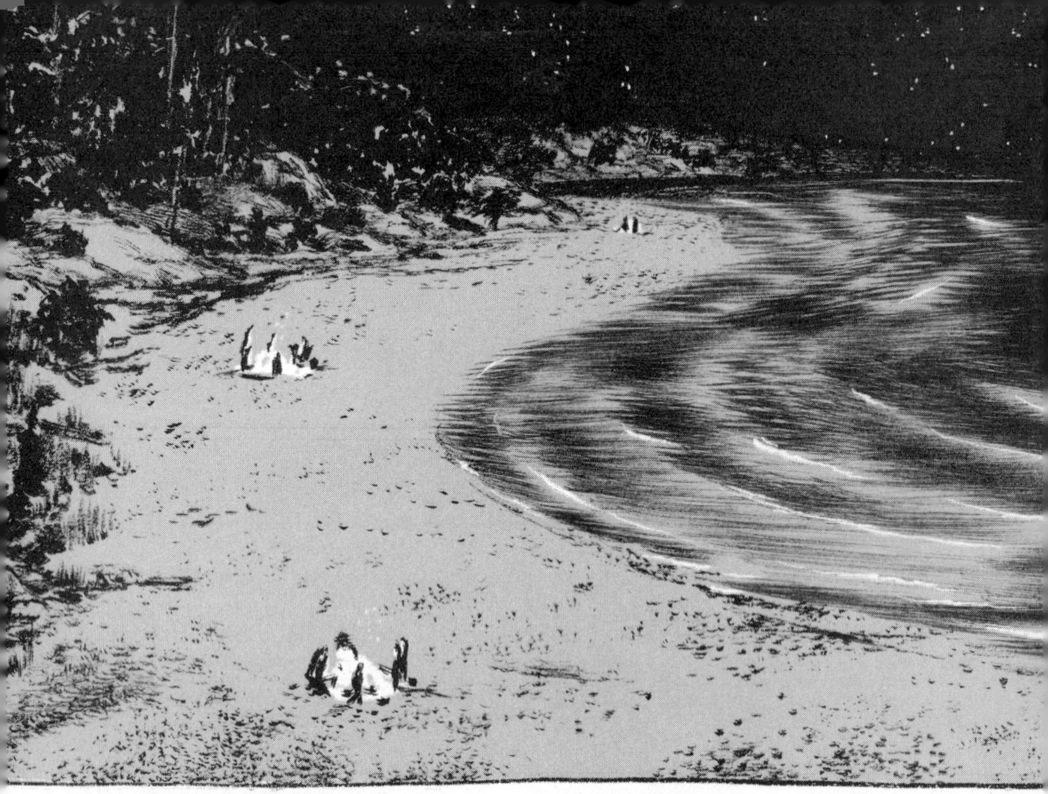

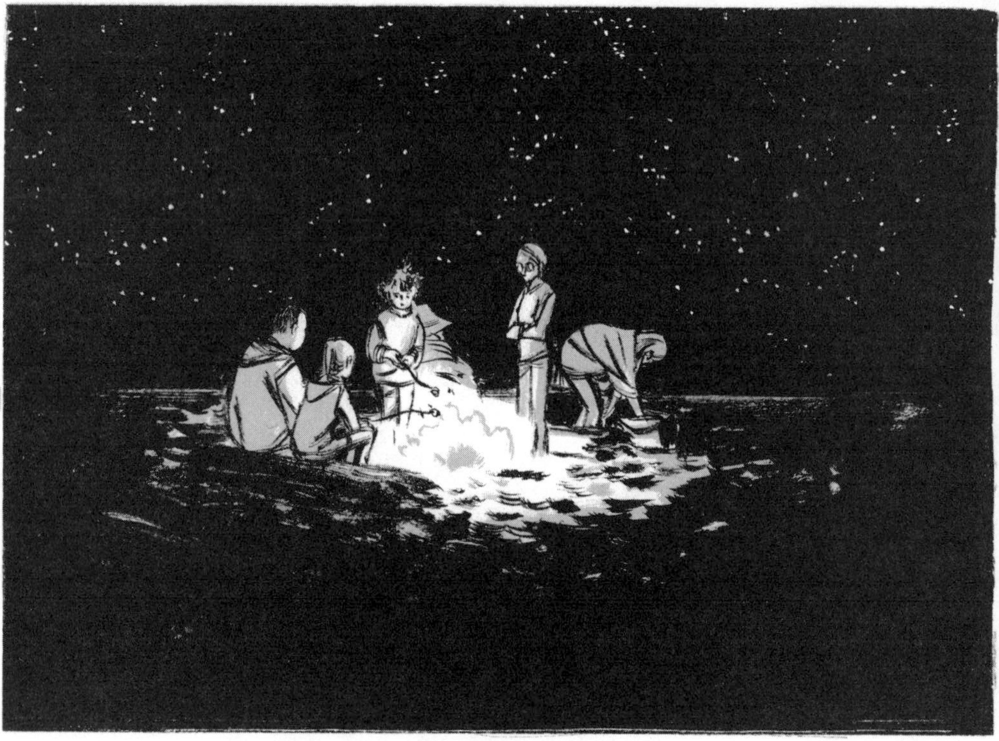

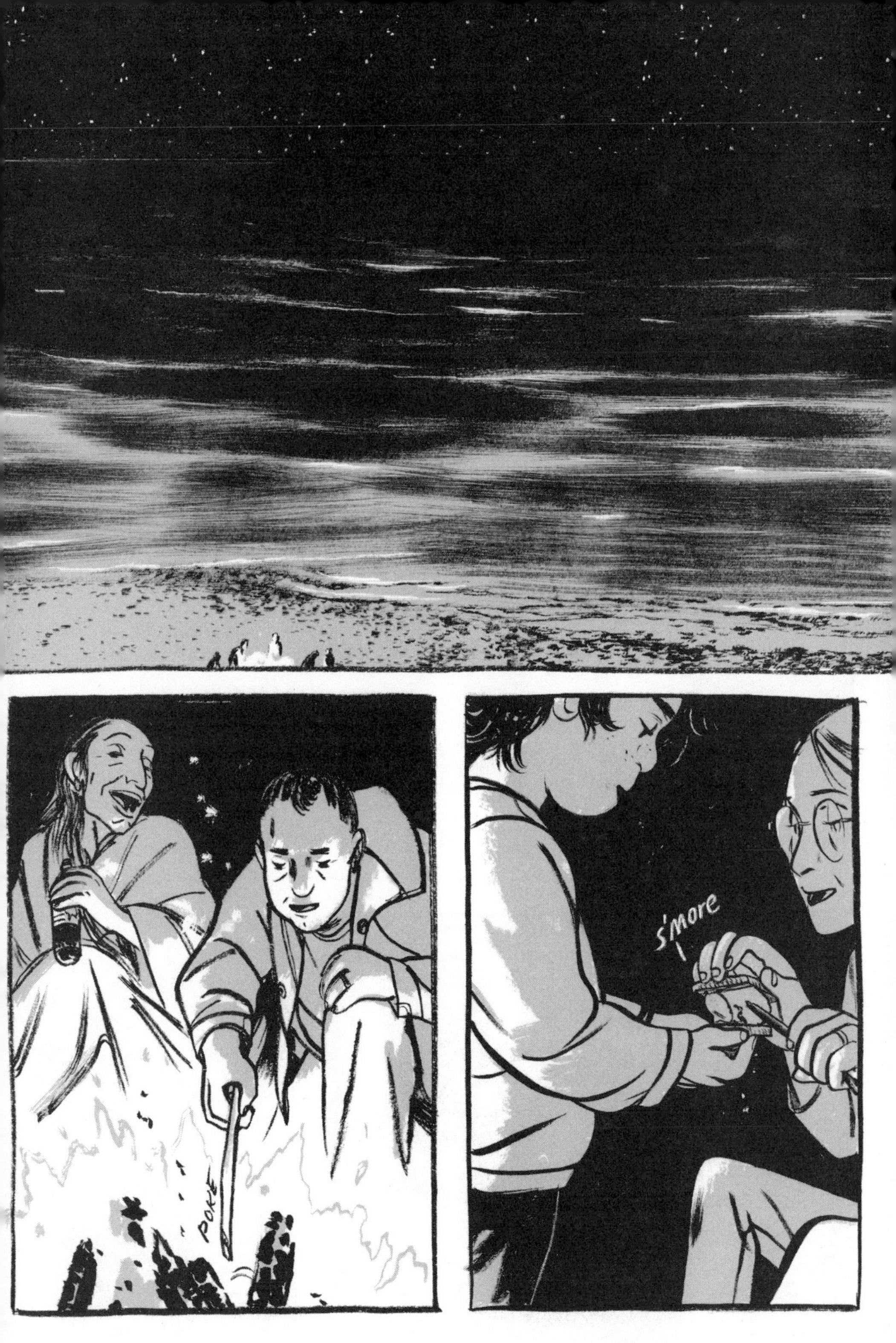
POKE
s'more

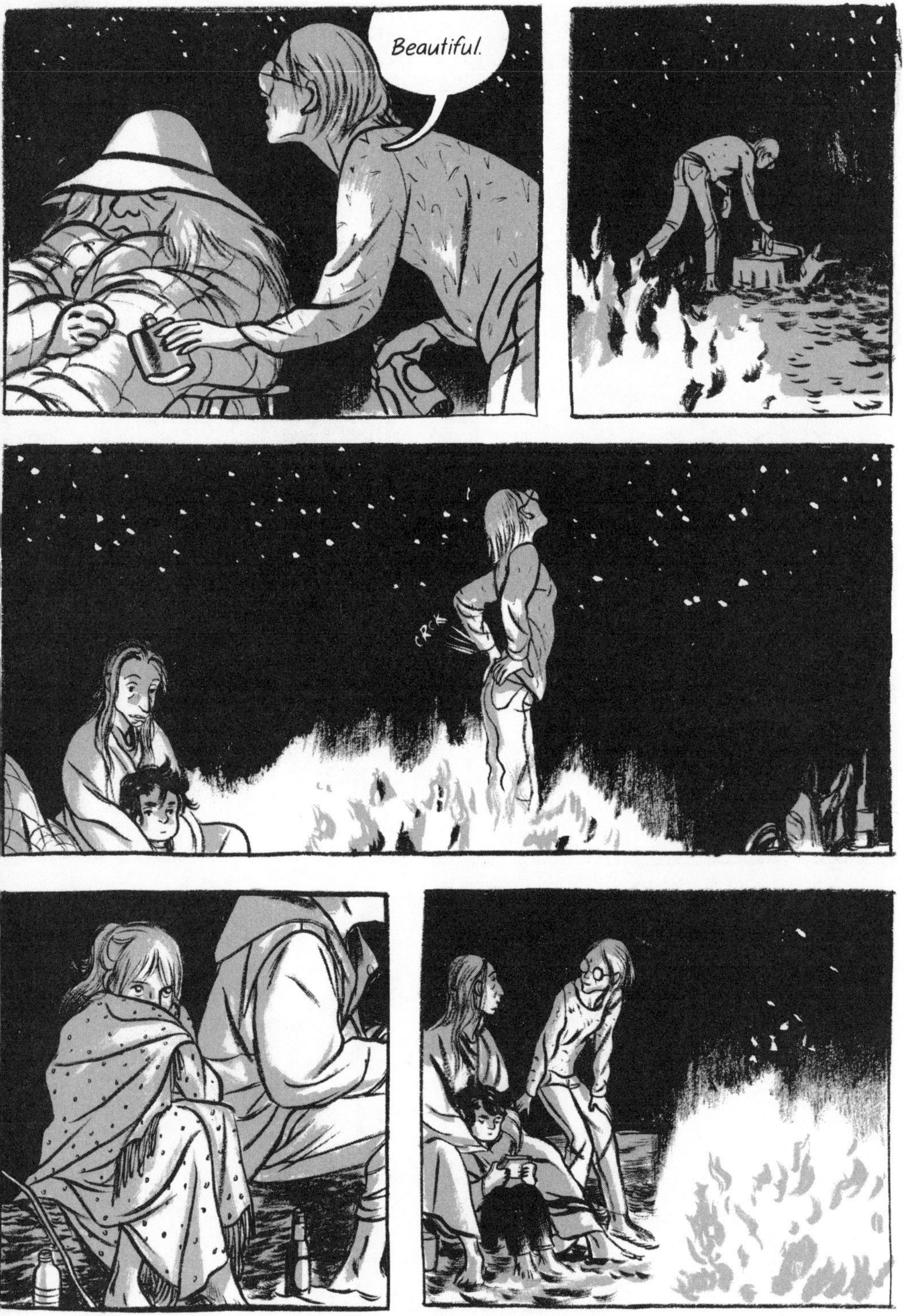
Beautiful.
CRCK

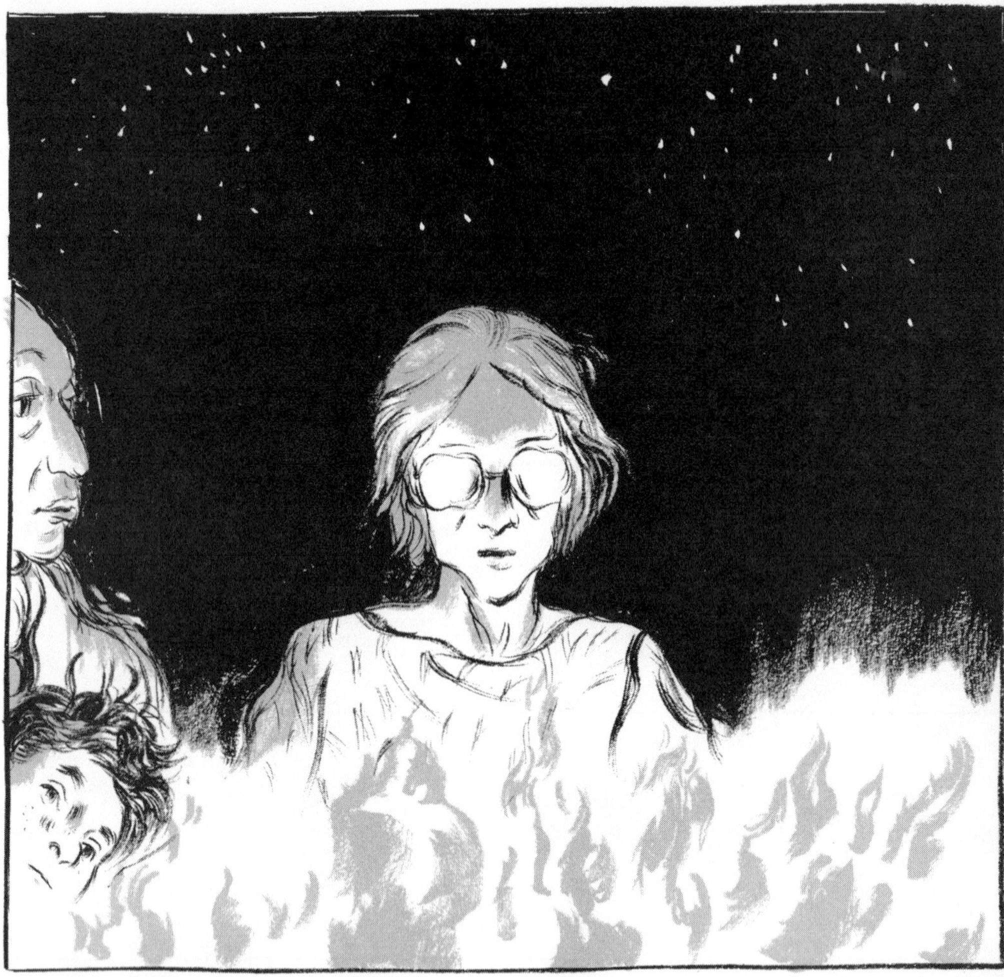

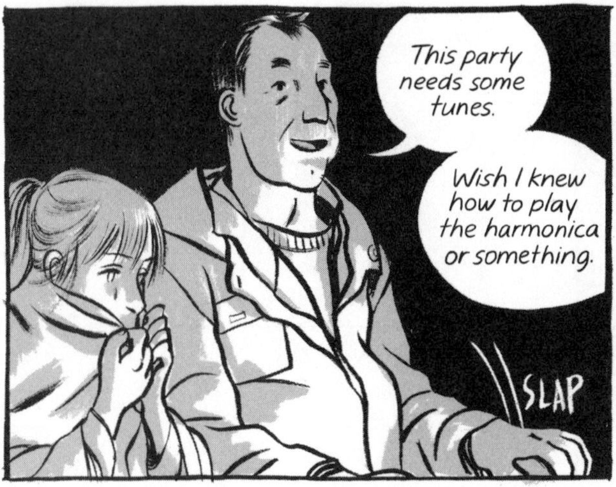
This party needs some tunes.
Wish I knew how to play the harmonica or something.
SLAP

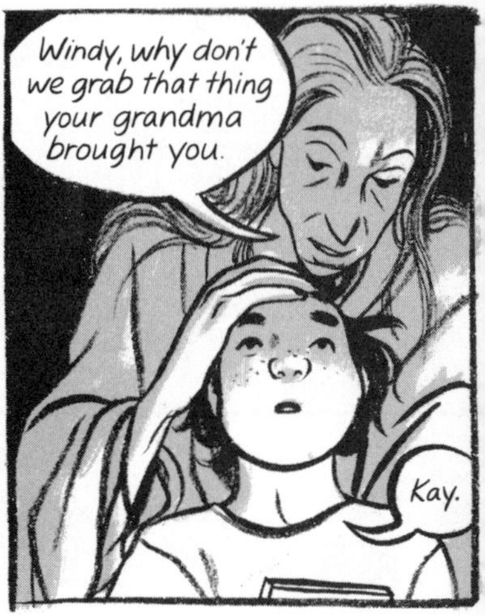
Windy, why don't we grab that thing your grandma brought you.
Kay.

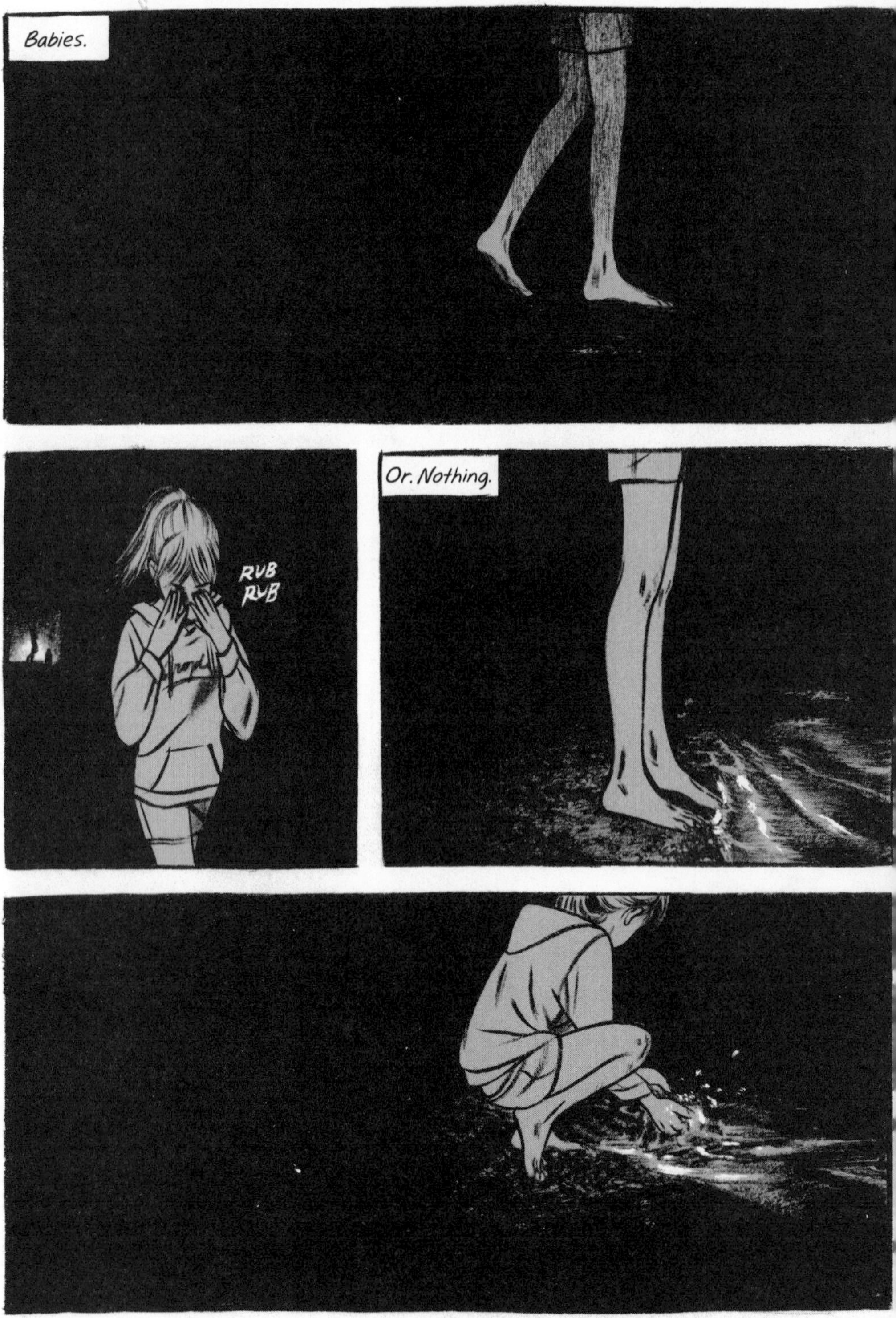
Babies.
RUB
RUB
Or. Nothing.

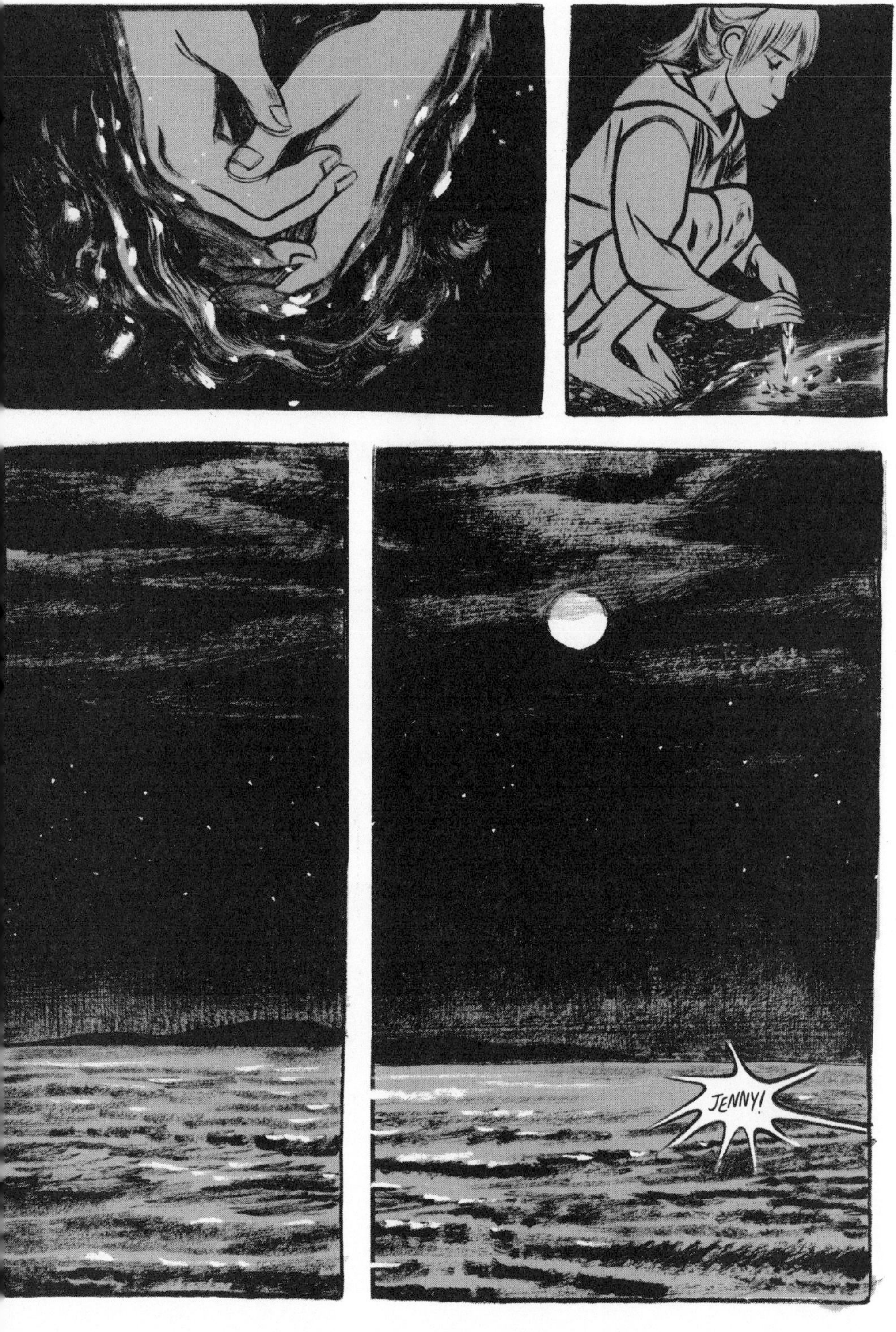
JENNY!

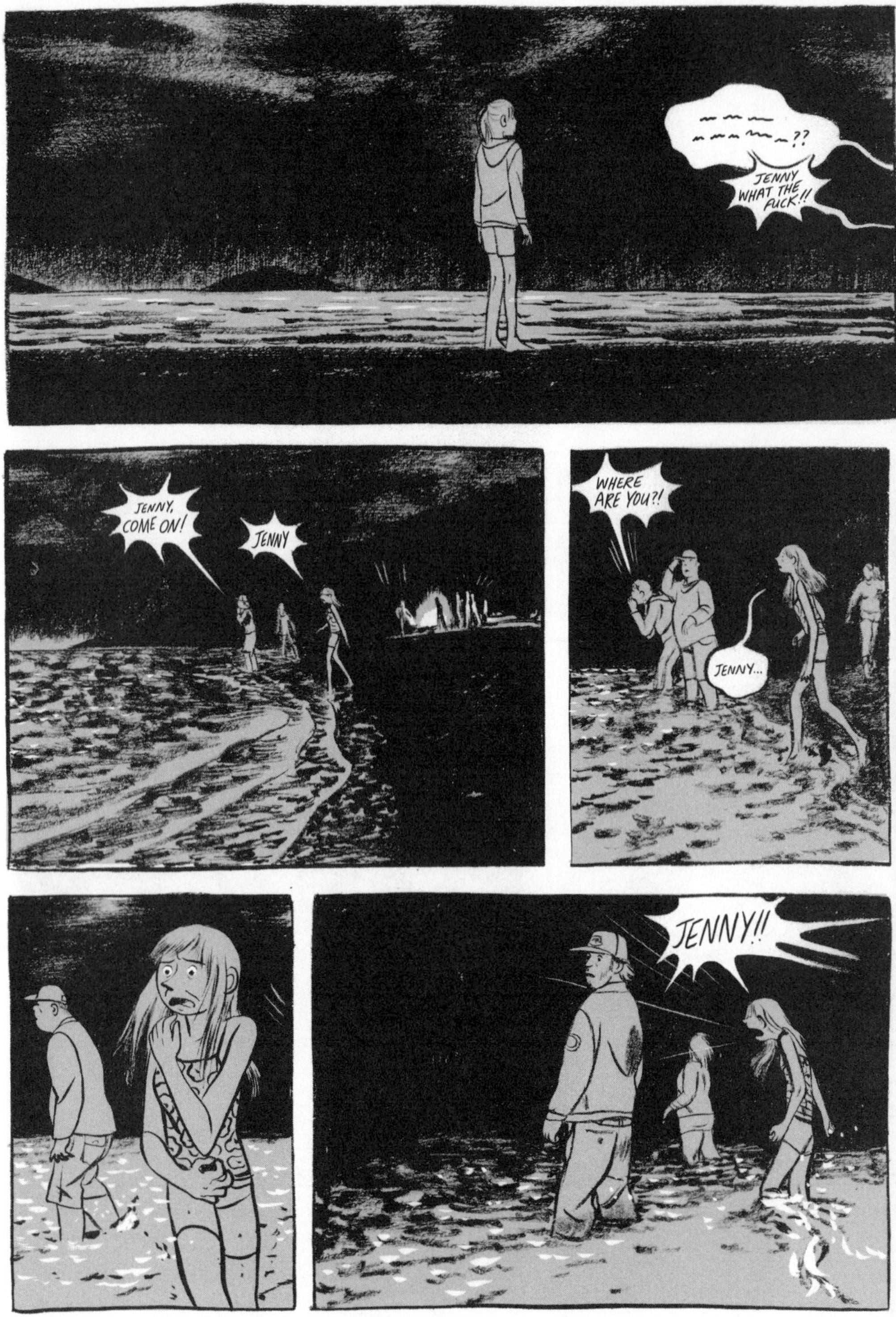

JENNY WHAT THE FUCK!!
JENNY, COME ON!
JENNY
WHERE ARE YOU?!
JENNY...
JENNY!!

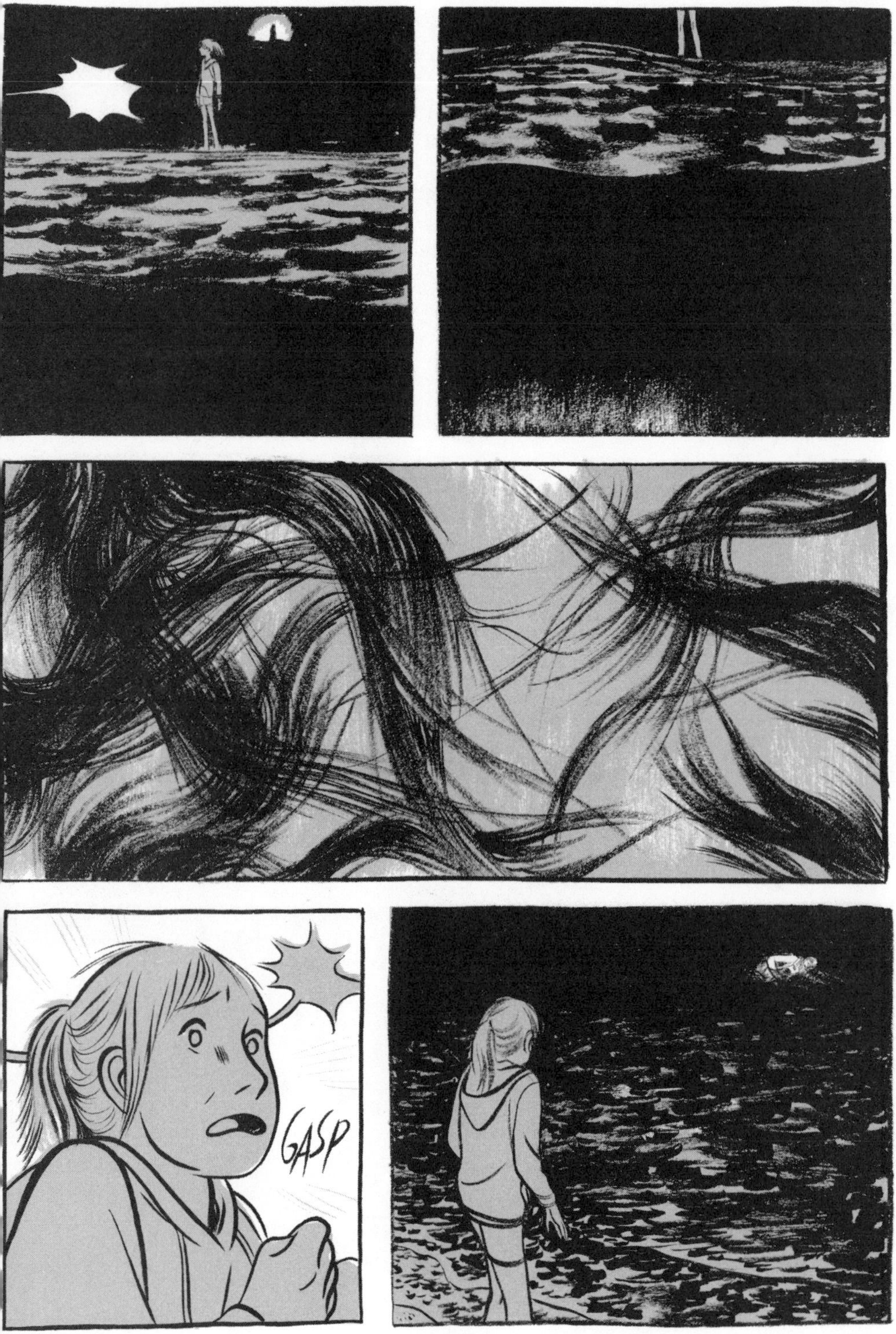
GASP

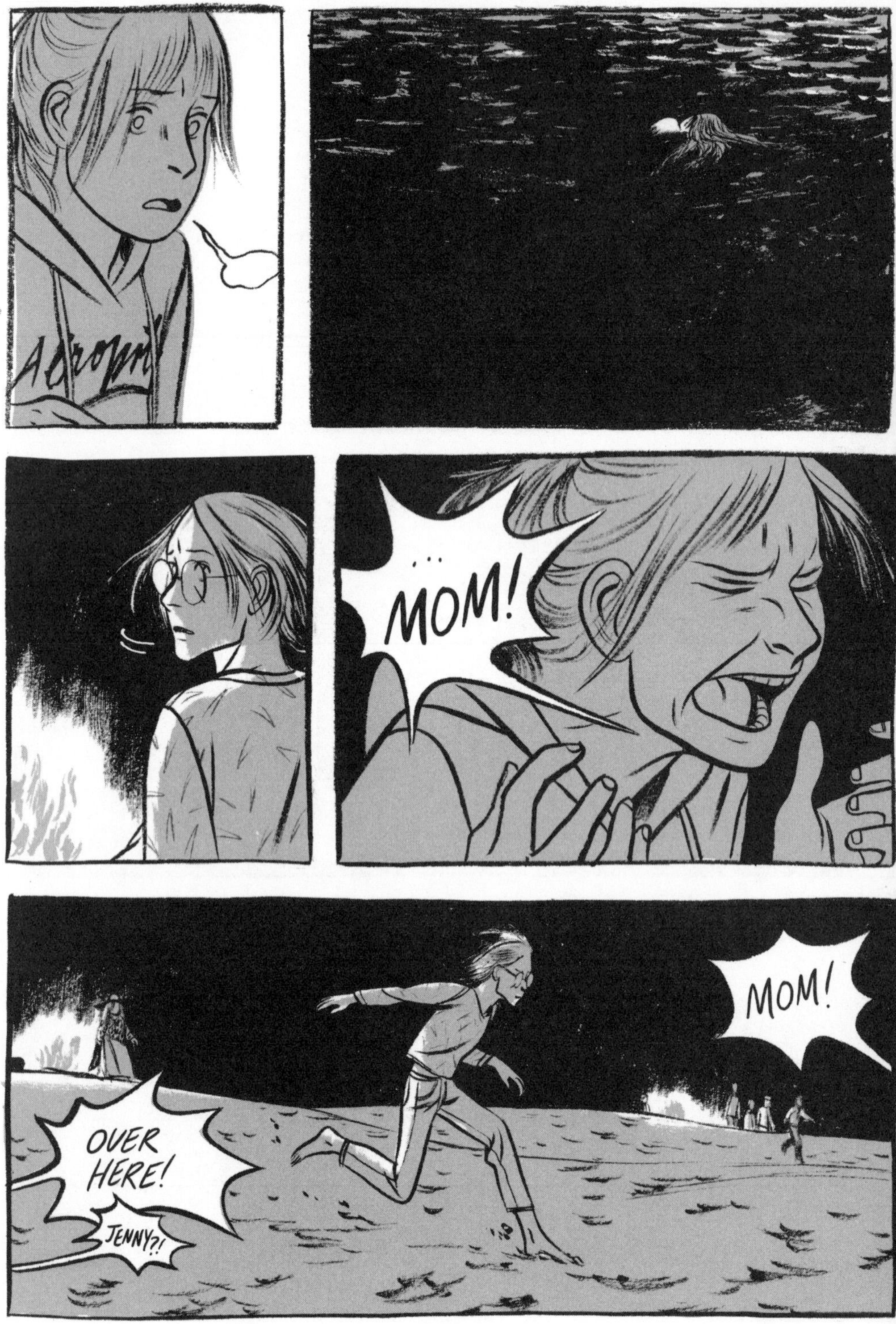
... MOM!
MOM!
OVER HERE!
JENNY?!

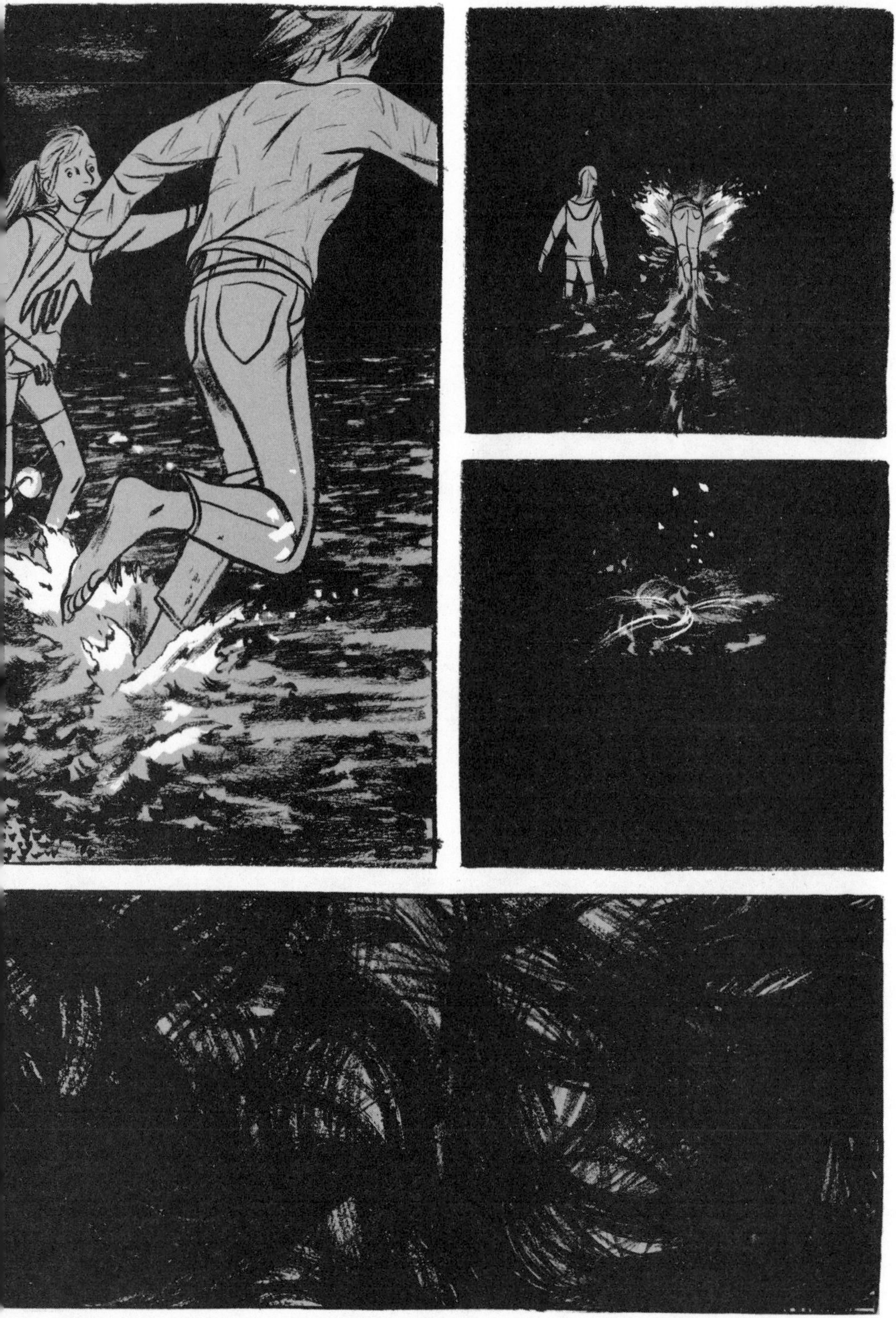

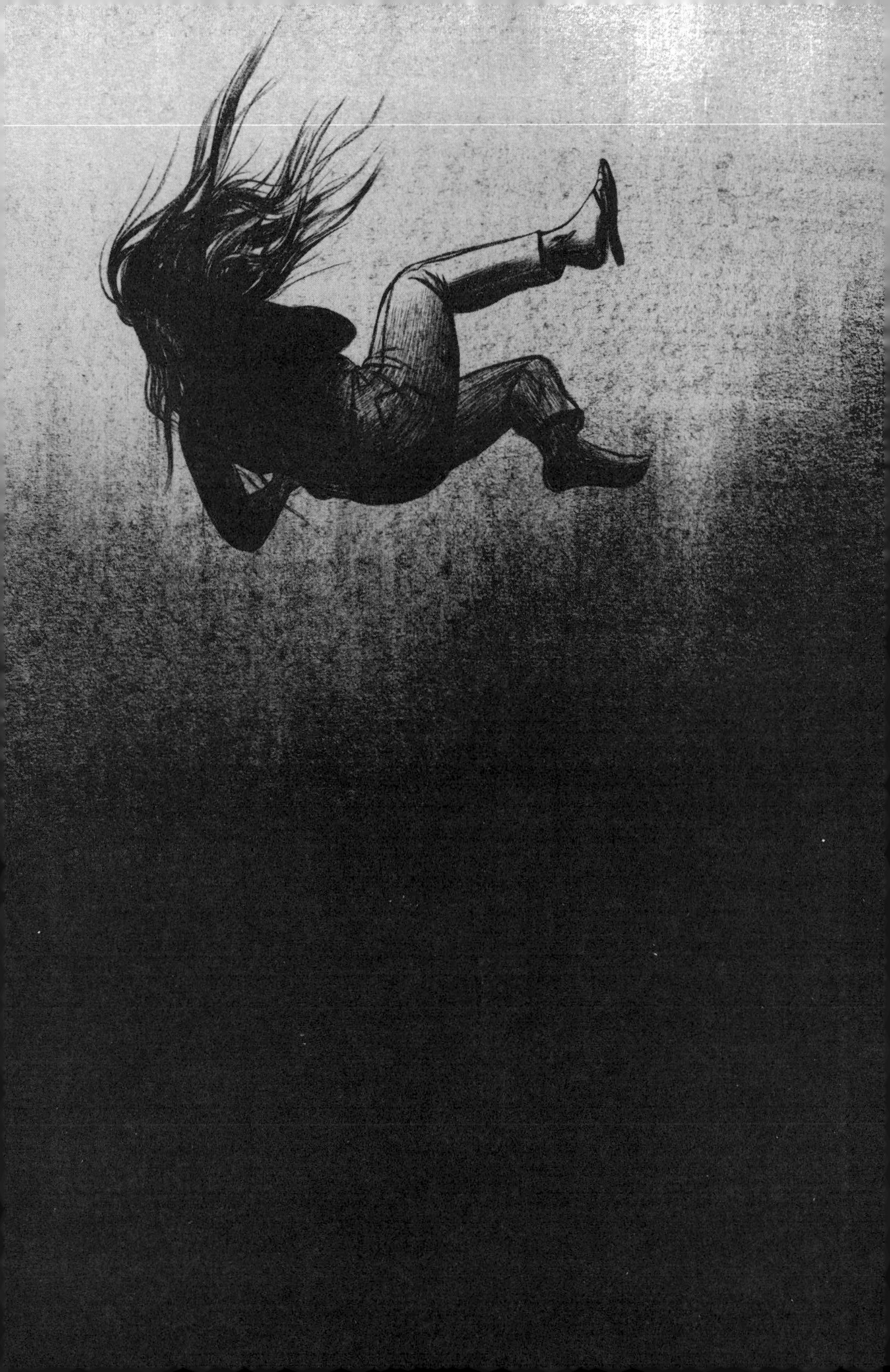

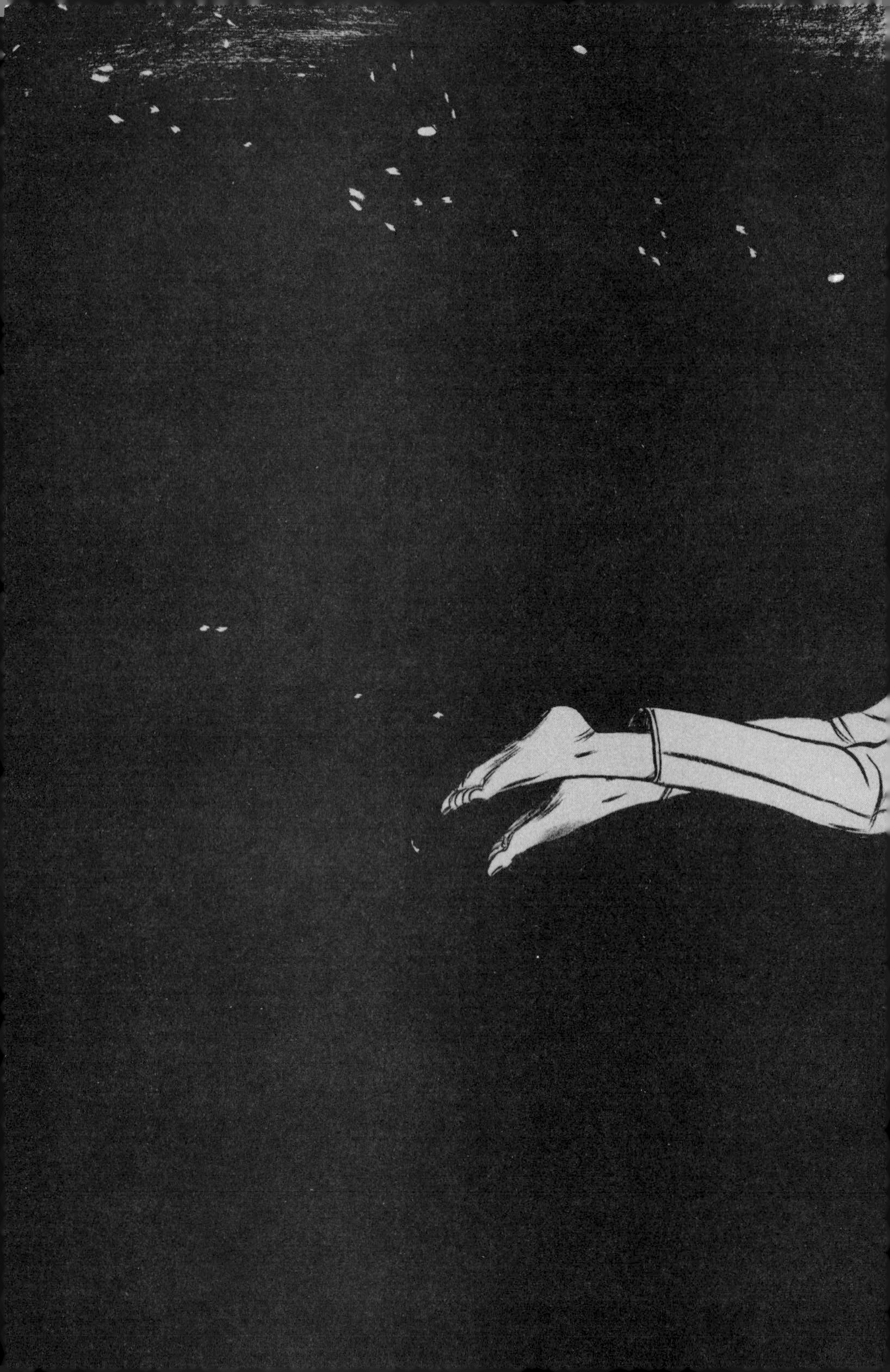

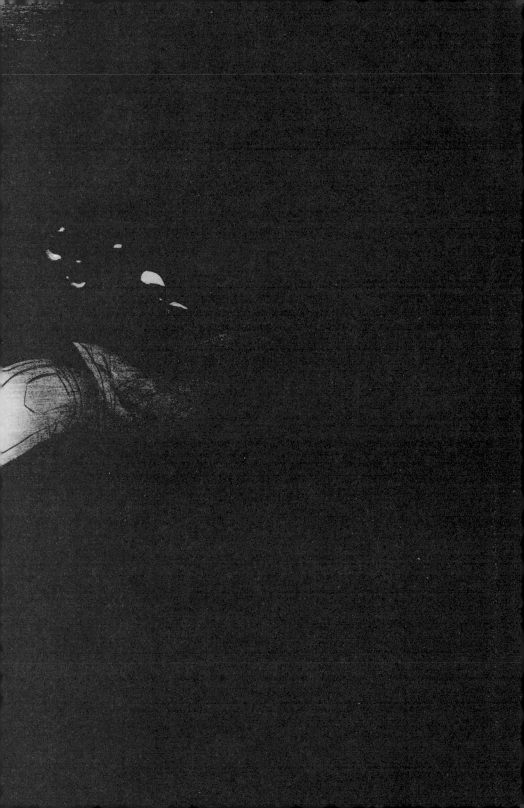

My mom told me.
Used to tell me all the time.
That she dreamed of me before I was born.

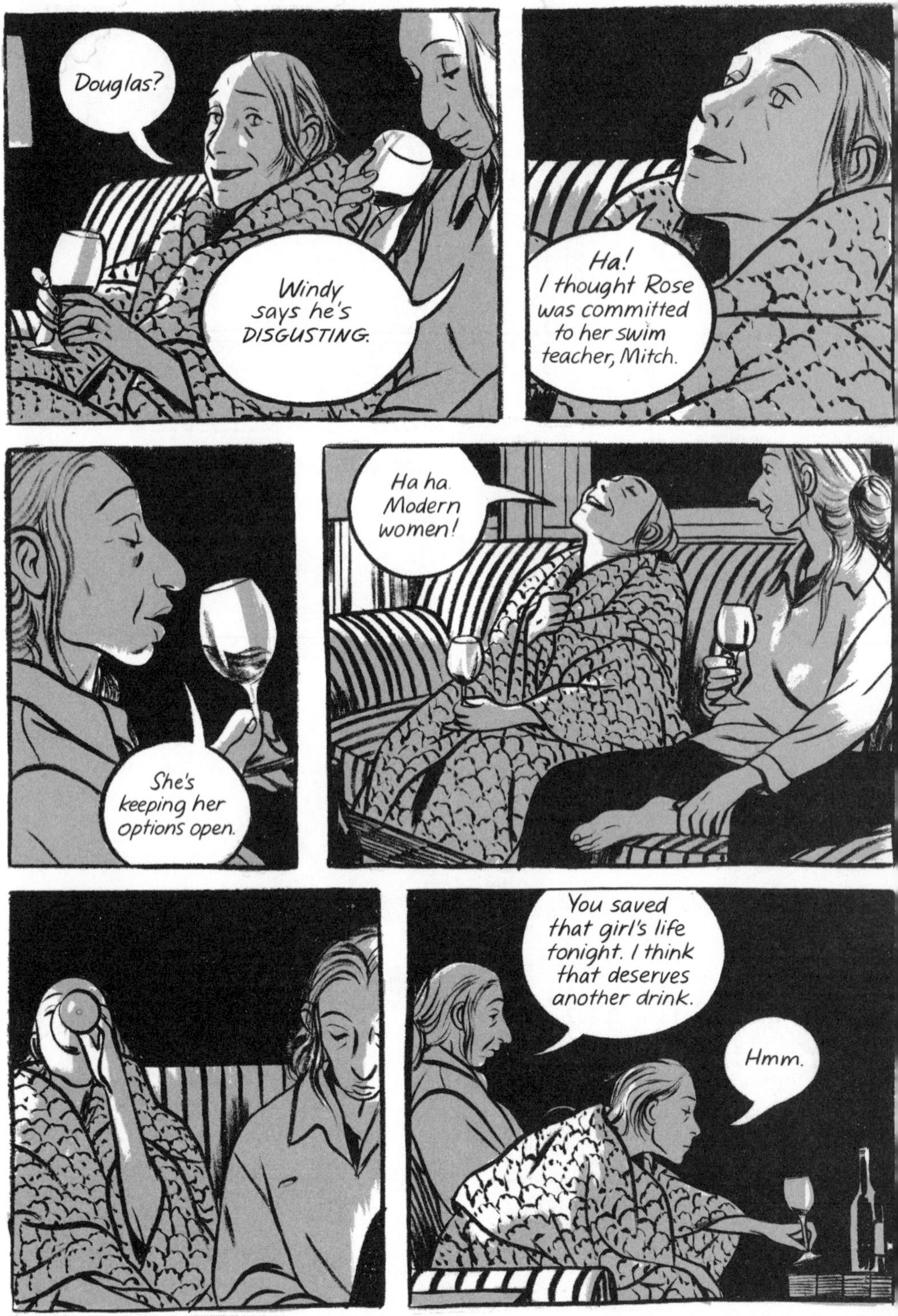
Douglas?
Windy says he's DISGUSTING.
Ha! I thought Rose was committed to her swim teacher, Mitch.
She's keeping her options open.
Ha ha. Modern women!
You saved that girl's life tonight. I think that deserves another drink.
Hmm.

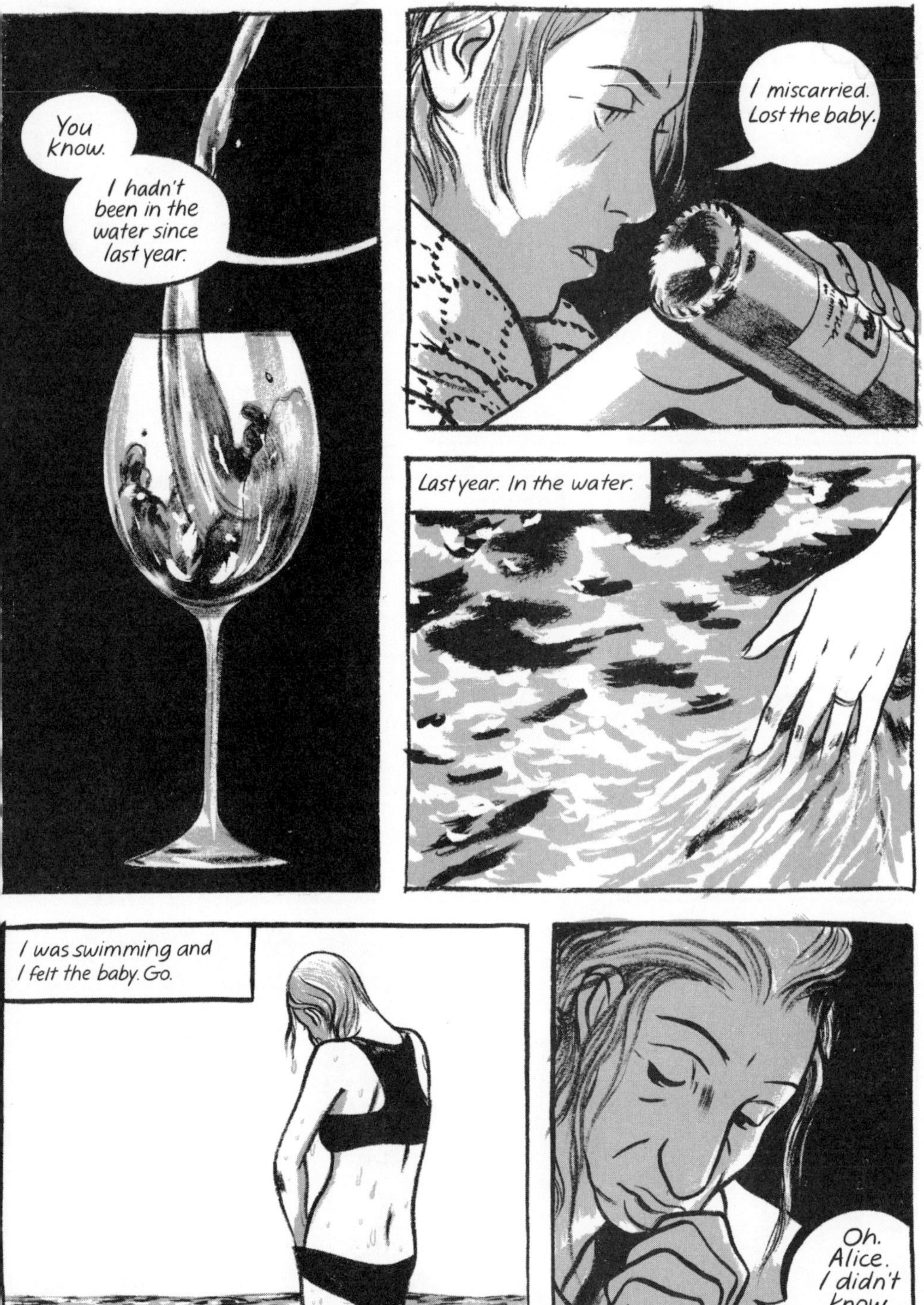
You know.
I hadn't been in the water since last year.
I miscarried. Lost the baby.
Last year. In the water.
I was swimming and I felt the baby. Go.
Oh. Alice. I didn't know.

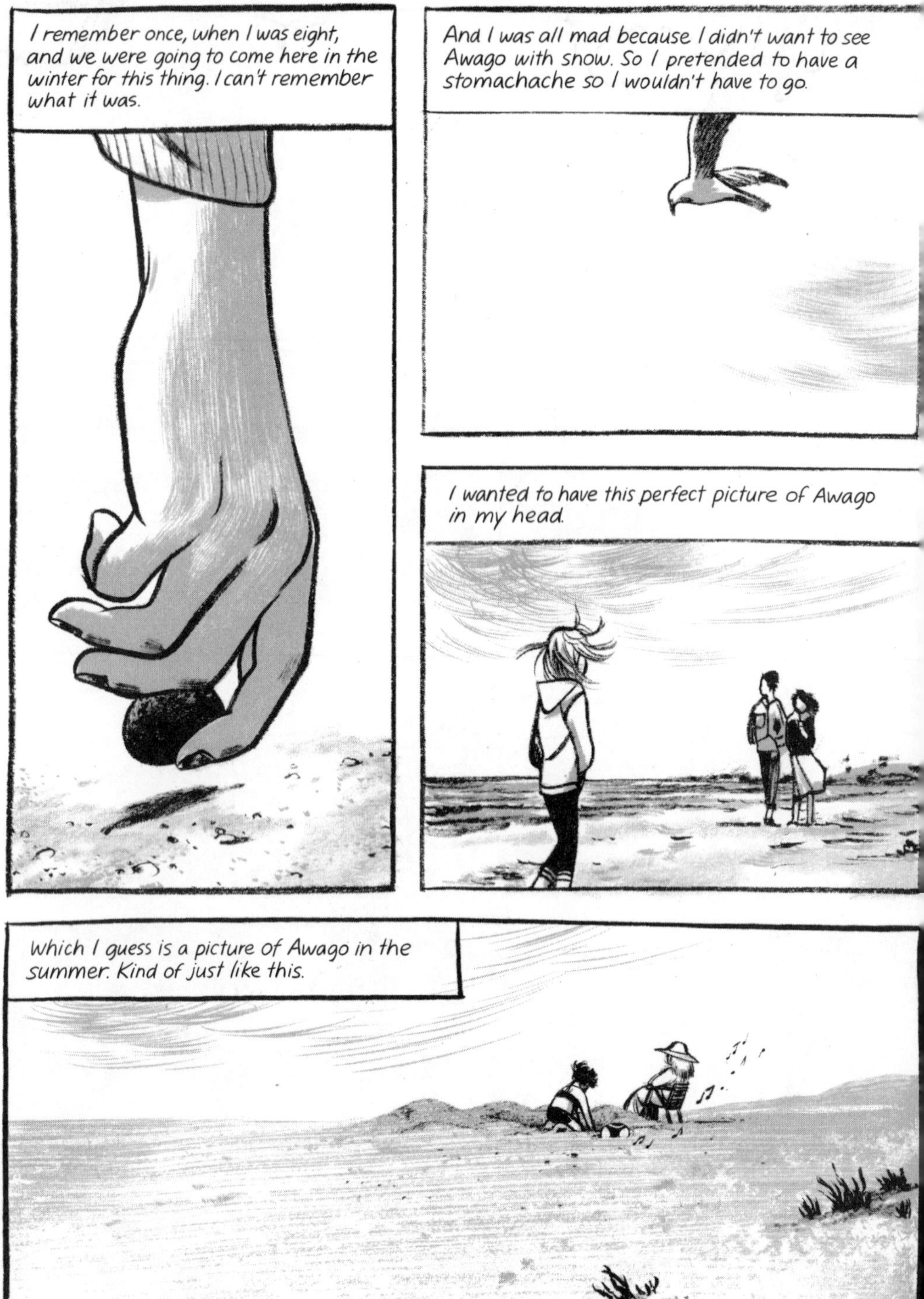
I remember once, when I was eight, and we were going to come here in the winter for this thing. I can't remember what it was.
And I was all mad because I didn't want to see Awago with snow. So I pretended to have a stomachache so I wouldn't have to go.
I wanted to have this perfect picture of Awago in my head.
Which I guess is a picture of Awago in the summer. Kind of just like this.

304

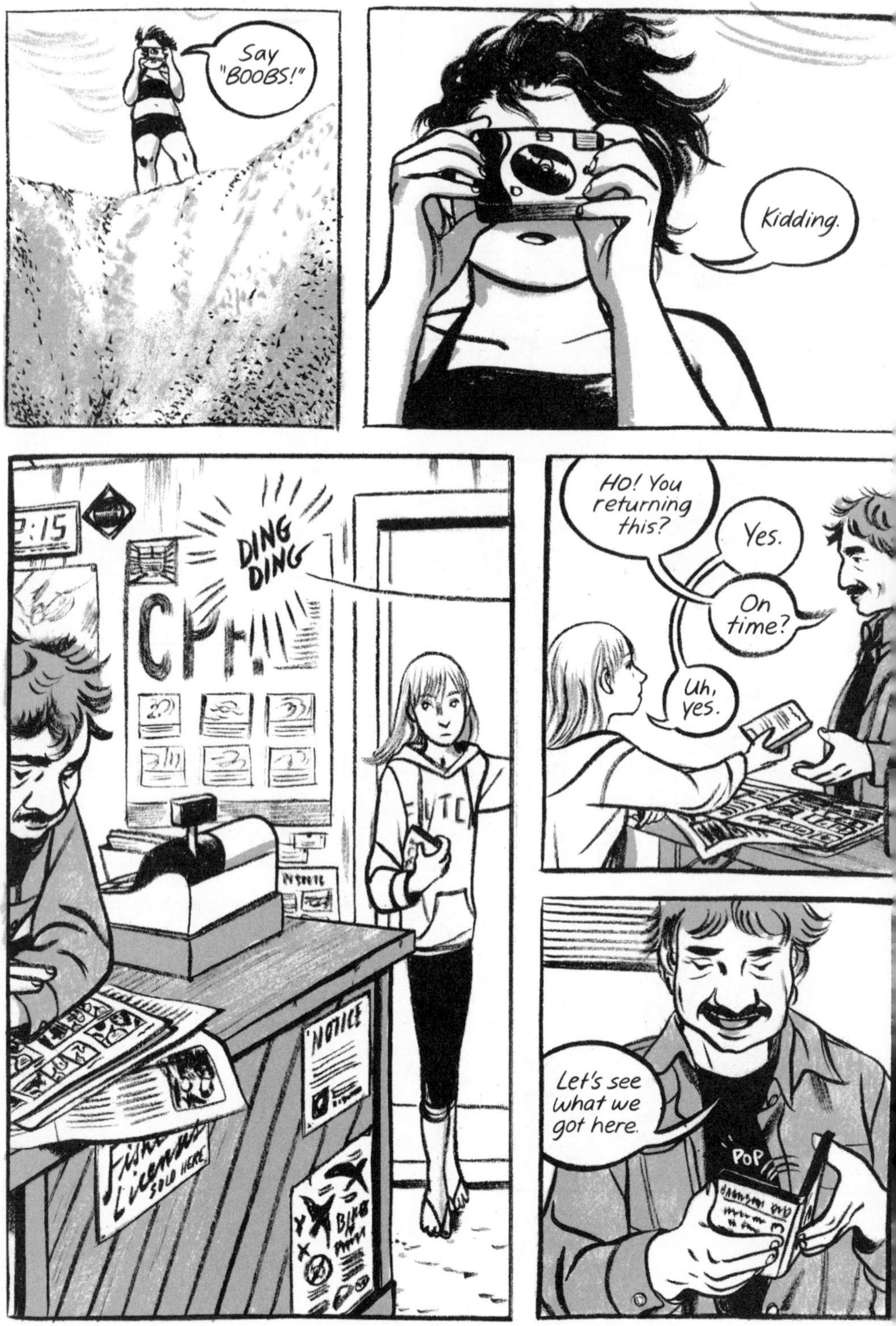
Say "BOOBS!"
Kidding.
DING DING
HO! You returning this?
Yes.
On time?
Uh, yes.
Let's see what we got here.
POP

308

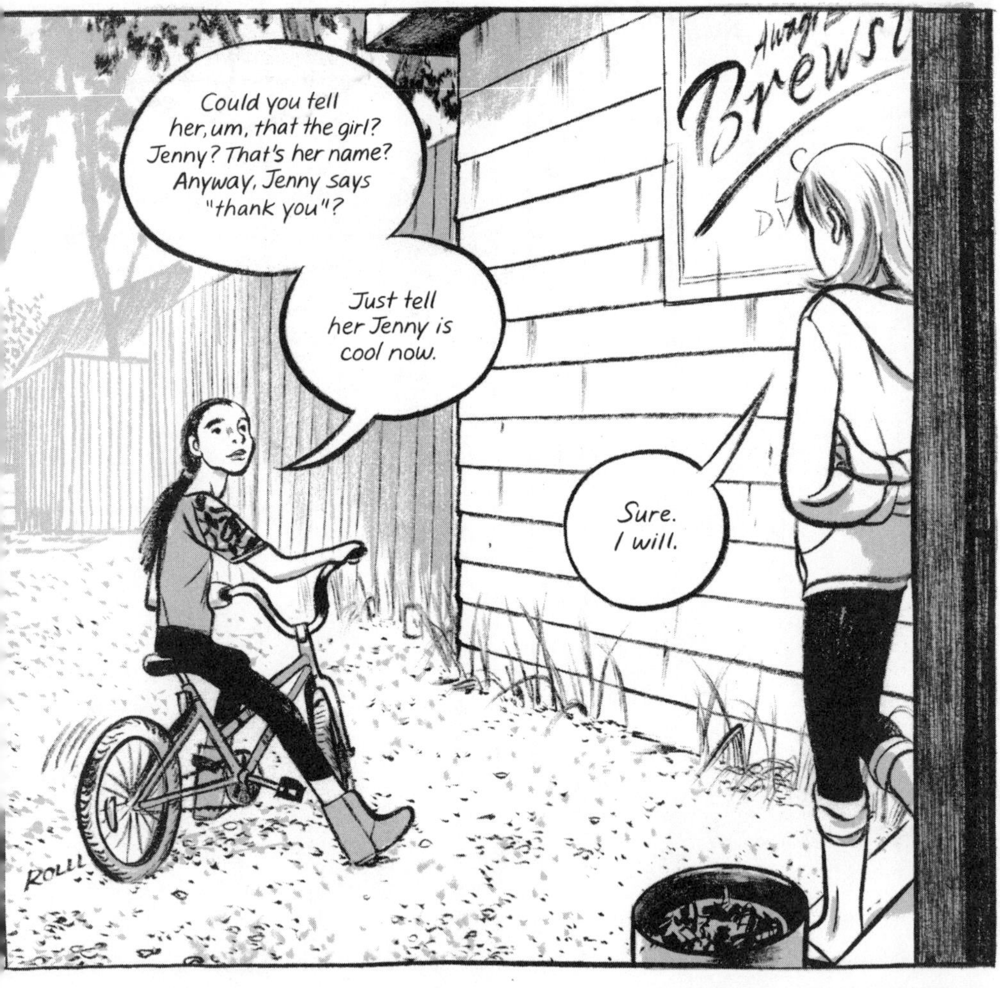
Could you tell her, um, that the girl? Jenny? That's her name? Anyway, Jenny says "thank you"?
Just tell her Jenny is cool now.
Sure. I will.
ROLL

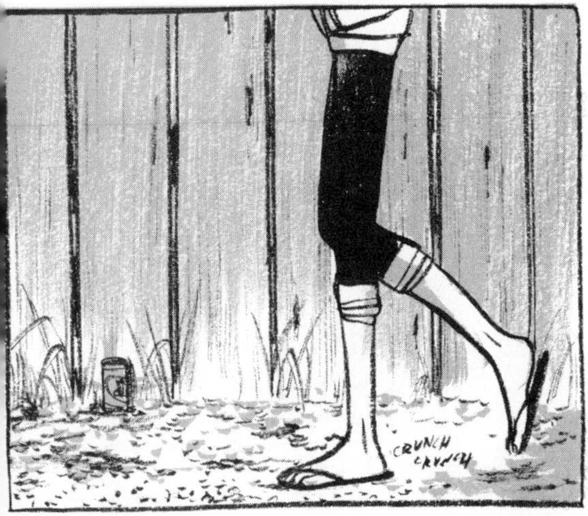
CRUNCH CRUNCH

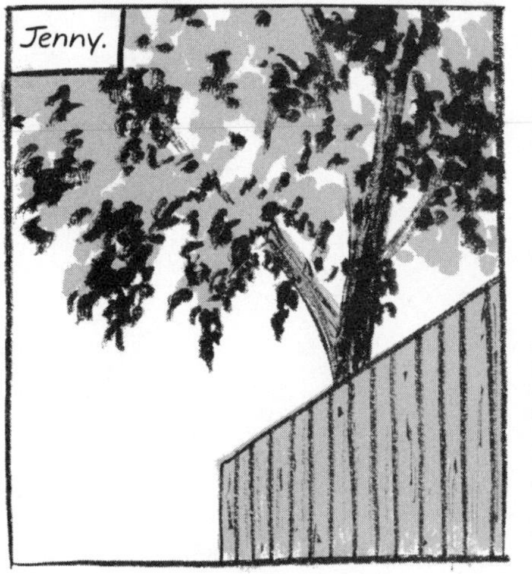
Jenny.

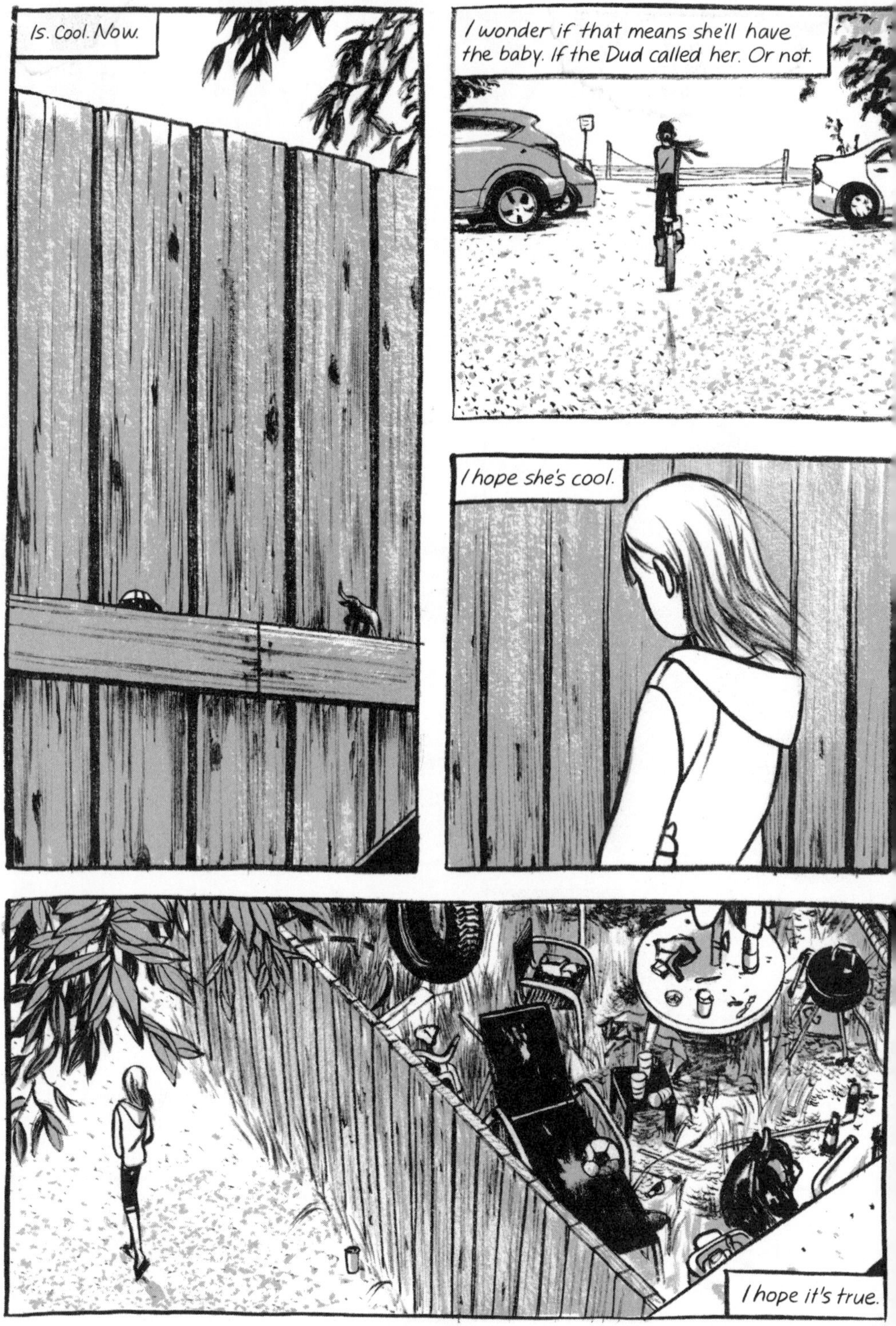
Is. Cool. Now.
I wonder if that means she'll have the baby. If the Dud called her. Or not.
I hope she's cool.
I hope it's true.

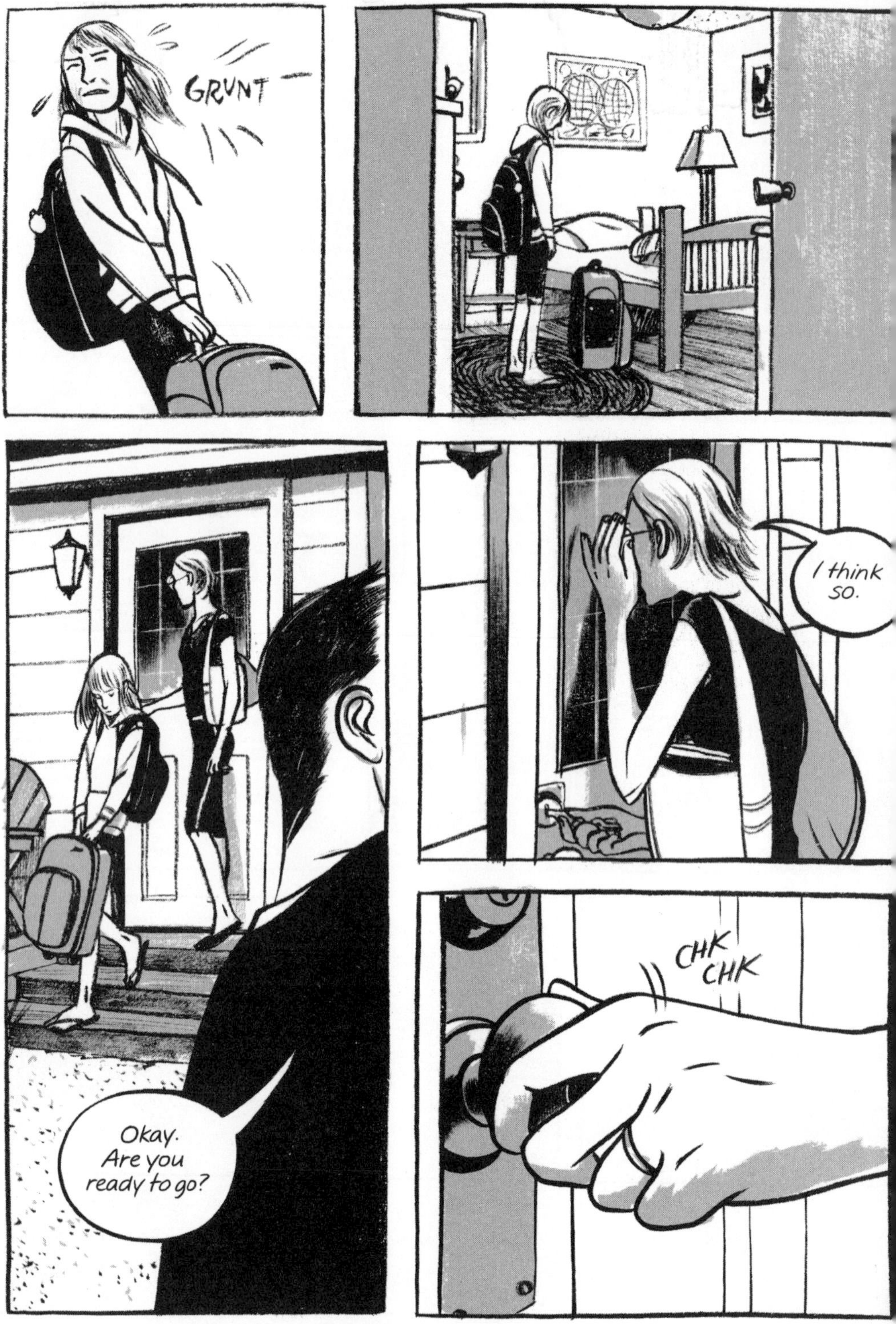
GRUNT
Okay.
Are you
ready to go?
I think
so.
CHK
CHK

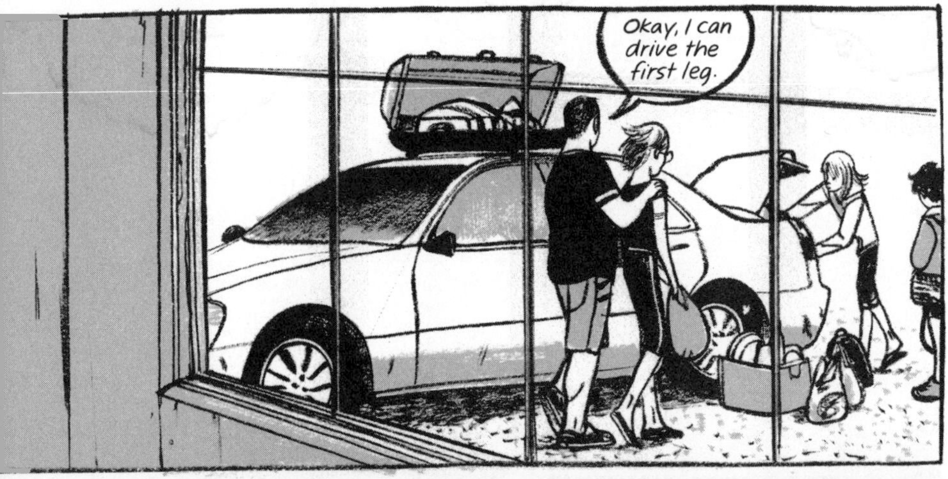
Okay, I can drive the first leg.

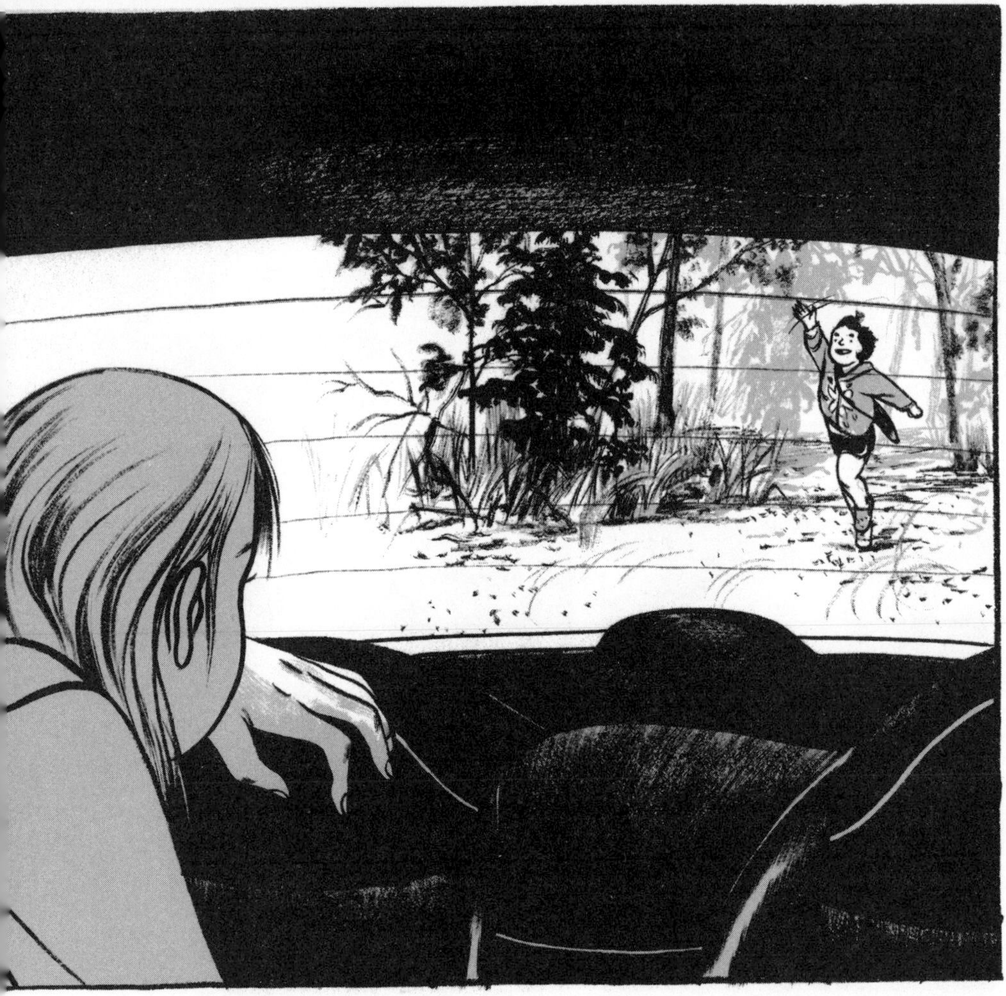

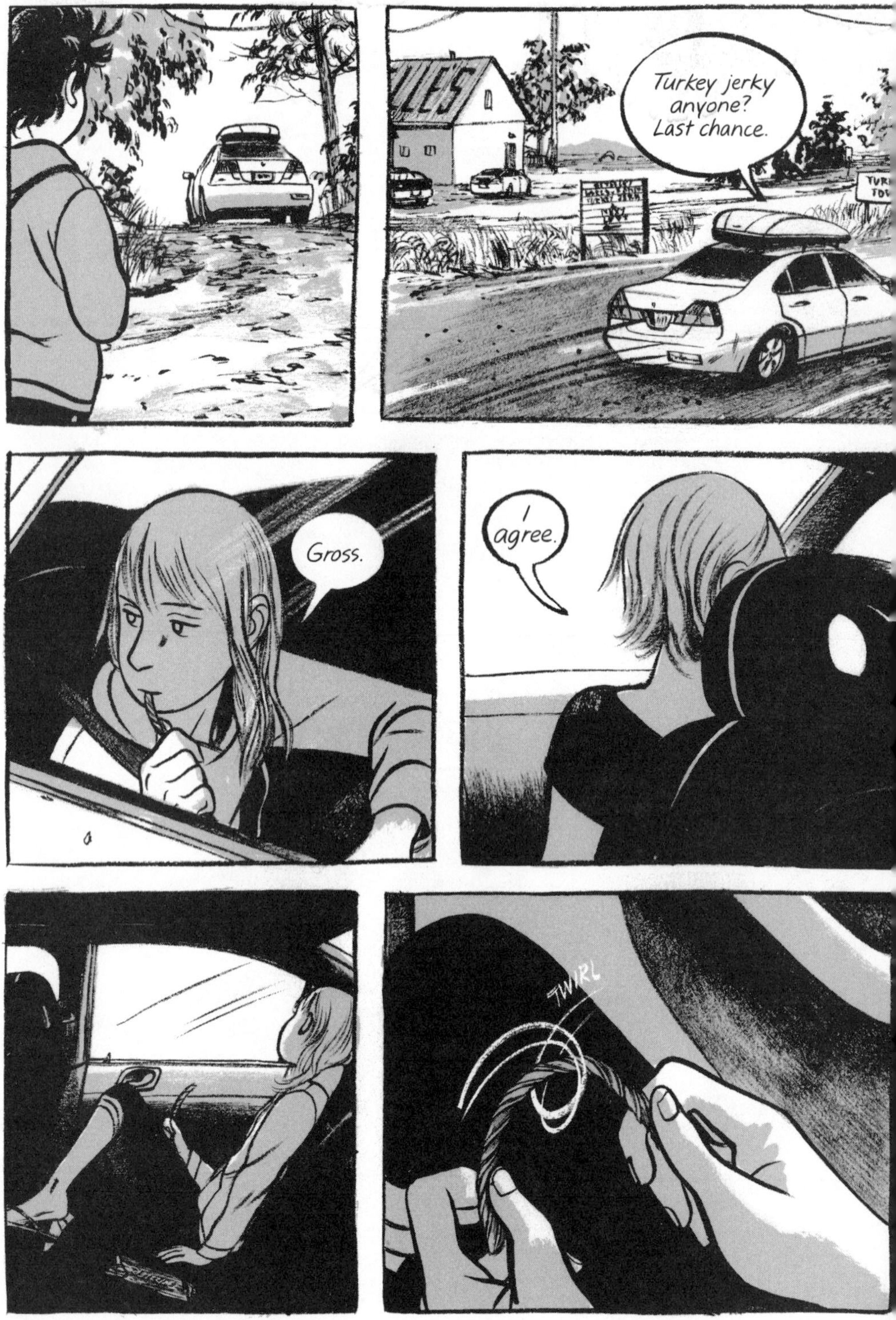
Turkey jerky anyone? Last chance.
Gross.
I agree.
TWIRL

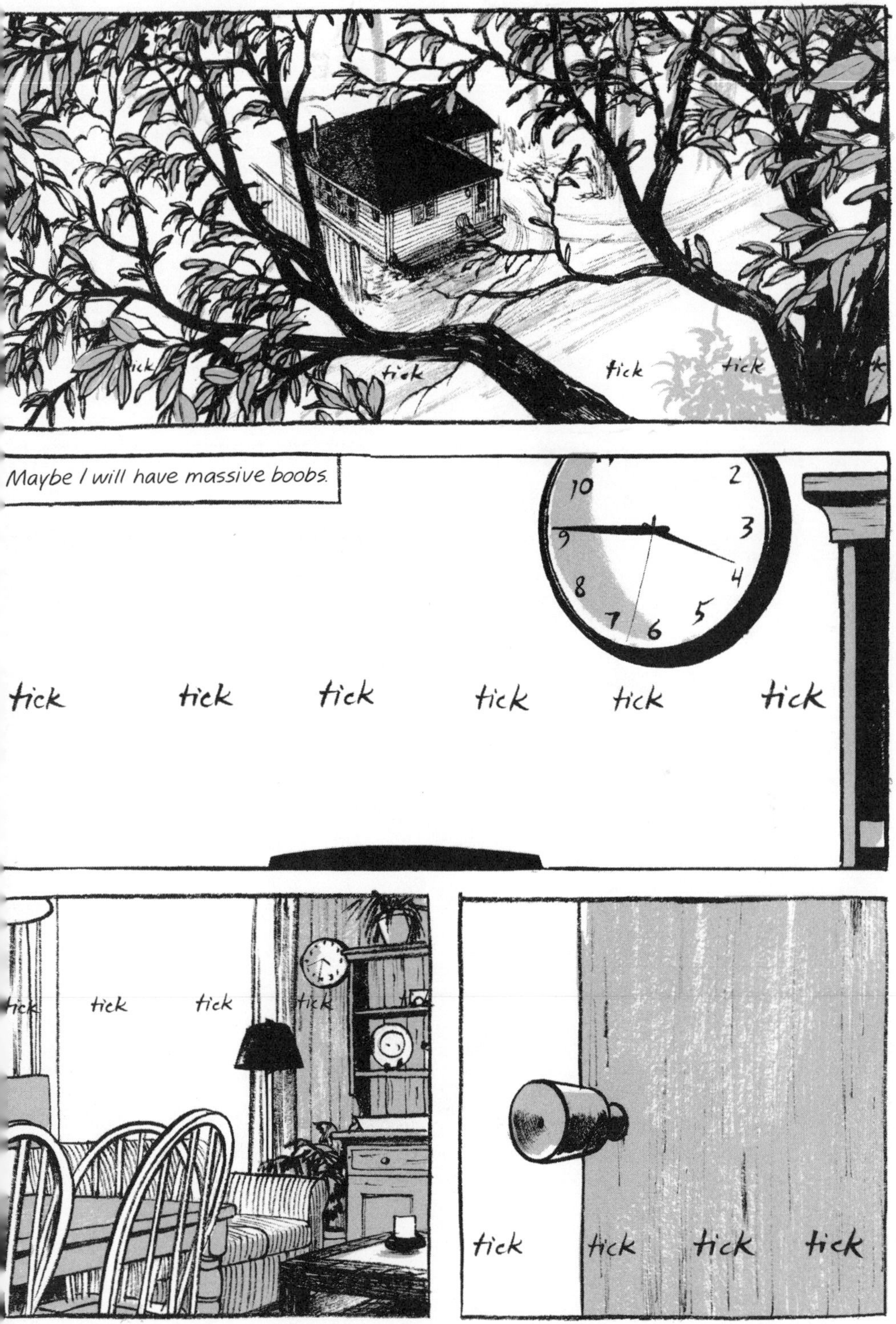
tick
tick
tick
tick
Maybe I will have massive boobs.
tick tick tick tick tick tick
tick tick tick
tick tick tick tick

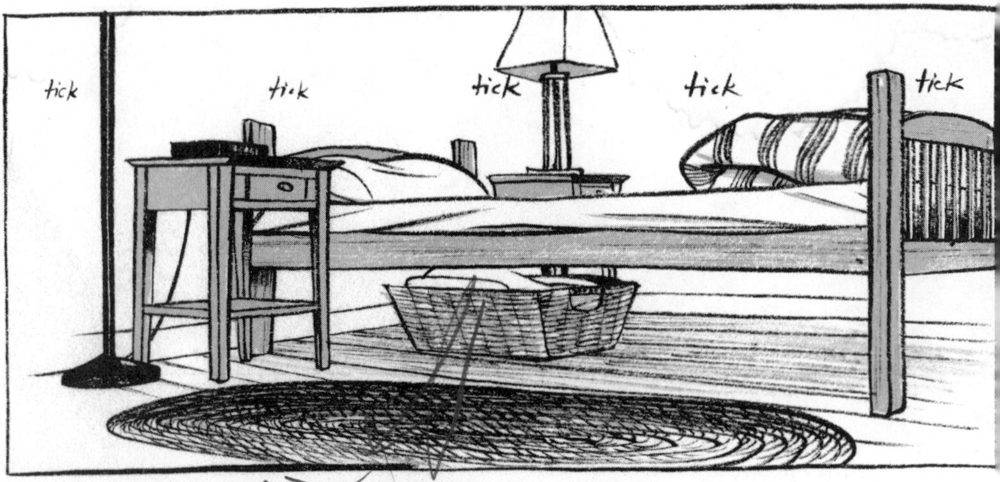
tick
tick
tick
tick
tick

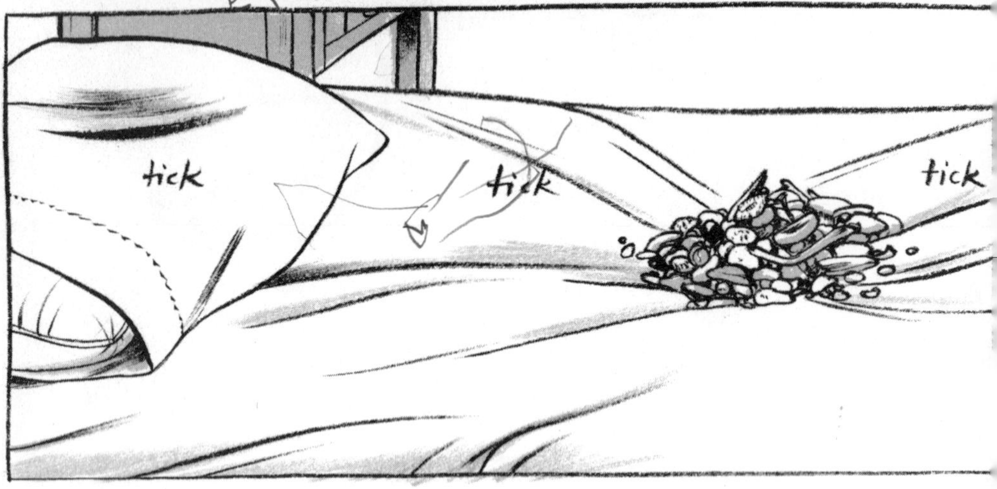
tick
tick
tick

tick.

Boobs would
be cool.

*For Julia K. & Abi S.*

*To the Tamaki families; Sam Weber; Heather Gold; The Kelk family;*
*Tom Upchurch; Zoe Whittall; Anna Yoken for the manga help;*
*Sam Hiyate and Allison McDonald of The Rights Factory; Mark Siegel*
*and Calista Brill at First Second; Shelley Tanaka, Patsy Aldana,*
*and Sheila Barry at Groundwood Books; and Rush.*

**First Second**

Text copyright © 2014 by Mariko Tamaki
Art copyright © 2014 by Jillian Tamaki

Published by First Second
First Second is an imprint of Roaring Brook Press,
a division of Holtzbrinck Publishing Holdings Limited Partnership
175 Fifth Avenue, New York, New York 10010

Cataloging-in-Publication Data is on file at the Library of Congress.

Hardcover ISBN 978-1-62672-094-7
Paperback ISBN 978-1-59643-774-6

First Second books may be purchased for business or promotional use. For information
on bulk purchases please contact Macmillan Corporate and Premium Sales Department
at (800) 221-7945 x 5442 or by email at specialmarkets@macmillan.com.

FIRST
EDITION

First edition 2014
Book design by Rob Steen and Colleen AF Venable

Printed in the United States of America

Hardcover: 10 9 8 7 6 5 4 3 2 1
Paperback: 10 9 8 7 6 5 4 3 2 1